THE TIME OF
TROUBLES II

Baen Books by HARRY TURTLEDOVE

The Time of Troubles I
The Time of Troubles II
The Bridge of the Separator (forthcoming)

The War Between the Provinces series:
Sentry Peak
Marching Through Peachtree
Advance and Retreat

The Fox novels:
Wisdom of the Fox
Tale of the Fox

3 x T
The Case of the Toxic Spell Dump
Thessalonica
Alternate Generals, editor
Alternate Generals II, editor
Alternate Generals III, editor
The Enchanter Completed, editor
Down in the Bottomlands (with L. Sprague de Camp)

THE TIME OF TROUBLES II

HARRY TURTLEDOVE

THE TIME OF TROUBLES II

This is a work of fiction. All the characters and events portrayed in this book are fictional, and any resemblance to real people or incidents is purely coincidental.

A Baen Book

Baen Publishing Enterprises
P.O. Box 1403
Riverdale, NY 10471
www.baen.com

ISBN-13: 978-1-4165-0899-1
ISBN-10: 1-4165-0899-6

Cover art by Gary Ruddell
Map art by Christine Levis

First printing, in this format, September 2005

Library of Congress Cataloging-in-Publication Data

Turtledove, Harry.
  The time of troubles II / Harry Turtledove.
     p. cm.
   ISBN 1-4165-0899-6 (hc)
  1. Marshals--Fiction. I. Title: Time of troubles 2. II. Title: Time of troubles two. III. Title.

  PS3570.U76T563 2005
  813'.54--dc22

                                              2005016175

Production & design by Windhaven Press, Auburn, NH (www.windhaven.com)
Printed in the United States of America

10   9   8   7   6   5   4   3   2   1

CONTENTS

THE TIME OF TROUBLES II

THE THOUSAND CITIES

THE TIME OF TROUBLES, VOL. 3

✦ 1

Abivard son of Godarz stared through sea mist to the east over the strait called the Cattle Crossing toward Vides-sos the city. The sun gleamed off the gilded globes the Videssians had set on spires atop the countless temples they had built to honor Phos, their false god. Abivard's left hand twisted in the gesture Makuraners used to invoke *the* God, the only one they reverenced.

"Narseh, Gimillu, the lady Shivini, Fraortish eldest of all, let that city fall into my hands," he murmured. He'd lost track of how many times he'd beseeched the Prophets Four to intercede with the God on his behalf, on behalf of Makuran, on behalf of Sharbaraz King of Kings. As yet his prayers remained unanswered.

Beside him Roshnani, his wife, said, "It seems close enough to reach out and pluck, like a ripe fig from a tree."

"Scarcely the third part of a farsang from one side of that water to the other," he agreed, setting a hand on her shoulder. "Were it land, a man could walk thrice so far in an hour's time. Were it land—"

"It is not land," Roshnani said. "No point wasting time think-ing what you might do if it were."

"I know," he answered. They smiled at each other. Physically they were very different: she short, round-faced, inclined to plump-ness; he lean and angular, with brooding eyes beneath bristling

3

brows. But they shared a commonsense practicality unusual both in their own folk—for Makuraners were given to extravagant melodramatics—and in the devious, treacherous Videssians. After a decade and more of marriage no one knew Abivard's mind better than Roshnani, himself often included.

The sun beat down on his head. It was not nearly so fierce as the summer sun that blazed down on Vek Rud domain, where he'd grown to manhood. Still, he felt its heat: he'd lost the hair at the back of his crown. Godarz had boasted a full head to his dying day, but the men of his mother, Burzoe's, family, those who lived long enough, went bald. He would rather not have followed in their footsteps, but the choice did not seem to be his.

"I wonder how the domain fares these days," he murmured. Formally, he was still its *dihqan*—its overlord—but he hadn't seen it for years, not since just after Sharbaraz had overthrown Smerdis, who had stolen the throne after Sharbaraz's father, Peroz King of Kings—along with Abivard's father, Godarz, along with a great host of other nobles, very nearly along with Abivard himself—had fallen in an attack gone disastrously awry against the Khamorth nomads who roamed the Pardrayan plain north of Makuran.

His younger brother, Frada, ran Vek Rud domain these days. Sharbaraz had flung Abivard against the Empire of Videssos when the Videssians had overthrown Likinios, the Avtokrator who'd helped restore the King of Kings to his throne in Mashiz. Videssian civil strife made triumphs come easy. And so, these days, all of Videssos' westlands lay under the control of Makuran through the armies Abivard commanded. And so—

Abivard kicked angrily at the beach on which he walked. Sand spurted under the sole of his sandal. "Back in Mashiz that last third of a farsang looks easy to cross to Sharbaraz. What a tiny distance, he's written to me. May his days be long and his realm increase, but—"

"And who has done more than you to increase his realm?" Roshnani demanded, then answered her own question: "No one, of course. And so he has no cause to complain of you."

"If I do not give the King of Kings what he requires, he has cause to complain of me," Abivard answered. "His Majesty does not understand the sea." Through Makuran's long history, few men had ever had occasion to understand the sea. A handful of fishing boats sailed on the landlocked Mylasa Sea, but, before

Videssos' recent collapse, the writ of the King of Kings had not run to any land that touched the broad, interconnected waters of the ocean. Sharbaraz thought of a third of a farsang and saw only a trivial obstacle. Abivard thought of this particular third of a farsang and saw—

Oars rhythmically rising and falling, a Videssian war dromon centipede-walked down the middle of the Cattle Crossing. The choppy little waves splashed from the greened bronze beak of its ram; Abivard could see the dart thrower mounted on its deck and the metal siphons that spit liquid fire half a bowshot. Videssos' banner, a gold sunburst on blue, snapped in the breeze from a flagstaff at the stern.

He did not know how many such dromons Videssos possessed. Dozens, certainly. Hundreds, probably. He did know how many he possessed. None. Without them his army could not leap over that last third of a farsang. If he tried getting a force across in the few fishing boats and merchantmen he did command—most of those had fled away from the westlands whither he could not pursue them—there would be a great burning and slaughter, and the green-blue waters of the Cattle Crossing would redden with blood for a while.

And so, as he had for almost two years, he stared longingly through sea mist over the water toward Videssos the city. He had studied the single seawall and the great double land wall not only with his eyes but also through detailed questioning of scores of Videssians. Could he but put his siege engines alongside those walls, he thought he could breach them. No foreign foe had ever sacked Videssos the city. Great would be the loot from that plundering.

"Let me but put them alongside," he muttered.

"May the God grant that you do," Roshnani said. "May she grant you the wisdom to see how it can be accomplished."

"Yes, may he," Abivard said. They both smiled. The God, being of unlimited mutability, was feminine to women and masculine to men.

But then Abivard turned his gaze back toward the capital of the Empire of Videssos. Roshnani's head swung that way, too. "I know what you're looking for," she said.

"I expected you would," Abivard answered. "Old Tanshar gave me three prophecies. The first two came true years ago, but I have yet to find a silver shield shining across a narrow sea." He laughed. "When Tanshar spoke those words, I'd never seen any sea, let alone a narrow one. But with so much that glitters in Videssos the city, I've never yet seen light sparking from a silver shield. Now I begin to wonder if the Cattle Crossing was the sea he meant."

"I can't think of any other that would be," Roshnani said, "but then, I don't know everything there is to know about seas, either. Pity we can't ask Tanshar what he meant."

"He didn't even know what he'd said in the prophetic fit, so strongly did it take him," Abivard said. "I had to tell him, once his proper, everyday senses came back." He sighed. "But even had he known, we couldn't call him back from his pyre." He kicked at the sand again, this time with a frustration different from that of a man thwarted of his prey. "I wish I could recognize the answers that spring from foretelling more readily than by spotting them as they've just passed. I shall have to speak to my present wizard about that."

"Which one?" Roshnani asked. "This new Bozorg or the Videssian mage?"

Abivard sighed again. "You have a way of finding the important questions. We've spent so long in Videssos since Likinios' fall, we've come to ape a lot of imperial ways." He chuckled. "I'm even getting a taste for mullet, and I ate no sea fish before these campaigns began."

"Nor I," Roshnani said. "But it's more than things like fish—"

As if to prove her point, Venizelos, the Videssian steward who had served them since they had drawn near the imperial capital, hurried up the beach toward them. The fussy little man had formerly administered an estate belonging to the Videssian logothete of the treasury. He'd changed masters as readily as the estate had. If the Videssians ever reclaimed this land, Abivard had few doubts that Venizelos would as readily change back.

The steward went down on one knee in the sand. "Most eminent sir," he said in Videssian, "I beg to report the arrival of a letter addressed to you."

"I thank you," Abivard answered in Makuraner. He probably would have used Videssian himself had he and Roshnani not been talking about the Empire and its influence on their lives.

He'd learned that speech in bitter exile in Serrhes, after Smerdis had driven Sharbaraz clean out of Makuran. Then he'd wondered if he'd see his homeland again or be forced to lived in Videssos forevermore.

He shook his mind off the past and followed Venizelos away from the beach, back toward the waiting dispatch rider. The suburb of Across, so called from its position relative to Videssos the city, was a sad and ragged town these days. It had gone back and forth between Makuran and Videssos several times in the past couple of years. A lot of its buildings were burned-out shells, and a lot of the ones that had escaped the fires were wrecks nonetheless.

Most of the people in the streets were Makuraner soldiers, some mounted, some afoot. They saluted Abivard with clenched fists over their hearts; many of them lowered their eyes to the ground as Roshnani walked past. That was partly politeness, partly a refusal to acknowledge her existence. By ancient custom, Makuraner noblewomen lived out their lives sequestered in the women's quarters first of their fathers' houses, then of their husbands'. Even after so many years of bending that custom to the breaking point, Roshnani still found herself an object of scandal.

The dispatch rider wore a white cotton surcoat with the red lion of Makuran embroidered on it. His whitewashed round shield also bore the red lion. Saluting Abivard, he cried, "I greet you in the name of Sharbaraz King of Kings, may his years be many and his realm increase!"

"In your person I greet his Majesty in return," Abivard answered as the horseman detached a leather message tube from his belt. The lion of Makuran was embossed there, too. "I am delighted to be granted the boon of communication from his flowing and illustrious pen."

No matter how well the Makuraner language lent itself to flowery flights of enthusiasm, Abivard would have been even more delighted had Sharbaraz let him alone and allowed him to get on with the business of consolidating his gains in the westlands of Videssos. Mashiz lay a long way away; why the King of Kings thought he could run the details of the war at such a remove was beyond Abivard.

"Why?" Roshnani had said once when he had complained about that. "Because he is King of Kings, that's why. Who in

Mashiz would presume to tell the King of Kings he cannot do as he desires?"

"Denak might," Abivard had grumbled. His sister was Sharbaraz's principal wife. Without Denak, Sharbaraz would have stayed mured up forever in Nalgis Crag stronghold. He honored her still for what she had done for him, but in their years of marriage she'd borne him only daughters. That made her influence on him less than it might have been.

But Sharbaraz might well not have heeded her had she given him sons. Even in the days when he had still been fighting Smerdis the usurper, he'd relied most of all on his own judgment, which, Abivard had to admit, was often good. Now, after more than a decade on the throne, Sharbaraz did solely as his will dictated—and so, inevitably, did the rest of Makuran.

Abivard opened the message tube and drew out the rolled parchment inside. It was sealed with red wax that, like the tube and the messenger's surcoat and shield, bore the lion of Makuran. Abivard broke the seal and unrolled the parchment. His lips moved as he read: "Sharbaraz King of Kings, whom the God delights to honor, good, pacific, beneficent, to our servant Abivard who does our bidding in all things: Greetings. Know that we are imperfectly pleased with the conduct of the war you wage against Videssos. Know further that, having brought the westlands under our hand, you are remiss in not extending the war to the very heart of the Empire of Videssos, which is to say, Videssos the city. And know further that we expect a movement against the aforementioned city the instant opportunity should present itself and that such opportunity should be sought with the avidity of a lover pursuing his beloved. Last, know also that our patience in this regard, appearances to the contrary notwithstanding, can be exhausted. The crown stands in urgent need of the last jewel remaining to the downfallen Empire of Videssos. The God grant you zeal. I end."

Roshnani stood beside him, also reading. She was less proficient at the art than he was, so he held the parchment till she was through. When she was, she let out an indignant snort. Abivard's glance warned her to say nothing where the dispatch rider could hear. He was sure she wouldn't have even without that look, but some things one did without thought.

"Lord, is there a reply?" the dispatch rider asked.

"Not one that has to go back on the instant," Abivard answered. "Spend the night here. Rest yourself; rest your horse. When morning comes, I'll explain to the King of Kings how I shall obey his commands."

"Let it be as you say, lord," the dispatch rider answered submissively.

To the messenger Abivard was *lord*, and a great lord at that: brother-in-law to the King of Kings, conqueror of Videssos' westlands, less exalted by blood than the high nobles of the Seven Clans, perhaps, but more powerful and prestigious. To every man of Makuran but one he was somebody with whom to reckon. To Sharbaraz King of Kings he was a servant in exactly the same sense as a sweeper in the royal palace in Mashiz was a servant. He could do more things for Sharbaraz than a sweeper could, but that was a difference of degree, not of kind. Sometimes he took his status for granted. Sometimes, as now, it grated.

He turned to Venizelos. "See that this fellow's needs are met, then join us back at our house."

"Of course, most eminent sir," Venizelos said in Videssian before falling into the Makuraner language to address the dispatch rider. These days Abivard was so used to lisping Videssian accents that he hardly noticed them.

The house where he and Roshnani stayed stood next to the ruins of the palace of the hypasteos, the city governor. Roshnani was still spluttering furiously when she and Abivard got back to it. "What does he want you to do?" she demanded. "Arrange a great sorcery so all your men suddenly sprout wings and fly over the Cattle Crossing and down into Videssos the city?"

"I'm sure the King of Kings would be delighted if I found a wizard who could work such a spell," Abivard answered. "Now that I think on it, I'd be delighted myself. It would make my life much easier."

He was angry at Sharbaraz, too, but was determined not to show it. The King of Kings had sent him irritating messages before, then had failed to follow up on them. As long as he stayed back in Mashiz, real control of the war against Videssos remained in Abivard's hands. Abivard didn't think his sovereign would send out a new commander to replace him. Sharbaraz knew beyond question that he was loyal and reliable. Of whom else could the King of Kings say that?

Then he stopped worrying about what, if anything, Sharbaraz thought. The door—which, but for a couple of narrow, shuttered windows, was the only break in the plain, to say nothing of dingy and smoke-stained, whitewashed facade of the house—came open, and his children ran out to meet him.

Varaz was the eldest, named for Abivard's brother who had fallen on the Pardrayan steppe with Godarz, with so many others. He had ten years on him now and looked like a small, smoothfaced, unlined copy of Abivard. By chance, even his cotton caftan bore the same brown, maroon, and dark blue stripes as his father's.

"What have you brought me?" he squealed, as if Abivard had just come back from a long journey.

"The palm of my hand on your backside for being such a greedy thing?" Abivard suggested, and drew back his arm as if to carry out that suggestion.

Varaz set his own hand on the hilt of the little sword—not a toy but a boy-sized version of a man's blade—that hung from his belt. Abivard's second living son grabbed his arm to keep him from spanking Varaz. Shahin was three years younger than his brother, between them lay another child, also a boy, who'd died of a flux before he had been weaned.

Zarmidukh grabbed Abivard's left arm in case he thought of using that one against Varaz. Unlike Shahin, who as usual was in deadly earnest, she laughed up at her father. In all her five years she'd found few things that failed to amuse her.

Not to be outdone, Gulshahr toddled over and seized Varaz's arm. He shook her off, but gently. She'd had a bad flux not long before and was still thin and pale beneath her swarthiness. When she grabbed her brother again, he shrugged and let her hold on.

"Our own little army," Abivard said fondly. Just then Livania, the Videssian housekeeper, came out to see what the children were up to. Nodding to her, Abivard added, "And the chief quartermaster."

He'd spoken in the Makuraner language. She answered in Videssian: "As far as that goes, supper is nearly ready." She hadn't understood the Makuraner tongue when Abivard's horsemen had driven the Videssians out of Across, but now she was fairly fluent.

"It's octopus stew," Varaz said. The name of the main ingredient came out in Videssian; as Makuran was a nearly landlocked country, its language had no name for many-tentacled sea creatures. All Abivard's children used Videssian as readily as their own tongue, anyhow. And why not? All of them save Varaz had been born in formerly Videssian territory, and all of them had spent far more time there than back in Makuran.

Abivard and Roshnani glanced at each other. Both of them were easily able to control their enthusiasm for octopus. As far as Abivard was concerned, the beasts had the texture of leather with very little redeeming flavor. He would have preferred mutton or goat or beef. The Videssians ate less red meat than did Makuraners at any time, though, and years of war had diminished and scattered their herds. If the choice lay between eating strange beasts that crawled in tide pools and going hungry, he was willing to be flexible.

The stew *was* tasty, full of carrots and parsnips and cabbage leaves and flavored with garlic and onions. Abivard, his family, Livania, and Venizelos ate in the central courtyard of the house. A fountain splashed there; that struck Abivard, who had grown up in a dry country, as an extravagant luxury.

On the other hand, no bright flowers bloomed in the courtyard, as they would have in any Makuraner home this side of a hovel. Livania had started an herb garden. Most of the plants that grew in it were nondescript to the eye, but their spicy scents cut through the city and camp stinks of smoke and men and animals and garbage and ordure.

Abivard snapped his fingers. "Have to find artisans to repair that broken sewage main or the smell will get worse and the men will start coming down sick by companies. We've been lucky we haven't had anything much going through them, because we've stayed in one place a long time."

"That's true, most eminent sir," Venizelos said gravely. "If once a few men are taken ill with a disease, it can race through a host like fire."

"May it not come to pass." Abivard twisted his left hand in a sign intended to avert any evil omen.

"When do we get to fight the Videssians again, Father?" Varaz asked, once more setting hand to sword hilt.

"That's up to Maniakes Avtokrator more than it is up to me," Abivard answered. "We can't get at his soldiers right now—"

However much Sharbaraz doesn't care for the notion, he added to himself. "—and he won't come to us. What does that leave?"

Varaz frowned, seriously considering the question. The past couple of years Abivard had taken to asking him more and more questions of that sort to get him used to thinking like an officer. Some of his answers had been very good. Once or twice Abivard thought they were probably better than the ones the officer facing the real situation had come up with.

Now Varaz said, "If we can't go over the Cattle Crossing and Maniakes won't cross over here to fight us, we have to find some other way to get at his army and beat it."

"Wishing for something you can't reach doesn't make it fall into your lap," Abivard answered, reminded that his eldest son was still a boy, after all. "There is another way for us to get to Videssos the city, but it's not one we can take. It would mean bringing an army over the Pardrayan steppe, all the way around the Videssian sea, and then down into Videssos from the north. How would we defend ourselves from the nomads if we tried that, or keep the army supplied on the long journey it would have to take?"

"We keep our armies supplied here in Videssos," Varaz said, reluctant to abandon his notion.

"Yes, but here in Videssos they grow all sorts of things," Abivard said patiently. "This coastal lowland is as rich as the soil of the Thousand Cities between the Tutub and the Tib, I think. And they have towns here, with artisans to make every kind of thing an army needs. It's different on the steppe."

"What's it like?" Shahin asked. He knew Videssos and little else.

"It's—vast," Abivard said. "I was only out there once, on the campaign of Peroz King of Kings, the one that failed. Nothing but farsang after farsang of rolling grassland, none of it very rich but so much of it that the nomads can pasture great flocks out there. But it has no cropland, no towns, no artisans except for the few among the Khamorth—and all they know is connected to the herds one way or another."

"If the country is that bad, why did Peroz King of Kings want it?" Varaz asked.

"Why?" Across a decade and more remembered anger smoldered in Abivard's voice. "I'll tell you why, Son. Because the Videssians spread gold among the Khamorth clans, bribing them to cross the Degird River into Makuran. You can never be too sure about Videssians."

"Well! I like that," Livania said indignantly.

Abivard smiled at her. "I didn't mean people like you and Venizelos. I meant the people in the palaces." He waved east, toward the imperial residence in Videssos the city. "They are devious, they are underhanded, they will cheat you three different ways in a minute's time if they see the chance—and they commonly do see it."

"But didn't Maniakes Avtokrator help put Sharbaraz King of Kings, may his years be many and his realm increase, back on the throne?" Varaz persisted.

"Yes, he did," Abivard said. "But that was your mother's idea."

Varaz had heard the story before. He looked proud, not astonished. Abivard thought Shahin had heard it, too, but he must not have understood what it meant, for, with his smaller sisters, he stared at Roshnani with enormous eyes. "*Your* idea, mother?"

"Smerdis' men had beaten us," she said. "They'd driven us away from Mashiz and across the Thousand Cities to the edge of the badlands that run between them and the border of the Videssian westlands. We were doomed if we stayed where we were, so I thought we couldn't do worse and might do better if we took refuge with the Videssians."

"And look what's become of that," Abivard added, driving the lesson home. "A lot of people—men mostly, but a surprising lot of women, too—think women are foolish just because they're women. They're wrong, all of them. If Sharbaraz hadn't taken your mother's advice, he probably wouldn't be King of Kings today."

Varaz pondered that with the same careful attention he'd given Abivard's question on strategy. Shahin just nodded and accepted it; he was still at the age when his parents' words had the authority of the Prophets Four. Maybe, if he heard such things often enough when he was small, he would pay more heed to his principal wife once he grew to be a man.

With luck, he would have a principal wife worth heeding. Abivard glanced fondly over at Roshnani.

Twilight deepened to darkness. Servants lit torches. They drew moths to join the clouds of mosquitoes that buzzed in the courtyard. Because the coastal lowlands were so warm and damp, the droning pests flourished there in swarms unknown back at Vek Rud domain. Every so often a nightjar or a bat would dive out of the night, seize a bug, and vanish again. There were more bugs, though, than creatures to devour them.

Livania put Zarmidukh and Gulshahr to bed, then came back for Shahin, who made his usual protests over going to sleep but finally gave in. Varaz, grave in the responsibility of approaching adulthood, went off without a fuss when his own turn came half an hour or so later. Roshnani chuckled under her breath. Abivard understood why: in another couple of weeks—or couple of days, for that matter—Varaz was liable to forget his dignity and go back to squawking.

"Will there be anything more, most eminent sir?" Venizelos asked.

"Go to bed," Abivard told him. "Roshnani and I won't be up much longer ourselves." Roshnani nodded agreement to that. As the two of them got up and headed for their bedchamber, the torches that had been lighted were doused. The stink of hot tallow filled the courtyard. The servants left a torch burning near the entrance to the house. Abivard paused there to light a clay lamp filled with olive oil.

Roshnani said, "I'd sooner burn that stuff than cook with it or sop bread in it the way the Videssians do."

"I'm not fond of it, either," Abivard answered. "But you'll notice all the children love it." He rolled his eyes. "They should, seeing how Livania stuffs it into them every chance she gets. I think she's trying to turn them into Videssians from the stomach out."

"I wonder if that's a kind of magic our wizards don't know." Roshnani laughed, but the fingers of her left hand twisted in the sign to turn aside the evil idea.

She and Abivard walked down the hall to their bedchamber. He set the lamp on a little table by his side of the bed. The bed had a tall frame enclosed by gauzy netting. There were usually fewer mosquitoes inside the netting than outside. Abivard supposed that was worthwhile. He pulled off his caftan and lay down on the bed. Sweet-smelling straw rustled beneath him; the leather straps supporting the mattress creaked a little.

After Roshnani lay down beside him, he blew out the lamp through the netting. The room plunged into darkness. He set a hand on her hip. She turned toward him. Had she turned away or lay still, he would have rolled over and gone to sleep without worrying about it. As it was, they made love—companionably, almost lazily—and then, separating to keep from sticking to each other once they were through, fell asleep together.

The Videssian in the blue robe with the cloth-of-gold circle on the left breast went down on one knee before Abivard. "By the lord with the great and good mind, most eminent sir, I beg you to reconsider this harsh and inhuman edict," he said. The early-morning sun gleamed off his shaved pate as if it were a gilded dome topping one of false Phos' temples.

"Rise, holy sir," Abivard answered in Videssian, and the hierarch of Across, a plump, middle-aged cleric named Artanas, grunted and got to his feet. Abivard fixed him with what he hoped was a baleful stare. "Now, see here, holy sir. You should be glad you are allowed to practice your religion in any way at all and not come whining to me about it. You will obey the decree of Sharbaraz King of Kings, may his days be long and his realm increase, or you will not be allowed to worship and you will be subject to the penalties the decree ordains." He set a hand on the hilt of his sword to make sure Artanas got the idea.

"But, most eminent sir," Artanas wailed, "forcing us to observe heretical rituals surely condemns us to Phos' eternal ice. And the usages of the Vaspurakaner heretics are particularly repellent to us."

Abivard shrugged. "If you disobey, you and all who worship with you will suffer." In the abstract, Sharbaraz had been clever to force the Videssian temples in the westlands to conform to Vaspurakaner usages if they wanted to stay open: it had split them away from the Empire of Videssos' central ecclesiastical authority. As for the Vaspurakaners themselves—"As I say, holy sir, count yourself lucky. In the land of Vaspurakan we require the worship of the God, not your false spirits of good and evil."

"That serves the Vaspurakaners right for their longtime treachery against the true faith," said Artanas, who did not object when the Makuraners interfered with someone else's belief, only when they meddled with his own.

For his part, Abivard was not sure the King of Kings was acting rightly in imposing the cult of the God in Vaspurakan. He did not doubt for a moment that faith in the God was the only guarantor of a happy afterlife, but he also had no reason to doubt the fanaticism of the Vaspurakaners for their own faith: all the followers of Phos struck him as being passionately wedded to their own version of error, whatever it happened to be. If one pushed them too far, they were liable to snap.

That same thought also applied to Artanas, though Abivard didn't care to admit as much to himself. Sharbaraz might have done better not to meddle in any matters of religion till after the war against Videssos had been won. But if Abivard did not carry out the policies the King of Kings had set forth, word of his failure would soon head for Mashiz—after which, most likely, he would, too, in disgrace.

He said, "We shall attend closely to what you preach, holy sir. I am not schooled in your false beliefs, but we have men who are. No matter what you say or where you say it, some of them will hear you. If you do not preach the doctrine you are ordered to preach, you will suffer the consequences. Perhaps I shall send to Mashiz for a special persuader."

Artanas' skin, already a couple of shades paler than Abivard's, went almost fish-belly white. Sweat gleamed on his shaved skull. Makuraner torturers and their skill in torment were legendary in Videssos. Abivard found that amusing, for Videssian torturers enjoyed a similar reputation in Makuran. He did not tell that to the Videssian hierarch.

"You ask me to preach what I know to be untrue," Artanas said. "How in good conscience can I do that?"

"Your conscience is not my concern," Abivard answered. "Your actions are. If you do not preach of Vaspur the Firstborn and the place of the Vaspurakaners as his chiefest descendants, you shall answer to me."

Artanas tried another tack: "The people here, knowing the Vaspurakaners' claims to be ignorant, empty, ignoble, and impious, will not heed this preaching and may rise up not only against me but also against you."

"That is my affair, not yours," Abivard said. "Where the armies of Videssos have not been able to stand against the brave war-riors of Makuran for lo these many years, why should we fear a rabble of peasants and artisans?"

The local prelate glared at him, then said, "Videssian arms won a great victory against the barbarians of Kubrat earlier this year, or so I have heard."

Abivard had heard that, too, and didn't care for it. He knew more than he'd ever wanted to learn about nomad horsemen pouring down out of the north. After the Khamorth had destroyed the flower of Peroz King of Kings' army out on the steppe, they'd raided over the Degird and into Makuran. The flocks and fields of his own domain had come under attack. Since Videssian meddling out on the steppe had set the clans in motion, he was anything but sorry to see the Empire having nomad troubles of its own and anything but glad to see those troubles overcome.

Making his voice hard, he said, "We are stronger than the barbarians, just as we are stronger than you Videssians. Heed what I say, holy sir, in your services and sermons, or you will learn at first hand how strong we are. Do you understand me?" When Artanas did not say no, Abivard made an abrupt gesture of dismissal. "Get you gone."

Artanas left. Abivard knew that the hierarch remained rebellious. That edict of Sharbaraz's imposing Vaspurakaner usages on the Videssian westlands had already sparked riots in a couple of towns. Abivard's men had put them down, true, but he wished they hadn't had the need.

Since Sharbaraz was King of Kings, the God was supposed to have blessed him with preternatural wisdom and foresight. If the God had done that, the results were moderately hard to notice. And here the sun was, not a third of the way up the sky from rising, and Abivard already felt like having a mug of wine or maybe two.

Hoping to escape any more importunate Videssians, he went out to the encampment of his own troops, not far from the field fortifications Maniakes had run up in a vain effort to hold the armored horsemen away from Across. The Videssian works were not so strong as they might have been; Maniakes, realizing they were too little, too late, had neither completed them nor defended what his engineers had built. Abivard was grateful for the wasted effort.

Back among the Makuraners, Abivard came as close to feeling at home as he could within sight of Videssos the city. The lean, swarthy men in caftans who groomed horses or sat playing dice in what shade they could find were of his kind. His own language filled his ears. Many of the warriors of the army he and Sharbaraz had so painstakingly rebuilt spoke with a northwestern accent like his own. When Sharbaraz had been a rebel, the Northwest had rallied to him first.

But even in the camp not all was as it would have been near Vek Rud domain or near Mashiz or between the Tib and the Tutub. A lot of the servants and most of the camp women were Videssians who had been scooped up as his army had traveled back and forth through the westlands. Some of those women had children seven and eight and nine years old. The children used a weird jargon of their own, with mostly Videssian words but a grammar closer to that of the Makuraner tongue. Only they could understand most of it.

And here came the man Abivard perhaps least wanted to see when he was fed up with things Videssian. He couldn't even show it, as he could with Artanas. "I greet you, eminent Tzikas," he said, and presented his cheek for the Videssian officer to kiss, a token that he reckoned Tzikas' rank but little lower than his own.

"I greet you, Abivard son of Godarz, brother-in-law to Sharbaraz King of Kings, may his years be many and his realm increase," Tzikas answered in Makuraner that was fluent and only slightly lisping. He kissed Abivard's cheek just as a minor noble from Mashiz might have, though that was not a practice the Videssians followed among themselves.

"Have you learned anything new and interesting from the other side, eminent sir?" Abivard asked, pointing with his chin east over the Cattle Crossing toward Videssos the city.

Tzikas shook his head. He was a solidly made middle-aged man with a thick head of graying hair and a neatly trimmed gray beard. He seemed quite ordinary till one looked at his eyes. When one did, one discovered they had already looked through one, weighed one's soul, measured it, and assigned one to one's proper pigeonhole in the document file of his mind. The turncoat Videssian was, Abivard had reluctantly been forced to conclude, nearly as clever as he thought he was—no mean assessment.

"Too bad," Abivard said. "Anything I can find out about what Maniakes is planning for this summer will help. I've seen him in action. If he has steady troops behind him, he'll be difficult."

"That pup?" Tzikas made a dismissive gesture that irritated Abivard, who was not far from Maniakes' age. "He has a habit of striking too soon and of thinking he's stronger than he really is." His face clouded. "It cost us dear in the Arandos valley not long after he took the crown."

Abivard nodded, though Tzikas was rewriting things in his memory. For years the garrison Tzikas commanded at Amorion, at the west end of the valley, had held off Abivard's force: Abivard had developed a healthy respect for the Videssian general's skill. But at last Amorion had fallen—before Maniakes' army, pushing west up the line of the Arandos, could reinforce it. Abivard's men had beaten Maniakes after that, but it had not been the Avtokrator's fault that Amorion had at last been taken.

What Abivard said was, "If he's as hasty and headstrong as you say, eminent sir, how did he smash the Kubratoi as he did?"

"Easy enough to win a fine name for yourself fighting savages," Tzikas answered. "What you get from it, though, won't help you much when you come up against soldiers with discipline and generals who can see farther than the ends of their noses."

Abivard took his own nose between thumb and forefinger for a moment. It was of generous size, though in no way outlandish for a man of Makuran. He hoped he could see past the end of it. "You do have a point," he admitted. "Fighting the Khamorth is nothing like coming up against you Videssians, I must say. But I worry about Maniakes. He made fewer mistakes against me last year than he had before—and tried to accomplish less, which is almost another way of saying the same thing, considering how unsteady his soldiers were. I fear he may be turning into a good commander."

Tzikas' lip curled. "Him? Not likely."

The first question that came to Abivard's mind was, *No? Then why did you fail when you tried overthrowing him this past winter?* He didn't ask it; on the orders of his sovereign, he was treating Tzikas with every courtesy in the hope that Tzikas would prove a useful tool against Maniakes. Had many Videssian garrisons in the westlands been left, Tzikas might have persuaded their commanders to go over to Makuran, as he had. But the only Videssian troops here these days were raiding bands largely immune to the renegade general's blandishments.

A traitor Tzikas might be; a fool he was not. He seemed to have a gift for plucking thoughts from the heads of those with whom he conversed. As if to answer the question Abivard had not asked, he said, "I would have toppled the pervert from the throne had his protective amulet not warded him just long enough to reach his wizard and gain a counterspell against my mage's cantrip."

"Aye, so you've said," Abivard replied. To his way of thinking, an effective conspirator would have known about that amulet and found some way to circumvent it. Saying that to Tzikas, though, would surely have offended him. If only Tzikas took similar care when speaking to Abivard.

Again the Videssian replied to what Abivard had not said: "I know you Makuraners think nothing of first cousins marrying, or uncles and nieces, or even brothers and sisters among the Seven Clans." He pulled a face. "Those usages are not ours, and no one will convince me they are not perverse. When Maniakes bedded his uncle's daughter, that was incest, plain as day."

"So you've said," Abivard repeated. "More than once, in fact. Has not your Mobedhan Mobedh, or whatever you call your chief priest, given leave for that marriage?"

"Our patriarch," Tzikas answered, reminding him of the Videssian word. "Yes, he has." Tzikas' lip curled again, more this time. "And no doubt he gained a fitting reward for the dispensation." Abivard picked up the meaning of that Videssian term from the context. Tzikas went on: "I stand with true righteousness no matter what the patriarch might say."

He looked very righteous himself. He was never less believable than when he donned that mantle of smug virtue, for it did not fit him well. He'd made his play, it hadn't worked, and now he seemed to want a special commendation for pure and noble motives. As far as Abivard was concerned, if one tried killing a man by magic, one's motives were unlikely to be pure or noble—odds were, one just wanted what he had.

Tzikas said, "How I admire Sharbaraz King of Kings, may his days be long and his realm increase, for maintaining the imperial dignity of the true heir to the throne of Videssos, Hosios the son of Likinios Avtokrator."

"How generous of you to recognize Hosios' claim," Abivard answered tonelessly. If he had to listen to much more of Tzikas' fulsome good cheer, he'd need a steaming down at the closest bathhouse. The real Hosios was long years dead, executed with his father when Genesios had butchered his way to the Videssian throne. As far as Abivard knew, three different Videssians had played Hosios at Sharbaraz's bidding. There might have been more. If one started to think one really was an Avtokrator rather than a puppet—

"I would recognize any claim in preference to that of Maniakes," Tzikas said seriously. But that was too much of a courtier's claim even for him to stomach. Shaking his head, he corrected himself: "No, were I to choose between Maniakes and Genesios, I would choose Maniakes."

Abivard knew that he ought to despise Genesios, too. The man had, after all, murdered not only Likinios, the benefactor of Makuran, but also all his family. But had it not been for Genesios, he would not be able to look over the Cattle Crossing and see Videssos the city. Under what passed for the murderer's reign, Videssos had dissolved in multicornered civil war, and more than one town in the westlands had welcomed the Makuraners in the hope that they would bring peace and order to replace the bloody chaos engulfing the Empire.

When Tzikas saw that Abivard was not going to respond to his preferences for the Videssian throne, he changed the subject, at least to some degree: "Brother-in-law to the King of Kings, when may I begin constituting my promised regiment of horsemen in the service of Hosios Avtokrator?"

"Soon," Abivard answered, as he had the last time Tzikas had asked that question, and the time before that, and the time before *that.*

"I have heard there is no objection in Mashiz to the regiment," Tzikas said delicately.

"Soon, eminent sir, soon," Abivard repeated. Tzikas was right; Sharbaraz King of Kings was happy to see a body of Videssian troops help give the current Hosios' claim to the throne legitimacy. The hesitation lay on Abivard's part. Tzikas was already a traitor once; what was to keep him from becoming a traitor twice?

Roshnani had used a homelier analogy: "A man who cheats *with* a woman and then marries her will cheat *on* her afterward—not always, maybe, but most of the time."

"I trust I shall not have to appeal directly to Sharbaraz King of Kings, may his years be many and his realm increase," Tzikas said exactly as a Makuraner noble might have—the Videssians knew how to squeeze, too.

"Soon I said, and soon I meant," Abivard replied, wishing that some hideous disease—another bout of treason, perhaps—would get Tzikas out of his hair. For the Videssian renegade to use the word *trust* when he was so manifestly unworthy of it grated. What grated even more was that Tzikas, who was so perceptive elsewhere, seemed blind to Abivard's reasons for disliking him.

"I shall take you at your word," Tzikas said, "for I know the nobles of Makuran are raised to ride, to fight, and to tell the truth."

That was what the Videssians said of Makuraners. The men of Makuran, for their part, were told that Videssians sucked in mendacity with their mothers' milk. Having dealt with men from both sides of the border, Abivard had come to the reluctant conclusion that those of either nation would lie when they thought that was to their benefit or sometimes merely for the sport of it, those who worshiped the God about as readily as those who followed Phos.

"Everything I can do, I will," Abivard said. *Eventually,* he added to himself. He did not enjoy being imperfectly honest with Tzikas, but he did not relish the prospect of the Videssian's commanding troops, either. To take the moral advantage away from Tzikas, he went on: "Have you had any luck in finding ship's carpenters, or whatever the proper name for them is? If we are going to beat Maniakes, to beat Videssos once and for all, we'll have to get our men over the Cattle Crossing and assault Videssos the city. Without ships—"

Tzikas sighed. "I am making every effort, brother-in-law to the King of Kings, but my difficulties in this regard, unlike yours concerning horsemen, are easy to describe." Abivard raised an eyebrow at that jab. Unperturbed, Tzikas went on, "Videssos separates land and sea commands. Had a drungarios fallen into your clutches, he could have done better by you, for such matters fall within his area of responsibility. As a simple soldier, though, I fear I am ignorant of the art of shipbuilding."

"Eminent sir, I certainly did not expect you to do the carpentry on your own," Abivard answered, working hard to keep his face straight. Tzikas' describing himself as a simple anything would have drawn a laugh from any Makuraner—and probably from most of the Videssians—who had ever had to deal with him. "Learning where to gather the men with the requisite trades is something else again."

"So it is, in the most literal sense of the word," Tzikas said. "Most of the men who practice these trades have left the westlands in the face of your victorious advance, whether by their own will or at the urging of their city governors or provincial chiefs."

Such urging, Abivard knew, had probably been at a sword's point. "The Videssians dug a hole and pulled it in after themselves," he said angrily. "I can see them over there in Videssos the city, but I can't touch them no matter what I try. But they can still touch me—some of their seaborne raids have hurt."

"They have a capacity you lack," Tzikas agreed. "I would help you remedy that lack were it in my power, but unfortunately it is not. You, on the other hand, have the ability to allow me to recruit a suitable number of horsemen who—" Without apparent effort, he turned the tables on Abivard.

By the time Abivard managed to break away, he'd decided he would gladly let Tzikas recruit his long-desired cavalry regiment provided that the Videssian swore a frightful oath to take that regiment far, far away and never come nagging any man of Makuran again.

Abivard missed Tanshar. He'd always gotten along well with the fortune-teller and wizard who'd lived for so long in the village below Vek Rud stronghold. But Tanshar now was five years dead. Abivard had been searching ever since for a mage who could give him results that matched Tanshar's and not make him feel like an idiot for asking an occasional question.

Whether the wizards who traveled with the army suited him or not, it had a fair contingent. Battle magic rarely did an army any good. For one thing, the opposition's sorcerers were likely to block the efforts of one's own mages. For another, no magic was very effective in the heat of battle. When a man's passions were roused to fever pitch as he fought for his life, he scarcely sensed spells that might have laid him low had they taken him at his ease.

The wizards, then, did more in the way of finding lost rings—and occasionally lost toddlers—for the camp women than they did in hurling sorcerous fireballs at Maniakes' men. They foretold whether pregnant women would bear boys or girls—not with perfect accuracy but better than they could have done by random guessing. They helped heal sick men and sick horses and with luck helped keep camp diseases from turning into epidemics. And, being men, they boasted about all the other things they might do if only they got the chance.

Every so often Abivard summoned one of them to see if he could make good on his boasts. One hot, sticky high-summer day he had called to his residence the mage named Bozorg, a young, eager fellow who had not accompanied the army in all its campaigns in the Videssian westlands but was newly arrived from Mashiz.

Bozorg bowed very low before Abivard, showing he recognized that his own rank was low compared with that of the general. Venizelos fetched in wine made tangy with the juice of oranges and lemons, a specialty of the coastal lowlands. Over the past couple of years Abivard had grown fond of it. Bozorg's lips puckered in an expression redolent of distaste.

"Too sour for me," he said, and then went on, "unlike my gracious and generous host, whose kindness is a sun by day and a full moon by night, illuminating by its brilliance all it touches. I am honored beyond my poor and humble worth by his invitation and shall serve him with all my heart, all my soul, and all my might, be my abilities ever so weak and feeble."

Abivard coughed. They didn't lay compliments on with a trowel in the frontier domain where he'd grown up. The Videssians weren't in the habit of quite such cloying fulsomeness, either; their praise tended to have a sardonic edge to it. But at the court of Mashiz flattery knew no bounds.

Bozorg must have expected him to take it for granted, too, for he continued. "How may I serve the valiant and noble lord whose puissance causes Videssos to tremble, whose onset is like that of the lion, who strikes with the swiftness of the goshawk, at whose approach the pale easterners who know not the God slink away like jackals, who overthrows city walls like an earthquake in human form, who—"

Abivard's patience ran thin. "If you'll give me a chance to get a word in edgewise, I'll tell you what I have in mind." He was glad Roshnani wasn't listening to Bozorg; he would have been a long time living down *earthquake in human form.*

"Your manner is harsh and abrupt," Bozorg said sulkily. Abivard glared at him. He'd sent looks less hostile toward the Videssian generals whose armies he'd overthrown. Bozorg wilted. Shifting from foot to foot, he admitted, "I am of course here to serve you, lord."

"That's a relief," Abivard said. "I thought you'd come to stop up my ears with treacle." Bozorg assumed a deeply wounded expression. He hadn't practiced it enough; it looked plastered on rather than genuine. Abivard did him a favor: he ignored it. After pausing to marshal his thoughts, he went on, "What I need from you, if you can give it to me, is some sort of picture of what Maniakes has in mind to do to us this year or next year or whenever he decides he's strong enough to face us in open battle."

Now Bozorg really did look worried. "Lord, this is no easy task you set me. The Avtokrator of the Videssians will surely have his plans hedged around with the finest sorcery he can obtain from those small fragments of the Empire still under his control."

"If what I wanted were simple, I could give silver arkets or Videssian goldpieces to any local hedge wizard," Abivard said, looking down his long nose at the mage from Mashiz. "You, sirrah, come recommended for both talent and skill. If I send you back to the capital because you have not the spirit to essay what I ask of you, you shall get no more such recommendations in the future."

"You misunderstand me, lord," Bozorg said quickly. "It is not to be doubted I shall attempt this task. I did but warn you that the God does not guarantee success, not against the wizards Maniakes Avtokrator has under his command."

"Once we're born, the only thing the God *guarantees* is that we'll die and be judged on how we have lived our lives," Abivard answered. "Between those two moments of birth and death we strive to be good and true and righteous. Of course we can't succeed all the time; only the Prophets Four came close, and so the God revealed himself to them. But we must strive."

Bozorg bowed. "My lord is a Mobedhan Mobedh of piety," he said. Then he gulped; had he laid his flattery on with a trowel again? Abivard contented himself with folding his arms across his chest and letting out an impatient sigh. Hastily the wizard said, "If my lord will excuse me for but a moment, I shall fetch in the magical materials I shall require in the conjuration."

He hurried out of Abivard's residence, returning a moment later with two dust-covered leather saddlebags. He set them down on a low table in front of Abivard, undid the rawhide laces that secured them, and took out a low, broad bowl with a glistening white glaze, several stoppered jars, and a squat jug of wine.

After staring at the jug, he shook his head. "No," he said. "That is wine of Makuran. If we are to learn what the Avtokrator of the Videssians has in his mind, Videssian wine is a better choice."

"I can see that," Abivard said with a judicious nod. He raised his voice: "Venizelos!" When the steward came into the chamber, he told him, "Fetch me a jar of Videssian wine from the cellar." Venizelos bowed and left, returning shortly with an earthenware jar taller and slimmer than the one Bozorg had brought from Mashiz. He set it on the table in front of the wizard, then disappeared as if made to vanish by one of Bozorg's cantrips.

Abivard wondered if a Videssian mage might not serve better than a Makuraner one, too. He shook his head. He couldn't trust Panteles, not for this.

Bozorg used a knife to cut through the pitch sealing the stopper in place. When the stopper was freed, he yanked it out and poured the white bowl nearly full of wine as red as blood. He also poured a small libation onto the floor for each of the Prophets Four.

He opened one of the jars—there was no pitch on its stopper— and spilled out a glittering powder from it into the palm of his hand. "Finely ground silver," he explained, "perhaps a quarter of an arket's worth. When polished, silver makes the finest mirrors: Unlike bronze or even gold, it adds no color of its own to the images it reflects. Thus, it also offers the best hope of an accurate and successful sorcerous view of what lies ahead."

So saying, he sprinkled the silver over the wine, chanting as he did so. It was not the ritual Tanshar had used in his scrying but seemed a shoot from a different branch of the same tree.

The powdered silver did not sink but stayed on the surface of the wine; Abivard got the idea that the incantation Bozorg had made had something to do with that. The mage said, "Now we wait for everything to become perfectly still." Abivard nodded; that, too, was akin to what the wizard from the village under Vek Rud stronghold had done.

"Will you tell me what you see?" he asked. "When the bowl is ready, I mean."

Bozorg shook his head. "No. This is a different conjuration. You will look into the bowl yourself and see—whatever is there to be seen. I may see something in the depths of the wine, too, but it will not be what you see."

"Very well," Abivard said. Waiting came with dealing with wizards. Bozorg studied the surface of the wine with a hunting hawk's intensity. At last, with a sudden sharp gesture, he beckoned Abivard forward.

Holding his breath so he wouldn't spoil the reflective surface, Abivard peered down into the bowl. Though his eyes told him the floating specks of silver were not moving, he somehow sensed them spinning, spiraling faster and faster till they seemed to cover the wine with a mirror that gave back first his face and the beams of the ceiling and then—

He saw fighting in mountain country, two armies of armored horsemen smashing against each other. One of the forces flew the red-lion banner of Makuran. Try as he would, he could not make out the standards under which the other side fought. He wondered if this was a glimpse of the future or of the past: he'd sent his mobile force into the southeastern hill country of the Videssian westlands, trying to quell raiders. His success had been less complete than he'd hoped.

Without warning, the scene shifted. Again he saw mountains. These, at a guess, were in hotter, drier country than those of the previous vision: the hooves of the horses strung out in the line of march kicked up sand at every step. The soldiers atop those horses were unmistakably Videssians. Off in the distance—to the south?—the sun sparkled off a blue, blue sea filled with ships.

There was another shift of scene. He saw more fighting, this time between Makuraners and Videssians. In the middle distance a town with a mud-brick wall stood on a hill that rose abruptly from flat farmland. *That's somewhere in the land of the Thousand Cities,* Abivard thought. The settlements there were so ancient that these days they sat atop mounts built up of centuries' worth of accumulated rubble. Again, he might have been seeing the future or the past. Videssians under Maniakes had fought Smerdis' Makuraners between the Tutub and the Tib to help return Sharbaraz to the throne.

The scene shifted once more. Now he had come full circle, for he found his point of vision back at Across, staring over the Cattle Crossing toward Videssos the city. He could see none of the dromons that had held his army away from the imperial capital. Suddenly, something flashed silver across the water. He knew that signal: the signal to attack. He would—

The wine in the bowl bubbled and roiled as if coming to a boil. Whatever it had been about to show Abivard vanished then; it was once more merely wine. Bozorg smacked his right fist into his left palm in frustration. "My scrying was detected," he said, angry at himself or at the Videssian mage who had thwarted him or maybe both at once. "The God grant you saw enough to suit you, lord."

"Almost," Abivard said. "Aye, almost. You confirmed for me that the 'narrow sea' of a prophecy I had years ago is indeed the Cattle Crossing, but whether the prophecy proves to be for good or ill I still do not know."

"I would hesitate before I sought to learn that, lord," Bozorg said. "The Videssian mages will now be alerted to my presence and watchful lest I try to sneak another scrying spell past them. For now, letting them ease back into sloth is the wiser course."

"Let it be as you say," Abivard answered. "I've gone without knowing the answer to that riddle for a long time now. A little longer won't matter—if in fact I can learn it before the event itself. Sometimes foreseeing is best viewed from behind, if you take my meaning."

Before, Bozorg had shown him flattery. Now the wizard bowed with what seemed genuine respect. "Lord, if you know so much, the God has granted you wisdom beyond that of most men. Knowing the future is different from being able to change it or even to recognize it until it is upon you."

Abivard laughed at himself. "If I were as wise as all that, I wouldn't have asked for the glimpses you just showed me. And if you were as wise as all that, you wouldn't have spent time and effort learning how to show me those glimpses." He laughed again. "And if the Videssians were as wise as all that, they wouldn't have tried to keep me from seeing those glimpses, either. After all, what can I do about them if the future is already set?'

"Only what you have seen—whatever that may be—is certain, lord," Bozorg warned. "What happened before, what may come after—those are hidden and so remain mutable."

"Ah. I understand," Abivard replied. "So if I saw, say, a huge Videssian army marching on me, I would still have the choice of either setting an ambush against it or fleeing to save my skin."

"Exactly so." Bozorg's head bobbed up and down in approval. "Neither of those is preordained from what you saw by the scrying: they depend on the strength of your own spirit."

"Even if I do set the ambush, though, I also have no guarantee ahead of time that it will succeed," Abivard said.

Bozorg nodded again. "Not unless you saw yourself succeeding."

Abivard plucked at his beard. "Could a man who was, say, both rich and fearful have a scryer show him great chunks of his life to come so he would know what dangers to avoid?"

"Rich, fearful, foolish men have indeed tried this many times over the years," Bozorg said with a scornful curl of his lip worthy of Tzikas. "What good does it do them? Any danger they do so see is one they cannot avoid, by the very nature of things."

"If I saw myself making what had to be a dreadful error," Abivard said after more thought, "when the time came, I would struggle against that course with all my might."

"No doubt you would struggle," Bozorg agreed, "and no doubt you would also fail. Your later self, having knowledge that the you who watched the scryer lacked, would assuredly find some reason for doing that which was earlier reckoned a disaster in the making—or might simply forget the scrying till, too late, he realized that the foretold event had come to pass."

Abivard chewed on that for a while, then gave it up with a shake of his head. "Too complex for my poor, dull wits. We might as well be a couple of Videssian priests arguing about which of the countless ways to worship their Phos is the single right and proper one. By the God, good Bozorg, I swear that one flyspeck on a theological manuscript of theirs can spawn three new heresies."

"They know not the truth and so are doomed to quarrel endlessly over how the false is false," Bozorg said with a distinct sniff, "and to drop into the Void once their foolish lives have passed."

Abivard was tempted to lock Bozorg and Artanas the hierarch in a room together to see which—if either—came out sane. Sometimes, though, one had to sacrifice personal pleasure for the good of the cause.

Bozorg bowed. "Will there be anything more, lord?"

"No, you may go," Abivard answered. "Thank you for your service to me."

"It is my pleasure, my privilege, my honor to serve a commander of such great accomplishment, one who excites the admiration of all who know of him," Bozorg said. "Truly you are the great wild boar of Makuran, trampling down and tearing all her foes." With a final bow the wizard reassembled his sorcerous paraphernalia, loaded it back into the saddlebags in which it had traveled from Mashiz, and took his leave.

As soon as his footsteps faded down the hall, Abivard let out a long sigh. This sorcerer wasn't a Tanshar in the making, either, being both oily as what the Videssians squeezed from olives and argumentative to boot. Abivard shrugged. If Bozorg proved competent, he'd overlook a great deal.

Abivard's marshals sprang to their feet to greet him. He went down their ranks accepting kisses on the cheek. A couple of his subordinates were men of the Seven Clans; under most circumstances he would have kissed them on the cheek, not the other way around. They might even have given him trouble about that had he been placed in command of them—were his sister not Sharbaraz's principal wife. As brother-in-law to the King of Kings, he unquestionably outranked them. They might resent that, but they could not deny it.

Romezan was a scion of the Seven Clans, but he had never given Abivard an instant's trouble over rank. Thick-shouldered rather than lean like most Makuraners, he was a bull of a man, the tips of whose waxed mustaches swept out like a bull's horns. All he wanted was more of Videssos than Makuran had yet taken. As he did at every officers' gathering, he said, "How can we get across that miserable little stretch of water, lord?"

"I could piss across it, I think, if I stood on the seashore there," another general said. Kardarigan was no high noble; like Abivard, he was a *dihqan* from the Northwest, one of so many young men forced into positions of importance when their fathers and brothers had died on the Pardrayan steppe.

Romezan leered at him. "You're not hung so well as that." Laughter rose from the Makuraner commanders.

"How do you know?" Kardarigan retorted, and the laughter got louder. The generals had reason to make free with their merriment. Up to the Cattle Crossing they'd swept all before them. Sharbaraz might be unhappy because they'd not done more, but they knew how much they had done.

"We must have marble in our heads instead of brains," Abivard said, "not being able to figure out how to beat the Videssians, even if only for a little while, and get our men and engines across to the eastern shore. Can we but set our engines against the walls of Videssos the city, we will take it." How many times had he said that?

"If that accursed Videssian traitor had built us a navy instead of stringing us along with promises, we might have been able to do it by now," Romezan said.

That accursed Videssian traitor. Abivard wondered what Tzikas would have done had he heard the judgment against him. Whatever he thought, he wouldn't have shown it on the outside. It would have to hurt, though. The Makuraners might use him, but he would never win their trust or respect.

A messenger, his face filthy with road dust, came hurrying up to Abivard. Bowing low, he said, "Your pardon, lord, but I bear an urgent dispatch from the *marzban* of Vaspurakan."

"What does Vshnasp want with me?" Abivard asked. Up till then Sharbaraz's governor of Vaspurakan had done his best to pretend that Abivard did not exist.

He accepted the oiled-leather message tube, opened it, and broke the wax seal on the letter inside with a thumbnail. As he read the sheet of parchment he'd unrolled, his eyebrows climbed toward his hairline. When he was through, he raised his head and spoke to his expectantly waiting officers: "Mikhran *marzban* requests—begs—our aid. Vshnasp *marzban* is dead. The Vaspurakaners have risen against him and against the worship of the God. If we don't come to his rescue at once, Mikhran says, the whole province will be lost."

A bivard stormed through the corridors of his residence. Venizelos started to say something to him but got a good look at his face and flattened himself against the wall to let his master pass.

Roshnani was embroidering fancy flowers on a caftan of winter-weight wool. She glanced up when Abivard came into the chamber where she was working, then bent her head to the embroidery once more.

"I told anyone who would listen that we should have left the Vaspurakaners to their own misguided cult," he ground out. "But no! We have to ram the God down their throats, too! And now look what it's gotten us."

"Yes, you told anyone who would listen," Roshnani said. "No one back in Mashiz listened. Are you surprised? Is this the first time such a thing has happened? Of course it's not. Besides, with Vshnasp over them, it's no wonder the Vaspurakaner princes decided to revolt."

"All the Vaspurakaners style themselves princes—the God alone knows why," Abivard said, a little less furious than he had been a moment before. He looked thoughtfully at his wife—his principal wife, he supposed he should have thought, but he'd been away from the others so long that he'd almost forgotten them. "Do you mean the Vaspurakaners would have rebelled even if we hadn't tried to impose the God on them?"

Roshnani nodded. "Aye, though maybe not so soon. Vshnasp had a reputation in Mashiz as a seducer. I don't suppose he would have stopped that just because he was sent to Vaspurakan."

"Mm, likely not," Abivard agreed. "Things were better with the old ways firmly in place, don't you think?"

"Better for men, certainly," Roshnani said, unusual sharpness in her voice. "If you ask the wives who spent their lives locked away in the women's quarters of strongholds and saw no more of the world than what the view out their windows happened to give, you might find them singing a different tune." She gave him a sidelong smile—she had never been one to stay in a bad humor. "Besides, husband of mine, are you not pleased to be on the cutting edge of fashion?"

"Now that you mention it, no," Abivard answered. Roshnani made a face at him. Like it or not, though, he and Sharbaraz *were* on the cutting edge of fashion. Giving their principal wives leave to emerge on occasion from the women's quarters had set long-frozen Makuraner usage on its ear. At first, ten years ago now, men had called noblewomen who appeared in public harlots merely for letting themselves be seen. But when the King of Kings and his most successful general set a trend, others would and did follow it.

"Besides," Roshnani said, "even under the old way, a man determined enough might find out how to sneak into the women's quarters for a little while, or a woman to sneak out of them."

"Never mind that," Abivard said. "Vshnasp won't sneak in now, nor women out to him. If such sneakings were what touched off the Vaspurakaner revolt, I wish some of the princes had caught him inside and made him into a eunuch so he would stay there without endangering anyone's chastity, including his own."

"You *are* angry at him," Roshnani observed. "A man says he wants to see another man made a eunuch only when his rage is full and deep."

"You're right, but that doesn't matter, either," Abivard answered. "Vshnasp is in the God's hands now, not mine, and if the God should drop his miserable soul into the Void . . ." He shook his head. Vshnasp *didn't* matter. He had to remember that. The hideous mess the late *marzban* of Vaspurakan had left behind was something else again.

As she often did, his wife thought along with him. "How

much of our force here in the westlands will you have to take
to Vaspurakan to bring the princes back under the rule of the
King of Kings?" she asked.

"Too much," he said, "but I have no choice. We ought to hold
the Videssian westlands, but we must hold Vaspurakan. We draw
iron and silver and lead from the mines there and also a little
gold. When times are friendlier than this, we draw horsemen,
too. And if we don't control the east-west valleys, Videssos will.
Whoever does control them has in his hands the best invasion
routes to the other fellow's country."

"Maniakes has Vaspurakaner blood, not so?" Roshnani said.

Abivard nodded. "He does, and I wouldn't be the least surprised
to find the Empire behind this uprising, either."

"Neither would I," Roshnani said. "It's what I'd do in his sandals. He doesn't dare come fight us face to face, so he stirs up
trouble behind our backs." She thought for a moment. "How large
a garrison do you purpose leaving behind here in Across?" Her
voice was curiously expressionless.

"I've been chewing on that," Abivard answered. The face he
made said that he didn't like what he'd been chewing. "I don't
think I'm going to leave anyone. We'll need a good part of the
field force to put down the princes, and on the far side of the
Cattle Crossing the Videssians have soldiers to spare to gobble
up any small garrison I leave here. Especially after they beat
the Kubratoi earlier this summer, I don't want to hand them
a cheap victory that would make them feel they can meet us
and win. It's almost sorcery: if they feel that, it's halfway to
being true."

He waited for Roshnani to explode like a covered pot left too
long in the fire. She surprised him by nodding. "Good," she said.
"I was going to suggest that, but I was afraid you'd be angry at
me. I think you're right—you'd be throwing away any men you
leave here."

"I think I'll name you my second in command," Abivard said,
and that got him a smile. He gave it back, then quickly sobered.
"After we leave, though, the Videssians will come back anyhow.
One of my officers is bound to write to Sharbaraz about that,
and Sharbaraz is bound to write to me." He rolled his eyes. "One
more thing to look forward to."

✦　　✦　　✦

A wagon rolled up in front of the residence that had belonged to the Videssian logothete of the treasury. Abivard's children swarmed aboard it with cries of delight. "A house that moves!" Shahin exclaimed. None of them remembered what living in such a cramped space for weeks at a time was like. They'd find out. Roshnani did remember all too well. She climbed into the wagon with much less enthusiasm than her offspring showed.

Venizelos, Livania, and the rest of the Videssian servants stood in front of the house. The steward went to one knee in front of Abivard. "The lord with the great and good mind grant you health and safety, most eminent sir," the steward said.

"I thank you," Abivard answered, though he noted that Venizelos had not prayed that Phos grant him success. "Perhaps one day we'll see each other—I expect so, at any rate."

"Perhaps," was all Venizelos said. He did not want to think about the Makuraners' return to Across.

Abivard handed him a small heavy leather sack, gave Livania another, and went down the line of servants with more. Their thanks were loud and effusive. He could have forced them to go along with him. For that matter, he could have had them killed for the sport of it. The coins inside the sack were silver arkets of Makuran, not Videssian goldpieces. The servants would probably grumble about that once he was out of earshot. Again, though, he could have done far worse.

He swung up onto his horse, a stalwart bay gelding. With knees and reins, he urged the animal into a walk. The wagon driver, a skinny fellow named Pashang, flicked the reins of the two-horse team. Clattering, its ungreased axles squealing, the wagon rattled after Abivard.

Abivard's soldiers had broken camp many times. They were used to it. The loose women they'd picked up and the Videssian servants they'd swept up were another matter altogether. The army was late setting out. Abivard willingly forgave that on the first day. Afterward, he'd start jettisoning stragglers. He also suspected that the racket his force made could be heard in Videssos the city on the far side of the Cattle Crossing.

That didn't much worry him. If Maniakes couldn't hear the Makuraner army departing, he'd be able to see it. If he didn't watch personally, the captains of those accursed dromons would notice that the camp at the edge of Across had been abandoned.

Abivard had thought about leaving men behind to light fires and simulate one more night's occupancy. What point was there to it, though? Already, very likely, men were slipping into little rowboats they'd hidden from the Makuraners and hurrying across the strait to tell the Avtokrator everything they knew. He wouldn't have been a bit surprised to learn that Venizelos was one of those men.

At last, far more slowly than he'd hoped, his force shook itself out into something that approximated its future line of march. Light cavalry, archers riding unarmored horses and wearing no more protection than helms and leather jerkins themselves, formed the vanguard, the rear guard, and scouting parties to either flank.

Within that screen of light cavalry rode the heavy horsemen who made the red lion of Makuran so feared. Neither riders nor horses were armored now, for Abivard did not expect battle any time soon. The weight of iron warriors and beasts carried into battle was plenty to exhaust the horses if they tried bearing it day in, day out. The riders still bore their long lances in the sockets on the right side of their saddles, though, even if their armor was wrapped and stored in the supply wagons.

Those, along with the wagons carrying noncombatants, made up the core of the army in motion. If Abivard suddenly had to fight, he would maneuver to put his force between the baggage train and the foe, regardless of the direction from which the foe came.

He ordered the army southwest on the first day's march, away from the coast. He did not want Maniakes' dromons watching every move he made and reporting back to the Avtokrator. He assumed that Maniakes already knew he was heading off to avenge Vshnasp. How fast was he going, and by what route? That was his business, not Maniakes'.

Peasants who had been busy in the fields took one look at the outriders to Abivard's army and did their best to make themselves invisible. Any who lived near high ground fled there. Those who didn't either hid in their houses or ran off with their wives and families and beasts of burden and whatever they could carry on their backs or those of their oxen and donkeys and horses.

"Take what you need from those who have run away," Abivard told his men, "but don't go setting fires for the sport of it." Some of the warriors grumbled; incendiarism was one of the sports that made war entertaining.

All was quiet the first night on the march and the second. On the third night someone—a couple of someones—sneaked past the sentries and lobbed arrows into the Makuraner camp. The archers wounded two men and escaped under cover of darkness.

"They will not play the game that way," Abivard declared when the unwelcome news reached him. "Tomorrow we burn everything along the line of march."

"Well done, lord," Romezan boomed. "We should have been doing that all along. If the Videssians fear us, they'll leave us alone."

"But if they hate us, they'll keep on hitting back at us no matter what we do," Kardarigan said. "It's a fine line we walk between being frightful and being despised."

"I was willing to treat them mildly," Abivard answered, "but if they shoot at us from ambush out of the night, I won't waste much sympathy on them, either. Actions have consequences."

Smoke from a great burning rose the next day. Abivard supposed that sailors on Videssian dromons, looking in from the waters of the Videssian Sea, could use that smoke to figure out where his army was. That made him regret having given the order, but only a little: Maniakes would have learned his whereabouts soon enough, anyhow.

When darkness fell, several more men shot at the encamped Makuraners. This time Abivard's troops were alert and ready. They swarmed out into the night after the bowmen and caught three of them. The Videssians were a long time dying. Most of the soldiers slept soundly through their shrieks.

Abivard ordered another day of burning when morning came. Kardarigan said, "If we trade frightfulness for frightfulness, where will this end?"

"We can hurt the Videssian in the westlands worse than they can hurt us," Abivard told him. "The sooner they get that idea, the sooner we can stop giving them lessons."

"Videssians are supposed to be a clever folk—you'd certainly think so from hearing them talk about themselves," Romezan added. "If they're too stupid to see that raids against the armies of the King of Kings are more trouble than they're worth, whose hard luck is it? Not ours, by the God. Drop me into the Void if I can work up much sympathy for 'em."

For the next couple of days the local Videssians left the Makura-ner army alone as it passed through their land. Abivard didn't know what happened after that; maybe his men outrode the news of what they did to the countryside when someone harassed them. Whatever the reason, the Videssians again took to shooting at the army by night.

The next day the Makuraners sent pillars of smoke billowing up to the sky. The day after that the Videssians caught two men from the vanguard away from the rest, cut their throats, and left them where the rest of the Makuraners would find them. That afternoon a medium-size Videssian village abruptly ceased to be.

"Lovely sort of fighting," Kardarigan remarked as Abivard's army made camp for the night. "I wish Maniakes would come forth and meet us. Fighting a real battle against real soldiers would be a relief."

"Wait till we get to Vaspurakan," Abivard told him. "The princes will be happy enough to oblige you."

Dispatches from Mikhran reached Abivard every day. The *marzban* kept urging him not to delay, to rush, to storm, to come to his rescue. All that proved to Abivard was that Mikhran hadn't yet received his first letter promising aid. He began to wonder if his courier had gotten through. If the Videssians harassed his army, what did they do to lone dispatch riders? On the other hand, if they habitually ambushed couriers, how did the ones Mikhran sent keep reaching him?

The army forded the Eriza River not far south of its head-waters. The Eriza would grow to become a stream of consid-erable importance, joining the Arandos to become the largest river system in the Videssian westlands. A bridge spanned the river a couple of farsangs south of the ford, or, rather, a bridge had spanned it. Abivard remembered watching it go up in flames as the Videssians had tried to halt his army's advance in one of the early campaigns in the westlands. It had yet to be repaired.

Tzikas remembered the bridge burning, too; he'd ordered it set afire. "You didn't know about the ford then, brother-in-law to the King of Kings," he said, still proud of his stratagem.

"That's so, eminent sir," Abivard agreed. "But if I'd pressed on instead of swinging south, I would have found out about it. The local peasants would have given it away, if for no other reason than to keep us from eating them out of house and home."

"Peasants." Tzikas let out a scornful snort amazingly like the one his horse would have produced. "That's hardly a fit way to run a war."

"I thought you Videssians were the ones who seized whatever worked and we Makuraners were more concerned with honor," Abivard said.

"Give me horsemen, brother-in-law to the King of Kings," Tzikas answered. "I will show you where honor lies and how to pursue it. How can you deny me now, when we shall no longer be facing Videssians but heretical big-nosed men of Vaspurakan? Let me serve the King of Kings, may his years be long and his realm increase, and let me serve the cause of Hosios Avtokrator."

Whatever the topic of conversation, Tzikas was adept at turning it toward his own desires. "Let us draw closer to Vaspurakan," Abivard said. The Videssian turncoat scowled at him, but what could he do? He lived on sufferance; Abivard was under no obligation to give him anything at all, let alone his heart's desire.

And while Tzikas scornfully dismissed the Vaspurakaners as heretics now, might he not suddenly develop or discover the view that they were in fact his coreligionists? Down under the skin, weren't Phos worshipers Phos worshipers come what may? If he did something of that sort, he would surely do it at the worst possible moment, too.

"You do not trust me," Tzikas said mournfully. "Since the days of Likinios Avtokrator, may Phos' light shine upon him, no one has trusted me."

There were good and cogent reasons for that, too, Abivard thought. He'd met Likinios. The Videssian Emperor had been devious enough for any four other people he'd ever known. If anyone could have been confident of outmaneuvering Tzikas at need, he was the man. After fighting against Tzikas, after accepting him as a fugitive upon his failure to assassinate Maniakes, Abivard thought himself justified in exercising caution where the Videssian was concerned.

Seeing that he would get no immediate satisfaction, Tzikas gave Abivard a curt nod and rode off. His stiff back said louder than words how indignant he was at having his probity questioned constantly.

Romezan watched him depart, then came up to Abivard and asked, "Who stuck the red-hot poker up his arse?"

"I did, I'm afraid," Abivard answered. "I just don't want to give him the regiment he keeps begging of me."

"Good," Romezan said. "The God keep him from being at my back the day I need help. He'd stand there smiling, hiding a knife in the sleeve of his robe. No thank you."

"Sooner or later he *will* write to Sharbaraz," Abivard said gloomily. "Odds are, too, that his request will get me ordered to give him everything his cold little heart desires."

"The God prevent!" Romezan's fingers twisted in an apotropaic sign. "If that does happen, he could always have an accident."

"Like the one Maniakes almost had, you mean?" Abivard asked. Romezan nodded. Abivard sighed. "That could happen, I suppose, though the idea doesn't much appeal to me. I keep hoping he'll want to be useful in some kind of way where I won't have to watch my back every minute to make sure he's not sliding that knife you were talking about between my ribs."

"The only use he's been so far is to embarrass Maniakes," Romezan said. "He doesn't even do that well anymore; the more the Videssians hear about how we came to acquire him, the more they think we're welcome to him."

"The King of Kings puts great stock in Videssian traitors," Abivard said. "Having had his throne usurped by treachery, he knows what damage it can do to a ruler."

"If the King of Kings is so fond of Videssian traitors, why don't we ship Tzikas off to Mashiz?" Romezan grumbled. But that was no answer, and he and Abivard both knew it. If Sharbaraz King of Kings expected them to encourage and abet Videssian traitors, they had to do it no matter how much Tzikas raised their hackles.

The road swung up from the coastal lowlands onto the central plateau. Resaina lay near the northern edge of the plateau, about a third of the way from the crossing of the Eriza to Vaspurakan. Like most good-sized Videssian towns, it had a Makuraner garrison quartered within its walls.

A plump, graying fellow named Gorgin commanded the garrison. "I've heard somewhat of the Vaspurakaners' outrages, lord," he said. "By the God, it does my heart good to see you ready to chastise them with all the force at your command."

Abivard sliced a bite of meat from the leg of mutton Gorgin had served him—cooked with garlic in the Videssian fashion instead of Makuraner style with mint. He stabbed the chunk and brought it to his mouth with the dagger. While chewing, he remarked, "I notice you do not volunteer the men of your command to join in this chastisement."

"I have not enough men here to hold down the city and the countryside against a real revolt," Gorgin answered. "If you take some of my soldiers from me, how shall I be able to defend Resaina against any sort of trouble whatever? These mad easterners riot at the drop of a skullcap. If someone who fancies himself a theologian rises among 'em, I won't be able to put 'em down."

"Are you enforcing the edict ordering their holy men to preach the Vaspurakaner rite?" Abivard asked.

"Aye, I have been," Gorgin told him. "That's one of the reasons I feared riots. Then, a few weeks ago, the Videssians, may they fall into the Void, stopped complaining about the rite."

"That's good news," Abivard said.

"I *thought* so," Gorgin replied gloomily. "But now my spies report the reason why they accept the Vaspurakaners' rituals: it's because the men from the mountains have revolted against us. The Videssians admire them for doing it because they'd like to get free of our yoke, too."

"You're right," Abivard said. "I don't fancy that, not even a little bit. What are we supposed to do about it, though? If we order them to go back to their old rituals, we not only disobey Sharbaraz King of Kings, may his days be long and his realm increase, we also make ourselves look ridiculous to the Videssians."

"We don't want that, let me tell you," Gorgin said. "They're hard enough to govern even when they know they have good reason to fear us. When they're laughing at us behind our backs, they're impossible. They'll do any harebrained thing to stir up trouble, but half the time their schemes end up not being harebrained at all. They find more ways to drive me crazy than I'd ever imagined." He shook his head with the bewildered air of a man who knew he was in too deep.

"After we beat the Vaspurakaners, the Videssians will see that the revolt didn't amount to anything," Abivard answered. "As soon as they realize that, the princes will look like heretics again, not heroes."

"The God grant it be so," Gorgin said.

A moment later Abivard discovered that not all Videssians willingly accepted the Vaspurakaner liturgy. "Torture! Heresy! Mayhem!" a man shrieked as he ran into Gorgin's residence.

The garrison commander jerked as if stuck by a pin, then exchanged a glance full of apprehension with Abivard. Both men got to their feet. "What have they gone and done now?" Gorgin asked, plainly meaning, *What new disaster has fallen on my head?*

But the disaster had fallen on the head of a Videssian priest, not that of Gorgin. The fellow sat in an antechamber, his shaved scalp and part of his forehead puffy and splashed here and there with dried blood. "You see?" cried the Videssian who had brought him in. "Do you see? They captured him, kidnapped him, however you like, and then they—" He pointed.

Abivard did see. The swelling and the blood came from the words that had been tattooed into the priest's head. Abivard read Videssian only haltingly. After some study, he gathered that the words came from a theological text attacking the Vaspurakaners and their beliefs. The priest would wear those passages for the rest of his life.

"Do you see?" Gorgin exclaimed, as the local had before him. "Every time you think you have their measure, the Videssians do something like this. Or something not like this but just as hideous, just as unimaginable, in a different way."

"We may even be able to make this outrage work to our advantage," Abivard said. "Take this fellow out and show him off after he heals. We can make him out to be a martyr to his version—our version—of the Videssians' false faith. When you take the heads of the men who did this, people will say they had it coming."

"Mm, yes, that's not bad," Gorgin said after a moment's thought. He looked at the priest who had just become, however unwillingly, a walking religious tract. "If he'd let his hair grow out, after a while you'd only be able to see a little of that."

He and Abivard had both been using their own language, assuming that the Videssian priest did not speak it. He proved them wrong, saying in fair Makuraner, "A bare scalp is the mark of the good god's servant. I shall wear these lying texts with pride, as a badge of holiness."

"On your head be it," Abivard said. The priest merely nodded.

Gorgin stared at him as if he'd said something horrid. After a moment he realized he had.

The Videssian central plateau put Abivard in mind of the country not far from Vek Rud domain. It was a little better watered and a little more broken up by hills and valleys than the territory in which he'd grown up, but it was mostly herding country, not farmland, and so had a familiar feel to it.

He didn't think much of the herds of cattle and flocks of sheep moving slowly over the grasslands. Any *dihqan* back in Makuran would have been ashamed to admit he owned such a handful of ragged, scraggly beasts. Of course, the flocks and herds of Makuran hadn't been devastated by years of civil war and invasion.

The Videssians certainly thought like their Makuraner counterparts. As soon as they got wind of the approach of Abivard's army, they tried to get their animals as far out of the way as they could. Foraging parties had to scatter widely to bring in the beasts that helped keep the army fed.

"That's the way," Romezan said when the soldiers led in a good many sheep one afternoon when the highlands of Makuran were beginning to push their way up over the western horizon. "If they won't give us what we need, we'll bloody well take it—and we'll take so much, we'll make the Videssians, crazed as they are with their false Phos, take starvation for a virtue because they'll see so much of it."

"These lands are subject to the rule of Sharbaraz King of Kings and so may not be wantonly oppressed," Abivard reminded him. But then he softened that by adding, "If the choice lies between our doing without and theirs, we ought not to be the ones going hungry."

From the west Mikhran *marzban* still bombarded him with letters urging haste. From the east he heard nothing. He wondered if Maniakes had retaken Across and whether Venizelos had resumed his post as steward to the logothete of the treasury.

Farrokh-Zad, one of Kardarigan's lieutenants, said, "Let your spirits not be cast down, lord, for surely this fool of a Maniakes, seeing us departed, will overreach himself as has been his habit of old. After vanquishing the vile Vaspurakaners, with their noses like sickles and their beards like thickets of wire, we shall return and take from the Videssian whatever paltry parts of the westlands he may steal from us. For are we not the men of Makuran, the mighty men whom the God delights to honor?"

He puffed out his chest, twirled the waxed tip of his mustache, and struck a fierce pose, dark eyes glittering. He was younger than Abivard and far more arrogant: Abivard had been on the point of laughing at his magniloquent bombast when he realized that Farrokh-Zad was in earnest.

"May Fraortish eldest of all ask the God to grant your prayers," Abivard said, and let it go at that. Farrokh-Zad nodded and rode off, a procession of one. Abivard stared after him. Farrokh-Zad probably hadn't set foot in Makuran since his beard had come in fully, but being away hadn't seemed to change his attitudes in the slightest. Those had probably set as hard as cast bronze before he had gotten big enough to defy his mother.

About half the officers in the army were like that; Romezan was a leader among them. They clung to the usages they'd always known even when those usages fit like a boy's caftan on a grown man. Abivard snorted. He was in the other faction, the ones who had taken on so many foreign ways that they hardly seemed like Makuraners anymore. If they ever did go home to stay, they were liable to be white crows in a black flock. But then, Abivard thought, he'd been getting around Makuraner traditions since the day he had decided to let Roshnani come along when he and Sharbaraz had launched their civil war against Smerdis the usurper.

Such concerns vanished a little later, for an armored rider approached the Makuraner army from the west, carrying a white-painted shield of truce. He was not a Videssian, although the army was still on what had been Videssian soil, but a warrior of Vaspurakan—a noble, by his horse and his gear.

Abivard had the fellow brought before him. He studied the Vaspurakaner with interest: he was not a tall man but thick-shouldered, with a barrel chest and strong arms. Abivard would not have cared to wrestle with him; he made even the bulky Romezan svelte by comparison. His features were strong and heavy, with bushy eyebrows that came together above a nose of truly majestic proportions. His thick beard, black lightly frosted with gray, spilled down over the front of his scale mail shirt and grew up to within a finger's breadth of his eyes. He looked brooding and powerful.

When he spoke, Abivard expected a bass rumble like falling

rocks. Instead, his voice was a pleasant, melodious baritone: "I greet you, Abivard son of Godarz, brother-in-law to Sharbaraz King of Kings, may his years be many and his realm increase," he said in Makuraner fluent enough but flavored by a throaty accent quite different from the Videssian lisp to which Abivard had grown used. "I am Gazrik son of Bardzrabol, and I have authority to speak for the princes of Vaspurakan."

"I greet you, Gazrik son of Bardzrabol," Abivard said, doing his best to imitate the way the Vaspurakaner pronounced his name and that of his father. "Speak, then. Enlarge yourself; say what is in your mind. My ears and my heart are open to you."

"You are as gracious as men say, lord, than which what compliment could be higher?" Gazrik replied. He and Abivard exchanged another round of compliments, and another. Abivard offered wine; Gazrik accepted. He took from a saddlebag a round pastry made with chopped dates and sprinkled over with powdered sugar; Abivard pronounced it delicious, and did not tell him the Videssians called such Vaspurakaner confections "princes' balls." At last, the courtesies completed, Gazrik began to come to the point. "Know, lord, that the cause of peace would be better served if you turned this host of yours aside from Vaspurakan, the princes' land, the heroes' land."

"Know, Gazrik son of Bardzrabol, the cause of peace would be better served if you left off your rebellion against Mikhran *marzban* and handed over to him the vile and vicious wretches responsible for the assassination of his predecessor, Vshnasp *marzban*."

Gazrik shook his head; Abivard was reminded of a black bear up in the Dilbat Mountains in back of Mashiz unexpectedly coming upon a man. The Vaspurakaner said, "Lord, we do not repent that Vshnasp *marzban* is dead. He was an evil man, and his rule over us was full of evils."

"Sharbaraz King of Kings set him over you. You were in law bound to obey him," Abivard answered.

"Had he stayed in law, obey him we would have," Gazrik said. "But you, lord, if a man took women all unwilling from your women's quarters for his own pleasure, what would you do?"

"I do not know that Vshnasp did any such thing," Abivard said, deliberately not thinking of some of the reports he'd heard. "A man's enemies will lie to make him seem worse than he is."

Gazrik snorted, not a horselike sound but almost the abrupt, coughing roar of a lion. Abivard had rarely heard such scorn. "Have that however you will, lord," the Vaspurakaner said. "But I tell you this also: any man who seeks to lead the princes away from Phos who first made Vaspur, that man shall die and spend eternity in Skotos' ice. If you help those who would force this on us, we shall fight you, too."

Uneasily, Abivard answered, "Sharbaraz King of Kings has ordained this course. So he has ordered; so shall it be."

"No," Gazrik said—just the one word, impossible to contradict. He went on in an earnest voice: "We were loyal subjects to the King of Kings. We paid him tribute in iron and silver and gold; our soldiers fought in his wars. We would do this again, did he not interfere in our faith."

Abivard hoped his frown concealed what he was thinking, for he agreed with Gazrik and had tried to persuade Sharbaraz to follow the course the Vaspurakaner had suggested. But the King of Kings had not agreed, which meant Abivard had to conform to the policy Sharbaraz had set regardless of what he thought of it. Abivard said, "The Videssians make all their subjects worship in the same way: as they have one empire, so they also have one religion. Sharbaraz King of Kings has decreed this a good arrangement for Makuran as well. Let all worship the God; let all acknowledge the power of the King of Kings."

Gazrik stared down his nose at him—and a fine nose for staring down it was, too. With magnificent contempt the Vaspurakaner said, "And if the Avtokrator of the Videssians chose to leap off a cliff, would Sharbaraz King of Kings likewise cast himself down from a promontory?" By his tone, he hoped it would be so.

Several of the Makuraner generals behind Abivard growled angrily. "Hold your tongue, you insolent dog!" Romezan said.

"Some day we may meet without shield of truce, noble from the Seven Clans," Gazrik answered. "Then we shall see which of us teaches the other manners." He turned back to Abivard. "Brother-in-law to the King of Kings, Mikhran *marzban* holds only the valley containing the fortress of Poskh, and not all of that. If he will withdraw and leave us in peace, we will give him leave to go. This will let you turn back to the east and go on with your war against Videssos. But if he would stay and you would go on, we shall have war between us."

The trouble was that Abivard saw the course Gazrik proposed

as most expedient for Makuran. He exhaled slowly and angrily. He could either obey Sharbaraz in spite of thinking him mistaken or rebel against the King of Kings. He'd seen enough of rebellion both in Makuran and in a Videssos too ravaged by uprising after uprising to oppose the forces of the King of Kings.

And so, wishing he could do otherwise, he said, "Gazrik son of Bardzrabol, if you are wise, you will disband your armies, have your men go home to the valleys where they were born, and beg Sharbaraz King of Kings to show you mercy on the grounds that you rebelled against his appointed *marzban* only because of the outrages he committed against your women. Then perhaps you will have peace. If you continue in arms against Sharbaraz King of Kings, know that we his soldiers shall grind you as the millstones grind wheat into flour, and the wind will blow you away like chaff."

"We have war now," Gazrik said. "We shall have more. You will pay in blood for every foot you advance into the princes' land." He bowed in the saddle to Romezan. "When the time comes, we shall see who speaks of insolence and of dogs. Skotos hollows a place in the eternal ice for you even now."

"May the Void swallow you—and so it shall," Romezan shouted back. Gazrik wheeled his horse and rode away without another word.

Soli, on the eastern bank of the Rhamnos River, was the last town in Videssian territory through which Abivard's army passed before formally entering Vaspurakan. The stone bridge over the river had been destroyed in one of the campaigns in the war between Makuran and Videssos, or perhaps in a round of Videssian civil war. But the Makuraner garrison commander, an energetic officer named Hushang, had spanned the ruined arch with timbers. Horses snorted nervously as their hooves drummed on the planks, but they and the heavily laden supply wagons crossed without difficulty.

Abivard did not feel he was entering a new world when he reached the west bank of the Rhamnos. The mountains grew a little higher and the sides of the valleys seemed a little steeper than they had on the Videssian side of the river, but the difference as yet was small. As for the people, folk of Vaspurakaner blood were far from rare east of the Rhamnos. The marketplace at Soli had been full of dark, stocky men, many of them in the three-peaked cap with multicolored streamers that was the national headdress of Vaspurakan.

"That's an ugly hat, isn't it, Father?" Varaz said one evening as a Vaspurakaner rode away after selling some sheep to the Makuraner army. "If you're not going to wear a helmet, you should wear a pilos the way we do." His hand went to the felt cap shaped like a truncated cone that sat on his own head.

"Well, I don't much fancy the caps the Vaspurakaners wear, I admit," Abivard told him, "but it's the same as it is with horses and women: not everybody thinks the same ones are beautiful. The other day I found out what the Vaspurakaners call the pilos." Varaz waited expectantly. Abivard told him: "A chamber pot that goes on the head."

He'd expected his son to be disgusted. Instead Varaz giggled. For boys of a certain age the line between disgusting and hilarious was a fine one. "Do they really call it that, Father?" Varaz demanded. Regretting he'd mentioned it, Abivard nodded. Varaz giggled even louder. "Wait till I tell Shahin."

Abivard decided not to put on a pilos for the next several weeks without upending it first.

He and the army pressed on toward the valley of Poskh. At first, in spite of what Gazrik had threatened, no one opposed them. The Vaspurakaner *nakharars*—nobles whose status was much like that of the *dihqans* of Makuran—stayed shut up in their gray stone fortresses and watched the Makuraners pass. To show them that he rewarded restraint with restraint, he kept the plundering by his men to a minimum.

That wasn't easy; the valleys of Vaspurakan were full of groves with apricots and plums and peaches just coming to juicy ripeness, full of sleek cattle and strong if not particularly handsome horses, full of all sorts of growing things.

Most of the valleys ran from east to west. Abivard chuckled as he passed from one into the next. A great many Makuraner armies had gone into battle heading east, roaring through Vaspurakan into the Videssian westlands. But never before in all the days of the world had the minstrels had the chance to sing of a Makuraner army moving into battle from the east: out of Videssos and into Vaspurakan.

His riders were entering the valley that held the town and

fortress of Khliat when the princes first struck at them. It was not an attack of horsemen against horsemen; that his force would have faced gladly. But the Vaspurakaners were less eager to face them. And so, instead of couching lances and charging home on those unlovely horses of theirs, they pushed rocks down the mountainside, touching off an avalanche they hoped would bury their foes without their having to face them hand to hand.

But they were a bit too eager and began shoving the boulders too soon. The rumble and crash of stone striking stone drew the Makuraners' eyes to the slopes above them. They reined in frantically, except for some in the van who galloped forward, hoping to outrun the falling rocks.

Not all escaped. Men shouted and wailed in agony as they were struck; horses with broken legs screamed. But the army, as an army, was not badly harmed.

Abivard stared grimly ahead toward the walls of Khliat as his men labored to clear boulders from the track so that the supply wagons could go forward. The sun sparkled off the weapons and armor of the warriors on those walls.

He turned to Kardarigan. "Take your soldiers and burn the fields and orchards here. If the Vaspurakaners will not face us in battle like men, let them learn the cost of cowardice as we taught it to the Videssians."

"Aye, lord," the great captain said dutifully, if without great enthusiasm. Before long flames were licking through the branches of the fruit trees. Great black clouds of smoke rose into the blue dome of the sky. Horses rode through wheatfields, trampling down the growing grain. Then the fields were fired, too. Come winter, Khliat would be a hungry place.

The Vaspurakaners shut up in the fortress shouted curses at Abivard's men, some in the Makuraner tongue, some in Videssian, but most in their own language. Abivard understood hardly a word of that, but it sounded fierce. If the sound had anything to do with the strength of the curse, Vaspurakaner was a fine language in which to wish harm on one's foes.

"The gloves have come off," Romezan said. "From now on we fight hard for everything we get." He sounded delighted at the prospect.

He also proved as good a prophet as any since the Four. Khliat was not well placed to keep invaders from moving west; that

showed that it had been built in fear of Makuran rather than
Videssos. Abivard and his army were able to skirt it, brush aside
the screen of Vaspurakaner horsemen trying to block the pass
ahead, and force their way into the valley of Hanzith.

As soon as he saw the shape of the mountains along the jagged
boundary between earth and sky, Abivard was certain he'd been
this way before. And yet he was just as certain that he'd never
passed through this part of Vaspurakan before in all his life. It
was puzzling.

No—it would have been puzzling had he had more than a
couple of heartbeats to worry about it. No cavalry screen lay
athwart the valley here; the Vaspurakaners had assembled an
army of their own to block his progress toward the valley and
fortress of Poskh. The riders were too many to be contained in
the pair of fortresses controlling the valley of Hanzith. Their tents
sprawled across what had been cropland, a few bright silk, more
dun-colored canvas hard to tell at a distance from dirt.

When the Makuraners forced their way into the valley, horns
cried the alarm up and down its length. The Vaspurakaners rushed
to ready themselves for battle. Abivard ordered his own lightly
armed horsemen ahead to buy time for himself and the rest of
his heavy horse to do likewise.

If you rode everywhere in iron covering you from head to
toe, if you draped your horse in what amounted to a blanket
and headpiece covered with iron scales, and if you then tried
to travel, you accomplished but one thing: You exhausted the
animals. You saved that gear till you really needed it. This was
one of those times.

Supply wagons rattled forward. Warriors crowded around them.
Drivers and servants passed their armor out to them. They helped
one another fasten the lashings and catches of their suits: chain
mail sleeves and gloves, finger-sized iron splints covering the torso,
a mail skirt, and iron rings on the legs, all bound to leather.

Abivard set his helmet back on his head after attaching to it a
mail aventail to protect the back of his neck and a mail veil to
ward his face below the eyes. Sweat streamed from every pore.
He understood how a chicken felt when it sweltered in a stew
pot. Not for nothing did the Videssians call Makuraner heavy
cavalry "the boiler boys."

He felt as if he were carrying Varaz on his shoulders when he walked back to his horse and grunted with the effort of climbing into the saddle. "You know," he said cheerfully as he mounted, "I've heard of men who've had their hearts give out trying this."

"Go ahead, lord," someone said close by. With metal veils hiding features and blurring voices, it was hard to tell who. "Make me feel old."

"I'm not the one doing that," Abivard answered. "It's the armor."

He surveyed the Vaspurakaners mustering against him. They did not have his numbers, but most of them and their horses wore armor like that of his heavy horsemen and their mounts. Iron was plentiful and cheap in Vaspurakan; every village had a smith or two, and every fortress had several of them, mostly busy making armor. Merchants sold Vaspurakaner cuirasses in Mashiz, and he'd seen them in the marketplaces of Amorion, Across, and other Videssian towns.

"Come on!" he shouted to his men. "Fast as you can." Who deployed first and by how much would say a lot about how and where the battle was fought.

Vaspurakaner horsemen began trotting toward his screening force of light cavalry before he had more than half his force of heavy horse ready for action. The Makuraners whooped and made mock charges and shot arrows at the oncoming princes. One or two Vaspurakaner horses screamed; one or two riders slid from their saddles. Most kept right on coming, almost as if the foes before them weren't there. Their advance had a daunting inevitability to it, as if the Makuraners were trying to hold back the sea.

Lances in the first ranks of the Vaspurakaner force swung from vertical down to horizontal. The princes booted their horses up from a slow trot to a quick one. Up ahead steel flashed from drawn swords as the Makuraner light cavalry readied itself to receive the charge.

It broke. Abivard had known it would break. Some of the Makuraners were speared out of their saddles, and some were ridden down by men and horses too heavily armed and armored to withstand. Most of his light horse simply scattered to either flank. The men were brave, but asking them to stop such opponents for long was simply expecting too much.

They had already done as much as he'd wanted them to do, though: they'd bought time. Enough of his own heavy horsemen had armed themselves to stand up against the Vaspurakaners. He waved the riders ahead, trotting at their fore. If they could hold the princes in place for a while, he'd soon have enough men to do a proper job of crushing them.

Next to him a proud young man carried the red-lion banner of Makuran. The Vaspurakaners fought under a motley variety of standards, presumably those of the *nakharars* who headed their contingents. Abivard saw a wolf, a bear, a crescent moon . . . He looked farther down their battle line. No, he couldn't make out what was on those banners.

He stared at them nonetheless. Those indecipherable standards set against these particular notched mountains—this was the first of the scenes Bogorz had shown him. The wizard had lifted the veil into the future, but so what? Abivard had no idea whether he was destined to win or lose this battle and hadn't realized he was in the midst of what he had foreseen till it was too late to do anything about it.

"Get moving!" he called to his men. The momentum that came from horse, rider, and weight of armor was what gave his lancers their punch. The last thing he wanted was to be stalled in place and let the Vaspurakaners thunder down on him. To meet them on even terms he had to have as much power in his charge as they did.

The collision sounded like a thousand smiths dumping their work on a stone floor all at the same time and then screaming about what they'd done. The fight, as it developed, was altogether devoid of subtlety: two large bands of men hammering away at each other to see which would break first.

Abivard speared a Vaspurakaner out of the saddle. His lance shattered against a second man's shield. He yanked out his long, straight sword and lay about him. The Videssians, whose archers and javelin men were between his heavy and light forces in armor and other gear, had delighted in feints and stratagems. He'd smashed through them all. Now the Vaspurakaners were trying to smash him.

One of the princes swung at him with the ruined stump of a lance much like the one he'd thrown away. He took the blow in the side. "*Aii!*" he said. The finger-sized iron splints of his armor and the leather and padding beneath them kept him from having broken bones—at least, no fractured ribs stabbed at him like knives when he breathed—but he knew he'd have a great dark bruise when he took off his corselet after the fight was done.

He slashed at the Vaspurakaner backhanded. The fellow was wearing a chain mail veil like his own. That meant Abivard's sword didn't carve a slab off his face, but the blow surely broke his nose and probably his teeth, too. The Vaspurakaner screamed, clutched at his hurt, and reeled away before Abivard could finish him.

Locked in a hate-filled embrace, the two armies writhed together, neither able to force the other back or break through. Now the lightly-armed Makuraners whom the men of Vaspurakan had so abruptly shoved aside came into their own. From either wing those of them who had not fled plied the Vaspurakaners with arrows and rushed stragglers four and five against one. The princes had no similar troops to drive them back.

A shout of "Hosios Avtokrator!" rose from the Makuraner left. That had to be Tzikas; none of the Makuraners cared a candied fig about Sharbaraz's puppet. But Tzikas, even without the prestige of Makuraner rank or clan, was able to lead by courage and force of personality. He slew a Vaspurakaner horseman, then swarmed in among the princes. Makuraners followed, wedging the breach in the line open wider. The men of Vaspurakan began falling back, which encouraged the Makuraners to press ahead even harder than they had before.

In the space of what seemed only a few heartbeats, the fight went from battle to rout. Instead of pressing forward as doughtily as their opponents, the Vaspurakaners broke off and tried to flee. As often happens, that might have cost them more casualties than it saved. Abivard hacked down a couple of men from behind; how could you resist with your foes' back to you?

Some of the Vaspurakaners made for the castles in the valleys, which kept their gates open wide till the Makuraners got too close for comfort. Other princes rode up into the foothills that led to the ranges separating one valley from another. Some made stands up there, while others simply tried to hide from the victorious Makuraners.

Abivard was not interested in besieging the Vaspurakaner castles. He was not even interested in scouring the valley of Hanzith clean of foes. For years, for centuries, Vaspurakan had been full of men with no great love for Makuran. The King of Kings had derived great profit from it even so. Sharbaraz could derive great profit again—once his *marzban* was freed to control the countryside. Getting Mikhran out of the castle of Poskh came first.

The valley of Poskh ran southwest from Hanzith. Abivard pushed his way through the pass a little before sunset. He saw the fortress, gray and massive in the distance, with the Vaspurakaners' lines around it. They hadn't sealed it off tightly from the outside world, but supply wagons would have had a rugged time getting into the place.

"Tomorrow we attack," Romezan said, sharpening the point of his lance on a whetstone. "The God grant I meet that churlish Vaspurakaner envoy. I shall have somewhat to say to him of manners."

"I'm just glad we hurt the Vaspurakaners worse than they hurt us," Abivard said. "It could have gone the other way about as easily—and even if we free Mikhran, will that do all we want?"

"How not?" Romezan said. "We'll get him out of the fortress, join forces with his men, thump the Vaspurakaners a few times, and remind them they'd better fear the God." He slammed his thick chest with one fist; the sound was almost like stone on wood.

"They may fear the God, but are they going to worship him?" Abivard asked. "We ruled them for a long time without demanding that. Now that we have demanded it, can we make them obey?"

"Either they obey or they go into the Void, which would prove to 'em the truth of our religion if only they could come back whence none returneth." Romezan was a typical man of the Seven Clans: he took his boyhood learning and beliefs as a given and expected everyone also to take them the same way. Within his limits he was solid.

"We should be trying to keep the princes quiet so we can fight Videssos, not antagonizing them, too," Abivard said. "We should—" He shook his head. "What's the use? We have our orders, so we follow them." He wasn't so different from Romezan, after all.

If Gazrik was in the fight the next day, Abivard didn't know it. With his force attacking the Vaspurakaners who besieged the fortress of Poskh, with Mikhran and his fellow Makuraners sallying from the fortress to grind the princes between two stones, the battle was easier than the previous fighting had been. Had he commanded the Vaspurakaners, he would have withdrawn in the night rather than accept combat on such terms. Sometimes headlong courage was its own punishment.

By noon his soldiers were gathering in the mounts of unhorsed Vaspurakaners and plundering bodies of weapons and armor, rings and bracelets, and whatever else a man might think of some value. One soldier carefully removed the red-dyed plumes from a prince's helm and replaced the crest of his own headgear with them.

Abivard had seen and heard and smelled the aftermath of battle too often for it to astonish or horrify him. It was what happened. He rode over the field till he found Mikhran *marzban*. He did not know the new Makuraner governor of Vaspurakan by sight, but like him, Mikhran had a standard-bearer nearby displaying the banner of their country.

"Well met, lord," Mikhran said, realizing who he must be. The *marzban* was a few years younger than he, with a long, thin face made to hold worried wrinkles. That face had already acquired a good many and probably would gain more as the years went by. "Thank you for your aid; without it, I should have come to know the inside of that castle a great deal better than I wanted."

"Happy to have helped," Abivard answered. "I might have been doing other things with my force, I admit, but this was one that needed doing."

Mikhran nodded vigorously. "Aye, lord, it was. And now that you have freed me from Poskh valley and Poskh fortress, our chances of regaining rule over all of Vaspurakan are—" Abivard waited for him to say something like *assured* or *very good indeed*. Instead, he went on, "—not much different from what they were while I was holed up in there."

Abivard looked at him with sudden liking. "You are an honest man."

"No more than I have to be," the *marzban* answered with a wintry smile. "But whatever else I may be, I am not a blind man, and only a blind man could fail to see how the princes hate us for making them worship the God."

"That is the stated will of Sharbaraz King of Kings, may his years be many and his realm increase," Abivard said. "The King of Kings feels that as he is the sole ruler of Makuran and as this land has come under Makuraner sway, it should be brought into religious conformity with the rest of the realm: one realm, one faith, one loyalty." He looked around at the scattered bodies and the spilled blood now turning black. "That one loyalty seems, um, a trifle hard to discover at the moment."

Mikhran's mournful features, which had corrugated even further as Abivard set forth the reasoning of the King of Kings, eased a bit when he admitted that the reasoning might not be perfect. "The one loyalty the princes have is to their own version of Phos' faith. It got them to murder Vshnasp *marzban* for trying to change it." He paused meditatively. "I don't think, though, that was what made them cut off his privates and stuff them into his mouth before they flung his body out into the gutter."

"They did that?" Abivard said. When Mikhran nodded, his gorge tried to rise. None of the *marzban's* dispatches had gone into detail about how Vshnasp had met his untimely demise. Picking his words with care, Abivard observed, "I've heard Vshnasp *marzban* was of . . . somewhat lustful temperament."

"He'd swive anything that moved," Mikhran said, "and if it didn't move, he'd shake it. Our nobles would have served him the same way had he outraged their womenfolk as he did those of the *nakharars* here."

"No doubt you're right. Gazrik said as much," Abivard answered, thinking what he'd do if anyone tried outraging Roshnani. Of course, anyone who tried outraging Roshnani might end up dead at her hands; she was nobody to take lightly nor one who shrank from danger.

"I warned him." Mikhran's words tolled like a sad bell. "He told me to go suck lemons; he'd go get something else sucked himself." He started to say something more, then visibly held his tongue. *He got that, all right, and just as he deserved,* was what ran through Abivard's mind. No, Mikhran *marzban* couldn't say that no matter how loudly he thought it.

Abivard sighed. "You proved yourself wiser than the man who was your master. So what do we do now? Must I spend the rest of this year going from valley to valley and thrashing the princes? I will if I must, I suppose, but it will lead to untold mischief in the Videssian westlands. I wish I knew what Maniakes was doing even now."

"Part of the problem solved itself when Vshnasp's genitals ceased to trouble the wives and daughters of the Vaspurakaner nobles," Mikhran said. "The *nakharars* would willingly return to obedience, save that . . ."

Save that we have to obey Sharbaraz King of Kings. Again Abivard supplied a sentence Mikhran *marzban* didn't care to speak aloud. Disobeying the King of Kings was not something to be contemplated casually by any of his servants. In spite of the God's conveyance of preternatural wisdom to the King of Kings, Sharbaraz wasn't always right. But he always thought he was.

Mikhran opened a saddlebag, reached in, and pulled out a skin of wine. He undid the strip of rawhide holding it closed, then poured a tiny libation for each of the Prophets Four down onto the ground that had already drunk so much blood. After that he took a long swig for himself and passed the skin to Abivard.

The wine went down Abivard's throat smooth as silk, sweet as one of Roshnani's kisses. He sighed with pleasure. "They know their grapes here, no doubt about that," he said. On the hillsides in the distance were vineyards, the dark green of the grapevines' leaves unmistakable.

"That they do." Mikhran hesitated. Abivard gave him back the wineskin. He swigged again, but that wasn't what he'd wanted. He asked, "What will the King of Kings expect from us now?"

"He will expect us to restore Vaspurakan to obedience, nothing less," Abivard answered. The golden wine mounted swiftly to his head, not least because he was so worn from the morning's fighting. He went on. "He will also expect us to have it done by yesterday, or perhaps the day before."

Mikhran *marzban's* slightly pop-eyed expression said he hadn't just stepped over an invisible line, he'd leapt far beyond it. He wished he'd held his tongue, a useless wish if ever there was one. But perhaps his frankness or foolishness or whatever one wanted to call it had finally won the *marzban's* trust. Mikhran said, "Lord, while we are putting down this rebellion in Vaspurakan, what will the Videssians be doing?"

"I was wondering the same thing myself. Their worst, unless I'm badly mistaken," Abivard said. He listened to himself in astonishment, as if he were someone else. If his tongue and wits were running a race, his tongue had taken a good-sized lead.

But Mikhran *marzban* nodded. "Which would Sharbaraz King

of Kings, may his days be long and his realm increase, sooner have: war here and Videssos forgotten or peace here and Videssos conquered?"

"Both," Abivard replied without hesitation. But in spite of his tongue's running free as an unbroken colt, he knew what Mikhran was driving at. The *marzban* didn't want to be the one to have to say it, for which Abivard could hardly blame him: Mikhran was not Sharbaraz's brother-in-law and enjoyed no familial immunity to the displeasure of the King of Kings. How much did Abivard enjoy? He suspected he'd find out. "If we give up trying to compel the princes to follow the God, they'll be mild enough to let me get back to fighting the Videssians."

When Mikhran had said the same thing earlier, he had spoken of it as an obvious impossibility. Abivard's tone was altogether different. Now Mikhran said, "Lord, do you think we can do such a thing and keep our heads on our shoulders once the King of Kings learns of it?"

"That's a good question," Abivard observed. "That's a very good question." It was *the* question, and both men knew it. Since Abivard didn't know what the answer was, he went on: "The other question, the one that goes with it, is, *What is the cost of not doing it?* You summed that up well, I think: we will have warfare here, and we will lose the gains we made in Videssos."

"You are right, lord; I'm certain of it," Mikhran said, adding, "You will have to draft with great care the letter wherein you inform the King of Kings of the course you have chosen." After a moment, lest that seem too craven, he added, "Of course I shall also append my signature and seal to the document once you have prepared it."

"I was certain you would," Abivard lied. And yet it made sense that he should be the one to write to Sharbaraz. For better or worse—for better *and* worse—he was brother-in-law to the King of Kings; his sister Denak would help ease any outburst of wrath from Sharbaraz when he learned that for once not all his wishes would be gratified. But surely Sharbaraz would see that the change of course would only do Makuran good.

Surely he would see that. Abivard thought of the latest letter he'd gotten from the King of Kings, back in Across. Sharbaraz had not seen wisdom then. But the red-lion banner had never before flown above Across. Makuran had struggled for centuries to dominate Vaspurakan. Persecutions of the locals had always failed. Surely Sharbaraz would remember that. Wouldn't he?

Mikhran said, "If the God be kind, we will be so well advanced on our new course, and will have gained such benefits from it by the time Sharbaraz King of Kings, may his years be many and his realm increase, receives your missive that he will be delighted to accept what we have done."

"If the God be kind." Abivard's left hand twisted in the gesture that invoked the Prophets Four. "But your point is well taken. Let us talk with their chief priests here; let us see what sort of arrangements we can work out to put the uprising behind us. Then, when we have at least the beginnings of good news to report, will be time enough to write."

"If we have even the beginnings of good news to report," Mikhran said, suddenly gloomy. "If not, we only bring more trouble down on our heads."

At first Abivard had a hard time imagining more trouble than Vaspurakan aflame with revolt and the Videssian westlands unguarded by his mobile force because of that revolt. But then he realized that those were troubles pertaining to Makuran as a whole. If Sharbaraz grew angry at how affairs in Vaspurakan were being handled contrary to his will, he would be angry not at Makuran in general but at Abivard in particular.

Nevertheless—"Are we agreed on our course?" he asked.

Mikhran *marzban* looked around the battlefield before answering. Most of the Makuraner dead had been taken away, but some still sprawled in death alongside the Vaspurakaners whose defeat they would not celebrate. He asked a question in his turn: "Can we afford more of this?"

"We cannot," Abivard answered, his purpose firming. "We'll treat with the princes, then, and see what comes of that." He sighed. "And then we'll tell Sharbaraz King of Kings of what we've done and see what comes of *that*."

The fortified town of Shahapivan lay in a valley south of Poskh. Abivard approached it by himself, holding before him a white-painted shield of truce. "What do you want, herald?" a Vaspurakaner called from the walls. "Why should we talk to any Makuraner after what you have done to our people and to our worship of the lord with the great and good mind who made us before all other men?"

"I am not a herald. I am Abivard son of Godarz, brother-in-law to Sharbaraz King of Kings, may his days be long and his realm increase. Is that reason enough to talk with me?"

He had the satisfaction of watching the jaw of the fellow who'd spoken to him drop. All the princes close enough to hear stared down at him. They argued in their own language. He'd learned a few Vaspurakaner curses but nothing more. Even if he did not speak the tongue, though, he easily figured out what was going on: some of the warriors believed him, while others thought he was a liar who deserved to have his presumption punished.

Presently a man with a gilded helmet and a great mane of a beard spilling down over his chest leaned out and said in fluent Makuraner, "I am Tatul, *nakharar* of Shahapivan valley. If you truly care to do the land of the princes a service, man of Makuran, take up your soldiers and go home with them."

"I do not wish to speak with you, Tatul *nakharar*," Abivard answered. Several of the Vaspurakaners up on the wall growled like wolves at that. The growls spread as they translated for their comrades who knew only their own tongue. Abivard went on, "Is not the chief priest of Shahapivan also chief priest of all those who worship Phos by your rite?"

"It is so." Pride rang in Tatul's voice. "So you would have speech with the marvelously holy Hmayeak, would you?"

"I would," Abivard answered. "Let him come to my camp, where I will treat him with every honor and try to compose the differences between us."

"No," the *nakharar* said flatly. "This past spring Vshnasp, who has now gone to the eternal ice, sought to foully murder the marvelously holy Hmayeak, upon whom Phos' light shines with great strength. If you would be illuminated by the good god's light reflected from his shining soul, enter into Shahapivan alone and entirely by yourself. Give yourself over into our hands and perhaps we shall find you worth hearing."

Tatul's smile was broad and unpleasant. Some of the Vaspurakaners on the wall laughed. "I am not Vshnasp," Abivard said. "I agree."

"You—agree?" Tatul said as if he'd forgotten what the Makuraner word meant. The princes on the wall of Shahapivan gaped. After a moment Tatul added, "Just like that?"

"I'm sorry," Abivard said politely. "Must I fill out a form?" When she found out he was going into Shahapivan alone, Roshnani would roast him over a slow fire. She, however, was back at the baggage train, while he was up here in front of the city gate. He dug the knife in a little deeper. "Or are you afraid I'll take Shahapivan all by myself?"

Tatul disappeared from the wall. Abivard wondered whether that meant the *nakharar* was coming down to admit him or had decided he was witstruck and so not worth the boon of a Vaspurakaner noble's conversation. He had almost decided it was the latter when, with a metallic rasp of seldom used hinges, a postern gate close by the main gate of Shahapivan swung open. There stood Tatul. He beckoned Abivard forward.

The gate was just tall and wide enough to let a single rider through at a time. When Abivard looked up as he passed through the gateway, he saw a couple of Vaspurakaners peering down at him through the iron grid that screened the murder hole. He heard a fire crackling up there. He wondered what the princes kept in the cauldron above it, what they would pour down through the grid onto anyone who broke down the gate. Boiling water? Boiling oil? Red-hot sand? He hoped he wouldn't find out.

"You have spirit, man of Makuran," Tatul said as Abivard emerged inside Shahapivan. Abivard was wondering what kind of idiot he'd been to come here. Hundreds of hostile Vaspurakaners stared at him, their dark, deep-set eyes seeming to burn like fire. They were quiet, quieter than a like number of Makuraners, far quieter than a like number of Videssians. That did not mean they would not use the weapons they carried or wore on their belts.

A bold front seemed Abivard's only choice. "I am here as I said I would be. Take me now to Hmayeak, your priest."

"Yes, go to him," Tatul said. "Here, by yourself, you shall not be able to serve him as Vshnasp served so many of our priests: you shall not cut out his tongue to keep him from speaking the truth of the good god, you shall not break his fingers to keep him from writing that truth, you shall not gouge out his eyes to keep him from reading Phos' holy scriptures, you shall not soak his beard with oil and set it alight, saying it gives forth Phos' holy light. None of these things shall you do, general of Makuran."

"Vshnasp did them?" Abivard asked. He did not doubt Tatul; the *nakharar's* list of outrages sounded too specific for invention.

"All—and more," Tatul answered. A servitor brought him a horse. He swung up into the saddle. "Come now with me."

Abivard rode with him, looking around curiously as Tatul led him through the narrow, winding streets of Shahapivan. Mashiz, the capital of Makuran, was also a city sprung from the mountains, but it was very different from the Vaspurakaner town. Though of the mountains, Mashiz looked east to the Thousand Cities on the floodplain of the Tutub and the Tib. Its builders worked in timber and in baked and unbaked brick as well as in stone.

Shahapivan, by contrast, might have sprung directly from the gray mountains of Vaspurakan. All the buildings were of stone: soft limestone, easily worked, took the place of mud brick and cheap timber, while marble and granite were for larger, more impressive structures.

The princes had not done much to enliven their town with plaster or paint, either. Even coats of whitewash were rare. The locals seemed content to live in the midst of gray.

They were not gray themselves. Men swaggered in caftans of fuller cut than Makuraners usually wore and dyed in stripes and dots and swirling patterns of bright colors. Their three-pointed tasseled hats looked silly to Abivard, but they made the most of them, shaking and tossing their heads as they talked so that the tassels, like their darting hands, helped punctuate what they said.

Peasant women and merchants' wives crowded the marketplaces, dickering and gossiping. The sun sparkled from their jewelry: polished copper bracelets and gaudy glass beads on those who were not so wealthy, massy silver necklaces or chains strung with Videssian goldpieces on those who were. Their clothes were even more brilliant than those of their menfolk. Instead of the funny-looking hats the men preferred, they wore cloths of linen or cotton or shimmering silk on their heads. They pointed at Abivard and let loose with loud opinions he could not understand but did not think complimentary.

Amid all those fiery reds, sun-bright yellows, vibrant greens, and blues of sky and water, the Vaspurakaner priests stood out by contrast. Unlike Videssian blue-robes, they wore somber black. They did not shave their heads, either, but gathered their hair, whether black or gray or white, into neat buns at the napes of their necks. Some of their beards, like Tatul's, reached all the way down to their waists.

The temples where they served Phos were like those of their Videssian counterparts in that they were topped with gilded globes. Otherwise, though, those temples were very much of a piece with the rest of the buildings of Shahapivan: square, solid structures with only upright rectangular slits for windows, having the look of being made much more for strength and endurance than for beauty and comfort. Abivard noted how many temples there were in this medium-size city. No one could say the Vaspurakaners did not take their misguided faith seriously.

They were in general a sober folk, given to minding their own business. Swarms of Videssians would have followed Tatul and Abivard through the streets. The same might have been true of Makuraners. It was not true here. The Vaspurakaners let their *nakharar* deal with Abivard.

He had expected Tatul to lead him to the finest temple in Shahapivan. When the *nakharar* reined in, though, he did so in front of a building that had seen not just better days but better centuries. Only the gilding on its globe seemed to have been replaced at any time within living memory.

Tatul glanced over to Abivard. "This is the temple dedicated to the memory of the holy Kajaj. He was martyred by you Makuraners—chained to a spit and roasted over coals like a boar—for refusing to abjure the holy faith of Phos and Vaspur the Firstborn. We reverence his memory to this day."

"I did not kill this priest," Abivard answered. "If you blame me for that or even if you blame me for what Vshnasp did, you are making a mistake. Would I have come here if I did not want to compose the differences between you princes and Sharbaraz King of Kings?"

"You are a brave man," Tatul said. "Whether you are a good man, I do not yet know enough to judge. For evil men can be brave. I have seen this. Have you not also?"

"Few men are evil in their own eyes," Abivard said.

"There you touch another truth," Tatul said, "but not one I can discuss with you now. Wait here. I shall go within and bring out to you the marvelously holy Hmayeak."

"I had thought to go with you," Abivard said.

"With the blood of Vaspurakaner martyrs staining your hands?" Tatul's eyebrows leapt up toward the rim of his helmet. "You would render the temple ritually unclean. We sometimes sacrifice a sheep to the good god: its flesh, burned in fire, gives Phos' holy light. But for that, though, blood and death pollute our shrines."

"However you would have it." When Abivard shrugged, his corselet made small rattling and clinking sounds. "I await him here, then."

Tatul strode into the temple. When he returned shortly afterward, the black-robed priest he brought with him was a surprise. Abivard had looked for a doddering, white-bearded elder. But the marvelously holy Hmayeak was in his vigorous middle years, his thick black beard only lightly threaded with gray. His shoulders would have done a smith credit.

He spoke to Tatul in the throaty Vaspurakaner language. The *nakharar* translated for Abivard: "The holy priest says to tell you he does not speak your tongue. He asks if you would rather I interpret or if you prefer to use Videssian, which he does know."

"We can speak Videssian if you like," Abivard said directly to

Hmayeak. He suspected that the priest was trying to annoy him by denying knowledge of the Makuraner tongue and declined to give him satisfaction by showing irk.

"Yes, very well. Let us do that." Hmayeak spoke slowly and deliberately, maybe to help Abivard understand him, maybe because he was none too fluent in Videssian himself. "Phos has taken for his own the holy martyrs you men of Makuran have created." He sketched the sun-circle that was his sign of piety for the good god, going in the opposite direction from the one a Videssian would have used. "How now will you make amends for your viciousness, your savagery, your brutality?"

"They were not mine. They were not those of Mikhran *marzban*. They were those of Vshnasp *marzban*, who is dead." Abivard was conscious of how much he wasn't saying. The policy of which Hmayeak complained had been Vshnasp's, true, but it also had been—and still was—Sharbaraz's. And Vshnasp was not merely dead but slain by the Vaspurakaners. For Abivard to overlook that was as much as to admit that the *marzban* had had it coming.

"How will you make amends?" Hmayeak repeated. He sounded cautious; he might not have expected Abivard to yield so much so soon. To him Vaspurakan was not just the center of the universe but the whole universe.

To Abivard it was but one section of a larger mosaic. He answered, "Marvelously holy sir, I cannot bring the dead back to life, neither your people who died for your faith nor Vshnasp *marzban*." *If you push me too hard, you'll make me remember how Vshnasp died.* Could Hmayeak read between the lines?

"Phos has the power to raise the dead," Hmayeak said in his deliberate Videssian, "but he chooses not to use it, so that we do not come to expect it of him. If Phos does not use this power, how can I expect a mere man to do so?"

"What do you expect of me?" Abivard asked.

Hmayeak looked at him from under thick, bushy bristling brows. His gaze was very keen yet almost childlike in its straightforward simplicity. Maybe he deserved to be called *marvelously holy*; he did not seem half priest, half politician, as so many Videssian prelates did.

"You have come to me," he replied. "This is brave, true, but it also shows you know your people have done wrong. It is for you to tell me what you will do, for me to say what is enough."

Almost, Abivard warned him aloud against pushing too hard. But Hmayeak sounded not like a man who was pushing but like one stating what he saw as a truth. Abivard decided to accept that and see what sprang from it. "Here is what I will do," he said. "I will let you worship in your own way so long as you pledge to remain loyal to Sharbaraz King of Kings, may his days be long and his realm increase. If you for your priesthood make this pledge and if the *nakharars* and warriors of Vaspurakan abide by it, the rebellion here shall be as if it had never been."

"You will seek no reprisals against the leaders of the revolt?" That was not Hmayeak speaking, but Tatul.

"I will not," Abivard said. "Mikhran *marzban* will not. But all must go back to being as it was before the revolt. Where you have driven Makuraner garrisons from towns and fortresses, you must let them return."

"You ask us to put on once more the chains of slavery we have broken," Tatul protested.

"If it comes to war between Vaspurakan and Makuran, you will lose," Abivard said bluntly. "You lived contentedly under the arrangement you had before, so why not go back to it?"

"Who will win in a war among Vaspurakan and Makuran—and Videssos?" Tatul shot back. "Maniakes, I hear, is not Genesios—he is not altogether hopeless at war. And Videssos follows Phos, as we do. The Empire might be glad to aid us against your false faith."

Abivard scowled for a moment before replying. Tatul, unlike Hmayeak, could see beyond the borders of his mountainous native land. If the past offered any standard for judgment, he was liable to be right, too—if Videssos had the strength to act as he hoped. "Before you dream such dreams, Tatul," Abivard said slowly, "remember how far from Vaspurakan any Videssian soldiers are."

"Videssos may be far." Tatul pointed toward the northeast. "The Videssian Sea is close."

That made Abivard scowl again. The Videssian Sea, like all the seas bordering the Empire, had only Videssian ships upon it. If Maniakes wanted badly enough to send an army to Vaspurakan, he could do so without fighting his way across the Makuraner-held westlands.

Hmayeak held up his right hand. The middle finger was stained with ink. The priest said, "Let us have peace. If we are allowed to worship as we please, it is enough. Videssos as our master would try to force what it calls orthodoxy upon us, just as the Makuraners try to make us follow the God and the Prophets Four. You know this, Tatul; it has happened before."

Grudgingly, the *nakharar* nodded. But then he said, "It might not happen this time. Maniakes is of the princes' blood, after all."

"He is not of our creed," Hmayeak said. "The Videssians could never stomach an Avtokrator who acknowledged Vaspur the Firstborn. If he comes to drive away the men of Makuran, be sure he will be doing it for himself and for Videssos, not for us. Let us have peace."

Tatul muttered under his breath. Then he rounded on Abivard again. "Will the King of Kings agree to the arrangement you propose?"

If he has a drop of sense in his head or concealed anywhere else about his person. But Abivard could not say that. "If I make the arrangement, he will agree to it," he said, and hoped he was not lying.

"Let it be as he says," Hmayeak told Tatul. "Vshnasp excepted, the Makuraners seldom lie, and he has made a good name for himself in the wars against Videssos. I do not think he is deceiving us." He spoke in Videssian so that Abivard could understand.

"I shall do as I say," Abivard declared. "May the Prophets Four turn their backs on me and may the God drop me into the Void if I lie."

"I believe you will do as you say," Tatul answered. "I do not need the marvelously holy Hmayeak to tell me you are honorable; by your words today you have convinced me. Would Vshnasp have trusted himself among us? It is to laugh. No, you have honor, brother-in-law to the King of Kings. But has Sharbaraz honor?"

"He is the King of Kings," Abivard declared. "He is the font of honor."

"Phos grant it be so," Tatul said, and sketched his god's sun-sign above his heart.

Roshnani stood, hands on hips, outside the wagon in which she had traveled so many farsangs through the Videssian west-lands and Vaspurakan. Facing her might have been harder than entering Shahapivan. "Husband of mine," she said sweetly, "you are a fool."

"Suppose I say something like *No doubt you're right, but I got away with it*?" Abivard answered. "If I do that, can we take the argument as already over? If I tell you I won't take such chances again—"

"You'll be lying," Roshnani interrupted. "You've come back, so we can argue. That takes a lot of cattle away from the stampede, if you know what I mean. But if you hadn't come back, we would have had a furious fight, let me tell you that."

"If I hadn't come back—" Abivard was tired. He got a quarter of the way through that before realizing it made no logical sense.

"Never mind," Roshnani said. "I gather the Vaspurakaners agreed. If they hadn't, they would have started sending you out in chunks." When Abivard didn't deny it, his principal wife asked the same question the *nakharar* Tatul had: "Will Sharbaraz King of Kings agree?"

Abivard could be more direct with her than he had been with the Vaspurakaner. "Drop me into the Void if I know," he said. "If the God is kind, he'll be so happy to hear we've brought the Vaspurakaner revolt under control without getting tied down in endless fighting here that he won't care how we did it. If the God isn't kind—" He shrugged.

"May she be so," Roshnani said. "I shall pray to the lady Shivini to intercede with her and ensure that she will grant your request."

"It will be as it is, and when we find out how that is, we shall deal with it as best we can," Abivard said, a sentence dismissing all fortune-telling if ever there was one. "Right now I wouldn't mind dealing with a cup of wine."

Roshnani played along with the joke. "I predict one lies in your future."

Sure enough, the wine appeared, and the world looked better for it. Roast mutton with parsnips and leeks improved Abivard's attitude, too. Then Varaz asked, "What would you have done if they'd tried to keep you in Shahapivan, Father?"

"What would I have done?" Abivard echoed. "I would have fought, I think. I wouldn't have wanted them to throw me into some cell in the citadel and do what they wanted with me for as long as they wanted. But after that your mother would have been even more upset with me than she really was."

Varaz thought that through and then nodded without saying anything more; he understood what his father meant. But Gulshahr, who was too young to follow conversations as closely as Varaz could, said, "Why would Mama have been upset, Papa?"

Abivard wanted to speak no words of evil omen, so he answered, "Because I would have done something foolish—like this." He tickled her ribs till she squealed and kicked her feet and forgot about the question she'd asked.

He drank more wine. One by one the children got sleepy and went off to their cramped little compartments in the wagon. Abivard got sleepy, too. Yawning, he walked with neck bent—to keep from bumping the roof—down to the little curtain-screened chamber he shared with Roshnani. Several carpets and sheepskins on the floor made sleeping soft; when winter came, he and Roshnani would sleep under several of them rather than on top.

There was no need now. Vaspurakan did not get summer heat to match that of Vek Rud domain, where Abivard had grown to manhood. When you stepped out into the sunshine on a hot day there, within moments you felt your eyeballs start to dry out. It was warm here in the valley of Shahapivan, but not so warm as to make you wonder if you had walked into a bake oven by mistake.

Abivard would have rolled over and gone to sleep—or even gone to sleep without rolling over first—but Roshnani all but molested him after she pulled the entry curtain shut behind her. Afterward he peered through the darkness at her and said, "Not that I'm complaining, mind you, but what was that in aid of?"

Like his, her voice was a thread of whisper: "Sometimes you can be very stupid. Do you know that I spent this whole day wondering whether I would ever see you again? *That* is what that was in aid of."

"Oh." After a moment Abivard said, "You're giving me the wrong idea, you know. Now, whenever I see a hostile city, I'll have an overpowering urge to go into it and talk things over with whoever is in command."

She poked him in the ribs. "Don't be more absurd than you can help," she said, her voice sharper than it usually got.

"I obey you as I would obey Sharbaraz King of Kings, may his years be many and his realm increase," Abivard said with an extravagant gesture that was wasted in the darkness. He paused again, then added, "As a matter of fact, I'd sooner obey you. You have better sense."

"I should hope so," Roshnani said.

Panteles went to one knee before Abivard, one step short of the full prostration the Videssian wizard would have granted to Maniakes. "How may I serve you, most eminent sir?" he asked, his dark eyes eager and curious.

"I have a question I'd like answered by magical means," Abivard said.

Panteles coughed and brought a hand up to cover his mouth. Like his face, his hands were thin and fine-boned: quick hands, clever hands. "What a surprise!" he exclaimed now. "And here I'd thought you'd summoned me to cook you up a stew of lentils and river fish."

"One of the reasons I don't summon you more often is that viper you keep in your mouth and call a tongue," Abivard said. Far from abashing Panteles, that made him preen like a peacock. Abivard sighed. Videssians were sometimes sadly deficient in notions of servility and subordination. "I presume you can answer such a question."

"Oh, I can assuredly answer it, most eminent sir," Panteles replied. He didn't lack confidence: Abivard sometimes thought that if Videssians were half as smart as they thought they were, they would rule the whole world, not just the Empire. "Whether knowing the answer will do you any good is another question altogether."

"Yes, I've started to see that prophecy is about as much trouble as it's worth," Abivard said. "I'm not asking for divination, only for a clue. Will Sharbaraz King of Kings approve of the arrangement I've made here in Vaspurakan?"

"I can tell you this," Panteles said. By the way he flicked an imaginary speck of lint from the sleeve of his robe, he'd expected something more difficult and complicated. But then he leaned forward like a hunting dog taking a scent. "Why do you not ask your own mages for this service, rather than me?"

"Because news that I've put the question is less likely to get from you to Sharbaraz than it would be from a Makuraner wizard," Abivard answered.

"Ah." Panteles nodded. "Like the Avtokrator, the King of Kings is sensitive when magic is aimed his way, is he? I can understand that."

"Aye." Abivard stopped there. He thought of Tzikas, who had tried to slay Maniakes by sorcery and had been lucky enough to escape after his attempt had failed. Sovereigns had good and cogent reasons for wanting magicians to leave them alone.

"A simple yes or no will suffice?" Panteles asked. Without waiting for an answer, he got out his paraphernalia and set to work. Among the magical materials was a pair of the round Vaspurakaner pastries covered with powdered sugar.

Pointing to them, Abivard said, "You need princes' balls to work your spell?"

"They are a symbol of Vaspurakan, are they not?" Panteles said. Then he let out a distinctly unsorcerous snort. He cut one of the pastries in half, setting each piece in a separate bowl. Then he poured pale Vaspurakaner wine over the two halves.

That done, he cut the other pastry in half. Those halves he set on the table, close by the two bowls. He tapped the rim of one bowl and said, "You will see a reaction here, most eminent sir, if the King of Kings is likely to favor the arrangement you have made."

"And I'll see one in the other bowl if he opposes?" Abivard asked. Panteles nodded. Abivard found another question: "What sort of reaction?"

"Without actually employing the cantrip, most eminent sir, I cannot say, for that will vary depending on a number of factors: the strength of the subject's feelings, the precise nature of the question, and so on."

"That makes sense, I suppose," Abivard said. "Let's see what happens."

With another nod Panteles began to chant in a language that after a moment Abivard recognized as Videssian, but of so archaic a mode that he could understand no more than every other word. The wizard made swift passes with his right hand, first over the bowl where Sharbaraz's approval would be indicated. Nothing happened there. Abivard sighed. He hadn't really expected the King of Kings to be happy about his plan. But how unhappy would Sharbaraz be?

Panteles shifted his attention to the princes' ball soaking in the other bowl. Almost at once the white wine turned the color of blood. The wizard's eyebrows—so carefully arched, Abivard wondered if he plucked them—flew upward, but he continued his incantation. The suddenly red wine began to bubble and steam. Smoke started rising from the Vaspurakaner pastry in the bowl with it.

And then, for good measure, the other half of that princes' ball, the one not soaked in wine, burst into flame there on the table. With a startled oath Panteles snatched up the jar of Vaspurakaner wine and poured what was left in it over the pastry. For a moment Abivard wondered if the princes' ball would keep burning anyhow, as the fire some Videssian dromons threw would continue to burn even when floating on the sea. To his relief, the flaming confection suffered itself to be extinguished.

"I believe," Panteles said with the ostentatious calm that masks a spirit shaken to the core, "I believe, as I say, Sharbaraz has heard ideas he's liked better."

"Really?" Abivard deliberately made his eyes go big and round. "I never would have guessed."

The messenger shook his head. "No, lord," he repeated. "So far as I know, the Videssians have not gone over the strait to Across."

Abivard kicked at the dirt in front of his wagon. He wanted Maniakes to do nice, simple, obvious things. If the Avtokrator of the Videssians had moved to reoccupy the suburb just on the far side of the Cattle Crossing, Abivard would have had no trouble figuring out what he was up to or why. As things were—"Well, what *have* the Videssians done?"

"Next to nothing, lord," the messenger answered. "I have seen as much—or, rather, as little—with my own eyes. Their warships remain ever on patrol. We have had reports they are fighting the barbarians to the north again, but we do not know that for a fact. They seem to be gathering ships at the capital, but it's getting late in the year for them to set out on a full-scale campaign."

"That's so," Abivard agreed. Before too long, storms would make the seas deadly dangerous and the fall rains would turn the roads into muck through which one couldn't move swiftly and sometimes couldn't move at all. Nobody in his right mind, or even out of it, wanted to get stuck in that kind of mess. And after the fall rains came snow and then another round of rain . . . He thought for a while. "Do you suppose Maniakes aims to wait till the rains start and then take back Across, knowing we'll have trouble moving against him?"

"Begging your pardon, lord, but I couldn't even begin to guess," the messenger said.

"You're right, of course," Abivard said. The messenger was a young man who knew what his commander had told him and what he'd seen with his own eyes. Expecting him to have any great insights into upcoming Videssian strategy was asking too much.

More dust flew up as Abivard kicked again. If he pulled out of Vaspurakan now, the settlement he'd almost cobbled together here would fall apart. It was liable to fall apart anyhow; the Vaspurakaners, while convinced of his good faith, still didn't trust Mikhran, who had served under the hated Vshnasp and who formally remained their governor. Abivard could make them believe he'd go against Sharbaraz's will; Mikhran couldn't.

"Is there anything else, lord?" the messenger asked.

"No, not unless you—" Abivard stopped. "I take that back. How was your journey across the westlands? Did you have any trouble with Videssians trying to make sure you never got here?"

"No, lord, nothing of the sort," the messenger answered. "I had a harder time prying remounts out of some of our stables than I did with any of the Videssians. In fact, there was this one girl—" He hesitated. "But you don't want to hear about that."

"Oh, I might, over a mug of wine in a tavern," Abivard said. "This isn't the time or the place for such stories, though; you're right about that. Speaking of wine, have yourself a mug or two, then go tell the cook to feed you till you can't eat any more."

He stared thoughtfully at the messenger's back as the youngster headed off to refresh himself. If the Videssians weren't doing more to harass lone Makuraners traveling through their territory, they didn't think Maniakes had any plans for this year. Maybe that was a good sign.

Rain pattered down on the cloth roof of the wagon. Abivard reminded himself to tell his children not to poke a forefinger up there against the fabric so that water would go through and run down it. He reminded them of that at the start of every rainy season and generally had to punctuate the reminders with swats on the backside till they got the message.

The rain wasn't hard yet, as it would be soon. So far it was just laying the dust, not turning everything into a quagmire. Probably it would ease up by noon, and they might have a couple of days of sun afterward, perhaps even a couple of days of summerlike heat.

From outside the wagon, Pashang the driver called out to Abivard: "Lord, here comes a Vaspurakaner; looks like he's looking for you." After a moment he added, "I wouldn't want him looking for me."

No one had ever accused Pashang of being a hero. All the same, Abivard belted on his sword before peering out. As raindrops splashed his face, he wished the pilos he was wearing had a brim.

He quickly discovered that donning the sword had been a useless gesture. The Vaspurakaner was mounted on an armored horse and wore full armor. He'd greased it with tallow; water beaded on his helmet and corselet but did not reach the iron.

"I greet you, Gazrik son of Bardzrabol," Abivard said mildly. "Do you come in search of me armed head to foot?"

"Not in search of you, brother-in-law to the King of Kings." Gazrik shook his head. Water sprayed out of his beard. "You treated me with honor, there when I bade you turn aside from Vaspurakan. You did not heed me, but you did not scorn me, either. One of your marshals, though, called me dog. I hoped to find him on the field when our force fought yours, but Phos did not grant me that favor. And so I have come now to seek him out."

"We were enemies then," Abivard reminded him. "Now there is truce between Makuran and Vaspurakan. I want that truce to grow stronger and deeper, not to see it broken."

Gazrik raised a thick, bushy eyebrow. "You misunderstand me, Abivard son of Godarz. This is not a matter of Vaspurakan and Makuran; this is a matter of man and man. Did a *nakharar* show me like insult, I would seek him out as well. Is it not the same among you? Or does a noble of Makuran suffer his neighbor to make his name into a thing of reproach?"

Abivard sighed. Gazrik was making matters as difficult as he could, no doubt on purpose. The Vaspurakaner knew whereof he spoke, too. Makuraner nobles were a proud and touchy lot, and the men of one domain often fought those of the next on account of some slight, real or imagined.

"Give me the name of the lout who styled me insolent dog," Gazrik said.

"Romezan son of Bizhan is a noble of the Seven Clans of Makuran," Abivard answered, as if to a backward child. By blood, Romezan was more noble than Abivard, who was but of the *dihqan* class, the minor nobility . . . but who was Sharbaraz's brother-in-law and marshal.

In any case, the distinction was lost on Gazrik, who judged by different standards. "No man not a prince of Vaspurakan can truly be reckoned of noble blood," he declared; like Abivard, he was explaining something so obvious to him, it hardly needed explanation. He went on, "Regardless, I care nothing for what blood he bears, for I purpose spilling it. Where in this camp of yours can I find him?"

"You are alone here," Abivard reminded him.

Gazrik's eyebrows twitched again. "And so? Would you keep a hound from the track? Would you keep a bear from the honey tree? Would you keep an insulted man from vengeance? Vshnasp excepted, you Makuraners are reputed to have honor; you yourself have shown as much. Would you throw that good name away?"

What Abivard would have done was throw Gazrik out of the encampment. That, though, looked likely to cause more problems than it solved. "You will not attack Romezan without warning?"

"*I* am a man of honor, brother-in-law to the King of Kings," Gazrik said with considerable dignity. "I wish to arrange a time and place where the two of us can meet to compose our differences."

By composing their differences, he meant that one of them would start decomposing. Makuraner nobles were known to settle disputes in that fashion, although a mere *dihqan* would rarely presume to challenge a man of the Seven Clans. By Gazrik's bearing, though, he reckoned all non-Vaspurakaners beneath him and was honoring Romezan by condescending to notice himself insulted.

Abivard pointed to a sprawling silk pavilion a couple of furlongs away. Peroz King of Kings might have taken a fancier one into the field when he went over the Degird on his ill-fated expedition against the Khamorth, but not by much—and

Romezan, however high his blood, was not King of Kings. "He dwells there."

Gazrik's head turned toward the pavilion. "It is very fine," he said. "I have no doubt some other man of your army will draw enjoyment from it once Romezan needs it no more."

He bowed in the saddle to Abivard, then rode off toward Romezan's tent. Abivard waited uneasily for shouts and screams to break out, as might have happened had Gazrik lied about going simply to deliver a challenge. But evidently Gazrik had spoken the truth. And if Romezan acknowledged him as noble enough to fight, the man of the Seven Clans would grant his foe every courtesy—until the appointed hour came, at which point he would do his considerable best to kill him.

Abivard wished kingdoms and empires could settle their affairs so economically.

It was a patch of dirt a furlong in length and a few yards wide: an utterly ordinary patch of ground, one occasionally walked across by a Vaspurakaner or even a Makuraner but not one to have had itself recorded in the memories of men, not till today.

From now on, though, minstrels would sing of this rather muddy patch of ground. Whether the minstrels who composed the boldest, most spirited songs would wear pilos or three-crowned caps would be determined today.

Warriors from Makuran and Vaspurakan crowded around the long, narrow strip of ground, jostling one another and glaring suspiciously when they heard men close by speaking the wrong language, whichever that happened to be. Sometimes the glares and growls persisted; sometimes they dissolved in the excitement of laying bets.

Abivard stood in the middle of the agreed-upon dueling ground. When he motioned Romezan and Gazrik toward him from the opposite ends of the field, the throng of spectators fell into expectant silence. The noble of the Seven Clans and the Vaspurakaner *nakharar* slowly approached, each on his armored steed. Both men were armored, too. In their head-to-toe suits of mail and lamellar armor, they were distinguishable from each other only by their surcoats and by the red lion painted on Romezan's small, round shield. The Makuraner's chain mail veil hid the waxed spikes of his mustache, while Gazrik's veil came down over his formidable beard.

"You are both agreed combat is the only way you can resolve the differences between you?" Abivard asked. With faint raspings of metal, two heads bobbed up and down. Abivard persisted: "Will you not be satisfied with first blood here today?"

Now, with more rasping noises, both heads moved from side to side. "A fight has no meaning, be it not to the death," Romezan declared.

"In this, if in no other opinion, I agree with my opponent," Gazrik said.

Abivard sighed. Both men were too stubborn for their own good. Each saw it in the other, not in himself. Loudly, Abivard proclaimed, "This is a fight between two men, each angry at the other, not between Makuran and Vaspurakan. Whatever happens here shall have no effect on the truce now continuing between the two lands. Is it agreed?"

He pitched that question not to Romezan and Gazrik but to the crowd of spectators, a crowd that could become a brawl at any minute. The warriors nodded in solemn agreement. How well they would keep the agreement when one of their champions lay dead remained to be seen.

"May the God grant victory to the right," Abivard said.

"No, Phos and Vaspur the Firstborn, who watches over his children, the princes of Vaspurakan," Gazrik said, sketching his deity's sun-circle above his left breast with a gauntleted hand. Many of the Vaspurakaners among the spectators imitated his gesture. Many of the Makuraners responded with a gesture of their own to turn aside any malefic influence.

"Ride back to your own ends of the field here," Abivard said, full of misgivings but unable to stop a fight both participants wanted so much. "When I signal, have at each other. I tell you this: in spite of what you have said, you may give over at any time, with no loss of honor involved." Romezan and Gazrik nodded. The nods did not say, *We understand and agree.* They said, *Shut up, get out of the way, and let us fight.*

Romezan, Abivard judged, had a better horse than did Gazrik, who was mounted on a sturdy but otherwise unimpressive gelding of Vaspurakaner stock. Other than that, he couldn't find a copper's worth of difference between the two men. He knew how good a warrior Romezan was; he did not know Gazrik, but the Vaspurakaner gave every impression of being able to handle himself.

Abivard raised his hand. Both men leaned forward in the saddle, couching their lances. He let his hand fall. Because their horses wore ironmongery like their own, neither Romezan nor Gazrik wore spurs. They used reins, voice, their knees, and an occasional boot in the ribs to get their beasts to do as they required. The horses were well trained. They thundered toward each other, dirt fountaining up under their hooves.

Each rider brought up his shield to protect his left breast and most of his face. *Crash!* Both lances struck home. Romezan and Gazrik flew over their horses' tails as the crowd shouted at the clever blows. The horses galloped down to the far ends of the field. Each man's retainers caught the other's beast.

Gazrik and Romezan got slowly to their feet. They moved hesitantly, as if half-drunk; the falls they'd taken had left them stunned, in the shock of collision Gazrik's lance had shivered. He threw aside the stub and drew his long, straight sword. Romezan's lance was still intact. He thrust at Gazrik: he had a great advantage in reach now.

Clang! Gazrik chopped at the shaft of the lance below the head, hoping to cut off that head as if it belonged to a convicted robber. But the lance had a strip of iron bolted to the wood to thwart any such blow.

Poke, poke. Like a cat toying with a mouse, Romezan forced Gazrik down the cleared strip where they fought, not giving him the chance to strike a telling blow of his own—until, with a loud cry, the Vaspurakaner used his shield to beat aside the questing lance head and rushed at his foe.

Romezan could not backpedal as fast as Gazrik bore down on him. He whacked Gazrik in the ribs with the shaft of the lance, trying to knock his foe off balance. That was a mistake. Gazrik chopped at the shaft again and this time hit it below the protective strip of iron. The shaft splintered. Cursing, Romezan threw it down and yanked out his sword.

All at once both men seemed tentative. They were used to fighting with swords from horseback, not afoot like a couple of infantrymen. Instead of going at each other full force, they would trade strokes, each draw back a step as if to gauge the other's strength and speed, and then approach for another short clash.

"Fight!" somebody yelled from the crowd, and in an instant a hundred throats were baying the word.

Romezan was the one who pressed the attack. Gazrik seemed content to defend himself and wait for a mistake. Abivard thought Romezan fought the same way he led his men: straight ahead, more than bravely enough, and with utter disregard for anything but what lay before him. Tzikas had used flank attacks to maul his troopers a couple of times.

Facing only one enemy, Romezan did not need to worry about an attack from the side. Iron belled on iron as he hacked away at Gazrik. Sparks flew as they did when a smith sharpened a sword on a grinding wheel. And then, with a sharp snap, Gazrik's blade broke in two.

Romezan brought up his own sword for the killing stroke. Gazrik, who had self-possession to spare, threw the stub and hilt of his ruined weapon at the Makuraner's head. Then he sprang at Romezan, both hands grabbing for his right wrist.

Romezan tried to kick his feet out from under him and did, but Gazrik dragged him down, too. They fell together, and their armor clattered about them. Gazrik pulled out a dagger and stabbed at Romezan, trying to slip the point between the lamellae of his corselet. Abivard thought he'd succeeded, but Romezan did not cry out and kept fighting.

Gazrik had let go of Romezan's sword arm to free his own knife. Romezan had no room to swing the sword or cut with it. He used it instead as a knuckle-duster, smashing Gazrik in the face with the jeweled and weighted pommel. The Vaspurakaner groaned, and so did his countrymen.

Romezan hit him again. Now Gazrik wailed. Romezan managed to reverse the blade and thrust it home point first, just above the chain mail veiling that warded most but not all of Gazrik's face. Gazrik's body convulsed, and his feet drummed against the dirt. Then he lay still.

Very slowly, into vast silence, Romezan struggled to his feet. He took off his helmet. His face was bloody. He bowed to Gazrik's corpse, then to the grim-featured Vaspurakaners in the crowd. "That was a brave man," he said, first in his own language, then in theirs.

Abivard hoped that would keep the Vaspurakaners in the crowd calm. No swords came out, but a man said, "If you call him brave now, why did you name him a dog before?"

Before Romezan answered, he shed his gauntlets. He wiped his forehead with the back of his hand, mixing sweat and grime and blood but not doing much more. At last he said, "For the same reason any man insults his foe during war. What have you princes called us? But when the war was over, I was willing to let it rest. Gazrik came seeking me; I did not go looking for him."

Though you certainly did on the battlefield, and though you were glad to fight him when he came to you, Abivard thought. But Romezan had given as good an answer as he could. Abivard said, "The general of Makuran is right. The war is over. Let us remember that, and let this be the last blood shed between us."

Along with his countrymen, he waited to see if that would be reply enough or if the Vaspurakaners, in spite of his words and Romezan's, would make blood pay for blood. He kept his own hand away from the hilt of his sword but was ready to snatch it out in an instant.

For a few heartbeats the issue hung in the balance. Then, from the back of the crowd, a few Vaspurakaners turned and trudged back toward the frowning gray walls of Shahapivan, their heads down, their shoulders bent, the very picture of dejection. Had Abivard had any idea who they were, he would have paid them a handsome sum of silver arkets or even of Videssian goldpieces. Their peaceful, disappointed withdrawal gave their countrymen both the excuse and the impetus to leave the site of the duel without trying to amend the result.

Abivard permitted himself the luxury of a long sigh of relief. Things could hardly have gone better: Not only had Romezan beaten his challenger, he'd managed to do it in a way that didn't reignite the princes' rebellion.

He walked up to his general. "Well, my great boar of Makuran, we got by with it."

"Aye, so we did," Romezan answered, "and I stretched the dog dead in the dirt, as he deserved." He laughed at Abivard's flabbergasted expression. "Oh, I spoke him fair for his own folks, lord. I'm no fool: I know what needed doing. But a dog he was, and a dead dog he is, and I enjoyed every moment of killing him." Just for a moment his facade of bravado cracked, for he added, "Except for a couple of spots where I thought he was going to kill me."

"How did you live, there when he was stabbing at you through your suit?" Abivard asked. "I thought he pierced it a couple of times, but you kept on."

Romezan laughed. "Aye, I did, and do you know why? Under it I wore an iron heart guard, the kind foot soldiers put on when they can't afford any other armor. You never know, thought I, when such will come in handy, and by the God I was right. So he didn't kill me, and I did kill him, and that's all that matters."

"Spoken like a warrior," Abivard said. Romezan, as best he could tell, had no great quantity of wit, but sometimes, as now, the willingness to take extra pains and a large helping of straight-forward courage sufficed.

Fall drew on. Abivard thought hard about moving back into the Videssian westlands before the rains finished turning the roads to mud but in the end decided to hold his mobile force in Vaspurakan. If the princes broke their fragile accord with Makuran, he didn't want to give them the winter in which to consolidate themselves.

Also weighting his judgment was how quiet Maniakes had been. Instead of plunging ahead regardless of whether he had the strength to plunge, as he had before, the Videssian Avtokra-tor was playing a cautious game. In a way that worried Abivard, for he wasn't sure what Maniakes was up to. In another way, though, it relieved him: even if he kept the mobile force here in Vaspurakan, he could be fairly sure the Avtokrator would not leap upon the westlands.

Keeping the mobile force in Vaspurakan also let him present to Sharbaraz the settlement he'd made with the princes as a reconquest and occupation of their land. He made full use of that aspect of the situation when at last he wrote a letter explaining to the King of Kings all he'd done. If one didn't read that letter with the greatest of care, one would never notice that the Vaspurakaners still worshiped at their old temples to Phos and that Abivard had agreed not to try to keep them from doing so.

"The King of Kings, may his days be long and his realm increase, is a very busy man," he said when he gave the carefully crafted letter to Mikhran *marzban* for his signature. "With any luck at all, he'll skim through this without even noticing the fine points of the arrangement." He hoped that was true, considering what

Panteles had told him about how Sharbaraz was likely to react if he did notice. He didn't mention that to the *marzban*.

"It would be fine, wouldn't it?" Mikhran said, scrawling his name below Abivard's. "It would be very fine indeed, and I think you have a chance of pulling it off."

"Whatever he does, he'll have to do it quickly," Abivard said. "This letter should reach him before the roads get too gloppy to carry traffic, but not long before. He'll need to hurry if he's going to give any kind of response before winter or maybe even before spring. I'm hoping that by the time he gets around to answering me, so many other things will have happened that he'll have forgotten all about my letter."

"That would be fine," Mikhran repeated. "In fact, maybe you should even arrange for your messenger to take so long that he gets stuck in the mud and makes your letter later still."

"I thought about that," Abivard said. "I've decided I dare not take the risk. I don't know who else has written to the King of Kings and what he or they may have said, but I have to think some of my officers will have complained about the settlement we've made. Sharbaraz needs to have our side of it before him, or he's liable to condemn us out of hand."

The *marzban* considered that, then reluctantly nodded. "I suppose you're right, lord, but I fear this letter will be enough to convict us of disobedience by itself. The Vaspurakaners are not worshiping the God."

"They aren't assassinating *marzbans* and waylaying soldiers, either," Abivard returned. "Sharbaraz will have to decide which carries the greater weight."

There the matter rested. Once the letter was properly signed and sealed, a courier rode off to the west with it. It would pass through the western regions of Vaspurakan and the Thousand Cities before it came to Mashiz—and to Sharbaraz's notice. As far as Abivard could see, he was obviously doing the right thing. But Panteles' magic made him doubt the King of Kings would agree.

Several days after the letter left his hands he wished he had it back again so he could change it—or so he could change his mind and not send it at all. He even started to summon Panteles to try to blank the parchment by sorcery from far away but ended up refraining. If Sharbaraz got a letter with no words from him, he'd wonder why and would keep digging till he found out. Better to give him something tangible on which to center his anger.

Abivard slowly concluded that he would have to give Tzikas something tangible, too. The Videssian turncoat had fought very well in Vaspurakan; how in justice could Abivard deny him a command commensurate with his talent? The plain truth was, he couldn't.

"But oh, how I wish I could," he told Roshnani one morning before a meeting with Tzikas he'd tried but failed to avoid. "He's so—polite." He made a gesture redolent of distaste.

"Sometimes all you can do is make the best of things," Roshnani said. She spoke manifest truth, but that did not make Abivard feel any better about the way Tzikas smiled.

Tzikas bowed low when Abivard approached his pavilion. "I greet you, brother-in-law to the King of Kings, may his days be long and his realm increase. May he and his kingdom both prosper."

"I greet you, eminent sir," Abivard answered in Videssian far more ragged than it had been a few months before. Don't use a language and you will forget it, he'd discovered.

Tzikas responded in Makuraner, whether just for politeness' sake or to emphasize how much he was himself a man of Makuran, Abivard couldn't guess. *Probably both,* he thought, and wondered whether Tzikas himself knew the proportions of the mix. "Brother-in-law to the King of Kings, have I in some way made myself odious to you? Tell me what my sin is and I shall expiate it, if that be in my power. If not, I can do no more than beg forgiveness."

"You have done nothing to offend me, eminent sir." Abivard stubbornly stuck to Videssian. His motives were mixed, too: not only did he need the practice, but by using the language of the Empire he reminded Tzikas that he remained an outsider no matter what services he'd rendered to Makuran.

The Videssian general caught that signal: Tzikas was sometimes so subtle, he imagined signals that weren't there, but not today. He hesitated, then said, "Brother-in-law to the King of Kings, would I make myself more acceptable in your eyes if I cast off the worship of Phos and publicly accepted the God and the Prophets Four?"

Abivard stared at him. "You would do such a thing?"

"I would," Tzikas answered. "I have put Videssos behind me; I have wiped her dust from the soles of my sandals." As if to emphasize his words, he scraped first one foot and then the other against the soil of Vaspurakan. "I shall also turn aside from Phos; the lord with the great and good mind has proved himself no match for the power of the God."

"You are a—" Abivard had to hunt for the word he wanted but found it—"a *flexible* man, eminent sir." He didn't altogether mean it as a compliment; Tzikas' flexibility, his willingness to adhere to any cause that looked advantageous, was what worried Abivard most about him.

But the Videssian renegade nodded. "I am," he declared. "How could I not be when unswerving loyalty to Videssos did not win me the rewards I had earned?"

What Tzikas had was unswerving loyalty to Tzikas. But if that could be transmuted into unswerving loyalty to Makuran . . . it would be a miracle worthy of Fraortish eldest of all. Abivard chided himself for letting the nearly blasphemous thought cross his mind. Tzikas was a tool, like a sharp knife, and, like a sharp knife, he would cut your hand if you weren't careful.

Abivard had no trouble seeing that much. What lay beyond it was harder to calculate. One thing did seem likely, though: "Having accepted the God, you dare not let the Videssians lay hands on you again. What do they do to those who leave their faith?"

"Nothing pretty, I assure you," Tzikas answered, "but no worse than what they'd do to a man who tried to slay the Avtokrator but failed."

"Mm, there is that," Abivard said. "Very well, eminent sir. If you accept the God, we shall make of that what we can."

He did not promise Tzikas his regiment. He waited for the renegade to beg for it or demand it or try to wheedle it out of him, all ploys Tzikas had tried before. But Tzikas, for once, did not push. He answered only, "As you say, brother-in-law to the King of Kings, Videssos shall reject me as I have rejected her. And so I accept the God in the hope that Makuran will accept me in return." He bowed and ducked back inside his pavilion.

Abivard stared thoughtfully after him. Tzikas had to know that, no matter how fervently and publicly he worshiped the God, the grandees of Makuran would never stop looking on him as a foreigner. They might one day come to look on him as a foreigner who made a powerful ally, perhaps even as a foreigner to whom one might be wise to marry a daughter. From Tzikas' point of view that would probably constitute acceptance.

Sharbaraz already thought well of Tzikas because of his support for the latest "Hosios Avtokrator." Add the support of the King of Kings to the turncoat's religious conversion and he might even win a daughter of a noble of the Seven Clans as a principal wife. Abivard chuckled. Infusing some Videssian slyness into those bloodlines would undoubtedly improve the stock. As a man who knew a good deal about breeding horses, he approved.

Roshnani laughed when he told her the conceit later that day, but she did not try to convince him he was wrong.

The first blizzard roared into Vaspurakan from out of the northwest without warning. One day the air still smelled sweet with memories of fruit just plucked from trees and vines; the next, the sky turned yellow-gray, the wind howled, and snow poured down. Abivard had thought he knew everything about winter worth knowing, but that sudden onslaught reminded him that he'd never gone through a hard season in mountain country.

"Oh, aye, we lose men, women, families, flocks to avalanches every year," Tatul said when he asked. "The snow gets too thick on the hillsides, and down it comes."

"Can't you do anything to stop that?" Abivard inquired.

The Vaspurakaner shrugged, as Abivard might have had he been asked what he could do about Vek Rud domain's summer heat. "We might pray for less snow," Tatul answered, "but *if* the lord with the great and good mind chooses to answer that prayer, the rivers will run low the next spring, and crops well away from them will fail for lack of water."

"Nothing is ever simple," Abivard murmured, as much to himself as to the *nakharar*. Tatul nodded; he took the notion for granted.

Abivard made sure all his men had adequate shelter against the cold. He wished he could imitate a bear and curl up in a cave till spring came. It would have made life easier and more pleasant. As things were, though, he remained busy through the winter. Part of that was routine: he drilled the soldiers when weather permitted and staged inspections of their quarters and their horses' stalls when it did not.

And part was anything but routine. Several of his warriors—most of them light cavalry with no family connections, but one a second son of a *dihqan*—fell so deep in love with Vaspurakaner women that nothing less than marriage would satisfy them. Each of those cases required complicated dickering between the servants of the God and the Vaspurakaner priests of Phos to determine which holy men would perform the marriage ceremony.

Some of the soldiers were satisfied with much less than marriage. A fair number of Vaspurakaner women brought claims of rape against his men. Those were hard for him to decide, as they so often came down to conflicting claims about what had really happened. Some of his troopers said the women had consented and were now changing their minds; others denied association of any sort with them.

In the end he dismissed about half the cases. In the other half he sent the women back to their homes with silver—more if their attackers had gotten them with child—and put stripes on the backs of the men who, he was convinced, had violated them.

The *nakharar* Tatul came out from the frowning walls of Shahapivan to watch one of the rapists take his strokes. Encountering Abivard there for the same reason, he bowed and said, "You administer honest justice, brother-in-law to the King of Kings. After Vshnasp's wicked tenure here, this is something we princes note with wonder and joy."

Craack! The lash scored the back of the miscreant. He howled. No doubt about his guilt: he'd choked his victim and left her for dead, but she had not died. Abivard said, "It's a filthy crime. My sister, principal wife to the King of Kings, would not let me look her in the face if I ignored it." *Craack!*

Tatul bowed again. "Your sister is a great lady."

"That she is." Abivard said no more than that. He did not tell Tatul how Denak had let herself be ravished by one of Sharbaraz's guards when the usurper Smerdis had imprisoned the rightful King of Kings in Nalgis Crag stronghold, thereby becoming able to pass messages to and from the prisoner and greatly aiding in his eventual escape. His sister would have had special reason to spurn him had he gone soft here. *Craack!*

After a hundred lashes the prisoner was cut down from the frame. He screamed one last time when a healer splashed warm salt water on his wrecked back to check the bleeding and make the flesh knit faster.

Once all the Vaspurakaner witnesses were gone and the punished rapist had been dragged off to recover from his whipping, Farrokh-Zad came up to Abivard. Unlike Tatul, Kardarigan's fiery young subordinate did not approve of the sentence Abivard had handed down. "There's a good man who won't be of any use in a fight for months, lord," he grumbled. "Sporting with a foreign slut isn't anything big enough to have stripes laid across your back on account of it."

"I think it is," Abivard answered. "If the Vaspurakaners came to your domain in Makuran and one of their troopers forced your sister's legs apart, what would you want done to him?"

"I'd cut his throat myself," Farrokh-Zad answered promptly.

"Well, then," Abivard said.

But Farrokh-Zad didn't see it even after Abivard spelled it out in letters of fire a foot in front of his nose. As far as Farrokh-Zad was concerned, anyone who wasn't a Makuraner deserved no consideration: whatever happened, happened, and that was all there was to it. The time Abivard had spent in Videssos and Vaspurakan had convinced him that foreigners, despite differences of language and faith, were at bottom far closer to the folk of Makuran than he'd imagined before he had left Vek Rud domain. Plainly, though, not all his countrymen had drawn the same lesson.

Maybe that gloomy thought was what brought on the next spell of gloomy weather. However that was, a new blizzard howled in the next afternoon. Had Abivard scheduled the rapist's chastisement for that day, the fellow might have frozen to death while taking his lashes. Abivard wouldn't have missed him a bit.

With storms like that, you could only stay inside whatever shelter you had, try to keep warm—or not too cold—and wait till the sun came out again. Even then, you wouldn't be comfortable, but at least you could emerge from your lair and move about in a world gone white.

The fall and spring rains stopped all traffic on the roads for weeks at a time. While it was raining, a road was just a stretch of mud that ran in a straight line. You could move about in winter provided that you had the sense to find a house or a caravanserai while the blizzard raged.

During a lull a courier rode into Shahapivan valley from out
of the west. He found Abivard's wagon and announced himself,
saying, "I bring a dispatch from Sharbaraz King of Kings, may
his days be long and his realm increase." He held out a message
tube stamped with the lion of Makuran.

Abivard took it with something less than enthusiasm. After
undoing the stopper, he drew out the rolled parchment inside and
used his thumbnail to break the red wax seal, also impressed with
a lion from Sharbaraz's signet, that held the letter closed. Then,
having no better choice, he opened it and began to read.

He skipped quickly through the grandiloquent titles with which
the King of Kings bedizened the document: he was after meat. He
also skipped over several lines' worth of reproaches; he'd heard
plenty of those already. At last he came to the sentence giving
him his orders: "You are to come before us at once in Mashiz to
explain and suffer the consequences for your deliberate defiance
of our will in Vaspurakan." He sighed. He'd feared as much.

✦ IV

Mikhran *marzban* put a hand on Abivard's shoulder. "I should be going with you. You came to my rescue, you promulgated this policy for my benefit, and you, it seems, will have to suffer the consequences alone."

"No, don't be a fool—stay here," Abivard told him. "Not only that: keep on doing as we've been doing till Sharbaraz directly orders you to stop. Keep on then, too, if you dare. If the princes rise up against us, we aren't going to be able to conquer Videssos."

"What—?" Mikhran hesitated but finished the question: "What do you suppose the King of Kings will do to you?"

"That's what I'm going to find out," Abivard answered. "With luck, he'll shout and fuss and then calm down and let me tell him what we've been doing and why. Without luck—well, I hope I'll have reason to be glad he's married to my sister."

The *marzban* nodded, then asked, "Whom will you leave in command of the army here?"

"It has to be Romezan," Abivard answered regretfully. "He's senior, and he has the prestige among our men from killing Gazrik. I'd give the job to Kardarigan if I could, but I can't."

"He may have more prestige among us, but the princes won't be happy to see him in charge of our warriors," Mikhran said.

"I can't do anything about that, either," Abivard said. "You're

89

in overall command here, remember: over Romezan, over everyone now that I'm not going to be around for a while. Use that power well and the Vaspurakaners won't notice that Romezan leads the army."

"I'll try," Mikhran said. "But I wasn't part of this army, so there's no guarantee they'll heed me as they would one of their own."

"Act so natural about it that they never think to do anything else," Abivard advised him. "One of the secrets to command is never giving the men you're leading any chance to doubt you have the right. That's not a magic Bogorz knows, or Panteles either, but it's nonetheless real even so."

"Vshnasp spoke of that kind of magic, too," Mikhran said, "save that he said that so long as you never seemed to doubt a woman would come to your bed, in the end she would not doubt it, either. I'd sooner not emulate his fate."

"I don't expect you to seduce Romezan—for which I hope you're relieved," Abivard said, drawing a wry chuckle from the *marzban*. "I only want you to keep him under some sort of rein till I return. Is that asking too much?"

"Time will tell," Mikhran replied in tones that did not drip optimism.

Roshnani, understanding why Abivard had been recalled to Mashiz, shared his worries. Like him, she had no idea whether they would be returning to Vaspurakan. Their children, however, went wild with excitement at the news, and Abivard could hardly blame them. Now, at last, they were going back to Makuran, a land that had assumed all but legendary proportions in their minds. And why not? They'd heard of it but had hardly any memories of seeing it.

When the King of Kings ordered his general to attend him immediately, he got what he desired. The day after his command reached Shahapivan, Pashang got the wagon in which Abivard and his family traveled rattling westward. With them rode an escort of fourscore heavy cavalry, partly to help clear the road at need and partly to persuade bandits that attacking the wagon would not be the best idea they'd ever had.

Past Maragha, the mountains of Vaspurakan began dwindling down toward hills once more and then to a rolling steppe country that was dry and bleak and cool in the winter, dry and bleak and blazing hot in summertime.

"I don't like this land," Abivard said when they stopped at one of the infrequent streams to water the horses.

"Nor I," Roshnani agreed. "The first time we went through it, after all—oh, south of here, but the same kind of country—was when we were fleeing the Thousand Cities and hoping the Videssians would give us shelter."

"You're right," he exclaimed. "That must be it, for this doesn't look much different from the badlands west of the Dilbat Mountains, the sort of country you'd find between strongholds. And yet the hair stood up on the back of my neck, and I didn't know why."

After a few days of crossing the badlands, days in which the only life they saw outside their own company was a handful of rabbits, a fox, and, high in the sky, a hawk endlessly circling, green glowed on the western horizon, almost as if the sea lay ahead. But Abivard, these past months, had turned his back on the sea. He pointed ahead, asking his children if they knew what the green meant.

Varaz obviously did but looked down on the question as being too easy for him to deign to answer. After a small hesitation Shahin said, "That's the start of the Thousand Cities, isn't it? The land between the rivers, I mean, the, the—" He scowled. He'd forgotten their names.

"The Tutub and the Tib," Varaz said importantly. Then, all at once, he lost some of that importance. "I'm sorry, Papa, but I've forgotten which one is which."

"That's the Tutub just ahead," Abivard answered. "The Tib marks the western boundary of the Thousand Cities."

Actually, the two rivers were not quite the boundaries of the rich, settled country. The canals that ran out from them were. A couple of the Thousand Cities lay to the east of the Tutub. Where the canals brought their life-giving waters, everything was green and growing, with farmers tending their onions and cucumbers and cress and lettuces and date-palm trees. A few yards beyond the canals the ground lay sere and brown and useless.

Roshnani peered out of the wagon. "Canals always seem so—wasteful," she said. "All that water on top of the ground and open to the thirsty air. *Qanats* would be better."

"You can drive a *qanat* through rock and carry water underground," Abivard said. Then he waved a hand. "Not much rock here. When you get right down to it, the Thousand Cities don't have much but mud and water and people—lots of people."

The wagon and its escort skirted some of the canals on dikes running in the right direction and crossed others on flat, narrow bridges of palm wood. Those were adequate for getting across the irrigation ditches; when they got to the Tutub, something more was needed, for even months away from its spring rising, it remained a formidable river.

It was spanned by a bridge of boats with timbers—real timbers from trees other than date palms—laid across them. Men in rowboats brought the bridge across from the western bank of the Tutub so that Abivard and his companions could cross over it. He knew there were other, similar bridges north and south along the Tutub and along the Tib and on some of their tributaries and some of the chief canals between them. Such crossings were quick to make and easy to maintain.

They were also useful in time of war: if you did not want your foes to cross a stretch of water, all you had to do was make sure the bridge of boats did not extend to the side of the river or canal he held. In the civil war against Smerdis the usurper's henchmen, who controlled most of the Thousand Cities, had greatly hampered Sharbaraz's movements by such means.

The folk who dwelt between the Tutub and the Tib were not of Makuraner blood, though the King of Kings had ruled the Thousand Cities from Mashiz for centuries. The peasants were small and swarthy, with hair so black that it held blue highlights. They wore linen tunics, the women's ankle-length, those of the men reaching down halfway between hip and knee. They would stare at the wagon and its escort of grim-faced fighting men, then shrug and get back to work.

When the wagon stopped at one of the Thousand Cities for the night, Pashang would invariably have to urge the team up a short but steep hill to reach the gate. That puzzled Varaz, who asked, "Why are the towns here always on top of hills? They aren't like that in Videssos. And why aren't there any hills without towns on them? This doesn't look like country where there should be hills. They stick up like warts."

"If it weren't for the people who live between the Tutub and the Tib, there wouldn't be any hills," Abivard answered. "The Thousand Cities are old; I don't think any man of Makuran knows just how old. Maybe they don't know here, either. But when Shippurak—this town here—was first built, it was on the same level as the plain all around; the same with all the other cities, too. But what do they use for building here?"

Varaz looked around. "Mud brick mostly, it looks like."

"That's right. It's what they have: lots of mud, no stone to speak of, and only date palms for timber. And mud brick doesn't last. When a house would start crumbling, they'd knock it down and build a new one on top of the rubble. When they'd been throwing rubbish into the street for so long that they had to step up from inside to get out through their doors, they'd do the same thing—knock the place down and rebuild with the new floor a palm's breadth higher, maybe two palm's breadths higher, than the old one. You do that again and again and again and after enough years go by, you have yourself a hill."

"They're living on top of their own rubbish?" Varaz said. Abivard nodded. His son took another look around, a longer one. "They're living on top of a *lot* of their own rubbish." Abivard nodded once more.

The city governor of Shippurak, a lean black-bearded Makuraner named Kharrad, greeted Abivard and his escort with wary effusiveness, for which Abivard blamed him not at all. He was brother-in-law to the King of Kings and the author of great victories against Videssos, and that accounted for the effusiveness. He was also being recalled to Mashiz under circumstances that Kharrad obviously did not know in detail but that just as obviously meant he had fallen out of favor to some degree. But how much? No wonder the city governor was wary.

He served up tender beans and chickpeas and boiled onions and twisted loaves of bread covered with sesame and poppy seeds. He did not act scandalized when Abivard brought Roshnani to the supper, though his own wife did not appear. When he saw that Roshnani would stay, he spoke quietly to one of his secretaries. The man nodded and hurried off. The entertainment after supper was unusually brief: only a couple of singers and harpers. Abivard wondered if a troupe of naked dancing girls had suddenly been excised from the program.

Kharrad said, "It must be strange returning to the court of the King of Kings, may his years be many and his realm increase, after so long away."

"I look forward to seeing my sister," Abivard answered. Let the city governor make of that what he would.

"Er—yes," Kharrad said, and quickly changed the subject. He didn't want to make anything of it, not where Abivard was listening to him.

Kharrad's reception was matched more or less exactly by other local leaders in the Thousand Cities over the next several days. The only real difference Abivard noted was that a couple of the city governors came from the ranks of the folk they controlled, having been born between the Tutub and the Tib. They did not receive Roshnani as if they were doing her a favor but as a matter of course and had their own wives and sometimes even their daughters join the suppers.

"Most of the time," one of them said after what might have been a cup too many of date wine, "you Makuraners are too stuffy about this. My wife nags me, but what can I do? If I offend her, she nags me. If I offend a man under the eye of the King of Kings, he makes me wish I was never born and maybe hurts my family, too. But you, brother-in-law to the King of Kings, you are not offended. My wife gets to come out and talk like a civilized human being, so she is not offended, either. Everyone is happy. Isn't that the way it ought to be?"

"Of course it is," Roshnani said. "Women's quarters were a mistake from the beginning. I wish Sharbaraz King of Kings, may his days be long and his realm increase, would outlaw them altogether."

"Yes, by the God!" the city governor's wife exclaimed. "May she plant that idea firmly in his Majesty's mind and heart."

A little farther down the low table Turan, the commander of the troopers escorting Abivard and his family, choked on his date wine. "Sweeter than I'm used to," he wheezed, wiping his mouth on the sleeve of his caftan.

That was true; Abivard found the sticky stuff cloying, too. He didn't think it was why Turan had swallowed wrong. Some nobles did ape Sharbaraz and himself and give their principal wives more freedom than upper-crust Makuraner women had customarily enjoyed. Others, though, muttered darkly about degeneration. Abivard did not think he would have to guess twice to figure out into which camp the escort commander fell.

They crossed the Tib on a bridge of boats much like the one

they'd used to cross the Tutub and enter the land between the rivers. Only a narrow strip of cultivated land ran along the western bank of the Tib. Canals could not reach far there, for the country soon began to slope up toward the Dilbat Mountains in whose foothills sat Mashiz.

Abivard pointed to the city and the smoke rising from it. "That's where we're going," he said. His children squealed excitedly. To them Mashiz was more nearly a legend than Videssos the city. They'd seen the capital of the Empire of Videssos misted in sea haze on the far side of the Cattle Crossing. Mashiz was new and therefore fascinating.

"That's where we're going," Roshnani agreed quietly. "How we'll come out again is another matter."

To enter Mashiz the cavalrymen escorting Abivard and his family donned their armor and decked their horses out in chamfrons and iron-studded blankets, too. They carried the lances that had stayed bundled in the bed of a wagon since they'd crossed the Tutub. It was a fine warlike display, making Abivard seem to be returning to the capital of his homeland in triumph. He wished reality were a better match for appearance.

People stared at the jingling martial procession that hurried through the streets toward the palace of the King of Kings. Some pointed, some cheered, and some loudly wondered what was being celebrated and why. Even when the horsemen shouted out Abivard's name, not everyone knew who he was. *So much for fame,* he thought with wry amusement.

In the market squares his escort had to slow from a trot to a walk. They fumed, but Abivard took that as a good sign. If so many people were buying and selling things that they crowded the squares, Makuran had to be prosperous.

The palace of the King of Kings was different from its equivalent in Videssos the city, which Abivard had so often watched with longing. The Avtokrator of the Videssians and his court had a good many buildings scattered among lawns and groves. Here in Mashiz, the King of Kings' palace lay all under one roof, with a dark stone wall surrounding it and turning it into a citadel in the heart of the city.

To preserve the outwall's military usefulness, the square around it was bare of buildings for a bowshot. When Smerdis the usurper had held Mashiz, Abivard had fought his way to the palace against soldiers and sorcery. Now, years later, summoned by the man he'd helped place on the throne, he approached with hardly less apprehension.

"Who comes?" called a sentry from above the gates. Oh, he knew, but the forms had to be observed.

"Abivard son of Godarz, returned to Mashiz from Videssos and Vaspurakan at the order of Sharbaraz King of Kings, may his days be long and his realm increase."

"Enter, Abivard son of Godarz, obedient to the command of Sharbaraz King of Kings," the sentry said. He called to the gate crew. With squeaks from hinges that needed oiling, the gates swung open. Abivard entered the palace.

Almost at once an army of servitors swarmed upon and overwhelmed his little army of warriors. Stablemen and grooms vanquished the riders. They waited impatiently for the cavalry-men to dismount so they could lead the horses off to the stables. Their armored riders accompanied them, reduced to near impo-tence by having to use their own legs to move from one place to another.

Higher-ranking servants saw to Abivard and Roshnani. A plump eunuch said, "If you will please to come with me, brother-in-law to the King of Kings, yes, with your excellent family, of course. Oh, yes," he went on, answering a question Abivard had been on the point of asking, "your conveyance and your driver will be attended to: you have the word of Sekandar upon it." He preened slightly so they would know he was Sekandar.

"How soon will we be able to see the King of Kings?" Abivard asked as the chamberlain led them into the palace itself.

"That is for the puissant Sharbaraz, may his years be many and his realm increase, to judge," Sekandar answered.

Abivard nodded and kept on following the eunuch but worried down where—he hoped—it did not show. If the King of Kings seldom left the palace and listened to the advice of Sekandar and others like him, how could he have any notion of what was true? Once, Sharbaraz had been a fighting man who led fighting men and took pleasure in their company. Now . . . Would he even acknowledge who Abivard was?

The apartment in which the eunuch installed Abivard and his family was luxurious past anything he had known in Videssos, and it was luxury of a familiar sort, not the icons and hard furniture of the Empire. Carpets into which his feet sank deep lay on the floor; thick, fat cushions were scattered in the corners of the rooms to support one's back while sitting. They had other uses, too; Varaz grabbed one and clouted Shahin with it. Shahin picked up his own, using it first for defense, then for offense.

"They're used to chairs," Abivard said. "They won't know how comfortable this can be till they try it for a while."

Roshnani was speaking to her sons in standard tones of exasperation. "Try not to tear the palace down around our ears *quite* yet, if you please." She seamlessly made a shift in subject to reply to her husband: "No, they won't." As if making a shameful confession, she added, "Nor will I, as a matter of fact. I got to like chairs a good deal. My knee clicks and my back crackles whenever I have to get up from the floor."

"So Videssos corrupted you, too?" Abivard asked, not quite joking.

"Life in the Empire could be very pleasant," his wife answered, as if defying him to deny it. "Our food is better, but they do more with the rest of life than we do."

"Hmm," Abivard said. "My backside starts turning to stone if I sit in a chair too long. I don't know; I think their towns are madhouses myself, far worse than Mashiz or any of the Thousand Cities. They're too fast, too busy, too set on getting ahead even if they have to cheat to do it. Those are all the complaints we've had about Videssians for hundreds of years, and if you ask me, they're all true."

Roshnani didn't seem to feel like arguing the point. She looked at the chambers in which the palace servitors had established them. "We are going nowhere, fast or slow; the God knows we shan't be busy, and the only way we can get ahead is if the King of Kings should will it."

"As is true of anyone in Makuran," Abivard said loudly for the benefit of anyone in Makuran who might be listening. Without seeming to, though, his wife had not only won the argument but pointed out that, palace though this might be for Sharbaraz, for Abivard and his kin it was a prison.

Winter dragged on, one storm following another till it looked as if the world would stay cold and icy forever. With each passing day Abivard came more and more to realize how right Roshnani had been.

He and his family saw only the servants who brought them food, hot water for bathing, and clothes once they had been laundered. He tried to bribe them to carry a note to Turan, the commander of the guard company that had escorted him to Mashiz. They took his money, but he never heard back from the officer. Their apologies sounded sincere but not sincere enough for him to believe them.

But having nothing better to do with his time and no better place to spend his money, he eventually tried getting a note to Denak. His sister never wrote back, either, at least not with a letter that reached his hands. He wondered whether his note or hers had disappeared. His, he suspected. If she knew what Sharbaraz was doing to him, she would make the King of Kings change his ways.

If she could—"Does she still have the influence she did in the early days of her marriage?" Roshnani asked after the Void had swallowed Abivard's letter. "Sharbaraz will have seen—not to put too fine a point on it, will have had—a lot of women in the years between."

"I know," Abivard said glumly. "As I knew him—" The past tense hurt but was true. "—as I knew him, I say, he always acknowledged his debts. But after a while any man could grow resentful, I suppose."

Varaz said, "Why not petition the King of Kings yourself, Father? Any man of Makuran has the right to be heard."

So, no doubt, his pedagogue had taught him. "What you learned and what is real aren't always the same thing, worse luck," Abivard answered. "The King of Kings is angry at me. That's why he would not hear my petition."

"Oh," Varaz said. "You mean the way Shahin won't listen to me after we've had a fight?"

"You're the one who won't listen to me," Shahin put in.

Having the advantage in age, Varaz took the lofty privilege of ignoring his younger brother. "*Is* that what you mean, Papa?" he asked.

"Yes, pretty much," Abivard answered. When you got down to it, the way Sharbaraz was treating him was childish. The idea of the all-powerful King of Kings in the guise of a bad-tempered small boy made him smile. Again, though, he fought shy of mentioning it out loud. You never could tell whose ear might be pressed to a small hole behind one of the tapestries hanging on the wall. If the King of Kings was angry at him, there was no point making things worse by speaking plain and simple truths in the hearing of his servants.

"I don't like this place," Zarmidukh declared. She was too young to worry about what other people thought when she spoke her mind. She said what she thought, whatever that happened to be. "It's boring."

"It's not the most exciting place I've ever been," Abivard said, "but there are worse things than being bored."

"I don't know of any," Zarmidukh said darkly.

"You're lucky," Abivard told her. "I do."

Someone rapped on the door. Abivard looked at Roshnani. It wasn't any of the times the palace servitors usually made an appearance. The knock came again, imperiously—or perhaps he was reading too much into it. "Who can it be?" he said.

With her usual practicality Roshnani answered, "The only way to find out is to open the door."

"Thank you so much for your help," he said. She made a face at him. He got up and went over to the door, his feet sinking deep into the thick carpet as he walked. He took hold of the handle and pulled the door open.

A eunuch with hard, suspicious eyes in a face of almost unearthly beauty looked him up and down as if to say he'd taken much too long getting there. "You are Abivard son of Godarz?" The voice was unearthly, too: very pure and clear but not in a register commonly used by either men or women. When Abivard admitted who he was, the eunuch said, "You will come with me at once," and started down the halls without waiting to see if he followed.

The guards who stood to either side of the doorway did not acknowledge his passing. Not even their eyes shifted as he walked by. Roshnani closed the door. Had she come after him unbidden, the guards would not have seemed as if they were carved from stone.

He did not ask the eunuch where they were going. He didn't think the fellow would tell him and declined to give him the pleasure of refusing. They walked in silence through close to half a farsang's worth of corridors. At last the eunuch stopped. "Go through this doorway," he said imperiously. "I await you here."

"Have a pleasant wait," Abivard said, earning a fresh glare. Pretending he didn't notice it, he opened the door and went in.

"Welcome to Mashiz, brother of mine," Denak said. She nodded when Abivard closed the door after himself. "That is wise. The fewer people who hear what we say, the better."

Abivard pointed to the maidservant who sat against the wall, idly painting her nails one by one from a pot of red dye and examining them with attention more careful than that she seemed to be giving Denak. "And yet you brought another pair of ears here?" he asked.

Denak assumed an exasperated expression, which brought lines to her face. Abivard hadn't seen much of her after Sharbaraz had taken Mashiz. He knew he'd aged in the intervening decade, but realizing that his sister had also aged came hard. She said, "I am principal wife to the King of Kings. It would be most unseemly for any man to see me alone. Most unseemly."

"By the God, I'm your brother!" Abivard said angrily.

"And that is how I managed to arrange to see you at all," Denak answered. "I think it will be all right, or not too bad. Ksorane is about as likely to tell me what Sharbaraz says as the other way around, or so I've found. Isn't that right, dear?" She waved to the girl.

"How could the principal wife to Sharbaraz King of Kings, may his days be long and his realm increase, be wrong?" Ksorane said. She put another layer of paint on the middle finger of her left hand.

Denak's laugh was as sour as vinegar. "Easily enough, by the God. I've found that out many a time and oft." If she'd said one word more, Abivard would have bet any amount any man cared to name that the maidservant, trusted or not, would have taken her remark straight to Sharbaraz. Even as things were, he worried. But Denak seemed oblivious, continuing, "As you have now found for yourself—is it not so, brother of mine?"

In spite of Denak's assurances, Abivard found it hard to speak his mind before someone he did not know. Cautiously, he answered, "Sometimes a man far from the field of action does not have everything he needs to judge whether his best interests are being followed."

Denak laughed again, a little less edgily this time. "You shouldn't be a general, brother of mine; the King of Kings should send you to Videssos the city as ambassador. You'd win from Maniakes with your honeyed words everything our armies haven't managed to take."

"I've spoken with Maniakes, when he came close to Across in one of the Videssians' cursed dromons," Abivard said. "I wish the God would drop all of those into the Void. We found no agreement. Nor, it seems, does Sharbaraz King of Kings find agreement with what I did in Vaspurakan. I wish he would summon me and say as much himself, so I might answer."

"People don't get everything they wish," Denak answered. "I know all about that, too." Her hopeless anger tore at Abivard. But then she went on, "This once, though, I got at least part of what I want. When the King of Kings heard you'd ignored his orders about Vaspurakan, he didn't only want to take your head from your shoulders—he wanted to give you over to the torturers."

As Abivard had learned after he had taken the Videssian westlands for Sharbaraz, the parents and nursemaids of the Empire used the ferocious talents of Makuraner torturers to frighten naughty children into obeying. He bowed very low. "Sister of mine, I am in your debt. My children are young to be fatherless. I should not complain about being unable to see the King of Kings."

"Of course you should," Denak said. "After him, you are the most powerful man in Makuran. He has no business to treat you so, no right—"

"He has the right: he is the King of Kings," Abivard said. "After the King of Kings, no man in Makuran is powerful. I was the most powerful Makuraner outside Makuran, perhaps." Now his grin came wry. "Once back within it, though . . . he may do with me as he will."

"In your mind you have no power next to Sharbaraz," Denak answered. "Every day courtiers whisper into his ear that you have too much. I can go only so far in making him not listen. He might pay me more heed if—"

If I had a son. Abivard filled in the words his sister would not say. Sharbaraz had several sons by lesser wives, but Denak had given him only girls. If she had a boy, he would become the heir, for she remained Sharbaraz's principal wife. But what were the odds of that? Did he still call her to his bed? Abivard could not ask, but his sister did not sound as if she expected to bear more children.

As if picking that thought from his mind, Denak said, "He treats me with all due honor. As he promised, I am not mewed up in the women's quarters like a hawk dozing with a hood over its eyes. He does remember—everything. But honor alone is not enough for a man and a wife."

She did speak as if Ksorane weren't there. At last Abivard imitated her, saying, "If Sharbaraz remembers all you did for him—and if he does, I credit him—why, by the God, doesn't he remember what I've done and trust my judgment?"

"I'd think that would be easy for you to see," Denak told him. "Come what may, *I* can't steal the throne from him. *You* can."

"I helped put him on the throne," Abivard protested indignantly. "I risked everything I had—I risked everything Vek Rud domain had—to put him on the throne. I don't want it. Till you spoke of it just now, the idea that I would want it never once entered my mind. If it entered his—"

He started to say, *He's mad.* He didn't, and fear of the maid-servant's taking his words to Sharbaraz wasn't what stopped him. For the King of Kings was not mad to fear usurpation. After all, he'd been usurped once already.

"He's wrong." That was better. Abivard reminded himself that he was speaking with Sharbaraz's wife as well as his own sister. But Denak *was* his sister, and how much he'd missed her over the years suddenly rose up in him like a choking cloud. "You *know* me, sister of mine. You know I would never do such a thing."

Her face crumpled. Tears made her eyes bright. "I knew you," she said. "I know the brother I knew would be loyal to the right-ful King of Kings through . . . anything." She held her hands wide apart to show how all-encompassing *anything* was. But then she went on. "I *knew* you. It's been so long . . . Time changes people, brother of mine. I know that, too. I should."

"It's been so long," Abivard echoed sadly. "I can't make Shar-baraz's years many; only the God grants years. But since the days of Razmara the Magnificent, who has increased the realm of the King of Kings more than I?"

"No one." Denak's voice was sad. One of the tears ran down her cheek. "And don't you see, brother of mine, every victory you won, every city you brought under the lion of Makuran, gave him one more reason to distrust you."

Abivard hadn't seen that, not with such brutal clarity. But it was clear enough—all too clear—when Denak pointed it out to him. He chewed on the inside of his lower lip. "And when I disobeyed him in Vaspurakan—"

Denak nodded. "Now you understand. When you disobeyed him, he thought it the first step of your rebellion."

"If it was, why did I come here with all my family at his order?" Abivard asked. "Once I did that, shouldn't he have realized he was wrong?"

"So I told him, though not in those words." One corner of his sister's mouth bent up in a rueful, knowing smile. "So many people tell the King of Kings he is right every moment of every waking hour of every day that when he was already inclined to think so himself, he became . . . quite convinced of it."

"I suppose so." Abivard had noted that trait in Sharbaraz even when he was a hunted rebel against Smerdis. After a decade and more on the throne at Mashiz he might well have come to think of himself as infallible. What Abivard wanted to say was, *He's only a man, after all.* But of all the things Ksorane could take back to Sharbaraz from his lips, that one might do the most damage.

Denak said, "I have been trying to get him to see you, brother of mine. So far . . ." She spread her hands again. He knew how much luck she'd had. But he also knew he still kept his head on his shoulder and all his members attached to his body. That was probably his sister's doing.

"Tell the King of Kings I did not mean to anger him," he said wearily. "Tell him I am loyal—why would I be here otherwise? Tell him in Vaspurakan I was doing what I thought best for the realm, for I was closer to the trouble than he. Tell him—" *Tell him to drop into the Void if he's too vain and puffed up with himself to see that on his own.* "Tell him once more what you've already told him. The God willing, he will hear."

"I shall tell him," Denak said. "I have been telling him. But when everyone else tells him the opposite, when Farrokh-Zad and Tzikas write from Vaspurakan complaining of how mild you were to the priests of Phos—"

"Tzikas wrote from Vaspurakan?" Abivard broke in. "Tzikas wrote *that* from Vaspurakan? If I see the renegade, the traitor, the wretch again, he is a dead man." His lips curled in what looked like a smile. "I know just what I'll do if I see him again, the cursed Videssian schemer. I'll send him as a present for Maniakes behind a shield of truce. We'll see how he likes *that*." Merely contemplating the idea gave him great satisfaction. Whether he'd ever get the chance to do anything about it was, worse luck, another question altogether.

"I'll pray to the God. May she grant your wish," Denak said. She got to her feet. Abivard rose, too. His sister took him in her arms.

Ksorane, about whom Abivard had almost entirely forgotten, let out a startled squeak. "Highness, to touch a man other than the King of Kings is not permitted."

"He is my brother, Ksorane," Denak answered in exasperated tones.

Abivard did not know whether to laugh or cry. He and Denak had criticized Sharbaraz King of Kings almost to, maybe even beyond, the point of lese majesty, and the serving woman had spoken not a word of protest. Indeed, by her manner she might not even have heard. Yet a perfectly innocent embrace drew horrified anger.

"The world is a very strange place," he said. He went back into the hall. If the eunuch had moved while he had been talking with his sister, it could not have been by more than the breadth of a hair. With a cold, hard nod the fellow led him back through the maze of corridors to the chambers where he and his family were confined.

The guards outside the chamber opened his door. The beautiful eunuch, who had said not a word while guiding him to his private prison, disappeared with silent steps. The door closed behind Abivard, and everything was just as it had been before Denak had summoned him.

When Sharbaraz King of Kings did not call him, Abivard grew furious at his sister. Rationally, he knew that was not only pointless but stupid. Denak might plead for him, as she had been pleading for him, but that did not mean that Sharbaraz would have to hear. By everything Abivard knew of the King of Kings, he was very good at not hearing.

Winter dragged on. The children at first grew restive at being cooped up in a small place like so many doves in a cote, then resigned themselves to it. That worried Abivard more than anything else he'd seen since Sharbaraz had ordered him to Mashiz.

Over and over he asked the guards who kept him and his family from leaving their rooms and the servants who fed them and removed the slop jars and brought fuel what was going on in Vaspurakan and Videssos. He rarely got answers, and the ones he did get formed no coherent pattern. Some people claimed there was fighting; others, that peace prevailed.

"Why don't they just say they don't know?" he demanded of Roshnani after yet another rumor—that Maniakes had slain himself in despair—reached his ears.

"You're asking a lot if you expect people to admit how ignorant they are," she answered. She had adapted to captivity better than he had. She worked on embroidery with thread borrowed from the servants and seemed to take so much pleasure from it that Abivard was more than once tempted to get her to teach him the stitches.

"I admit how ignorant I am here," he said. "Otherwise I wouldn't ask so many questions."

Roshnani loosened the hoop that held a circle of linen taut while she worked on it. She shook her head. "You don't understand. The only reason you're ignorant is that you're shut up here. You can't know what you want to find out. Too many people don't want to find out anything and just repeat what they happen to hear without thinking about it."

He thought about that, then slowly nodded. "You're probably right," he admitted. "It doesn't make this easier to bear, though."

In the end he did learn to embroider and concentrated his fury in producing the most hideous dragon he could imagine. He was glad he had only the rudiments of the craft, for if he could have matched Roshnani's skill, he would have given the dragon Sharbaraz's face.

Some of his imaginings along those lines disturbed him. In his mind he formed a picture of his army swarming out of Vaspurakan to rescue him that felt so real, he was shocked and disappointed when no one came battering down the door. As it had a way of doing, hope outran reality.

Among themselves, the servants began to talk of rain rather

than snow. Abivard noted that he wasn't feeding the braziers as much charcoal as he had been or sleeping under such great piles of rugs and furs and blankets. Spring was coming. He, on the other hand, had nowhere to go, nothing to do.

"Ask Sharbaraz King of Kings, may his years be many and his realm increase, if he will free my family and let them go back to Vek Rud domain," he told a guard—and whoever might be listening. "If he wants to punish me, that is his privilege, but they have done nothing to deserve his anger."

Sharbaraz's privilege, though, was whatever he chose to make it. If the message got to him, he took no notice of it.

As one dreary day dragged into the next, Abivard began to understand Tzikas better. Unlike the Videssian renegade, he had done nothing to make his sovereign nervous about his loyalty—so he still believed, at any rate. But Sharbaraz had gotten nervous anyhow, and the results—

"How am I supposed to command another Makuraner army after this?" he whispered to Roshnani in the darkness after their children—and, with luck, any lurking listeners—had gone to bed.

"What would you do, husband of mine, if you got another command?" she asked, even more softly than he had spoken. "Would you go over to the Videssians to pay back the King of Kings for what he's done?"

She had been thinking about Tzikas, too, then. Abivard shook his head. "No. I am loyal to Makuran. I would be loyal to Sharbaraz, if he would let me. But even if I had no grievance against him before, I do now. How could he let me lead troops without being afraid that I would try to take the vengeance I deserve?"

"He has to trust you," Roshnani said. "In the end I think he will. Did not your wizard see you fighting in the land of the Thousand Cities?"

"Bogorz? Yes, he did. But was he looking into the past or the future? I didn't know then, and I don't know now."

Bogorz had seen another image, too: Videssians and ships, soldiers disembarking at an unknown place at an equally unknown time. How much that had to do with the rest of his vision, Abivard could not begin to guess. If the wizard had shown him a piece of the future, it was a useless one.

Roshnani sighed. "Not knowing is hard," she agreed. "The way we're treated here, for instance: by itself, it wouldn't be bad. But since we don't know what will come at the end of it, how can we help but worry?"

"How indeed?" Abivard said. He hadn't told her that Sharbaraz had wanted to take his head—and worse. *What point to that?* he'd asked himself. Had the King of Kings chosen to do it, Roshnani could not have stopped him, and if he hadn't, Abivard would have made her fret without need. He seldom held things back from her but kept that one to himself without the slightest trace of guilt.

She snuggled against him. Though the night was not so chilly as the nights had been, he was glad of her warmth. He wondered if they would still be in this chamber when nights, no less than days, were sweaty torments and skin did nothing but stick to skin. If they were meant to be, they would, he decided. He could do nothing about it one way or the other. Presently he gave up and fell asleep.

The door to the chamber opened. Abivard's children stared. It wasn't the usual time. Abivard stared, too. He'd been shut up so long, he found a change of routine dangerous in and of itself.

Into the room came the beautiful eunuch who had conducted him to Denak. "Come with me," he said in his beautiful, sexless voice.

"Are you taking me to see my sister again?" Abivard asked, climbing to his feet.

"Come with me," the eunuch repeated, as if it were none of Abivard's business where he was going till he got there, and perhaps not then, either.

Having no choice, Abivard went with him. As he walked out the door, he reflected that things could hardly be worse. He'd thought that before, too, every now and then. Sometimes he'd been wrong, which was something he would rather not have remembered.

He quickly realized that the eunuch was not leading him down the same halls he had traveled to visit Denak. He asked again where they were going, but only stony silence answered him. Though the eunuch said not a word, hatred bubbled up from him like steam from a boiling pot. Abivard wondered if that was hatred for him in particular or for any man lucky enough to have a beard and all parts complete and in good working order.

Several times they passed other people in the hall: some servants, some nobles. Abivard was tempted to ask them if they knew where he was going and what would happen to him when he got there. The only thing holding him back was a certainty that one way or another the eunuch would pay him back for his temerity.

He hadn't been in the palace for years before the summons had come that had led him to become much more intimately acquainted with one small part of it than he'd ever wanted to be. All the same, the corridors through which he was traveling began to look familiar.

"Are we going to—?" he asked, and then stopped with the question incomplete. The way the eunuch's back stiffened told him plainer than words that he'd get no answer. This once, though, it mattered less than it might have under other circumstances. Sooner or later, regardless of what the eunuch told him, he would know.

Without warning, the hallway turned and opened out into a huge chamber whose roof was supported by rows of columns. Those columns and the long expanse of carpet running straight ahead from the entrance guided the eye to the great throne at the far end of the room. "Advance and be recognized," the eunuch told Abivard. "I presume you still recall the observances."

By his tone, he presumed no such thing. Abivard confined himself to one tight nod. "I remember," he said, and advanced down the carpet toward the throne where Sharbaraz King of Kings sat waiting.

Nobles standing in the shadows stared at him as he strode forward. The walls of the throne room looked different from the way he remembered them. He could not turn his head—not without violating court ritual—but flicked his eyes to the right and the left. Yes, those wall hangings were definitely new. They showed Makuraner triumphs over the armies of Videssos, triumphs where he had commanded the armies of the King of Kings. The irony smote him like a club.

The eunuch stepped aside when the carpet ended. Abivard strode out onto the polished stone beyond the woven wool and prostrated himself before Sharbaraz. He wondered how many thousands of men and women had gone down on their bellies before the King of Kings in the long years since the palace had been built. Enough, certainly, to give a special polish to the patch of stone where their foreheads touched.

Sharbaraz let him stay prostrate longer than he should have. At last, he said, "Rise."

"I obey, Majesty," Abivard said, getting to his feet. Now he was permitted to look upon the august personage of the King of Kings. His first thought was, *He's gone fat and soft.* Sharbaraz had been a lion of a warrior when he and Abivard had campaigned together against Smerdis the usurper. He seemed to have put on a good many more pounds than the intervening time should have made possible.

"We are not well pleased with you, Abivard son of Godarz," he declared. Even his voice sounded higher and more querulous than it had. His face was pale, as if he never saw the sun. Abivard knew he was pale, too, but he'd been imprisoned; Sharbaraz had no such excuse. Though Abivard hadn't seen himself in a mirror any time lately, he would have bet he didn't carry those dark, pouchy circles under his eyes.

He strangled the scorn welling up in him. No matter how Sharbaraz looked, he remained King of Kings. Whatever he decreed, that would be Abivard's fate. *Walk soft,* Abivard reminded himself. *Walk soft.* "I grieve to have displeased you, Majesty," he said. "I never intended to do that."

"We *are* displeased," Sharbaraz said, as if passing sentence. Perhaps he was doing just that; several of the courtiers let out soft sighs. Abivard wondered if the execution would be performed in the throne room for their edification. The King of Kings went on, "We trusted you to obey our commands pertaining to Vaspurakan, as we expect to be obeyed in all things."

In the old days as a rebel against Smerdis he hadn't been so free with the royal *we.* Hearing it from a man with whose humanity and fallibility he was all too intimately acquainted irked Abivard. With a sudden burst of insight he realized that Sharbaraz was trying to overawe him precisely because they had once been intimates: to subsume the remembered man in the present King of Kings. As such ploys often did, it had an effect opposite to the one Sharbaraz had intended.

Abivard said, "I pray your pardon, Majesty. I served Makuran as best I could."

"The affair appears otherwise to us," the King of Kings replied.

"In disobeying our orders, you damaged the realm and brought both it and us into disrepute."

"I pray your pardon," Abivard repeated. He might have known—indeed, he had known—Sharbaraz would say that. Disobedience was a failure no ruler could tolerate, and as he and Roshnani had agreed, being right was in a way worse than being wrong.

But Sharbaraz said, "In our judgment you have now been punished enough for your transgressions. We have summoned you hither to inform you that Makuran once more has need of your services."

"Majesty?" Abivard had been half expecting—more than half expecting—the King of Kings to order him sent to the headsman or the torturers. If he'd frightened Sharbaraz, he could expect no better fate. Now, though, with courtiers murmuring approval in the background, the King of Kings had . . . pardoned him? "What do you need of me, Majesty?" Whatever it was, it couldn't be much worse than going off to meet the chopper.

"We begin to see why you had such difficulties in bringing Videssos the city under the lion of Makuran," Sharbaraz answered. It wasn't an apology—not quite—but it was closer to one than Abivard had ever heard from the King of Kings, who went on, not altogether comfortably, "We also see that Maniakes Avtokrator exemplifies in his person the wicked deviousness our lore so often attributes to the men of Videssos."

"In what way, Majesty?" Abivard asked in lieu of screaming, *By the God, what's he gone and done now?* He made himself keep his voice low and calm as he twisted the knife just a little. "As you will remember, I had not had much chance to learn what passes outside Mashiz." He hadn't had much chance to learn what passed outside the chamber in which Sharbaraz had locked him away, but the King of Kings already knew that.

Sharbaraz said, "Our one weakness is in ships. We have come to realize how serious a weakness it is." Abivard had realized that the instant he had seen how Videssian dromons kept his army from getting over the Cattle Crossing; he was glad Sharbaraz had been given a similar revelation, no matter how long delayed it was. The King of Kings went on. "Taking a sizable fleet, Maniakes has sailed with it to Lyssaion in the Videssian westlands and there disembarked an expeditionary force."

"Lyssaion, Majesty?" Abivard frowned, trying to place the town on his mental map of the westlands. At first he had no luck, for he was thinking of the northern coastline, the one on the Videssian Sea and closest to Vaspurakan. Then he said, "Oh, on the southern coast, the one by the Sailor's Sea—the far southwest of the westlands."

He stiffened. He should have realized that at once—after all, hadn't Bozorg shown him Videssians coming ashore somewhere very like there and then heading up through the mountains? He'd had knowledge of Maniakes' plan for most of a year—and much good that had done him.

"Yes," Sharbaraz was saying, his words running parallel to Abivard's thoughts. "They landed there, as I told you. And they have been pushing northwest ever since—pushing toward the land of the Thousand Cities." He paused, then said what was probably the worst thing he could think of: "Pushing toward Mashiz."

Abivard took that in and blended it with the insight he now had—too late—from Bogorz's scrying. "After Maniakes beat the Kubratoi last year, he was too quiet by half," he said at last. "I kept expecting him to do something against us, especially when I pulled the field force out of the Videssian westlands to fight in Vaspurakan." *I wouldn't have had to do that but for your order to suppress the worship of Phos*—another thing he couldn't tell the King of Kings. "But he never moved. I wondered what he was up to. Now we know."

"Now we know," Sharbaraz agreed. "We never took Videssos the city in war, but the Videssians have sacked Mashiz. We do not intend this to happen again."

Undoubtedly, the King of Kings intended to sound fierce and martial. Undoubtedly, his courtiers would assure him he sounded very fierce and martial, indeed. *He's afraid*, Abivard realized, and a chill ran through him. *He did well enough when the war was far away, but now it's coming here, almost close enough to touch. He's been comfortable too long. He's lost the stomach for that kind of fight. He had it once, but it's gone.*

Aloud, he repeated, "How may I serve you, Majesty?"

"Take up an army." Sharbaraz's words were quick and harsh. "Take it up, I say, and rid the realm of the invader. Makuran's honor demands it. The Videssians must be repulsed."

Does Maniakes know he's putting him in fear? Abivard wondered.

Or is he striking at our vitals tit for tat, as we have struck at his? Command of the sea lets him pick his spots.

"What force have you for me to use against the imperials, Majesty?" he asked—a highly relevant question. Was Sharbaraz sending him forth in the hope he would be defeated and killed?

"Take up the garrisons from as many of the Thousand Cities as suits you," Sharbaraz answered. "With them to hand, you will far outnumber the foe."

"Yes, Majesty, but—" Contradicting the King of Kings before the whole court would not improve Abivard's standing here. True, *if* he took up all the garrisons from the Thousand Cities, he would have far more men in the field than Maniakes did. Being able to do anything useful with them was something else again. Almost all of them were foot soldiers. Simply mustering them would take time. Getting them in front of Maniakes' fast-moving horsemen and bringing him to battle would take not only time but great skill—and even greater luck.

Did Sharbaraz understand that? Studying him, Abivard decided he did. It was one of the reasons he was afraid. He'd sent his best troops, his most mobile troops, into Videssos and Vaspurakan and had left himself little with which to resist a counterthrust he hadn't thought Maniakes would be able to make.

"Using the canals between the Tutub and the Tib will also let you delay the enemy and perhaps turn him back altogether," Sharbaraz said. "We remember well how the usurper whom we will not name put them to good use against us in the struggle for the throne."

"That is so, Majesty," Abivard agreed. It was also the first thing the King of Kings had said that made sense. If he could take up the garrisons from the cities between the rivers and put them to work wrecking canals and flooding the countryside, he might get more use from them than he would if he tried to make them fight the Videssians. It still might not net everything Sharbaraz hoped for; the Videssians were skilled engineers and expert at corduroying roads through unspeakable muck. But it would slow them down, and slowing them was worth doing.

"Also," Sharbaraz said, "for cavalry to match the horsemen Maniakes brings against us, we give you leave to recall Tzikas from Vaspurakan. His familiarity with the foe will win many

Videssians to our side. Further, you may take Hosios Avtokrator with you when you go forth to confront the foe."

Abivard opened his mouth, then closed it again. Sharbaraz was living in a dream world if he thought any Videssian would abandon Maniakes for his pretender. But then, insulated by the court *from* reality, in many ways Sharbaraz *was* living in a dream world.

Tzikas was a different matter. Unlike Sharbaraz's puppet, he did have solid connections within the Videssian army. If he got down to the land of the Thousand Cities soon enough, he might help solidify whatever force Abivard had managed to piece together from the local garrisons. Abivard suspected that Sharbaraz didn't know he knew what Tzikas had been saying about him; that meant Denak's maidservant was more reliable than Abivard had thought.

"Speak!" the King of Kings exclaimed. "What say you?"

"May it please you, Majesty, but I would sooner not have the eminent Tzikas—" Abivard gave the title in Videssian to emphasize the turncoat's foreignness. "—under my command." *About the only thing I'd like less would be the God dropping all Makuran into the Void.*

For a wonder, Sharbaraz took the hint "Perhaps another commander, then," he said. Abivard had feared he'd insist; he didn't know what he would have done then. Arranged for Tzikas to have an accident, maybe. If any man ever deserved an accident, Tzikas was the one.

"Perhaps so, Majesty," Abivard answered. Curse it, how did you tell the King of Kings he'd made a harebrained suggestion? You couldn't not if you wanted to keep your head on your shoulders. From what he'd seen, the Avtokrator of the Videssians had a similar problem, perhaps in less acute form.

Sharbaraz said, "We are confident you will hold the enemy far away from us and far away from Mashiz, preserving our complete security."

"The God grant it be so," Abivard said. "The men of Makuran have beaten the Videssians many times during your glorious reign." He had led Sharbaraz's troops to a lot of those victories, too. Now the King of Kings suddenly recalled that: he needed one more victory, or maybe more than one. Abivard went on, "I shall do all I can for you and for Makuran. The Videssians, though, I must say, fight with more spirit for Maniakes than they ever did for Genesios."

"We are confident," the King of Kings repeated. "Go forth, Abivard son of Godarz: go forth and defeat the foe. Then return in triumph to the bosom of your wife and family."

Almost, Abivard missed the meaning lurking there. That made the surge of fury all the more ferocious when it came. Sharbaraz was going to hold Roshnani and his children hostage to guarantee he would neither rebel once he had an army under his command again nor go over to the Videssians.

He thinks he is. Abivard said, "Majesty, my wife and children have always taken the field with me, ever since the days when you guested at Vek Rud stronghold."

The days when you were first a prisoner whom I helped rescue and then a rebel against the King of Kings ruling in Mashiz, he meant. From behind him came the faintest of murmurs: Sharbaraz's courtiers took the point. By the way the countenance of the King of Kings darkened, so did he. He tried to put the best face on it that he could: "We think only for their safety. Here in Mashiz all their needs will be met, and they will be in no danger from vicious marauding Videssians."

Abivard looked Sharbaraz in the face. That was not quite a discourtesy, or did not have to be, but the way he held Sharbaraz's eyes certainly was. "If you rely on me to protect you and your capital, Majesty, surely you can rely on me to protect my kin."

The murmur behind him got louder. He wondered how long it had been since someone had defied the King of Kings, no matter how politely, in his own throne room. Generations, probably. By the dazed expression on Sharbaraz's face, it had never happened to him before.

He tried to rally, saying, "Surely we know better than you the proper course in this affair, that which would be most expedient for all Makuran."

Abivard shrugged. "I have enjoyed the company of my wife and children all through the winter. May it please you, Majesty, I would just as soon return to them in the chambers you so generously granted us." *If I don't take them with me, I won't go out.*

"It does not please us," Sharbaraz answered in a hard voice. "We place the good of the realm ahead of that of any one man."

"The good of the realm will not be harmed if I take my family with me." Abivard gave the King of Kings a sidelong look. "I will have one more reason to repel the Videssians if my wife and children are at my side."

"That is not our view of the matter," Sharbaraz said.

The murmurs behind Abivard were almost loud enough now for him to make out individual voices and words. People would speak of this scandal for years. "Perhaps, Majesty, you would be better served with a different general in command of these garrison troops," he said.

"Had we wanted a different general, be sure we should have selected one," the King of Kings replied. "We are aware we have a great many from among whom we may choose. Rest assured you were not picked at random."

You're the one who's done best. That was what he meant. Abivard felt like laughing in his face. If he wanted Abivard and no one else, that limited his choices. He couldn't do anything dreadful to Roshnani or the children, not if he expected Abivard to serve him. What better way to get Abivard to do what he said he would not do and go over to Videssos?

How long had it been since the King of Kings had wanted someone to do something but had not gotten his way? By the frustrated glare on Sharbaraz's face, a long time. "Do you presume to disobey our will?" he demanded.

"No, Majesty," Abivard said. *Yes, Majesty—again.* "Loose me against the Videssians and I will do everything I can to drive them from the realm. So the King of Kings has ordered; so shall it be. My family will watch as I oppose Maniakes with every fiber of my being."

And if my family isn't there to watch—well, it doesn't matter then, anyhow, for I won't be there doing the fighting. Abivard smiled at his brother-in-law. No, Sharbaraz was not giving the orders here. How long would he need to realize as much?

He was not stupid. Arrogant, certainly, and stubborn, and long accustomed to having others leap to fulfill his every wish, but not stupid. "It shall be as you say," he replied at length. "You and your family shall go forth against Maniakes. But as you have set the terms under which you deign to fight, so you have also set for yourself the terms of the fight. We shall look for victory from you, nothing less."

"If you send forth a general expecting him to fail, you've sent forth the wrong general," Abivard answered. A nasty chill of worry ran down his back. Again he wondered if Sharbaraz was setting him up to fail so he could justify eliminating him.

No. Abivard could not believe it. The King of Kings needed no such elaborate justifications. Once Abivard was away from his army and in Mashiz, Sharbaraz could have eliminated him whenever he chose.

The King of Kings gestured brusquely. "We dismiss you, Abivard son of Godarz." It was as abrupt an end to an audience as could be imagined. The hum of talk behind Abivard made him think the courtiers never had imagined anything like it.

He prostrated himself once more, symbolizing the submission he'd subverted. Then he rose and backed away from Sharbaraz's throne until he could turn around without causing a scandal—*a bigger scandal than I've caused already,* he thought, amused by the contrast between ritual and substance.

The beautiful eunuch fell in beside him. They walked out of the throne room together, neither of them saying a word. Once they were in the hallway, though, the eunuch turned blazing eyes on Abivard. "How dare you defy the King of Kings?" he demanded, his voice beautiful no more but cracking with rage.

"How dare I?" Abivard echoed. "I didn't dare leave my family behind in his clutches, that's how." No doubt every word he said would go straight back to Sharbaraz, but he got the idea that words would go back to Sharbaraz whether he said anything or not. If he didn't, the eunuch would invent something.

"He should have given you over to the torturers," the eunuch hissed. "He should have given you over to the torturers when first you came here."

"He needs me," Abivard answered. The beautiful eunuch recoiled, almost physically sickened at the idea that the King of Kings could need anyone. Abivard went on, "He needs me in particular. You can't pick just anyone and order him to go out and win your battles for you. Oh, you could, but you wouldn't care for the results. If people can win battles for you, giving them to the torturers is wasteful."

"Do not puff yourself up like a pig's bladder at me," the eunuch snarled. "All your pretensions are empty and vain, foolish and insane. You shall pay for your presumption; if not now, then in due course."

Abivard did not answer, on the off chance that keeping quiet would prevent the beautiful eunuch from growing more angry at him still. He was even gladder than he had been while facing down Sharbaraz that he'd managed to pry his family out of the palace. If the eunuch was any indication, the servitors to the King of Kings distrusted and feared him even more than Sharbaraz did.

And for what? The only thing he could think of was that he'd been too successful at doing Sharbaraz's bidding. If the King of Kings was lord over all the realm of Makuran, could he afford such successful servants? Evidently he didn't think so.

"I hope you lose," the beautiful eunuch said. "No matter how you boast, Sharbaraz King of Kings, may his years be many and his realm increase, is rash in putting his faith in you. The God grant that the Videssians bewilder you, befuddle you, and beat you."

"An interesting prayer," Abivard answered. "Should the God grant it, I expect Maniakes would be here a few days later to burn Mashiz around your ears. Shall I tell Sharbaraz you wished for that?"

The eunuch glared again. They had come to hallways Abivard knew. In a moment they rounded a last corner and came up to the guarded door behind which Abivard had passed the winter. At the beautiful eunuch's brusque gesture, the guardsmen opened the door. Abivard went in. The door slammed shut.

Roshnani pounced on him. "Well?" she demanded.

"I was summoned before the King of Kings," he told her.

"And?"

"There's more to the world than this suite of rooms," Abivard told her. She hugged him. Their children squealed.

In early spring even the parched country between Mashiz and the westernmost tributaries of the Tib bore a thin carpet of green that put Abivard in mind of the hair on top of a balding man's head: you could see the bare land beneath, as you could see the bald man's scalp, and you knew it would soon prevail over the temporary covering.

For the first few farsangs out of the capital, though, such fine distinctions were the last thing on Abivard's mind, or his principal wife's, or those of their children. Breathing fresh air, seeing the horizon farther than a wall away—those were treasures beside which the riches in the storerooms of the King of Kings were pebbles and lumps of brass by comparison.

And happy as they were to escape their confinement, Pashang, their driver, was more joyful yet. They had been confined in genteel captivity: mewed up, certainly, but in comfort and with plenty to eat. Pashang had gone straight to the dungeons under the palace.

"The God only knows how far they go, lord," he told Abivard as the wagon rattled along. "They're getting bigger all the time, too, for Sharbaraz has gangs of Videssian prisoners driving new tunnels through the rock. He uses 'em hard; when one dies, he just throws in another one. I was lucky they didn't put me in one of those gangs, or somebody else would be driving you now."

"We took a lot of Videssian prisoners," Abivard said in a troubled voice. "I'd hoped they were put to better use than that."

Pashang shook his head. "Didn't look so to me, lord. Some of those poor buggers, they'd been down underground so long, they were pale as ghosts, and even the torchlight hurt their eyes. Some of 'em, they didn't even know Maniakes was Avtokrator in Videssos; they were trying to figure out what year of Genesios' reign they were in."

"That's . . . alarming to think about," Abivard said. "I'm glad you're all right, Pashang; I'm sorry I couldn't protect you as I would have liked."

"What could you do, when you were in trouble yourself?" the driver answered. "It could have been worse for me, too. I know that. They just held me in a cell and didn't try to work me to death, till they finally let me out." He glanced down at his hands. "First time in more years'n I can remember I don't have calluses from the reins. I'll blister, I suppose, then get 'em back."

Abivard set a hand on his shoulder. "I'm glad you'll have the chance."

The soldiers who had accompanied him to the capital now accompanied him away from it. Their fate had been milder than his and far milder than Pashang's. They'd been quartered apart from the rest of the troops in Mashiz, as if they carried some loathsome and contagious illness, and they'd been subjected to endless interrogations designed to prove that either they or Abivard was disloyal to the King of Kings. After that failed, they'd been left almost as severely alone as Abivard had.

One of them rode up to him as he was walking back to the wagon from a call of nature. The trooper said, "Lord, if we weren't angry at Sharbaraz before we got into Mashiz, we are now, by the God."

He pretended he hadn't heard. For all he knew, the trooper was an agent of the King of Kings, trying to entrap him into a statement Sharbaraz could construe as treasonous. Abivard hated to think that way, but everything that had happened to him since he had been recalled from Vaspurakan warned him that he'd better.

When he came to Erekhatti, one of the westernmost of the Thousand Cities, he got his next jolt: the sort of men Sharbaraz expected him to forge into an army with which to vanquish

Maniakes. The city governor assembled the garrison for his inspection. "They are bold men," the fellow declared. "They will fight like lions."

What they looked like to Abivard was a crowd of tavern toughs or, at best, tavern bouncers: men who would probably be fierce enough facing foes smaller, weaker, and worse armed than themselves but who could be relied on to panic and flee under any serious attack. Though almost all of them wore iron pots on their heads, a good quarter were armed with nothing more lethal than stout truncheons.

Abivard pointed those men out to the city governor. "They may be fine for keeping order here inside the walls, but they won't be enough if we're fighting real soldiers—and we will be."

"We have spears stored somewhere, I think," the governor said doubtfully. After a moment he added, "Lord, garrison troops were never intended to go into battle outside the city walls, you know."

So much for fighting like lions, Abivard thought. "If you know where those spears are, dig them up," he commanded. "These soldiers will do better with them than without."

"Aye, lord, just as you desire, so shall it be done," the governor of Erekhatti promised. When Abivard was ready to move out the next morning with the garrison in tow, the spears had not appeared. He decided to wait till afternoon. There was still no sign of the spears. Angrily, he marched out of Erekhatti. The governor said, "I pray to the God I did not distress you."

"As far as I'm concerned, Maniakes is welcome to this place," Abivard snarled. That got him a hurt look by way of reply.

The next town to which he came was called Iskanshin. Its garrison was no more prepossessing than the one in Erekhatti—less so, in fact, for the city governor of Iskanshin had no idea where to lay his hands on the spears that might have turned his men from bravos into something at least arguably resembling soldiers.

"What am I going to do?" Abivard raved as he left Iskanshin. "I've seen two cities now, and I have exactly as many men as I started out with, though three of those are down with a flux of the bowels and useless in a fight."

"It can't all be this bad," Roshnani said.

"Why not?" he retorted.

"Two reasons," she said. "For one, when we were forced through the Thousand Cities in the war against Smerdis, they defended themselves well enough to hold us out. And second, if they were all as weak as Erekhatti and Iskanshin, Videssos would have taken the land between the Tutub and the Tib away from us hundreds of years ago."

Abivard chewed on that. It made some of his rage go away—some, but not all. "Then why aren't these towns in any condition to meet an attack now?" he demanded not so much of Roshnani as of the world at large.

The world didn't answer. The world, he'd found, never answered. His wife did: "Because Sharbaraz King of Kings, may his years be many and his realm increase, decided the Thousand Cities couldn't possibly be in any danger and so scanted them. And one of the reasons he decided the Thousand Cities were safe for all time was that a certain Abivard son of Godarz had won him a whole great string of victories against Videssos. How could the Videssians hope to trouble us after they'd been beaten again and again?"

"Do you know," Abivard said thoughtfully, "that's not the answerless question it seems to be when you ask it that way. Maniakes has started playing the game by new rules. He's written off the westlands for the time being, which is something I never thought I'd see from an Avtokrator of the Videssians. But the way he's doing it makes a crazy kind of sense. If he can strike a blow at our heart and drive it home, whether we hold the westlands won't matter in the long run, because we'll have to give them up to defend ourselves."

"He's never been foolish," Roshnani said. "We've seen that over the years. If this is how he's fighting the war, it's because he thinks he can win."

"Far be it from me to argue," Abivard exclaimed. "By all I've seen here, I think he can win, too."

But his pessimism was somewhat tempered by his reception at Harpar, just east of the Tib. The city governor there did not seem to regard his position as an invitation to indolence. On the contrary: Tovorg's garrison soldiers, while not the most fearsome men Abivard had ever seen, all carried swords and bows and looked to have some idea what to do with them. If they ever got near horsemen or in among them, they might do some damage, and they might not run in blind panic if enemy troopers moved toward them.

"My compliments, Excellency," Abivard said. "Compared to what I've seen elsewhere, your warriors deserve to be recruited into the personal guard of the King of Kings."

"You are generous beyond my deserts, lord," Tovorg answered, cutting roast mutton with the dagger he wore on bis belt. "I try only to do my duty to the realm."

"Too many people are thinking of themselves first and only then of the realm," Abivard said. "To them—note that I name no names—whatever is easiest is best."

"You need name no names," the city governor of Harpar said, a fierce gleam kindling in his eyes. "You come from Mashiz, and I know by which route. Other towns between the rivers are worse than those you have seen."

"You do so ease my mind," Abivard said, to which Tovorg responded with a grin that showed his long white teeth.

He said, "This was of course my first concern, lord." Then he grew more serious. "How many peasants shall I rout out once you have moved on, and how much of the canal system do you think we'll have to destroy?"

"I hope it doesn't come to that, but get ready to rout out as many as you can. Destroying canals will hurt the cropland but not your ability to move grain to the storehouses—is that right?"

"There it might even help," Tovorg said. "We mostly ship by water in these parts, so spreading water over the land won't hurt us much. What we eat next year is another question, though."

"Next year may have to look out for itself," Abivard answered. "If Maniakes gets here, he'll wreck the canals as best he can instead of just opening them here and there to flood the land on either side of the banks. He'll burn the crops he doesn't flood, and he'll burn Harpar, too, if he can get over the walls or through them."

"As we did in the Videssian westlands?" Tovorg shrugged. "The idea, then, is to make sure he doesn't come so far, eh?"

"Yes," Abivard said, wondering as he spoke where he would find the wherewithal to stop Maniakes. Harpar's garrison was a start but no more. And they were infantry. Positioning them so they could block Maniakes' progress would be as hard as he'd warned Sharbaraz.

"I will do everything I can to work with you," Tovorg said. "If the peasants grumble—if they try to do anything more than grumble—I will suppress them. The realm as a whole comes first."

"The realm comes first," Abivard repeated. "You are a man of whom Makuran can be proud." Tovorg hadn't asked about rewards. He hadn't made excuses. He'd just found out what needed doing and promised to do it. If things turned out well afterward, he undoubtedly hoped he would be remembered. And why not? A man was always entitled to hope.

Abivard hoped he would find more city governors like Tovorg.

"There!" A mounted scout pointed to a smoke cloud. "D'you see, lord?"

"Yes, I see it," Abivard answered. "But so what? There are always clouds of smoke on the horizon in the Thousand Cities. More smoke here than I ever remember seeing before."

That wasn't strictly true. He'd seen thicker, blacker smoke rising from Videssian cities when his troops had captured and torched them. But that smoke had lasted only until whatever was burnable inside those cities had burned itself out. Between the Tutub and the Tib smoke was a fact of life, rising from all the Thousand Cities as their inhabitants baked bread, cooked food, fired pots, smelted iron, and did all the countless other things requiring flame and fuel. One more patch of it struck Abivard as nothing out of the ordinary.

But the scout spoke with assurance: "There lies the camp of the Videssians, lord. No more than four or five farsangs from us."

"I've heard prospects that delighted me more," Abivard said. The scout showed white teeth in a grin of sympathetic understanding.

Abivard had known for some time the direction from which Maniakes was coming. Had the refugees fleeing before the Videssian Avtokrator been mute, their presence alone would have warned him of Maniakes' impending arrival, as a shift in the wind foretells a storm. But the refugees were anything but mute. They were in fact voluble and volubly insistent that Abivard throw back the invader.

"Easy to insist," Abivard muttered. "Telling me how to do it is harder."

The refugees had tried that, too. They'd bombarded him with plans and suggestions till he had tired of talking with them. They were convinced that they had the answers. If he'd had as many horsemen as there were people in all the Thousand Cities put together, the suggestions—or some of them—might have been good ones. Had he even had the mobile force he'd left behind in Vaspurakan, he might have been able to do something with a few of the half-bright schemes. As things were—

"As things are," he said to no one in particular, "I'll be lucky if I don't get overrun and wiped out." Then he called to Turan. The officer who had commanded his escort on the road from Vaspurakan down to Mashiz was now his lieutenant general, for he'd found no man from the garrison forces of the Thousand Cities whom he liked better for the role. He pointed to the smoke from Maniakes' camp, then asked, "What do you make of our chances against the Videssians?"

"With what we've got here?" Turan shook his head. "Not good. I hear the Videssians are better than they used to be, and even if they weren't, it wouldn't much matter. If they hit us a solid blow, we'll shatter. By any reasonable way of looking at things, we don't stand a chance."

"Exactly what I was thinking," Abivard said, "almost word for word. If we can't do anything reasonable to keep Maniakes from rolling over us, we'll just have to try something unreasonable."

"Lord?" Turan stared in blank incomprehension. Abivard took that as a good sign. If his own lieutenant couldn't figure out what he had in mind, maybe Maniakes wouldn't be able to, either.

The night was cool only by comparison to the day that had just ended. Crickets chirped, sawing away like viol players who knew no tunes and had only one string. Somewhere off in the distance a fox yipped. Rather closer, the horses from Maniakes' army snorted and occasionally whickered on the picket lines where they were tied.

Stars blazed down from the velvety black dome of the sky. Abivard wished the moon were riding with them. Had he been able to see his way here, he wouldn't have fallen down nearly so often. But had the moon been in the sky, Videssian sentries might well have seen him and his comrades, and that would have been disastrous.

He tapped Turan—he hoped it was Turan—on the shoulder. "Get going. You know what to do."

"Aye, lord." The whisper came back in the voice of his lieutenant.

That took one weight off his mind, leaving no more than ninety or a hundred.

Turan and the band he led slipped away. To Abivard they seemed to be making an appalling amount of noise. The Videssians not far away—not far away at all—appeared to notice nothing, though. Maybe the crickets were drowning out Turan's racket. *Or maybe,* Abivard thought, *you're wound as tight as a youth going into his first battle, and every little noise is loud in your ears.*

Had he had better officers, he wouldn't have been out here himself, nor would Turan. But if you couldn't trust someone else to do the job properly, you had to take care of it for yourself. Had Abivard been younger and less experienced, he would have found crouching there in the bushes exciting. How often did a commanding general get to lead his own raiding party? *How many times does a commanding general* want *to lead his own raiding party?* he wondered, and came up with no good answer.

He hunkered down, listening to the crickets, smelling the manure—much of it from the farmers themselves—in the fields. Waiting came hard, as it always did. He was beginning to think Turan had somehow gone astray when a great commotion broke out among the Videssians' tethered horses. Some of the animals whinnied in excitement as the lines holding them were cut; others screamed in pain and panic when swords slashed their sides. Turan and his men ran up and down the line, doing as much harm in as short a time as they could.

Mingled with the cries of the horses were those of the sentries guarding them. Some of those cries were cut off abruptly as Turan's followers cut down the Videssians. But some sentries survived and fought and helped raise the alarm for their fellows in the tents off to the side of the horse lines.

The watch fires burning around those tents showed men bursting forth from them, helms jammed hastily onto heads, sword blades glittering. "Now!" Abivard shouted. The warriors who had stayed behind with him started shooting arrows into the midst of the Videssians. At night and at long range they could hardly aim, but with enough arrows and enough targets, some were bound to strike home. Screams said that some did.

Abivard plucked arrow after arrow from his bow case, shooting as fast as he could. This was a different sort of warfare from the one to which he was accustomed. Normally he hunted with the bow but in battle charged with the lance. Using archery against men felt strange.

Strange or not, he saw Videssians topple and fall. Hurting one's foe was what war was all about, so he stopped worrying about how he was doing it. He also saw more Videssians, urged on by cursing officers, trot out toward him and his men.

He gauged their numbers—many more than he had. "Back, back, back!" he yelled. Most of the soldiers he had with him were men from the city garrisons, not Turan's troopers. They saw nothing shameful about retreat. Very much the reverse; he heard a couple of them grumbling that he'd waited too long to order it.

They ran back toward the rest. Most of them wore only tunics, so Abivard in their midst felt himself surrounded by ghosts. When they'd gotten across the biggest canal between Maniakes' camp and their own, some of them attacked its eastern bank with a mattock. Water poured out onto the fields.

The Makuraners raised a cheer when Abivard and his little band returned after losing only a couple of men. "That was better than a flea bite," he declared. "We've nipped their finger like an ill-mannered lapdog, perhaps. The God willing, we'll do worse when next we meet." His men cheered again more loudly.

"The God willing," Roshnani said when he'd returned to the wagon giddy with triumph and date wine, "you won't feel compelled to lead another raid like that any time soon." Abivard did not argue with her.

Abivard hoped Maniakes would be angry enough at the lapdog nip he'd given him to lunge straight ahead without worrying about the consequences. A couple of years before Maniakes would have been likely to do just that; he'd had a way of leaping before he looked. And if he was heading straight for Mashiz, as Sharbaraz had thought—as Sharbaraz had feared—Abivard's army lay directly across his path. That hadn't been easy to arrange, since it involved maneuvering infantry against cavalry.

But to Abivard's dismay, Maniakes did not try to bull his way straight to Mashiz. Instead, he moved north toward the Mylasa Sea, up into the very heart of the land of the Thousand Cities.

"We have to follow him," Abivard said when a scout brought the unwelcome news that the Avtokrator had broken camp. "If he gets around us, our army might as well fall into the Void for all the help it will be to the realm."

As soon as he put his army on the road, he made another unpleasant discovery. Up till that time his forces had been impeding Maniakes' movements by destroying canals. Now, suddenly, the boot was on the other foot. The floods that spilled out over the fields and gardens of the lands between the rivers meant that he had to move slowly in pursuit of the Videssians.

While his men were struggling with water and mud, a great pillar of smoke rose into the sky ahead of him. "That's not a camp," Abivard said grimly. "That's not the ordinary smoke from a city, either. It's the pyre of a town that's been sacked and burned."

So indeed it proved to be. Just as the sack was beginning, Maniakes had gathered up a couple of servants of the God and sent them back to Abivard with a message. "He said this to us with his own lips and in our tongue so we could not misunderstand," one of the men said. "We were to tell you this is repayment for what Videssos has suffered at the hands of Makuran. We were also to tell you this was only the first coin of the stack."

"Were you?" Abivard said.

The servants of the God nodded together. Abivard's pedagogue had given him a nodding acquaintance with logic and rhetoric and other strange Videssian notions. Years of living inside the Empire and dealing with its people had taught him more. Not so the servants of the God, who didn't know what to do with a rhetorical question.

Sighing, Abivard said, "If that's how Maniakes intends to fight this war, it will be very ugly indeed."

"He said you would say that very thing, lord," one of the servants of the God said, scratching himself through his dirty yellow robe. "He said to tell you, if you did, that to Videssos it was already ugly and that we of Makuran needed to be reminded wars aren't always fought on the other man's soil."

Abivard sighed again. "Did he tell you anything else?"

"He did, lord," the other holy man answered. "He said he would leave the Thousand Cities if the armies of the King of Kings, may his days be long and his realm increase, leave Videssos and Vaspurakan."

"Did he?" Abivard said, and then said no more. He had no idea whether Maniakes meant that as a serious proposal or merely as

a ploy to irk him. Irked he was. He had no intention of sending
Sharbaraz the Avtokrator's offer. The King of Kings was inflamed
enough without it. The servants of the God waited to hear what
he would say. He realized he would have to respond. "If we can
destroy Maniakes here, he'll be in no position to propose anything."

Destroying Maniakes, though, was beginning to look as hard to
Abivard as stopping the Makuraners formerly had to have looked
to the Videssian Emperor.

Up on its mound the city of Khurrembar still smoked. Videssian siege engines had knocked a breach in its mud-brick wall,
allowing Maniakes' troopers in to sack it. One of these days the
survivors would rebuild. When they did, so much new rubble
would lie underfoot that the hill of Khurrembar would rise higher
yet above the floodplain.

Surveying the devastation of what had been a prosperous city,
Abivard said, "We must have more cavalry or Maniakes won't
leave one town between the Tutub and the Tib intact."

"You speak nothing but the truth, lord," Turan answered, "but
where will we come by horsemen? The garrisons hereabouts
are all infantry. Easy enough to gather together a great lump
of them, but once you have it, what do you do with it? By
the time you move it *here*, the Videssians have already ridden
there."

"I'd even take Tzikas' regiment now," Abivard said, a telling
measure of his distress.

"Can we pry those men out of Vaspurakan?" Turan asked. "As
you say, they'd come in handy now, whoever leads them."

"Can we pry them loose?" Abivard plucked at his beard. He
hadn't meant it seriously, but now Turan was forcing him to think
of it that way. "The King of Kings was willing—even eager—to
give them to me at the start of the campaign. I still despise Tzikas, but I could use his men. Perhaps I'll write to Sharbaraz—and
to Mikhran *marzban*, too. The worst they can tell me is no, and
how can hearing that make me worse off?"

"Well said, lord," Turan said. "If you don't mind my telling you
so, those letters shouldn't wait."

"I'll write them today," Abivard promised. "The next interesting question is, Will Tzikas want to come to the Thousand Cities

when I call him? Finding out should be interesting. So should finding out how reliable he proves if he gets here. One more thing to worry about."

Turan corrected him: "Two more."

Abivard laughed and bowed. "You are a model of precision before which I can only yield." His amusement vanished as quickly as it had appeared. "Now, to keep from having to yield to Maniakes' men—"

"Yield to them?" Turan said. "We can't keep up with them, which is, if you ask me, a worse problem than that. The Videssians, may they fall into the Void, move over the land of the Thousand Cities far faster than we can."

"Over the land of the Thousand Cities—" Abivard suddenly leaned forward and kissed Turan on the cheek, as if to suggest his lieutenant were of higher rank than he. Turan stared till he began to explain.

Abivard laughed out loud. The rafts that now transported his part of the army up a branch of the Tib had carried beans and lentils down to the town where he'd commandeered them. With the current of the river, though, and with little square sails raised, they made a fair clip—certainly as fast as horses went if they alternated walk and trot as they usually did.

"Behold our fleet!" he said, waving to encompass the awkward vessels with which he hoped to steal a march on Maniakes. "We can't match the Videssians dromon for dromon on the sea, but let's see them match us raft for raft here on the rivers of the Thousand Cities."

"No." Roshnani sounded serious. "Let's not see them match us."

"You're right," Abivard admitted. "Like a lot of tricks, this one, I think, is good for only one use. We need to turn it into a victory."

The flat, boring countryside flowed by on either bank of the river. Peasants laboring in the fields that the canals from the stream watered looked up and stared as the soldiers rafted north, then went back to their weeding. Off to the east another one of the Thousand Cities went up in smoke. Abivard hoped Maniakes would spend a good long while there and sack it thoroughly. That would keep him too busy to send scouts to the river to spy this makeshift flotilla. With luck, it would also let Abivard get well ahead of him.

Abivard also hoped Maniakes would continue to take the part of the army still trudging along behind him—now commanded by Turan—for the whole. If all went perfectly, Abivard would smash the Avtokrator between his hammer and Turan's anvil. If all went well, Abivard's part of the army would be able to meet the Videssians on advantageous terms. If all went not so well, something else would happen. The gamble, though, struck Abivard as worthwhile.

One advantage of the rafts that he hadn't thought of was that they kept moving through the night. The rafters took down the sails but used poles to keep their unwieldy craft away from the banks and from shallow places in the stream. They seemed so intimately acquainted with the river, they hardly needed to see it to know where they were and where the next troublesome stretch lay.

As with sorcery, Abivard admired and used the rafters' abilities without wanting to acquire those abilities himself. Even had he wanted to acquire them, the rafters weren't nearly so articulate as mages were. When Varaz asked one of them how he'd learned to do what he did, the fellow shrugged and answered, "Spend all your years on the water. You learn then. You learn or you drown." That might have been true, but it left Varaz unenlightened.

Abivard's concern was not for the rafts themselves but for the stretch of fertile ground along the eastern bank of the river: he did not want to discover Videssian scouts riding there to take word of what he was doing back to Maniakes.

He did not see any scouts. Whether they were there at some distance, he could not have said. When the rafts came ashore just south of the city of Vepilanu, he acted on the assumption that he had been seen, ordering his soldiers to form a line of battle immediately. He visualized Videssian horsemen thundering down on them, wrecking them before they had so much as a chance to deploy.

Nothing of the sort happened, and he let out a silent sigh of relief where his half-trained troopers couldn't see it. "We'll take our positions along the canal," he told the garrison troops, pointing to the broad ditch that ran east from the river. "If the Videssians want to go any farther north, they'll have to go through us."

The soldiers cheered. They hadn't done any fighting yet; they didn't know what that was like. But they had done considerable foot slogging and then had endured the journey by raft. Those trials had at least begun to forge them into a unit that might prove susceptible to his will ... provided that he didn't ask too much.

He knew that the field army he had commanded in the Videssian westlands would have smashed his force like a dropped pot. But the field army also had spent a lot of time smashing Videssian forces. What he still did not know was how good an army Maniakes had managed to piece together from the rubble of ten years of almost unbroken defeats.

For two days his soldiers stood to arms when they had to and spent most of the rest of their time trying to spear carp in the canal and slapping at the clouds of mosquitoes, gnats, midges, and flies that buzzed and hovered and darted above it. Some of them soon began to look like raw meat. Some of them came down with fevers, but not too many: most were native to the land and used to the water. Abivard hoped that more of the Videssians would sicken and that the ones who did would sicken worse. The Videssians had better, more skilled healers than his own people had but he didn't think they could stop an epidemic; diseases could be more deadly than a foe to an army.

The Videssian scouts who discovered his army showed no sign of illness. They rode along the southern bank of the canal, looking for a place to cross. Abivard wished he'd given them an obvious one and then tried to ambush Maniakes' forces when they used it. Instead, he'd done his best to make the whole length of the canal seem impassable.

"You can't think of everything all the time," Roshnani consoled him when he complained about that.

"But I have to," he answered. "I feel the weight of the whole realm pressing down on my shoulders." He paused to shake his head and slap at a mosquito. "Now I begin to understand why Maniakes and even Genesios wouldn't treat with me while I was on Videssian soil: they must have felt they were all that stood between me and ruin." His laugh rang bitter. "Maniakes has managed to put that boot on my foot."

Roshnani sounded bitter, too, but for a different reason. Lowering her voice so that only Abivard could hear, she said, "I wonder what Sharbaraz King of Kings feels now. Less than you, or I miss my guess."

"I'm not doing this for Sharbaraz," Abivard said. "I'm doing it for Makuran." But what helped Makuran also helped the King of Kings.

Abivard had not seen the Videssian banner, gold sunburst on blue, flying anywhere in the westlands of the Empire for years. To see that banner now in among the Thousand Cities came as a shock. He peered across the canal at the Videssian force that had come up to challenge his. The first thing that struck him was how small it was. If this was as much of the Videssian army as Maniakes had rebuilt, he was operating on a shoestring. One defeat, maybe two, and he'd have nothing left.

He must have known that, too, but he didn't let on that it bothered him. His troopers rode up and down along the canal as the scouts had the day before, looking for a place to force a crossing and join battle with their Makuraner foes. There weren't many of them, but they did look like good troops. Like Abivard's field force, they had a way of responding to commands instantly and without wasted motion. Abivard judged that they would do the same in battle.

A couple of times the Videssians made as if to cross the canal, but Abivard's men shot swarms of arrows at them, and they desisted. The garrison troops walked tall and puffed out their chests with pride. Abivard was glad of that but did not think the archery was what had thwarted the Videssians. He judged that Maniakes was trying to make him shift troops back and forth either to expose or to create a weakness along his line. Declining to be drawn out, he sat tight, concentrating his men at the fords about which the peasants told him. If Maniakes wanted to come farther, he would have to do it on Abivard's terms.

As the sun set, the Videssians, instead of forcing another attack, made camp. Abivard thought about trying to disrupt them again but decided against it. For one thing, he suspected that Maniakes would have done a better job of posting sentries than he had before. And for another, he did not want to make the Videssians move. He wanted them to stay where they were so he could pin them between the force he had with him and the rest of his army which was still slowly slogging up from the south.

He looked east and west along the canal. As far as his eye could see, the campfires of his own host blazed. That encouraged him; the numbers that had seemed to be useless when he had begun assembling the garrison troops into an army proved valuable after all, in defense if not in attack.

"Will we fight tomorrow?" Roshnani and Varaz asked together. His wife sounded concerned, his elder son excited.

"It's up to Maniakes now," Abivard answered. "If he wants to stay where he is, I'll let him—till the other half of my men come up. If he tries to force a crossing before then, we'll have a battle on our hands."

"We'll beat him," Varaz declared.

"Will we beat him?" Roshnani asked quietly.

"Mother!" Now Varaz sounded indignant. "Of course we'll beat him! The men of Makuran have been beating Videssians for as long as I've been alive, and they've never beaten us, not once, in all that time."

Above his head Abivard and Roshnani exchanged amused looks. Every word he'd said was true, but that truth was worth less than he thought. His life did not reach over a great stretch of time, and Maniakes' army was better and Abivard's worse than had been true in any recent encounters.

"If Maniakes attacks us, we'll give him everything he wants," Abivard promised. "And if he doesn't attack us, we'll give him everything he wants then, too. The only thing is, that will take longer."

When it grew light enough to see across the canal, sentries came shouting to wake Abivard, who'd let exhaustion overwhelm him at a time he gauged by the moon to be well after midnight. Yawning and rubbing sand from his eyes with his knuckles, he stumbled out of his tent—the wagon hadn't gone aboard the raft—and walked down to the edge of the water to see why the guards had summoned him.

Already drawn up in battle array, the Videssian army stood, impressively silent, impressively dangerous-looking, in the brightening morning light. As he stood watching them, they sat on their horses and stared over the irrigation channel toward him.

Yes, that was Maniakes at their head. He recognized not only the imperial armor but also the man who wore it. To Maniakes he was just another Makuraner in a caftan. He turned away from the canal and called orders. Horns blared. Drums thumped.

Men began tumbling out of tents and bedrolls, looking to their weapons.

Abivard ordered archers right up to the bank of the canal to shoot at the Videssians. Here and there an imperial trooper in the front ranks slid off his horse or a horse bounded out of its place in line, squealing as an arrow pierced it.

A return barrage would have hurt Abivard's unarmored infantry worse than their shooting had harmed the Videssians. Instead of staying where he was and getting into a duel of arrows with the Makuraners, though, Maniakes, with much loud signaling from trumpets and pipes, ordered his little army into motion, trotting east along the southern bank of the canal. Abivard's troops cheered to see the Videssians ride off, perhaps thinking they'd driven them away. Abivard knew better.

"Form line of battle facing east!" he called, and the musicians with the army blew great discordant blasts on their horns and thumped the drums with a will. The soldiers responded as best they could: not nearly so fast as Abivard would have expected from trained professionals, not nearly so raggedly as they would have a few weeks before.

Once they had formed up, he marched all of them after Maniakes except for a guard he left behind at the ford. He knew he could not match the speed of cavalry with men afoot but hoped that, if the Videssians forced a crossing, he could meet them at a place of his choosing, not theirs.

He found such a place about half a farsang east of the encampment: rising ground behind a north-south canal flowing into—or perhaps out of—the larger one that ran east-west. There he established himself with the bulk of his force, sending a few men ahead to get word of what was happening farther east. If one of his detachments was battling to keep Maniakes from fording the bigger canal, Abivard would order more troops forward to help. If it was already too late for that . . .

The canal behind which he'd positioned his men was perhaps ten feet wide and hardly more than knee-deep. It would not have stopped advancing infantry; it wouldn't do anything but slow oncoming horses a little. Abivard's foot soldiers stood in line at the crest of their little rise. Some grumbled about having missed breakfast, and others boasted of what they would do when they finally came face to face with Maniakes' men.

That was harmless and, since it helped them build courage, might even have helped. What he feared they would do, on facing soldiers trained in a school harder than garrison duty, was run as if demons like those the Prophets Four had vanquished were after them.

"These are the tools Sharbaraz gave me," Abivard muttered, "and I'm the one he'll blame if they break in my hand." Already, though, he'd drawn Maniakes away from the straight road to Mashiz, and so Sharbaraz, with luck, was breathing easier on his throne.

He shaded his eyes against the sun and peered eastward. Dust didn't rise up from under horses' hooves in this well-irrigated country as it did most places, but the glitter of sun off chain mail was unmistakable. So was the group of men fleeing his way. Maniakes' troopers had found and forced a ford.

Abivard yelled like a man possessed, readying his army against the imminent Videssian attack as best he could. Maniakes' horsemen grew with alarming speed from glints of sun off metal to toy soldiers that somehow moved of their own accord to real warriors. Abivard watched his own men for signs of panic as the Videssians, horns blaring, came up to the canal behind which his force waited.

Water splashed and sprayed upward when the imperials rode into the canal. Just for an instant the Videssians seemed to be wreathed in rainbows. Then, as if tearing a veil, they galloped through them, up onto the rising ground that led to Abivard's position.

"Shoot!" Abivard shouted. His own trumpeters echoed and amplified the command. The archers in his army snatched arrows from their quivers, drew their bows to the ear, and let fly at the oncoming Videssians. The thrum of bowstrings and the hissing drone of arrows through the air put Abivard in mind of horseflies.

Like horseflies, the arrows bit hard. Videssians tumbled from the saddle. Horses crashed to the ground. Other horses behind them could not swerve in time and fell over them, throwing more riders.

But the Videssians did not press their charge with the thundering drumroll of lances Abivard's field force would have used. Instead, their archers returned arrows at long range. Some of their javelin men did ride closer so they could hurl the light spears at the Makuraners. That done, the riders would gallop back out of range.

Except for helmets and wicker shields, Abivard's men had no armor to speak of. When an arrow struck, it wounded. Near Abivard a man moaned and clutched at a shaft protruding from his belly. Blood ran between his fingers. His feet kicked at the ground in agony. The soldiers on either side of him gaped in horror and dismay. No, garrison duty had not prepared them for anything like this.

But they did not run. They dragged their stricken comrade out of the line and then returned to their own places. One of them stuffed the wounded man's arrows into his own bow case and went back to shooting at the Videssians with no more fuss than if he'd just straightened his caftan after making water.

The Videssians wore swords on their belts but did not come close enough to use them. Abivard's spirits rose. He shook his fist at Maniakes, who stayed just out of arrow range. The Avtokrator was finding out that facing Makuraners was a different business from beating barbarians. Where was the dash, the aggressiveness the Videssians had shown against the Kubratoi? Not here, not if they couldn't make a better showing than this against the inexperienced troops Abivard commanded.

Maniakes' one abiding flaw as a commander had been that he thought he could do more than he could. If he couldn't make his men go forward against garrison troops, he'd soon get a rude surprise as the rest of Abivard's army came up to try to cut off his escape. Before this fight began Abivard had had scarcely any hope of accomplishing that. Now, seeing how tentative the Videssians were . . .

It was almost as if Maniakes had no particular interest in winning the fight but merely wanted to keep it going. When that thought crossed Abivard's mind, his head went up like a fox's on catching the scent of rabbit—or, rather, like a rabbit's on catching the scent of fox.

He didn't see anything untoward. There, at the front, the Videssians were keeping up their halfhearted archery duel with his soldiers. Because they were so much better armored than their foes, they were causing more casualties than they suffered. They were not causing nearly enough, though, to force Abivard's men from their position, nor were they trying to bull their way through the line. What exactly *were* they doing?

Abivard peered south, wondering if Maniakes had gotten into a fight here so he could sneak raftloads of Videssians over the large canal and into the Makuraner rear. He saw no sign of it. Had the Avtokrator's sorcerers come up with something new in the line of battle magic? There was no sign of that, either: no cries of alarm from the mages with Abivard's force, no Makuraner soldiers suddenly falling over dead.

A moment before his head would have turned in that direction anyhow, Abivard heard sudden shouts of alarm from the north. The horsemen riding down on his army came behind a banner bearing a gold sunburst on a field of blue. Maniakes' detachment must have crossed the large canal well to the east before his own men had moved so far. They'd trotted right out of his field of view—but they were back now.

"I *thought* Maniakes had more men than that," Abivard said, as much to himself as to anyone else. While he'd been trying to trap the Videssians between the two pieces of his army, they'd been trying to do the same thing to him. The only difference was that they'd managed to spring their trap.

The battle was lost—no help for that now. The only thing left was to save as much as he could from the wreck. "Hold fast!" he shouted to his men. "Hold fast! If you run from them, you're done for."

One advantage of numbers was having reserves to commit. He sent all the men in back of the line up to the north to face the oncoming Videssians squarely; if he'd tried swinging around the troops that already were engaged, he would have lost everything in confusion and in the certainty of being hit from the flank.

Maniakes' Videssians held back no more. The Avtokrator had kept Abivard in play until his detached force could reach the field. Now he pressed forward as aggressively as he had before he'd had the resources to let him get by with a headlong attack. This time, he did.

The Videssians, instead of stopping short and plying Abivard's army with arrows, charged up with drawn swords and got in among the garrison troops, hacking down at them from horseback. Abivard felt a certain somber pride in his men, who performed better than he'd dared hope. They fell—by scores, by hundreds they fell—but they did not break. They did what they could to fight back, stabbing horses and dragging Videssians out of the saddle to grapple with them in the dirt.

On the northern flank the blow fell at about the same time as it did in the east. It fell harder in the north, for the soldiers there had not gotten a taste of fighting but were rushed up to plug a gap. Still, the Videssians did not have it all their own way there, as they might have hoped. They did not—they could not—break through into the rear of the Makuraner line and roll up Abivard's men like a seamstress rolling up a line of yarn.

He rode north, figuring to show himself where he was most needed. He wished he'd had a few hundred men from the field force up in Vaspurakan with him. They would have sent the Videssians reeling off in dismay. No, he wouldn't have minded—well, he didn't think he would have minded—if Tzikas had been at the head of the regiment. The Videssian renegade could hardly have made things worse.

"Hold as firm as you can!" Abivard yelled. Telling his soldiers to yield no ground at all was useless now; they *were* retreating, as any troops caught in a like predicament would have done. But there were retreats and retreats. If you kept facing the foe and hurting him wherever you could, you had a decent chance of coming whole through a lost battle. But if you turned tail and ran, you would be cut down from behind. You couldn't fight back that way.

"Rally on the baggage train!" Abivard commanded. "We won't let them have that, will we, lads?"

That order surely would have made the field army fight harder. All the booty those soldiers had collected in years of triumphant battle traveled in the baggage train; if they lost it, some of them would have lost much of their wealth. The men who had come from the city garrisons were poorer and had not spent years storing up captured money and jewels and weapons. Would they battle to save their supplies of flour and smoked meat?

As things turned out, they did. They used the wagons as small fortresses, fighting from inside them and from the shelter they gave. Abivard had hoped for that but had not ordered it for fear of being disobeyed.

Again and again the Videssians tried to break their tenuous hold on the position, to drive them away from the baggage train so they could be cut down while flying or forced into the big canal and drowned.

The Makuraners would not let themselves be dislodged. The fight raged through the afternoon. Abivard broke his lance and was reduced to clouting Videssians with the stump. Even with its scale mail armor, his horse took several wounds. *He* had an incentive to hold the baggage wagons: his wife and family were sheltering among them.

Maniakes drew his troops back from combat about an hour before sunset. At first Abivard thought nothing of that, but the Avtokrator of the Videssians did not send them forward again. Instead, singing a triumphant hymn to their Phos, they rode off toward the nearest town.

Abivard ordered his horn players to blow the call for pursuit. He had the satisfaction of seeing several Videssians' heads whip around in alarm. But despite the defiant horn calls, he was utterly unable to pursue Maniakes' army, and he knew it. The mounted foes were faster than his own foot soldiers, and despite the protection they'd finally gotten from the wagons of the baggage train, his men had taken a far worse drubbing. He began riding around to see just how bad things were.

A soldier sat stolidly while another one sewed up his wounded shoulder. He nodded to Abivard. "You must be one tough general, lord, if you beat them buggers year in and year out. They can fight some." He laughed at his own understatement.

"You can fight some yourself," Abivard answered. Though beaten, the garrison troops had done themselves proud. Abivard knew that was so and also knew that Sharbaraz King of Kings would not see it the same way. Having done his best to make victory impossible, Sharbaraz now insisted that nothing less would do. If the miracle inexplicably failed to materialize, he would not blame himself—not while he had Abivard.

Weary soldiers began lighting campfires and seeing about supper. Abivard grabbed a lump of hard bread—that better described the misshapen object the cook gave him than would a neutral term such as *loaf*—and a couple of onions and went from fire to fire, talking with his men and praising them for having held their ground as well as they had.

"Aye, well, lord, sorry it didn't work out no better than it did," one of the warriors answered, picking absently at the black blood on the edges of a cut that ran from just below his ear to near the corner of his mouth. "They beat us, is all."

"Maybe next time we beat them," another warrior put in. He drew a dagger from his belt. "Give you a chunk of mutton sausage—" He held it up. "—for half of one of those onions."

"I'll make that trade," Abivard said, and did. Munching, he reflected that the soldier might well be right. If his army got another chance against the Videssians, they might well beat them. Getting that chance would be the hard part. He'd stolen a march on Maniakes once, but how likely was he to be able to do it twice? When you had one throw of the dice and didn't roll the twin twos of the Prophets Four, what did you do next?

He didn't know, not in any large sense of the word, not with the force he had here. On a smaller scale, what you did was keep your men in good spirits if you could so that they wouldn't brood on this defeat and expect another one in the next fight. Most of the men with whom he talked didn't seem unduly downhearted. Most of them in fact seemed happier about the world than he was.

When he finally got back to his tent, he expected to find everyone asleep. As it had the night before, the moon told him it was past midnight. Snores from soldiers exhausted after the day's marching and fighting mingled with the groans of the wounded. Out beyond the circles of light the campfires threw, crickets chirped. Mosquitoes buzzed far from the fires and close by. Every so often someone cursed as he was bitten.

Seeing Pashang beside the fire in front of the tent was not a large surprise, nor was having Roshnani poke her head out when she heard his approaching footsteps. But when Varaz stuck his head out, too, Abivard blinked in startlement.

"I'm angry at you, Papa," his elder son exclaimed. "I wanted to go and fight the Videssians today, but Mama wouldn't let me—she said you said I was too little. I could have hit them with my bow; I know I could."

"Yes, you probably could," Abivard agreed gravely. "But they could have hit you, too, and what would you have done when the fighting got to close quarters? You're learning the sword, but you haven't learned it well enough to hold off a grown man."

"I think I have," Varaz declared.

"When I was your age, I thought the same thing," Abivard told him. "I was wrong, and so are you."

"I don't think I am," Varaz said.

Abivard sighed. "That's what I said to my father, too, and it got me no further with him than you're getting with me. Looking back, though, he was right. A boy can't stand against men, not if he hopes to do anything else afterward. Your time will come—and one fine day, the God willing, you'll worry about keeping your son out of fights he isn't ready for."

Varaz looked eloquently unconvinced. His voice had years to go before it started deepening. His cheeks bore only fine down. To expect him to think of the days when he'd be a father himself was to ask too much. Abivard knew that but preferred argument to breaking his son's spirit by insisting on blind obedience.

There was, however, a time and place for everything. Roshnani cut off the debate, saying, "Quarrel about it tomorrow. You'll get the same answer, Varaz, because it's the only one your parents can give you, but you'll get it after your father has had some rest."

Abivard hadn't let himself think about that. Hearing the word made him realize how worn he was. He said, "If you two don't want my footprints on your robes, you'd best get out of the way."

Before long he was lying in the crowded tent on a blanket under mosquito netting. Then, no matter how his body craved sleep, it would not come. He had to fight the battle over again, first in his own mind and then, softly, aloud for his principal wife.

"You did everything you could," Roshnani assured him.

"I should have realized Maniakes had split his army, too," he said. "I thought it looked small, but I didn't know how many men he really had, and so—"

"Only the God knows all there is to know, and only she acts in perfect rightness on what she does know," Roshnani said. "This once, the Videssians were luckier than we."

Everything she said was true and in perfect accord with Abivard's own thoughts. Somehow that helped not at all. "The King of Kings, may his years be long and his realm increase, entrusted me with this army to—"

"To get you killed or at best ruined," Roshnani broke in quietly but with terrible venom in her voice.

He'd had those thoughts, too. "To defend the realm," he went on, as if she hadn't spoken. "If I don't do that, nothing else I do, no matter how well I do it, matters anymore. Any soldier would say the same. So will Sharbaraz."

Roshnani stirred but did not speak right away. At last she said, "The army still holds together. You'll have your chance at revenge."

"That depends," Abivard said. Roshnani made a questioning noise. He explained: "On what Sharbaraz does when he hears I've lost, I mean."

"Oh," Roshnani said. On that cheerful note they fell asleep.

When Abivard emerged from the wagon the next morning, Er-Khedur, the town north and east of the battle site, was burning. His mouth twisted into a thin, bitter line. If his army couldn't keep the Videssians in check, why should the part of the garrison of Er-Khedur he'd left behind?

He didn't realize he'd asked the question aloud till Pashang answered it: "They did have a wall to fight from, lord."

That mattered less in opposing the Videssians than it would have against the barbarous Khamorth, perhaps less than it would have in opposing a rival Makuraner army. The Videssians were skillful when it came to siegecraft. Wall or no wall, a handful of half-trained troops would not have been enough to keep them out of the city.

Abivard thought about going right after the imperials and trying to trap them inside Er-Khedur. Reluctantly, he decided not to. They'd just mauled his army once; he wanted to drill his troops before he put them into battle again. And he doubted the Videssians would tamely let themselves be trapped. They had no need to stay and defend Er-Khedur, they could withdraw and ravage some other city instead.

The Videssians didn't have to stay and defend any one point in the Thousand Cities. The chief reason they were there was to do as much damage as they could. That gave them more freedom of movement than Abivard had had when he was conquering the westlands from the Empire. He'd wanted to seize land intact first and destroy it only if he had to. Maniakes operated under no such restraints.

And how were the westlands faring these days? As far as Abivard knew, they remained in the hands of the King of Kings. Dominating the sea as he did, Maniakes hadn't had to think about freeing them before he invaded Makuran. Now each side in the war had forces deep in the other's territory. He wondered if that had happened before in the history of warfare. He knew of no songs that suggested that it had. Groundbreaking was an uncomfortable sport to play, as he'd found out when ending Roshnani's isolation from the world.

If he couldn't chase right after Maniakes, what could he do? One thing that occurred to him was to send messengers south over the canal to find out how close Turan was with the rest of the assembled garrison troops. He could do more with the whole army than he could with this battered piece of it.

The scouts rode back late that afternoon with word that they'd found the host Turan commanded. Abivard thanked them and then went off away from his men to kick at the rich black dirt in frustration. He'd come so close to catching Maniakes between the halves of the Makuraner force; that the Videssians had caught him between the halves of theirs seemed most unfair.

He posted sentries out as far as a farsang from his camp, wanting to be sure Maniakes could not catch him by surprise. He had considerably more respect for the Videssian Avtokrator now than he'd had when his forces had been routing Maniakes' at every turn.

When he said as much, Roshnani raised an eyebrow and remarked, "Amazing what being beaten will do, isn't it?" He opened his mouth, then closed it, discovering himself without any good answer.

Turan's half of the Makuraner army reached the canal a day and a half later. After the officer had crossed over and kissed Abivard's cheek by way of greeting, he said, "Lord, I wish you could have waited before you started your fight."

"Now that you mention it, so do I," Abivard answered. "We don't always have all the choices we'd like, though."

"That's so," Turan admitted. He looked around as if gauging the condition of Abivard's part of the army. "Er—lord, what do we do now?"

"That's a good question," Abivard said politely, and then proceeded not to answer it. Turan's expression was comical, or would have been had the army's plight been less serious. But here, unlike in his conversations with his wife, Abivard understood he would have to make a reply. At last he said, "One way or another we're going to have to get Maniakes out of the land of the Thousand Cities before he smashes it all to bits."

"We just tried that," Turan answered. "It didn't work so well as we'd hoped."

"One way or another, I said," Abivard told him. "There is something we haven't tried in fullness, because as a cure it's almost worse than the sickness of invasion."

"What's that?" Turan asked. Again Abivard didn't answer, letting his lieutenant work it out for himself. After a while Turan did. Snapping his fingers, he said, "You want to do a proper job of flooding the plain."

"No, I don't *want* to do that," Abivard said. "But if it's the only way to get rid of Maniakes, I *will* do it." He laughed wryly. "And if I do, half the Thousand Cities will close their gates to me because they'll think I'm a more deadly plague than Maniakes ever was."

"They're our subjects," Turan said in a that-settles-it tone.

"Yes, and if we push them too far, they'll be our *rebellious* subjects," Abivard said. "When Genesios ruled Videssos, he had a new revolt against him every month, or so it seemed. The same could happen to us."

Now Turan didn't answer at all. Abivard started to try to get him to say something, to say anything, then suddenly stopped. One of the things he was liable to say was that Abivard might lead a revolt himself. Abivard didn't want to hear that. If he did hear it, he would have to figure out what to do about Turan. If he let his lieutenant say it without responding, he would in effect be guilty of treasonous conspiracy. If Turan wanted to take word of that back to Sharbaraz, he could. But if Abivard punished him for saying such a thing, he would cost himself an able officer.

And so, to forestall any response, Abivard changed the subject "Do your men still have their fighting spirit?"

"They did till they got here and saw bodies out in the sun starting to stink," Turan said. "They did till they saw men down with festering wounds or out of their heads from fever. They're garrison troops. Most of 'em never saw what the aftermath of a battle—especially a lost battle—looks like before. But your men seem to be taking it pretty well."

"Yes, and I'm glad of that," Abivard said. "When we'd beat the Videssians, they'd go all to pieces and run every which way. I thought my own raw troops would do the same thing, but they haven't, and I'm proud of them for it."

"I can see that, since it would have been your neck, too, if they did fall apart," Turan said judiciously. "But you can fight another battle with 'em, and they're ready to do it, too. My half of the army will be better for seeing that."

"They are ready to fight again," Abivard agreed. "That surprises me, too, maybe more than anything else." He waved toward the northeast, the direction in which Maniakes' army had gone. "The only question is, Will we be able to catch up with the Videssians and bring them to battle again? It's because I have my doubts that I'm thinking so hard of flooding the land between the Tutub and the Tib."

"I understand your reasons, lord," Turan said, "but it strikes me as a counsel of desperation, and there are a lot of city governors it would strike the same way. And if they're not happy—" He broke off once more. They'd already been around to that point on the wheel.

Abivard didn't know how to keep them from going around again, either. But before he had to try, a scout interrupted the circle, crying, "Lord, cavalry approach from out of the north!"

Maybe Maniakes hadn't been satisfied to beat just one piece of the Makuraner army, after all. Maybe he was coming back to see if he could smash the other half, too. Such thoughts ran through Abivard's mind in the couple of heartbeats before he shouted to the trumpeters: "Blow the call for line of battle!"

Martial music rang out. Men grabbed weapons and rushed to their places more smoothly than he would have dared hope a couple of weeks before. If Maniakes was coming back to finish the job, he'd get a warm reception. Abivard was pleased to see how well Turan's troops moved along with his own, who had been blooded. The former squadron commander had done well with as large a body of men.

"Sharbaraz!" roared the Makuraner troops as the onrushing cavalry drew near. A few of them yelled "Abivard!" too, making their leader proud and apprehensive at the same time.

And then they got a better look at the approaching army. They cried out in wonder and delight, for it advanced under the red-lion banner of the King of Kings. And its soldiers also cried Sharbaraz's name, and some few of them the name of their commander as well: "Tzikas!"

✦ VI

O ne of the lessons Abivard's father, Godarz, had drilled into him was not asking the God for anything he didn't really want, because he was liable to get it anyhow. He'd forgotten that principle on this campaign, and now he was paying for it.

The look on Turan's face probably mirrored the one on his own. His lieutenant asked, "Shall we welcome them, lord, or order the attack?"

"A good question." Abivard shook his head, as much to suppress his own temptation as for any other reason. "Can't do that, I'm afraid. We welcome them. Odds are, Tzikas doesn't know I know he sent those letters complaining of me to Sharbaraz."

If the Videssian renegade did know that, he gave no sign of it. He rode out in front of the ranks of his own horsemen and through the foot soldiers—who parted to give him a path—straight up to Abivard. When he reached him, he dismounted and went down on one knee in what was, by Videssian standards, the next closest thing to an imperial greeting. "Lord, I am here to aid you," he declared in his lisping Makuraner.

Abivard, for his part, spoke in Videssian: "Rise, eminent sir. How many men have you brought with you?" He gauged Tzikas' force. "Three thousand, I'd guess, or maybe a few more."

"Near enough, lord," Tzikas answered, sticking to the language of the land that had adopted him. "You gauge numbers with marvelous keenness."

"You flatter me," Abivard said, still in Videssian; he would not acknowledge Tzikas as a countryman. Then he showed his own fangs, adding, "I wish you had been so generous when you discussed me with Sharbaraz King of Kings, may his days be long and his realm increase."

A Makuraner, thus caught out, would have shown either anger or shame. Tzikas proved himself foreign by merely nodding and saying, "Ah, you found out about that, did you? I wondered if you would."

Abivard wondered what he was supposed to make of that. It sounded as if in some perverse way it was a compliment. However Tzikas meant it, Abivard didn't like it. He growled, "Yes, I found out about it, by the God. It almost cost me my head. Why shouldn't I bind you and give you to Maniakes to do with as he pleases?"

"You could do that." Though Tzikas continued to speak Makuraner, even without his accent Abivard would have had no doubt he was dealing with a Videssian. Instead of bellowing in outrage or bursting into melodramatic tears, the renegade sounded cool, detached, calculating, almost amused. "You could—if you wanted to put the realm in danger or, rather, in more danger than it's in already."

Abivard wanted to hit him, to get behind the calm mask he wore to the man within . . . if there was a man within. But Tzikas, like a rider controlling a restive horse, had known exactly where to flick him with the whip to get him to jump in the desired direction. Abivard tried not to acknowledge that, saying, "Why should removing you from command of your force here have anything to do with how well the troopers fight? You're good in the field, but you're not so good as all that."

"Probably not—not in the field," Tzikas answered, sparring still. "But I am very good at picking the soldiers who go into my force, and, brother-in-law to the King of Kings, I am positively a genius when it comes to picking the officers who serve under me."

Abivard had learned something of the subtle Videssian style of fighting with words while in exile in the Empire and later in treating with his foes. Now he said, "You may be good at picking those who serve under you, eminent sir, but not in picking those under whom you serve. First you betrayed Maniakes, then me. Beware falling between two sides when both hate you."

Tzikas bared his teeth; that had pierced whatever armor he had put around his soul. But he said, "You may insult me, you may revile me, but do you want to work with me to drive Maniakes from the land of the Thousand Cities?"

"An interesting choice, isn't it?" Abivard said, hoping to make Tzikas squirm even more. Tzikas, though, did not squirm but merely waited to see what Abivard would say next—which required Abivard to decide what he *would* say next. "I still think I should take my chances on how your band performs without you."

"Yes, that is what you would be doing," the renegade said. "I've taught them everything I know—everything."

Abivard did not miss the threat there. What Tzikas knew best was how to change sides at just the right—or just the wrong—moment. Would the soldiers he commanded go over to Maniakes if something—even something like Maniakes, if Abivard handed Tzikas to him—happened to him? Or would they simply refuse to fight for Abivard? Would they perhaps do nothing at all except obey their new commander?

Those were all interesting questions. They led to an even more interesting one: *could Abivard afford to find out?*

Reluctantly, he decided he couldn't. He desperately needed that cavalry to repel the Videssians, and Tzikas, if loyal, made a clever, resourceful general. The trouble was, he made a clever, resourceful general even if he wasn't loyal, and that made him more dangerous than an inept traitor. Abivard did his best not to worry about that. His best, he knew, would not be good enough.

Hating every word, he said, "If you keep your station, you do it as my hunting dog. Do you understand, eminent sir? I need not give you to the Avtokrator to be rid of you. If you disobey me, you are a dead man."

"By the God, I understand, lord, and by the God, I swear I will obey your every command." Tzikas made the left-handed gesture every follower of the Prophets Four used. He probably meant it to reassure Abivard. Instead, it only made him more suspicious. He doubted Tzikas' conversion as much as he doubted everything else about the renegade.

But he needed the horsemen Tzikas had led down from Vaspurakan, and he needed whatever connections Tzikas still had inside Maniakes' army. Treachery cut both ways, and Tzikas still hated Maniakes for being Avtokrator in place of someone more deserving—someone, for instance, like Tzikas.

Abivard chuckled mirthlessly. "What amuses you, lord?" Tzikas asked, the picture of polite interest.

"Only that one person, at least, is safe from your machinations," Abivard said. One of Tzikas' disconcertingly mobile eyebrows rose in silent question. With malicious relish Abivard explained: "You may want my post, and you may want Maniakes' post, but Sharbaraz King of Kings, may his years be many and his realm increase, is beyond your reach."

"Oh, indeed," Tzikas said. "The prospect of overthrowing *him* never once entered my mind." By the way he said it and by his actions, the same did not apply to Abivard or Maniakes.

Abivard watched glumly as, off in the distance, another of the Thousand Cities went up in flames. "This is madness," he exclaimed. "When we took Videssian towns, we took them with a view to keeping them intact so they could yield revenue to the King of Kings. A burned city yields no one revenue."

"When we went into Videssos, we went as conquerors," Turan said. "Maniakes isn't out for conquest. He's out for revenge, and that changes the way he fights his war."

"Well put," Abivard said. "I hadn't thought of it in just that way, but you're right, of course. How do we stop him?"

"Beat him and drive him away," his lieutenant answered. "No other way to do it that I can think of."

That was easy to say, but it had proved harder to do. Being uninterested in conquest, Maniakes didn't bother garrisoning the towns he took: he just burned them and moved on. That meant he kept his army intact instead of breaking it up into small packets that Abivard could have hoped to defeat individually.

Because the Videssian force was all mounted, Maniakes moved through the plain between the Tutub and the Tib faster than Abivard could pursue him with an army still largely made up of infantry. Not only that, he seemed to move through the land of the Thousand Cities faster than Abivard's order to open the canals and flood the plain reached the city governors. Such inundations as did take place were small, hindered Maniakes but little, and were repaired far sooner that they should have been.

Abivard, coming upon the peasants of the town of Nashvar doing everything they could to make a broken canal whole once more, angrily confronted the city governor, a plump little man named Beroshesh. "Am I to have my people starve?" the governor wailed, making as if to rend his garment. His accented speech proclaimed him a local man, not a true Makuraner down from the high plateau to the west.

"Are you to let all the Thousand Cities suffer because you do not do all you can to drive the enemy from our land?" Abivard returned.

Beroshesh stuck out his lower lip, much as Abivard's children did when they were feeling petulant. "I do as much as any of my neighbors, and you cannot deny this, lord. For you to single me out—where is the justice there? Eh? Can you answer?"

"Where is the justice in not rallying to the cause of the King of Kings?" Abivard answered. "Where is the justice in your ignoring the orders that come from me, his servant?"

"In the same place as the justice of the order to do ourselves such great harm," Beroshesh retorted, not retreating by so much as the width of a digit. "If you could by some great magic make all my fellow officials obey to the same degree, this would be another matter. All would bear the harm together, and all equally. But you ask me to take it all on my own head, for the other city governors are lazy and cowardly and will not do any such thing, not unless you stand over them with whips."

"And what would they say of you?" Abivard asked in a mild voice. Beroshesh, obviously convinced he was the soul of virtue, donned an expression that might better have belonged on the face of a bride whose virginity was questioned. Abivard wanted to laugh. "Never mind. You needn't answer that."

Beroshesh did answer, at considerable length. After a while Abivard stopped listening. He wished he had a magic that could make all the city governors in the Thousand Cities obey his commands. If there were such a magic, though, Kings of Kings would have been using it for hundreds of years, and rebellions against them would have been far fewer.

Then he had another thought. He sat up straighter in his chair and took a long pull at the goblet of date wine a serving girl had set before him. The stuff was as revoltingly sweet as it always had been. Abivard hardly noticed. He set down the goblet and pointed a finger at Beroshesh, who reluctantly stopped talking. Quietly, thoughtfully, Abivard said, "Tell me, do your mages do much with the canals?"

"Not mine, no," the city governor answered, disappointing him. Beroshesh went on, "My mages, lord, are like you: they are men of the high country and so do not know much about the way of this land. Some of the wizards of the town, though, do repair work on the banks now and again. Sometimes one of them can do at once what it would take a large crew of men with mattocks and spades days to accomplish. And sometimes, magic being what it is, not. Why do you ask?"

"Because I was wondering whether—" Abivard began.

Beroshesh held up his right hand, palm out. Bombastic he might have been, but he was not stupid. "You want to work a magic to open the canals all at once. Tell me if I am not correct, lord."

"You are right," Abivard answered. "If we gathered wizards from several cities here, all of them, as you say, from the land of the Thousand Cities so they knew the waters and the mud and what to do with them . . ." His voice trailed away. Knowing what one wanted to do and being able to do it were not necessarily identical.

Beroshesh looked thoughtful. "I do not know whether such a thing has ever been essayed. Shall I try to find out, lord?"

"Yes, I think you should," Abivard told him. "If we have here a weapon against the Videssians, don't you think we ought to learn whether we can use it?"

"I shall look into it," Beroshesh said.

"So shall I," Abivard assured him. He'd heard that tone in functionaries' voices before, whenever they made promises they didn't intend to keep. "I will talk to the mages here in town. You find out who the ones in nearby cities are and invite them here. Don't say too much about why or spies will take the word to Maniakes, who may try to foil us."

"I understand, lord," Beroshesh said in a solemn whisper. He looked around nervously. "Even the floors have ears."

Considering how much of the past of any town hereabouts lay right under one's feet, that might have been literally true. Abivard wondered whether those dead ears had ever heard of a scheme like his. Then, more to the point, he wondered whether Maniakes had. The Avtokrator had surprised Makuran and had surprised Abivard himself. Now, maybe, Abivard would return the favor.

✦ ✦ ✦

Abivard had never before walked into a room that held half a dozen mages. He found the prospect daunting. In his world, with the mundane tools of war, he was a man to be reckoned with. In their world, which was anything but mundane, he held less power to control events than did the humblest foot soldier of his army.

Even so, the wizards reckoned him a man of importance. When he nerved himself and went in to them, they sprang to their feet and bowed very low, showing that they acknowledged he was far higher in rank than they. "We shall serve you, lord," they said, almost in chorus.

"We shall all serve the King of Kings, may his days be long and his realm increase," Abivard said. He waved to the roasted quails, bread and honey, and jars of date wine on the sideboard. "Eat. Drink. Refresh yourselves." By the cups some of the mages were holding, by the gaps in the little loaves of bread, by the bird bones scattered on the floor, they hadn't needed his invitation to take refreshment.

They introduced themselves, sometimes between mouthfuls. Falasham was fat and jolly. Glathpilesh was also fat but looked as if he hated the world and everyone in it. Mefyesh was bald and had the shiniest scalp Abivard had ever seen. His brother, Yeshmef, was almost as bald and almost as shiny but wore his beard in braids tied with yellow ribbons, which gave him the look of a swarthy sunflower. Utpanisht, to whom everyone, even Glathpilesh, deferred, was ancient and wizened; his grandson, Kidinnu, was in the prime of life.

"Why have you summoned us, lord?" Glathpilesh demanded of Abivard in a voice that suggested he had better things to do elsewhere.

"Couldn't you have found that out by magic?" Abivard said, thinking, *If you can't, what are you doing here?*

"I could have, aye, but why waste time and labor?" the wizard returned. "Magic is hard work. Talk is always easy."

"Listening is easier yet," Falasham said so good-naturedly that even dour Glathpilesh could not take offense.

"You know the Videssians have invaded the land of the Thousand Cities," Abivard said. "You may also know they've beaten the army I command. I want to drive them off, if I can find a way."

"Battle magic," Glathpilesh said scornfully. "He wants battle magic to drive off the Videssians. He doesn't want much, does he?" His laugh showed what he thought of what Abivard wanted.

In a creaking voice Utpanisht said, "Suppose we let him tell us what he wants? That might be a better idea than having us tell him." Glathpilesh glared at him and muttered something inaudible but subsided.

"What I want is not battle magic," Abivard said with a grateful nod to Utpanisht. "The passion of those involved will have nothing to do with diluting the power of the spell." He laughed. "And I won't try to explain your own business to you anymore, either. Instead, I'll explain what I do want." He spent the next little while doing just that.

When he was finished, none of the magicians spoke for a moment. Then Falasham burst out with a high, shrill giggle. "This is not a man with small thoughts, whatever else we may say of him," he declared.

"Can you do this thing?' Abivard asked.

"It would not be easy," Glathpilesh growled.

Abivard's hopes soared. If the bad-tempered mage did not dismiss the notion as impossible out of hand, that might even mean it was easy. Then Yeshmef said, "This magic has never been done, which may well mean this magic cannot be done." All the other wizards nodded solemnly. Mages were conservative men, even more likely to rely on precedent than were servants of the God, judges, and clerks.

But Utpanisht, whom he would have expected to be the most conservative of all, said, "One reason it has not been done is that the land of the Thousand Cities had never faced a foe like this Videssian and his host. Desperate times call out for desperate remedies."

"*Can* call out for them," Mefyesh said. To Abivard's disappointment, Utpanisht did not contradict him.

Kidinnu said, "Grandfather, even if we can work this magic, should we? Will it not cause more harm than whatever the Videssian does?"

"It is not a simple question," Utpanisht said. "The harm from this Maniakes lies not only in what he does now but in what he may do later if we do not check him now. That could be very large indeed. A flood—" He shrugged. "I have seen many floods in my years here. We who live between the rivers know how to deal with floods."

Kidinnu bowed his head in acquiescence to his grandfather's reasoning. Abivard asked his question again: "Can you do this thing?"

This time the wizards did not answer him directly. Instead, they began arguing among themselves, first in the Makuraner language and then, by the sound of things because they didn't find that pungent enough, in the guttural tongue the folk of the Thousand Cities used among themselves. Mefyesh and Yeshmef didn't find even their own language sufficiently satisfying, for after one hot exchange they pulled each other's beards. Abivard wondered if they would yank out knives.

At last, when the wrangling died down, Utpanisht said, "We think we can do this. All of us agree it is possible. We still have not made up our minds about what method we need to use."

"That is because some of these blockheads insist on treating canals as if they were rivers," Glathpilesh said, "when any fool—but not any idiot, evidently—can see they are of two different classes."

Falasham's good nature was fraying at the edges. "They hold flowing water," he snapped. "Spiritually and metaphorically speaking, that makes them rivers. They aren't lakes. They aren't baths. What are they, if not rivers?"

"Canals," Glathpilesh declared, and Yeshmef voiced loud agreement. The row started up anew.

Abivard listened for a little while, then said sharply, "Enough of this!" His intervention made all the wizards, regardless of which side they had been on, gang up against him instead. He'd expected that would happen and was neither disappointed nor angry. "I admit you are all more learned in this matter that I could hope to be—"

"He admits the sun rises in the east," Glathpilesh muttered. "How generous!"

Pretending he hadn't heard that, Abivard plowed ahead: "But how you work this magic is not what's important. That you work it is. And you must work it soon, too, for before long Maniakes will start wondering why I've stopped here at Nashvar and given up on pursuing him." *Before long Sharbaraz King of Kings will*

*start wondering, too, and likely decide I'm a traitor, after all. Or
if he doesn't, Tzikas will tell him I am.*

Kidinnu said, "Lord, agreeing on the form this sorcery must
take is vital before we actually attempt it."

That made sense; Abivard wasn't keen on the idea of going
into battle without a plan. But he said, "I tell you, we have no
time to waste. By the time you leave this room, hammer out your
differences." All at once, he wished he hadn't asked Beroshesh to
set out such a lavish feast for the mages. Empty bellies would
have sped consensus.

His uncompromising stand drew more of the wizards' anger.
Glathpilesh growled, "Easier for us to agree to turn you into a
cockroach than on how to breach the canals."

"No one would pay you to do that to me, though," Abivard
answered easily. Then he thought of Tzikas and then of Sharbaraz.
Well, the wizards didn't have to know about them.

Yeshmef threw his hands in the air. "Maybe my moron of a
brother is right. It has happened before, though seldom."

Glathpilesh was left all alone. He glared around at the other
five wizards from the Thousand Cities. Abivard did not like the
look on his face—had being left all alone made him more stubborn? If it had, could the rest of the mages carry on with the
conjuration by themselves? Even if they could, it would surely be
more difficult without their colleague.

"You are all fools," he snarled at them, "and you, sirrah—" He
sent Yeshmef a look that was almost literally murderous. "—fit
for nothing better than bellwether, for you show yourself to be
a shambling sheep without bollocks." He breathed heavily, jowls
wobbling; Abivard wondered whether he would suffer an apo-
plectic fit in his fury.

He also wondered whether the other wizards would want to work
with Glathpilesh after his diatribe. There, at least, he soon found
relief, for the five seemed more amused than outraged. Falasham
said, "Not bad, old fellow." And Yeshmef tugged at his beard as
if to show he still had that which enabled him to grow it.

"Bah," Glathpilesh said, sounding angry that he had been unable
to anger his comrades. He turned to Abivard and said "Bah"
again, perhaps so Abivard would not feel left out of his disapproval. Then he said, "None of you has the wit the God gave a
smashed mosquito, but I'll work with you for no better reason

than to keep you from going astray without my genius to show you what needs doing."

"Your generosity, as usual, is unsurpassed," Utpanisht said in his rusty-hinge voice.

Glathpilesh spoiled that by swallowing its irony. "I know," he answered. "Now we'll see how much I regret it."

"Not as much as the rest of us, I promise," Mefyesh said.

Falasham boomed laughter. "A band of brothers, the lot of us," he declared, "and we fight like it, too." Remembering the fights he'd had with his own brothers, Abivard felt better about the prospects for the mages' being able to work together than he had since he'd walked into the room.

Having wrangled about how to flood the canals, the wizards spent a couple of more days wrangling over how best to make that approach work. Abivard didn't listen to all those arguments. He did stop in to see the wizards several times a day to make sure they were moving forward rather than around and around.

He also sent Turan out with some of the assembled garrison troops and some of the horsemen Tzikas had brought from Vaspurakan. "I want you to chase Maniakes and to be obvious and obnoxious about doing it," he told his lieutenant. "But by the God, don't catch him, whatever you do, because he'll thrash you."

"I understand," Turan assured him. "You want it to look as if we haven't forgotten about him so he won't spend too much time wondering what we're doing here instead of chasing him."

"That's it," Abivard said, slapping him on the back. He called to a servant for a couple of cups of wine. When he had his, he poured libations to the Prophets Four, then raised the silver goblet high and proclaimed, "Confusion to the Avtokrator! If we can keep him confused for a week, maybe a few days longer, he'll be worse than confused after that."

"If we make it so he can't stay here, he might have a hard time getting back to Videssos, too," Turan said with a predatory gleam in his eye.

"So he might," Abivard said. "That would have been more likely before we had to pull our mobile force out of Videssos and into Vaspurakan last year, but . . ." His voice trailed away. What point was there to protesting orders straight from the King of Kings?

Turan's force set out the next day with horns blowing and

banners waving. Abivard watched them from the city wall. They looked impressive; he didn't think Maniakes would be able to ignore them and go on sacking towns. Stopping that would be an added benefit of Turan's sortie.

From up there Abivard could see a long way across the floodplain of the Tutub and the Tib. He shook his head in mild bemusement. How many centuries of accumulated rubbish lay under his feet to give him this vantage point? He was no scholar; he couldn't have begun to guess. But if the answer proved less than the total of his own toes and fingers, he would have been astonished.

The vantage point would have been even more impressive had there been more to see. But the plain was as flat as if a woman had rolled it with a length of dowel before putting it on the griddle to bake—and the climate of the land of the Thousand Cities made that seem possible. Here and there, along a canal or a river, a few lines of date palms rose up above the fields. Most of the countryside, though, was mud and crops growing on top of mud.

Aside from the palms, the only breaks in the monotony were the hillocks on which the cities of the floodplain grew. Abivard could see several of them, each crowned with a habitation. All were as artificial as the one on which he stood. A great many people had lived in the land between the Tutub and the Tib for a long, long time.

He thought of the hill on which Vek Rud stronghold sat. There was nothing man-made about that piece of high ground: the stronghold itself was built of stone quarried from it. Here, all stone, right down to the weights the grain merchants used on their scales, had to be brought in from outside. *Mud,* Abivard thought again. He was sick of mud.

He wondered if he would ever see Vek Rud domain again. He still thought of it as home, though it had scarcely seen him since Genesios had overthrown Likinios and given Sharbaraz both the pretext and the opportunity he had needed to invade Videssos. How were things going up in the far northwest of Makuran? He hadn't heard from his brother, who was administering the domain for him, in years. Did Khamorth raiders still strike south over the Degird River and harass the domain, as they had since Peroz King of Kings had thrown away his life and his army out on the Pardrayan steppe? Abivard didn't know, and throughout his early years he'd expected to live out his whole life within the narrow confines of the domain and to be happy doing it, too.

As he seldom did, he thought about the wives he'd left behind in the women's quarters of Vek Rud stronghold. Guilt pierced him; their confines were far narrower than those he would have known even had he remained a *dihqan* like any other. When he'd left the domain, he'd never thought to be away so long. And yet, many if not most of his wives would have taken a proclamation of divorce as an insult, not as liberation. He shook his head. Life was seldom as simple as you wished it would be.

That thought made him feel kinder toward the wrangling wizards who labored to create a magic that would make the canals of the floodplain between the Tutub and the Tib spill their waters onto the land. Even the little he understood about sorcery convinced him they were undertaking something huge and complex. No wonder, then, if they quarreled as they figured out how to go about it.

Things they would need for the spell kept coming in: sealed jars with water from canals throughout the land of the Thousand Cities, each one neatly labeled to show from which canal it had come; mud from the dikes that kept the canals going as they should; wheat and lettuce and onions nourished by the water in the canals.

All those Abivard instinctively understood—they had to do with the waterways and the land they would inundate. But why the wizards also wanted oddments such as several dozen large quail's eggs, as many poisonous serpents, and enough pitch to coat the inside of a couple of wine jars was beyond him. He knew he'd never make a mage and so didn't spend a lot of time worrying about the nature of the conjuration the wizards would try.

What did worry him was *when* the wizards would try it. Short of lighting a bonfire under their chambers, he didn't know what he could do to make them move faster. They knew how important speed was here, but one day faded into the next without the spell being cast.

As he tried without much luck to hustle the wizards along, a messenger arrived from Mashiz. Abivard received the fellow with something less than joy. He wished the wizards had flooded the land of the Thousand Cities, for that would have kept the messenger from arriving. The timing was right for Sharbaraz King of Kings to have heard of his defeat at Maniakes' hands.

Sure enough, the letter was sealed with the lion of the King of Kings stamped into red wax. Abivard broke the seal, waded through the grandiose titles and epithets with which Sharbaraz bedizened his own name, and got to the meat of the missive: "We are once more displeased that you should take an army and lead it only into defeat. Know that we question your judgment in dividing your force in the face of the foe and that we are given to understand this contravenes every principle of the military art. Know further that any more such disasters associated with your name shall have a destructive and deleterious effect on our hopes and expectations for complete victory over Videssos."

"Is there a reply, lord?" the messenger asked when Abivard had rolled up the parchment and tied it with a bit of twine.

"No," he said absently, "no reply. Just acknowledge that you gave it to me and I read it."

The messenger saluted and left, presumably to make his return to Mashiz. Abivard shrugged. He saw no reason to doubt that the canals would remain unflooded till the man had returned—and maybe for a long time afterward, too.

He undid the twine that bound up Sharbaraz's letter and read it over again. That brought on another shrug. The tone was exactly as he'd expected, with petulance the strongest element. No mention—not even the slightest notion—that any of the recent reverses might have been partly the fault of the King of Kings. Sharbaraz's courtiers were undoubtedly encouraging him to believe he could do no wrong, not that he needed much in the way of encouragement along those lines.

But the letter was as remarkable for what it didn't say as for what it did. In with the usual carping criticism and worries lay not the slightest hint that Sharbaraz was thinking about changing commanders. Abivard had dreaded a letter from the King of Kings not least because he'd looked for Sharbaraz to remove him from his command and replace him, perhaps with Turan, perhaps with Tzikas.

Could he have taken orders from the Videssian renegade? He didn't know and was glad he didn't have to find out. Did Sharbaraz trust him? Or did the King of Kings merely distrust

Tzikas even more? If the latter, it was, in Abivard's opinion, only sensible of his sovereign.

He took the letter to Roshnani to find out whether she could see in it anything he was missing. She read it through, then looked up at him. "It could be worse," she said, as close as she'd come to praising Sharbaraz for some time.

"That's what I thought." Abivard picked up the letter from the table where she'd laid it, then read it again himself. "And if I lose another battle, it *will* be worse. He makes that clear enough."

"All the more reason to hope the wizards do succeed in flooding the plain," his principal wife answered. She cocked her head to one side and studied him. "How are they coming, anyhow? You haven't said much about them lately."

Abivard laughed and gave her a salute as if she were his superior officer. "I should know better than to think being quiet about something is the same as concealing it from you, shouldn't I? If you really want to know what I think, it's this: if Sharbaraz's courtiers were just a little nastier, they'd make pretty good sorcerers."

Roshnani winced. "I hadn't thought it was that bad."

All of Abivard's frustration came boiling out. "Well, it is. If anything, it's worse. I've never seen such backbiting. Yeshmef and Mefyesh ought to have their heads knocked together; that's what my father would have done if I quarreled like that with a brother of mine, anyhow. And as for Glathpilesh, I think he delights in being hateful. He's certainly made all the others hate him. The only ones who seem like good and decent fellows are Utpanisht, who's too old to be as useful as he might be, and his grandson, Kidinnu, who's the youngest of the lot and so not taken seriously—not that Falasham would take anything this side of an outbreak of pestilence seriously."

"And these were the good wizards?" Roshnani asked. At Abivard's nod, she rolled her eyes. "Maybe you should have recruited some bad ones, then."

"Maybe I should have," Abivard agreed. "I'll tell you what I've thought of doing: I've thought of making every mage in this crew shorter by a head and showing the heads to the next lot I recruit. That might get their attention and make them work fast." He regretfully spread his hands. "However tempting that is, though, gathering up a new lot would take too long. For better or worse, I'm stuck with these six."

He supposed it was poetic justice, then, that only a little while after he had called the six mages from the land of the Thousand Cities every name he could think of, they sent him a servant who said, "Lord, the wizards say to tell you they are ready to begin the conjuration. Will you watch?"

Abivard shook his head. "What they do wouldn't mean anything to me. Besides, I don't care how the magic works. I care only that it works. I'll go up on the city wall and look out over the fields to the canals. What I see there will tell the tale one way or the other."

"I shall take your words to the mages, lord, so they will know they may begin without you," the messenger said.

"Yes. Go." Abivard made little impatient brushing motions with his hands, sending the young man on his way. When the fellow had gone, Abivard walked through Nashvar's twisting, crowded streets to the wall. A couple of garrison soldiers stood at the base to keep just anyone from ascending it. Recognizing Abivard, they lowered their spears and stepped aside, bowing as they did so.

He had not climbed more than a third of the mud-brick stairs when he felt the world begin to change around him. It reminded him of the thrum in the ground just before an earthquake, when you could tell it was coming but the world hadn't yet started dancing under your feet.

He climbed faster. He didn't want to miss whatever was about to happen. The feeling of pressure grew until his head felt ready to burst. He waited for others to exclaim over it, but no one did. Up on the wall sentries tramped along, unconcerned. Down on the ground behind him merchants and customers told one another lies that had been passed down from father to son and from mother to daughter for generations uncounted.

Why was he, alone among mankind, privileged to feel the magic build to a peak of power? Maybe, he thought, because he had been the one who had set the sorcery in motion and so had some special affinity for it even if he was no wizard. And maybe, too, he was imagining all this, and nobody else felt it because it wasn't really there.

He couldn't make himself believe that. He looked out over the broad, flat floodplain. It seemed no different from the way it had the last time he'd seen it: fields and date palms and peasants in loincloths down in a perpetual stoop, weeding or manuring or gathering or trying to catch little fish in streams or canals.

Canals . . . Abivard looked out at the long straight channels that endless labor had created and more endless labor now maintained. Some of the fishermen, tiny as ants in the distance, suddenly sprang to their feet. One or two of them, for no apparent reason, looked back toward Abivard up on the city wall of Nashvar. He wondered if they had some tiny share of magical ability, enough at any rate to sense the rising power of the spell.

Would it never stop rising? Abivard thought he would have to start pounding his temples with his fists to let out the pressure inside. And then, all at once, almost like an orgasm, came release. He staggered and nearly fell, feeling as if he'd suddenly been emptied.

And all across the floodplain, as far as he could see, the banks of canals were opening up, spilling water over the land in a broad sheet that sparkled silver as the sunlight glinted off it. Thin in the distance came the cries of fishers and farmers caught unaware by the flood. Some fled. Some splashed in the water. Abivard hoped they could swim.

He wondered how widely through the land of the Thousand Cities canal banks were crumbling and water was pouring out over the land. For all he knew for certain, the flood might have been limited to the narrow area he could see with his own eyes.

But he didn't believe it. The flood *felt* bigger than that. Whatever he'd felt inside himself, whatever had made him feel he was about to explode like a sealed pot in a fire, was too big to be merely a local marvel. He had no way to prove that—not yet—but he would have sworn by the God it was so.

People began running out of Nashvar toward the breached canals. Some carried mattocks, others hoes, others spades. Wherever they could reach a magically broken bank, they started to repair it with no more magic than that engendered by diligent work.

Abivard scowled when he saw that. It made perfect sense—the peasants didn't want to see their crops drowned and all the labor they'd put into them lost—but it took him by surprise all the same. He'd been so intent on covering the floodplain with water, he hadn't stopped to think what the people would do when that happened. He'd realized that they wouldn't be delighted; that they'd immediately try to set things right hadn't occurred to him.

He'd pictured the land between the Tutub and the Tib underwater, with only the Thousand Cities sticking up out of it on their artificial hillocks like islands from the sea. With the certainty that told him the flood stretched farther than his body's eyes could reach, he now saw in his mind's eye men—aye, and probably women, too—pouring out of the cities all across the floodplain to repair what the great conjuration had wrought.

"But don't they want to be rid of the Videssians?" Abivard said out loud, as if someone had challenged him on that very point.

The folk who lived—or had lived—in cities Maniakes and his army had sacked undoubtedly hoped every Videssian ever born would vanish into the Void. But the Videssians had sacked but a handful of the Thousand Cities. In all the other towns, they were no more than a hypothetical danger. Flood was real and immediate—and familiar. The peasants wouldn't know, or care, what had caused it They would know what to do about it.

That worked against Makuran and for Videssos. The land between the Tutub and the Tib would, Abivard realized, come back to normal faster than he had expected. And, during the time when it wasn't normal, he would have as much trouble moving as Maniakes did. Maybe, though, Turan could strike a blow at some of the Videssians if they'd grown careless and split their forces.

Less happy than he'd thought he'd be, Abivard descended from the wall and walked back toward the city governor's residence. There he found Utpanisht, who looked all but dead from exhaustion, and Glathpilesh, who was methodically working his way through a tray of roasted songbirds stuffed with dates. Fragile bones crunched between his teeth as he chewed.

Swallowing, he grudged Abivard a curt nod. "It is accomplished," he said, and reached for another songbird. More tiny bones crunched.

"So it is, for which I thank you," Abivard answered with a bow. He could not resist adding, "And done well, in spite of its not being done as you first had in mind."

That got him a glare; he would have been disappointed if it hadn't. Utpanisht held up a bony, trembling hand. "Speak not against Glathpilesh, lord," he said in a voice like wind whispering through dry, dry straw. "He served Makuran nobly this day."

"So he did," Abivard admitted. "So did all of you. Sharbaraz King of Kings owes you a debt of gratitude."

Glathpilesh spit out a bone that might have choked him had he swallowed it. "What he owes us and what we'll get from him are liable to be two different things," he said. His shrug made his flabby jowls wobble. "Such is life: what you get is always less than you deserve."

Such a breathtakingly sardonic view of life would have annoyed Abivard most of the time. Now he said only, "Regardless of what Sharbaraz does, I shall reward all six of you as you deserve."

"You are generous, lord," Utpanisht said in that dry, quavering voice.

"Just deserts, eh?" Glathpilesh said with his mouth full. He studied Abivard with eyes that, while not very friendly, were disconcertingly keen. "And will Sharbaraz King of Kings, may his days be long and his realm increase—" He made a mockery of the honorific formula. "—reward you as you deserve?"

Abivard felt his face heat. "That is as the King of Kings wishes. I have no say in the matter."

"Evidently not," Glathpilesh said scornfully.

"I am sorry," Abivard told him, "but your wit is too pointed for me today. I'd better go and find the best way to take advantage of what your flood has done to the Videssians. If we had a great fleet of light boats ... but I might as well wish for the moon while I'm at it."

"Use well the chance you have," Utpanisht told him, almost as if prophesying. "Its like may be long in coming."

"That I know," Abivard said. "I did not do all I could with our journey by canal. The God will think less of me if I let this chance slip, too. But—" He grimaced. "—it will not be so easy as I thought when I asked you to flood the canals for me."

"When is anything ever as easy as you think it will be?" Glathpilesh demanded. He pointed to the tray of songbirds, which was empty now. "There. You see? As I said, you never get all you want."

"Getting all I want is the least of my worries," Abivard answered. "Getting all I need is another question altogether."

Glathpilesh eyed him with sudden fresh interest and respect. "For one not a mage—and for one not old—to know the difference between those two is less than common. Even for mages, *need* shades into *want* so that we must ever be on our guard against disasters spawned from greed."

To judge from the empty tray in front of him, Glathpilesh was intimately acquainted with greed, perhaps more intimately acquainted than he realized—no one needed to devour so many songbirds, but he'd certainly wanted them. The only disaster to which such gluttony could lead, though, Abivard thought, was choking to death on a bone, or perhaps getting so wide that you couldn't fit through a door.

Utpanisht said, "May the God grant you find a way to use our magic as you had hoped and drive the Videssians and their false god from the land of the Thousand Cities."

"May it be as you say," Abivard agreed. He was less sure it would be that way now than he had been when he had decided to use the flood as a weapon against Maniakes. But no matter what else happened, the Videssians would not be able to move around on the plain between the Tutub and the Tib as freely as they had been doing. That would reduce the amount of damage they could inflict.

"It had better be as Utpanisht says," Glathpilesh said. "Otherwise a lot of time and effort will have gone for nothing."

"A lot of time," Abivard echoed. The wizards, as far as he was concerned, had wasted a good deal of it all by themselves. They, no doubt, would vehemently disagree with that characterization and would claim they had spent time wisely. But whether wasted or spent, time had passed—quite a bit of it. "Not much time is left for this campaigning season. We've held Maniakes away from Mashiz for the year, anyhow."

That was exactly what Sharbaraz King of Kings had sent him out to do. Sharbaraz had expected he'd do it by beating the Videssians, but making them shift their path, making them fight even if he couldn't win, and then using water as a weapon seemed to work as well.

"As harvest nears, the Videssians will leave our land, not so?" Utpanisht said. "They are men; they must harvest like other men."

"The land of the Thousand Cities grows enough for them to stay here and live off the countryside if they want to," Abivard said, "or it did before the flood, at any rate. But if they do stay here, who will bring in the harvests back in their homeland? Their women will go hungry; their children will starve. Can Maniakes make them go on while that happens? I doubt it."

"And I as well," Utpanisht said. "I raised the question to be certain you were aware of it."

"Oh, I'm aware of it," Abivard answered. "Now we have to find out whether Maniakes is—and whether he cares."

With the countryside flooded around them, the Videssians no longer rampaged through the land of the Thousand Cities. Not even their skill at engineering let them do that. Instead, they stayed near the upper reaches of one of the Tutub's tributaries, from which they could either resume the assault they had carried on through the summer or withdraw back into the westlands of their own empire.

Abivard tried to force them to the latter course, marching out and joining up with Turan's force before moving—sometimes single file along causeways that were the only routes through drowned farmlands—against the Videssians. He sent a letter off to Romezan up in Vaspurakan, asking him to use the cavalry of the field force to attack Maniakes once he got back into Videssos. The garrisons holding the towns in the Videssian westlands weren't much better equipped for mobile warfare than were those that had held down the Thousand Cities.

Word came from out of Videssian-held territory that Maniakes' wife, Lysia—who was also his first cousin—not only was with the Avtokrator but had just been delivered of a baby boy. "There—do you see?" Roshnani said when Abivard passed the news to her. "You're not the only one who takes his wife on campaign."

"Maniakes is only a Videssian bound for the Void," Abivard replied, not without irony. "What he does has no bearing on the way a proper Makuraner noblewoman should behave."

Roshnani stuck out her tongue at him. Then she grew serious once more. "What's she like—Lysia, I mean?"

"I don't know," Abivard admitted. "He may take her on campaigns with him, but I've never met her." He paused thoughtfully. "He must think the world of her. For the Videssians, marrying your cousin is as shocking as letting noblewomen out in public is for us."

"I wonder if that's part of the reason he's brought her along," Roshnani mused. "Having her with him might be safer than leaving her back in Videssos the city while he's gone."

"It could be so," Abivard said. "If you really want to know,

we can ask Tzikas. He professed to be horrified about Maniakes'
incest—that's what he called it—when he came over to us. The
only problem is, Tzikas would profess anything if he saw as
much as one chance in a hundred that he might get something
he wants by doing it."

"If I thought you were wrong, I would tell you," Roshnani said.
She thought for a moment, then shook her head. "If finding out
about Lysia means asking Tzikas, I'd rather not know."

Abivard gave the Videssian renegade such praise as he could:
"He hasn't done anything to me since he came here from
Vaspurakan."

Roshnani tempered even that: "Anything you know of, you
mean. But you didn't know everything he was doing to you
before, either."

"I'm not saying you're wrong, either, mind you, but I am learning," Abivard answered. "Tzikas doesn't know it, but slipping a few
arkets to his orderlies means I read everything he writes before
it goes into a courier's message tube."

Roshnani kissed him with great enthusiasm. "You *are* learning," she said.

"I should be clever more often," Abivard said. That made her
laugh and, as he'd hoped, kiss him again.

The closer his army drew to Maniakes' force, the more Abivard
worried about what he'd do if the Videssians chose battle instead
of retreat. Tzikas' regiment of veteran cavalry stiffened the men
he already had, and half of those garrison soldiers had fought
well even if they had lost in the end. He was still leery of the
prospect of battle and suddenly understood why the Videssians
had been so hesitant about fighting his army after losing to it a
few times. Now he felt the pinch of that sandal on his foot.

In the fields the peasants of the Thousand Cities worked stolidly
away at repairing the damage from the breaches in the canals he'd
had the wizards make. He wanted to shout at them, try to make
them see that in so doing they were also helping to turn Maniakes
loose on their land once more. He kept quiet. From long, often
unhappy experience, he knew a peasant's horizon seldom reached
farther than the crop he was raising. There was some justification
for that way of thinking, too: if the crop didn't get raised, nothing
else mattered, not to the peasant who stood to starve.

But Abivard saw farther. If Maniakes got loose to rampage

over the land between the Tutub and the Tib once more, these particular peasants might escape, but others, probably more, would suffer.

He found himself glancing at the sun more often than usual. Like anyone else, he looked to the sky to find out what time it was. Nowadays, though, he paid more attention to where in the sky the sun was rising and setting. The sooner autumn came, the happier he would be. Maniakes would have to withdraw to his own land then . . . wouldn't he?

If he did intend to withdraw, he gave no sign of it. Instead, he sent out horsemen to harass Abivard's soldiers and slow their already creeping advance even further. With Abivard's reluctant blessing, Tzikas led his cavalry regiment in a counterattack that sent the Videssians back in retreat.

When the renegade tried to push farther still, he barely escaped an ambush Maniakes' troopers set for him. On hearing that, Abivard didn't know whether to be glad or sorry. Seeing Tzikas fall into the hands of the Avtokrator he'd tried to slay by sorcery would have been the perfect revenge on him even if Abivard had decided not to hand him over to Maniakes.

"Why can't you?" Turan asked when Abivard grumbled about that. "I wish you would have after he came down here, no matter what he said about his regiment." He paused thoughtfully. "The cursed Videssian's not a coward in battle, whatever else you want to say about him. Arrange for him to meet about a regiment's worth of Videssians with maybe half a troop of his own at his back. That'll settle him once and for all."

Abivard pondered the idea. It brought a good deal of temptation with it. In the end, though, and rather to his own surprise, he shook his head. "It's what he would do to me were our places reversed."

"All the more reason to do it to him first," Turan said.

"Thank you, but no. If you have to become a villain to beat a villain, the God will drop you into the Void along with him."

"You're too tenderhearted for your own good," Turan said. "Sharbaraz King of Kings, may his days be long and his realm increase, would have done it without blinking an eye, and he wouldn't have needed me to suggest it to him, either."

That was both true and false. Sharbaraz, these days, could be as ruthless as any man ever born when it came to protecting his throne . . . yet he had not put Abivard out of the way when he had had the chance. Maybe that meant a spark of humanity did still lurk within the kingly facade he'd been building over the past decade and more.

Turan looked sly. "If you want to keep your hands clean, lord, I expect I could arrange something or other. You don't even have to ask. I'll take care of it."

Abivard shook his head again, this time in annoyance. If Turan had quietly arranged for Tzikas' untimely demise without telling him about it, that would have been between his lieutenant and the God. But for Turan to do that after Abivard had said he didn't want it done was a different matter. What would have been good service would have turned into villainy.

"You've got more scruples than a druggist," Turan grumbled as he walked off, as disappointed with Abivard as Abivard was with him.

The next day Tzikas returned to camp to give Abivard the details of his skirmish with the Videssians. "The enemy, at least, thought I was a man of Makuran," he said pointedly. " 'There's that cavalry general of theirs, curse him to the ice,' they said. A good many of them have fallen into the Void now, eternal oblivion their fate."

He said all the right things. He'd let his beard grow out so that it made his face seem more rectangular, less pinched in at the jaw and chin. He wore a Makuraner caftan. And he still was, to Abivard, a foreigner, a Videssian, and so not to be trusted because of who he was, let alone because of his letters to Sharbaraz King of Kings.

But he'd done decent service here. Abivard acknowledged that, saying, "I'm glad you beat them back. Knowing a cavalry regiment is here and able to do its job will make Maniakes think twice about getting pushy so late in the year."

"Yes," Tzikas said. "Your magic helped there, too, even if not quite so much as you'd hoped." His lips twisted in a grimace no Makuraner could have matched, an expression of self-reproach that was quintessentially Videssian: he was berating himself for being less underhanded than he would have wanted. "Had the magic I essayed worked even half so well, I, not Maniakes, would be Avtokrator now."

"And I might be trying to figure out how to drive you from

the land of the Thousand Cities," Abivard answered. His gaze sharpened. Here was a chance to get a look at the way Tzikas' mind worked. "Or would you have tried such a bold thrust if you had the Videssian throne under your fundament?"

"No, not I," Tzikas said at once. "I would have held on to what I had, strengthened that, and then begun to wrest back what was mine. I would have had no need to hurry, for I could have held out in Videssos the city forever, so long as my fleet kept you from crossing over from the westlands. Once my plans were ripe, I'd have struck and struck hard."

Abivard nodded. It was a sensible, conservative plan. That mirrored the way Tzikas had opposed Makuran back in the days when he'd been the best of the Videssian generals in the westlands—and the one who had paid the most attention to fighting the invaders and the least to the endless rounds of civil war engulfing the Empire after Genesios had murdered his way to the Videssian throne. Only in treachery, it seemed, was Tzikas less than conservative, although by Videssian standards, even that might not have been so.

"But Maniakes has thrown us back on our heels," Abivard argued. "Would your scheme have done so much so soon?"

"Probably not," Tzikas said. "But it would have risked less. Maniakes, whining pup that he is, has a way of overreaching that will bring him down in the end—you mark my words."

"I always mark your words, eminent sir," Abivard answered. Tzikas scowled at his use of the Videssian title. Abivard didn't care. He also didn't think Tzikas was right. Maniakes, unlike a lot of generals, kept getting better at what he did.

"By the God," Tzikas replied, again reminding Abivard that he had bound himself to Makuran for better or for worse—*or until he sees a chance for some new treachery,* Abivard thought—"we should push straight at Maniakes with everything we have and force him out of the land of the Thousand Cities."

"I'd love to," Abivard said. "The only problem with the plan is that everything we have hasn't been enough to force him out of the Thousand Cities."

Tzikas didn't answer, not with words. He simply donned another of those characteristically Videssian expressions, this one saying that, had he been in charge of things, they would have gone better.

Before Abivard could get angry at that, he realized there was another problem with the scheme the Videssian renegade had proposed. Like Tzikas' plan for fighting Makuran had he been Avtokrator, this one lacked imagination; it showed no sense of where the enemy's real weakness lay.

Slowly Abivard said, "Suppose we do force Maniakes away from the Tutub. What happens next? Where does he go?"

"He falls back into the westlands. Where else can he go?" Tzikas said. "Then, I suppose, he makes for the coast, whether north or south I couldn't begin to guess. And then he sails away, and Makuran is rid of him till the spring campaigning season, by which time, the God willing, we shall be better prepared to face him here in the land of the Thousand Cities than we were this year."

"My guess is he'll go south," Abivard said. "To reach the coast of the Videssian Sea, he'd have to skirt Vaspurakan, where we have a force that should be coming out to hunt him anyhow, and he controls none of the ports along that coast. But he's taken Lyssaion, which means he has a gateway out on the coast of the Sailors' Sea."

"Clearly reasoned," Tzikas agreed. From a Videssian that was no small praise. "Yes, I suppose he likely will escape to the south, and we shall be rid of him—and we shall not miss him one bit."

"Do you play the Videssian board game?" Abivard asked, continuing, "I was never very good at it, but I liked it because it leaves nothing to chance but rests everything on the skill of the players."

"Yes, I play it," Tzikas answered. By the predatory look that came into his eyes, he played well. "Perhaps you would honor me with a game one day."

"As I say, you'd mop the floor with me," Abivard said, reflecting that Tzikas would no doubt enjoy mopping the floor with him, too. "But that's not the point. The point is, you can hurt the fellow playing the other side, sometimes hurt him a lot, just by putting one of your pieces between his piece and where it's trying to go."

"And so?" Tzikas said, right at the edge of rudeness. But then his manner changed. "I begin to see, lord, what may be in your mind."

"Good," Abivard told him, less sardonically than he'd intended.

"If we can set an army on his road down to Lyssaion, that will cause him all manner of grief. And unless I misremember, delaying him on the road to Lyssaion really matters at this season of the year."

"You remember rightly, lord," Tzikas said. "The Sailors' Sea turns stormy in the fall and stays stormy through the winter. No captain would want to risk taking his Avtokrator and the best soldiers Videssos has back to the capital by sea, not in a few weeks, not when he'd know he was only too likely to lose them all. And that would mean—"

"That would mean Maniakes would have to try to cross the westlands to get home," Abivard said, interrupting not from irritation but from excitement. "He'd have to capture each town along the way if he wanted to encamp in it, and the winter there is hard enough that he'd have to try—he couldn't very well live under canvas till spring came. So if we can get between him and Lyssaion, we don't even have to win a battle—"

"A good thing, too, with these odds and sods under your command," Tzikas broke in. Now he was being rude but not inaccurate.

"And whose fault is it that Sharbaraz King of Kings, may his years be many and his realm increase, wouldn't trust me with better?" Abivard retorted. The prospect of discomfiting Maniakes made him better able to tolerate Tzikas, so that came out as badinage, not rage. He went on, "If you think they're bad now, you should have seen them when I first got them. Eminent sir, they're brave enough, and they are starting to learn their trade."

"I'd cheerfully trade them for a like number of real soldiers nonetheless," Tzikas said, again impolite but again correct.

Abivard said, "It's settled, then. We advance against Maniakes and demonstrate in front of him, with luck making him abandon his base here. And as he moves south, we have a force waiting to engage him. We don't have to win; we simply have to keep him in play till it's too late for him to sail out of Lyssaion."

"That's it," Tzikas said. He bowed to Abivard. "A plan worthy of Stavrakios the Great." The Videssian renegade suddenly suffered a coughing fit; Stavrakios was the Avtokrator who'd smashed every Makuraner army he had faced and had occupied Mashiz. When Tzikas could speak again, he went on: "Worthy of the great heroes of Makuran, I should have said."

"It's all right," Abivard said magnanimously. In a way he was relieved Tzikas had slipped. The cavalry officer did do an alarmingly good job of aping the Makuraners with whom he'd had to cast his lot. It was just as well he'd proved he remained a Videssian at heart.

Abivard wasted no time sending a good part of his army south along the Tutub. Had he seriously intended to defeat Maniakes as the Avtokrator headed for Lyssaion, he would have gone with that force. As things were, he sent it out under the reliable Turan. He commanded the rest of the Makuraner army, the part demonstrating against Maniakes in his lair.

His force included almost all of Tzikas' cavalry regiment. That left him nervous in spite of the accord he seemed to have reached with the Videssian renegade. Having betrayed Maniakes and Abivard both, was he now liable to betray one of them to the other? Abivard didn't want to find out.

But Tzikas stayed in line. His cavalry fought hard against the Videssian horsemen who battled to hold them away from Maniakes' base. He reveled in fighting for his adopted country against the men of his native land and worshiped the God more ostentatiously than did any Makuraner.

Maniakes once more took to breaking canals to keep Abivard's men at bay. Flooding was indeed a two-edged sword. Wearily, Abivard's soldiers and the local peasants worked side by side to repair the damage so the soldiers could go on and the peasants could save something of their crops.

And then, from the northeast, the smoke from a great burning rose into the sky, as it so often had in the land of the Thousand Cities that summer. More wrecked canals kept Abivard's men from reaching the site of that burning for another couple of days, but Abivard knew what it meant: Maniakes was gone.

Abivard glared at the peasant in some exasperation. "You saw the Videssian army leave?" he demanded. The peasant nodded. "And which way did they go? Tell me again," Abivard said.

"That way, lord." The peasant pointed east, as he had before.

Everyone with whom Abivard had spoken had said the same thing. Yes, the Videssians were gone. Yes, the locals were glad—although they seemed less glad to see a Makuraner army arrive to take the invaders' place. And yes, Maniakes and his men had gone east. No one had seen them turn south.

He's being sneaky, Abivard thought. *He'll go out into the scrub country between the Tutub and Videssos and stay there as long as he can, maybe even travel south a long way before he comes back to the river for water.* You could travel a fair distance through that semidesert, especially when the fall rains—the same rains that would be storms on the Sailors' Sea—brought the grass and leaves to brief new life.

But you could not travel all the way down to Lyssaion without returning to the Tutub. Even lush scrub wouldn't support an army's horses indefinitely, and there weren't enough water holes to keep an army of men from perishing of thirst. And when Maniakes came back to the Tutub, Abivard would know exactly where he was.

True, Maniakes' army could move faster than his. But that army, burdened by a baggage train, could not outrun the scouting detachments Abivard sent galloping southward to check the likely halting places along the Tutub. If the scouts came back, they would bring news of where the Videssians were. And if one detachment did not come back, that would also tell Abivard where the Videssians were.

All the detachments came back. None of them had found Maniakes and his men. Abivard was left scratching his head. "He hasn't vanished into the Void, however much we wish he would," he said. "Can he be mad enough to try crossing the Videssian westlands on horseback?"

"I don't know anything about that, lord," answered the scout to whom he'd put the question. "All I know is I haven't seen him."

Snarling, Abivard dismissed him. The scout hadn't done anything wrong; he'd carried out the orders Abivard had given him, just as his fellows had. Abivard's job was to make what the scouts had seen—and what they hadn't seen—mean something. But what?

"He hasn't gone south," he said to Roshnani that evening. "I don't want to believe that, but I haven't any choice. He can't have chosen to fight his way across the westlands. I *won't* believe that; even if he made it, he'd throw away most of his army in the doing, and he hasn't got enough trained men to use them up so foolishly."

"Maybe he headed into Vaspurakan to try to rouse the princes against our field force again," Roshnani suggested.

"Maybe," Abivard said, unconvinced. "But that would tie him down in long, hard fighting and make him winter in Vaspurakan. I have trouble thinking he'd risk so much with such a distance and so many foes between him and country he controls."

"I'm no general—the God knows that's so—but I can see that what you say makes sense," Roshnani said. "But if he hasn't gone south and he hasn't gone into the Videssian westlands and he hasn't gone to Vaspurakan, where is he? He hasn't gone west, has he?"

Abivard snorted. "No, and that's not his army camped around us, either." He plucked at his beard. "I wonder if he could have gone north, up into the mountains and valleys of Erzerum. He might find friends up there no matter how isolated he was."

"From what the tales say, you can find anything up in Erzerum," Roshnani said.

"The tales speak true," Abivard told her. "Erzerum is the rubbish heap of the world." The mountains that ran from the Mylasa Sea east to the Videssian Sea and the valleys set among them were as perfectly defensible a terrain as had ever sprung from the mind and hand of the God. Because of that, almost every valley there had its own people, its own language, its own religion. Some were native, some survivors whose cause had been lost in the outer world but who had managed to carve out a shelter for themselves and hold it against all comers.

"The folk in some of those valleys worship Phos, don't they?" Roshnani asked.

"So they do," Abivard said. "What I'd like to see is Videssos pushed back into one of those valleys and forgotten about for the rest of time." He laughed. "It won't happen any time soon. And the Videssians would like to see us penned back there for good. That won't happen, either."

"No, of course not," Roshnani said. "The God would never allow such a thing; the very idea would appall her." But she didn't let Abivard distract her, instead continuing with her own train of thought: "Because some of them worship Phos, wouldn't they be likely to help Maniakes?"

"Yes, I suppose so," Abivard agreed. "He might winter up there. I have to say, though, I don't see why he would. He couldn't keep it a secret the winter long, and we'd be waiting for him to try to come back down into the low country when spring came."

"That's so," Roshnani admitted. "I can't argue with a word of it. But if he hasn't gone north, south, east, or west, *where is he?*"

"Underground," Abivard said. But that was too much to hope for.

He made his own arrangements for the winter, billeting his troops in several nearby cities and overcoming the city governors' remarkable lack of enthusiasm for keeping them in supplies. "Fine," he told one such official when the man flatly refused to aid the soldiers. "When the Videssians come back next spring, if they do, we'll stand aside and let them burn your town without even chasing them afterward."

"You couldn't do anything so heartless," the city governor exclaimed.

Abivard looked down his nose at him. "Who says I can't? If you don't help feed the soldiers, sirrah, why should they help protect you?"

The soldiers got all the wheat and vegetables and poultry they needed.

Only a couple of days after Abivard had won that battle a messenger reached him with a letter from Romezan. After the usual greetings the commander of the field forces came straight to the point: "I regret to tell you that the cursed Videssians, may they and their Avtokrator fall into the Void and be lost forever, slipped past my army, which was out hunting them. Following the line of the Rhamnos River, they reached Pityos, on the Videssian Sea, and took it by surprise. With the port in their hands, ships came and carried them away; my guess is that they have returned to Videssos the city by now, having also succeeded in embarrassing us no end. By the God, lord, I shall have my revenge on them."

"Is there a reply, lord?" the messenger asked when Abivard rolled up the message parchment once more.

"No, no reply," Abivard answered. "Now I know where the Videssians disappeared to, and I rather wish I didn't."

Winter in the land of the Thousand Cities meant mild days, cool nights, and occasional rain—no snow to speak of, though there were a couple of days of sleet that made it all but impossible to go outside without falling down. Abivard found that a nuisance, but his children enjoyed it immensely.

Although Maniakes would not be back till the following spring, if then, Abivard did not let his army rest idle. He drilled the foot soldiers every day the ground was dry enough to let them maneuver. The more he worked with them, the happier he grew. They would make decent fighting men once they had enough practice marching and got used to the idea that the enemy could not easily crush them so long as they stood firm.

And then, as the winter solstice approached, Abivard got the message he'd been waiting for and dreading since Sharbaraz had ordered him into the field against Maniakes with a force he knew to be inadequate: a summons to return to Mashiz at once.

He looked west across the floodplain toward the distant Dilbat Mountains. News of the order had spread very fast. Turan, who had rejoined him after Maniakes had escaped, came up beside him and said, "I'm sorry, lord. I don't know what else you could have done to hold the Videssians away from Mashiz."

"Neither do I," Abivard said wearily. "Nothing would have satisfied the King of Kings, I think."

Turan nodded. He couldn't say anything to that. No, there was one thing he could say. But the question, *Why don't you go into rebellion against Sharbaraz?* was not one a person could ask his commander unless that person was sure his answer would be something like, *Yes, why don't I?* Abivard had never let—had been careful never to let—anyone get that impression.

Every now and then he wondered why. These past years he'd generally been happiest when farthest away from Sharbaraz. But he'd helped Sharbaraz cast down one usurper simply because Smerdis had been a usurper. Having done that, how could he think of casting the legitimate King of Kings from a throne rightfully his? The brief answer was that he couldn't, not if he wanted to be able to go on looking at himself in the mirror.

And so, without hope and without fear, he left the army in Turan's hands—better his than Tzikas', Abivard judged—and obeyed Sharbaraz's order. He wanted to leave Roshnani and his children behind, but his principal wife would not hear of it. "Your brother and mine can avenge us if we fall," she said. "Our place is at your side." Glad of her company, Abivard stopped arguing perhaps sooner than he should have.

The journey across the land of the Thousand Cities showed the scars the Videssian incursion had left behind. Several hills were topped by chaired ruins, not living towns. Soon, Abivard vowed, those towns would live again. If he had anything to say about it, money and artisans from the Videssian westlands would help make sure they lived again—that appealed to his sense of justice.

Whether he would have anything to say about it remained to be seen. The letter summoning him to Mashiz hadn't been so petulant as some of the missives he'd gotten from Sharbaraz. That might mean the King of Kings was grateful he'd kept Maniakes from sacking the capital. On the other hand, it might also mean Sharbaraz was dissembling and wanted him back in Mashiz before doing whatever dreadful things he would do.

As usual, Roshnani thought along with him. When she asked what he thought awaited them in Mashiz, he shrugged and answered, "No way to judge till we get there." She nodded, if not satisfied, then at least knowing that she knew as much as her husband.

They crossed the Tib on a bridge of boats that the operator dragged back to the western bank of the river after they went over it. That sort of measure was intended to make life difficult for invaders. Abivard doubted it would have thwarted Maniakes long.

After they left the land of the Thousand Cities, they went up into the foothills of the Dilbat Mountains toward Mashiz. Varaz said, "They're not going to lock us up in one suite of rooms through the whole winter again, are they, Father?"

"I hope not," Abivard answered truthfully, "but I don't know for certain."

"They'd better not," Varaz declared, and Shahin nodded.

"I wish they wouldn't, too," Abivard said, "but if they do, what can you do about it—aside from driving everyone crazy, I mean?"

"What we should do," Varaz said, with almost the force of someone having a religious revelation, "is drive the palace servants and the guards crazy, not you and Mother and—" He spoke with the air of one yielding a great concession. "—our sisters."

"If I told you I thought that an excellent plan, I would probably be guilty of lese majesty in some obscure way, and I don't want that," Abivard said, "so of course I won't tell you any such thing." He set a finger alongside his nose and winked. Both his sons laughed conspiratorial laughs.

There ahead stood the great shrine dedicated to the God. Abivard had seen the High Temple in Videssos the city at a shorter remove, though here no water screened him from reaching the shrine if he so desired. Again, whether Sharbaraz's minions would keep him from the shrine was a different matter.

Away from the army, Abivard was just another traveler entering Mashiz. No one paid any special attention to his wagon, which was but one of many clogging the narrow streets of the city. Drivers whose progress he impeded cursed him with great gusto.

Abivard had studied from afar the palaces in Videssos the city. They sprawled over an entire district, buildings set among trees and lawns and gardens. But then, as he knew all too well, Videssos the city was a fortress, the mightiest fortress in the world.

Mashiz was not so lucky, and the palace of the King of Kings had to double as a citadel.

The wheels of the wagon rattled and clattered off the cobbles of the open square surrounding the wall around the palace. As he had the winter before, Abivard identified himself to the guards at the gate. As before, the valves of the gate swung wide to let him and his family come in, then closed with a thud that struck him as ominous.

And as before, and even more ominously, grooms led the horses away from the stables, while a fat eunuch in a caftan shot through with silver threads took charge of Pashang. The wagon driver sent Abivard a look of piteous appeal. "Where are you taking him?" Abivard demanded.

"Where he belongs," the eunuch answered, sexless voice chillier than the cutting breeze that blew dead brown leaves over the cobbles.

"Swear by the God you are not taking him to the dungeon," Abivard said.

"It is no business of yours where he goes," the eunuch told him.

"I choose to make it my business." Abivard set a hand on the hilt of his sword. Even as he made the gesture, he knew how foolish it was. If the eunuch so much as lifted a finger, the palace guards would kill him. Sharbaraz would probably reward them for doing it.

The finger remained unlifted. The eunuch licked his lips; his tongue was very pink against the pale, unweathered flesh of his face. He looked from Abivard to Pashang and back again. At last he said, "Very well. He shall dwell in the stables with your horses. By the God, I swear that to be true; may it drop me into the Void if I lie. There. Are you satisfied?"

"I am satisfied," Abivard answered formally. Men used masculine pronouns when speaking of the God, women feminine; it had never occurred to Abivard that eunuchs would refer to him—for so Abivard conceived of his deity—in the neuter gender. He turned to Pashang. "Make sure they feed you something better than oats."

"The God go with you and keep you safe, lord," Pashang said, and started to prostrate himself as if Abivard were King of Kings. With a snort of disgust the eunuch hauled him to his feet and led him away. Pashang waved clumsily, like a bear trained to do as much in hopes of winning a copper or two.

Another eunuch emerged from the stone fastness of the palace. "You will come with me," he announced to Abivard.

"Will I?" Abivard murmured. But that question had only one possible answer. His family trailing behind him, he did follow the servitor into the beating heart of the kingdom of Makuran.

He knew—knew only too well—every turn and passageway that would lead him to the suite where he and his family had been politely confined the winter before. As soon as the eunuch turned left instead of right, he breathed a long if silent sigh of relief. He glanced over to Roshnani. She was doing the same thing.

The chambers to which the fellow did lead them were in a wing far closer to the throne room than the place they had been before. Abivard would have taken that as a better sign had not two tall, muscular men in mail shirts and plume-crested helms stood in front of the doorway.

"Are we prisoners here?" he demanded of the eunuch.

"No," that worthy replied. "These men are but your guard of honor."

Abivard plucked a hair from his beard as he thought that over. The winter before no one in the palace had pretended he was anything but a prisoner. That had had the virtue of honesty, if no other. Would Sharbaraz lie, though, if he thought it served his purpose? The answer seemed obvious enough.

"Suppose we go in there," Abivard said. "Then suppose we want to come out and walk through the halls of the palace here. What would the guards do? On your oath by the God."

Before answering, the eunuch held a brief, low-voiced colloquy with the soldiers. "They tell me," he said carefully, "that if you came out for a stroll, as you say, one of them would accompany you while the other remained on guard in front of your door. By the God, lord, that is what they say."

The guardsmen nodded and gestured with their left hands to confirm his words. "We have no choice," Roshnani said. She had picked up Gulshahr, who was tired from all the walking she'd done.

"You're right," Abivard said, though there had been that unspoken choice: rebelling rather than coming to Mashiz a second time after what had happened before. But rebellion was no longer possible, not here, not now. Lion trainers, to thrill a crowd, would stick their heads into the mouths of their beasts day after day. But the lions they worked with were tame. One could form a pretty good notion of what they would do from day to day. With Sharbaraz—

"Does it suit you, lord?" the eunuch asked.

"For now it suits me," Abivard said, "but I want an audience with the King of Kings as soon as may be."

Bowing, the eunuch said, "I shall convey your request to those better able than I to make certain it is granted."

Abivard had no trouble translating that for himself. He might gain an audience with Sharbaraz tomorrow, or he might have to wait till next spring. No way to guess which—not yet.

"Please let me or another of the servitors know whatever you may be lacking or what may conduce toward your pleasure," the eunuch said. "Rest assured that if it be within our power, it shall be yours."

Abivard paused thoughtfully. No one had spoken to him like that last winter. Maybe he hadn't been summoned back here in disgrace, after all. Then again, maybe he had. He did his best to find out: "I would like to see my sister Denak, principal wife to the King of Kings as soon as I can, to thank her for her help." Let the eunuch make of that what he would.

Whatever he made of it he concealed, saying as he had before, "I shall take your words to those better able to deal with them than I."

One of the guardsmen in front of the door opened it and gestured for Abivard and his family to go through and enter the suite of rooms set aside for them. Full of misgivings, he went in. The door closed. The rooms had carpets and pillows different from the ones that had been in the suite of the winter before. Other than that, was there any difference from that year to this?

The latch clicked. Abivard opened the door. He stepped out into the corridor. The guards who'd been standing watch when he had gone into the chamber were gone, but the ones who'd taken their place looked enough like them to be their cousins.

He took a couple of steps down the hall. One of the guards came after him; the fellow's mail shirt jingled as he walked. Abivard kept on going. The soldier came after him but did not call him back or try to stop him. It was exactly as the eunuch had said it would be. That left Abivard disconcerted; he wasn't used to having promises from Sharbaraz or his servitors kept.

After a while he turned and asked the guard, "Why are you following me?"

"Because I have orders to follow you," the fellow answered at once. "Don't want you winding up in any mischief, lord, and I don't want you getting lost here, either."

"I can see how I might get lost," Abivard admitted; one palace hallway looked much like another one. "But what sort of mischief am I liable to get into?"

"Don't ask me, lord—I've no idea," the guardsman said with a grin. "I figure anybody can if he tries, though."

"You sound like a man with children," Abivard said, and the guard laughed and nodded. Seeing the people set to keep an eye on him as ordinary human beings was strange for Abivard.

And then, around a corner, came one who would never have children but who had assuredly gotten Abivard into mischief: the beautiful eunuch who'd escorted him first to his sister and then to Sharbaraz.

He gave Abivard a look of cold indifference. That was one of the friendlier looks Abivard had received from him. Abivard said, "You might thank me."

"Thank you?" The eunuch's voice put Abivard in mind of silver bells. "Whatever for?"

"Because the Videssians didn't burn Mashiz down around your perfect, shell-like ears, for starters," Abivard said.

The beautiful eunuch's skin was swarthy, like that of most Makuraners, but translucent even so; Abivard could watch the tips of those ears turn red. "Had you brought Maniakes' head hither or even sent it on pickled in salt, you might have done something worthy of gratitude," the eunuch said. "As things are, however, I give you—this—as token of my esteem." He turned his back and walked away.

Staring after him, the guard let out a soft whistle. "You put Yeliif's back up—literally, looks like."

"Yeliif?" But Abivard realized who the fellow had to mean. "Is that what his name is? I never knew till now."

"You never knew?" Now the guardsman stared at him. "You made an enemy of Yeliif without knowing what you were doing?

Well, the God only knows what you could have managed if you'd really set your mind to it."

"I didn't make him an enemy," Abivard protested. "He made himself an enemy. I never laid eyes on him till the King of Kings summoned me here last winter. If I never lay eyes on him again, I won't be sorry."

"Can't blame you there," the guardsman said, but he dropped his voice as he did it. "Not a drop of human kindness in dear Yeliif, from all I've seen. They say losing their balls makes eunuchs mean. I don't know if that's what bothers him, but mean he is. And it might not matter whether you set eyes on him again or not. Sooner or later you're going to have to eat some of the food that goes into your room there."

"What?" Abivard said, his wits working more slowly than they should, and then, a moment later, "Oh. Now, that's a cheerful thought."

He didn't think the beautiful eunuch would poison him. Had Yeliif wanted to do that, he could have managed it easily the winter before. Then Sharbaraz probably would have given him anything this side of his stones back for doing the job. Abivard didn't think he was as deeply disgraced now as he had been then. Now the King of Kings might be annoyed rather than relieved at his sudden and untimely demise.

Or, on the other hand, Sharbaraz might not. You never could tell with the King of Kings. Sometimes he was brilliant, sometimes foolish, sometimes both at once—and sorting the one out from the other was never easy. That made living under him . . . interesting.

Someone knocked on the door to the suite in which Abivard and his family were quartered. The winter before that would have produced surprise and alarm, for it was not time for the servants to bring in a meal, being about halfway between luncheon and dinner. Now, though, people visited at odd hours; sometimes Abivard almost managed to convince himself he was a guest, not a prisoner.

He could, for instance, bar the door on the inside. He'd done so the first several days after he'd arrived in Mashiz. After that, though, he gave it up. If Sharbaraz wanted to kill him badly enough to send assassins in after him, he'd presumably send assassins with both the wit and the tools to break down the door. And so, of late, Abivard had left it unbarred. As yet, he also remained unmurdered.

He doubted Sharbaraz would send out a particularly polite assassin, and so he opened the door at the knock with no special qualms. When he discovered Yeliif standing in the hallway, he wondered if he'd made a mistake. But the eunuch was armed with nothing but his tongue—which, while poisonous, was not deadly in and of itself. "For reasons beyond my comprehension and far beyond your deserts," he told Abivard, "you are summoned before Sharbaraz King of Kings, may his days be long and his realm increase."

"I'm coming," Abivard answered, turning to wave quickly to Roshnani. As he closed the door after himself, he asked, "So what are these reasons far beyond your deserts or my comprehension?"

The beautiful eunuch started to answer, stopped, and favored him with a glare every bit as toxic as his usual speech. Without a word, he led Abivard through the maze of hallways toward the throne room.

This time, Abivard not being isolated as if suffering from a deadly and infectious disease, the journey took far less time than it had when he'd finally been summoned into Sharbaraz's presence the winter before. At the entrance to the throne room Yeliif broke his silence, saying, "Dare I hope you remember the required procedure from your last appearance here?"

"Yes, thank you very much, Mother, you may dare," Abivard answered sweetly. If Yeliif was going to hate him no matter what he did, he had no great incentive to stay civil.

Yeliif turned and, back quiveringly straight, stalked down the aisle toward the distant throne on which Sharbaraz sat. Not many nobles attended the King of Kings this day. Those who were there, as best Abivard could guess from their faces, were not anticipating the spectacle of a bloodbath, as the courtiers and nobles emphatically had been the last time Abivard had come before his sovereign.

Yeliif stepped to one side, out of the direct line of approach. Abivard advanced to the paving slab prescribed for prostration and went to his knees and then to his belly to honor Sharbaraz King of Kings. "Majesty," he murmured, his breath fogging the shiny marble of the slab.

"Rise, Abivard son of Godarz," Sharbaraz said. He did not keep Abivard down in a prostration any longer than was customary, as he had in the previous audience. When he spoke again, though, he sounded far from delighted to see his brother-in-law: "We are deeply saddened that you permitted Maniakes and his Videssian bandits not only to inflict grievous damage upon the land of the Thousand Cities but also, having done so, to escape unharmed, seize one of the towns in the Videssian westlands now under our control, and thence flee by sea to Videssos the city."

He was saddened, was he? Abivard almost said something frank and therefore unforgivable. But Sharbaraz was not going to trap him like that, if such was his aim. Or was he simply blind to mistakes he'd helped make? Would the likes of Yeliif tell him about them? Not likely!

"Majesty, I am also saddened, and I regret my failure," Abivard said. "I rejoice, however, that through the campaigning season Mashiz had no part of danger and remained altogether safe and secure."

Sharbaraz squirmed on the throne. He was vain, but he wasn't stupid. He understood what Abivard didn't say; those unspoken words seemed to echo in the throne room. *You sent me out to find my own ragtag army. You wanted to hold my family hostage while I did it. And now you complain because I didn't bring you Maniakes weighted down with chains? Be thankful he didn't visit you in spite of everything I did.*

Behind Abivard a faint, almost inaudible hum rose. The courtiers and nobles in the audience could catch those inaudible echoes, too, then.

Sharbaraz said, "When we send a commander out against the foe, we expect him to meet our requirements and expectations in every particular."

"I regret my failure," Abivard repeated. "Your Majesty may of course visit any punishment he pleases upon me to requite that failure."

Go ahead. Are you so blind to honor that you'll torment me for failing to do the impossible? More murmurs said the courtiers had again heard what he had meant along with what he had said. The trouble was, the King of Kings might not have. The only subtleties Sharbaraz was liable to look for were those involving danger to him, which he was apt to see regardless of whether it was real. Kings of Kings often died young, but they always aged quickly.

"We shall on this occasion be clement, given the difficulties with which you were confronted on the campaign," Sharbaraz said. It was as close as he was ever likely to come to admitting he'd been at fault.

"Thank you, Majesty," Abivard said without the cynicism he'd expected to use. Deciding to take advantage of what seemed to be Sharbaraz's good humor, he went on, "Majesty, will you permit me to ask a question?"

"Ask," the King of Kings said. "We are your sovereign; we are not obliged to answer."

"I understand this, Majesty," Abivard said, bowing. "What I would ask is why, if you were not dissatisfied—not too dissatisfied, perhaps I should say—with the way I carried out the campaign in the land of the Thousand Cities this past summer, did you recall me from my army to Mashiz?"

For a moment Sharbaraz did not look like a ruler who used the royal *we* as automatically as he breathed but like an ordinary man taken aback by a question he hadn't looked for. At last he said, "This course was urged upon us by those here at court, that we might examine the reasons behind your failure."

"The chief reason is easy to see," Abivard answered. "We saw it, you and I, when you sent me out against Maniakes last spring: Videssos has a fleet, and we have not. That gives the Avtokrator a great advantage in choosing when and where to strike and in how he can escape. Had we not already known as much, the year's campaign would have shown it."

"Had we had a fleet—" Sharbaraz said longingly.

"Had we had a fleet, Majesty," Abivard interrupted, "I think I should have laid Videssos the city at your feet. Had we had a fleet, I—or Mikhran *marzban*—could have chased Maniakes after he swooped down on Pityos. Had we had a fleet, he might never have made for Pityos, knowing our warships lay between Pityos and the capital. Had we had a fleet—"

"The folk of Makuran are not sailors, though," Sharbaraz said—an obvious truth. "Getting them into a ship is as hard as getting the Videssians out of one, as you no doubt will know better than we."

Abivard's nod was mournful. "Nor do the Videssians leave any ships behind for their fisherfolk to crew for us. They are not fools, the imperials, for they know we would use any ships and sailors against them. Could we but once get soldiers over the Cattle Crossing—" He broke off. He'd sung that song too many times to too many people.

"We have no ships. We are not sailors. Not even our command can make the men of Makuran into what they are not," Sharbaraz said. Abivard dipped his head in agreement. The King of Kings went on. "Somewhere we must find ships." He spoke as if certain his will could conjure them up, all difficulties notwithstanding.

"Majesty, that would be excellent," Abivard said. He'd been saying the same thing since the Makuraner armies had reached the coasts of the Videssian westlands. He'd been saying it loudly since the Makuraner armies had reached the Cattle Crossing, with Videssos the city so temptingly displayed what would have been an easy walk away . . . if men could walk on water, which they couldn't, save in ships. Wanting ships and having them, though, were two different things.

Thinking of ships seemed to make Sharbaraz think of water in other contexts, although he didn't suggest walking on it. He said, "We wish you had not loosed the waters of the canals that cross the land of the Thousand Cities, for the damage the flooding did has reduced the tax revenues we shall be able to gather in this year."

"I regret my failure," Abivard said for the third time. But that wooden repetition of blame stuck in his craw, and he added, "Had I not arranged to open the canals, Maniakes Avtokrator might now be enjoying those extra tax revenues."

Behind him one of the assembled courtiers, against all etiquette, laughed for a moment. In the deep, almost smothering quiet of the throne room that brief burst of mirth was all the more startling. Abivard would not have cared to be the man who had so forgotten himself. Everyone near him would know who he was, and Yeliif would soon learn—his job was to learn of such things, and Abivard had no doubt he was very good at it. When he did . . . Abivard had found out what being out of favor at court was like. He would not have recommended it to his friends.

Sharbaraz's expression was hooded, opaque. "Even if this be true, you should not say it," he replied at last, and then fell silent again.

Abivard wondered how to take that nearly oracular pronouncement. Did the King of Kings mean he shouldn't publicly acknowledge Videssos' strength? Or did he mean he thought Maniakes would keep whatever Makuraner revenue he got his hands on? Or was he saying that it wasn't true, and even if it was, it wasn't? Abivard couldn't tell.

"I did what I thought best at the time," he said. "I think it did help Maniakes decide he couldn't spend the winter between the Tutub and the Tib. We have till spring to prepare the land of the Thousand Cities against his return, which the God prevent."

"So may it be," Sharbaraz agreed. "My concern is, will he do the same thing twice running?"

"Always a good question, Majesty," Abivard said. "Maniakes has a way of learning from his mistakes that many have said to be unusual."

"So I have heard," Sharbaraz said.

He said nothing about learning from his own mistakes. Was that because he was sure he learned or because he assumed he made no mistakes? Abivard suspected the latter, but some questions not even he had the nerve to put to the King of Kings.

He did press Sharbaraz a little, asking, "Majesty, will you grant me leave to return to the land of the Thousand Cities so I can go back to training the army I raised from the troops you had me gather together last year? I must say I am also anxious at being so far from them when one of my commanders does not enjoy my full confidence."

"What?" Sharbaraz demanded. "Who is that?"

"Tzikas, Majesty—the Videssian," Yeliif answered before Abivard could speak. "The one who helped alert you to unreliability before." *To Abivard's unreliability*, he meant.

Sharbaraz said, "Ah, the Videssian. Yes, I remember now. No, he needs to remain in his place. He is one general who cannot plot against me."

Abivard had had that same thought himself. "As you say, Majesty," he replied. "I do not ask that he be removed. I want only to go and join him and make sure that the cavalry he leads is working well with the infantry from the city garrisons. And just as he keeps an eye on me, I want to keep an eye on him."

"What you want is not my chiefest concern," the King of

Kings answered. "I think more of my safety and of the good of Makuran."

In that order, Abivard noted. It wasn't anything he hadn't already understood. In a way, having Sharbaraz come right out and own up to it made things better rather than worse—no pretending now. Abivard said, "Letting the army go soft and its pieces grow apart from each other serves neither of those purposes, Majesty."

Sharbaraz hadn't expected his army to amount to anything. The King of Kings had thrown him and the garrison soldiers at the Videssians in the way a man throws a handful of dirt on a fire when he has no water: in the hope it would do some good, knowing he'd lose little if it didn't. He hadn't expected them to turn into an army, and he hadn't expected the army to seem so important for the battles of the coming campaigning season.

What you expected, though, wasn't always what you got. With Videssian mastery of the sea, Maniakes was liable to land his armies anywhere when spring brought good weather. If he did strike again for the land of the Thousand Cities, that makeshift army Abivard had patched together would be the only force between the Videssians and Mashiz. At that, Sharbaraz would be better off than he had been, for he'd had no shield the year before.

When the King of Kings did not answer right away, Abivard grasped his dilemma. An army worth something as a shield was also worth something as a sword. Sharbaraz did not merely fear Maniakes and the Videssians; he also feared any army Abivard was able to make effective enough to confront the invaders. An army effective enough to do that could threaten Mashiz in its own right.

At last Sharbaraz King of Kings said, "I believe you have officers who know their business. If you did not, you could not have done what you did against the Videssians. They will hold your army together for you until spring comes and the general is needed in the field. So shall it be."

"So shall it be," Abivard echoed, bowing, acquiescing. Sharbaraz still did not trust him as far as he should have, but he did trust him more than he had the winter before. Abivard chose to look on that as progress—not least because looking on it any other way would have made him scream in frustration or despair or rage or maybe all three at once.

He expected the King of Kings to dismiss him after rendering his decision. Instead, after yet another hesitation Sharbaraz said, "Brother-in-law of mine, I am asked by Denak my principal wife—your sister—to tell you that she is with child. Her confinement should come in the spring."

Abivard bowed again, this time in surprise and delight. From what Denak had said, Sharbaraz seldom summoned her to his bedchamber these days. One of those summonses, though, seemed to have borne fruit.

"May she give you a son, Majesty," Abivard said—the usual thing, the polite thing, the customary thing to say.

But nothing was simple, not when he was dealing with Sharbaraz. The King of Kings sent him a hooded look, though what he said—"May the God grant your prayer"—was the appropriate response. Here, for once, Abivard needed no time to figure out how he had erred. The answer was simple: he hadn't.

But Denak's pregnancy complicated Sharbaraz's life. If his principal wife did bear a son, the boy automatically became the heir presumptive. And if Denak bore a boy, Abivard became uncle to the heir presumptive. Should Sharbaraz die, that would make Abivard uncle to the new King of Kings and a very important man, indeed. The prospect of becoming uncle to the new King of Kings might even—probably would in the eyes of the present King of Kings—give Abivard an incentive for wanting Sharbaraz dead.

Almost, Abivard wished Denak would present the King of Kings with another girl. Almost.

Now Sharbaraz dismissed Abivard from the audience. Abivard prostrated himself once more, then withdrew, Yeliif appearing at his side as if by magic as he did so. The beautiful eunuch stayed silent till they left the throne room, and that suited Abivard fine.

Afterward, in the hallway, Yeliif hissed, "You are luckier than you deserve, brother-in-law to the King of Kings." He made Abivard's title, in most men's mouths one of respect, into a reproach.

Abivard had expected nothing better. Bowing politely, he said, "Yeliif, you may blame me for a great many things, and in some of them you will assuredly be right, but that my sister is with child is not my fault."

By the way Yeliif glared at him, everything was his fault. The eunuch said, "It will cause Sharbaraz King of Kings, may his days be long and his realm increase, to forgive too readily your efforts to subvert his position on the throne."

"What efforts?" Abivard demanded. "We went through this last winter, and no one, try as everybody here in Mashiz would, was able to show I've been anything but loyal to the King of Kings, the reason being that I *am* loyal."

"So you say," Yeliif answered venomously. "So you claim."

Abivard wanted to pick him up and smash him against the stone of the wall as if he were an insect to crush underfoot. "Now you listen to me," he snapped, as he might have at a soldier who hesitated to obey orders. "The way you have it set up in your mind is that, if I win victories for the King of Kings, I'm a traitor because I'm too successful and you think the victories are aggrandizing me instead of Sharbaraz, whereas if I lose, I'm a traitor because I've thrown victory away to the enemies of the King of Kings."

"Exactly," Yeliif said. "Precisely."

"Drop me into the Void, then!" Abivard exclaimed. "How am I supposed to do anything right if everything I can possibly do is wrong before I try it?"

"You cannot," the beautiful eunuch said. "The greatest service you could render Sharbaraz King of Kings would be, as you say, to drop into the Void and trouble the realm no more."

"As far as I can tell, the next time I trouble the realm will be the first," Abivard said stubbornly. "And if you ask me, there can be a difference between serving the King of Kings and serving the realm."

"No one asked you," Yeliif said. "That is as well, for you lie."

"Do I?" Such an insult from a whole man would have made Abivard challenge him. Instead, he stopped walking and studied Yeliif. Eunuchs' ages were generally hard to judge, and Yeliif powdered his face, making matters harder yet, but Abivard thought he might be older than he seemed at first glance. Doing his best to sound innocent, he said, "Tell me, were you here in the palace to serve Peroz King of Kings?"

"Yes, I was." Pride rang in Yeliif's voice.

"Ah. How lucky for you." Abivard bowed again. "And tell me, when Smerdis usurped the throne after Peroz died, did you serve him, too, while he held Mashiz and kept Sharbaraz prisoner?"

Yeliif's eyes blazed hatred. He did not reply, which Abivard took to mean he had won the argument. As he realized a moment later, that might have done him more harm than good.

✦ ✦ ✦

"It's not as bad as it could be," Roshnani said one day about a week after Abivard's audience with the King of Kings.

"No, it's not," Abivard agreed, "although I don't think our children would say that you're right." Even though they could go though the corridors of the palace, the children still felt very much confined. Most of the time that would have been Abivard's chief concern. Now, though, he burst out, "What drives me mad is that it's so useless. Sharbaraz King of Kings, may his years be many and his realm increase—" He generally used the full honorific formula, for the benefit of any unseen listeners. "—has declared his trust in me and admits I did little wrong and much right during the campaigning season just past. I wish he would let me go back to the army I built."

"He trusts you—but he doesn't trust you," Roshnani said with a rueful smile. "That's better than it was, too, but it's not good enough." She raised her voice slightly. "You've shown your loyalty every way a man can." Yes, she, too, was mindful of people who might not even be there but who were noting her words for the King of Kings if they were.

"The only good thing I can see about having to stay here," Abivard said, also pitching his voice to an audience wider than one person, "is that, if the God is kind, I'll get the chance to see my sister and give her my hope for a safe confinement."

"I'd like to see her, too," Roshnani said. "It's been too long, and I didn't get the chance when we were here last winter."

They smiled at each other, absurdly pleased with the game they were playing. It put Abivard in mind of the skits the Videssians performed during their Midwinter's Day festivals, when the players performed not only for themselves but also for the people watching them. Here, though, everything he and his principal wife said was true, only the intonation changing for added effect.

Roshnani went on, "It's not as if I couldn't go through the corridors to see her, either, in the women's quarters or outside them. Thanks to Sharbaraz King of Kings, may his days be long and his realm increase—" No, Roshnani didn't miss a trick, not one. "—women are no longer confined as straitly as they used to be."

Take that, Abivard thought loudly at whatever listeners he and Roshnani had. If there were listeners, they probably would not

take it gladly. From all he'd seen, people at the court of the King
of Kings hated change of any sort more than anyone else in the
world did. Abivard was not enthusiastic about change; what sensible man was? But he recognized that change for the better was
possible. Sharbaraz's courtiers rejected that notion out of hand.

"To the Void with them," he muttered, this time so quietly
that Roshnani had to lean forward to catch his words. She nodded but said nothing; the unseen audience did not have to know
everything that went on between the two principal players.

A couple of days later Yeliif came to the door. To Abivard's
surprise, the beautiful eunuch wanted to speak not to him but
to Roshnani. As always, Yeliif's manners were flawless, and that
made the message he delivered all the more stinging. "Lady,"
he said, bowing to Roshnani, "for you to be honored by an
audience with Denak, principal wife to Sharbaraz King of
Kings, is not, cannot be, and shall not be possible, for which
reason such requests, being totally useless, should in future be
dispensed with."

"And why is that?" Roshnani asked, her voice dangerously calm.
"Is it that my sister-in-law does not wish to see me? If she will
tell me how I offended her, I will apologize or make any other
compensation she requires. I will say, though, that she was not
ashamed to stay with me in the women's quarters of Vek Rud
domain after Sharbaraz King of Kings made her his principal
wife."

That shot went home; Yeliif's jaw tightened. The slight shift of
muscle and bone was easily visible beneath his fine, beardless skin.
The eunuch answered, "So far as I know, lady, you have not given
offense. But we of the court do not deem it fitting for a lady of
your quality to expose herself to the stares of the vulgar multitude
in her traversal of the peopled corridors of the palace."

Abivard started to explode—he thought Denak and Roshnani
had put paid to that attitude, or at least its public expression,
years before. But Roshnani's raised hand stopped him before he
began. She said, "Am I to understand, then, that my requests to
see Denak do not reach her?"

"You may understand whatever you like," Yeliif replied.

"And so may you. Stand aside now, if you please." Roshnani
advanced on the beautiful eunuch. Yeliif did stand aside; had he
not done so, she would have stamped on his feet and walked over

or through him—that was quite plain. She opened the door and started out through it.

"Where are you going?" Yeliif demanded. "What are you doing?" For the first time his voice was less than perfectly controlled.

Roshnani took a step out into the hall, as if she'd decided not to answer. Then, at the last minute, she seemed to change her mind—or maybe, Abivard thought admiringly, she'd planned that hesitation beforehand. She said, "I am going to find Sharbaraz King of Kings, may his years be many and his realm increase, wherever he is, and I am going to put in his ear the tale of how his courtiers seek to play havoc with the new customs for noble-women he himself, in his wisdom, chose to institute."

"You can't do that!" Now Yeliif sounded not just imperfectly controlled but appalled.

"No? Why can't I? I abide by the customs the King of Kings began; don't you think he'd be interested to learn that you don't?"

"You cannot interrupt him! It is not permitted."

"You cannot keep my messages from reaching Denak, but you do," Roshnani said sweetly. "Why, then, can't I do what cannot be done?"

Yeliif gaped. Abivard felt like snickering. Roshnani's years of living among the Videssians had made her a dab hand at chopping logic into fine bits, as if it were mutton or beef to be made into sausage. The beautiful eunuch wasn't used to argument of that style and plainly had no idea how to respond.

Roshnani gave him little chance, in any case. When she said she would do something, she would do it. She started into the hallway. Yeliif dashed out after her. "Stop her!" he shouted to the guards who were always posted outside the suite of rooms.

Abivard went out into the hall, too. The guards were armored and had spears to his knife. Even so, the only way he would let them lay hands on Roshnani was over his dead body.

But he needn't have worried. One of the soldiers said to Yeliif, "Sir, our orders say she is allowed to go out." He did his best to sound regretful—the eunuch was a powerful figure at court—but couldn't keep amusement from his voice.

Yeliif made as if to grab Roshnani himself but seemed to think better of it at the last minute. That was probably wise on his part; Roshnani made a habit of carrying a small, thin dagger somewhere about her person and might well have taken it into her head to use the knife on him.

He said, "Can we not reach agreement on this, thereby preventing an unseemly display bound to upset the King of Kings?"

Abivard had no trouble reading between the lines there: an unseemly display would leave Yeliif in trouble with Sharbaraz because the eunuch had permitted it to happen. Roshnani saw that, too. She said, "If I am allowed to see Denak today, then very well. If not, I go out searching for the King of Kings tomorrow."

"I accept," Yeliif said at once.

"Don't think to cheat by delaying and getting the guards' orders changed," Roshnani told him, rubbing in her victory. "Do you know what will happen if you try? One way or another I'll manage to get out and go anyway, and when I do, you'll pay double."

The threat was probably idle. The palace was Yeliif's domain, not Roshnani's. Nevertheless, the beautiful eunuch said, "I have made a bargain, and I shall abide by it," and beat a hasty retreat. Roshnani went back into the chamber. So did Abivard, shutting the door behind him. He did his best to imitate the fanfare horn players blew to salute a general who had won a battle. Roshnani laughed out loud. From the other side of the closed door, so did one of the guardsmen.

"You ground him for flour in the millstones," Abivard said.

"Yes, I did—for today." Roshnani was still laughing, but she also sounded worn. "Will he stay ground, though? What will he do tomorrow? Will I have to go out looking for the King of Kings and humiliate myself if I find him?"

Taking her in his arms, Abivard said, "I don't think so. If you show you're willing to do whatever you have to, very often you end up not needing to do it."

"I hope this is one of those times," Roshnani said. "If the God is kind, she'll grant it be so."

"May he do that," Abivard agreed. "And if not, Sharbaraz King of Kings, may his years be many and his realm increase, will at least have learned that one of his principal servants is a liar and a cheat."

By what Yeliif had said, he'd learned that he and Roshnani did indeed have listeners. With any luck at all, some of them would report straight to the King of Kings.

✦　　✦　　✦

Abivard had guessed that Yeliif would break his promise, but he didn't. Not long after breakfast the next day he came to the suite of rooms where Abivard and his family were staying and, as warmly as if he and Roshnani had not quarreled the day before, bade her accompany him to see her sister-in-law, "who," he said, "is in her turn anxious to see you."

"Nice to know that," Roshnani said. "If you'd delivered my requests sooner, we might have found out before."

Yeliif stiffened and straightened up, as if a wasp had stung him at the base of the spine. "I thought we might agree to forget yesterday's unpleasantness," he said.

"I may not choose to do anything about it," Roshnani told him, "but I never, ever forget." She smiled sweetly.

The beautiful eunuch grimaced, then shook himself as if using a counterspell against a dangerous sorcery. Maybe that was what he thought he was doing. His manner, which had been warm, froze solid. "If you will come with me, then?" he said.

Roshnani came with condescension that, if it wasn't queenly, would have made a good imitation.

Abivard stayed in the suite and kept his children from injuring themselves and one another. For no visible reason Varaz seemed to have decided Shahin was good for nothing but being punched. Shahin fought back as well as he could, but that often wasn't well enough. Abivard did his best to keep them apart, which wasn't easy. At last he asked Varaz, "How would you like it if I walloped you for no reason at all whenever I felt like it?"

"I don't know what you're talking about," Varaz said. Abivard had heard that tone of voice before. His son meant every word of the indignant proclamation, no matter how unlikely it sounded to Abivard. Varaz wasn't old enough—and was too irked—to be able to put himself in his brother's shoes. But he also knew Abivard would wallop him if he disobeyed, and so desisted.

Worry over Roshnani also made Abivard more likely to wallop Varaz than he would have been were he calm. Abivard, knowing that, tried to hold his temper in check. It wasn't easy, not when he trusted Yeliif not at all. But he could no more have kept Roshnani from going to see Denak than he could have held some impetuous young man out of battle. He sighed, wishing relations between husband and wife could be managed by orders given and received as they were on the battlefield.

Then he wished he hadn't thought of the battlefield. Time seemed elastic now, as it did in the middle of a hot fight. An hour or two seemed to go by; then he looked at a shadow on the floor and realized that only a few minutes had passed. A little later an hour did slide past without his even noticing. Servants startled him when they brought in smoked meats and saffron rice for his luncheon; he'd thought it still midmorning.

Roshnani came back not long after the servitors had cleared away the dishes. "I wouldn't have minded eating more, though they fed me there," she said, and then, "Ah, they left the wine. Good. Pour me a cup, would you, while I use the pot. Not something you do in the company of the principal wife of the King of Kings, even if she is your sister-in-law." She undid the buckles on her sandals and kicked the shoes across the room, then sighed with pleasure as her toes dug into the rug.

Abivard poured the wine and waited patiently till she got a chance to drink it. Along with wanting to ease herself, she also had to prove to her children that she hadn't fallen off the edge of the world while she had been gone. But finally, wine in hand, she sat down on the floor pillows and got the chance to talk with her husband.

"She looks well," she said at once. "In fact, she looks better than well. She looks smug. The wizards have made the same test with her that Tanshar did with me. They think she'll bear a boy."

"By the God," Abivard said softly, and then, "May it be so."

"May it be so, indeed," Roshnani agreed, "though there are some here at court who would sing a different song. I name no names, mind you."

"Names?" Abivard's voice was the definition of innocence. "I have no idea who you could mean." Off in a corner of the room the children were quarreling again. Instead of shouting for them to keep quiet as he usually would have, Abivard was grateful. He used their racket to cover his own quiet question: "So her bitterness is salved, is it?"

"Some," Roshnani answered. "Not all. She wishes—and who could blame her?—this moment had come years before." She spoke so softly, Abivard had to bend so his head was close to hers.

"No one could blame her," he said as softly. But he had a harder time than usual blaming Sharbaraz here. The King of Kings could pick and choose among the most beautiful women of Makuran.

Given that chance, should anyone have been surprised he took advantage of it?

Roshnani might have been thinking along with him, for she said, "The King of Kings needs to get an heir for the realm on his principal wife if he can, just as a *dihqan* needs to get an heir for his domain. Failing in this is neglecting your plain duty."

"It's more enjoyable carrying out some duties than others," Abivard observed, which won him a snort from Roshnani. He went on, "What news besides that of the coming boy?" The wizards' predictions weren't always right, but maybe speaking as if they were would help persuade the God to let this one be.

"Denak notes she will have more influence over the King of Kings for the next few months than she has enjoyed lately," Roshnani said; in her voice Abivard could hear echoes of his sister's weary, disappointed tones. "How long this lasts afterward will depend on how wise the wizards prove to be. May the lady Shivini prove them so."

Now Abivard echoed her: "Aye, may that be so." Then he remembered the six squabbling sorcerers he'd assembled in Nashvar. If he'd needed a curative for the notion that mages were always preternaturally wise and patient, they'd given him one.

Roshnani said, "Your sister thinks Sharbaraz will soon give you leave to go back to your command in the land of the Thousand Cities."

"It's not really the command I want," Abivard said. "I want to be back at the head of the field force and take it into the Videssian westlands again. If we're on the move there, maybe we can keep Maniakes from attacking the Thousand Cities this year." He paused and laughed at himself. "I'm trying to spin moonshine into thread, aren't I? I'll be lucky to have any command at all; getting the one I particularly want is too much to ask."

"You deserve it," Roshnani said, her voice suddenly fierce.

"I know I do," he answered without false modesty. "But that has only so much to do with the price of wine. What does Tzikas deserve? To have his mouth pried open and molten lead poured down his gullet by us and the Videssians both. What will he get? The way to bet is that he'll get to die old and happy and rich, even if nobody on whichever side of the border on which he ends up trusts him as far as I could throw him. Where's the justice there?"

"He will drop into the Void and be gone forever while you spend eternity in the bosom of the God," Roshnani said.

"That's so—or I hope that's so," Abivard said. It did give him some satisfaction, too; the God was as real to him as the pillow on which he sat. But—"I won't see him drop into the Void, and where's the justice *there*, after what he's done to me?"

"That I can't answer," his principal wife said with a smile. She held up a forefinger. "But Denak said to tell you to remember your prophecy whenever you feel too downhearted."

Abivard bowed low as he sat, bending almost double. He would never see a silver shield shining across a narrow sea if he remained commander in the land of the Thousand Cities. "I may have been wrong," he said humbly. "There may be some use to foretelling, after all. Knowing I *will* see what was foretold lets me bear up under insults meanwhile."

"Under some insults, for some time, certainly," Roshnani replied. "But Tanshar didn't say when you would see these things. You're a young man still; it might be thirty years from now."

"It might be," Abivard agreed. "I don't think it is, though. I think it's connected to the war between Makuran and Videssos. That's what everything about it has seemed to mean. When it comes, whatever it ends up meaning, it will decide the war, one way or the other." He held up a hand, palm out. "I don't know that for a fact, but I think it's true even so."

"All right," Roshnani said. "You should also know you're going back to the land of the Thousand Cities for a while, because you didn't see the battle Bogorz's scrying showed you."

"That's true; I didn't," Abivard admitted. "Or I don't think I did, anyhow. I don't remember seeing it." The frown gave way to a sheepish laugh. "Is it a true prophecy if it happens but no one notices?"

"Take that one to the Videssians," Roshnani said. "They'll spend so much time arguing over it, they won't be ready to invade us when the campaigning season starts."

By her tone of voice, she was only half joking. From his time spent among the Videssians, Abivard thoroughly understood that. If a problem admitted of two points of view, some Videssians would take the one and some the other, as far as he could tell for the sake of disputation. And if a problem admitted of only one point of view, some Videssians would take that and some the other, again for the sake of disputation.

Roshnani said, "If we understand the prophecies rightly, you'll beat Maniakes in the land of the Thousand Cities. If you don't beat him there, you won't have the chance to go back into the Videssian westlands and draw near Videssos the city, now, will you?"

"I don't see how I would, anyhow," Abivard said. "But then, I don't see everything there is to see, either."

"Do you see that for once you worry too much?" Roshnani said. "Do you see that?"

Abivard held up his hand again, and she stopped. Genuine curiosity in his voice, he said, "*Could* Sharbaraz have ordered me slain last winter? Could I have died with the prophecies unfulfilled? What would have happened if he'd given the order? Could the headsman have carried it out?"

"There's another question the Videssians would exercise themselves over for years," Roshnani answered. "All I can tell you is that I not only don't know, I'm glad we didn't have to find out. If you have to hope for a miracle to save yourself, you may not get it."

"That's true enough," Abivard said. The children's game broke down in a multisided squabble raucous enough to make him get up and restore order. He kept on wondering, though, all the rest of the day.

✦ VIII

I f you were going to be in the land of the Thousand Cities, the very beginning of spring was the time to do it. The weather hadn't yet grown unbearably hot, the flies and mosquitoes weren't too bad, and a steady breeze from the northwest helped blow smoke away from the cities instead of letting it accumulate in foglike drifts, as could happen in the still air of summer.

Beroshesh, the city governor of Nashvar, did a magnificent job of concealing his delight at Abivard's return. "Are you going to flood us out again?" he demanded, and then, remembering his manners, added, "Lord?"

"I'll do whatever needs doing to drive the Videssians from the domain of Sharbaraz King of Kings, may his years be many and his realm increase," Abivard answered. Casually, he asked, "Have you heard the news? Sharbaraz's principal wife is with child, and the wizards believe it will be a boy."

"Congratulations are due her, I'm sure, but why do you—?" Beroshesh stopped the rather offhanded question as he remembered who Sharbaraz's principal wife was and what relation she held to Abivard. When he spoke again, his tone was more conciliatory: "Of course, lord, I shall endeavor to conform to any requirements you may have of me."

"I knew you would," Abivard lied politely. Then, finding a truth he could tell, he went on, "Turan and Tzikas both tell me you have done well in keeping the army supplied through the winter."

"Even with the ravages of the Videssians, the land of the Thousand Cities remains rich and fertile," Beroshesh said. "We had no trouble supplying the army's wants."

"So I heard, and as I say, I'm glad of it," Abivard told him. The floodplain was indeed rich and fertile if, even after all the damage it had suffered through the previous year, it still yielded surplus enough to feed the army on top of the peasantry.

"What do you expect Maniakes to do this season?" Beroshesh asked. "Will he come here at all? Will he come from north or south or straight out of the east?"

"Good question," Abivard said enthusiastically, making as if to applaud. "If you should have a good answer for it, please let me know. Whichever way he comes, though, I'll fight him. Of that I'm sure." He hesitated. "Fairly sure." He couldn't know for certain the scrying Bogorz had shown him would come to pass in this campaigning season, but that did seem to be the way to bet.

Beroshesh said, "Lord, you have been fighting this Maniakes for many years. Do you not know in your mind what will be in his?"

That was a legitimate question. In fact, it was better than a legitimate question; it was a downright clever question. Abivard gave it the careful thought it deserved before answering, "My best guess is that he'll do whatever he doesn't think we'll expect him to do. Whether that means setting out from Lyssaion again or picking a new way to get at us, I can't really tell, I fear. Trying to fathom the way Videssians think is like looking into several mirrors reflecting one from another, so that after a while what's reflection and what's real blur together."

"If the God be kind, the barbarians who infest his—southern—frontier, is it?' Beroshesh hesitated.

"Northern frontier," Abivard said, not unkindly. There was no reason for a city governor to have any clear notion of Videssian geography, especially for the lands on the far side of the imperial capital.

"Yes, the northern frontier. Thank you, lord. If they were to attack Maniakes, he could hardly assail us here and defend against them at the same time, could he?"

"It's not something I'd want to try, I'll tell you that," Abivard said "Yes, the God would be kind if he turned the Kubratoi—that's what the barbarians call themselves—loose on Videssos again. The only trouble is, Maniakes beat them badly enough to make them thoughtful about having another go at him."

"Pity," Beroshesh murmured. He clapped his hands loudly. "How much you know about these distant peoples! Surely you and they must have worked together closely when you forced your way to the very end of the Videssian westlands."

"I wish we would have," Abivard said. No, Beroshesh didn't know much about how the Empire of Videssos was made and how it operated. "But Videssos the city, you see, kept the Kubratoi from crossing over to join us, and the Videssian navy not only kept us from going over the Cattle Crossing to lay siege to the city, it also kept the Kubratoi from going over to the westlands in the boats they make. Together, we might have crushed Videssos, but Maniakes and his forces and fortress held us apart."

"Pity," Beroshesh said again. He pointed to a silver flagon. "More wine?"

It was date wine. "No, thank you," Abivard said. He would drink a cup for politeness' sake but had never been fond of the cloying stuff.

Quite seriously Beroshesh asked, "Could you not put your soldiers on barges and in skin boats and cross this Cattle Crossing without the Videssians' being the wiser till you appeared on the far shore?"

Beroshesh had never seen the sea, never seen a Videssian war galley. Abivard remembered that as he visualized a fleet of those swift, maneuverable, deadly galleys descending on rafts and round skin boats trying to make their way over the Cattle Crossing. He saw in his mind's eye rams sending some of them to the bottom and dart-throwers and fire-throwers wrecking many more. He might get a few men across alive, but even fewer in any condition to fight; he was all too sure of that.

Out of respect for Beroshesh's naïveté, he didn't laugh in the city governor's face. All he said was, "That has been discussed, but no one seems to think it would turn out well."

"Ah," Beroshesh said. "Well, I didn't want to take the chance that you'd overlooked something important."

Abivard sighed.

"Lord!" A member of the city garrison of Nashvar came running up to Abivard. "Lord, a messenger comes with news of the Videssians."

"Thank you," Abivard said. "Bring him to me at once." The guardsman bowed and hurried away.

Waiting for his return, Abivard paced back and forth in the room Beroshesh had returned to him when he had come back to Nashvar. Soon, instead of having to guess, he would know how Maniakes intended to play the game this year and how he would have to respond.

The soldier came back more slowly than he'd hoped, leading the messenger's horse. The messenger probably would have gotten there sooner without the escort, but after so long a wait, a few minutes mattered little, and the member of the garrison got to enjoy his moment in the light.

Bowing low to Abivard, the messenger cried, "Lord, the Videssians come down from the north, from the land of Erzerum, where treacherous local nobles let them land and guided them through the mountains so they could descend on the land of the Thousand Cities!"

"Down from the north," Abivard breathed. Had he bet on which course Maniakes would take, he would have expected the Avtokrator to land in the south and move up from Lyssaion once more. He knew nothing but relief that he'd committed no troops to backing his hunch. He wouldn't have to double back against his foe's move.

"I have only one order for the city governors in the north," he told the messenger, who poised himself to hear and remember it. "That order is, *Stand fast!* We will drive the invaders from our soil."

"Aye, lord!" the messenger said, and dashed off, his face glowing with inspiration at Abivard's ringing declaration. Behind him Abivard stood scratching his head, wondering how he was going to turn that declaration into reality. Words were easy. Deeds mattered more but were harder to produce on the spur of the moment.

The first thing that needed doing was reassembling the army. He sent messengers to the nearby cities where he'd billeted portions of his infantry. The move would undoubtedly delight the governors of those cities and just as undoubtedly dismay Beroshesh, for it would mean Nashvar would have to feed all his forces till they moved against Maniakes.

As the soldiers from the city garrisons whom Abivard had hastily gathered together the spring before began returning to

Nashvar, they found ways to let him know they were glad he was back to command them. It wasn't that they obeyed him without grumbling; the next army to do that for its leader would be the first. But whether they grumbled or not, they did everything he asked of them and did it promptly and well.

And they kept bringing tidbits here and tidbits there to the cook who made the meals for him and Roshnani and their children, so that they ended up eating better than they had at the palace in Mashiz. "It's almost embarrassing when they do things like this," Abivard said, using a slender dagger to spear from its shell a snail the cook had delicately seasoned with garlic and ginger.

"They're fond of you," Roshnani said indignantly. "They ought to be fond of you. Before you got hold of them, they were just a bunch of tavern toughs—hardly anything better. You made an army out of them. They know it, and so do you."

"Well, put that way, maybe," Abivard said. A general whom his men hated wouldn't be able to accomplish anything. That much was plain. A general whom his men loved . . . was liable to draw the watchful attention of the King of Kings. Abivard supposed that was less an impediment for him than it might have been for some other marshals of Makuran. He already enjoyed—if that was the word—Sharbaraz's watchful attention.

Seeing how much better at their tasks the soldiers were than they had been the spring before gratified Abivard as much as their affection did. He'd done his job and given them the idea that they could go out and risk maiming and death for the good of a cause they didn't really think about. He sometimes wondered whether to be proud or ashamed of that.

Sooner than he'd hoped, he judged the army ready to use against Maniakes. Sharbaraz King of Kings had been right in thinking the officers Abivard had left behind could keep the men in reasonably good fighting trim. That pleased Abivard and irked him at the same time: was he really necessary?

Turan and Tzikas were getting along well, too. Again, Abivard didn't know what to make of that. Had the Makuraner suc-cumbed to Tzikas' charm? Abivard would have been the last to deny that the Videssian renegade had his full share of that—and then some.

"He's a fine cavalry officer," Turan said enthusiastically after he, Tzikas, and Abivard planned the move they'd be making in a couple of days. "Having commanded a cavalry company myself, I was always keeping an eye on the officers above me, seeing how they did things. Do you know what I mean, lord?" He waited for Abivard to nod, then went on, "And Tzikas, he does everything the way it's supposed to be done."

"Oh, that he does." Abivard's voice was solemn. "He's a wonderful officer to have for a superior. It's only when you're *his* superior that you have to start watching your back."

"Well, yes, there is that," Turan agreed. "I hadn't forgotten about it. Just like you, I made sure I had his secretary in my belt pouch, so a couple of letters never did travel to Mashiz."

"Good," Abivard said. "And good for you, too."

However much Abivard loathed him, Tzikas had done a fine job making the cavalry under his command work alongside the infantry. That wasn't how the men of Makuran usually fought. Light cavalry and heavy horse worked side by side, but infantry was at best a scavenger on the battlefields where it appeared. Those were few and far between; in most fights cavalry faced cavalry.

"I didn't think Videssian practice so different from our own," Abivard remarked after watching the horsemen practice a sweep from the flank of the foot soldiers. "Or to put it another way, you didn't fight against us like this when you were on the other side in the westlands."

"By the God, I am a Makuraner now," Tzikas insisted. But then his pique, if it had been such, faded. "No, Videssians did not fight that way. Cavalry rules their formations no less than ours." He was playing the role of countryman to the hilt, Abivard thought. Thoughtfully, the renegade went on, "I've just been wondering how best to use the two arms together now that you and Turan have made these infantrymen into real soldiers. This is the best answer I found."

Abivard nodded—warily. He heard the flattery there: not laid on as thickly as was the usual Videssian style but perhaps more effective on account of that. Or it would have been more effective had he not suspected everything Tzikas said. Didn't Tzikas understand that? If he did, he concealed it well.

And he had other things on his mind, too, saying, "This year we'll teach Maniakes not to come into Makuran again."

"I hope so," Abivard said; that had the twin virtues of being true and of not committing him to anything.

✦   ✦   ✦

He moved the army out of Nashvar a few days later. Beroshesh had assembled the artisans and merchants of the town to cheer the soldiers on their way. How many of those were cheers of good luck and how many were cheers of good riddance, Abivard preferred not to try to guess.

Along with the chorus of what might have been support came another, shriller, altogether unofficial chorus of the women and girls of the town, many with visibly bulging bellies. That sort of thing, Abivard thought with a mental sigh, was bound to happen when you quartered soldiers in a town over a winter. Some lemans were accompanying the soldiers as they moved, but others preferred to stay with their families and scream abuse at the men who had helped make those families larger.

Scouts reported that Maniakes and the Videssians were moving southwest from Erzerum toward the Tib River and leaving behind them the same trail of destruction they'd worked the year before. Scouts also reported that Maniakes had more men with him than he'd brought on his first invasion of Makuran.

"I have to act as if they're right and hope they're wrong," Abivard said to Roshnani when the army camped for the night. "They often are—wrong, I mean. Take a quick look at an army from a distance and you'll almost always guess it's bigger than it is."

"What do you suppose he plans?' Roshnani asked. "Fighting his way down the Tib till he can strike at Mashiz?"

"If I had to guess, I'd say yes," Abivard answered, "but guessing what he has in mind gets harder every year. Still, though, that would be about the second worst thing I can think of for him to do."

"Ah?" His principal wife raised an eyebrow. "And what would be worse?'

"If he struck down the Tib and at the same time sent envoys across the Pardrayan steppe to stir up the Khamorth tribes against us and send them over the Degird River into the northwest of the realm." Abivard looked grim at the mere prospect. So did Roshnani. Both of them had grown up in the Northwest, not far from the frontier with the steppe. Abivard went on, "Likinios played that game, remember—Videssian gold was what made Peroz King of Kings move into Pardraya, what made him meet his end, what touched off our civil war. Couple that with the Videssian invasion of the land of the Thousand Cities and—"

"Yes, that would be deadly dangerous," Roshnani said. "I see it. We'd have to divide our forces, and we might not have enough to be able to do it."

"Just so," Abivard agreed. "Maniakes doesn't seem to have thought of that ploy, the God be praised. When Likinios used it, he didn't think to invade us himself at the same time. From what I remember of Likinios, he was always happiest when money and other people's soldiers were doing his fighting for him."

"Maniakes isn't like that," Roshnani said.

"No, he'll fight," Abivard said, nodding. "He's not as underhanded as Likinios was, but he's learning there, too. As I say, I'm just glad he hasn't yet learned everything there is to know."

Hurrying west across the floodplain from the Tutub to the Tib brought Abivard's army across the track of devastation Maniakes had left the summer before. In more than one place he found peasants repairing open-air shrines dedicated to the God and the Prophets Four that the Videssians had made a point of wrecking.

"He had some men who spoke Makuraner," one of the rural artisans told Abivard. "He had them tell us he did this because of what Makuran does to the shrines of his stupid, false, senseless god. He pays us back, he says."

"Thank you, Majesty," Abivard murmured under his breath. Once again Sharbaraz's order enforcing worship of the God in Vaspurakan was coming back to haunt Makuran. The peasant stared at Abivard, not following what he meant. If the fellow hoped for an explanation, he was doomed to disappointment.

Tzikas' horsemen rode ahead of the main force, trying to let Abivard know where the Videssians were at any given time. Every so often the cavalry troopers would skirmish with Maniakes' scouts, who were trying to pass to the Avtokrator the same information about Abivard's force.

And then, before too long, smoke on the northern horizon said the Videssians were drawing close. Tzikas' scouts confirmed that they were on the eastern bank of the Tib; they'd been either unwilling or unable to cross the river. Abivard took that as good news. He would, however, have liked it better had he had it from men who owed their allegiance to anyone but Tzikas.

Because Maniakes was staying on the eastern side of the Tib, Abivard sent urgent orders to the men in charge of the bridges of boats across the river to withdraw those bridges to the western bank. He hoped that would help him but did not place sure trust in the success of the ploy: being skilled artificers, the Videssians might not need boats to cross the river.

But Maniakes, who had not gone out of his way to look for a fight the summer before, seemed more aggressive now, out not just to destroy any town in the land of the Thousand Cities but also to collide with the Makuraner army opposing him.

"I think the scouts are right—they do have more men than they did last year," Turan said unhappily. "They wouldn't be pushing so hard if they didn't."

"Whereas we still have what we started last year with—minus casualties, whom I miss, and plus Tzikas' regiment of horse, whom I wouldn't miss if they fell into the Void this minute," Abivard said, Tzikas not being in earshot to overhear. "Now we get to find out whether that will be enough."

"Oh, we can block the Videssians," Turan said, "provided they don't get across to the far side of the river. If they do—"

"They complicate our lives," Abivard finished for him. "Maniakes has been complicating my life for years, so I have no reason to think he'll stop now." He paused thoughtfully. "Come to that, I've been complicating his life for a good many years now, too. But I intend to be the one who comes out on top in the end." After another pause he went on. "The question is, Does he intend to do any serious fighting this year, or is he just raiding to keep us off balance, the way he was last summer? I think he really wants to fight, but I can't be certain—not yet."

"How will we know?" Turan asked.

"If he gets across the river somehow—and he may, because the Videssians have fine engineers—he's out to harass us like last year," Abivard answered. "But if he comes straight at us, he thinks he can beat us with the new army he's put together, and it'll be up to us to show him he's wrong."

Turan glanced at the long files of foot soldiers marching toward the Tib. They were lean, swarthy men, some in helmets, some in baggy cloth caps, a few with mail shirts, most wearing leather vests or quilted tunics to ward off weapons, almost all of them with wicker shields slung over their shoulders, armed with spears or swords or bows or, occasionally, slings. "He's not the only one who's put a new army together," Abivard's lieutenant said quietly.

"Mm, that's so." Abivard studied the soldiers, too. They seemed confident enough, and thinking you could hold off a foe was halfway to doing it. "They've come a long way this past year, haven't they?"

"Aye, lord, they have," Turan said. He looked down at his hands before going on. "They've done well learning to work with cavalry, too."

"Learning to work with Tzikas' cavalry, you mean," Abivard said, and Turan, looking uncomfortable, nodded. Abivard sighed. "It's for the best. If they didn't know what to do, we'd be in a worse position than we are now. If only Tzikas weren't commanding that regiment of horse, I'd be happy."

"He was—harmless enough this past winter," Turan said, giving what praise he could.

"For which the God be praised," Abivard said. "But he's wronged me badly, and he knows it, which might tempt him to betray me to the Videssians. On the other hand, he tried to kill Maniakes, so he wouldn't be welcomed back with open arms, not unless the Avtokrator of the Videssians is stupider than I know he is. How badly would Tzikas have to betray me, do you suppose, to put himself back into Maniakes' good graces?"

"It would have to be something spectacular," Turan said. "I don't think betraying you would be coin enough to do the job, truth to tell. I think he'd have to betray Sharbaraz King of Kings himself, may his years be many and his realm increase, to buy Maniakes' favor once more."

"How would Tzikas betray the King of Kings?" Abivard said, gesturing with his right hand to turn aside the evil omen. Then he held up that hand. "No, don't tell me if you know of a way. I don't want to think about it." He stopped. "No, if you know of a way, you'd better say you do. If you can think of one, without a doubt Tzikas can, too."

"I can't, the God be praised," Turan said. "But that doesn't mean Tzikas can't."

Abivard positioned his men along the Tib, a little north of one of the boat bridges drawn up on the far side of the river. If the Videssians did seek to cross to the other side, he hoped he could either get across himself in time to block them or at least pursue and harass them on the western side.

But Maniakes showed no intention of either crossing to the west bank or swinging east and using the superior speed with which his army could move to get around Abivard's force. His scouts came riding down to look over the position Abivard had established and then, after skirmishing once more with Tzikas' horsemen, went galloping back to give the Videssian Avtokrator the news.

Two days later the whole Videssian army came into sight just after the first light of day. With trumpets and drums urging them to ever greater speed, Abivard's troops formed their battle line. Abivard had Tzikas' horsemen on his right flank and split the infantry in which he had the most confidence in two, stationing half his best foot soldiers in the center and the other half closest to the Tib to anchor the line's left.

For some time the two armies stood watching each other from beyond bowshot. Then, without Abivard's order, one of the warriors from Tzikas' regiment rode out into the space between them. He made his horse rear, then brandished his lance at the Videssians as he shouted something Abivard couldn't quite make out.

But he didn't need to understand the words to know what the warrior was saying. "He's challenging them to single combat!" Abivard exclaimed. "He must have watched that Vaspurakaner who challenged Romezan the winter before last."

"If none of them dares come out or if this fellow wins, we gain," Turan said. "But if he loses—"

"I wish Tzikas hadn't let him go forth," Abivard said. "I—"

He got no further than that, for a great shout arose from the Videssian ranks. A mounted man came galloping toward the Makuraner, who couched his lance and charged in return. The Videssian's mail shirt glittered with gilding. So did his helm, which also, Abivard saw, had a golden circlet set on it.

"That's Maniakes!" he exclaimed in a hoarse voice. "Has he gone mad to risk so much on a throw of the dice?"

The Avtokrator had neither lance nor javelin, being armed instead with bow and arrows and a sword that swung from his belt. He shot at the Makuraner, reached over his shoulder for another arrow, set it in his bow, let fly, and grabbed for yet another shaft. He'd shot four times before his foe came close.

At least two, maybe three, of the shafts went home, piercing the Makuraner champion's armor. The fellow was swaying in the saddle when he tried to spear Maniakes off his horse. The lance stroke missed. The Avtokrator of the Videssians drew his sword and slashed once, twice, three times. His foe slipped off his horse and lay limp on the ground.

Maniakes rode after the Makuraner's mount, caught it by the reins, and began to lead it back toward his own line. Then, almost as an afterthought, he waved toward the Makuraner cavalry and toward the fallen champion. *Pick him up if you like,* he said with gestures.

He spoke the Makuraner tongue. He might have said that to his opponents with words, but his own men were cheering so loudly, no words would have been heard. As he rejoined his soldiers, a couple of Makuraners rode out toward the man who had challenged the Videssian army. The imperials did not attack them. They heaved the beaten man up onto one of their horses and rode slowly back to their position on the right.

"If Maniakes didn't kill that fellow, we ought to take care of the job," Turan said.

"Isn't that the sad and sorry truth?" Abivard agreed. "All right—he was brave. But he couldn't have done us more harm than by challenging and losing, not if he tried to murder you and me both in the middle of the battle. It disheartened us—and listen to the Videssians! If they were still wondering whether they could beat us, they aren't anymore."

He wondered whether Tzikas hadn't set up the whole thing. Could the Videssian renegade, despite his fervent protestations of loyalty and his worship of the God, have urged a warrior forward while sure he would lose, in the hope of regaining favor back in Videssos? The answer was simple: of course he could. But the next question—would he?—required more thought.

He had everything he could want in Makuran—high rank, even the approval of Sharbaraz King of Kings. Why would he throw that away? The only answer that occurred to Abivard was the thrill that had to go with treason successfully brought off. He shook his head. Videssians were connoisseurs of all sorts of subtle refinements, but could one become a connoisseur of treason? He didn't think so. He hoped not.

Abivard got no more time to think about it, for as soon as the cavalrymen had returned with their would-be champion, horns sounded up and down the Videssian line. The imperials rode forward in loose order and began plying the Makuraners with arrows, as they had at the battle by the canal the summer before.

As before, Abivard's men shot back. He waved. Horns rang out on his army's right wing. He had cavalry now. Were they loyal? They were: Tzikas' men thundered at the Videssians.

Maniakes must have been expecting that. After the fact, Abivard realized he'd advertised it in his deployment—but given the position he had had to protect, he'd found himself with little choice.

A regiment of Videssians, armed with their usual bows and javelins, peeled off from the left wing of Maniakes' army and rode to meet the Makuraners. Being less heavily armed and armored than Tzikas' horsemen, the Videssians could not stop their charge in its tracks as a countercharge by a like number of Makuraners might well have done. But they did blunt it, slow it, and keep it from smashing into their comrades on the flank. That let the rest of the Videssians assail Abivard's foot soldiers.

Maniakes' men did not hold back as they had in the battle by the canal. Then they'd wanted to keep the Makuraners in play till their fellows could circle around and hit Abivard's force from an unexpected direction. Now they were coming straight at Abivard and the assembled city garrison troops, plainly confident that no such army could long stand in their way.

Because they wore mail shirts and their foes mostly did not, their archery was more effective than that of Abivard's men. They drew close enough to ply the front ranks of the Makuraners with javelins and hurt them doing it.

"Shall we rush at them, lord?" Turan shouted above the screams and war cries of the fight.

Abivard shook his head. "If we do that, we're liable to open up holes in our line, and if they once pour into holes like that, we're done for. We just have to hope we can stand the pounding."

He wished Maniakes hadn't overthrown the Makuraner champion. That had to have left his own men glum and the Videssians elated. But when you were fighting for your life, weren't you too busy to worry about what had happened a while ago? Abivard hoped so.

When arrows and javelins failed to make the Makuraners break and run, the Videssians drew swords and rode straight into the line Abivard had established. They slashed down at their enemies on foot; some of them tried to use their javelins as the Makuraner heavy horse used lances.

The Makuraners fought back hard not only against Maniakes' men but also against the horses they rode. Those poor beasts were not armored like the ones atop which Tzikas' men sat; they were easy to slash and club and shoot. Their blood splashed on the ground with that of their riders; their screams rose to the sky with those of wounded men on both sides.

Abivard rushed reserves to a dangerously thin point in the line. He had tremendous pride in his troops. This was not a duty they'd expected to have a year before. They were standing up to the Videssians like veterans. Some of them were veterans now; by the end of the battle they'd all be veterans.

"Don't let them through!" Abivard shouted. "Stand your ground!"

Rather to Abivard's surprise, they stood their ground and kept standing it. Maniakes did have more men with him than he'd brought the year before, but Tzikas' cavalry regiment neutralized a good part of his increased numbers. The rest were not enough to force a breakthrough in Abivard's line.

The stalemate left Abivard tempted to attack in turn, allowing openings to develop in his position in the hope of trapping a lot of Videssians. He had little trouble fighting down the temptation. He found it too easy to imagine himself on the other side of the battlefield, looking for an opportunity. If Maniakes spotted one, he'd take full advantage of it. Abivard knew that. Most important, then, was not giving the Avtokrator the chance.

As fights had a way of doing, this one seemed to go on forever. Had the sun not shown him it was but midafternoon, Abivard would have guessed the battle had lasted three or four days. Then, little by little, Videssian pressure eased. Instead of attacking, Maniakes' men broke contact and rode back toward the north, back the way they had come. Tzikas' men made as if to pursue—the foot soldiers could hardly do so against cavalry—but a shower of arrows and a fierce countercharge said the Videssians remained in good order. The pursuit quickly stalled.

"By the God, we threw them back," Turan said in tones of wonder.

"By the God, so we did." Abivard knew he sounded as surprised as his lieutenant. He couldn't help that. He *was* surprised.

Maybe his soldiers were surprised, and maybe they weren't. Surprised or not, they knew what they'd accomplished. Above and through the moans of the wounded and the shriller shrieks of hurt horses rose a buzz that swelled to a great cheer. The cheer had but one word: "Abivard!"

"Why are they shouting my name?" he demanded of Turan. "They're the ones who did it."

His lieutenant looked at him. "Sometimes, lord, you can be too modest."

The soldiers evidently thought so. They swarmed around Abivard, still calling his name. Then they tried to pull him down from his horse, as if he were a Videssian to be overcome. Turan's expression warned him he had better yield to the inevitable. He let his feet slide out of the stirrups. As Turan leaned over and grabbed hold of his horse's reins, he let himself slide down into the mass of celebrating soldiers.

They did not let him fall. Instead, they bore him up so he rode above them on a stormy, choppy sea of hands. He waved and shouted praise the foot soldiers didn't hear because they were all shouting and because they were passing him back and forth so everyone could carry him and have a go at dropping him.

At last he did slip down through the sea of hands. His feet touched solid ground. "Enough!" he cried; being upright somehow put fresh authority in his voice. Still shouting his praises, the soldiers decided to let him keep standing on his own.

"Command us, lord!" they shouted. A man standing near Abivard asked, "Will we go after the Videssians tomorrow?" Somewhere in the fighting a sword had lopped off the fleshy bottom part of his left ear; blood dried black streaked that side of his face. He didn't seem to notice.

Abivard suffered a timely coughing fit. When he did answer, he said, "We have to see what they do. The trouble is, we can't move as fast as they do, so we have to figure out where they're going and get there first."

"You'll do that, lord!" the soldier missing half an ear exclaimed. "You've done it already, lots of times."

Twice, to Abivard's way of thinking, didn't constitute lots of times. But the garrison troops were cheering again and shouting for him to lead them wherever they were supposed to go. Since he'd been trying to figure out how to bring about exactly that effect, he didn't contradict the wounded man. Instead he said, "Maniakes wants Mashiz. Mashiz is what he's wanted all along. Are we going to let him have it?"

"No!" the soldiers yelled in one great voice.

"Then tomorrow we'll move south and cut him off from his goal," Abivard said. The soldiers shouted louder than ever. If he'd told them to march on Mashiz instead of defending it, he thought they would have done just that.

He shoved the idea down into some deep part of his mind where he wouldn't have to think about it. That wasn't hard. The aftermath of battle had given him plenty to think about. They'd fought, the Videssians had retreated, and now his men were going to retreat, too. He wondered if there had ever been a battlefield before where both sides had abandoned it as soon as they could.

The secretary was a plump, fastidious little man named Gyanarspar. More than a bit nervously, he held out a sheet of parchment to Abivard. "This is the latest the regimental commander Tzikas has ordered me to write, lord," he said.

Abivard quickly read through the letter Tzikas had addressed to Sharbaraz King of Kings. It was about what he might have thought Tzikas would say but not what he'd hoped. The Videssian renegade accused him of cowardice for not going after Maniakes' army in the aftermath of the battle by the Tib and suggested that a different leader—coyly unnamed—might have done more.

"Thank you, Gyanarspar," Abivard said. "Draft something innocuous to take the place of this tripe and send it on its way to the King of Kings."

"Of course, lord—as we have been doing." The secretary bowed and hurried out of Abivard's tent.

Behind him Abivard kicked at the dirt. Tzikas made a fine combat soldier. If only he'd been content with that! But no, not Tzikas. Whether in Videssos or in Makuran, he wanted to go straight to the top, and to get there he'd give whoever was ahead of him a good boot in the crotch.

Well, his spiteful bile wasn't going to get to Sharbaraz. Abivard had taken care of that. The silver arkets he lavished on Gyanarspar were money well spent as far as he was concerned. The King of

Kings hadn't tried joggling his elbow nearly so much or nearly so hard since Abivard had started making sure the scurrilous things Tzikas said never reached his ear.

Gyanarspar, the God bless him, didn't aspire to reach the top of anything. Some silver on top of his regular pay sufficed to keep him sweet. Abivard suddenly frowned. How was he to know whether Tzikas was also bribing the secretary to let his letters go out as he wrote them? Gyanarspar might think it clever to collect silver from both sides at once.

"If he does, he'll find he's made a mistake," Abivard told the wool wall of the tent. If Sharbaraz all at once started sending him more letters full of caustic complaint, Gyanarspar would have some serious explaining to do.

At the moment, though, Abivard had more things to worry about than the hypothetical treachery of Tzikas' secretary. Maniakes' presence in the land of the Thousand Cities was anything but hypothetical. The Avtokrator hadn't tried circling around Abivard's forces and striking straight for Mashiz, as had been Abivard's greatest worry. Instead, Maniakes had gone back to his tactics of the summer before and was wandering through the land between the Tutub and the Tib, destroying everything he could.

Abivard kicked at the dirt yet again. He couldn't chase Maniakes over the floodplain any more than he could have pursued him after the battle by the Tib. He didn't know what he was supposed to do. Was he to travel back to Nashvar and have the contentious local wizards break the banks of the canals again? He was less convinced than he had been the year before that that would accomplish everything he wanted. He also knew Sharbaraz would not thank him for any diminution in revenue from the land of the Thousand Cities. And two years of flooding in a row were liable to put the peasants in an impossible predicament. They weren't highest on his list of worries, but they were there.

Sitting there and doing nothing did not appeal to him, either. He might be protecting Mashiz where he was, but that didn't do the rest of the realm any good. While he kept Maniakes from falling on the capital with fire and sword, the Avtokrator visited them upon other cities instead. Sharbaraz's realm was being diminished, not increasing, while that happened.

"I can keep Maniakes from breaking past me and driving into Mashiz," Abivard said to Roshnani that night. "I think I can do that, at any rate. But keep him from tearing up the land of the Thousand Cities? How? If I venture out against him, he *will* break around me, and then I'll have to chase his dust back to the capital."

For a moment he was tempted to do just that. If Maniakes put paid to Sharbaraz, the King of Kings wouldn't be able to harass him anymore. Rationally, he knew that wasn't a good enough reason to let the realm fall into the Void, but he was tempted to be irrational.

Roshnani said, "If you can't beat the Videssians with what you have here, can you get what you need to beat them somewhere else?"

"I'm going to have to try to do that, I think," Abivard replied. If his principal wife saw the same possible answer to his question that he saw himself, the chance that answer was right went up a good deal. He went on, "I'm going to send a letter to Romezan, asking him to move the field force out of Videssos and Vaspurakan and to bring it back here so we can drive Maniakes away. I hate to do that—I know it's what Maniakes wants me to do—but I don't see that I have any choice."

"I think you're right." Roshnani hesitated, then asked the question that had to be asked: "What will Sharbaraz think, though?"

Abivard grimaced. "I'll have to find out, won't I? I don't intend to ask him for permission to recall Romezan; I'm going to do that on my own. But I will write him and let him know what I've done. If he wants to badly enough, he can countermand my order. I know just what I'll do if he does that."

"What?" Roshnani asked.

"I'll lay down my command and go back to Vek Rud domain, by the God," Abivard declared. "If the King of Kings isn't satisfied with the way I defend him, let him choose someone who does satisfy him: Tzikas, maybe, or Yeliif. I'll go back to the Northwest and live out my days as a rustic *dihqan*. No matter how far Maniakes goes into Makuran, he'll never, ever reach the Vek Rud River."

He waited with some anxiety to see how Roshnani would take that. To his surprise and relief, she shoved aside the plates off which they'd eaten supper so she could lean over on the carpet they shared and give him a kiss. "Good for you!" she exclaimed. "I wish you would have done that years ago, when we were in the Videssian westlands and he kept carping because you couldn't cross to attack Videssos the city."

"I felt as bad about that as he did," Abivard said. "But it's only gotten worse since then. Sooner or later everyone has a breaking point, and I've found mine."

"Good," Roshnani said again. "It would be fine to get back to the Northwest, wouldn't it? And even finer to get out from under a master who's abused you too long."

"He'd still be my sovereign," Abivard said. But that wasn't what Roshnani had meant, and he knew it. He wondered how well his resolve would hold up if Sharbaraz put it to the test.

The letters went out the next day. Abivard thought about delaying the one to Sharbaraz, to present the King of Kings with troop movements too far along for him to prevent when he learned of them. In the end Abivard decided not to take that chance. It would give Yeliif and everyone else at court who was not well inclined toward him a chance to say he was secretly gathering forces for a move of his own against Mashiz. If Sharbaraz thought that and tried to recall him, it might force him to move against Mashiz, which he did not want to do. As far as he was concerned, beating Videssos was more important.

"All I want," he murmured, "is to ride my horse into the High Temple in Videssos the city and to see the expression on the patriarch's face when I do."

When he'd spent a couple of years in Across, staring over the Cattle Crossing at the Videssian capital, that dream had seemed almost within his grasp. Now here he was with his back against the Tib, doing his best to keep Maniakes Avtokrator from storming Mashiz. War was a business full of reversals, but going from the capital of the Empire of Videssos to that of Makuran in the space of a couple of years felt more like an upheaval.

"Ships," he said, turning the word into a vile curse. Had he had some, he would long since have ridden in triumph into Videssos the city. Had Makuran had any, Maniakes would not have been able to leap the length of the Videssian westlands and bring the war home to the land of the Thousand Cities. And after a moment's reflection, he found yet another reason to regret Makuran's lack of a navy: "If I had a ship, I could put Tzikas on it and order it sunk."

That bit of whimsy kept him happy for an hour, until Gyanarspar came into his tent with a parchment in his hand and a worried expression on his face. "Lord, you need to see this and decide what to do with it," he said.

"Do I?" If Abivard felt any enthusiasm for the proposition, he concealed it even from himself. But he held out his hand, and Gyanarspar put the parchment into it. He read Tzikas' latest missive to the King of Kings with incredulity that grew from one sentence to the next. "By the God!" he exclaimed when he was through. "About the only thing he doesn't accuse me of is buggering the sheep in the flock of the King of Kings."

"Aye, lord," Gyanarspar said unhappily.

After a bit of reflection Abivard said, "I think I know what brought this on. Before, his letters to Sharbaraz King of Kings, may his days be long and his realm increase, got action—action against me. This year, though, the letters haven't been getting through to Sharbaraz. Tzikas must think that they have—and that the King of Kings is ignoring them. And so he decided to come up with something a little stronger." He held his nose. This letter, as far as he was concerned, was strong in the sense of stale fish.

"What shall we do about it, lord?" Gyanarspar asked.

"Make it disappear, by all means," Abivard said. "Now, if we could only make Tzikas disappear, too."

Gyanarspar bowed and left. Abivard plucked at his beard. Maybe he could sink Tzikas even without a ship. He hadn't wanted to before, when the idea had been proposed to him. Now—Now he sent a servant to summon Turan.

When his lieutenant stepped into the tent, he greeted him with, "How would you like to help make the eminent Tzikas a hero of Makuran?"

Turan was not the swiftest man in the world, but he was a long way from the slowest. After a couple of heartbeats of blank surprise his eyes lit up. "I'd love to, lord. What have you got in mind?"

"That scheme you had a while ago still strikes me as better than most: finding a way to send him out with a troop of horsemen against a Videssian regiment. When it's over, I'll be very embarrassed I used such poor military judgment."

Turan's predatory smile said all that needed saying there. But then the officer asked, "What changed your mind, lord? When I suggested this before, you wouldn't hear me. Now you like the idea."

"Let's just say Tzikas has been making a little too free with his opinions," Abivard answered, at which Turan nodded in grim amusement. Abivard turned practical: "We'll need to set this up with the Videssians. When we need to, we can get a message to them, isn't that right?"

"Aye, lord, it is," Turan said. "If we want to exchange captives, things like that, we can get them to hear us." He smiled again. "For the chance of getting their hands on Tzikas, after what he tried to do to Maniakes, I think they'll hear us, as a matter of fact."

"Good," Abivard said. "So do I. Oh, yes, very good indeed. You will know and I will know and our messenger will know, and a few Videssians, too."

"I don't think they'd give us away, lord," Turan said. "If things were a little different, they might, but I think they hate Tzikas worse than you do. If they can get their hands on him, they'll keep quiet about hows and whys."

"I think so, too," Abivard said. "But there is one other person I'd want to know before the end."

"Who's that?" Turan sounded worried. "The more people who know about a plot like this, the better the chance it'll go wrong."

"'Before the end,' I said," Abivard replied. "Don't you think it would be fitting if Tzikas figured out how he'd ended up in his predicament?"

Turan smiled.

After swinging away from the Tib to rampage through the floodplain, Maniakes' army turned back toward the west, as if deciding it would attack Mashiz after all. Abivard spread his own force out along the river to make sure the Videssians could not force a crossing without his knowing about it.

He spread his cavalry particularly wide, sending the horsemen out not only to scout against the Videssians but also to nip at them with raids. Tzikas was like a whirlwind, now here, now there, always striking stinging blows against the countrymen he'd abandoned.

"He *can* fight," Abivard said grudgingly one evening after the Videssian had come in with a couple of dozen of Maniakes' men as prisoners. "I wonder if I really should—"

Roshnani interrupted him, her voice very firm: "Of course you should. Yes, he can fight. Think of all the other delightful things he can do, too."

His resolve thus stiffened, Abivard went on setting up the trap that would give Tzikas back to the Videssians. Turan had been right: once his messenger met Maniakes', the Avtokrator proved eager for the chance to get his hands on the man who had nearly toppled him from his throne.

When the arrangements were complete, Abivard sent most of Tzikas' cavalry force under a lieutenant against a large, ostentatious Videssian demonstration to the northeast. "That should have been my mission to command," Tzikas said angrily. "After all this time and all this war against the Videssians, you still don't trust me not to betray you."

"On the contrary, eminent sir," Abivard replied. "I trust you completely."

Against a Makuraner that would have been a safe reply. Tzikas, schooled in Videssian irony, gave Abivard a sharp look. Abivard was still kicking himself when, as if on cue in a Videssian Midwinter's Day mime show, a messenger rushed up, calling, "Lords, the imperials are breaking canals less than a farsang from here!" He pointed southeast, though a low rise obscured the Videssians from sight.

"By the God," Tzikas declared, "I shall attend to this." Without paying Abivard any more attention, he hurried away. A few minutes later, leading the couple of hundred heavy horsemen left in camp, he rode off, the red-lion banner of Makuran fluttering at the head of his force.

Abivard watched him go with mingled hope and guilt. He still wasn't altogether pleased at the idea of getting rid of Tzikas this way, no matter how necessary he found it. And he knew Makuraners would suffer in the trap Maniakes was setting. He hoped they would make the Videssians pay dearly for every one of them they brought down.

But most of all he hoped the scheme would work.

Only a remnant of the cavalry troop came back later that afternoon. A good many of the warriors who did return were wounded. One of the troopers, seeing Abivard, cried out, "We were ambushed, lord! As we engaged the Videssians who were wrecking the waterway, a great host of them burst out of the ruins of a village nearby. They cut us off and, I fear, had their way with us."

"I don't see Tzikas," Abivard said after a quick glance up and down the battered column. "What happened to him? Does he live?"

"The Videssian? I don't know for certain, lord," the soldier answered. "He led a handful of men on a charge straight into the heart of the foe's force. I didn't see him after that, but I fear the worst."

"May the God have given him a fate he deserved," Abivard said, a double-edged wish if ever there was one. He wondered if Tzikas had attacked the Videssians so fiercely to try to make them kill him instead of taking him captive. Had he done to Maniakes what Tzikas had done, he wouldn't have wanted the Avtokrator to capture him.

The next day Tzikas' Makuraner lieutenant, a hot-blooded young hellion named Sanatruq, returned with most of the cavalry regiment after having beaten back the large Videssian movement. He was very proud of himself. Abivard was proud of him, too, but rather less so: he knew Maniakes had made the movement to draw out most of the Makuraner cavalry so that, when Tzikas led out the rest, he would face overwhelming odds.

"He was overwhelmed?" Sanatruq said in dismay. "Our lord? It is sad—no, it is tragic! How shall we carry on without him?" He reached down to the ground, pinched up some dust, and rubbed it on his face in mourning.

"I give the regiment to you for now," Abivard said. "Should the God grant that Tzikas return, you'll have to turn it over to him, but I fear that's not likely."

"I shall avenge his loss!" Sanatruq cried. "He was a brave leader, a bold leader, a man who fought always at the fore, in the days when he was against us and even more after he was with us."

"True enough," Abivard said; it was likely to be the best memorial Tzikas got. Abivard wondered what Maniakes was having to say to the man who'd tried to murder him with magic. He suspected it was something Tzikas would remember for the rest of his life, however long—or short—that turned out to be.

Whatever Maniakes was saying to Tzikas, he wasn't staying around the Tib to do it. He went back into the central region of the land of the Thousand Cities, doing his best to make Abivard's life miserable in the process. Abivard had had a vague hope that the cooperation between the Avtokrator and himself over Tzikas might make a broader truce come about, but that didn't happen. Both he and the Avtokrator had wanted to be rid of the Videssian renegade, and that had let them work together in ways they couldn't anywhere else.

Sanatruq proved to have all the energy Tzikas had had as a cavalry commander but less luck. The Videssians beat back his raids several times in a row, till Abivard almost wished he had Tzikas back again.

"Don't say that!" Roshnani exclaimed one day when he was irked enough to complain out loud. Her hand moved in a gesture designed to turn aside evil omens. "You know you'd go for his throat if he chanced to walk in here right now."

"Well, so I would," Abivard said. "All right, then, I don't wish Tzikas to come walking into the tent right now."

That was true enough. He did want to find out what had happened to the Videssian renegade, though. Had he fallen in the fight where he'd unexpectedly been so outnumbered, or had he fallen into Maniakes' hands instead? If he was a captive, what was Maniakes doing with—or to—him now?

When the Videssians had invaded the land of the Thousand Cities, they hadn't brought all the laborers and servants they'd needed. Instead, as armies will, they'd taken men from the cities to do their work for them and rewarded those men with not enough food and even less money. They'd also ended up with the usual number of camp followers.

Laborers and camp followers were not permanent parts of an army, though. They came and went—or sometimes they stayed behind as the army came and went. Abivard ordered his men to bring in some of them so he could try to learn Tzikas' fate.

And so, a few days later, he found himself questioning a small, swarthy woman in a small, thin shift that clung to her wherever she would sweat—and in summer in the land of the Thousand Cities, there were very few places a woman or even a man would not sweat.

"You say you saw them bring him into the Videssian camp?" Abivard asked. He put the question in Videssian first and only afterward in Makuraner. The woman, whose name was Eshkinni, had learned a fair amount of the language of the Empire (and who could say what else?) in her time in the invaders' camp but used the tongue of the floodplain, of which Abivard knew a bare handful of words, in preference to Makuraner.

Eshkinni tossed her head, making the fancy bronze earrings she wore clatter softly. She had a necklace of gaudy glass beads and more bronze bangles on her arms. "I to see him, that right," she said. "They to drag him, they to curse him with their god, they to say Avtokrator to do to him something bad."

"You are sure this was Tzikas?" Abivard persisted. "Did you hear them say the name?"

She frowned, trying to remember. "I to think maybe," she said. She wiggled a little and stuck out her backside, perhaps hoping to distract him from her imperfect memory. By the knowing look in her eye, some time as a camp follower probably hadn't taught her much she hadn't already known.

Abivard, however, cared nothing for the charms she so calculatingly flaunted. "Did Maniakes come out and see this captive, whatever his name was?"

"Avtokrator? Yes, he to see him," Eshkinni said. "Avtokrator, I to think Avtokrator old man. But he not old . . . not too old. Old like you, maybe."

"Thank you so much," Abivard said. Eshkinni nodded as if his gratitude had been genuine. He couldn't be properly sardonic in a language not his own, even if Videssian was made for shades of irony. And he thought she had seen Maniakes; the Avtokrator and Abivard really were about of an age. He tried another question: "What did Maniakes say to the captive?"

"He to say he to give him what he have to come to him," Eshkinni answered. Abivard frowned, struggling through the freshet of pronouns and infinitives, and then nodded. Had he had Tzikas in front of him, he would have said very much the same thing, though he probably would have elaborated on it a good deal. For that matter, Maniakes might well have elaborated on it; Abivard realized that Eshkinni wasn't giving him a literal translation.

He asked, "Did Maniakes say what he thought Tzikas had coming to him?" He itched to know, an itch partly gleeful, partly guilty.

But Eshkinni shook her head. Her earrings clinked again. Her lip curled; she was plainly bored with this whole proceeding. She tugged at her shift not to get rid of the places where it clung to her but to emphasize them. "You to want?" she asked, twitching her hip to leave no possible doubt about what she was offering.

"No, thank you," Abivard said politely, though he felt like exclaiming, *By the God, no!* Polite still, he offered an explanation: "My wife is traveling with me."

"So?" Eshkinni stared at him as if that had nothing to do with anything. In her eyes and in her experience, it probably didn't. She went on. "Why for big fancy man to have only one wife?" She sniffed as an answer occurred to her. "To be same reason you no to want me, I to bet. You no to have beard, I to wonder if you a—" She couldn't come up with the Videssian word for *eunuch* but made crotch-level cutting motions to show what she meant.

"No," Abivard said, sharply now. But she had done him a service, so he reached into a pouch he wore on his belt and drew from it twenty silver arkets, which he gave her. Her mood improved on the instant; it was far more than she would have hoped to realize by opening her legs for him.

"You to need to know any more things," she declared, "you to ask me. I to find out for you, you to best believe I to do." When she saw Abivard had nothing more to ask her then, she walked off, rolling her haunches. Abivard remained unstirred by the charms thus advertised, but several of his troopers appreciatively followed Eshkinni with their eyes. He suspected she might enlarge upon her earnings.

Later that day he asked Turan, "What would you do if you had Tzikas in your clutches?"

His lieutenant gave a pragmatic answer: "Cast him in irons so he couldn't escape, then get drunk to celebrate."

Abivard snorted. "Aside from that, I mean."

"If I found a pretty girl, I might want to get laid, too," Turan said, and then, grudgingly, seeing the warning on Abivard's face, "I suppose you mean after that. If I were Maniakes, the next thing I'd do would be to squeeze him dry about whatever he'd done while he was here. After that I'd get rid of him, fast if he'd done a good job of singing, slow if he hadn't—or maybe slow on general principles."

"Yes, that sounds reasonable," Abivard agreed. "I suspect I'd do much the same myself. Tzikas has it coming, by the God." He thought for a minute or so. "Now we have to tell Sharbaraz what happened without letting him know we made it happen. Life is never dull."

He learned how true that was a few days later, when one of his cavalry patrols came across a westbound rider dressed in the light tunic of a man from the land of the Thousand Cities. "He didn't sit his horse quite the way most of the other folk here do, so we thought we'd look him over," the soldier in charge of the patrol said. "And we found—this." He held out a leather message tube.

"Did you?" Abivard turned to the captured courier, asking in Videssian, "And what is—this?"

"I don't know," the courier answered in the same language; he was one of Maniakes' men, sure enough. "All I know is that I was supposed to get through your lines and carry it to Mashiz, then bring back Sharbaraz's answer if he had one."

"Were you?" Abivard opened the tube. Save for being stamped with the sunburst of Videssos rather than Makuran's lion, it seemed ordinary enough. The rolled-up parchment inside was sealed with scarlet wax, an imperial prerogative. Abivard broke the seal with his thumbnail.

He read Videssian, but haltingly; he moved his lips, sounding out every word. "Maniakes Avtokrator to Sharbaraz King of Kings: Greetings," the letter began. A string of florid salutations and boasts followed, showing that the Videssians could match the men of Makuran in such excess as well as in war.

After that, though, Maniakes got down to cases faster than most Makuraners would have. In his own hand—which Abivard recognized—he wrote, "I have the honor to inform you that I am holding as a captive and condemned criminal a certain Tzikas, a renegade formerly in your service, whom I had previously condemned. For the capture of this wretch I am indebted to your general Abivard son of Godarz, who, being as vexed by Tzikas' treacheries as I have been myself, arranged to have me capture him and dispose of him. He shall not be missed when he goes, I assure you. He—"

Maniakes went on at some length to explain Tzikas' iniquities. Abivard didn't read all of them; he knew them too well. He crumpled up the parchment and threw it on the ground, then stared at it in genuine, if grudging, admiration. Maniakes had more gall than even he'd expected. The Avtokrator had used him to help get rid of Tzikas and now was using Sharbaraz to help get rid of him because of Tzikas! If that wasn't effrontery, Abivard didn't know what was.

And only luck had kept the plan from working or at least had delayed it. If the Videssian courier had ridden more like a local—

Abivard picked up the sheet of parchment, unfolded it as well as he could, and summoned Turan. He translated the Videssian for his lieutenant, who did not read the language. When he was through, Turan scowled and said, "May he fall into the Void! What a sneaky thing to do! He—"

"Is Avtokrator of the Videssians," Abivard interrupted. "If he weren't sneaky, he wouldn't have the job. My father could go on for hours at a time about how devious and underhanded the Videssians were, and he—" He stopped and began to laugh. "Do you know, I can't say whether he ever had anything more to do with them than skirmishing against them. But however he knew or heard, he was right. You can't trust the Videssians when your eye's not on them, nor sometimes when it is."

"You're too right there." Now Turan laughed, though hardly in a way that showed much mirth. "I wish Maniakes were out of the land of the Thousand Cities. Then my eye wouldn't be on him."

Later that evening Roshnani found a new question to ask: "Did Maniakes' letter to the King of Kings actually come out and say he was going to put Tzikas to death?"

"It said he wouldn't be missed when he went," Abivard answered after a little thought. "If that doesn't mean the Avtokrator is going to kill him, I don't know what it does mean."

"You're right about that," Roshnani admitted, sounding for all the world like Turan. "The only trouble is, I keep remembering the Videssian board game."

"What has that got to do with—?" Abivard stopped. While he'd liked that game well enough during the time he had lived in Across, he'd hardly thought of it since leaving Videssian soil. One salient feature—a feature that made the game far more complex and difficult than it would have been, otherwise—was that captured pieces could return to the board, fighting under the banner of the player who had taken them.

Abivard had used Tzikas exactly as if he were a board-game piece. For as long as the Videssian renegade had been useful to

Makuran after failing to assassinate Maniakes, Abivard had hurled him against the Empire he'd once served. Once Tzikas was no longer useful, Abivard had not only acquiesced in but arranged his capture. But that didn't necessarily mean he was gone for good, only that Videssos had recaptured him.

"You don't suppose," Abivard said uneasily, "Maniakes would give him a chance to redeem himself, do you? He'd have to be crazy, not just foolish, to take a chance like that."

"So he would," Roshnani said. "Which doesn't mean he wouldn't try it if he thought he could put sand in the axles of our wagon."

"If Tzikas does fight us, he'll fight as if he thinks the Void is a short step behind him—and he'll be right," Abivard said. "If he's not useful to Maniakes, he's dead." He rubbed his chin. "I'm still more worried about Sharbaraz."

IX

L ord," the messenger said with a bow as he presented the message tube, "I bring you a letter from Sharbaraz King of Kings, may his years be many and his realm increase."

"Thank you," Abivard lied, taking the tube. As he opened it, he reflected on what he'd said to Roshnani a few days before. When you were more worried about what your own sovereign would do to hamstring your campaign than you were about the enemy, things weren't going as you had hoped when you'd embarked on that campaign.

He broke the seal, unrolled the parchment, and began to read. The familiar characters and turns of phrase of his own language were a pleasant relief after struggling through the Videssian intricacies of the dispatch from Maniakes he'd intercepted before it could get to Sharbaraz.

He waded through the list of Sharbaraz's titles and pretensions with amused resignation. With every letter, the list got longer and the pretensions more pretentious. He wondered when the King of Kings would simply declare he was the God come down to earth and let it go at that. It would save parchment, if nothing else.

After the bombast Sharbaraz got down to the meat: "Know that we are displeased you have presumed to summon our good and loyal servant Romezan from his appointed duties so that he might serve under you in the campaign against the usurper

Maniakes. Know further that we have sent under our seal orders to Romezan, commanding him in no way to heed your summons but to continue on the duties upon which he had been engaged prior to your illegal, rash, and foolish communication."

"Is there a reply, lord?' the messenger asked when Abivard looked up from the parchment.

"Hmm? Oh." Abivard shook his head. "Not yet, anyhow. I have the feeling Sharbaraz King of Kings has a good deal more to say to me than I can answer right at this moment."

He read on. The next chunk of the letter complained about his failure to drive the Videssians out of the land of the Thousand Cities and keep them from ravaging the floodplain between the Tutub and the Tib. He wished he were in a building of brick or sturdy stone, not a tent. That would have let him pound his head against a wall. Sharbaraz didn't care for what was going on now but didn't want him to do anything about it, either. *Lovely,* he thought. *No matter what I do, I end up getting blamed.* He'd seen that before, too, more times than he cared to remember.

"Know also," Sharbaraz wrote, "that we are informed you not only let the general Tzikas fall into the hands of the foe but also connived at, aided, and abetted his capture. We deem this an act both wretched and contemptible and one for which only a single justification and extenuation may be claimed: which is to say, your success against the Videssians without Tzikas where you failed with him. Absent such success during this campaigning season, you shall be judged most harshly for your base act of betrayal."

Abivard let out a sour laugh there. He was being blamed for betraying Tzikas, oh yes, but had Tzikas ever been blamed for betraying him? On the contrary—Tzikas had found nothing but favor with the King of Kings. And Sharbaraz had ordered him to go out and win victories or face the consequences, all without releasing Romezan's men, who might have made such victory possible.

"Have you a reply, lord?" the messenger asked again.

The one that came to mind was scatological. Abivard suppressed it. With Maniakes in the field against him, he had no time for fueling a feud with the King of Kings, especially since in such a feud he was automatically the loser unless he rebelled, and if he started a civil war in Makuran, he handed not only the land of the Thousand Cities but also Vaspurakan to the Empire of Videssos. He understood that from direct experience: Makuran held the Videssian westlands because of the Empire's descent into civil war during Genesios' reign.

"Lord?" the messenger repeated.

"Yes, I do have a reply," Abivard said. He called for a servant to fetch parchment, pen, and ink. When he got them, he wrote his own name and Sharbaraz's, then meticulously copied all the titles with which the King of Kings adorned himself—he didn't want Yeliif or someone like him imputing disloyalty because of disrespect. When that was finally done, halfway down the sheet, he got to his real message: *Majesty, I will give you the victory you desire even if you do not give me the tools I need to make it.* He signed his name, rolled up the message, and stuffed it into the tube. He did not care whether the messenger read it.

When the fellow had ridden off, Abivard turned and looked west toward the Dilbat Mountains and Mashiz. Half of him wished he had the letter back; he knew he'd promised more than he could deliver and knew he would be punished for failing to deliver. But the other half of him did not care. The promise aside, he'd told Sharbaraz nothing but the truth, a rarity in the palace at Mashiz. He wondered if the King of Kings would recognize it when he heard it.

He told Roshnani what he'd done. She said, "It's not enough. You said you would resign your command if Sharbaraz counter-manded your order to Romezan. He has." She cocked her head to one side and waited to hear how he would answer.

"I know what I said." He didn't want to meet her eye. "Now that it's happened, though . . . I can't. I wish I could, but I can't. Talking of it was easy. Doing it—" Now he waited for the storm to burst on his head.

Roshnani sighed. "I was afraid you would find that was so." She smiled wryly. "To tell you the truth, I thought you would find that was so. I wish you hadn't. You have to beat Maniakes once to make the King of Kings shut up, and that won't be easy. But you have to do it anyway, so I don't see you've made yourself any worse off in Mashiz than you were already."

"That's what I thought," Abivard said, grateful that his wife was accepting his change of heart with no more than private disappointment. "That's what I hoped, at any rate. Now I have to figure out how to give myself the best chance of making my boast come true."

Maniakes seemed to have given up on the notion of assaulting Mashiz and was going through the land of the Thousand Cities as he had the year before, burning and destroying. Flooding the plain between the Tutub and the Tib had proved less effective than Abivard had hoped. If he was going to stop the Videssians, he'd have to move against them and fight them where he could.

He left the encampment along the Tib with a certain amount of trepidation, sure that Sharbaraz would interpret his move as leaving Mashiz uncovered. He was, though, so used to being in the bad graces of the King of Kings that making matters a little worse no longer worried him as much as it once had.

He wished he had more cavalry. His one effort to use Tzikas' regiment as a major force in its own right had been at best a qualified success. If he tried it again, Maniakes was all too likely to anticipate his move and pinch off and destroy the regiment.

"You can't do the same thing to Maniakes twice running," he told Turan, as if his lieutenant had disagreed with him. "If you do, he'll punish you for it. Why, if we had another traitor to feed him, we'd have to do it a different way this time, because he'd suspect a trap if we didn't."

"As you say, lord," Turan answered. "And what new stratagem will you use to surprise and dazzle him?"

"That's a good question," Abivard said. "I wish I had a good answer to give you. Right now the best I can think of is to close with him—if he'll let us close with him—and see what sorts of chances we get."

To make sure the Videssians did not take him by surprise, he decided to use his cavalry not so much as an attacking force but as screens and scouts, sending riders much farther out ahead of his main body of foot soldiers than usual. Sometimes he thought more of them were galloping back and forth with news and orders than were actually keeping track of Maniakes' army, but he found he had no trouble staying informed about where the Videssians were going and even, after he'd been watching them for a while, guessing what they were liable to do next. He vowed to shadow his foes more closely in future fights, too.

Maniakes' force did not move as quickly as it might have. Every day Abivard drew closer. Maniakes did not turn and offer battle but made no move to avoid it, either. He might have been saying, *If you're sure this is what you want, I'll give it to you.* Abivard still wondered that the Videssians had such confidence; he was used to imperial armies that fled before his men.

The only exception to that rule, he remembered with painful irony, had been the men under Tzikas' command. But the army Abivard commanded now, he silently admitted, was only a shadow of the striking force he'd once led. And the Videssians had gotten used to the idea that they could win battles. He knew how much difference that made.

He began putting his horsemen into larger bands to skirmish with the Videssians. If Maniakes would accept battle, he intended to give it to the Avtokrator. His foot soldiers, having stood up to Maniakes' cavalry twice, were loudly certain they could do it again. He would let them have their chance. If he didn't fight the Videssians, he had no hope of beating them.

After a few days of small-scale clashes he drew his army up in a battle line on gently rising ground not far from Zadabak, one of the Thousand Cities, inviting an attack if Maniakes cared to make it. And Maniakes, sure enough, brought the Videssians up close to look over the Makuraner position and camped for the night close enough to make it clear he intended to fight when morning came.

Abivard spent much of the night exhorting his soldiers and making final dispositions for the battle to come. His own disposition was somewhere between hopeful and resigned. He was going to make the effort to drive the Videssians from the land of the Thousand Cities. If the God favored him, he would succeed. If not, he would have done everything he could with the force Sharbaraz had allowed him. The King of Kings might blame him but would have trouble doing so justly.

When morning came, Abivard scowled as his troops rose from their bedrolls and went back into line. They faced east, into the rising sun, which meant the Videssians had the advantage of the light, being able to see his forces clearly instead of having to squint against glare. If the fight quickly went against the Makuraners, that would be an error over which Sharbaraz would have every right to tax him.

He summoned Sanatruq and said, "We have to delay the general engagement till the sun is higher in the sky."

The cavalry commander gauged the light and nodded. "You want me to do something about that, I take it."

"Your men can move about the field faster than the foot soldiers, and they're lancers, not archers; the sun won't bother them so much," Abivard answered. "I hate to ask you to make a sacrifice like that—I feel almost as if I'm . . . betraying you." He'd almost said *treating you as I did Tzikas.* But Sanatruq didn't know about that, and Abivard didn't want him to learn. "I wish we had more cavalry, too."

"So do I, lord," Sanatruq said feelingly. "For that matter, I wish we had more infantry." He waved toward the slowly forming line, which was not so long as it might have been. "But we do what we can with what we have. If you want me to throw my men at the Videssians, I'll do it."

"The God bless you for your generous spirit," Abivard said, "and may you—may we all—come through safe so you can enjoy the praise you will have earned."

Sanatruq saluted and rode off to what was left of his regiment. Moments later they trotted toward the ranks of the Videssians. As they drew near, they lowered their lances and went from trot up to thunderous gallop. The Videssians' response was not so swift as it might have been; perhaps Maniakes did not believe the small force would attack his own till the charge began.

Whatever the reason, the Makuraner heavy horse penetrated deep into the ranks of the Videssians. For a few shining moments Abivard, who was peering into the sun, dared to hope that the surprise assault would throw his enemies into such disorder that they would withdraw or at least be too shaken to carry out the assault they'd obviously intended.

A couple of years before he probably would have been right, but no more. The Videssians took advantage of their superior numbers to neutralize the advantage the Makuraners had in armor for men and horses and in sheer weight of metal. The imperials did not shrink from the fight but carried on with a businesslike competence that put Abivard in mind of the army Maniakes' father had led to the aid of Sharbaraz King of Kings during the last years of the reign of the able but unlucky and unloved Avtokrator Likinios.

Sanatruq must have known, or at least quickly seen, that he had no hope of defeating the Videssians. He fought on for some time after that had to have become obvious, buying the foot soldiers in Abivard's truncated battle line the time needed so that the archers would no longer be hampered by shooting straight into the sun.

When at last the choice was continuing the unequal struggle to the point of destruction or pulling back and saving what he could of his force, the cavalry commander did pull back, but more toward the north than to the west, so that if Maniakes chose to pursue, he could do so only by pulling men away from the force with which he wanted to assail Abivard's line of infantrymen.

To Abivard's disappointment, Maniakes did not divide his force in that way. The Avtokrator had learned the trick or acquired the wisdom of concentrating on what he really wanted and not frittering away his chances of gaining it by going after three other things at the same time. Abivard wished his foe would have proved more flighty.

Horns blaring, the Videssians moved across the plain and up the gently sloping ground against Abivard's men. The horsemen plied Abivard's soldiers with arrows, raising their shields to ward themselves from the Makuraners' reply. Here and there a Videssian or a horse would go down, but only here and there. More lightly armed infantrymen were pierced than their opponents.

Some Videssians, brandishing javelins, rode out ahead of their main force. They pelted Abivard's men with the throwing spears from close range. He itched to order his troops forward against them but deliberately restrained himself. Infantry charging cavalry opened gaps into which the horsemen could force their way, and if they did that, they could break his whole army to pieces in the same way a wedge, well driven home, would split a large, thick piece of wood.

He suspected that Maniakes was trying to provoke him into a charge for that very reason. The javelin men stayed out there in front of his own army, temptingly close, as if itching to be assailed. "Hold fast!" Abivard shouted, over and over. "If they want us so badly, let them come and get us."

Had he ever imagined that the Videssians lacked the stomach for close combat, their response when they saw their foes refusing to be lured out of their position would have disabused him of the notion forever. Maniakes' men drew their swords and rode forward against the Makuraners. If Abivard would not hand them a breach in the Makuraner line, they'd manufacture one for themselves.

The Makuraners thrust with spears at their horses, used big wicker shields to turn aside their slashes, and hit back with clubs and knives and some swords of their own. Men on both sides cursed and gasped and prayed and shrieked. Though not Makuraner heavy cavalry, the Videssians used the weight of their horses to force Abivard's line to sag back in the center like a bent bow.

He rode to where the battle raged most fiercely, not only to fight but to let the soldiers from the garrisons of the Thousand Cities, men who up till the summer before had never expected to do any serious fighting, know he was with them. "We can do it!" he called to them. "We can hold the imperials back and drive them away."

Hold the Makuraners did, and well enough to keep the Videssians from smashing through their line. Maniakes sent a party to try to outflank Abivard's relatively short line but had little luck there. The ground at the unanchored end was soft and wet, and his horsemen bogged down. His whole attack bogged down not far from victory. He kept feeding men into the fight till he was heavily engaged all along the line.

"Now!" Abivard said, and a messenger galloped away. The fight went on, for *now* did not translate to *immediately.* He wished he'd arranged some special signal, but he hadn't, and he would just have to wait till the messenger got where he was going.

He also had to worry about whether he'd waited too long before releasing the rider. If the battle was lost here before he could put his scheme into play, what point was there to having had the idea in the first place?

Actually, the battle didn't look as if it would be lost or won any time soon. It was a melee, a slugging match, neither side willing to go back, neither able to force its way forward. Abivard had not expected the Videssians to make that kind of fight. Perhaps Maniakes had not expected the Makuraners, the former garrison troops, to withstand it if he did.

If he hadn't, he found himself mistaken. His men hewed and cursed at Makuraners who hewed and cursed back, the two armies locked together as tightly as lovers. And with them locked together thus, Zadabak's gates came open and a great column of foot soldiers, all yelling like fiends, rushed down the artificial hill and across the gently sloping flatlands below toward the Videssians.

Maniakes' men yelled, too, in surprise and alarm. Now, instead of trying to fight their way forward against the Makuraners, they found themselves taken in the flank and forced to a sudden, desperate defense. The horns directing their movements blared urgent orders that often were impossible to fulfill.

"Let's see how you like it!" Abivard shouted at the Videssians. He'd had a year and a half of having to react to Maniakes' moves and hadn't liked it a bit. As men will, he'd conveniently forgotten that for some years before he'd driven the Videssians back across the length of the westlands. "Let's see!" he yelled again. "What are you made of? Have you got bollocks, or are you just the bunch of prancing, mincing eunuchs I think you are?"

If word of that taunt ever got back to Yeliif, he was in trouble. But then, he was in trouble with the beautiful eunuch no matter what he said or did, so what did one taunt matter? Along with his soldiers, he screamed more abuse at the Videssians.

To his surprise and disappointment Maniakes' men did not break at the new challenge. Instead, they turned to meet it, the soldiers on their left facing outward to defend themselves against the Makuraner onslaught. Romezan's veterans might have done better, but not much. Instead of the Videssians' having their line rolled up, they only had it bent in, as Abivard's had been not long before.

The Videssian horns blared anew. Now, as best they could, the imperials did break off combat with their foes, disengaging, pulling back. They had the advantage there; even moving backward, they were quicker than their foes. They regrouped out of bowshot, shaken but not broken.

Abivard cursed. Just as his men had proved better and steadier than Maniakes had thought, so the Videssians had outdone what he had thought they could manage. The end result of that was a great many men on both sides dead or maimed for no better reason than that each commander had underestimated the courage of his opponents.

"We rocked them!" Turan shouted to Abivard.

"Aye," Abivard said. But he'd needed to do more than rock the Videssians. He'd needed to wreck them. That hadn't happened. As before up at the canal, he'd come up with a clever stratagem and one that hadn't failed, not truly . . . but one that hadn't succeeded to the extent he'd hoped, either.

And now, as then, Maniakes enjoyed the initiative once more. If he wanted, he could ride away from the battle. Abivard's men would not be able to keep up with his. Or, if he wanted, he could renew the attack on the battered Makuraner line in the place and manner he chose.

For the moment he did neither, simply waiting with his force, perhaps savoring the lull as much as Abivard was. Then the Videssian ranks parted and a single rider approached the Makuraners, tossing a javelin up into the air and catching it as it came down again. He rode up and down between the armies before shouting in accented Makuraner: "Abivard! Come out and fight, Abivard!"

At first Abivard thought of the challenge only as a reversal of the one his men had hurled at Maniakes before the fight by the Tib. Then he realized it was a reversal in more ways than one, for the warrior offering single combat was none other than Tzikas.

He wasted a moment admiring the elegance of Maniakes' scheme. If Tzikas slew him, the Avtokrator profited by it—and could still dispose of Tzikas at his leisure. If, on the other hand, he slew Tzikas, Maniakes would still be rid of a traitor but would not suffer the onus of putting Tzikas to death himself. No matter what happened, Maniakes couldn't lose.

Admiration, calculation—they did not last long. There rode Tzikas, coming out from the enemy army, a legitimate target at last. If he killed the renegade—the double renegade—now, the only thing Sharbaraz could do would be to congratulate him. And since he wanted nothing so much as to stretch Tzikas' body lifeless in the dirt, he spurred his horse forward, shouting, "Make way, curse you!" to the foot soldiers standing between him and his intended prey.

But the sight of Tzikas back serving the Videssians once more after renouncing not only them but their god inflamed the members of the Makuraner cavalry regiment that had fought so long and well under his command. Before Abivard could charge the man who had betrayed Maniakes and him both, a double handful of horsemen were thundering at the Videssian. Tzikas had shown himself no coward, but he'd also shown himself no fool. He galloped back to the protection of the Videssian line.

All the Makuraner cavalrymen screamed abuse at their former

leader, reviling him in the foulest ways they knew. Abivard started to join them but in the end kept silent, savoring a more subtle revenge: Tzikas had failed in the purpose to which Maniakes had set him. What was the Avtokrator of the Videssians likely to do with—or to—him now? Abivard didn't know but enjoyed letting his imagination run free.

He did not get to enjoy such speculation long. Videssian horns squalled again. Shouting Maniakes' name—conspicuously not shouting Tzikas' name—the Videssian army rode forward again. Fewer arrows flew from their bows, and fewer from those of the Makuraners as well. A lot of quivers were empty. Picking up shafts from the ground was not the same as being able to refill those quivers.

"Stand fast!" Abivard called. He had never seen a Videssian force come into battle with such grim determination. Maniakes' men were out to finish the fight one way or the other. His own foot soldiers seemed steady enough, but how much more pounding could they take before they broke? In a moment he'd find out.

Swords slashing, the Videssians rode up against the Makuraner line. Abivard hurried along the line to the place that looked most threatening. Trading strokes with several Videssians, he acquired a cut—luckily a small one—on the back of his sword hand, a dent in his helmet, and a ringing in the ear by the dent. He thought he dealt out more damage than that, but in combat, with what he saw constantly shifting, he had trouble being sure.

Peering up and down the line, he saw the Videssians steadily forcing his men back despite all they could do. He bit his lip. If the Makuraners did not hold steady, the line would break somewhere. When that happened, Maniakes' riders would pour through and cut up his force from in front and behind. That was a recipe for disaster.

Forcing the enemy back seemed beyond his men's ability now that his stratagem had proved imperfectly successful. What did that leave him? He thought for a moment of retreating back into Zadabak, but then glanced over toward the walled city atop its mound of ancient rubbish. Retreating uphill and into the city was liable to be a nightmare worse than a Videssian breakthrough down here on the flatlands.

Which left . . . nothing. The God did not grant man's every prayer. Sometimes, even for the most pious, even for the most virtuous, things went wrong. He had done everything he knew how to do here to beat the Videssians and had proved to know not quite enough. He wondered if he would be able to retreat on the flat without tearing the army to pieces. He didn't think so but had the bad feeling he would have to try it anyhow before long.

Messengers rode and ran up to him, reporting pressure on the right, pressure on the left, pressure in the center. He had a last few hundred reserves left and fed them into the fight more in the spirit of leaving nothing undone than with any serious expectation that they would turn the tide. They didn't, which left him facing the same dilemma less than half an hour later, this time without any palliative to apply.

If he drew back with his left, he pulled away from the swamp anchoring that end of the line and gave the Videssians a free road into his rear. If he drew back with his right, he pulled away from Zadabak and its hillock. He decided to try that rather than the other plan, hoping the Videssians would fear a trap and hesitate to push between his army and the town.

A few years before the ploy might have given Maniakes pause, but no more. Without wasted motion or time he sent horsemen galloping into the gap Abivard had created for him. Abivard's heart sank. Whenever he'd been beaten before, here in the land of the Thousand Cities, he'd managed to keep his army intact, ready to fight another day. For the life of him, he didn't see how he was going to manage that this time.

More Videssian horn calls rang out. Abivard knew those calls as well as he knew his own. As people often do, though, at first he heard what he expected to hear, not what the trumpeters blew. When his mind as well as his ear recognized the notes, he stared in disbelief.

"That's *retreat*," Turan said, sounding as dazed as Abivard felt.

"I know it is," Abivard answered. "By the God, though, I don't know why. We were helpless before them, and Maniakes surely knew it."

But the flankers who should have gotten around to Abivard's rear and started the destruction of the Makuraner army instead reined in and, obedient to the Avtokrator's command, returned to their own main body. And then that main body disengaged from Abivard's force and rode rapidly off toward the southeast, leaving Abivard in possession of the field.

"I don't believe it," he said. He'd said it several times by then. "He had us. By the God, he *had* us. And he let us get away. No, he didn't just let us get away. He ran from us even though we couldn't make him run."

"If battle magic worked, it would work like that," Turan said. "But battle magic doesn't work or works so seldom that it's not worth the effort. Did he up and go mad all of a sudden?"

"Too much to hope for," Abivard said, to which his lieutenant could only numbly nod. He went on, "Besides, he knew what he was doing, or thought he did. He handled that retreat as smoothly as any other part of the battle. It's only that he didn't need to make it ... did he?"

Turan did not answer that. Turan could not answer that any more than Abivard could. They waited and exclaimed and scratched their heads but came to no conclusions.

In any other country they would have understood sooner than they could on the floodplain between the Tutub and the Tib. On the Pardrayan steppe, on the high plateau of Makuran, in the Videssian westlands, an army on the move kicked up a great cloud of dust. But the rich soil hereabouts was kept so moist, little dust rose from it. They did not know the army was approaching till they saw the first outriders off to the northeast.

Spying them gave rise to the next interesting question: whose army were they? "They can't be Videssians, or Maniakes wouldn't have run from them," Abivard said. "They can't be our men, because these are our men." He waved to his battered host.

"They can't be Vaspurakaners or men of Erzerum, either, or Khamorth from off the steppe," Turan said. "If they were any of those folk Maniakes would have welcomed them with open arms."

"True. Every word of it true," Abivard agreed. "That leaves nobody, near as I can see. By the kind of logic the Videssians love so well, then, that army there doesn't exist." His shaky laugh said what such logic was worth.

He did his best to make his army ready to fight at need. Seeing the state his men were in, he knew how forlorn that best was. The army from which Maniakes had fled drew closer. Now Abivard could make out the banners that army flew. As with the

Videssian horn calls, recognition and understanding did not go together.

"They're *our* men," he said. "Makuraners, flying the red lion."

"But they can't be," Turan said. "We don't have any cavalry force closer than Vaspurakan or the Videssian westlands. I wish we did, but we don't."

"I know," Abivard said. "I wrote to Romezan, asking him to come to our aid, but the King of Kings, in his wisdom, counter-manded me."

Still wondering, he rode out toward the approaching horsemen. He took a good-sized detachment of his surviving cavalry with him, still unsure this wasn't some kind of trap or trick—though why Maniakes, with a won battle, would have needed to resort to tricks was beyond him.

A party to match his separated itself from the main body of the mysterious army. "By the God," Turan said softly.

"By the God," Abivard echoed. That burly, great-mustached man in the gilded armor— Now, at last, Abivard rode out ahead of his escort. He raised his voice: "Romezan, is it really you?"

The commander of the Makuraner mobile force shouted back: "No, it's just someone who looks like me." Roaring laughter, he spurred his horse, too, so that he and Abivard met alone between their men.

When they clasped hands, Romezan's remembered strength made every bone in Abivard's right hand ache. "Welcome, wel-come, three times welcome," Abivard said most sincerely, and then, lowering his voice though no one save Romezan was in earshot, "Welcome indeed, but didn't Sharbaraz King of Kings, may his days be long and his realm increase, order you to stay in the westlands?"

"He certainly did," Romezan boomed, careless of who heard him, "and so here I am."

Abivard stared. "You got the order—and you disobeyed it?"

"That's what I did, all right," Romezan said cheerfully. "From what you said in your letter, you needed help, and a lot of it. Sharbaraz didn't know what was happening here as well as you did. That's what I thought, anyhow."

"What will he do when he finds out, do you think?" Abivard asked.

"Nothing much—there are times when being of the Seven Clans

works for you," Romezan answered. "If the King of Kings gives us too hard a time, we rise up, and he knows it."

He spoke with the calm confidence of a man born into the high nobility, a man for whom Sharbaraz was undoubtedly a superior but not a figure one step—and that a short one—removed from the God. Although Abivard's sister was married to the King of Kings, he still retained much of the awe for the office, if not for the man who held it for the moment, that had been inculcated in him since childhood. When he thought it through, he knew how little sense that made, but he didn't—he couldn't—always pause to think it through.

Romezan said, "Besides, how angry can Sharbaraz be once he finds out we've made Maniakes run off with his tail between his legs?"

"How angry?" Abivard pursed his lips. "That depends. If he decides you came here to join forces with me, not so you could go after Maniakes, he's liable to be very angry indeed."

"Why on earth would he think that?" Romezan boomed laughter. "What does he expect the two of us would do together, move on Mashiz instead of twisting Maniakes' tail again?"

"Isn't this a pleasant afternoon?" Abivard said. "I don't know that I've seen the sun so bright in the sky since, oh, maybe yesterday."

Romezan stared at him, the beginning of a scowl on his face. "What *are* you talking about?" he demanded. Fierce as fire in a fight, he wasn't the fastest man Abivard had ever seen in pursuit of an idea. But he wasn't a fool, either; he did eventually get where he was going. After a couple of heartbeats the scowl vanished. His eyes widened. "He truly is liable to think that? Why, by the God?"

For all his blithe talk a little while before about going into rebellion, Romezan drew back when confronted with the actual possibility. Having drawn back himself, Abivard did not think less of him for that. He said, "Maybe he thinks I'm too good at what I do."

"How can a general be too good?" Romezan asked. "There's no such thing as winning too many battles."

His faith touched Abivard. Somehow Romezan had managed to live for years in the Videssian westlands without acquiring a bit of subtlety. "A general who is too good, a general who wins all his battles," Abivard said, almost as if explaining things to Varaz, "has no more foes to beat, true, but if he looks toward the throne on which his sovereign sits . . ."

"Ah," Romezan said, his voice serious now. Yes, talking of rebellion had been easy when it had been nothing but talk. But he went on, "The King of Kings suspects *you*, lord? If you're not loyal to him, who is?"

"If you knew how many times I've put that same question to him." Abivard sighed. "The answer, as best I can see, is that the King of Kings suspects everyone and doesn't think anyone is loyal to him, me included."

"If he truly does think that way, he'll prove himself right one of these days," Romezan said, tongue wagging looser than was perfectly wise.

Wise tongue or not, Abivard basked in his words like a lizard in the sun. For so long everyone around him had spoken nothing but fulsome praises of the King of Kings—oh, not Roshnani, but her thought and his were twin mirrors. To hear one of Sharbaraz's generals acknowledge that he could be less than wise and less than charitable was like wine after long thirst.

Romezan was looking over the field. "I don't see Tzikas anywhere," he remarked.

"No, you wouldn't," Abivard agreed. "He had the misfortune to be captured by the Videssians not so long ago." His voice was as bland as barley porridge without salt: how could anyone imagine *he'd* had anything to do with such a misfortune? "And, having been captured, the redoubtable Tzikas threw in his lot with his former folk and was most definitely seen not more than a couple of hours ago, fighting on Maniakes' side again." That probably wasn't fair to the unhappy Tzikas, who had problems of his own—a good many of them self-inflicted—but Abivard couldn't have cared less.

"The sooner he falls into the Void, the better for everybody," Romezan growled. "Never did like him, never did trust him. The idea that a Videssian could ape Makuraner manners—and to think we'd think he was one of us . . . not right, not natural. How come Maniakes didn't just up and kill him after he caught him? He owes him a big one, eh?"

"I think he was more interested in hurting us than in hurting Tzikas, worse luck," Abivard said, and Romezan nodded. Abivard went on, "But we'll hurt him worse than the other way around. I've been so desperately low in cavalry till you got here, I couldn't take the war to Maniakes. I had to let him choose his moves and then respond."

"We'll go after him." Romezan looked over the field once more. "You took him on with just foot soldiers, pretty much, didn't you?" Abivard nodded. Romezan let out a shrill little whistle. "I wouldn't like to try that, not with infantry alone. But your men seem to have given the misbelievers everything they wanted. How did you ever get infantry to fight so well?"

"I trained them hard, and I fought them the same way," Abivard said. "I had no choice: it was use infantry or go under. When they have confidence in what they're doing, they make decent troops. Better than decent troops, as a matter of fact."

"Who would have thought it?" Romezan said. "You must be a wizard to work miracles no one else could hope to match. Well, the days of needing to work miracles are done. You have proper soldiers again, so you can stop wasting your time on infantry-men."

"I suppose so." Oddly, the thought saddened Abivard. Of course cavalry was more valuable than infantry, but he felt a pang over letting the foot soldiers he'd trained slip back into being nothing more than garrison troops once more. It seemed a waste of what he'd made them. Well, they'd be *good* garrison troops, anyhow, and he could still get some use out of them in this campaign.

Romezan said, "Let's clean up this field here, patch up your wounded, and then we'll go chase ourselves some Videssians."

Abivard didn't need to hear that notion twice to like it. He hadn't been able to chase the Videssians in all his campaigning through the land of the Thousand Cities. He'd put himself where they would be a couple times, and he'd lured them into coming to him, too. But to go after them, knowing he could catch them . . . "Aye," he said. "Let's."

Maniakes very quickly made it clear that he did not intend to be brought to bay. He went back to the old routine of wrecking canals and levees behind him to slow the Makuraner pursuit. Even with that, though, not all was as it had been before Romezan had come to the land of the Thousand Cities. The Videssians did not enjoy the luxury of leisure to destroy cities. They had to content themselves with burning crops and riding through fields to trample down grain: wreckage, yes, but of a lesser sort.

Abivard wrote a letter to Sharbaraz, announcing his victory over Maniakes. Romezan also wrote one with Abivard looking over his shoulder as he drafted it and offering helpful suggestions. It apologized for disobeying the orders he'd gotten from the King of Kings and promised that if forgiven, he'd never again make such a heinous blunder. After reading it, Abivard felt as if he'd eaten too much fruit that had been too sweet to begin with and then had been candied in honey.

Romezan shook his head as he stamped his signet—a wild boar with great tushes—into the hot wax holding the letter closed. "If someone sent me a letter like this, I'd throw up."

"So would I," Abivard said. "But it's the sort of thing Sharbaraz likes to get. We've both seen that: tell the truth straight out and you're in trouble, load up your letter with this nonsense and you get what you want."

The same courier carried both letters off toward the west, toward a Mashiz no longer in danger from the Videssian army, toward a King of Kings who was likely to care less about that than about his orders, no matter how foolish, being obeyed. Abivard wondered what sort of letter would come out of the west, out of the shadows of the Dilbat Mountains, out of the shadows of a court life only distantly connected to the real world.

He also wondered when he would hear that Tzikas had been put to death. When he did not hear of the renegade's premature—though not, to his way of thinking, untimely—demise, he wondered when he would hear of Tzikas' leading the rear guard against his own men.

That did not happen, either. The longer either of those things took to come about, the more unhappy he got. He'd handed Tzikas over to Maniakes in the confident expectation—which Maniakes had fostered—that the Avtokrator would put him to death. Now Maniakes was instead holding on to him: to Abivard it seemed unfair.

But he knew better than to complain. If the Avtokrator had managed to trick him, that was his own fault, no one else's. Maybe he'd get the chance to pay Maniakes back one day soon. And maybe he wouldn't have to rely on trickery. Maybe he'd run the Videssians to earth as if they were a herd of wild asses and ride them down. Amazing, the thoughts to which the arrival of a real cavalry force could give rise.

Sharbaraz King of Kings did not delay in replying to the letters he'd gotten from Abivard and Romezan. When Abivard received a messenger from the King of Kings, he did so with all the enthusiasm he would have shown going off to get a rotting tooth pulled from his head.

By the same token, the leather message tube the fellow handed him might as well have been a venomous serpent. He opened it, broke the seal on the parchment, and unrolled it with no small trepidation. As usual, Sharbaraz had made his scribe waste several lines with his titles, his accomplishments, and his hopes. He seemed to take forever to get to the gist . . .

"We are, as we have said, angered that you should presume to summon to your aid the army commanded by Romezan son of Bizhan, which we had purposed using for other tasks during this campaigning season. We are further vexed with the aforesaid Romezan son of Bizhan for hearkening to your summons rather than ignoring it, as was our command, the aforesaid Romezan being separately admonished in a letter directed specifically to him.

"Only one possible circumstance can mitigate the disobedience the two of you have demonstrated both individually and collectively, the aforementioned circumstance being complete and overwhelming victory against the Videssians violating the land of the Thousand Cities. We own ourselves delighted one such victory has been gained and look forward either to Maniakes' extermination or to his ignominious retreat. The God grant that you soon have the opportunity to inform me of one or the other of these happy results."

As messengers did, this one asked Abivard, "Is there a reply, lord?"

"Wait a bit," Abivard answered. He read the letter again from top to bottom. It was no more vituperative in the second reading than it had been in the first. Abivard stepped out of the tent and spotted Pashang coming by, swigging on a jug of date wine. "Go find Romezan and fetch him to me," he told the driver.

"Aye, lord," Pashang said, and went off for Romezan. His pace was slower than Abivard would have desired; Abivard wondered how much of the wine he'd had.

But he did find Romezan and bring him back. The Makura-ner general was waving a parchment as he approached; Abivard assumed that that was because he'd just gotten his letter from the King of Kings, too. And so it proved. Romezan called, "There, you see? I told you that you worry too much."

"So you did," Abivard admitted. By the way Romezan was act-ing, his letter wasn't actively painful, either. Turning to the mes-senger, Abivard said, "Please tell Sharbaraz King of Kings we'll do everything we can to obey him." Romezan nodded vigorously.

The messenger bowed. "It shall be as you say, lords." To him Abivard and Romezan were figures almost as mighty as Sharbaraz himself: the one brother-in-law to the King of Kings, the other a great noble of the Seven Clans. Abivard clicked his tongue between his teeth. It all depended on how, and from what sta-tion, you looked at life.

When the fellow was gone, Abivard turned to Romezan in some bemusement. "I had expected the King of Kings to be angry at us," he said.

"I told you," Romezan answered. "Victory atones for any num-ber of sins."

"It's not that simple," Abivard insisted to Roshnani over stewed kid that night. "The more victories I won in the Videssian west-lands, the more suspicious of me Sharbaraz got. And then here, in the land of the Thousand Cities, I couldn't satisfy him no matter what I did. If I lost, I was a bungling idiot. But if I won, I was setting myself up to rebel against him. And if I begged for some help to give me a chance to win, why then I was obviously plotting to raise up an army against him."

"Until now," his principal wife said.

"Until now," Abivard echoed. "He didn't fall on Romezan like an avalanche, either, and Romezan flat disobeyed his orders. Till now he's screamed at me even though I've done everything he told me to do. I don't understand this. What's wrong with him?" The incongruity of the question made him laugh as soon as it had passed his lips, but he'd meant it, too.

Roshnani said, "Maybe he's finally come to see you really do want to do what's best for him and for Makuran. The years pile up on him the same as they do on everyone else; maybe they're getting through."

"I wish I could believe that—that's he's grown up at last, I mean,"

Abivard said. "But if he has, it's very sudden. I think something else is going on, but for the life of me I have no idea what."

"Well, let's see if we can figure it out," Roshnani said, logical as a Videssian. "Why is he ignoring things that would have made him angry if he were acting the way he usually does?"

"The first thing I thought of is that he's trying to lull Romezan and me into feeling all calm and easy when he really does intend to fall on us like an avalanche," Abivard said. "But if that's so, we'll have to look out for people trying to separate us from the army in the next few days, either that or people trying to murder us right in the middle of it. That could be, I suppose. We'll have to keep an eye out."

"Yes, that certainly is possible," Roshnani agreed. "But again, it's not the way he's been in the habit of behaving. Maybe he really is pleased with you."

"That would be even more out of character," Abivard said, his voice bitter. "He hasn't been, not for years."

"He was . . . better this past winter than the one before," Roshnani said. Odd for her to be defending the King of Kings and for Abivard to be assailing him. "Maybe he's warming up to you again. And then—" She paused before going on thoughtfully. "And then, your sister is drawing nearer to her time every day. Maybe he remembers the family connection."

"Maybe." Abivard sounded imperfectly convinced, even to himself. "And maybe he remembers that, if he does have a boy, all he has to do is die for me to become uncle and maybe regent to the new King of Kings."

"Absent assassins, that doesn't add up," Roshnani said, to which Abivard had to nod. His principal wife sighed. "Day by day we'll see what happens."

"So we will," Abivard said. "One of the things that will happen, by the God, is that I'll drive Maniakes out of the land of the Thousand Cities."

With Romezan's cavalry added to the infantry he'd trained, Abivard knew he had a telling advantage over the force Maniakes had operating between the Tutub and the Tib. Making the telling advantage actually tell was another matter altogether. Maniakes proved an annoyingly adroit defender.

What irked Abivard most was the Avtokrator's mutability. When

Maniakes had had the edge in numbers and mobility, he'd pressed it hard. Now that his foes enjoyed it, he was doing everything he could to keep them from getting the most out of it.

Wrecked canals, little skirmishes, nighttime raids on Abivard's camp—much as Abivard had raided him the year before—all added up to an opponent who might have smeared butter over his body to make himself too slippery to be gripped. And whenever Maniakes got the chance, he would storm another town on the floodplain; another funeral pyre rising from an artificial hillock marked a success for him, a failure for Makuran.

"Never have liked campaigning in this country," Romezan said. "I remember it from the days when Sharbaraz was fighting Smerdis. Too many things can go wrong here."

"Oh, yes, I remember that, too," Abivard said. "And, no doubt, so does Maniakes. He's giving us as much grief as we can handle, isn't he?"

"That he is," the cavalry general said. "He doesn't care about proper battle, does he, not so long as he can have a good time raiding?"

"That's what he's here for," Abivard agreed. "It's worked, too, hasn't it? You're not fighting him in the Videssian westlands, and I'm not sitting in Across going mad trying to figure out how to get to Videssos the city."

"You're right, lord," Romezan said, using the title as one of mild, perhaps even amused, respect. "I wish you'd found a way, too; I'd be lying if I said anything else."

"We haven't got any ships, curse it," Abivard said. "We can't get any ships. Our mages couldn't conjure up the number of ships we'd need. Even if they could, it would be battle magic and liable to fall apart when we needed it most. And even if it didn't, the Videssians are a hundred times the sailors we are. They could sink magical ships the same as any others, I fear."

"You're probably right," Romezan admitted. "What we really need—"

"What we really need," Abivard interrupted, "is a mage who could make a giant silvery bridge over the Cattle Crossing into Videssos the city so our warriors could cross dryshod and not have to worry about Videssians in ships. The only trouble with that is—"

"The only trouble with that is," Romezan said, interrupting

in tarn, "a mage who could bring off that kind of conjuration wouldn't be interested in helping the King of Kings. He'd want to be King of Kings himself or, more likely, king of the world. So it's a good thing there's no such mage."

"So it is," Abivard said with a laugh. "Or it's mostly a good thing, anyhow. But it does mean we'll have to do more of the work ourselves—no, all of the work ourselves, or as near as makes no difference."

A couple of days later a scout brought back a piece of news he'd been dreading and hoping for at the same time: at the head of a troop of Videssian cavalry Tzikas had delivered a formidable attack against Romezan's horsemen. As long as Tzikas stayed in his role, he made a formidable opponent to whichever side he didn't happen to be on at the moment. Since he refused to stay in his role for long, odds were good he wouldn't stay on that particular side forever.

When Abivard passed the news on to Roshnani, she asked, "What are you going to do if he wants to serve Makuran again one day?"

"By the God!" He clapped a hand to his forehead. "You're a step ahead of me there. He probably will want to come back to us one day, won't he?"

"Sooner rather than later," Roshnani guessed. "He's only defamed you, and you don't rule Makuran. He's tried to murder the Avtokrator, and he's renounced Videssos' god for ours. He has to be biding his time in that camp; he can't be happy or comfortable there."

"He's probably renounced the God again for Phos," Abivard said, "or maybe for Skotos, the Videssians' dark god. When he does finally die, I expect there'll be a war in the heavens over whether to torment his soul forever in Skotos' snow and ice or drop it into the Void and make it as if it had never been." The idea struck him as deliciously blasphemous.

At the urging of both Romezan and Turan, Abivard dealt with Tzikas' reappearance in the field by ordering his men to try to kill the renegade whenever they saw him, regardless of what that meant to the rest of the fight. The command struck him as safe enough: Tzikas would not be commanding any vital part of whatever forces were engaged, for Maniakes would not be so stupid as to trust him with anything vital. Abivard remained disappointed that Maniakes had allowed Tzikas to keep breathing, but the Avtokrator must have decided to squeeze whatever use against Makuran he could from the traitor.

Abivard would have loved to squeeze Tzikas—by the neck, if at all possible. Doing that, though, meant catching up to the Videssians. His army, despite the addition of Romezan's cavalry, still moved more slowly than did Maniakes'.

And then the Avtokrator halted on the east side of a large canal that ran north and south through the land of the Thousand Cities. He kept cavalry patrols along the bank of the canal in strength enough to stop Abivard from getting a detachment across it or gaining control of a big enough stretch of bank to let his whole army cross. The Videssians not on patrol resumed the depredations that had grown too familiar over the past couple of campaigning seasons.

Abivard moved more forces forward, expecting to make Maniakes withdraw from the line of the canal; he could not hope to hold it against several simultaneous strong crossings. But Maniakes did not withdraw. Nor did he bring the whole of his army back to the canal to fight the Makuraners once they crossed. He went on about the business of plunder and rapine as if Abivard and his men had fallen into the Void.

"He's making a mistake," Abivard said in glad surprise at a council of war. "How best do we make him pay?"

"Get across the water, smash his patrols, hammer the rest of his army," Romezan said. Abivard looked to his other officers. Sanatruq, who had commanded the cavalry till Romezan had arrived, nodded. So did Turan. So, in the end, did Abivard. Romezan was never going to be accused of subtlety, but you didn't need to be subtle all the time. Sometimes you just had to get in there and do what needed doing. This looked to be one of those times.

As best he could, Abivard readied his host to cross with overwhelming strength and speed. The canal was half a bowshot wide and, peasants said, better than waist-deep everywhere. The Videssians could make getting over it expensive. But instead of concentrating against his force, they rode back and forth, back and forth, along the eastern bank of the canal.

He chose a late-afternoon attack: let the Videssians fight with the sun in their faces for a change. He formed his army with the infantry in the center and the cavalry on both wings. He commanded the right, Romezan the left, and Turan the foot soldiers in the center.

Horns blared. Standard-bearers waved the red-lion banners of Makuran and the smaller flags and streamers marking regiments and companies. Shouting Sharbaraz's name, the army moved forward and splashed down into the canal.

The muddy water was just the temperature of blood. The muck on the bottom had not been stirred up since the last time the canal had been dredged out, however many years before that might have been. When hooves and feet roiled it, a horrible stench rose. Choking a little, Abivard rode farther out into the canal.

He looked back over his shoulder. The rest of the horsemen on the right were following him into the water, shouting abuse at the Videssians on the far bank as they came. Maniakes' men quietly sat their horses and waited for the onslaught. Had they been Abivard's, he would have had them doing more: if nothing else, riding up to the edge of the canal and plying their foes with arrows. But they simply waited and watched. Maybe the might of the Makuraner force had paralyzed them with dread, he thought.

His head swam. He shook it and sent a curse down to the stinking muck that surely made every man who had to endure it reel in the saddle. If the God was kind, he would grant that no one would get woozy enough to fall off his horse and drown in the dirty water.

Here came the bank of the canal after what seemed like much too long in it. Abivard hoped no leeches were clinging to him or to his horse. He spurred the animal up onto solid ground once more. The red disk of the sinking sun glared into his face.

For a moment he simply accepted that, as one does with any report from the eyes. Then he gave a great cry of amazement and alarm, echoed by the more alert among the soldiers he led. They had ridden into the canal with the sun at their backs. Here they were, coming out with it in their eyes.

Abivard looked back over his shoulder again. Here came the whole army up out of the canal. There, on the far bank, the Videssians still sat on their horses, quietly, calmly, as if nothing in the least out of the ordinary had happened. No, not quite like that: a couple of them were sketching circles over the left side of their chests, the gesture they used when invoking their god.

Seeing that made Abivard's wits, stunned till then, begin to work once more: Whether well or poorly he could not guess, but thought started replacing the blank emptiness between his ears. He shouted the first word that came into his mind: "Magic!" A moment later he amplified it: "The Videssians have used magic to keep us from crossing the canal and giving them what they deserve!"

"Aye!" Hundreds, then thousands of voices took up that cry and others like it. Like sunshine burning away fog, fury ousted fear. That did Abivard's heart good. The angrier his men were, the less likely whatever crafty spell the Videssians had used was to seize and hold them. Passion weakened sorcery. That was why both battle magic and love philters failed more often than they succeeded.

"Are we going to let them get away with this outrage?" Abivard shouted. "Are we going to let them blind us with treacherous battle magic?"

"No!" the troopers roared back. "No, by the God! We'll pay them back for the affront!" someone shouted. Had Abivard known who, he would cheerfully have paid the fellow a pound of silver; a paid shill could have done no better.

"Battle magic fails!" Abivard cried. "Battle magic fades! Battle magic feeds on fears. Angry men don't let themselves be seduced. Now that we know what we're up against, we'll show the Videssians their charms and spells are useless. And when we've crossed the canal, we'll punish them doubly for seeking to befool us with their wizards' games."

His men roared approval at him. The cavalrymen brandished their lances. Foot soldiers waved clubs and swung swords. Encouraged by their fury, he booted his horse in its armored flanks and urged it toward the canal once more.

The animal went willingly. Whatever the wizards of Videssos had done, it didn't disturb the beasts. The horse snorted a little as its hooves stirred up the muck on the bottom of the canal, but that was only because new noxious bubbles rose to the surface and burst foully and flatulently.

There, straight ahead, were the same Videssians who had watched Abivard cross the canal—or, rather, try to cross the canal—before. This time, the battle magic having been spotted for what it was, he would ride upon them and spear them out of the saddle one after another. Not normally a man who delighted in battle for its own sake, he wanted to fight now, to purge the rage coursing through him at Maniakes' trickery.

Closer and closer to the Videssians he came. Here was the bank of the canal. Here was his horse setting foot on the bank. He couched his lance, ready to charge hard at the first Videssian he saw.

Here was . . . the setting sun, almost touching the western horizon, shining straight into his face.

Once more he led his army up onto the bank of the canal from which they'd departed. Once more he had no recollection of turning around. Once more he didn't think he *had* turned around. By the shouts and oaths coming from his men, they didn't think they'd turned around, either. But here they were. And there, on the far—the indisputably eastern—bank of the canal the Videssian cavalry patrols trotted back and forth or simply waited, staring into the sunset—the sunset that should have blinded them in the fighting—at the Makuraners who could not reach them.

Abivard gauged that treacherous sun. If he made another try, it would be in darkness. If the Videssians had one magic working, maybe they had more than one. He decided he dared not take the chance. "We camp here tonight," he declared. A moment later he sent messengers to seek Turan and Romezan and order them to his tent.

The first thing he wanted to find out was whether his officers had experienced anything different from his own mystifying trips into and out of the canal. They looked at each other and shook their heads.

"Not me, lord," Turan said. "I was in the canal. I was moving forward all the time. I never turned around—by the God, I didn't! But when I came up onto dry land, it was the same dry land I'd left. I don't know how and I don't know why, but that's what it was."

"And I the same, lord," Romezan said heavily. "I was in the canal. There, ahead, the Videssians sat their horses, waiting for me to spit them like a man putting meat and onions on a skewer to roast in the fire. I spurred my own mount ahead, eager to slaughter them—ahead, not back, I tell you. I came up onto the bank, and it was this bank. As Turan said, how or why I do not know—I am but a poor, stupid fighting man—but it was." He bowed to

Abivard. "Honor to your courage, lord. My bowels turned to jelly within me at the magic. I would never have been so brave as to lead our men into the canal that second time. And they followed you—I followed you—too." He bowed again.

"I don't think I believed it the first time, not all the way through," Abivard said. "And I thought an aroused army would be plenty to beat down Videssian battle magic." He laughed ruefully. "Only shows what I know, doesn't it?"

"What do our own brilliant mages have to say about this?" Turan asked. "I put the question to a couple of the wizards with the infantry: men from the Thousand Cities of the same sort as the ones who worked your canal magic last year, and all they do is gape and mumble. They're as baffled as we are."

Abivard turned to Romezan. "Till now we've had so little need of magic since you arrived, I haven't even thought to ask what sorts of sorcerers you have with you. Are Bozorg and Panteles still attached to the field force?"

"Aye, they are." Romezan hesitated, then said, "Lord, would you trust a Videssian to explain—more, to fight back against— Videssian sorcery? I've kept Panteles with us, but I've hesitated to use him."

"I can see that," Abivard agreed, "but I'd still like to find out what he has to say, and Bozorg, too. And Bozorg should be able to tell if he's lying. If we do decide to use him to try to fight the spell, Bozorg should be able to tell us if he's making an honest effort, too."

Romezan bowed. "This is wisdom. I know it when I hear it." He stepped out of the tent and bawled for a messenger. The man's sandals rapidly pattered away. Romezan came back in and folded broad arms across his chest. "They have been summoned."

Waiting gnawed at Abivard. He'd done too much of it, first in Across, then in the King of Kings' palace, to feel happy standing around doing nothing. He wanted to charge into the canal again—but if he came out once more on the bank from which he started, he feared he'd go mad.

The messenger needed a while to find the wizards in the confusion of a camp Abivard hadn't expected to have to make. At last, though, the fellow returned with them, each warily eyeing the other. They both bowed low to Abivard, acknowledging his rank as far superior to theirs.

"Lord," Bozorg said in Makuraner.

"Eminent sir," Panteles echoed in Videssian, putting Abivard in mind of Tzikas, who presented a problem of which he did not want to be reminded at the moment.

"I think the two of you may have some idea why I've called you here tonight," Abivard said, his voice dry.

Both wizards nodded. They looked at each other, respect mixed with rivalry. Bozorg spoke first: "Lord, whatever this spell may be, it is not battle magic."

"I figured that much out for myself," Abivard answered even more dryly. "If it had been, we would have gotten over on the second try. But if it's not battle magic, what is it?"

"If it were battle magic, it would have been aimed at your soldiers, and their attitude would indeed have influenced the spell," Bozorg said. "Since their attitude did not influence it, I conclude it pertains to the canal, whose emotional state is not subject to flux."

Panteles nodded. Romezan snorted. Turan grinned. Abivard said, "A cogent point, the next question being, What do we do about it?"

The wizards looked at each other again. Again Bozorg spoke for them: "As things stand now, lord, we do not know." Panteles nodded once more.

Romezan snorted again, on an entirely different note. "Glad to have you along, mages; glad to have you along." Panteles looked down at the ground. Bozorg, who had served at the palace of the King of Kings, glared.

Abivard sighed and waved to dismiss both mages. "Bend all your efforts to finding out what Maniakes' wizards have done. When you know—no, when you have even a glimmer—come to me. I don't care what I may be doing; I don't care what hour of the day or night it may be. With you or without you, I intend to keep trying to cross that canal. Come—do you understand?"

Both wizards solemnly nodded.

X

When the sun rose the next morning, Abivard proved as good as his word. He mustered his army, admiring the way the men held their spirit and discipline in the face of the frightening unknown. *Maybe,* he thought, *things will be different this time. The sun is in our face already. Videssian magic often has a lot to do with the sun. If we're already moving toward it, maybe they won't be able to shift us away.*

He thought about spreading that idea among the soldiers but in the end decided against it. Had he been more confident he was right, he might have chosen differently. He knew too well, though, that he was only guessing.

"Forward!" he shouted, raising a hand to his eyes to peer into the morning glare to try to see what the Videssians on the eastern bank of the canal were doing. The answer seemed to be, *Not much.* Maniakes did not have his army drawn up in battle array to meet the Makuraners. A few squadrons of cavalry trotted back and forth; that was all.

"Forward!" Abivard shouted again, and urged his horse down into the muddy water of the canal.

He kept his eye on the sun. *As long as I ride straight toward it, everything should be all right,* he told himself. The canal wasn't that wide. Surely he and his followers could not reverse themselves and go back up onto the bank from which they'd started: not without noticing. No, they couldn't do that ... could they?

Closer and closer came the eastern bank. The day, like all summer days in the land of the Thousand Cities, promised to be scorchingly hot. Already the sun glared balefully into Abivard's face. He blinked. Yes, the far bank was very close now. But the bank up onto which his dripping horse floundered was the western one, with the sun now unaccountably at his back.

And here came his army after him, storming up to overwhelm the place they'd just left. Their shouts of amazement and anger and despair said everything that needed saying. No, almost everything: the other thing that needed saying was that he and his army weren't going to be able to cross that cursed canal—the canal that might as well have been literally cursed—till they figured out and overcame whatever sorcery Maniakes was using to thwart them.

Glumly, Abivard ordered the army to reestablish the camp it had just struck. He spent the next couple of hours pacing through it, doing his best to lift the soldiers' sagging spirits. He knew that best would have been better had his own spirits been anywhere but at the bottom of the sea. But he did not have to show the men that, and he didn't.

At last he went back to his own pavilion. He didn't know exactly what he'd do there: getting drunk seemed as good a plan as any, since he couldn't come to grips with the Videssians. But when he got to the tent, he found Bozorg and Panteles waiting for him.

"I think I have the answer, eminent sir!" Panteles exclaimed in high excitement.

"I think this Videssian is out of his mind, lord: utterly mad," Bozorg declared, folding his arms across his chest. "I think he wants only to waste your time, to deceive you, and to give the victory to Maniakes."

"I think you are as jealous as an ugly girl watching her betrothed talking to her pretty sister," Panteles retorted—not a comparison a Makuraner was likely to use, not in a land of sequestered women, but a telling one even so.

"I think I'm going to knock your heads together," Abivard said judiciously. "Tell me whatever you have to tell me, Panteles. I'll judge whether it's trickery. If it is, I'll do as I think best."

Panteles bowed. "As you say, eminent sir. Here." He displayed a length of leather about as long as Abivard's forearm: most likely a piece cut from a belt. Joining the ends, he held them together with thumb and forefinger, then pointed to the resulting circle with his other hand. "How many sides does the strap have, eminent sir?"

"How many sides?" Abivard frowned. "What foolishness is this?" Maybe Bozorg had known what he was talking about. "It has two, of course: an inside and an outside."

"And a strap across the Videssian's backside," Bozorg added.

But Panteles seemed unperturbed. "Just so," he agreed. "You can trace it with your finger if you like." He held the leather circle out so Abivard could do just that. Abivard dutifully did, hoping against hope Panteles wasn't talking to hear himself talk, as Videssians often did. "Now—" Panteles said.

Bozorg broke in: "Now, lord, he shows you idiotic nonsense. By the God, he should be made to answer for his foolishness with the lash!"

Anything that could so anger the Makuraner mage was either idiotic nonsense, as he'd said, or exactly the opposite. "As I said, I will judge," Abivard told Bozorg. He turned to Panteles. "Go on. Show me this great discovery of yours, or whatever it is, and explain how it ties up all our troubles like a length of twine around a stack of cured hides."

"It's not my discovery, and I don't know if it ties up our troubles or not," Panteles said. Oddly, Abivard liked him more for that, not less. The more spectacular a claim, the less likely it was to be justified.

Panteles held up the length of leather once more and again shaped it into a continuous band. This time, though, he gave it a half twist before joining the two ends together between his thumb and index finger. Bozorg gestured as if to ward off the evil eye, hissing, "Trickery."

Panteles took no notice either of him or of Abivard's hand upraised in warning. The Videssian wizard said, "This was discovered in the Sorcerers' Collegium in Videssos the city some years ago by a certain Voimios. I don't know whether it's magic or not in any formal sense of the word. Maybe it's only trickery, as the learned Bozorg claims." Like any Videssian worth his salt, he used irony as a stiletto. "Whatever it is, it's interesting. How many sides does the strap have now?" He held it up so Abivard could trace out his answer as he had before.

"What do you mean, how many sides does it have?" Abruptly, Abivard regretted doubting Bozorg. "It has to have two sides, the same as it did before."

"Does it?" Panteles' smile was mild, benign. "Show me with your finger, eminent sir, if you'd be so kind."

With the air of someone humoring a madman, Abivard ran his finger around the outside of the strap. A moment later, he would run it around the inside, and a moment after that he would give Panteles what he deserved for making him the butt of what had to be a foolish joke.

But in tracing the length of leather with his finger, he somehow found himself back where he'd begun after having touched every finger's breadth of it. "Wait a moment," he said sharply. "Let me try that again." This time he paid closer attention to his work. But paying closer attention didn't seem to matter. Again he traced the entire length of leather and returned to his starting point.

"Do you see, eminent sir?" Panteles said as Abivard stared down at his own finger as if it had betrayed him. "Voimios' strap—that's the name it took on at the Sorcerers' Collegium—has only one side, not two."

"That's impossible," Abivard said. Then he looked at his finger again. It looked as if it knew better.

"You just made a continuous line from your starting point back to your starting point," Panteles said politely. "How could you do that if you went from one side to another? You just got there backward and were taken by surprise."

As Panteles had doubtless meant them to, the words hung in the air. "Wait," Abivard said. "Let me think. You're trying to tell me Maniakes' wizards have turned the canal into a strap of Voimios—is that what you called it?"

"Close enough, eminent sir," Panteles said.

"Drivel!" Bozorg said. He snatched the leather strap out of Panteles' hand and threw it to the ground. "It's a fraud, a fake, a trick. There's no magic whatever to it, only deception."

"What do you have to say to that?" Abivard asked Panteles.

"Eminent sir, I never claimed there was any magic in Voimios' strap," the Videssian wizard answered. "I offered it as analogy, not proof. Besides—" He stooped and picked up the length of leather

Bozorg had thrown down. "—this is a flat thing. To twist it so it has only one side, all you need do is this." He gave it the deft half twist that turned it baffling. "But if you were going to make it so that something with length and width and height turned back on itself the same way, the only twist I can imagine to do such a thing is a magical one."

Trying again and again to cross the canal and failing had already done more strange things to Abivard's imagination than he'd ever wanted. He turned to Bozorg. "Have *you* got a different idea how the Videssians could have turned us back on ourselves?"

"No, lord," Bozorg admitted. "But the one this Videssian puts forward is ridiculous on the face of it. His precious Voimios probably got some of his horse's harness on poorly, then spent the next twenty years cadging cups of wine on the strength of it."

"Are you denying what Panteles says is true, or are you only disparaging it?" Abivard asked pointedly.

The question had sharp teeth. Bozorg might have been furious, but he was no fool. He said, "What he said about the strap may be true, I suppose, no matter how absurd it sounds. But how could anyone take seriously this nonsense about twisting a canal back on itself?"

"I'd say some thousands of soldiers take the notion seriously, or would if they heard it," Panteles shot back. "It happened to them, after all."

"So it did," Abivard said. "I was one of them, and thinking of it still makes me shiver." He looked from Panteles to Bozorg and back again. "Do you think the two of you, working together—" He put special stress on those words. "—can find out whether what happened to the canal is the magical equivalent of a Voimios strap?"

Panteles nodded. A moment later, more grudgingly, Bozorg did, too. Panteles said, "Making a magic of this sort cannot have been easy for Maniakes' wizards. If the traces of the sorcery linger on this plane, we shall find them."

"And if you do?" Abivard asked. "What then?"

"Untwisting the canal should be easier for us than twisting it was for them—if that's what they did," Panteles answered. "Restoring a natural condition takes far less sorcery than changing away from what is natural."

"Mm, I can see the sense in that," Abivard said. "How soon

will you be able to find out if Maniakes has turned the canal into a strap of Voimios?"

Bozorg stirred. Abivard looked his way. He said, "Lord, do you feel easy about using a Videssian to fight the Videssians?"

Abivard had been wrestling with that question since he had realized magic was holding him away from Maniakes' army. He'd worried about it less since Panteles had started his elaborate theoretical explanation: any man dedicated enough to put so much effort into figuring out what might have gone into a spell wouldn't be content unless he could have a hand in unraveling it, too . . . would he?

"How say you, Panteles?" Abivard asked.

"Eminent sir, I say I never imagined turning a Voimios strap from an amusement into a piece of creative sorcery," Panteles answered. "To understand how that's done and then to figure out a spell to counter it—I'm lucky to be living in such exciting times, when anything seems possible."

His eyes gleamed. Abivard recognized the expression on his pinched, narrow face. Soldiers with that exalted look would ride to their deaths without flinching; minstrels who had it crafted songs that lived for generations. Panteles would go where knowledge and energy and inspiration took him and would pursue his target with the eagerness of a bridegroom going to his bride.

"I think it will be all right," Abivard said to Bozorg. "And if it isn't all right, I trust your skill to hold disaster away from us."

"Lord, you may honor me beyond my worth," the Makuraner mage murmured.

"I don't think so," Abivard said heartily. "And as I've told you, I expect you to work with him. If his idea turns out to be wrong-headed after all, I'll need to hear that from you so we can figure out what to try next."

He hoped with all his heart that Panteles and Bozorg would be able to find a way around—or through—Maniakes' magic. If they could, the sorcery would be a one-time wonder: if not, every time Makuraners tried to clash with Videssians, they would find themselves going back the way from which they had come. That would be a worse disaster than defeat in battle.

"What one mage has done, another may undo," Panteles declared. To that Bozorg assented with a cautious nod.

"Finding out what the mage has done can be interesting, though," Abivard remarked.

"Truth, eminent sir. I do not know if I have proposed the correct explanation, either," Panteles said. "One of the many things I need to learn—"

"Don't just stand there." Abivard realized he was being unfair, but urgency counted for more. "Go find out what you can by whatever means you can. I intend to send riders up and down the canal—provided they don't think they're riding north when they're riding south or the other way around. If we can force a crossing somewhere else—"

"Then the notion of the Voimios strap becomes moot," Panteles interrupted.

Abivard shook his head. "Not quite. Oh, we might be able to get around it this one time, but it would keep on being a trick Maniakes has and we don't. He could use it again, say, in a mountain pass where we didn't have any choice about how we tried to get at him. If we can, I want us to have a way to beat this spell so it doesn't stay in the Avtokrator's arsenal, if you take my meaning."

Both Panteles and Bozorg bowed as if to say they not only understood but agreed. Abivard waved them off to begin their investigation. At his shouted orders, horsemen did gather to ride off up and down the canal. But before they set out, one of them asked, "Uh, lord, how are we to know whether the spell still holds?"

Abivard wished he hadn't asked that. Sighing, he answered, "The only way I can think of is to ride out into the canal and try to cross it. If you do, you've passed the point where the Videssians' magic works. If you don't—"

One of the riders committed the enormity of interrupting the army commander: "If we don't—if we come back where we started from—and we haven't gone crazy before then, that's when we know."

The other horsemen nodded. The fellow had made a pretty fair joke, or what would have been a pretty fair joke under other circumstances, but none of them laughed or even smiled. Neither did Abivard; nor did he stand on his dignity or rank. He said, "That magic is plenty to drive anyone mad, so my best guess is that we've all gone mad already, and getting bitten by it one more time won't do any harm."

"You have a good way of looking at things, lord," said the fellow who had interrupted him. He rode south along the canal. Some men followed him; others headed north.

Was it a good way of looking at things? Abivard didn't know. If Maniakes' magic extended a good distance up and down the canal, some of those men were liable to have to endure having their world twisted several times, not once alone. You could grow used to almost anything . . . but to *that*?

Something else occurred to him: was the canal folded back on itself for the Videssians, too? If they tried to cross from east to west to attack him, what would happen? Would they make it over to his side of the canal, or would they, too, end up riding out onto the bank from which they'd departed? The question was so intriguing, he almost summoned Bozorg and Panteles so he could ask it. All that restrained him was the thought that they already had enough to worry about.

And so did he. The riders he'd sent north along the canal came back perhaps sooner than he'd expected with the news that the spell, whether it was some larger version of Voimios' strap or not, extended in that direction as far as they'd traveled. They hadn't traveled so far as he'd hoped, but the fear on their faces said they'd gone into the canal as often as they could stand.

Men who'd ridden south began coming back to Abivard's camp, too, not all at once like those who'd gone the other way but a few at a time, some going back into the canal after others could bear it no more. Whether they came soon or late, they had the same news as the men who had traveled north: when they tried to go east over the canal, they found themselves unable.

Last of all to return was the fellow who had suggested that going into the canal would make a man crazy. By the time he came back, the sun was setting in the west. Abivard had begun to wonder whether he'd gone into the canal and never come out.

He shook his fist at the sun, saying, "I've seen that thing too many times—may it drop into the Void. I tried to ride away from it a dozen times, maybe more, this afternoon, and I ended up coming right back at it every one of them. Sorry lord; that spell goes on a long way south."

"No cause for you to be sorry," Abivard answered. "I'd call you a hero for braving the canal more than anyone else did."

"A hero?" The rider shook his head. "I'll tell you what I'd call me, and that's a bloody fool. By your leave, lord, I'll go off and polish my armor—keep it from rusting as best I can, eh?" Abivard nodded permission. Sketching a salute, the soldier strode off.

Abivard muttered something foul under his breath. Maniakes' mages could certainly hold the spell in place for half a day's ride, or perhaps a bit less, to either side of his own position. That meant that shifting camp wasn't likely to do much good, because the Videssians were liable either to move or to extend the spell to his new position.

If he couldn't go around the twisted canal, he'd have to go through it. Going through it meant beating Maniakes' magic. Between them, Bozorg and Panteles would have to come up with some answers.

Summoning them to his tent, Abivard said, "Can you cut through the spell and let us cross?"

"Cutting a Voimios strap is less easy than it sounds, eminent sir," Panteles said. "When you do cut one lengthwise, do you know what you get?"

"I was going to say two thinner ones, but that would be too simple and obvious, wouldn't it?" Abivard said, and Panteles nodded. "All right, what do you get?" Abivard asked. "A bowl of oxtail soup? Three arkets and a couple of coppers? A bad case of the itch?"

Panteles gave him a reproachful look; maybe mighty Makuraner marshals, to his way of thinking, weren't allowed to be absurd. He reached into a pouch he wore on his belt and pulled out a Voimios strap made from thin leather and sewn together at the ends so he didn't need to hold them between his long, thin, agile thumb and forefinger. "See for yourself, eminent sir, and you will better understand the difficulty we face."

"All right, I will." Abivard drew a sharp dagger, poked it through the leather, and began to cut. He worked slowly, carefully, methodically; a pair of shears would have been better for the job, but he had none. When he got the sharp strap cut nearly all the way around, he thought Panteles had been lying to him, for it did look as if it might split in two, as a simple ring would have. But then he made the last cut, and exclaimed in surprise: he still had one twisted strap, but twice as long and half as wide as it had been before.

"This shows some of the complications we face," Panteles said.

"Some means of countering the magic are caught up in its twists and prove to be of no use against it."

"Yes, I see," Abivard said. "This is what happens when you cut *with* the spell. But when you do this—" He cut the strap across instead of lengthwise. "—things look easier." He handed Panteles the simple length of leather.

The wizard took it and looked at it thoughtfully. "Yes, eminent sir, that is the effect we are trying to create. I shall do everything in my power to imitate the elegance of your solution." He rolled up the strap into a tight little cylinder, put it back in his belt pouch, and went away.

Abivard awaited results with growing impatience. Every day he and his army stayed stuck on the western side of the canal was another day in which Maniakes had free rein in the east. Maniakes had done enough—too much—damage even when Abivard had opposed him. Without opposition...

For a wonder, both Panteles and Bozorg looked pleased with themselves. "We can break this spell, lord," Bozorg said to Abivard.

Panteles shook his head. "No, eminent sir," he said. "Breaking it is the wrong way to express what we do. But we can, I think, cut across it as you did with the Voimios strap a few days ago. That will produce the desired effect, or so we believe."

"I say breaking is a better way to describe what we do," Bozorg said. He and Panteles glared at each other.

"I don't care what you call it or how you describe it," Abivard said. "So long as your spell—or whatever it is—works, names don't matter. Argue all you like about them—later."

A few Videssian horsemen still patrolled the eastern bank of the canal—not so many now, for Maniakes must have concluded that his spell was keeping Abivard trapped on the other side. At first the Avtokrator's disposition of his army had been cautious, but now he went about the business of destruction as if Abivard and his men were no longer anywhere near.

Maybe we'll give him a surprise, Abivard thought. *Or maybe we'll just end up here again, where we started. Have to find out, though. That's the worst thing that can happen, and how are we worse off if it does?*

Panteles and Bozorg began to chant, the one in Videssian and the other in the Makuraner language. Bozorg sprinkled sparkling crystals into a bowl of water, which turned bright yellow. Abivard looked out to the canal. The water there did not turn bright yellow but remained muddy brown.

Panteles, chanting still, held a knife over a small fire of fragrant wood till the blade glowed red. Then he plunged it into the bowl of yellow water. A hiss and a puff of strong-smelling steam rose from the water. Still holding the blade in his right hand, he took from his belt pouch a Voimios strap like the one he had given to Abivard to cut lengthwise.

He called on Phos. At the same time, either to complement or to confound his invocation, Bozorg called on the God through the Prophets Four. Panteles took the knife and cut the twisted strap of leather with it—cut it clean across, as Abivard had done, so that it became a plain strap once more, not one with the peculiar properties the Voimios strap displayed.

Abivard looked out toward the canal again. He didn't know what he would see. He didn't know if he would see anything. Maybe the spell would produce no visible effect. Maybe it wouldn't work—that was always possible, too.

Bozorg and Panteles stood as if they didn't know whether the spell was working, either. Watching them, Abivard forgot about the canal for a moment. When Panteles gave a sharp gasp, he stared at the Videssian, not at the muddy ditch. Then the Videssian mage pointed to it.

The surface of the canal roiled and bubbled. That was how it began. Slowly, slowly, over minutes, the water in the canal pulled away from itself: that was how Abivard described it to himself afterward. When the process was done, the muddy bottom of the canal lay exposed to the sun—it was as if someone had taken a knife to the waterway and cut it in two.

"The law of similarity," Panteles said in Videssian.

"Like yields like," Bozorg said in the Makuraner tongue—two ways of putting the same thought into words.

"Come on!" Abivard shouted to his warriors, who gaped at the gap in the canal. "Now we can reach the Videssians. Now we can make them pay for turning us the wrong way time after time." He sprang onto his horse. "Are we going to let them get away with what they did to us, or are we going to punish them?"

"Punish!" the Makuraner soldiers howled, savage as a pack of wolves on a cold winter night. Abivard had to boot his horse hard to make sure he entered the canal first. The going was slow, for the mud was thick and slimy and pulled at the horse's legs. But the beast went on.

In the water piled up to either side of the muddy, stinking canal bottom, Abivard saw a fish. It stared out at him, mouth opening and closing, as if it were a stupid old man. He wondered what it thought of him and then whether it thought at all.

Up toward the eastern bank of the canal he rode. Despite the magic of Panteles and Bozorg, he still feared he would somehow end up back on the west side of the canal again. But he didn't. Floundering and then gaining steadiness, his horse carried him up onto the eastern side at last.

Had the Videssian soldiers there wanted to make a fight of it, they might well have prevented his army from gaining a lodgment. The opening the two mages had made in the canal was not very wide, and only a few horses could get through it at any one time. A determined stand might have held up the whole Makuraner force.

But the Videssians, who had seemed taken aback by the wizards' success in breaking or breaking through their spell, also seemed startled that the Makuraners were exploiting that success so vigorously. Instead of staying and trying to hold back Abivard and his men, they rode off as fast as their horses would carry them. Maybe they were taking Maniakes the news of what had just happened. Had Abivard been Maniakes, he would have been less than delighted to see them come. As things were, he was delighted to see them go.

Later, he wished he had sent men straight after them. At the moment he was just glad he and his followers wouldn't have to fight them. Instead of pursuit, what he thought about was getting as many men across the canal as he could before either the sorcery Bozorg and Panteles had cobbled together or the two men themselves collapsed.

The bulk of the army did get across before Panteles, who had been swaying like a tree in a high wind, toppled to the ground. As he did, the suspended water in the canal came together with a wet slap. Some of the foot soldiers who were caught in it drowned; more, though, struggled forward and crawled out onto the eastern bank, wet and dripping but alive.

At first Abivard and his companions were so busy helping them to dry land, he had no time for thought. Then he realized the soldiers were reaching the eastern bank, not being thrown back to the west. The spell the Videssian and Makuraner mages had used, though vanished now, had left the canal permanently untwisted. It was, in short, as it had been before Maniakes' wizards had begun meddling with it.

By then Bozorg and some of the other men still on the western bank of the canal had flipped water into Panteles' face. Free of the burden of having to maintain the spell, the Videssian wizard managed to stay on his feet and even rejoin Abivard on the eastern side of the waterway.

"Well done!" Abivard greeted him.

"For which I thank you, eminent sir," Panteles answered. "The relationship between the Voimios strap and the nature of the spell laid on the canal did indeed prove to be close to that which I had envisioned. This conformation between theory and practice is particularly satisfying on those rare occasions when it may be observed."

"You were right," Bozorg said. "You were right, you were right, you were right. By the Prophets Four, I admit it." He spoke as a man might when publicly paying off a bet.

Panteles peered around. Now that the Makuraner army had reached it, the eastern bank of the canal seemed little different from the western: flat, muddy land with a lot of soldiers scattered across it. The Videssian wizard turned to Abivard. "Having gained this side of the canal, eminent sir, what will you do next?"

It was a good question and not one Abivard could answer on the spur of the moment. For the past several days getting across the canal had so consumed him, he'd lost track of the reasons for which he'd sought to do so. One thing, however, remained clear: "I am going to hunt Maniakes down and fight him when I do."

Romezan had never let that escape his mind. Already, with the last of the soldiers across the canal, still muddy and soaked, he was shouting, "Form up, the God curse you. Don't stand around there wasting time. The Videssian patrols rode off to the southeast. You think they went that way by accident? In a horse's pizzle they did! If that's not where we'll find Maniakes, I'll eat my scabbard, metal fittings and all."

Abivard thought he was right. Maniakes hadn't quite taken for granted the Makuraners' inability to cross the canal, but he had left behind a force too small to fight their whole army, especially after failing to fight when Abivard and the first few men following him had floundered up onto the bank the Videssians had been holding without effort. If they weren't going to fight, the only useful service they could perform was warning the Avtokrator. To do that, they'd have to go where he was. Abivard's army would follow them there.

He raised his voice, adding his outcry to Romezan's relentless shouts. The soldiers responded more slowly than he would have wanted but not, he supposed, more slowly than was to be expected after the trouble they'd had reaching the eastern bank of the canal.

And as the men shook themselves out into a line of march, excitement gradually began to seep into them. They cheered Abivard when he rode up and down the line. "Wasn't for you, lord, we'd *still* be stuck over there," somebody called. That made the cheers come louder.

Abivard wondered if Maniakes knew his magic had been defeated even before soldiers had ridden to him with the news. He would have a wizard—more likely wizards—with him. Breaking the Videssian spell probably would have produced a quiver of some sort in the world, a quiver a wizard could sense.

Because of that suspicion, Abivard reinforced what would have been his normal vanguard with picked fighting men who did not usually move at the very fore. He also spread his net of scouts and outriders farther around the army than he normally might have. If trouble threatened, he wanted warning as soon as he could get it.

"Be particularly careful and alert," he warned the scouts. "Tzikas is liable to be commanding the Videssian rear guard. If he is, you'll have to look for something nasty and underhanded. I wish I could guess what, but I can't. All I can tell you is, keep your eyes open."

For the first day after crossing the canal he wondered if Maniakes had bothered with a rear guard. His own army surged forward without resistance. They made so much progress, he almost felt as if they'd made up for all the time they'd spent trapped on the far side of the canal.

When he said that to Roshnani after they'd finally camped for the night, she gave him the look she reserved for times when he'd been especially foolish. "Don't be absurd," she said. "You can't make up that much time in one day, and you know it."

"Well, yes, so I do," he admitted, and gave her a look of his own. "I'd bet none of the great minstrels ever had a wife like you." His voice went falsetto: "No, you can't say his sword sang, dear. Swords don't sing. And was his armor really too heavy for ten ordinary men to lift, let alone wear? That doesn't sound very likely to me. Why don't you change it?"

Roshnani made as if to pick up the pot of saffron rice and black cherries that sat between them and dump it over his head. But she was laughing, too. "Wicked man," she said.

"Thank you," he said, making both of them laugh some more. But he quickly grew serious again. "If the magic this morning had failed, I don't know what I would have done. I don't know what the army would have done."

"The worst you could have done would have been to lay down your command and go back to Vek Rud domain. There are still times I wish you'd done it after Sharbaraz refused to let you summon Romezan."

"That worked out well in spite of Sharbaraz," Abivard answered. "Romezan is like me: he sees what the realm needs and goes ahead and takes care of it no matter what the King of Kings may think of the matter."

Roshnani sniffed. "The King of Kings is supposed to see what the realm needs and take care of it himself. He shouldn't need to rely on others to do that for him. If he can't do it, why is he the one to rule Makuran?"

She spoke in a low voice and looked around before the words left her mouth to make sure no servant—or even her children— could hear. Abivard understood that; unlike Romezan, he found the idea of criticizing the King of Kings daunting at best. And Roshnani wasn't just criticizing. She was suggesting Sharbaraz didn't belong on the throne if he didn't do a better job. And if he didn't belong on that throne, who did?

Abivard answered in a voice as soft as the one his principal wife had used: "I don't want to rebel against Sharbaraz King of Kings. Can you imagine me trying to lord it over the eunuchs in the palace? I only wish Sharbaraz would tend to ruling the realm and let all of us who serve him tend to our own soup without his always sticking his finger in and giving it a stir."

"He *is* the King of Kings, and he knows it," Roshnani said with a wintry sigh. "He knows it too well, maybe. Whenever he can stick his finger in, he feels he has to, as if he wouldn't be ruling if he didn't."

"I've spent a good part of the past ten years and more hoping—wishing—you were wrong," Abivard said, sighing, too. "I'm beginning to think you're right. Pound me on the head with a hammer often enough and ideas do sometimes get in. From brief acquaintance with his father, it's in his blood."

"It might not have been so bad if he hadn't had the throne stolen from him once," Roshnani said.

Abivard gulped down his wine. "It might not have been so bad," he said, spacing his words out to emphasize them, "if Smerdis had kept on being King of Kings and no one had ever found out Sharbaraz was hidden away in Nalgis Crag stronghold."

When the words were out of his mouth, he realized he'd spoken treason—retroactive treason, since Smerdis the usurper was long dead, but treason nonetheless. He waited to hear how Roshnani would react to it. Calmly, she said, "Had matters turned out so, you wouldn't be brother-in-law to the King of Kings, you know."

"Do you think I care?" he returned. "I don't think my sister would have been less happy if she'd stayed married to Pradtak of Nalgis Crag domain than she is married to Sharbaraz of Makuran. No more happy, maybe, but not less." He sighed again. "You can't tell about such things, though. Smerdis was busy paying the Khamorth tribute, if you'll remember. That would have touched off a revolt in the Northwest sooner or later. As well, maybe, that we had a proper King of Kings to head it."

"Maybe." Roshnani emptied her wine cup, too. "All these might-have-beens can make you dizzier than wine if you spend too much time thinking about them."

"Everything is simple now," Abivard said. "All we have to do is beat Maniakes."

First they had to come to grips with Maniakes. As Abivard had already discovered, that wasn't easy, not when Maniakes didn't care to be gripped. But having defeated the Avtokrator's best sorcery—or what he sincerely hoped was the Avtokrator's best sorcery—he pursued him with more confidence than he would have shown before.

In case his sincere hopes proved mistaken, he stopped ignoring Bozorg and Panteles and had the two wizards ride together in a wagon near his own. Sometimes they got on as well as a couple of brothers. Sometimes they quarreled—also like a couple of brothers. As long as they weren't working magic to do away with each other, Abivard pretended not to see.

He sent his part of cavalry out in a wide sweep, first to find Maniakes' army and then to slow it down so he could come up with the main body of his army and fight the Videssians. "This is what we couldn't do before," he said enthusiastically, riding along with Turan. "We can move horsemen out ahead and make the Videssians turn and fight, hold them in place long enough for the rest of us to come forward and smash them."

"If all goes well, we can," Turan said. "Their rear guard has been fighting hard, though, to keep us from getting hold of the main force Maniakes is leading."

"They can only do that for so long, though," Abivard said. "The land between the Tutub and the Tib isn't like the Pardrayan steppe: it doesn't go on forever. After a while you get pushed off the floodplain and out into the scrub country. You can't keep an army alive out there."

"We talked about that last winter," his lieutenant answered. "Maniakes didn't even try then. He just crossed the Videssian westlands till he came to a port, then sailed away, no doubt laughing at us. He could do the same again, every bit as easily."

"Yes, I suppose he could," Abivard said. "He could go on to Serrhes, too, in the interior, the way Sharbaraz did all those years ago. I don't think he'll do either one, though. When he came into the land of the Thousand Cities last year, he had doubts. He was tentative; he wasn't sure at first that his soldiers were reliable. He's not worried about that anymore. He knows his men can fight. If he sees a spot he likes, he'll give battle there. He aimed to wreck us when he came back this year."

"He almost did it a couple of times, too," Turan agreed. "And then, when that didn't work, he tried to drive us mad with the magic his wizards put on the canal." He chuckled. "That was such a twisted scheme, I wonder if Tzikas was the one who thought of it."

Abivard started to answer seriously before realizing Turan was joking. Joke or not, it wasn't the most unlikely notion Abivard had ever heard. As he'd learned from painful experience, Tzikas was devious enough to have done exactly what Turan had said.

Abivard soon had reason to pride himself on his own predictive powers. Not far from the headwaters of the Tutub, where the stream still flowed swift and foamy over stones before taking a generally calmer course, Maniakes chose a stretch of high ground and made it very plain to his pursuers that he intended to be pursued no more.

"We'll smash him!" Romezan shouted. "We'll smash him and be rid of him once and for all." After a moment he added, "Won't miss him a bit once he's gone, either."

"That would be very fine," Abivard agreed. "The longer I look at that position, though, the more I think we'll come out of it like lamb's meat chopped up for the spit if we're not careful."

"They're only Videssians," Romezan said. "It's not as if they're going to come charging down at us while we're advancing on them."

"No, I suppose not," Abivard said. "But an uphill charge—and it would be a long uphill charge—doesn't strike with so much force as one on level ground. And if I know anything about Maniakes, it's that he doesn't intend just to sit up there and await our charge. He'll do something to break it up and keep it from hitting as hard as it should."

"What can he do?" Romezan demanded.

"I don't know," Abivard said. "I wish I did."

"And I wish you wouldn't shy at shadows," Romezan said. "Maniakes is only a man, and soldier for soldier our horsemen are better than his. He can make a river flip—or he could till we figured out how to stop him—but he can't make his whole cursed army leap up in the air and land in our rear and on both flanks at the same time, now, can he?"

"No," Abivard admitted.

"Well, then," Romezan said triumphantly, as if he'd proved his point. Maybe he thought he had; he was as straightforward and aggressive in argument as he was in leading his cavalry into action.

Abivard shook his head. "Go straight into battle against the Videssians and you're asking to come to grief. And not all fields are as open and tempting as they look. Remember how Peroz King of Kings died, leading the flower of the soldiery of Makuran against the Khamorth across what looked like an ordinary stretch of steppe. If my horse hadn't stepped in a hole and broken a leg at the very start of that charge, I expect I would have died there, too, along with my father and my brother and three half brothers."

Romezan scowled but had no quick comeback. Every Makuraner noble family, whether from the Seven Clans or from the lesser nobility, had suffered grievous loss out on the Pardrayan steppe. After that fight how could you argue for a headlong charge and against at least a little caution?

Sanatruq remained impetuous even after Abivard's blunt warning. "What are we going to do, then, lord?" he demanded. "Did we find a way across the canal only to decide we needn't have bothered? If we're not going to fight the Videssians, we might as well have stayed where we were."

"I never said we weren't going to fight them," Abivard said. "But don't you think doing it on our terms instead of theirs matters?"

The argument should have been telling. The argument in fact was telling—to Abivard. Romezan let out a sigh. "I should have stayed in the Videssian westlands and sent Kardarigan to you with this part of the field army. The two of you would have got on better than you and I do, both of you being . . . cautious. But I thought a cautious man better there, where there were towns to guard, and a fighter better here, where there were battles to wage. Maybe I was wrong."

That hurt. Abivard turned away so Romezan wouldn't see him wince. And had Romezan not been intrepid enough to leave the westlands and disobey Sharbaraz's order against doing it, to say nothing of being intrepid enough to pitch right into the Videssians when he found them, Abivard would have been in no condition to hold this conversation now. Still—

"A baker thinks bread is the answer to every question," he said, "while a farrier is sure it's horseshoes. No wonder a battler wants to go straight into the fray. But I don't merely want to fight Maniakes—I want to crush him if we can. If thinking things over instead of wading straight in will help us do that, I'd sooner think."

Romezan's bow was anything but submissive. "There he is," he said, pointing toward the banner with a gold sunburst on blue that marked the Avtokrator's position. "He's got water right behind him, enough to keep him from getting thirsty but not enough to keep him from going over it if he has to. He's got the high ground. If he doesn't have plenty of food, I'll be amazed and so will you. He's got no reason to move, in other words. If we want him, we have to go at him. He's not going to come to us."

All those comments were true. Abivard had been studying the ground and said, "Don't you think the slope is less there on his right—our left?"

"If you say so, lord," Romezan answered, prepared to be magnanimous now that he scented victory. "Do you want the attack to go in on our left? We can do that, of course."

Abivard shook his head, and that made Romezan and Sanatruq look suspicious again. He said, "I want to make it seem as if the main attack is going in on our left. I want Maniakes to think that and to shift his forces to meet it. But once he's gone for the feint, I want the true attack to come from the right."

Romezan toyed with one spiky, waxed mustache tip. "Aye, lord, that's good," he said at last. "We give them something they don't expect that way."

"And you'll want the foot to hold the center, the way you've been doing lately?" Turan asked.

"Just so," Abivard agreed. As Romezan was in the habit of doing, the noble from the Seven Clans looked down his considerable nose at the mere mention of infantry. Before taking over the city garrisons Abivard would have done the same thing. He knew what these men were worth, though. They would fight and fight hard. He slapped Turan on the shoulder. "Get them ready."

"Aye, lord." His lieutenant hurried away.

Something else occurred to Abivard. "When we move against the Videssians, Romezan, I will command on the left and you on the right."

Romezan stared at him. "Lord . . . you would give me the honor of leading the chief attack? I am in your debt, but are you certain you do not damage your own honor with this generosity?"

"The realm comes first," Abivard said firmly. "Maniakes will see me there on the left. He'll recognize my banners, and he'll likely recognize me, too. When he sees me there, that will make him more certain the division of the army I command will be the one to try to smash him. He will reason as you do, Romezan:

how could I give up the place of honor to another? But honor lies in victory, and for victory over the Videssians I gladly give up this superficial honor."

Romezan bowed very low, as if Abivard were far superior to him in rank. "Lord, you could do worse than instructing the Seven Clans on the nature of honor."

"To the Void with that. If they want instruction, we've sent them enough Videssian slaves to serve them as pedagogues for the next hundred years. What we have now is a battle to fight." Abivard stared over toward the distant banners of Videssos that marked the Avtokrator's position. Outwitting Maniakes got trickier every time he tried it, but he'd managed to come up with something new. Like a boy with a new toy, he could hardly wait to try it.

"Let me understand you, lord," Romezan said. "You will want my men to hang back somewhat and not show their true courage—they should act as if the steepness of the ground troubles them."

"That's what I have in mind," Abivard agreed, his earlier quarrel with Romezan almost forgotten. "I'll press the attack on my flank as hard as I can and do everything I know how to do to draw as many Videssians to me as will come. Meanwhile, you, poor fellow, will be having all sorts of trouble—till the right moment comes."

"I won't be too soon, lord," Romezan promised. "And you can bet I won't be too late, either." He sounded very sure of himself.

For the first time since his recall from Across Abivard had a proper Makuraner army, not some slapped-together makeshift, to lead into battle against the Videssians. Since Likinios' overthrow, he'd won whenever he had led a proper army against them. Indeed, they'd fled before him time after time. He eyed his men. They seemed full of quiet confidence. They were used to beating the Videssians, too.

He rode to the front of the left wing. On this field he wanted his presence widely advertised. Banners blazoned with the red lion of Makuran fluttered all around him. *Here I am, the commander of this host,* they shouted to the Videssians up on their low rise. *I'm going to lead the main attack—of course I am. Pay me plenty of attention.*

Maniakes, by his own banners, led from the center of his army, the most common Videssian practice. He'd invited battle, which meant he felt confident, too. He'd beaten the Kubrati barbarians. He'd beaten Abivard more often than not—when Abivard had been leading a patchwork force. Did that really make him think he could beat the Makuraner field army? If it did, Abivard intended to show him he was wrong.

Abivard nodded to the horn players. "Sound the advance," he said, and pointed up the slope toward the Videssians. Martial music blared forth. Abivard booted his horse in the ribs. It started forward.

He had to sacrifice a little of the full fury of a Makuraner charge because he was going uphill at the Videssians. He also had to be careful to make sure the horse archers he'd placed to link the heavy cavalry contingents he and Romezan commanded to Turan's infantry kept on linking the different units and didn't go rushing off on some brainstorm of their own. That might open gaps the Videssians could exploit.

Horn calls rang out along the Videssian line, too. Peering over the chain mail veil of his helmet, Abivard watched Maniakes' men ride forward to meet his. Whatever else they intended, the Videssians didn't aim to stand solely on the defensive.

Their archers started shooting at the oncoming Makuraner heavy cavalry. Here and there a man slid from his mount or a horse stumbled and went down, and as often as not, other horses would trip over those in the first ranks that had fallen. Had the Videssians done more damage with their archery, they might have disrupted the Makuraner charge.

But the riders of Makuran were armored in iron from head to foot. Their horses wore iron scales, too, sewn into or mounted in pockets on the blankets that covered their backs and sides, while iron chamfrons protected their heads and necks. Arrows found lodging places far less often than they would have against lightly warded men and animals.

No one now rode out between the armies with a challenge to single combat. In principle, such duels were honorable, even if Tzikas' attempts to use them both for and against Makuran had all but driven Abivard mad. But showy displays of honor had given way—on both sides, apparently—to a hard desire to fight things out to the end as soon as possible.

Lowering his lance, Abivard picked the Videssian he wanted to spear out of the saddle. The imperial saw him coming, saw the stroke was going to be unavoidable, and twisted in the saddle to try to turn the lance head with his small, round shield.

He gauged the angle well. Sparks spit as the iron point skidded across the iron facing of his shield. That deflection kept the point from his vitals. But the force of the blow still all but unhorsed him and meant his answering sword cut came closer to lopping off one of his mount's ears than to doing Abivard any harm.

"Sharbaraz!" Abivard shouted. He spurred his horse forward, using speed and weight against the Videssian. As the man—he *was* a good horseman and as game as they came—righted himself in the saddle, Abivard clouted him on the side of the head with the shaft of his lance. The blow caught the Videssian by surprise; it was one a Makuraner was far likelier to make with a broken lance than with a whole one, the point being so much more deadly than the shaft.

But Abivard knew from painful experience how much damage a blow to the head could do even if it didn't cave in a skull. The Videssian reeled. He held on to the sword but looked at it as if he hadn't the slightest idea what it was good for.

His opponent stunned, Abivard had the moment he needed to draw the lance back and slam it into the fellow's throat. Blood sprayed out, then gushed as he yanked the point free. The Videssian clutched at the shaft of the lance, but his grip had no strength to it. His hands slipped away, and he crumpled to the ground.

Another Videssian slashed at Abivard. Awkwardly, he blocked the blow with his lance. The imperial's blade bit into the wood. The soldier cursed horribly as he worked it free; his face was twisted with fear lest he be assailed while he could not use his weapon. He did manage to clear it before another Makuraner attacked him. What happened to him after that, Abivard never knew. As was often the way of battle, they were swept apart.

Abivard had plenty of fighting nonetheless. Because he had made no secret of his rank, the Videssians swarmed against him, trying to cut him down. He did eventually break his lance over the head of one of those Videssians. That blow didn't merely stun the man—it broke his neck. He slid off his horse like a sack of rice after a strap broke.

Throwing the stump of the lance at the nearest Videssian, Abivard yanked his sword free of the scabbard. He slashed an imperial's unarmored horse. The animal screamed and bucked. The soldier aboard it had all he could do to stay on. For the next little while he couldn't fight. Abivard counted that a gain.

Fighting in the first rank himself, he had less sight of the battlefield as a whole than he'd grown used to enjoying. Whenever he looked around to get a picture of what was happening, some Videssian was generally inconsiderate enough to try to take advantage of his lack of attention by puncturing or otherwise maiming him.

One thing he did discover: in Maniakes the Videssians now had a commander who could make them stand and fight. Throughout Genesios' reign the imperials had fled before the Makuraner field army. They'd fled through the early years of Maniakes' reign, too, but they fled no more.

Abivard, doing everything he could against them, felt their confidence, their cockiness. Whenever his men managed to hew their way a few feet forward, the Videssians, instead of panicking, rallied and pushed them back. Yes, the imperials had the advantage of terrain, but an advantage of that sort meant little unless the soldiers who enjoyed it were prepared to exploit it. The Videssians were.

"Here, come on!" one of their officers called, waving men forward. "Got to plug the holes, boys, or the wine dribbles out of the jar." Having learned Videssian, Abivard had often used his knowledge of the language to gain an edge on his foes. Now, overhearing that calm, matter-of-fact reaction to trouble, he began to worry. Warriors who didn't let themselves get fearful and flustered when things went wrong were hard to beat.

He listened for the Videssian horn calls, gauging how many of the enemy were being drawn from Maniakes' left to help deal with the trouble he was causing here. A fair number, he judged. Enough to let Romezan strike a telling blow on that flank? He'd find out.

Turan's foot soldiers poured volleys of arrows into the ranks of the Videssians. Maniakes' men shot back. Groans rose from the ranks of the infantry as one soldier after another fell. As usual, the Videssians suffered fewer casualties than they inflicted on their foes. Abivard thought kindly of the garrison troops he'd turned into real soldiers. If he'd left them in their cities, though, how many men who had died would still be alive today?

He knew no way to answer that question. He did know that a good many men and women in the Thousand Cities—and probably in Mashiz, too—who lived now would almost certainly have been dead had he not gathered the garrisons together and made the swaggering town toughs warriors instead.

As if struck by the same idea at the same time, Turan's soldiers rushed up at Maniakes' men while a couple of troops of imperials detached themselves from the main Videssian mass and rode down against their tormentors. Neither side, then, got what it wanted. The Makuraners who advanced kept the Videssians from getting in among their fellows, while the surge of the Makuraners upslope kept the imperials from galloping down on them and perhaps slashing their way through them.

And over on the right—what was happening over on the right? From where Abivard had placed himself, with so much of Maniakes' army between him and the division Romezan led, he could not tell. He was sure Romezan hadn't yet charged home with all the strength he had. Had he done so, Videssian horn calls—the God willing, dismayed Videssian horn calls—would have alerted Abivard as they summoned more imperials.

Romezan was still holding back, still waiting for Abivard, by the ferocity of his attack, to convince Maniakes that this was where the supreme Makuraner effort lay, that this was where the Videssians would have to bring all their strength if they were going to survive, that the other wing, without the presence of a supreme commander, could not deliver—could not imagine delivering—a strong blow of its own.

Abivard was the one who had to do the convincing, and the Avtokrator was a much more discriminating audience than he had been before. If you were going to act a part, it was best to do it to the hilt. Waving his sword, Abivard shouted to his men, "Press them hard! We'll bring Maniakes back to Mashiz in chains and throw him down at Sharbaraz's feet!"

He got a cheer from his soldiers, who did press the Videssians harder. As he slashed at an imperial with a heavy-featured, swarthy face that argued for Vaspurakaner blood, he felt the irony of the war cry he had just loosed. He wanted to give Maniakes to the King of Kings, but what had Sharbaraz given him lately? Humiliation, mistrust, suspicion—if Romezan hadn't disobeyed Sharbaraz, Abivard would not have been commanding these men.

But to the soldiers Sharbaraz King of Kings might as well have been Makuran incarnate. They knew little of Abivard's difficulties with him and cared less. When they shouted Sharbaraz's name, they shouted it from the bottoms of their hearts. Absurdly, Abivard felt almost guilty for inspiring them with a leader who was, were the truth known, something less than inspiring,

He shook his head, making the chain mail veil he wore clink and clatter. Inspiration and truth barely spoke to each other. Men picked up pieces of things they thought they knew and sewed them together into bright, shining patterns, patching thin spots and holes with hopes and dreams. And the patterns somehow glowed even if the bits of truth in them were invisibly small.

He was trying to make Maniakes see a pattern, too, a pattern like that of many past Makuraner attacks. It was a point of honor for a Makuraner commander to lead the chief assault of his army. Here was Abivard, commanding the army and ostentatiously leading an assault against the Videssians. If you brought over enough good troops to contain the force he led, you won the battle, didn't you? By the pattern of battles past, you did.

"Here I am," Abivard panted, slashing at an imperial soldier. The fellow took the blow on his shield. The tides of battle swept him away from Abivard before he could return a cut. "Here I am," Abivard repeated. "You have to pay attention to me, don't you, Maniakes?"

When would the big attack on the right go in? Romezan's instinct was to hit as hard as he could as soon as he could. Abivard marveled that he'd managed to restrain himself so long. The next thing to worry about was, would Romezan, restraining himself from striking too early, restrain himself so thoroughly that he struck too late? He'd said not, back when Abivard had given him his orders, but . . .

In the press of fighting—Videssians ahead of him, Makuraners behind him trying to move forward to get at the Videssians— Abivard found himself unable to send a messenger to Romezan. It was a disadvantage of leading from the front he hadn't anticipated. He had to rely on Romezan's good judgment—he had to hope Romezan had good judgment.

The longer the fight went on, the more he doubted that. Over here, on the left, his force and the Videssians facing them were locked together as tightly as two lovers in an embrace that went on and on and on. In the center Turan's foot soldiers, keeping their ranks tight, were doing a good job of holding and harassing their mounted foes. And over on the right—

"Something had better happen over on the right," Abivard said, "or the Videssians will beat us over here before we can beat them over there."

Nobody paid the least bit of attention to him. Most likely nobody heard him, not with the clangor of combat all around and the iron veil he wore over his mouth muffling his words. He didn't care. He was doing his best to make patterns, too, even if they weren't the ones he would have preferred to see.

"Come on, Romezan," he said. Nobody heard that, either. What he feared was that Romezan was among the multitude who didn't hear.

Then, when he'd all but given up hope for the attack from the noble of the Seven Clans, the Videssian horns that ordered the movements of imperial troops abruptly blared out a complicated series of new, urgent commands. The pressure against Abivard and his comrades eased. Even above the din of the field shouts of alarm and triumphant cries rang out on the right.

A great weight suddenly seemed to drop from Abivard. For one brief moment battle seemed as splendid, as glorious, as exciting as he'd imagined before he went to war. He wasn't tired, he forgot he was bathed in sweat, he no longer needed to climb down from his horse and empty his bladder. He'd made Maniakes bar the front door—and then had kicked the back door down.

"Come on!" he shouted to the men around him, who were suddenly moving forward again now that Maniakes had thinned his line to rush troops back to the other side to stem Romezan's advance. "If we drive them, they all perish!"

That was how it looked, anyhow. If the Makuraners kept up the pressure from both wings and the center at the same time, how could the Videssian invaders hope to withstand them?

Over the next couple of hours Abivard found out how. He began to think Maniakes should have been not the Avtokrator but a juggler. No traveling mountebank could have done a neater job of keeping so many sets of soldiers flying this way and that to prevent the Makuraners from turning an advantage into a rout.

Oh, the Videssians yielded ground, especially where Romezan had crumpled them on the right. But they didn't break and flee as they had in so many fights over the years, and they didn't quite let either Romezan's men or Abivard's find a hole in their line, tear through, and cut off part of their army. Whenever that looked like it would happen, Maniakes would find some reserves—or soldiers in a different part of the fight who weren't so heavily pressed—to throw into the opening and delay the Makuraners just long enough to let the Videssians contract and re-form their line.

Abivard tried to send men from his own force around to his left to see if he could get into the Videssians' rear by outflanking them if he couldn't bull his way through. That didn't work, either. For once, the lighter armor the Videssians wore worked to their advantage. Carrying less weight, their horses moved faster than those of Abivard's men, and, even starting later, they were able to block and forestall his force.

"All right, then," he cried, gathering the men together once more. "A last good push and we'll have them!"

He didn't know whether that was true; under Maniakes the Videssians fought as they hadn't since the days of Likinios Avtokrator. He did know that one more push was all his army had time to make. The sun was going down; darkness would be coming soon. He booted his horse forward. "This time, by the God, we take them!" he shouted.

And for a while he thought his army would take them. Back went the Videssians, back and back again, their ranks thinning, thinning, and no more reserves behind them to plug the gap. And then, with victory in Abivard's grasp, close enough for him to reach out and touch it, a hard-riding regiment of imperials came up and hurled themselves at his men, not only halting them but throwing them back. "Maniakes!" the last-minute rescuers and their commander cried. "Phos and Maniakes!"

Abivard's head came up when he heard that commander shout. He had to keep fighting for all he was worth to ensure that the Videssians didn't gain too great an advantage in their turn. But he looked this way and that . . . surely he'd recognized that voice.

Yes! There! "Tzikas!" he cried.

The renegade stared at him. "Abivard!" he said, and then, scornfully, "Eminent sir!"

"Traitor!" they roared together, and rode toward each other.

bivard slashed at Tzikas with more fury than science. The Videssian renegade—or possibly by now rerenegade—parried the blow with his own sword. Sparks flew as the iron blades belled off each other. Tzikas gave back a cut that Abivard blocked. They struck more sparks.

"You sent me to my death!" Tzikas screamed.

"You slandered me to the King of Kings," Abivard retorted. "You told nothing but lies about me and everything I did. I gave you what you deserved, and I waited too long to do it."

"You never gave me the credit I deserve," Tzikas said.

"You never give anyone around you anything but a kick in the balls, whether he deserves it or not," Abivard said.

As they spoke, they kept cutting at each other. Neither could get through the other's defense. Abivard looked around the field. To his dismay, to his disgust, the same held true of the Makuraners and the Videssians. Tzikas' ferocious counterattack had blunted his last chance for a breakthrough.

"You just saved the fight for a man you tried to murder by magic," Abivard said. If he couldn't slay Tzikas with his sword, he might at least wound him with words.

The renegade's face contorted. "Life doesn't always turn out to be what we think it will, by the God," he said, but at the same time he named the God he also sketched Phos' sun-circle above

288

his heart. Abivard got the idea that Tzikas had no idea which side he belonged on, save only—and always—his own.

A couple of other Videssians rode toward Abivard. He drew back. Wary of a trap, Tzikas did not press him. For once Abivard had no trap waiting. But were he Tzikas, he would have been wary, too. He heartily thanked the God he was not Tzikas, and he did not make Phos' sun-sign as he did so.

He looked over the field again in the fading light to see if he had any hope left of turning victory into rout. Try as he would, he saw none. Here were his banners, and there were those of the Videssians. Horsemen and foot soldiers still hewed at one another, but he did not think anything they did would change the outcome now. Instead of a battlefield, the fight looked more like a picture of a battle on a tapestry or wall painting.

Abivard frowned. That was an odd thought. He stiffened. No, not a picture of a battle—an image of a battle, an image he had seen before. This was the fight Panteles had shown him. He hadn't known, when he had seen it, whether he was looking on past or future. Now, too late to do him any good—as was often true of prophecy—he had the answer.

The Videssians withdrew toward their camp. They kept good order and plainly had plenty of fight left in them. After a last couple of attacks, as twilight began to fall, Abivard let them go.

From his right someone rode up calling his name. His hand tightened on the hilt of his sword. After a clash with Tzikas, he suspected everyone. The approaching horseman wore the full armor of the Makuraner heavy cavalry and rode an armored horse as well. Abivard remained cautious. Armor could be captured, and horses, too. And the chain mail veil the rider wore would disguise a Videssian in Makuraner clothing.

That veil also had the effect of disguising the voice. Not until the rider drew very close did Abivard recognize Romezan. "By the God," he exclaimed, "I wouldn't have known you from your gear. You look as if you've had a smith pounding on you."

If anything, that was an understatement. A sword stroke had sheared the bright, tufted crest from atop Romezan's helm. His surcoat had been cut to ribbons. Somewhere in the fighting he'd lost not only his lance but also his shield. Through the rents in his surcoat Abivard could see the dents in his armor. He had an arrow sticking out of his left shoulder, but by the way he moved his arm, it must have lodged in the padding he wore beneath his lamellar armor, not in his flesh.

"I *feel* as if a smith's been pounding on me," he said. "I've got bruises all over; three days from now I'll look like a sunset the court poets would sing about for years." He hung his head. "Lord, I fear I held off on the charge till too late. If I'd loosed my men at the Videssians sooner, we'd have had so much more time in which to finish the job of beating them."

"It's done," Abivard said; he was also battered and bruised and, as usual after a battle, deathly tired. He thought Romezan had held off till too late, too, but what good would screaming about it do now? "We hold the field where we fought; we can claim the victory."

"It's not enough," Romezan insisted, as hard on himself as he was on the foe. "You wanted to smash them, not just push them back. We could have done it, too, if I'd moved faster. I have to say, though, I didn't think Videssians could fight that well."

"If it makes you feel any better, neither did I," Abivard said. "For as long as I've been warring against them, when we send in the heavy cavalry, they give way. But not today."

"No, not today." Romezan twisted in the saddle, trying to find a way to make the armor fit more comfortably on his sore carcass. "You were right, lord, and I own it. They can be very dangerous to us."

"Right at the end I thought we would break through here on the left," Abivard said. "They threw the last of their reserves in to stop us, and they did. You'll never guess who was leading those reserves."

"No, eh?" All Abivard could see of Romezan was his eyes. They widened. "Not Tzikas?"

"The very same. Somehow Maniakes has found a way to keep him alive and keep him tame, at least for now, because he fought like a demon."

For the next considerable while Romezan spoke with pungent ingenuity. The gist of what he said boiled down to *how very unfortunate*, but he put it rather more vividly than that. When he'd calmed down to the point where he no longer seemed to be imitating a kettle boiling over, he said, "We may be sorry, but Maniakes also will be. Tzikas is more dangerous to the side he's

on than to the one he isn't on, because you never know when
he's going to go over to the other one."

"I've had the same notion," Abivard said. "But while he's being
good for Maniakes, he knows he has to be very good indeed or
the Avtokrator will stake him out for the crows and buzzards."

"If it were me, I'd do it whether he was being very good indeed
or not," Romezan said.

"So would I," Abivard agreed. "And next time I get the chance—
and there's likely to be a next time—I will . . . unless I don't."

"Do we pick up the fight tomorrow, lord?" Romezan asked. "If
it were up to me, I would, but it isn't up to me."

"I won't say yes or no till morning," Abivard answered. "We'll
see what sort of shape the army is in then and see what the
Videssians are doing, too." He yawned. "I'm so tired now, I might
as well be drunk. My head will be clearer come morning, too."

"Ha!" Romezan said in a voice so full of doubt, a Videssian
would have been proud to claim it. "I know you better than that,
lord. You'll have scouts wake you half a dozen times in the night
to tell you what they can see of the Videssian camp."

"After most fights I'd do just that," Abivard said. "Not tonight."

"Ha!" Romezan said again. Abivard maintained a dignified
silence.

As things worked out, scouts woke Abivard only four times
during the night. He couldn't decide whether that demolished
Romezan's point or proved it.

The news the scouts brought back was so utterly predictable, so
utterly normal, that Abivard could have neglected to send them
out and still have had almost as good a notion of what the Videssians were doing. The foe kept a great many fires going through
the first watch of the night, fewer in the second, and only those
near their guard positions for the third. Maniakes' men would
have done the same had they not just fought a great murdering
battle. They gave the Makuraners no clue to their intentions.

But when morning came, all that lay on the Videssian campsite
were the remains of the fires and a few tents, enough to create the
impression in dim light that many more were there. Maniakes and
his men had decamped at some unknown hour of the night.

Following them was anything but hard. An army of some
thousands of men could hardly slip without a trace through the

grass like an archer gliding ever closer to a deer. Thousands of men rode thousands of horses, which left tracks and other reminders of their presence.

And in retreat an army often discarded things its men would keep if they were advancing. The more things soldiers threw away, the likelier their retreat was to be a desperate one.

By that standard the Videssians did not strike Abivard as desperate. Yes, they were running away from Abivard and his men. But they were a long way from jettisoning everything that kept them from running faster.

Abivard did some jettisoning of his own: not without regret, he let Turan's foot soldiers fall behind. "The Videssians are all mounted," he told his lieutenant. "If you stay with us, we can't move fast enough to catch up with them. You follow behind. If it looks as if Maniakes is turning to offer battle again, we'll wait till you catch up to start fighting if we can."

"Meanwhile, we eat your dust," Turan said. A couple of years campaigning as an infantry officer seemed to have made him forget he'd served for years as a horseman before. But, however reluctantly, he nodded. "I see the need, lord, no matter how little I like it. I aim to surprise you, though, with how fast we can march."

"I hope you do," Abivard said. Then he summoned Sanatruq, having a use for an intrepid, aggressive young officer. "I am going to put the lightly armed cavalry in your hands. I want you to course ahead of the heavy horse, the way the hounds course ahead of the hunters when we're after antelope. Bring the Videssians to bay for me. Harass them every way you can think of."

Sanatruq's eyes glowed. "Just as you say, lord. And if Tzikas is still heading up Maniakes' rear guard, I have a small matter or two to discuss with him as well."

"We all have a small matter or two to discuss with Tzikas," Abivard said. He drew his sword. "I've been honing my arguments, you might say." Sanatruq grinned and nodded. He rode off, shouting to the Makuraner horse archers to stop whatever they were doing and get busy doing what he told them.

Be careful, Abivard thought as the light cavalry went trotting out ahead of the more heavily armored riders. Tzikas was liable to be trouble no matter how careful you were; that was why so many people had so much to discuss with him.

Almost as an afterthought, Abivard dashed off a quick letter to Sharbaraz, detailing not only the victory he had won over the imperials but also Tzikas' role in making that victory less than it should have been. *Let's see the cursed renegade try to get back into the good graces of the King of Kings after that,* he thought with considerable satisfaction.

The farther south Maniakes rode, the closer to the source of the Tutub he drew. The land rose. In administrative terms it was still part of the land of the Thousand Cities, but it was unlike the floodplain on which those cities perched. For one thing, the hills here were natural, not the end product of countless years of rubble and garbage. For another, none of the Thousand Cities was anywhere close by. A few farmers lived by the narrow stream of the Tutub and the even narrower tributaries feeding it. A few hunters roamed the wooded hills. For the most part, though, the land seemed empty, deserted.

Abivard wondered what Maniakes had in mind in such unpromising country. He understood why this part of the region remained unfamiliar to him: it wasn't worth visiting. He wished the Videssians joy of it. At an officers' council he said, "If they try to stay here, they'll starve, and in short order, too. If they try to leave, they'll have to cross a fair stretch of country worse than this before they come to any that's better."

Sanatruq said, "If they leave, we'll have driven them out of the land of the Thousand Cities. That was what Sharbaraz King of Kings, may his years be many and his realm increase, set us to do at the start of the campaigning season. I'm not sure anyone thought we could do it, but we've done it."

"We had a certain amount of expert help, for which I'm grateful," Abivard said to Romezan.

"You wanted to force battle," the noble of the Seven Clans said. "You were forcing battle when I rode up and found you. Anyone who goes out and fights the enemy deserves to win, so I was glad to give whatever little help I could." *Get in there and fight and worry later about what's supposed to happen next* should have been blazoned on Romezan's surcoat and painted in big letters on the front of his armor.

"Looks to me like good country for scouring with light cavalry," Abivard said, nodding to Sanatruq. "The rest of us can follow after they've developed whatever positions the Videssians are holding."

"What do you think the Videssians *are* doing here, lord?" Romezan asked. "Are they really finished for this campaigning season, or do they aim to give us one more boot in the crotch if we let 'em?"

"From what I know of Maniakes, I'd say he wants to hit us again if he finds the chance," Abivard said. "But I admit that's only a guess." He grinned at the noble of the Seven Clans. "You asked me just to hear me guess so you can twit me for it if I turn out to be wrong."

"Ha!" Romezan said. "I can figure you for foolish without getting as complicated as that."

Abivard waited till his subordinates were done laughing, then said, "We'll go ahead as if we're certain Maniakes is lying in wait for us. Better to worry and be wrong than not to worry—and be wrong." Not even Romezan could argue with him there.

Up close, the ground was worse than it appeared. The road through the highlands from which the Tutub sprang wound into little rocky valleys and over hillsides so packed with thorny, spiky scrub plants that going off it cut your speed not in half but to a quarter of what it was on the track.

No, that wasn't true. Going out into the scrub cut your speed to a quarter of what it would have been if the road had been unobstructed. The road, however, was anything but. The Videssians had thoughtfully sown it with caltrops, the exact equivalent for this terrain of breaking canals in the floodplain. Abivard's men had to slow down to clear the spikes, which let Maniakes' force increase its lead.

And to complicate things further, every so often the Videssians would post archers in the undergrowth by the side of the road and try to pot a few of the Makuraners who were picking up the caltrops. That meant Abivard had to send men after them, and that meant he lost still more time.

Seeing Maniakes getting ever farther ahead ate at him. He wanted to keep moving through the night. That made even Romezan raise an eyebrow. "In this wretched country," he rumbled, "it's hard enough to move during the day. At night—"

If Romezan didn't think it could be done, it couldn't. "But Maniakes is going to get away from us," Abivard said. "We haven't been able to slow him down no matter how we've tried. And if he can travel two or three more days, he'll strike the river that runs south and east to Lyssaion, and he'll have ships waiting there. Ships." As he often had of late, he made the word a curse.

"If we take Lyssaion, he may have ships, but he won't have anywhere they can land," Romezan said.

Abivard shook his head with real regret. "Too late in the year to besiege the place," he said, "and we haven't got the supplies with us to undertake a siege, anyhow." He waited to see whether Romezan would argue with that. The noble from the Seven Clans looked unhappy but kept quiet. Abivard went on, "We have driven him out of the land of the Thousand Cities. At the start of the campaigning season I would have been happy to settle for that."

"Generals who are happy to settle for less than the most they can get mostly don't end up with much," Romezan observed. That made Abivard bite his lip, for it was true.

Coming to a town in the middle of that rugged country was a surprise. The Videssians had burned the place in passing, but it had been little more than a village even before they had put it to the torch. They'd dumped dead animals into the wells that were probably the town's reason for being, too. After that, though, they seemed to have relented, for they stopped leaving caltrops in the roadway. That might, of course, have indicated a dearth of caltrops rather than a sudden surge in goodwill.

"Now we can make better time," Romezan said, noting the absence of the freestanding spiked obstructions. He shouted for the vanguard to speed up, then turned to Abivard, saying, "We'll catch the bastards yet; see if we don't."

"Maybe we will," Abivard replied. "The God grant we do." He scratched his head. "It's not like the Videssians to make things easy for us, though."

"They can't do everything right all the time," Romezan grunted. "When they squat over a slit trench, it's not rose petals that come out." He shouted again for more speed. Abivard pondered his analogy.

As the day went on, Abivard began to think the noble from the Seven Clans might have had a point. The army hadn't moved so fast since it had gotten into the uplands, and the Videssians couldn't be very far ahead. One more engagement and Maniakes might not be able to get his army back to Lyssaion.

And then, not long before Abivard was going to order his forces out of their column and into a line of battle despite the rugged terrain, a rider came galloping up the path from the southeast, from the Videssian force toward the Makuraners. He was shouting something in the Makuraner tongue as he drew near. Before long Abivard, who was riding at the front of the column, could make out what it was: "Stop! Hold up! It's a trap!"

Abivard turned to the horn players. "Blow halt," he commanded. "We have to find out what this means."

As the call rang out and the horsemen obediently reined in, Abivard studied the approaching horseman, who kept yelling at the top of his lungs. Because the fellow was bawling so hoarsely, Abivard needed longer than he should have to realize he recognized that voice. His jaw fell.

Before he could speak the name, Romezan beat him to it: "That's Tzikas. It can't be, but it is."

"It really is," Abivard breathed. By then he could see the renegade's face; Videssians usually didn't go in for chain mail veils. "What is he doing here? Did he try killing Maniakes one more time and botch it again? If he did kill him, he'd do us a favor, but if he killed him, he'd be back with the Videssian army, not coming up to ours."

Tzikas rode straight up to Abivard, as he had in battle a few days before. This time, though, he did not draw the sword that hung on his hip. "The God be praised," he said in his lisping Videssian accent. "I've gotten to you before you rode into the trap." The gelding on which he was mounted was blowing and foam-flecked; he'd come at a horse-killing pace.

"What are you talking about, Tzikas?" Abivard ground out. Nothing would have pleased him more than slaying the renegade. No one could stop him now, not with Tzikas coming alone to him in the midst of his army. But the Videssian never would have done such a thing without a pressing reason. Until Abivard found out what that reason was, Tzikas would keep breathing.

Tzikas wasn't breathing well now; gasping was more like it. "Trap," he said, pointing over his shoulder. "Magic. Back there."

"Why should I believe you?" Abivard said. "Why should I ever believe you?" He turned to the men of the vanguard, who were gaping at Tzikas as if he were a ghost walking among men. "Seize him! Drag him off his horse. Disarm him. The God alone knows what mischief he's plotting."

"You're mad!" Tzikas shouted as the Makuraners carried out Abivard's orders. "Why would I stick my head in the lion's mouth if I didn't wish you and the King of Kings well?"

"Escaping from Maniakes comes to mind," Abivard replied. "So does looking for another chance to drag my name through the dirt for Sharbaraz King of Kings, may his days be long and his realm increase." For a despised foreigner like Tzikas, he appended Sharbaraz's honorific formula.

"Why should I want to escape Maniakes when you're just as eager to do me in?" Tzikas asked bitterly. "He gloated about that—by the God, how he gloated about it."

"He gloated so hard and made you hate him so much that you commanded his rear guard, you rode out to challenge me to single combat, and your counterattack wrecked our last chance of beating him," Abivard said. "You were swearing by Phos then, or at least your hand was, though your mouth didn't tell it everything. By the God, Tzikas—" He put into the oath all the contempt he had in him. "—what would you have done if you'd decided you *liked* the Avtokrator?"

"My hand? I don't know what you're talking about," Tzikas said sullenly. It might even have been true. He went on, "Go ahead—mock me, slay me, however you please. And go ahead, run right after the Videssian army. Maniakes will give you a kiss on the cheek for helping him along. See if he doesn't."

He had, if not all the answers, enough of them to make Abivard doubt himself and his purpose. But then, Tzikas usually had a great store of answers, plenty to make you doubt yourself. Videssians bounced truth and lies back and forth, as if in mirrors, till you couldn't tell what you were seeing. Abivard sometimes wondered whether the imperials themselves could keep track.

One thing at a time, then. "What sort of magic is it, Tzikas?"

"I don't know," the renegade answered. "Maniakes didn't tell me. All I know is, I saw his wizards hard at work back there after he and his wife—his cousin who is his wife—had been closeted with them for a couple of hours before they started doing whatever they were doing. I didn't think it was for your health and well-being. I was commanding the rear guard—he'd come to trust me that far again. When I saw my chance, I galloped here. And look at the thanks you give me for it, too."

"You can check this, lord," Romezan rumbled. He'd listened to Tzikas with the same mixture of fascination and doubt Abivard felt.

"I know I can. I intend to," Abivard said. He turned to his men and said to one of them, "Fetch Bozorg and Panteles up here. If there's any magic up ahead, they'll sniff it out. And if there's not, Tzikas here will wish he'd stayed to suffer Maniakes' tender mercy when he finds out what we end up doing to him." As the soldier hurried off, Abivard shifted to the Videssian to ask a mocking question: "Do you follow that, eminent sir?"

"Perfectly well, thank you." Tzikas had sangfroid, no two ways about it. But then, a man would hardly arrive at a position where he could commit treason—let alone repeated treason—without a goodly helping of sangfroid.

Abivard fretted and stewed. While he waited, Maniakes and his army were getting farther away every moment. After what seemed an interminable delay, Bozorg and Panteles came trotting up behind the soldier Abivard had sent to bring them. He watched Tzikas watching the Videssian in his service and made up his mind not to let the two of them be alone together if he could help it.

No time to worry about that, though. Abivard spoke to the two mages: "This, as you know, is the famous and versatile Tzikas of the Videssian army, our army, the Videssians again, and now—maybe—ours once more."

"One of those transfers was involuntary on my part," Tzikas said. Yes, he had sangfroid and to spare.

As if he hadn't spoken, as if Bozorg and Panteles weren't staring wide-eyed at the famous and versatile Tzikas, whom they could not have expected to find returned to allegiance to the King of Kings—if he had returned to allegiance to the King of Kings—Abivard went on, "Tzikas says the Videssians are planning something unpleasantly sorcerous for us up ahead. I want you to find out whether that's so. If it is, I suppose Tzikas may have earned his life. If not, I promise he will keep it longer than he wants to but not long."

"Aye, lord," Bozorg said.

"It shall be as you say, eminent sir," Panteles added in Videssian.

Abivard wished he hadn't done that. The soldiers of the vanguard, from the lowliest trooper up through Romezan, looked from him to Tzikas and back again, tarring both of them with the same brush. Abivard didn't want Panteles getting any ideas, from any source, about disloyalty.

The two wizards worked together smoothly enough, more smoothly than they had when they had been trying to cross the canal, when Bozorg had reckoned the Voimios strap only a figment of Panteles' imagination and a twisted figment at that. Now, sometimes chanting antiphonally, sometimes pointing and gesturing down the road in the direction from which Tzikas had come, sometimes roiling the dust with their spells, they probed what lay ahead.

At last Bozorg reported, "Some sort of sorcerous barrier does lie ahead, lord. What may hide behind it I cannot say: it serves only to mask the sorceries on the farther side. But it is there."

"That's so," Panteles agreed. "No possible argument. There's a sorcerous fog bank, so to speak, dead ahead of us."

Abivard glanced over at Tzikas. The renegade affected not to notice that he was being watched. *I've told the truth,* his posture said. *I've always told the truth.* Abivard wondered if he really grasped the difference between the posture of truth and truth itself.

For the time being that was beside the point. He asked Bozorg, "Can you penetrate the fog bank to see what lies behind it?"

"Can we? Perhaps, lord," Bozorg said. "In fact, it is likely, as penetrating it tends toward a restoration of a natural state. The question of whether we should, however, remains."

"Drop me into the Void if I can see why," Abivard said. "It's there, and we need to find out what's on the other side of it before we send the army into what's liable to be danger. That's plain enough, isn't it?"

"Oh, it's plain enough," Bozorg agreed, "but is it wise? For all we know, trying to penetrate the sorcerous fog, or succeeding in penetrating it, may be the signal for the truly fearsome charm it conceals to spring to life."

"I hadn't thought of that." Abivard was certain his face looked as if he'd been sucking on a lemon. His stomach was as sour as if he'd been sucking on a lemon, too. "What are we supposed to do, then? Sit around here quivering and wait for the sorcerous fog bank to roll away? We're all liable to die of old age before that happens. If I were Maniakes, I'd make sure my wizards gave it a good long life, anyhow."

Neither Bozorg or Panteles argued with him. Neither of them sprang into action to break down the sorcerous fog, either. When Abivard glared at them, Panteles said, "Eminent sir, we have here risks in going ahead and also risks in doing nothing. Weighing these risks is not easy."

Abivard glanced over, not at Tzikas this time but at Romezan. The noble of the Seven Clans would have had only one answer: when in doubt, go ahead, and worry afterward about what happens afterward. Romezan reckoned Abivard a man of excessive caution. This time the two of them were likely to be thinking along the same lines.

"If you can pierce that fog, pierce it," Abivard told the two wizards. "The longer we stay stuck here, the farther ahead of us Maniakes gets. If he gets too far ahead, he escapes. We don't want that."

Panteles bowed, a gesture of respect the Videssians gave to any superior. Bozorg didn't. It wasn't that he minded acknowledging Abivard as being far superior to him in rank; he'd done that before. But to do it now would have been to acknowledge that he thought Abivard was right, and he clearly didn't.

Whether he thought him right or not, though, he obeyed. As at the twisted canal, Panteles took the lead in the answering magic; being a Videssian, he was likely to be more familiar with the sort of sorcery Maniakes' mages employed than Bozorg was.

"We bless thee, Phos, lord with the great and good mind, by thy grace our protector," Panteles intoned, "watchful beforehand that the great test of life may be decided in our favor."

Along with the other Makuraners who understood the Videssian god's creed, Abivard bristled at hearing it. Panteles said, "We have a fog ahead. We need Phos' holy light to pierce it."

Since Bozorg kept quiet, Abivard made himself stay calm, too. Panteles incanted steadily and then, with a word of command that might not have been Videssian at all—that hardly sounded like any human language—stabbed out his finger at what lay ahead. Abivard expected something splendid and showy, perhaps a ray of scarlet light shooting from his fingertip. Nothing of the sort happened, so it seemed the sort of gesture a father might have used to send an unruly son to his room after the boy had misbehaved.

Then Bozorg grunted and staggered as if someone had struck him a heavy blow, though no one stood near him. "No, by the God!" he exclaimed, and gestured with his left hand. "Fraortish eldest of all, lady Shivini, Gimillu, Narseh—come to my aid!"

He straightened and steadied. Panteles repeated Phos' creed. The two wizards shouted together, both crying out the same word that was not Videssian—it might not have been a word at all, not in the grammarians' sense of the term.

Abivard was watching Tzikas. The renegade started to sketch Phos' sun-circle but checked himself with the motion barely begun. Instead, his left hand twisted in the gesture Bozorg had used. *Almost forgot whose camp you were in, didn't you?* Abivard thought.

But Tzikas' return to the Makuraner fold did not seem to have been a trap or a snare. He'd warned of magic ahead, and magic ahead there had been. He'd done Abivard a service the general could hardly ignore. The last time they'd seen each other, Tzikas had done his best to kill him. That had been a more honest expression, no doubt, of how the renegade felt—not that Abivard had any great and abiding love for him, either.

The wizards, meanwhile, continued their magic. At length Abivard felt a sharp snap somewhere right in the middle of his head. By the way the soldiers around him exclaimed, he wasn't the only one. Afterward the world seemed a little clearer, a little brighter.

"We have pierced the sorcerous fog, revealing it for the phantasm it is," Panteles declared.

"And what lies behind it?" Abivard demanded. "What other magic was it concealing?"

Panteles and Bozorg looked surprised. In defeating the first magic, they'd forgotten for a moment what came next. More hasty incanting followed. In a voice that suggested he had trouble believing what he was saying, Bozorg answered, "It does not seem to be concealing any other magic."

"Bluff!" Romezan boomed. "All bluff."

"A bluff that worked, too," Abivard said unhappily. "We've wasted a lot of time trying to break through that screen of theirs. We were almost on their heels, but we're not, not anymore."

"Let's go after them, then," Romezan said. "The longer we stand around jabbering here, the farther away they get."

"That's so," Abivard said. "You don't suppose—" He glanced over at Tzikas, then shook his head. The renegade would not have come to the Makuraner army Abivard commanded for the sole purpose of delaying it. Maniakes could not have forced that from Tzikas, not when he knew Abivard was as eager as the Avtokrator to dispose of him . . . could he?

Romezan's gaze swung to Tzikas, too. "What do we do about him now?"

"Drop me into the Void if I know. He said there was magic being worked, and there was. He's no wizard or he would have tried to murder Maniakes himself instead of hiring someone to do it for him." That made Tzikas bite his lip. Abivard ignored him, continuing: "He had no way to know the magic wasn't worse than what it turned out to be, and so he warned us. That counts for something."

"Far as I'm concerned, it means we don't torture him—just hew off his head and have done," Romezan said.

"Your generosity is remarkable," Tzikas told him.

"What do you think we should do with you?" Abivard asked, curious to hear what the renegade would say.

Without hesitation Tzikas replied, "Give me back my cavalry command. I did nothing to give anyone the idea I don't deserve it."

"Nothing except slander me to Sharbaraz King of Kings, may his years be many and his realm increase," Abivard said. "Nothing except offer to slay me in single combat. Nothing except blunt my troops in battle and keep Maniakes from being wrecked. Nothing except—"

"I did what I had to do," Tzikas said.

How slandering Abivard to Sharbaraz counted as something he had had to do, he did not explain. Abivard wondered if he knew. The most likely explanation was that aggrandizing Tzikas was indeed something Tzikas had to do. Whatever the explanation, though, it was beside the point at the moment. "You will not lead cavalry in my army," Abivard said. "Until such time as I know you can be trusted, you are a prisoner, and you may thank the God or Phos or whomever you're worshiping on any particular day that I don't take Romezan's suggestion, which would without a doubt make my life easier."

"I find no justice anywhere," Tzikas said, melodrama throbbing in his voice.

"If you found justice, you *would* be short a head," Abivard retorted. "If you're going to whine because you don't find as much mercy as you think you deserve, too bad." He turned to some of his soldiers. "Seize him. Strip him and take away whatever weapons you find. Search carefully, search thoroughly, to make sure you find them all. Hold him. Do him no harm unless he tries to escape. If he tries, kill him."

"Aye, lord," the warriors said enthusiastically, and proceeded to give the command the most literal obedience imaginable, stripping Tzikas not only of his mail shirt but also, their pattings not satisfying them, of his undertunic and drawers as well, so that he stood before them clad in nothing more than irate dignity. Abivard groped for a word to describe his expression and finally found one in Videssian, for the imperials did more reveling in suffering for the sake of their faith than did Makuraners. Tzikas, now—Tzikas looked *martyred*.

For all their enthusiasm, the searchers found nothing out of the ordinary and suffered him to dress once more. Seeing that Tzikas was not immediately dangerous—save with his tongue, a weapon Abivard would have loved to cut out of him—the bulk of the army rode off in pursuit of Maniakes' force.

The Videssians, though, had used well the time their sorcerous smoke screen had bought them. "We aren't going to catch them," Abivard said, bringing his horse up to trot beside Romezan's. "They're going to make their way down to Lyssaion and get away to fight next spring."

He hoped Romezan would disagree with him. The noble from the Seven Clans was relentlessly optimistic, often believing something could be done long after a more staid man would have given up hope—and often being right, too. But now the wild boar of Makuran nodded. "I fear you're right, lord," he said. "These cursed Videssians are getting to be harder to step on for good and all than so many cockroaches. They'll be back to bother us again."

"We have driven them clean out of the land of the Thousand Cities," Abivard said, as he had before. "That's something. Even the King of Kings will have to admit that's something."

"The King of Kings won't have to do any such thing, and you know it as well as I do," Romezan retorted, tossing his head so that his waxed mustaches flipped back and slapped against his cheeks. "He *may*, if his mood is good and the wind blows from the proper quarter, but to have to? Don't be stupid . . . lord."

That came uncomfortably close to Abivard's own thoughts, so close that he took no offense at Romezan's blunt suggestion. It also sparked another thought in him: "My sister should long since have had her baby by now, and I should have had word, whatever the word was."

Now Romezan sounded reassuring: "Had anything bad happened, lord, which the God forbid, rest assured you would have heard of that."

"I won't say you're wrong," Abivard answered. "Sharbaraz by now probably would be glad to get shut of any family ties to me. But if Denak had another girl—" If, despite the wizards' predictions, she'd had another girl, she would not get another chance for a boy.

Romezan's hand twisted in a gesture intended to turn aside an evil omen. That touched Abivard. The noble of the Seven Clans might well have resented his low birth and Denak's and not wanted the heir of the King of Kings to spring from their line. Abivard was glad none of that seemed to bother him.

"All right, if we can't catch up to the Videssians, what do we do?" Romezan asked.

"Return in triumph to Mashiz, of course," Abivard said, and laughed at the expression on Romezan's face. "What we really need to do is pull back out of this rough country into the floodplain, where we'll have plenty of supplies. Not much to be gathered here."

"That's so," Romezan agreed. "Won't be so much down on the flat as there usually is, either, thanks to Maniakes. But you're right: more than here. One more question and then I shut up: have we won enough of a victory to satisfy the King of Kings?"

Sharbaraz had said that nothing less than complete and overwhelming defeat of the Videssians would be acceptable. Together, Abivard and Romezan had given him . . . something less than that. On the other hand, giving him the complete and overwhelming defeat of Maniakes probably would have frightened him. A general who could completely and overwhelmingly defeat a foreign foe might also, should the matter ever cross his mind, contemplate completely and overwhelmingly defeating the King of Kings. Maniakes had abandoned the land of the Thousand Cities under pressure from Abivard and Romezan. Would that satisfy Sharbaraz?

"We'll find out," Abivard said without hope and without fear.

The messenger from Mashiz reached the army as it was coming down from the high ground in which the Tutub originated. Abivard was still marching as to war, with scouts well out ahead of his force. There was no telling for certain that Maniakes hadn't tried circling around through the semidesert scrub country for another go at the land of the Thousand Cities. Abivard didn't think the Avtokrator would attempt anything so foolhardy, but one thing he'd become sure of was that you never could tell with Maniakes.

Instead of a horde of Phos-worshipping Videssians, though, the scouts brought back the messenger, a skinny little pockmarked man mounted on a gelding much more handsome than he was. "Lord, I give you the words of Sharbaraz King of Kings, may his years be many and his realm increase," he said.

"For which I thank you," Abivard replied, not wanting to say in public that the words of Sharbaraz King of Kings were nothing he looked forward to receiving.

With a flourish the messenger handed him the waterproof leather message tube. He popped it open. The sheet of parchment within was sealed with the lion of Makuran stamped into blood-red wax: Sharbaraz's insigne, sure enough. Abivard broke the seal with his thumbnail, let the fragments of wax fall to the ground, and unrolled the parchment.

As usual, Sharbaraz's titulature used up a good part of the sheet. The scribe who had taken down the words of the King of Kings had a large, round hand that made the titles seem all the more impressive. Abivard skipped over them just the same, running a finger down the lines of fine calligraphy till he came to words that actually said something instead of serving no other function than advertising the magnificence of the King of Kings.

"Know that we have received your letter detailing the joint action you and Romezan son of Bizhan fought against the Videssian usurper Maniakes in the land of the Thousand Cities, the aforesaid Romezan having joined you in defiance of our orders," Sharbaraz wrote. Abivard sighed. Once Sharbaraz got an idea, he never let go of it. Thus, Maniakes was still a usurper even though he was still solidly on the Videssian throne. Thus, too, the King of Kings was never going to forget—or let anyone else forget—that Romezan had disobeyed him.

"Know further that we are glad your common effort met with at least a modicum of success and grieved to learn that Tzikas, with his inborn Videssian treachery, presumed to challenge you to single combat, you having benefited him after his defection to our side," Sharbaraz continued.

Abivard looked down at the parchment in pleased surprise. Had the King of Kings sounded so reasonable more often, he would have been a better ruler to serve.

He went on, "And know also we are happy you succeeded in defeating the vile Videssian sorcery applied to the canal in the aforementioned land of the Thousand Cities and that we desire full details of the said sorcery forwarded to Mashiz so that all our wizards may gain familiarity with it." Abivard blinked. That wasn't just reasonable—it was downright sensible. He wondered if Sharbaraz was well.

"Having crossed the canal in despite of the said sorcery, you and Romezan son of Bizhan did well to defeat the usurper Maniakes in the subsequent battle, the traitor Tzikas again establishing himself as a vile Videssian dog biting the hand of those who nourished them upon his defection and making himself liable to ruthless, unhesitating extermination upon his recapture, should the aforementioned recapture occur."

Abivard was tempted to summon Tzikas and read him that part of the letter just to watch his face. But the Videssian had again muddied the waters by warning of Maniakes' sorcery, even if it had been no more than a smoke screen.

"Know further," Sharbaraz wrote, "that it is our desire to see the Videssians defeated or crushed or, those failing, at the very least driven from the land of the Thousand Cities so that they no longer infest the said land, ravaging and destroying both commerce and agriculture. Failure to accomplish this will result in our severest displeasure."

It is *accomplished,* Abivard thought. He had, for once, done everything the King of Kings had demanded of him. He reveled in the sensation, knowing it was unlikely to recur any time soon. And even doing anything Sharbaraz demanded of him wouldn't keep his sovereign satisfied: if he could do that, who knew what else, what other enormities, he might be capable of?

Sharbaraz went on with more instructions, exhortations, and warnings. At the bottom of the sheet of parchment, almost as an afterthought, the King of Kings added, "Know also that the God has granted us a son, whom we have named Peroz in memory of our father, Peroz King of Kings, who was born to us of our principal wife, Denak: your sister. Child and mother both appear healthy; the God grant that this should continue. Rejoicing reigns throughout the palace."

Abivard read through the last few lines several times. They still said what they had the first time he'd read them. Had Sharbaraz King of Kings had any true familial feelings for him, he would have put that news at the head of the letter and let all the rest wait. Had he followed the advice of Yeliif and those like him, though, he probably wouldn't have let Abivard know of his unclehood at all. It was a compromise, then—not a good one, as far as Abivard was concerned, but not the worst, either.

Sharbaraz's messenger, who had ridden along with him while he read the letter from the King of Kings, now asked him, as messengers were trained to do, "Is there a reply, lord? If you write it, I will deliver it to the King of Kings; if you tell it to me, he will have it as you speak it."

"Yes, there is a reply. I will speak it, if you don't mind," Abivard said. The messenger nodded and looked attentive. "Tell Sharbaraz King of Kings, may his days be long and his realm increase, I have driven Maniakes from the land of the Thousand Cities. And tell him I thank him for the other news as well." He fumbled in his belt pouch, pulled out a Videssian goldpiece with Likinios Avtokrator's face on it, and handed it to the messenger. "You men get blamed too often for the bad news you bring, so here is a reward for good news."

"Thank you, lord, and the God bless you for your kindness," the messenger said. He repeated Abivard's message to make sure he had it right, then kicked his horse up into a trot and headed back toward Mashiz with the reply.

For his part, Abivard wheeled his horse and rode to the wagons that traveled with the army. When he saw Pashang, he waved. Abivard then called for Roshnani. When she came out of the covered rear area and sat beside Pashang, Abivard handed the letter to her.

She read through it rapidly. He could tell when she came to the last few sentences, because she took one hand off the parchment, made a fist, and slammed it down on her leg. "That's the best news we've had in years!" she exclaimed. "In years, I tell you."

"What news is this, mistress?" Pashang asked. Roshnani told him of the birth of the new Peroz. The driver beamed. "That *is* good news." He nodded to Abivard. "Congratulations, lord—or should I say uncle to the King of Kings to be?"

"Don't say that," Abivard answered earnestly. "Don't even think it. If you do, Sharbaraz will get wind of it, and then we'll get to enjoy another winter at the palace, packed as full of delight and good times as the last two we had in Mashiz."

Pashang's hand twisted in the gesture Makuraners used to turn aside evil omens. "I'll not say it again any time soon, lord, I promise you that." He repeated the gesture; that first winter in Makuran had been far harder on him than on Abivard and his family.

Roshnani held out the letter to Abivard, who took it back from her. "The rest of this isn't so bad, either," she said.

"I know," he said, and lowering his voice so that only she and Pashang could hear, he added, "It's so good, in fact, I almost wonder whether Sharbaraz truly wrote it."

His principal wife and the driver both smiled and nodded, as if they'd been thinking the same thing. Roshnani said, "Having a son and heir come into the world is liable to do wonders for anyone's disposition. I remember how you were after Varaz was born, for instance."

"Oh?" Abivard said in a tone that might have sounded ominous to anyone who didn't know him and Roshnani well. "And how was I?"

"Dazed and pleased," she answered; looking back on it, he decided she was probably right. Pointing to the parchment, she went on, "The man who wrote that letter is about as dazed and pleased as Sharbaraz King of Kings, may his days be long and his realm increase, ever lets himself get."

"You're right," Abivard said in some surprise; he hadn't looked at it like that. *Poor bastard,* he thought. He would have said that to Roshnani, but he didn't want Pashang to hear it, so he kept quiet.

✦   ✦   ✦

Peasants in loincloths labored in the fields around the Thousand Cities, some of them bringing in the crops, others busy repairing the canals the Videssians had wrecked. Abivard wondered, with a curiosity slightly greater than idle, how the peasants would have gone about repairing the half twist Maniakes' mages had given that one canal.

No one in the land of the Thousand Cities came rushing out from the cities or in from the fields to clasp his hand and congratulate him for what he had done. He hadn't expected anyone to do that, so he wasn't disappointed. Armies got no credit from the people in whose land they fought.

Khimillu, city governor of Qostabash, the leading town the Videssians had not sacked in the area, turned red under his swarthy skin when Abivard proposed garrisoning troops there for the winter. "This is an outrage!" he thundered in a fine, deep voice. "What with the war, we are poor. How are we to support these men gobbling our food and fondling our women?"

However impressive Khimillu's voice, he was a short, plump man, a native of the Thousand Cities. That let Abivard look down his nose at him. "If you don't want to feed them, I suppose they'll just have to go away," he said, using a ploy that had proved effective in the land of the Thousand Cities. "Then, next winter, you can explain to Maniakes why you don't feel like feeding his troopers—if he hasn't burned this town down around your ears by then."

But Khimillu, unlike some other city governors, was made of stern stuff despite his unprepossessing appearance. "You will not do such a thing. You cannot do such a thing," he declared. Again unlike other city governors, he sounded unbluffably certain.

That being so, Abivard did not try to bluff him. Instead he said, "Maybe not. Here is what I can do, though: I can write to my brother-in-law, Sharbaraz King of Kings, may his years be many and his realm increase, and tell him exactly how you are obstructing my purpose here. Have one of your scribes bring me pen and ink and parchment; the letter can be on its way inside the hour. Does that suit you better, Khimillu?"

If the city governor had gone red before, he went white now. Abivard would not have had the stomach to endanger all of Qostabash because of his obstinacy. Getting rid of an obstreperous official, though, wouldn't affect the rest of the town at all. "Very well, lord," Khimillu said, suddenly remembering—or at least acknowledging—Abivard outranked him. "It shall be as you say, of course. I merely wanted to be certain you understood the predicament you face here."

"Of course you did," Abivard said. In another tone of voice that would have been polite agreement. As things were, he had all but called Khimillu a liar to his face. With some thousands of men at his back, he did not need to appease a city governor who cared nothing for those men once they had done him the services he had expected of them.

Blood rose once more to Khimillu's face. Red, white, red—he might have done for the colors of Makuran. Abivard wondered whether he should hire a taster to check his meals for as long as he stayed in Qostabash. In a tight voice the city governor said, "You could spread your men around through more cities hereabouts if the Videssians hadn't burned so many."

"We don't work miracles," Abivard answered. "All we do is the best we can. Your town is intact, and the Videssians have been driven away."

"Small thanks to you," Khimillu said. "For a very long time the Videssians were near, and you far away. Had they stretched out their hands toward Qostabash, it would have fallen like a date from a tree."

"It may yet fall like a date from a tree," Abivard said. The city governor's complaint had just enough truth in it to sting. Abivard had done his best to be everywhere at once between the Tutub and the Tib, but his best had not always been good enough. Still—"We *are* going to garrison soldiers here this winter, the better to carry on the war against Videssos when spring comes. If you try to keep us from doing that, I promise: you and this city will have cause to regret it."

"That is an outrage!" Khimillu said, which was probably true. "I shall write to Sharbaraz King of Kings, may his days be long and his realm increase, and inform him of what . . ."

His voice faded. Complaining to the King of Kings about what one of his generals was doing stood some chance of getting a city governor relief. Complaining to the King of Kings about what his brother-in-law was doing stood an excellent chance of getting a city governor transferred to some tiny village on the far side of the Sea of Salt, to the sort of place where no one cared if the taxes were five years in arrears because five years worth of taxes from it wouldn't have bought three mugs of wine at a decent tavern.

With the poorest of poor graces, Khimillu said, "Very well. Since I have no choice in the matter, let it be as you say."

"The troops do have to stay somewhere," Abivard said reasonably, "and Qostabash is the city that's suffered least in these parts."

"And thus we shall suffer on account of your troops," the governor returned. "I have trouble seeing the justice in that." He threw his hands in the air, defeated. "But you are too strong for me. Aye, it shall be as you desire in all things, lord."

Abivard rapidly discovered what he meant by that: not the wholehearted cooperation the words implied nor, really, cooperation of any sort. What Khimillu and the officials loyal to him did was stand aside and refrain from actively interfering with Abivard. Beyond that they did their best to pretend that neither he nor the soldiers existed. If that was how they viewed granting his desires in all things, he shuddered to think what would have happened had they opposed him.

"We should have loosed Khimillu against the Videssians," Abivard told Roshnani after they and their children had been installed in some small, not very comfortable rooms a good distance from the city governor's palatial residence. "He would have made them flee by irking them too much for them to stay." He chuckled at his own conceit.

"They've been irksome themselves lately," she said, thumping at a lumpy cushion to try to beat it into some semblance of comfort. When she leaned back against it, she frowned and punched it some more. At last satisfied, she went on, "And speaking of irksome, what do you aim to do about Tzikas?"

"Drop me into the Void if I know what to do with him," Abivard said, adding, "Or what to do to him," a moment later. "That last letter from the King of Kings seems to give me free rein, but if the traitor hadn't escaped from Maniakes and come to us, who knows how long we might have been entangled with the Videssians' magic? I do need to remember that, I suppose."

"But the Videssians' magic was only that screen, with nothing behind it," Roshnani said.

"Tzikas couldn't have known that . . . I don't think." Abivard drummed his fingers on his thigh. "The trouble is, if I leave Tzikas to his own devices, in two weeks' time he'll be writing to Sharbaraz, telling him what a wretch I am. Khimillu has a sense of restraint; Tzikas has never heard of one."

"I can't say you're wrong about that, and I wouldn't try," his principal wife said. "You still haven't answered my question: what are you going to do about him?"

"I don't know," Abivard admitted. "On the one hand, I'd like to be rid of him once for all so I wouldn't have to worry about him anymore. But I keep thinking he might be useful against Maniakes, and so I hold off from killing him."

"Maniakes evidently thought the same thing in reverse, or he would have killed Tzikas after you arranged to give him to the Avtokrator," Roshnani said.

"Maniakes got some use out of the traitor," Abivard said resentfully. "If it hadn't been for Tzikas, we would have crushed the Videssians in the battle on the ridge." He checked himself. "But to be honest, we got a couple of years of decent use out of him before he decided to try to convince the King of Kings he could do everything better than I can."

"And the Videssians got good use from him before that, when he sat at Amorion and held us away from the Arandos valley," Roshnani said.

"But he was doing that for himself more than for Genesios or Maniakes." Abivard laughed. "Tzikas has done more for—and to—both sides here than anyone else in the whole war. Nobody can possibly trust him now, but that doesn't mean he has no value."

"If you're going to use him against the Videssians, how do you propose to go about it?" Roshnani asked.

"I don't know that, either, not right now," Abivard admitted. "All I aim to do is keep him alive—however much I don't like the idea—keep him under my control, and wait and see what sorts of chances I get, if I get any. In my place, what would you do?"

"Kill him," Roshnani said at once. "Kill him now and then write to tell the King of Kings what you've done. If Sharbaraz likes it—and after his latest letter he might—fine. If he doesn't like it, well, not even the King of Kings can order a man back from the dead."

That was so. Abivard's chuckle came out wry. "I wonder what

Maniakes would say if he found out the chief marshal of Makuran had a wife who was more ruthless than he."

Roshnani smiled. "He might not be surprised. The Videssians give their women freer rein in more things than we do—why not in ruthlessness, too?" She looked thoughtful. "For that matter, who's to say Maniakes' wife who is also his cousin isn't more ruthless than he ever dreamed of being?"

"Now, there's an interesting idea," Abivard said. "Maybe one day, if we're ever at peace with Videssos and if Maniakes is still on his throne, you and his Lysia can sit down and compare what the two of you did to make each other's lives miserable during the war."

"Maybe we can," Roshnani replied. Abivard had meant it as a joke, but she took him seriously. After a moment he decided she had—or might have had—reason to do so. She went on, "Speaking of ruthlessness, I meant what I said about the Videssian traitor. I'd sooner find a scorpion in my shoe than him on my side."

Abivard spoke in sudden decision. "You're right, by the God. He's stung me too often, too. I've held back because I've thought of the use I could get from him, but I'll never feel safe with him still around to cook up schemes against me."

"Checking you at the battle where you should have crushed Maniakes should weigh in the scales, too," Roshnani said.

"Checking me? He came too close to killing me," Abivard said. "That's the last time he'll thwart me, though, by the God." He went to the door of the apartment and ordered the sentry to summon a couple of soldiers who had distinguished themselves in the summer's fighting. When they arrived, he gave them their orders. Their smiles were all glowing eyes and sharp teeth. They drew their swords and hurried away.

He had a servant fetch a jar of wine, with which he intended to celebrate Tzikas' premature but not untimely demise. But when the soldiers returned to give him their report, they had the look of dogs that had seen a meaty bone between the boards of a fence but hadn't been able to squeeze through and seize the morsel. One of them said, "We found out he has leave to go walking through the streets of Qostabash so long as he returns to his quarters by sunset. He's not quite an ordinary prisoner, the guards told me." His expression said more clearly than words what he thought of that.

"The guard is right, and the fault is mine," Abivard said. "I give you leave to look for him in the city and kill him wherever you happen to find him. Or if that doesn't suit you, wait till sunset and put an end to him then."

"If it's all the same to you, lord, we'll do that," the soldier said. "I'm just a farm boy and not used to having so many people around all the time. I might kill the wrong one by mistake, and that would be a shame." His comrade nodded. Abivard shrugged.

But Tzikas did not return to his quarters when the sun went down. When he didn't, Abivard sent soldiers—farm boys and others—through the bazaars and brothels of Qostabash looking for him. They did not find him. They did find a horse dealer who had sold him—or at least had sold someone who spoke the Makuraner language with a lisping accent—a horse.

"Drop me into the Void!" Abivard shouted when that news reached him. "The rascal saw his head going down on the block, and now he's gone and absconded—and he has most of the day's start on us, too."

Romezan was there to hear the report, too. "Don't take it too hard, lord," he said. "We'll run the son of a whore to earth; you see if we don't. Besides, where is he going to go?"

That was a good question. As Abivard thought about it, he began to calm down. "He can't very well run off to Maniakes' army, now, can he? Not anymore he can't, not with the Videssians gone to Lyssaion and probably back to Videssos the city by sea already. And if he doesn't run off to the Videssians, we'll hunt him down."

"You see?" Romezan said. "It's not so bad." He paused and fiddled with one spike of his mustache. "Pretty slick piece of work, though, wasn't it? Him figuring out the exact right time to slide away, I mean."

"Slick is right," Abivard said, angry at himself. "He never should have had the chance . . . but I did trust him, oh, a quarter of the way, because the warning he gave us was a real one." He paused. "Or I thought it was a real one. Still, the magical screen the Videssians had set up was just that—a screen, nothing more. But it delayed us almost as much as it would have if it had had deadly sorcery concealed behind it. We always thought Tzikas didn't know it was only a screen. But what if he did? What if

Maniakes sent him out to make us waste as much time as he possibly could and help the Videssian army get away?"

"If he did that," Romezan said, "if he did anything like that, we don't handle him ourselves when we catch him. We send him back to Mashiz in chains, under heavy guard, and let Sharbaraz's torturers take care of him a little at a time. That's what he pays them for."

"Most of the time I'd fight shy of giving anyone over to the torturers," Abivard said. "For Tzikas, especially if he did that, I'd make an exception."

"I should hope so," Romezan replied. "You're too soft some-times, if you don't mind my saying so. If I had to bet, I'd say it came from hauling a woman all over the landscape. She probably thinks it's a shame to see blood spilled, doesn't she?"

Abivard didn't answer, convincing Romezan of his own right-ness. The reason Abivard didn't answer, though, was that he was having to do everything he could to keep from laughing in his lieutenant's face. Romezan's preconceptions had led him to a conclusion exactly opposite the truth.

But that wouldn't matter, either. However Abivard had reached his decision, he wanted Tzikas dead now. He offered a good-sized reward for the return of the renegade alive and an even larger one for his head, so long as it was in recognizable condition.

When morning came, he sent riders out to the south and east after Tzikas. He also had dogs brought into the Videssian's quarters to take his scent and then turned loose to hunt him down wherever he might be. The dogs, however, lost the trail after the time when Tzikas bought his horse; not enough of his scent had clung to the ground for them to follow it.

The human hunters had no better luck. "Why couldn't you have turned bloodthirsty a day earlier than you did?" Abivard demanded of Roshnani.

"Why couldn't you?" she returned, effectively shutting him up.

Every day that went by the searchers spread their nets wider. Tzikas did not get caught in those nets, though. Abivard hoped he'd perished from bandits or robbers or the rigor of his flight. If he ever did turn up in Videssos again, he was certain to be trouble.

✦ XII

Mashiz grew nearer with every clop of the horses' hooves, with every squealing revolution of the wagon's wheels. "Summoned to the capital," Abivard said to Roshnani. "Nice to hear that without fearing it's going to mean the end of your freedom, maybe the end of your life."

"About time you've been summoned back to Mashiz to be praised for all the good things you've done, not blamed for things that mostly weren't your fault," Roshnani said, loyal as a principal wife should be.

"Anything that goes wrong is your fault. Anything that goes right is credited to the King of Kings." Abivard held up a hand. "I'm not saying a word against Sharbaraz."

"I'll say a word. I'll say several words," Roshnani replied.

He shook his head. "Don't. As much as I've complained about it, that's not his fault . . . well, not altogether his fault. It comes with being King of Kings. If someone besides the ruler gets too much credit, too much applause, the man on the throne feels he'll be thrown off it. It's been like that in Makuran for a long, long time, and it's like that in Videssos, too, though maybe not so bad."

"It isn't right," Roshnani insisted.

"I didn't say it was right. I said it was real. There's a difference," Abivard said. Because Roshnani still looked mutinous, he added, "I expect you'll agree with me that it's not right to lock up noblemen's wives in the women's quarters of a stronghold. But the custom of doing that is real. You can't pretend it's not there and expect all those wives to come out at once, can you?"

"No," Roshnani said unwillingly. "But it's so much easier and more enjoyable to dislike Sharbaraz the man doing as he pleases than Sharbaraz the King of Kings acting like a King of Kings."

"So it is," Abivard said. "Don't get me wrong: I'm not happy with him. But I'm not as angry as I was, either. The God approves of giving those who wrong you the benefit of the doubt."

"Like Tzikas?" Roshnani asked, and Abivard winced. She went on, "The God also approves of revenge when those who wrong you won't change their ways. She understands there will be times when you have to protect yourself."

"He'd better understand that," Abivard answered. They both smiled, as Makuraners often did when crossing genders of the God.

With the wind coming off the Dilbat Mountains from the west, Mashiz announced itself to the nose as well as to the eye. Abivard had grown thoroughly familiar with the city stink of latrines, smoke, horses, and unwashed humanity. It was the same coming from the capital of Makuran as it was in the land of the Thousand Cities and the same there as in Videssos.

For that matter, it was the same in Vek Rud stronghold and the town at the base of the high ground atop which the stronghold sat. Whenever people gathered together, other people downwind knew about it.

Once the wagon got into Mashiz, Pashang drove it through the city market on the way to the palace of the King of Kings. The going was slow in the market district. Hawkers and customers clogged the square, shouting and arguing and calling one another names. They cursed Pashang with great panache for driving past without buying anything.

"Madness," Abivard said to Roshnani. "So many strangers, all packed together and trying to cheat other strangers. I wonder how many of them have ever before seen the people from whom they buy and how many will ever see them again."

His principal wife nodded. "There are advantages to living in a stronghold," she said. "You know everyone around you. It can get poisonous sometimes—the God knows that's so—but it's for the good, too. A lot of people who would cheat a stranger in a heartbeat will go out of their way to do something nice for someone they know."

They rode through the open square surrounding the walls of the palace of the King of Kings. The courtiers within those walls led lives as ingrown in their own way as those of the inhabitants of the most isolated stronghold of Makuran. And very few of them, Abivard thought, were likely to go out of their way to do anything nice for anyone they knew.

The guards at the gate saluted Abivard and threw wide the valves to let him and his family come inside. Servitors took charge of the wagon—and of Pashang. The driver went with them with less fear and hesitation than he'd shown the winter before. Abivard was glad to see that, though he still wondered what sort of reception he himself was likely to get.

His heart sank when Yeliif came out to greet him; the only people he would have been less glad to see in the palace were, for different reasons, Tzikas and Maniakes. But the beautiful eunuch remained so civil, Abivard wondered whether something was wrong with him, saying only, "Welcome, Abivard son of Godarz, in the name of Sharbaraz King of Kings, may his days be long and his realm increase. Come with me and I shall show you to the quarters you have been assigned. If they prove unsatisfactory in any way, by all means tell me, that I may arrange a replacement."

He'd never said anything like that the past couple of years. Then Abivard's stays in the palace had been in essence house arrest. Now, as he and his family walked through the hallways of the palace, servants bowed low before them. So did most nobles he saw, acknowledging his rank as being far higher than theirs. A few high nobles from the Seven Clans kissed him on the cheek, claiming status only a little lower than his. He accepted that. Had he not done what he'd done, he would have been the one bowing before them.

No. Had he not done what he'd done, the nobles from the Seven Clans would either have fled up into the plateau country west of the Dilbat Mountains or would be trying to figure out what rank they had among Maniakes' courtiers. He'd earned their respect.

The suite of rooms to which Yeliif led him had two great advantages over those in which he'd stayed in the past two years. First was their size and luxury. Second, and better by far, was the complete absence of sentries, guards, keepers, what have you in front of the door.

"Sharbaraz King of Kings, may his days be long and his realm increase, will allow us to come and go as we please and to receive visitors likewise?" Abivard asked. Only after he'd spoken did he realize how great a capacity for irony he'd acquired in his years in Videssos.

Yeliif had never been to Videssos but was formidably armored against irony. "Of course," he replied, his limpid black eyes as wide and candid as if Abivard had enjoyed those privileges on his previous visits to the palace . . . and as if he had never urged drastic punishment for the disloyalty of which Sharbaraz so often suspected Abivard.

Abivard's tone swung from sardonic to bland: "Perhaps you could help me arrange a meeting with my sister Denak and even arrange for me to see my nephew, Peroz son of Sharbaraz."

"I shall bend every effort toward achieving your desire in that regard," the beautiful eunuch said, sounding as if he meant it. Abivard studied him in some bemusement; cooperation from Yeliif was so new and strange, he had trouble taking the idea seriously. And then, as politely as ever but with a certain amount of relish nonetheless, the eunuch asked, "And would you also like me to arrange for you a meeting with Tzikas?"

Abivard stared at him. So did Roshnani. So even did Varaz. Yeliif's small smile exposed white, even, sharply pointed teeth. "Tzikas is here—in the palace?" Abivard asked.

"Indeed he is. He arrived a fortnight before you," Yeliif answered. "Would you like me to arrange a meeting?"

"Not right now, thank you," Abivard said. If Tzikas had been there two weeks and had still kept his head on his shoulders, he was liable to keep it a good deal longer. Somehow or other he'd managed to talk Sharbaraz out of giving him over to the torturers. That meant he'd be getting ready to give Abivard another riding boot between the legs the first chance he saw.

Yeliif said, "The King of Kings was inclined toward severity in the matter of Tzikas until the Videssian enlightened him as to how, after a daring escape from Maniakes' forces, he saved your entire army from destruction at the hands of vicious Videssian sorcery."

"Did he?" Abivard said, unsure whether he meant Tzikas'

"enlightenment" of Sharbaraz or his alleged salvation of the
Makuraner force. The more he thought about it, the more he
wondered whether Maniakes hadn't known perfectly well that
Tzikas would flee back to the Makuraners and thus had given him
something juicy with which to flee. Maybe the magical preparations had looked worse than they were, to impress the renegade,
just as the sorcerous "fog bank" had impressed Abivard's wizards
till they had discovered that nothing lay behind it.

And maybe, too, Tzikas had known perfectly well that the
Videssians' magecraft was harmless and had gone back with the
specific intention of delaying Abivard's army as long as he could
and giving Maniakes a chance to get away. He'd certainly done
that whether he had intended to or not. And Tzikas, from what
Abivard had seen, seldom did things inadvertently.

"These quarters *are* satisfactory?" Yeliif asked.

"Satisfactory in every way," Abivard told him, that being the
closest he could come to applauding the lack of keepers. Roshnani nodded. So did their children, who would have more room
now than they had enjoyed in some time. Of course, after slow
travel in the wagon, any chamber larger than belt-pouch size felt
commodious to them.

"Excellent," the beautiful eunuch said, and bowed low, the first
such acknowledgment of superiority he'd ever granted Abivard.
"And rest assured I shall not forget to make arrangements for
you to see your sister and nephew." He slipped from the suite
and was gone.

Abivard stared after him. "Was that really the Yeliif we've
known and loathed the past couple of years?" he said to no one
in particular.

"It really was," Roshnani said, sounding as dazed as he was.
"Do you know what I wish we could borrow right now?"

"What's that?" Abivard asked.

"Sharbaraz's food taster, if he has one," his principal wife
answered. "And he probably does." Abivard thought about that,
then nodded, agreeing with both the need and the likelihood.

Yeliif used a suave and tasteful gesture to point out the door
through which Abivard was to enter. "Denak and young Peroz
await you within," he said. "I shall await you here in the hall and
return with you to your chamber."

"I can probably find my way back by myself," Abivard said.

"It is the custom," the eunuch answered, a sentence from which there could be no possible appeal.

Shrugging, Abivard opened the door and went inside. He didn't shut it in Yeliif's face, as he would have done before. Since the beautiful eunuch was not actively hostile, Abivard didn't want to turn him that way.

Inside the room waited not only his sister and her new baby but also the woman Ksorane. Not even her brother could be alone with the principal wife of the King of Kings, and tiny Peroz didn't count in such matters.

"Congratulations," he said to Denak. He wanted to run to his sister and take her in his arms but knew the serving woman would interpret that as uncouth familiarity no matter how closely they were related. He did the next best thing by adding, "Let me see the baby, please."

Denak smiled and nodded, but even that proved complicated. She could not simply hand Peroz to Abivard, for the two of them would touch each other if she did. Instead, she gave the baby to Ksorane, who in turn passed him to Abivard, asking as she did so, "You know how to hold them?"

"Oh, yes," he assured her. "My eldest will start sprouting his beard before many years go by." She nodded, satisfied. Abivard held Peroz in the crook of his elbow, making sure he kept the baby's head well supported. His nephew stared up at him with the confused look babies so often give the large, confusing world. Their eyes met. Peroz's blank stare was swallowed by a large, enthusiastic, toothless smile. Abivard smiled back, and that made the baby's smile get even wider. Peroz jerked and waved his arms around, not seeming quite sure they belonged to him.

"Don't let him grab your beard," Denak warned. "He's already pulled my hair a couple of times."

"I know about that, too," Abivard said. He held the baby for a while, then handed it back to the serving woman, who returned it to his sister. "An heir to the throne," he murmured, adding for Ksorane's benefit, "Though I hope Sharbaraz keeps it for many years to come." He remained unsure whether the woman's first loyalty lay with Denak or with the King of Kings.

"As do I, of course," Denak said; maybe she wasn't perfectly sure, either. But then she went on, "Yes, now I've had my foal.

And now I'm put back in the stable again and forgotten." She did not bother to disguise her bitterness.

"I'm sure the King of Kings gives you every honor," Abivard said.

"Honor? Yes, though I'd be worse than forgotten if Peroz had turned out to be a girl." Denak's mouth twisted. "I have everything I want—except about three quarters of my freedom." She held up a hand to keep Abivard from saying anything. "I know, I know. If I'd stayed married to Pradtak, I'd still be stuck away in the women's quarters, but I would rule his domain in spite of that. Here I can go about more freely, which looks well, but no one listens to me—no one." The lines new on her face these past few years grew deep and harsh.

"Do you want freedom," Abivard asked, "or do you want influence?"

"Both," Denak answered at once. "Why shouldn't I have both? If I were a man, I could easily have both. Because I'm not, I'm supposed to be amazed to have one. That's not the way I work."

Abivard knew as much. It had never been the way his sister worked. He pointed to Peroz, who was falling asleep in her arms. "You have influence there—and you'll have more as time goes by."

"Influence because I'm his mother," Denak said, looking down at the baby. "Not influence because I am who I am. Influence through a baby, influence through a man. It's not enough. I have wit enough to be a counselor to the King of Kings or even to rule in my own right. Will I ever have the chance? You know the answer as well as I do."

"What would you have me do?" Abivard said. "Shall I ask the God to remake the world so it pleases you better?"

"I've asked her that myself often enough," Denak said, "but I don't think she'll ever grant my prayer. Maybe, in spite of what we women call her, the God is a man, after all. Otherwise, how could she treat women so badly?"

Sitting off in a corner of the room, the serving woman yawned. Denak's complaints meant nothing to her. In some ways she was freer than the principal wife of the King of Kings.

Changing the subject seemed a good idea to Abivard. "What did Sharbaraz say when he learned you'd had a son?" he asked.

"He said all the right things," Denak answered: "that he was glad, that he was proud of me, that Peroz was a splendid little fellow and hung like a horse, to boot." She laughed at the expression on Abivard's face. "It was true at the time."

"Yes, I suppose it would have been," Abivard agreed, remembering how the genitals of his newborn sons had been disproportionately large for the first few days of their lives. "It surprised me."

"It certainly did—you should have seen your jaw drop," Denak said. She went on, "And how have you been? How has life been outside the walls of this palace?"

"I've been fairly well—not perfect but fairly well. We even beat the Videssians this year, not so thoroughly as I would have liked, but we beat them." Abivard shrugged. "That's how life works. You don't get everything you want. If you can get most of it, you're ahead of the game. Maybe Sharbaraz is starting to see that, too: I didn't know how he'd take it when we beat the Videssians without smashing them to bits, but he hardly complained about that."

"He has some sort of scheme afoot," Denak answered. "I don't know what it is." The set of her jaw said what she thought about not knowing. "Whatever it is, he thought it up himself, and he's doubly proud of it on account of that. When he turns it loose, he says, Videssos the city will tremble and fall."

"That would be wonderful," Abivard answered. "For a while there a couple of springs ago, I was afraid Mashiz would tremble and fall."

"He says he's taken a lesson from the Videssians," Denak added, "and they'll pay for having taught him."

"What's that supposed to mean?" Abivard asked.

"I don't know," Denak told him. "That's all he's said to me; that's all he will say to me." Her thinned lips showed how much she cared for her husband's silence. "When he talks about this lesson, whatever it is, he has the look on his face he puts on when he thinks he's been clever."

"Does he?" Abivard said. "All right." He wouldn't say more with Ksorane listening. Sharbaraz was not stupid. He knew that. Sometimes the schemes the King of Kings thought up were very clever indeed. And sometimes the only person Sharbaraz's schemes fooled was Sharbaraz himself. Worst of all was the impossibility of figuring out in advance which was which.

"I'm glad he's—content with you," Denak said. "That's much better than the way things have been."

"Isn't it?" Abivard agreed. He smiled at his sister. "And I'm glad for you—and for little Peroz there."

She looked down at the baby. Her expression softened. "I do love him," she said quietly. "Babies are a lot of fun, especially with so many servants around to help when they're cranky or sick. But . . . it's hard sometimes to think of him as just a baby and not as a new piece of the palace puzzle, if you know what I mean. And that takes away from letting myself enjoy him."

"Nothing is simple," Abivard said with great conviction. "Nothing is ever simple. If living up by the nomads hadn't taught me that, the civil war would have, that or living among Videssians for a while." He rolled his eyes. "You live among Videssians for a while, by the end of that time you'll have trouble remembering your own name, let alone anything else."

Ksorane began to fidget. Abivard took that as a sign that he'd spent about as much time with his sister as had been allotted to him. He said his good-byes. The serving woman got up and served as a conduit so Denak could pass him Peroz once more and he, after holding the baby for a little while, could pass it back again. He reached out his arms toward Denak, and she stretched the one not holding Peroz out to him. They couldn't touch. Custom forbade it. Custom was very hard. He felt defeated as he went out into the corridor.

Yeliif was waiting for him. *Custom again,* he thought—the beautiful eunuch had said as much. Abivard could have walked back alone, but having Yeliif with him now was more a mark of his status than a sign that he was something close to a prisoner.

As the two of them fell into stride, Abivard asked quite casually, "What sort of lessons has Sharbaraz King of Kings, may his years be many and his realm increase, taken from the Videssians?"

"Ah, you heard about that, did you?" Yeliif said. "From the lady your sister, no doubt."

"No doubt," Abivard agreed. They walked on a few steps, neither of them saying anything. Abivard poked a little harder: "You do know the answer?"

"Yes, I know it," the beautiful eunuch said, and said no more.

"Well?"

Yeliif didn't answer right away. Abivard had the pleasure of seeing him highly uncomfortable. At last the beautiful eunuch said, "While I do know the answer, I do not know whether I should be the one to reveal it to you. The King of Kings would be better in that role, I believe."

"Ah." They walked along a little farther. By way of experiment Abivard shifted into Videssian: "Does the eminent Tzikas know this answer, whatever it may be?"

"No, I don't believe he does," Yeliif answered in the same tongue, and then glared at him for being found out.

"That's something, anyhow," Abivard said in relief.

"Sharbaraz King of Kings, may his days be long and his realm increase, considered it, but I dissuaded him," Yeliif said.

"Did you? Good for you," Abivard said; the beautiful eunuch's action met with his complete approval. Something else occurred to Abivard: "Did he by any chance tell Hosios Avtokrator?" He kept all irony from his voice, as one had to do when speaking of "Hosios"; though the King of Kings had gone through several puppet Avtokrators of the Videssians without finding any of them effective in bringing Videssians over to Makuran, he kept on trying.

Or he had kept on trying, anyhow. Matching Abivard in keeping emotion from his voice, Yeliif said, "Hosios Avtokrator—" He did not say, *the most recent Hosios Avtokrator,* either. "—had the misfortune of suddenly departing this world late this past summer. The King of Kings ordered him mourned and buried with the pomp and circumstances he deserved."

"Died suddenly, you say?" Abivard murmured, and Yeliif nodded a bland nod in return. "How unfortunate." Yeliif nodded again. Abivard wondered whether the latest "Hosios," like at least one of his predecessors, had shown an unwonted and unwanted independence that had worried Sharbaraz or whether the King of Kings had simply decided to give up serving as puppet-master.

Then a really horrid thought struck him. "The King of Kings isn't planning on naming Tzikas Avtokrator if we ever do conquer Videssos the city, is he? Please tell me no." For once he spoke to the beautiful eunuch with complete sincerity.

"If he is, I have no knowledge of it," Yeliif answered. That relieved Abivard, but less than he would have liked. The eunuch said, "Myself, I do not believe that policy would yield good results." His doelike black eyes widened as he realized he'd agreed with Abivard.

"When can I hope for an audience with the King of Kings?" Abivard asked, hoping to take advantage of such unusual amiability from Yeliif.

"I do not know," the beautiful eunuch answered. "I shall pass on your request to him. It should not be an excessively long period. Better he should talk to you than to the Videssian."

"When I came to Mashiz, didn't you mock me with the news that Tzikas had gotten here first?" Abivard said.

"So I did," Yeliif admitted. "Well, we all make mistakes. Next to Tzikas, you are a pillar supporting Sharbaraz's every enterprise." He glanced toward Abivard. Those black eyes suddenly were not doelike but cold and hard and shiny as polished jet. "This should by no means be construed as a compliment, you understand."

"Oh, yes, I understand that," Abivard said, his voice as dry as the summer wind that blew dust into Vek Rud stronghold. "You loathe me as much as you ever did; it's just that you've discovered you loathe Tzikas even more."

"Precisely," the eunuch said. As far as Abivard could tell, he loathed everyone to some degree, save perhaps the King of Kings. Did that mean he loathed himself, too? No sooner had the question crossed Abivard's mind than he realized it was foolish. Being what he was, any hope of manhood taken from him by a knife, how could Yeliif help loathing himself? And from that, no doubt, all else sprang.

Abivard said, "If I were a danger to Sharbaraz, I would have shown as much a long time ago, wouldn't I? Tzikas, now..." A mutual loathing was as good a reason for an alliance as any, he thought, and better than most.

Yeliif eyed him with a look as close to approval as he'd ever won from him. "Those last two words, I believe, with their accompanying ellipsis, are the first sensible thing I have ever heard you say."

As compliments went, it wasn't much. Abivard was glad of it all the same.

Courtiers with elaborately curled hair and beards, with rouged cheeks, with caftans bound by heavy gold belts and shot through with gold and silver thread drew down their eyebrows—those whose eyebrows were gray or white had a way of drawing them down harder than did those whose brows remained dark—when Abivard and Roshnani came into the banquet hall arm in arm.

Custom died hard. Sharbaraz King of Kings had kept his word about allowing Denak to leave the women's quarters, a liberty the wives of nobles had not enjoyed till then. And for a while a good many nobles had followed their sovereign's lead. Evidently, though, the old ways were reasserting themselves, for only a couple of other women besides Roshnani were in the hall. Abivard looked around to see if his sister was among them. He didn't see her, but then, Sharbaraz hadn't yet entered, so that didn't signify anything.

He stiffened. Denak wasn't there, and neither was Sharbaraz, but there sat Tzikas, talking amiably with a Makuraner noble from the Seven Clans. To look at the Videssian renegade, he hadn't a care in the world. His gestures were animated; his face showed nothing but sincerity. Abivard knew, to his cost, how much that sincerity was worth. The noble, though, seemed altogether entranced. Abivard had seen that before, too.

To his dismay, the servant who led Roshnani and him to their places seated them not far from Tzikas. Brawling in the palace was unseemly, so Abivard ignored the Videssian renegade. He poured wine first for Roshnani, then for himself.

Sharbaraz came into the hall. Everyone rose and bowed low. The King of Kings entered alone. Sadness smote Abivard. He hoped Denak was not at Sharbaraz's side because little Peroz needed her. He doubted it, though. The King of Kings had given his principal wife more freedom than was customary, but custom pulled even on him. If he wasn't wholehearted about keeping such changes alive, they would perish.

Roshnani noted Denak's absence, too. "I would have liked to see my sister-in-law without having to go into the women's quarters to do it," she said. She didn't raise her voice but didn't go to any trouble to keep it down, either. A couple of courtiers gave her sidelong looks. She looked back unabashed, which seemed to disconcert them. They muttered back and forth to each other but did not turn their eyes her way again.

A soup of meatballs and pomegranate seeds started the feast. For amusement Abivard and Roshnani counted the seeds in their bowl; pomegranate seeds were supposed to bring good luck. When they both turned out to have seventeen, they laughed: neither one got to tease the other.

After the soup came a salad of beets in yogurt enlivened with mint. Abivard had never been fond of beets. They were far more tolerable here than in most of the dishes where they appeared.

Rice gorgeously stained and flavored with sour cherries and saffron followed the beets. Accompanying it was mutton cooked with onions and raisins. Roshnani mixed hers together with the rice. Abivard, who preferred to savor flavors separately, didn't.

The food, as usual in the palace, was splendid. He gave it less attention than was his habit, and he was moderate with his wine, calling for quince and rhubarb sherbets more often than he did for the captured Videssian vintages Sharbaraz served his grandees. He directed more attention to his ears than to his tongue, trying to catch what Tzikas was saying behind his back.

Tzikas had been saying things behind his back since not long after the Videssian had fled the Avtokrator he had formerly served. He hadn't thought Abivard knew about that—and indeed, Abivard hadn't known about it till almost too late. Now, though, he had to think Abivard would hear him, and that, to Abivard's way of thinking, would have been the best possible reason for him to keep his mouth shut.

Maybe Tzikas didn't know how to keep his mouth shut. Maybe he could no more stop intriguing than he could stop breathing: he might claim to worship the God, but he remained Videssian to the core. Or maybe he just did not really believe Abivard could overhear. Whatever the reason, his tongue rolled on without the least hesitation.

Abivard could not make out everything he said, but what he caught was plenty: "—my victory over Maniakes by the banks of the Tib—" Tzikas was saying to someone who hadn't been there and couldn't contradict him. He sounded most convincing, but then, he always did.

When Abivard turned toward Tzikas, Roshnani set a warning hand on his arm. He usually took her warnings more seriously than he did now. Smiling a smile that had little to do with amiability, he said, "When you came to Mashiz, Tzikas, you should have set up shop in the bazaar, not the palace."

"Oh?" Tzikas said, staring at him as if he'd just crawled out from under a flat stone. "And why is that?" No matter how he aped Makuraner ways, the renegade kept all his Videssian arrogance, remaining convinced that he was and had to be the cleverest man around.

Smiling, Abivard sank his barb: "Because then you could have sold your lies wholesale instead of doling them out one by one the way you do here."

Tzikas glowered at him. "I am not the one who handed my subordinate to the enemy," he said.

"True enough—you don't do things like that," Abivard agreed. "Your subordinates are safe from you. It's your superiors who have to have eyes in the backs of their heads. What would you have done if you had killed Maniakes by magic and made yourself Avtokrator of the Videssians?"

"Beaten you," Tzikas said. Yes, he had his own full measure and to spare of the overweening pride that singularly failed to endear the imperials to the men of Makuran.

But when Abivard said "I doubt it," that didn't merely spring from his angry reaction to the renegade's words. However skilled an intriguer Tzikas was, Abivard was convinced he had his measure in the field. Lightly, casually, he went on, "That wasn't what I meant, anyhow."

"What *did* you mean?" Now Tzikas sounded ominous, beginning to realize Abivard was scoring off him.

Abivard scored again: "I meant you'd be bored sitting on the throne with no one in Videssos to betray."

Tzikas glared at him; that had gotten to the renegade, even though the odds were good that it wasn't true. An intriguer would hardly stop intriguing because he'd schemed his way to the top. He'd sit up there and scheme against all those—and there would surely be some—who'd try to follow him and pull him down. And even if he saw no one who looked dangerous, he would probably destroy a courtier every now and then for the sport of it and to keep rivals wary.

"If you want me to prove what sort of liar you are, I will meet you when and where you like, with the weapons you like," Tzikas said.

Abivard beamed at him. "The first generous offer you've made! We've tried to kill each other before; now I can do it properly."

"It is forbidden," Yeliif said. Abivard and Tzikas both stared in startlement at the beautiful eunuch. Yeliif went on, "Sharbaraz

King of Kings, may his years be many and his realm increase, has let me know he requires both of you for the enterprise he contemplates beginning next spring."

"What *is* this fabled enterprise?" Tzikas demanded. *Good,* Abivard thought. *Yeliif wasn't lying to me—Tzikas doesn't know, either.* He would have been offended to the core had Sharbaraz enlightened the Videssian renegade while leaving him in the dark.

Yeliif sniffed. "When the proper time for you to gain that knowledge comes, rest assured it shall be provided to you. Until such time cherish the fact that you will be preserved alive to acquire the knowledge when the time comes."

"He certainly doesn't deserve to live to find out," Abivard said.

"At one time or another a good many have expressed the opinion that you yourself did not merit remaining among the living," the beautiful eunuch replied coldly. Abivard knew full well he had been among the leaders of those expressing that opinion.

Injustice still stung him. "Some people thought I was too successful, and so I had to be a traitor on account of that. But everyone knows Tzikas is a traitor. He doesn't even bother pretending not to be."

"So he doesn't," Yeliif said, favoring Tzikas with a glance as icy as any with which he had ever chilled Abivard. "But a known traitor has his uses, provided he is watched at all times. The King of Kings intends to get such use as he can from the renegade."

Abivard nodded. Where Tzikas was concerned, Sharbaraz had less to worry about than did Maniakes. Tzikas had already tried to steal the Videssian throne. Whatever else he might do, he could not set himself up as King of Kings of Makuran.

That didn't mean he could not aspire to any number of lesser but still prominent offices in Makuran, such as the one Abivard had. He'd already aspired to that office and done his best to throw Abivard out of it. He'd do the same again if he saw a chance and thought Sharbaraz would look the other way.

Abivard made a solemn resolution: regardless of whether Sharbaraz intended using Tzikas in this grand scheme of his, whatever it was, he was going to take out the Videssian renegade if he saw even the slightest chance of doing so. He could always apologize to the King of Kings afterward, and had no intention of granting Tzikas the same chance.

✦   ✦   ✦

Winter dragged on. The children got to go out into the courtyard now, as they hadn't in years gone by. Even Gulshahr was
old enough now to pack snow into a ball and throw it at her
brothers. Doing that left her squealing with glee.

Videssian captives tutored Varaz and Shahin. Abivard's sons
took to lessons with the same enthusiasm they would have shown
taking poison. He walloped them on the backside and kept them
at it.

"We already know how to speak Videssian," Varaz protested.
"Why do we have to know how to make speeches in it?"

"And all these numbers, too," Shahin added. "It's like they're all
pieces of a puzzle, and they're all scrambled up, and the Videssians
expect us to be able to put them together as easy as anything."
He stuck out his lower lip. "It's not fair." That was the worst
condemnation he could give to anything not to his liking.

"Being able to count past ten without having to take off your
shoes won't kill you," Abivard said. He rounded on Varaz. "You'll
be dealing with Videssians your whole life, most likely. Knowing
how to impress them when you talk won't do you any lasting
harm."

"When you first went into Videssos, did you know how to
speak the language there?" Varaz asked.

"Not so you'd notice," Abivard answered. "But remember, I grew
up in the far Northwest, and I never expected to go into Videssos
at all, except maybe as a soldier in an invading army." He folded
his arms across his chest. "You'll keep on with your lessons," he
declared as firmly as Sharbaraz promulgating a decree. The King
of Kings could make the whole of Makuran heed him. Abivard's
authority was less than that but did extend to his two boys.

They studied more than mathematics and rhetoric. They rode
ponies, shot bows suited to their strength, and began to learn
swordplay. They would acquire a Videssian veneer—Abivard was
convinced it would prove useful—but beneath it would have the
accomplishments of a proper Makuraner noble.

"The more different things you know how to do, the better off
you'll be," Abivard told them.

The man that thought called to mind, unfortunately, was Tzikas.
The Videssian renegade knew not only his own tongue but that
of Makuran as well. He could tell convincing stories in either

one. He was a talented soldier to boot. If he'd been only a little luckier, he would have been Avtokrator of the Videssians or perhaps commander of the Makuraner field army. No one had ever come closer to meeting both of those seemingly incompatible goals.

He was missing one thing, though. Abivard wasn't sure it had a name. *Steadfastness* was as close as he could come, that or *integrity*. Neither word felt quite right. Without the quality, though, Tzikas' manifold talents brought him less than they might have otherwise.

Yeliif said the same thing a different way a few days later. "He is a Videssian," the beautiful eunuch intoned, as if to say that alone irremediably spoiled Tzikas.

Abivard eyed Yeliif with speculation of a sort different from that which he usually gave the eunuch. In the matter of Tzikas, for once, they shared an interest. "I'd be happier if we never had to speak of him again," Abivard said, an oblique message but not so oblique that the beautiful eunuch couldn't follow up on it if he so desired.

Yeliif also looked thoughtful. If the notion of being on the same side as Abivard pleased him, he didn't let his face know about it. After a little while he said, "Didn't you tell me Tzikas has wavered back and forth between the God and the false faith of Phos?"

"I did. He has," Abivard answered. "In the next world he will surely fall into the Void and be forgotten. I wish he would be forgotten here and now, too."

"I wonder," Yeliif said in musing tones, "yes, I wonder what the Mobedhan Mobedh would say on hearing that Tzikas has wavered between the true faith and the false."

"That is an . . . intriguing question," Abivard answered after a moment's pause to weigh just how intriguing it was. "Sharbaraz has forbidden the two of us to quarrel, but if the chief servant of the God comes to him with a complaint that Tzikas is an apostate, he may have to listen."

"So he may," Yeliif agreed. "On the other hand, he may not. Dhegmussa is his servant in all things. But a man who will not notice his servants is less than perfectly wise."

Not a word passed Abivard's lips. For all he knew, the beautiful eunuch was playing a game different from the one that showed on the surface of his words. He might be hoping to get Abivard to call the King of Kings a fool and then report what Abivard had said to Sharbaraz. Abivard did think the King of Kings a fool, but he himself was not so foolish as to say so where any potential foe could hear him.

But Yeliif's idea was far from the worst he'd ever heard. Maybe Dhegmussa wouldn't be able to do anything; the Mobedhan Mobedh was far more the creature of the King of Kings than the Videssians' ecumenical patriarch was the Avtokrator's creature. Apostasy, though, was nothing to take lightly. And making Tzikas sweat was nearly as good as making him suffer.

"I'll talk with Dhegmussa," Abivard said. Something glinted in Yeliif's black, black eyes. Was it approval? Abivard hadn't seen it there often enough to be sure he recognized it.

The shrine in which Dhegmussa, chief servant of the God, performed his duties was the most splendid of its kind in all Makuran. That said, it was nowhere near so fine as several of the temples to Phos Abivard had seen in Videssian provincial towns and not worth mentioning in the same breath as the High Temple in Videssos the city. The Makuraners said, *The God lives in your heart, not on the wall.*

Dhegmussa lived in a small home next to the shrine, a home like that which a moderately successful shoemaker might have inhabited: whitewashed mud bricks forming an unimpressive facade but a fair amount of comfort inside.

"You honor me, marshal of Makuran," the Mobedhan Mobedh said, leading Abivard along a dim, gloomy hall at the end of which light from the courtyard shone. When they got there, Dhegmussa waved a regretful hand. "You must imagine how it looks in spring and summer, all green and full of sweet-smelling, bright-colored flowers. This brown, dreary mess is not what it should be."

"Of course not," Abivard said soothingly. Dhegmussa guided him across the court to a room heated by a couple of charcoal braziers. A servant brought wine and sweet cakes. Abivard studied the Mobedhan Mobedh as they refreshed themselves. Dhegmussa was about sixty, with a closely trimmed gray beard and a loud voice that suggested he was a trifle deaf.

He waited till Abivard had eaten and drunk, then left off the polite small talk and asked, "How may I serve you, marshal of Makuran?"

"We have a problem, holy one, with a man who, while claiming to worship the God, abandoned in time of danger the faith he had professed, only to return to it when that seemed safer than the worship for which he had given it up," Abivard answered.

"This sounds dolorous indeed," Dhegmussa said. "A man who blows whichever way the winds of expediency take him is not one to hold a position of trust nor one who has any great hope of escaping the Void once his life on earth is done."

"I have feared as much myself, holy one," Abivard said, calling up a sadness he did not truly feel.

They went back and forth a while longer. The servant brought more cakes, more wine. At last the Mobedhan Mobedh put the question he had studiously avoided up till then: "Who is this man for whose spiritual well-being you so justly fear?"

"I speak of Tzikas, the Videssian renegade," Abivard said, a reply that could not have surprised Dhegmussa in the least by then. "Can any man who dons and doffs religions as if they were caftans possibly be a reliable servant to Sharbaraz King of Kings, may his years be many and his realm increase?"

"It seems difficult," Dhegmussa said, and then said no more for a time.

When he remained silent, Abivard pressed the matter: "Can a man who chooses whether to swear by the God or by false Phos by who is listening to him at any given moment be believed when he swears by either one?"

"It seems difficult," Dhegmussa said again.

That was as far as he would go on his own. Abivard prodded him to go further: "Would you want such a man close to the King of Kings? He might corrupt him with his own needlessness, or, on the other hand, failing to corrupt the King of Kings, he might be moved to violence against him."

"Fraortish eldest of all, prevent it," the Mobedhan Mobedh said, his fingers twisting in a sign to avert the evil omen. Abivard imitated the gesture. But then, to his disappointment, Dhegmussa went on: "But surely the King of Kings is aware of the risks entailed in having this Videssian close by him."

"There are risks, holy one, and then there are risks," Abivard said. "You do know, of course, that Tzikas once tried to murder the Videssian Avtokrator by magic." One of the advantages of telling the truth was the casual ease with which he could bring out such horrors.

Dhegmussa suffered a coughing fit. When he could finally speak again, he said, "I had heard such a thing, yes, but discounted it as a scurrilous rumor put about by his enemies." He looked sidelong at Abivard, who was certainly no friend to Tzikas.

"It certainly is scurrilous," Abivard agreed cheerfully, "but rumor it is not. I was the one who received him in Across after he fled in a rowboat over the strait called the Cattle Crossing after his conjuration couldn't kill Maniakes. If he'd stayed in Videssos the city another hour, Maniakes' men would have had him." *And that would have made life simpler for both the Avtokrator and me,* Abivard thought. Ever since he'd rescued Sharbaraz from Nalgis Crag stronghold, though, it had become more and more obvious that his life, whatever else it might hold, would not contain much simplicity.

"You swear this to me?" Dhegmussa asked.

"By the God and the Prophets Four," Abivard declared, raising first the thumb and then the fingers of his left hand.

Still Dhegmussa hesitated. Abivard wanted to kick him to see if direct stimulation would make his wits work faster. The only reason he could conceive for Sharbaraz having named this man Mobedhan Mobedh was the assurance of having an amiable nonentity in the position. So long as everything went well, having a nonentity in an important place held advantages, chief among them that he was not likely to be dangerous to the King of Kings. But sometimes a man who would not or could not act was more dangerous than one who could and would.

Trying to avoid action, Dhegmussa repeated, "Surely Sharbaraz is familiar with the problems the Videssian represents."

"The problems, yes," Abivard said. "My concern is that he has not fully thought through the religious import of all these things. That's why I came to you, holy one." *Do I have to color the picture as well as draw it?*

Maybe he didn't. Dhegmussa said, "I shall suggest to the King of Kings the possible consequences of keeping near his person a man of such, ah, ambiguous qualities and the benefits to be gained by removing him from a position where he might influence not only the affairs of Makuran but also the spiritual life of the King of Kings."

That was less than Abivard had hoped to get from the Mobe-dhan Mobedh. He'd wanted Dhegmussa to rear up on his hind legs and bellow something like *Get rid of this man or put your soul in peril of falling into the Void.*

Abivard chuckled. Any Videssian priest who deserved his blue robe would have said something like that, or else something worse. The Videssian patriarch had come out and publicly condemned Maniakes for marrying his own first cousin. That wasn't so offensive to Makuraner morality as it was in Videssos, but even if it had been, the Mobedhan Mobedh would not—could not—have taken such an active role in opposing it. A Mobedhan Mobedh who criticized his sovereign too vigorously wasn't just packed off to a monastery. He was liable to be a dead man.

Mild reproof, then, Abivard supposed, was as much as he could reasonably have expected to get. He bowed and said, "Thank you, holy one." The novelty of having Dhegmussa express anything but complete and glowing approval of everything Sharbaraz did might make the King of Kings sit up and take notice.

If it didn't . . . Abivard had tried direct methods of getting rid of Tzikas before. He'd been too late the last time. If he had to try again, he wouldn't be.

This winter a knock on the door to Abivard's suite of rooms did not provoke the alarm it had the past two years, even if it came at an hour when Abivard wasn't particularly looking for visitors. But when he opened the door and found Yeliif standing there, a memory of that alarm stirred in him. The beautiful eunuch might join him in despising Tzikas, but that did not make him a friend.

Ceremony nonetheless had to be observed. Abivard offered his cheek for the eunuch to kiss: Yeliif had influence but, because of his mutilation, not rank. Then Abivard stepped aside, saying, "Enter. Use these my rooms as your own while you are here."

"You are gracious," Yeliif said without sardonic overtones but also without warmth. "I have the honor to bring you a message from Sharbaraz King of Kings, may his years be many and his realm increase."

"I am always glad to bask in the wisdom of the King of Kings," Abivard answered. "What clever thought would he impart to me today?"

"The same thought he imparted to me not long ago," Yeliif said; by his expression, he would sooner not have had that thought, whatever it was, thus imparted.

"Enlighten me, then, by all means," Abivard said. He glanced over to Roshnani, who was sitting cross-legged on the floor by a window, quietly embroidering. Had she raised an eyebrow, he would have know he'd sounded sarcastic. Since she didn't, he supposed he'd gotten by with that.

"Very well," the beautiful eunuch said. "Sharbaraz King of Kings, may his days be long and his realm increase, bade me tell you—and incidentally bade me bear in mind myself—that he requires Tzikas' service in the enterprise he has planned for the next campaigning season and that he forbids you either to harm Tzikas' person or to seek the Videssian's condemnation for any of the malfeasances he either has committed or may commit in future."

"Of course I obey the King of Kings," Abivard replied. *Better than he deserves, too.* "But Tzikas' obedience in such matters must be questionable at best. If he attacks me, am I to ignore it?"

"If he attacks you, his head shall answer for it," Yeliif said. "So the King of Kings has ordered. So shall it be."

"So shall it be," Abivard echoed. If Sharbaraz really meant that—more to the point, if Sharbaraz convinced Tzikas he really meant that—all would be well. If not, the Videssian was already trying to find a way out of the order. Abivard would have bet on the latter.

"The King of Kings is most determined in this matter," the eunuch said, perhaps thinking along with him, "and has made his determination perfectly clear to Tzikas."

"Tzikas listens to Tzikas, no one else." Abivard held up his hand before Yeliif could reply. "Never mind. He hasn't managed to kill me yet, no matter how often he's betrayed me. I expect I can survive him a while longer. What seems to matter here, though, is why Sharbaraz is insisting we both stay alive and don't try to do each other in. You've said you know."

"I do," Yeliif agreed. "And as I have also said before, it is not my place to enlighten you as to the intentions of the King of Kings. He shall do that himself when he judges the time ripe. Since I have delivered his message and been assured you understand it, I shall take my leave." He did exactly that, sliding away as gracefully as an eel.

Abivard closed the door after him and turned to Roshnani. "So much for Dhegmussa," he said with a shrug.

"Yeliif was right: the idea was worth trying," she answered. They both paused in some surprise at the idea of admitting that the beautiful eunuch had been right about anything. Roshnani went on: "I wonder as much as you do about what's important enough to be worth keeping Tzikas alive. I can't think of anything that important."

"This side of taking Videssos the city, neither can I," Abivard said.

"If you couldn't take Videssos the city, Sharbaraz has to be mad to think Tzikas will be able to do it," Roshnani said indignantly. Abivard pointed to the walls of their suite and then to the ceiling. He didn't know if Sharbaraz had placed listeners by the suite, but the King of Kings surely had done that the past two winters, so taking chances was foolish. Roshnani nodded, following what he'd meant. She went on, "The Videssians hate Tzikas, too, though, so I don't see how he'd be a help in taking their capital."

"Neither do I," Abivard said. Even if Sharbaraz wouldn't listen to Dhegmussa, his spies were going to get an earful of what Abivard thought of the renegade. Sooner or later, he kept telling himself, some dirt would have to stick to Tzikas. "They'd sooner kill him than me. I'm just an enemy, while he's a traitor."

"A traitor to them, a traitor to us, a traitor to them again," Roshnani said, getting into the spirit of the game. "I wonder when he'll betray us again."

"First chance he gets, or I miss my bet," Abivard answered. "Or maybe not—who knows? Maybe he'll wait till he can do us the most harm instead."

They spent the next little while contentedly running down Tzikas. If the listeners in the walls were paying any attention, they could have brought Sharbaraz enough dirt for him to order Tzikas executed five or six times over. After a while, though, Abivard gave up. No matter what the listeners told Sharbaraz, he wasn't going to send Tzikas to the chopping block. He already had all the dirt he needed to order Tzikas executed. The trouble was, the King of Kings wanted the renegade alive so he could figure in his scheme, whatever it was.

Abivard sat down beside Roshnani and slipped an arm around her. He liked that for its own sake. It also gave him the chance to put his head close to hers and whisper, "Whatever plan Sharbaraz has, if it's for taking Videssos the city, it won't work. He can't make ships sprout from thin air, and he can't make Makuraners into sailors, either."

"You don't need to tell me that," she answered, also whispering. "Do you think you were the only one who looked out over the Cattle Crossing from Across at the city—" She dropped into Videssian for those words; to the imperials, their capital was *the* city, incomparably grander than all others. "—on the far side?"

"I never caught you doing that," he said.

She smiled. "Women do all sorts of things their husbands don't catch them doing. Maybe it comes from having spent so much time in the women's quarters—they're as much for breeding secrets as for breeding babies."

"You've been out of the women's quarters since not long after we wed," he said. "You needn't blame that for being sneaky."

"I didn't intend 'blaming' it on anything," Roshnani answered. "I'm proud of it. It's saved us a good deal of trouble over the years."

"That's true." Abivard lowered his voice even further. "If it weren't for you, Sharbaraz wouldn't be King of Kings now. He never would have thought of taking refuge in Videssos for himself—his pride ran too deep for that, even so long ago."

"I know." Roshnani let out a small, almost silent sigh. "Did I save us trouble there or cost us trouble?" The listeners, if there were any, could not have heard her; Abivard scarcely heard her himself, and his ear was close to her mouth. And having heard her, he had no idea what the answer to her question was. Time would tell, he supposed.

Sharbaraz King of Kings had enjoined Abivard from trying to dispose of Tzikas. From what Yeliif had said, Sharbaraz had also enjoined Tzikas from trying to get rid of him. He wouldn't have given a counterfeit copper for the strength of that last prohibition, though.

After that one near disaster at the feast the palace servitors did their best to ensure that Abivard and Tzikas did not come close to occupying the same space at the same time. Insofar as that meant keeping them far apart at ceremonial meals, the servitors' diligence was rewarded. But Abivard was free to roam the corridors of the palace. And so, however regrettable Abivard found the prospect, was Tzikas.

They bumped into each other three or four days after Yeliif had delivered the message from Sharbaraz ordering Abivard not to run down the Videssian renegade. Message or not, that was almost literally what happened. Abivard was hurrying down a passageway not far from his suite of rooms when Tzikas crossed his path. He stopped in a hurry. "I'm sor—" Tzikas began, and then recognized him. "You!"

"Yes, me." Abivard's hand fell, as if of its own accord, to the hilt of his sword.

Tzikas did not flinch from him and was also armed. No one had ever accused the Videssian of cowardice in battle. Plenty of other things had been charged against him, but never that one. He said, "A lot of men have lodged accusations against me—all lies, of course. Not one of those men came to a good end."

"Oh, I don't know," Abivard answered. "Maniakes still seems to be flourishing nicely, however much I wish he weren't."

"His time approaches." For a man who had been condemned to death by both sides, who switched gods as readily as a stylish woman switched necklaces, his confidence was infuriating. "For that matter, so does yours."

Abivard's sword leapt halfway out of its scabbard. "Whatever else happens, I'll outlive you. By the God I swear it—and he's likely to remember me, because I worship him all the time."

Videssian skin being fairer than the Makuraner norm, Tzikas' flush was quite visible to Abivard, who skinned his lips back from his teeth, pleased at having made a hit. The renegade said, "My heart knows where the truth lies."

He was speaking the Makuraner tongue; he wouldn't have given Abivard that kind of opening in Videssian. And Abivard took advantage of it, saying, "Your heart knows all about lies, doesn't it, Tzikas?"

Now the Videssian snarled. His graying beard gave him the aspect of an angry wolf. He said, "Jeer all you like. I am a constant man."

"I should say so—you're false all the time." Abivard pointed rudely at Tzikas' face. "Even your beard is changeable. When you first fled to us, you wore it trimmed close, the way most Videssians do. Then you grew it out to look more like a Makuraner. But when I fought you down in the land of the Thousand Cities, after Maniakes got hold of you, you'd cut it short and shaved around the edges again. And now it's getting longer and bushier."

Tzikas brought a hand up to his chin. Maybe he hadn't noticed what he was doing with his beard, or maybe he was angry someone else had noticed. "After Maniakes got hold of me, you say?" His voice went ugly. "You gave me to him, intending that he kill me."

"He has even better reason to love you than I do," Abivard replied, "but I have to say I'm gaining on him fast. You're like a sock, Tzikas—you fit either foot. But whoever made you wove you with a dye that burns like fire. Whatever you touch goes up in flames."

"I'll send you up in flames—or down to the ice," Tzikas said, and snatched out his sword.

Abivard's sword cleared the scabbard at about the same instant The clash of metal on metal brought shouts from around corners—people knew what that sound was even if they couldn't tell whence it came. Abivard knew what it was, too: the answer to his prayers. Tzikas had drawn on him first. He could kill the renegade and truthfully claim self-defense.

He was bigger and younger than Tzikas. All he had to do, he thought, was cut the Videssian down. He soon discovered it wouldn't be so easy. For one thing, Tzikas was smooth and strong and quick. For another, the corridor was narrow and the ceiling low, cutting into his size advantage: He had no room to make the full-armed cuts that might have beaten their way through Tzikas' guard. And for a third, neither he nor the renegade was used to fighting on foot in any surroundings, let alone such cramped ones. They were both horsemen by choice and by experience.

Tzikas had a strong wrist and tried to twist the sword out of Abivard's hand. Abivard held on to his blade and cut at his foe's head. Tzikas got his sword up in time to block the blow. As they had been on horseback, they were well matched here.

"Stop this at once!" someone shouted from behind Abivard. He took no notice; had he taken any notice, he would have been spitted the next instant. Nor did Tzikas show any signs of trusting him to show restraint—and the renegade had reason, for once two enemies began to fight, getting them to stop before one was bleeding or dead was among the hardest things for individuals and empires both.

A servant behind Tzikas shouted for him to give over. He kept slashing away at Abivard nonetheless, his fencing style afoot taking on more and more of the manner in which he would have fought while horsed as he went on battling his foe. Abivard found himself making more thrusts than cuts, doing his best to adapt to the different circumstances in which he now found himself. But whatever he did, Tzikas kept beating aside his blade. Whatever else anyone said about the Videssian, he could fight.

None of the palace servitors was so unwise as to try to break up the fight by grabbing one of the contestants. If someone did try tackling Tzikas, Abivard was ready to run the renegade through, however unsporting that was. He had no doubt Tzikas would give him the same treatment if he got the chance.

One thing that would stop two parties from fighting each other was overwhelming outside force directed at them both. A shout of "Drop your sword or neither one of you comes out alive!" got Abivard's undivided attention. A squadron of palace guards, bows drawn, were rushing up behind Tzikas.

Abivard sprang back from Tzikas and lowered his sword, though he did not drop it. He hoped Tzikas might pursue the fight without checking and thus get himself pincushioned. To his disappointment, the Videssian looked over his shoulder instead. He also let his arm drop but still kept hold of his sword. "I'll kill you yet," he told Abivard.

"Only in your dreams," Abivard retorted, and started to raise his blade again.

By then, though, the guardsmen had gotten between them. "That will be enough of that," the squadron leader said as if talking to a couple of fractious boys rather than a pair of men far outranking him.

Very much like a fractious boy, Tzikas said, "He started it."

"Liar!" Abivard snapped.

The squadron leader held up a hand. "I don't care who started it. All I know is that Sharbaraz King of Kings, may his days be long and his realm increase, doesn't want the two of you brawling, no matter what. I'm going to split my men in two. Half of them will take one of you back to his lodging; the other half will take the other noble gentleman back to his. That way nothing can go wrong."

"Hold!" That ringing voice could have belonged to only one

man—or, rather, not quite man—in the palace. Yeliif strode through the guards, disgust manifest not only on his face but in every line of his body. He looked from Abivard to Tzikas. His eyes flashed contempt. "You fools," he said, making it sound like a revelation from the God.

"But—" Abivard and Tzikas said in the same breath. They glared at each other, angry at agreeing even in protest.

"Fools," Yeliif repeated. He shook his head. "How the King of Kings expects to accomplish anything working through such tools as you is beyond me, but he does, so long as you do not break each other before he can take you in hand."

Abivard pointed at Tzikas. "That tool will cut his hand if he tries to wield it."

"You know not whereof you speak," the beautiful eunuch snapped. "Now more than ever the King of Kings prepares to gather the fruits of what his wisdom long ago set in motion, and you seek in your ignorance to trifle with his design? You do not understand, either one of you. All is changed now. The ambassadors have returned."

✦ XIII

Abivard scratched his head. He hadn't known of any embassies going out, let alone any coming back. "What ambassadors?" he asked. "Ambassadors to Videssos? Do we have peace with the Empire, then?" That made no sense. If Sharbaraz had made peace with Videssos, what need had he for either a marshal or a Videssian traitor?

Yeliif rolled his eyes in theatrical scorn. "Since you seem intent on making a display of your ignorance, I shall merely confirm it, noting that you do not in fact know everything there is to know and noting further that the glorious vision of Sharbaraz King of Kings, may his years be many and his realm increase, vastly outranges your own."

"To the ice—uh, to the Void—with me if I know what you're talking about," Tzikas told the eunuch.

"Nor does that surprise me." Yeliif looked at the renegade as if he were something pallid and slimy that lived in the mud under flat stones by the bank of a creek that did not run clean. Abivard loathed Tzikas with a loathing both pure and hot, but that stare made him feel a moment's sympathy for the Videssian. "Your function is solely to serve the King of Kings, not to be privy to his plans."

"If we're going to be part of his plans, we ought to have some idea of what those plans are," Abivard said, and found Tzikas nodding along with him. Accusingly, he went on, "You've known for some time. Why haven't we gained the same knowledge?"

"Until the return of the ambassadors, the King of Kings judged the time unripe," Yeliif answered. Abivard found the hand that wasn't on his sword tightening into a fist. Yeliif knew the answers, while he didn't even know the questions. Until moments before he hadn't known there were any questions. It all struck him as most unfair.

"Now that the ambassadors are back, will the King of Kings let us know what they were doing while they were away?" Tzikas sounded as if he didn't care for having been left in the dark, either.

Not that that mattered to Yeliif. "In his own good time the King of Kings *will* inform you," he said. "It is, then, your task—and I speak to each of you in this instance—to be here to be informed at the time of the King of Kings' choosing and not to eliminate each other before that time. Do you understand?"

He sought to shame them, to make them feel like brawling boys. In no small measure he succeeded. Nevertheless, Abivard knew a stir of anger at being considered only insofar as he fit into Sharbaraz's plans. He said, "I do hope the King of Kings will let us know what he intends us to do before we have to do it, not afterward."

"He will do as he chooses, not as you seek to impose upon—" The perfect apologist for the King of Kings, Yeliif started to defend him before hearing everything Abivard had had to say. When he realized he'd made himself look foolish, the eunuch bared small, white, even teeth in something closer to a snarl than to a smile. "I don't know why you want to kill this Videssian," he said, pointing at Tzikas. "Living among his folk for so long has taught you to play meaningless games with words, just as they do."

"You insult me," Abivard said.

"No, you insult *me*," Tzikas insisted. "Twice, in fact. First you call me a Videssian when I am one no longer, and second you call *him*—" He pointed at Abivard. "—one when he manifestly is not. Were I a Videssian yet, I'd not want him as one."

"He didn't call me a Videssian," Abivard said, "and if he had, he would have insulted me, not you, by doing so."

Tzikas started to raise his sword. The palace guards made ready to pincushion him and Abivard both if they started fighting again.

Coldly, Yeliif said, "Do not be more stupid than you can help. I have told you that you and Abivard are required in the future plans of the King of Kings. When those plans are accomplished, you may fight if you so desire. Until then you are his. Remember it and comport yourselves accordingly." He swept away, the hem of his caftan brushing the floor.

"Put up your swords," the guards' leader said as he had before. Abivard and Tzikas reluctantly obeyed. The guard went on, "Now, I'm gonna do like I said before, split my men in half and take you noble gentlemen back where you belong."

"*You* wouldn't know about these ambassadors, would you?" Abivard asked him as they walked down the hallway.

"Who, me?" The fellow shook his head. "I don't know anything. That's not what I'm here for, knowing things. What I'm here for is to keep people from killing other people they're not supposed to kill. You know what I mean?"

"I suppose so," Abivard said, wondering where Sharbaraz had found such a magnificently phlegmatic man. A court officer who did not want to know things surely ranked as a freak of nature.

When Abivard walked into the suite of rooms, the soldiers stayed out in the hallway, presumably to make certain he did not go out hunting Tzikas. Roshnani stared at them till he shut the door after himself; too often in the past couple of years soldiers had stood in the hallways outside their rooms. She pointed past Abivard to the guards and asked, "What are they in aid of?"

"Nothing of any great consequence," he answered airily. "Tzikas and I had a go at settling our differences, that's all."

"Settling your—" Roshnani scrambled to her feet and took great care in inspecting him from all sides. At last, having satisfied herself almost against her will, she said, "You're not bleeding anywhere."

"No, I'm not. Neither is Tzikas, worse luck," Abivard said. "And if we go after each other again, we face the displeasure of the King of Kings—so I've been told, at any rate." He lowered his voice. "That and a silver arket will make me care an arket's worth."

Roshnani nodded. "Sharbaraz would have done better to take Tzikas' head himself." She tossed her own head in long-standing exasperation. "No plan of his could possibly be clever enough to justify keeping the renegade alive."

"If you expect me to argue with you, you'll be disappointed," Abivard said, to which they both laughed. He grew thoughtful. "Do you know anything about ambassadors returning?"

"I didn't know any ambassadors were out," his principal wife answered, "so I could hardly know they've come back." That was logical enough to satisfy the most exacting, finicky Videssian. Roshnani went on, "Where did you hear about them?"

"From Yeliif, after the guardsmen kept me from giving Tzikas everything he deserved. Whoever they are, wherever they went, however they came back here, they have something to do with Sharbaraz's precious plan."

"Whatever that may be," Roshnani said.

"Whatever that may be," Abivard echoed.

"Whatever it is, when will you find out about it?" Roshnani asked.

"Whenever Sharbaraz King of Kings, may his days be long and his realm increase, finds a day long enough for him to have the time to give to me," Abivard answered. "Maybe tomorrow, maybe next spring." On that cheerful note conversation flagged.

Nine days after Abivard and Tzikas tried to kill each other, Yeliif knocked on the door to Abivard's suite. When Abivard opened the door to let him in, he stuck his head out and looked up and down the hall. The guardsmen had been gone for a couple of days. "How may I help you?" Abivard asked warily; Yeliif as anything other than inimical still struck him as curious.

The beautiful eunuch said, "You are bidden to an audience with Sharbaraz King of Kings, may his days be long and his realm increase. You shall come with me this moment."

"I'm ready," Abivard said, though he wasn't, not really. It was, he thought sadly, typical of the King of Kings to leave him on a shelf, as it were, for weeks at a time and then, when wanting him, to want him on the instant.

"I am also bidden to tell you that Tzikas shall be there," Yeliif said. When Abivard did nothing more than nod, the eunuch also nodded thoughtfully, as if he'd passed a test. He said, "I *can* tell you—" Not *I am bidden to tell you*, Abivard noted. "—that Tus and Piran are attending the King of Kings."

"I'm sorry, but I don't know those names nor the men attached to them," Abivard said.

"They are the ambassadors whose recent return has provoked this audience," Yeliif answered.

"Are they?" Abivard said, interest quickening in his voice. Now, at last, he would get to find out just how harebrained Sharbaraz's grandiose plan, whatever it was, would turn out to be. He had no great expectations for it, only the small one of having his curiosity satisfied. In aid of which . . . "Ambassadors to whom?" he asked. "I didn't know we'd sent an embassy to Maniakes, even if he has been closer to Mashiz lately than he usually gets." He also remembered the Videssian ambassador Sharbaraz had imprisoned and let die but did not find mentioning him politic.

If Yeliif hadn't been born smiling that knowing, superior smile, he'd spent a lot of time practicing it, perhaps in front of a mirror of polished silver. "All will be made clear to you in due course," he said, and would say no more. Abivard felt like booting him in the backside as they walked down the corridor.

Tzikas had indeed been bidden to the audience: he stood waiting at the rear of the throne room. Someone—very likely Yeliif—had taken the sensible precaution of posting some palace guards back there. Their dour expressions were as well schooled as Yeliif's smile.

Abivard glared at Tzikas but, with the guards there, did no more. Tzikas glared back. Yeliif said, "The two of you shall accompany me to the throne together and prostrate yourselves before the King of Kings at the same time. No lapses shall be tolerated, if I make myself clear."

Without waiting to find out whether he did, he started down the aisle on the long walk toward the throne on which Sharbaraz sat. Abivard stayed by his right side; Tzikas quickly found a place on his left. It was as if each of them was using the eunuch to shield himself from the other. Under different circumstances the idea might have been funny.

A pair of men stood to one side of the throne of the King of Kings. Abivard presumed they were the mysterious Tus and Piran. Yeliif explained nothing. Abivard had expected no more. Then, at the appropriate moment, the beautiful eunuch stepped away, leaving Abivard and Tzikas side by side before the King of Kings.

They prostrated themselves, acknowledging their insignificance in comparison to their sovereign. Out of the corner of his eye

Abivard watched Tzikas, but he had already known that the ritual was almost the same among Videssians as among the folk of Makuran. The two men waited together, foreheads touching the polished marble floor, for Sharbaraz to give them leave to rise.

At last he did. "We are not pleased with the two of you," he said when Abivard and Tzikas had regained their feet. Abivard already knew that from the length of time the King of Kings had required them to stay on their bellies. Sharbaraz went on, "By persisting in your headstrong feud, you have endangered the plan we have long been maturing, a plan which, to work to its fullest extent, requires the service of both of you."

"Majesty, if we knew what this plan was, we would be able to serve you better," Abivard answered. He was sick to death of Sharbaraz's notorious plan. Sharbaraz was full of big talk that usually ended up amounting to nothing—except trouble for Abivard.

When Sharbaraz spoke again, his words did not seem immediately to the point: "Abivard son of Godarz, brother-in-law of mine, you will remember how our father, Peroz King of Kings, departed this world for the company of the God?"

He hadn't publicly acknowledged Abivard as his brother-in-law for a long time. Abivard noted that as he answered, "Aye, Majesty, I do: battling bravely against the Khamorth out on the Pardrayan steppe." Only the blind chance of his own horse's stepping in a hole and breaking a leg at the start of its charge had kept him out of the overwhelming disaster that had befallen the Makuraner army moments afterward.

"What you say is true but incomplete," Sharbaraz told him. "How did it happen that our father, Peroz King of Kings, saw the need to campaign against the Khamorth out on the steppe?"

"They were raiding us, Majesty, as you will no doubt remember," Abivard said. "Your father wanted to punish them as they deserved." He would not speak ill of the dead. Had Peroz flung out his net of scouts more widely, the plainsmen might not have trapped him and his host.

Sharbaraz nodded. "And why were they raiding us at that particular time?" he asked with the air of a schoolmaster leading a student through a difficult lesson step by step. Abivard had trouble figuring out what to make of that.

The answer, though, was plain enough: "Because the Videssians paid them gold to raid us." He glared at Tzikas.

"Not my idea." The Videssian renegade held up a hand, denying any responsibility. "Likinios Avtokrator sent the gold out where he thought it would do the most good."

"Likinios Avtokrator, whom we knew, was devious enough to have devised such a scheme for harming his foes without risking his own men or the land then held by the Empire of Videssos," Sharbaraz said. Abivard nodded; Likinios had lived up to all the Makuraner tales about calculating, cold-blooded Videssians. The King of Kings went on, "We have endeavored to learn even from our foes. Thus the ambassadors we sent forth two years ago, just now returned to us: Tus and Piran."

"Ambassadors to whom, Majesty?" Abivard asked. At last he could put the question to someone who might answer it.

But Sharbaraz did not answer it directly. Instead, he turned to the men now back from their two-year embassy and said, "Whose agreement did you bring back with you?"

Tus and Piran spoke together, denying Abivard the chance to figure out who was who: "Majesty, we brought back the agreement of Etzilios, khagan of Kubrat, Videssos' northern neighbor."

"By the God," Abivard murmured. He'd had that notion years before but hadn't thought it really could be done, If Sharbaraz had done it . . .

Tzikas' right hand started to shape Phos' sun-sign, then checked itself. The renegade murmured, "By the God," too. Abivard for once was not disgusted at his hypocrisy. He was too busy staring at Sharbaraz King of Kings. For once he'd been wrong about his sovereign.

Sharbaraz said, "Aye, two years ago I sent them forth. They had to traverse the mountains and valleys of Erzerum without revealing their mission to the petty princes there who might have betrayed us to Videssos. They had to travel over the Pardrayan steppe all around the Videssian Sea, giving the Videssian outpost on the northern shore there a wide berth. They could not sail over the Videssian Sea to Kubrat, for we have no ships capable of such a journey." He nodded to Abivard. "We now more fully appreciate your remarks on the subject."

One of the ambassadors—the taller and older of the two—said, "We shall have ships. The Kubratoi hollow out great tree trunks and mount masts and sails on them. With these single-trunk ships they have raided the Videssian coast again and again, doing no small damage to our common foe."

"Piran has the right of it," Sharbaraz said, letting Abivard learn who was who. "Brother-in-law of mine, when the campaigning season begins this coming spring, you shall lead a great host of the men of Makuran through the Videssian westlands to Across, where all our previous efforts were halted. Under Etzilios, the Kubratoi shall come down and besiege the city by land. And—"

"And—" Abivard committed the enormity of interrupting the King of Kings. "—and their one-trunk ships will ferry over our men and the siege gear to force a breach in the wall and capture the enemy's capital."

"Just so." Sharbaraz was so pleased with himself, he overlooked the interruption.

Abivard bowed low. "Majesty," he said with more sincerity in his voice than he had used in complimenting the King of Kings for some years, "this is a splendid conception. You honor me by letting me help bring it to reality."

"Just so," Sharbaraz said again. Abivard let out a small mental sigh. That the King of Kings had come up with a good idea did not keep him from remaining as full of himself as he'd grown in his years on the throne, even if it did give him better reason than usual for his pride.

"You have given me my role to play, Majesty, and I am proud to play it, as I told you," Abivard said. He turned toward Tzikas. "You have not said what the Videssian's role is to be or why he should have one." If the God was kind, he might yet be rid of Tzikas.

All Sharbaraz said was, "He will be useful to you."

That left Tzikas to speak for himself, which he did in his lisping Videssian accent: "I tell you, Abivard son of Godarz, as I long ago told Sharbaraz King of Kings, may his days be long and his realm increase, that I know a secret way into Videssos the city once your men get over the Cattle Crossing and reach the wall. I did not think what I knew was worth much, because I did not think you could cross to the city. The King of Kings remembered, though, for which I thank him." He, too, bowed to Sharbaraz.

"What is this secret way into Videssos the city?" Abivard asked.

Tzikas smiled. "I will tell you—when it is time for you to send men through it into the city."

"All right," Abivard said, his voice mild. He saw a hint of

surprise, almost of disappointment, on the Videssian renegade's face. *Expecting me to threaten and bluster, were you?* Abivard thought. Maybe the torturers could find a way to pull what Tzikas knew out of him. But maybe not; the renegade was nothing if not resourceful and might well contrive to kill himself without yielding his secret.

In the end, though, it wouldn't matter. Before Tus and Piran had returned to Mashiz, Sharbaraz had shown every sign of being willing, if not downright eager, to be rid of Tzikas, secret or no secret. Now, with the King of Kings' plan unfolding, what Tzikas knew—or what Tzikas said he knew, which might not be the same thing—took on new value.

But suppose everything went exactly as Tzikas hoped. Suppose, thanks to his knowledge of the wall and whatever weak points it had, the Makuraners got into Videssos the city. Suppose he was the hero of the moment.

Abivard smiled at the renegade. Suppose all that came true. It would not profit Tzikas for long. Abivard was as sure of that as he was of light at noon, dark at midnight. Once Tzikas' usefulness was over, he would disappear. Sharbaraz would never name him puppet Avtokrator of the Videssians, not when he couldn't be counted on to stay a puppet.

So let him have his moment now. Why not? It wouldn't last.

Sharbaraz said, "Now you see why we could permit no unseemly brawling between the two of you. Both of you are vital to our plans, and we should have been most aggrieved at having to go forward with only one. Until Videssos the city should fall, you are indispensable to us."

"I will do my best to live up to the trust you've placed in me," Tzikas answered, bowing once more to the King of Kings. Yes, Abivard judged, the renegade made a formidable courtier, and his command of the Makuraner language was excellent. It was not, however, perfect. Sharbaraz had said that Tzikas—and Abivard, too, for that matter—was indispensable until Videssos the city fell. He had not said a word about anyone's indispensability after Videssos the city fell. Abivard had noticed that. Tzikas, by all appearances, had not.

Yeliif reappeared between Abivard and Tzikas. One moment he was not there, the next he was. He was no mean courtier in his own right, arriving at the instant when Sharbaraz dismissed them.

As protocol required, Abivard and Tzikas prostrated themselves once more. For the first time in some years Abivard felt he was giving the prostration to a man who deserved such an honor.

After he and Tzikas rose, they backed away from the King of Kings till they could with propriety turn and walk away from his presence. The beautiful eunuch stayed between them. Abivard wondered if that was to ensure that the two of them didn't start fighting again no matter what instructions they'd had from Sharbaraz.

At the entrance to the throne room another eunuch took charge of Tzikas and led him away, presumably toward whatever chambers he had been allotted. Yeliif accompanied Abivard back to his own suite of rooms. "Now perhaps you understand and admit the King of Kings has a grander notion of things as they are and things as they should be than your limited imagination can encompass," Yeliif said.

"He certainly had one splendid idea there," Abivard said, which sounded like agreement but wasn't quite. He suppressed a sigh. With all the courtiers telling Sharbaraz how clever he was, the King of Kings would get—indeed, no doubt had long since gotten—the idea that all his thoughts were brilliant merely because he was the one who'd had them. That might help Sharbaraz follow through on a genuinely good notion like the one he'd had here but would make him pursue his follies with equal vigor.

"His wisdom approaches that of the God," the beautiful eunuch declared. Abivard didn't say anything to that. Sharbaraz was liable to have himself worshiped in place of the God if he kept hearing flattery like that. Abivard wondered what Dhegmussa would have to say about such a claim. He wondered if the Mobedhan Mobedh would have the spine to say anything at all.

When he got back to the rooms where he and his family were staying, he found Roshnani, as he'd expected, waiting impatiently to hear what news he'd brought. He gave that news to her, crediting the King of Kings for the scheme he'd developed. Roshnani listened with her usual sharp attention and asked several equally sharp questions. After Abivard had answered them all, she paid Sharbaraz the highest compliment Abivard had heard from her in years: "I wouldn't have believed he had it in him."

✦   ✦   ✦

Abivard greeted Romezan with a handclasp. "Good to see you," he said. "Good to see anyone who's ever gone out into the field and has some idea of what fighting is all about."

"Not many like that around the court, as I know better than I'd like," Romezan answered. He paced up and down the central room of Abivard's suite like a trapped animal. "That's why I'd rather be out in the field if I had any choice about it."

"Turan won't let the army fall into the Void while you're away from it," Abivard answered, "and I need your help working out exactly how to put the King of Kings' plan into effect."

"What exactly is the King of Kings' plan?" Romezan asked. "I've heard there is such a thing, but that's about all."

When Abivard told him, Romezan stopped pacing and listened intently. When Abivard was through, the noble from the Seven Clans whistled once, a low, prolonged note. Abivard nodded. "That's how I felt the first time I heard it, too," he said.

Romezan stared at him. "Do you mean to tell me you had nothing to do with this plan?" Abivard, truthfully enough, denied everything; even if he had once had the same idea, Sharbaraz was the one who'd made it real, or as real as it was thus far. Romezan whistled again. "Well, if he really did think of it all by his lonesome, more power to him. Splendid notion. Kills any number of birds with one stone."

"I was thinking the same thing," Abivard said. "What worries me is timing the attack and coordinating it with the Kubratoi to make sure they're doing their part when we come calling. They can't take Videssos the city by themselves; I'm sure of that. And we can't take it if we can't get to it. Working together, though—"

"Oh, aye, I see what you're saying," Romezan told him. "These are all the little things the King of Kings won't have bothered worrying about. They're also the sorts of things that make a plan go wrong if nobody bothers to think of them. And if that happens, it's not the fault of the King of Kings. It's the fault of whoever was in charge of the campaign."

"Something like that, yes." Abivard pointed to the walls and ceiling to remind Romezan that privacy was an illusion in the palace. Romezan tossed his head imperiously as if to answer that he did not care. Abivard went on, "We also want to make sure Maniakes is away from Videssos the city when we attack it: preferably bogged down fighting in the land of the Thousand Cities the way he has been the last couple of years."

"Aye, that would be good," Romezan agreed. "But if we don't move for Videssos the city till he's moved against us, that cuts down the time we'll have to try to take the place."

"I know," Abivard said unhappily. "Anything that makes one thing better has a way of making something else worse."

"True enough, true enough," Romezan said. "Well, that's life. And you're right that we'd be better off waiting for Maniakes to be out of Videssos the city and far away before we try to take it; if he's leading the defense, it's the same as giving the Videssians an extra few thousand men. I've fought him often enough now that I don't want to do it again."

"He is troublesome," Abivard said, knowing what an understatement that was. He laughed nervously. "I wonder if he has a secret plan of his own, too, one that will let him take Mashiz. If he holds our capital while we capture his, can we trade them back when the war is over?"

"You're full of jolly notions today, aren't you?" Romezan said, but then he added, "I do see what you're saying, so don't get me wrong about that. If we figure out everything we're going to do but nothing of what Maniakes is liable to try, we end up in trouble."

"Maniakes is liable to try almost anything, worse luck for us," Abivard answered. "We thought we had him penned away from the westlands for good till he ran around us by sea."

"Still doesn't seem right," Romezan grumbled. Like most other Makuraner officers, he had trouble taking the sea seriously, even though, had it not been there, every elaborate scheme to capture Videssos the city would have been unnecessary. Then, thoughtfully, he went on, "What are they like? The Kubratoi, I mean."

"How should I know?" Abivard answered almost indignantly. "I've never dealt with them, either. If we're going to ally with them, though, we probably could do worse than asking the ambassadors who made the arrangements in the first place."

"That's sensible," Romezan said, approval in his voice. He set a finger by the side of his nose. "Or, of course, we could always ask Tzikas."

"Ho, ho!" Abivard said. "You *are* a funny fellow." Both men laughed. Neither seemed much amused.

✦   ✦   ✦

"We shall tell you whatever we can," Piran said. Beside him Tus nodded. Both men sipped wine and ate roasted pistachios from a silver bowl a servant had brought them.

"The most important question is, What are they worth in a brawl?" Romezan said. "You've seen 'em; we haven't. By the God, I can't tell you three things about 'em."

Romezan's mind reached no farther than the battlefield, but Abivard had longer mental vision: "What are they like? If they make a bargain, will they keep it?"

Piran snorted. "They're just one band of cows in the huge Khamorth herd that stretches from the Degird River across the great Pardrayan plain to the Astris River and beyond—which means any one of 'em would sell his own grandmother to the village butcher if he thought her carcass would fetch two arkets."

"Sounds like all the Khamorth I've ever known," Romezan agreed.

Tus held up a finger like a village schoolmaster. "But," he said, "against Videssos they will keep a bargain."

"If they're of the Khamorth strain, they're liable to betray anyone for any reason or for no reason at all," Abivard said.

"Were they fighting another clan of Khamorth, you would be right," Tus said. "But Etzilios hates Maniakes for having beaten him and fears he will beat him again. With a choice between Videssos and Makuran, he will be a faithful ally for us."

"Nothing like fear to keep an alliance healthy," Romezan observed.

"If I were khagan of Kubrat—and the God be praised I'm not, nor likely to be—I'd look for allies against Videssos, too," Abivard said. "The Videssians have long memories, and their neighbors had better remember it."

"You sound as if you might mean us, not just the Kubratoi and the other barbarous nations of the farthermost east," Piran said.

"Of course I mean us," Abivard exploded. "Maniakes has spent the past two years trying to tear down the land of the Thousand Cities one mud brick at a time. He hasn't been doing that for his own amusement; he's been doing it to pay us back for having taken the westlands away from Videssos. If we can cut off the head by taking Videssos the city, the body—the Empire of Videssos—will die. If we can't, our grandchildren will be trying to figure out how to keep the Videssians from taking back everything Sharbaraz has won in his wars."

"That is why the King of Kings sent us on our long, hard journey," Tus said. "He agrees with you, lord, that we must uproot the Empire to keep it from growing back and troubling us again in later days."

"Will the Kubratoi horsemen and single-trunk ships be enough toward helping us get done what needs doing?" Abivard asked.

Piran said, "Their soldiers are much like Khamorth anywhere. They have a lot of warriors because the grazing is good south of the Astris. A few of their fighting men wear mail shirts in place of boiled leather. Some are loot from the Videssians; some are made by smiths there."

"What about the ships?" Romezan asked, beating Abivard to the question.

"I'm no sailor—" Piran began.

Abivard broke in: "What Makuraner is?"

"—but they looked to me as if they'd be dangerous. They carry a mast and a leather sail to mount on it, and they can hold a lot of warriors."

"That sounds like what we need to do the job, right enough," Romezan said, eyes kindling with excitement.

Abivard hoped he was right. Along with catapults and siege towers, ships were a projection of the mechanical arts into the art of war. In all such things the Videssians were uncommonly good. How he had resented those spider-striding galleys that had held him away from Videssos the city! He hadn't thought he could hate ships more than he'd hated those galleys. Now, though, after ships had let Maniakes bypass the Makuraner-held Videssian westlands and bring the war to the land of the Thousand Cities, he wondered where his greater antipathy lay.

"If we have ships to put their ships out of action—" He frowned. "Have the Kubratoi met the Videssians on the sea in these single-trunk ships?"

"We saw no such fights," Piran said. "Etzilios was at peace with Videssos while we were in Kubrat, you understand, not wanting to make Maniakes worry about him."

"I do understand." Abivard nodded. "Maniakes needs to think all's quiet behind him. He needs to invade the land of the Thousand Cities again, in fact. The farther he is from the capital when we launch our attack, the better off we'll be. If the God is kind, we'll be in Videssos the city before he can get back." He smiled wolfishly. "I wonder what he'll do then."

Harking back to his original question, Tus said, "Etzilios assured us, boasting and vaunting about what his people have done, that their ships had stood up against the Videssians in times past."

"I know they were raiding the Videssian coast when we were in Across," Romezan said. "They could hardly have done that if their ships didn't measure up, now, could they?"

"I suppose not," Abivard said. The wolfish smile remained. "The Videssians did have some other things to worry about then, though."

"Aye, so they did." Romezan's smile was more nearly reminiscent than lupine. "We scared them then. When we come back, we'll do more than scare them. Scaring people is for children. Winning wars is a man's proper sport."

"Well said!" Piran exclaimed. "The Kubratoi, like most nomads, would phrase that a little differently: they would say fighting wars is a man's proper sport. They will make allies worth having."

Allies worth betraying, Abivard thought. If all went well, if the Kubratoi and the Makuraners together took Videssos the city and extinguished the ancient Empire of Videssos, how long before they started quarreling over the bones of the carcass? Not long, Abivard was sure: Makuran had always had nomads on the frontier and never had had any use for them.

Something else occurred to him. To Romezan he said, "We'll be taking the part of the field army you brought out of Videssos to the land of the Thousand Cities, not so?"

"We'd better," Romezan declared. "If we're going to try to break into Videssos the city, we'll need everything we have. Kardarigan's chunk won't be enough by itself. Tell me you think otherwise and I'll be very surprised."

"I don't," Abivard assured him. "But while we're in Videssos, Maniakes is going to be in the land of the Thousand Cities. And do you know who will have to keep him busy there and make sure he doesn't sack our capital while we're busy sacking his?"

"Somebody had better do that," Romezan said. His eyes sparkled. "I know who—those foot soldiers you're so proud of, the city militiamen you trained into soldiers almost worth having."

"They *are* worth having," Abivard insisted. He started to get angry before he noticed that Romezan was grinning at him. "The proof of which is they'll be able to keep the Videssians busy here long enough for us to do what needs doing there."

"They'd better, or Sharbaraz will want both our heads and likely Turan's, too: he'll be commanding them, I suppose, so he won't be able to escape his share of the blame," Romezan said. He whistled a merry little tune he'd picked up in Videssos. "Of course, if your fancied-up city guards don't do their job, the King of Kings may not be able to take anybody's head, because Maniakes may not have left him with his. One way or another, the war ends next summer."

"Not 'one way or another,'" Abivard said. "The war ends next summer: our way."

Romezan, Tus, and Piran lifted their silver goblets of wine in a salute.

Prince Peroz stared up at Abivard, who in turn looked down at the little fellow who would one day rule him if he outlived Sharbaraz King of Kings. Peroz reached up and tried to grab hold of his beard. He hadn't taken that from his own children; he wouldn't take it from his future sovereign, either.

"He's starting to discover that he has hands," Abivard said to Denak, and then, "They change so fast when they're this small."

"They certainly do." His sister sighed. "I'd almost forgotten. It's been a while now since Jarireh was tiny. She's almost Varaz's age, you know."

"Is she well? Is she happy?" Abivard asked. His sister hardly ever mentioned his eldest niece. He wondered if Denak thought of Jarireh and her sisters as failures because they had not been boys and thus had not cemented their mother's place among the women of the palace.

"She is well," Denak said. "Happy? Who could be happy here at court?" She spoke without so much as glancing over at Ksorane, who sat in a corner of the room painting her eyelids with kohl and examining her appearance in a small mirror of polished bronze. Maybe, by now, Sharbaraz had heard all of Denak's complaints.

"If we take Videssos the city—" Abivard stopped. For the first time in a long while he let himself think about all the things that might happen if Makuran took Videssos the city. "If we take the city, Dhegmussa will offer up praise to the God from the High

Temple and Sharbaraz King of Kings, may his days be long and his realm increase, will quarter himself in Maniakes' palaces. He should bring you with him, for without you he never would have had the chance."

"I've given up thinking that what he should do and what he will do are one and the same," Denak answered. "He'll go to Videssos the city, no doubt, to see what you've done for him and, as you say, to vaunt himself by taking over the Avtokrator's dwelling. But I'll stay here in Mashiz, sure as sure. He'll take women who . . . amuse him, or else he'll amuse himself with frightened little Videssians." She sounded very sure, very knowing, very bitter.

"But—" Abivard began.

His sister waved him to silence. "Sharbaraz dreams large," she said. "He always has—I give him that much. Now he's dreamed large enough to catch you up in his webs again, the way he did when the crown of the King of Kings was new on his head. But I'm not part of his dreams anymore, not in any real way." She pointed to Peroz, who was beginning to yawn in Abivard's arms. "Sometimes I think he's a dream and, if I go to bed and then wake up, he'll be gone." She shrugged. "I don't even know why Sharbaraz summoned me that one night."

Ksorane set down the mirror and said, "Lady, he feared your brother and wanted a better bond with him if he could forge one."

Denak and Abivard both stared at her in surprise. The only previous time she'd spoken without being spoken to had been to keep them from touching each other. As if to pretend she hadn't done anything at all, she went back to ornamenting her eyelids.

Denak shrugged again. "Maybe she's right," she told Abivard, still as if Ksorane weren't there listening. "But whether she is or isn't, it doesn't matter as far as my going to Videssos the city. Peroz is part of Sharbaraz's dreams, but I'm not. I'll stay here in Mashiz." She was utterly matter-of-fact about it, as if foretelling the yield from a plot of land near Vek Rud stronghold. Somehow that made the prediction worse, not better.

Abivard rocked his nephew in his arms. The baby's eyes slid shut. His mouth made little sucking noises. Ksorane came up to take him and return him to his mother. "Wait a bit," Abivard told her. "Let him get a little more deeply asleep so he won't start howling when I hand him to you."

"You know something about children," Ksorane said.

"I'd be a poor excuse for a father if I didn't," he answered. Then he wondered how much Sharbaraz King of Kings knew about children. Not much, he suspected, and that saddened him. *Some things,* he thought, *should not be left to servants.*

After a while he did hand the baby to Ksorane, who returned it to Denak. Neither transfer disturbed little Peroz in the least. Looking down at him, Denak said, "I wonder what dreams he'll have, many years from now, up there on the throne of the King of Kings, and who will follow them and try to make them real for him."

"Yes," Abivard said. But what he was wondering was whether Peroz would ever sit on the throne of the King of Kings. So many babies died no matter how hard their parents struggled to keep them alive. And even if Peroz lived to grow up, his father had for a time lost the throne through disaster and treachery. Who could say now that the same would not befall the babe? No one, as Abivard knew only too well. One thing he had seen was that life did not come with a promise that it would run smoothly.

By the standards with which Abivard had become familiar while living in Vek Rud domain, Mashiz enjoyed a mild winter. It was chilly, but even the winds off the Dilbat Mountains were nothing like the ones that blew around Vek Rud stronghold. Those seemed to take a running start on the Pardrayan steppe and to blow right through a man because going around him was too much trouble.

They got mild days in Mashiz, as opposed to the endless, bone-numbing chill of the far Northwest. Every so often the wind would shift and blow off the land of the Thousand Cities. Whenever it did that for two days running, Abivard began to think spring had arrived at last. He could taste how eager he was for good weather that wasn't just a tease of the sort a dancing girl would give to a soldier who lusted after her but whom she wanted to annoy rather than bed.

As the sun swung northward from its low point in the sky, the mild days gradually came more often. But every time Abivard's hopes began to rise with the sap in the trees, a new storm would claw its way over the mountains and freeze those hopes once more.

Abivard did send messages both to the field army, ordering it to be ready to move out when the weather permitted, and to Turan, ordering him to prepare to defend the land of the Thousand Cities with foot soldiers from the city garrisons alone. He did not go into more detail than that in his message. In peacetime the Thousand Cities had a flourishing trade with Videssos. That news of what he intended might reach the Avtokrator struck him as far from impossible.

Varaz knew what Sharbaraz intended. He had even less patience than Abivard, being wild to leave the foothills for the flatlands to the east, the flatlands that were the gateway to Videssos. "You need to wait," his father told him. "Leaving too soon doesn't get us anywhere—or not soon enough, anyhow."

"I'm sick of waiting!" Varaz burst out, a sentiment with which Abivard had more than a little sympathy. "I've spent the last three winters waiting here in the palace. I want to get out, to get away. I want to go to the places where things will happen."

Pretty soon, Abivard thought, Varaz would be old enough to make things happen rather than just watching them happen. He was taller than his mother now. Before long, his beard would begin to grow and he would make the discovery every generation finds astounding: that mankind includes womankind and is much more interesting on account of it.

Abivard hadn't cared for being cooped up three winters running, either, even if conditions had improved from one winter to the next. He had borne it more easily than had his son, though. But Varaz was going to escape from Mashiz, to return first to the land of the Thousand Cities, then to Across, and then, if the God was willing, to enter Videssos the city.

"Count yourself lucky," Abivard told his elder son. "Your cousin Jarireh may never leave the palace till the day she marries."

"She's a girl, though," Varaz said. Had Roshnani heard the tone in which he said it, she probably would have boxed his ears. He went on, "Besides, her baby brother's going to be King of Kings."

"That won't help her get out and see the world—or at least I don't think it will," Abivard said. "It will make picking someone for her to marry harder than it would be, though."

"Marriage—so what?" Varaz said, nothing but scorn in his voice—he remained on the childish side of the great divide.

"Your family picks someone for you, the two of you go before the servant of the God, and that's it. That's how it works most of the time, anyhow."

"Are you making an exception for your mother and me?" Abivard asked dryly.

"Well, yes, but the two of you are different," Varaz said. "Mother goes out and *does* things, almost as if she were a man; she doesn't stay in the women's quarters all the time. And you *let* her."

"No," Abivard said. "I don't 'let' her. I'm glad she does. In a number of ways she's more clever than I am. I'm only lucky in that I'm clever enough to see she is more clever."

"I don't follow that," Varaz said. He quickly held up a hand. "I probably wouldn't follow it in Videssian, either, no matter how logical it's supposed to be, so don't bother trying."

Thus forestalled, Abivard threw his hands in the air. Varaz escaped from his presence and went dashing down a palace hallway. Watching him, Abivard sighed. No, waiting was never easy.

But even Sharbaraz had been forced to wait for his ambassadors to return. In another sense he'd had to wait more than a dozen years after the Empire of Videssos had fallen into civil strife to be able to assail its capital with any hope of success. In still another sense Makuran as a whole had been waiting centuries for this opportunity to come around.

Abivard snapped his fingers. Lands didn't wait—people did. And, like his son, he was very tired of waiting.

Pashang clucked to the horses and flicked the reins. The wagon rattled away from Mashiz. Abivard rode beside it on a fine black gelding, the gift of Sharbaraz King of Kings. Romezan rode another that might have been a different foal of the same mare. Around them, almost as splendidly mounted, trotted a company of heavy cavalry, their armor and that of their horses stowed in carts or on packhorses since they were traveling through friendly terri-tory and were not expecting to fight. One proud young horseman carried the red war banner.

Off to one side, with the group but not of it, rode Tzikas. Abivard had been warned of all the horrid things that would happen to him if anything at all happened to Tzikas. He was still trying to work out whether those horrid things were deterrent enough. For the moment they probably were. Once Videssos the city fell, Tzikas would be expendable. And if by some misfortune Videssos the city failed to fall, Sharbaraz would be looking for a scapegoat.

Tzikas no doubt was thinking along similar lines. Abivard glanced over toward him and wasn't surprised to find the Videssian renegade's eyes already on him. He stared at Tzikas for a little while, nothing but challenge in his gaze. Tzikas looked back steadily. Abivard let out a silent sigh. Enemies were so much easier to despise when they were cowards. Yet even though Tzikas was no coward, Abivard despised him anyhow.

He turned in the saddle and said to Romezan, "We're riding in the right direction now."

"How do you mean that?" Romezan returned. "Away from the palace? Out into the field? Toward the war?"

"Any of those will do," Abivard said. "They'll all do." If he had to pick one, *away from the palace* probably would fit his thought best. In the palace he was slave to the King of Kings, for all his achievements hardly higher in status than sweepers or captive Videssian pedagogues. Away from the palace, away from the King of Kings, he was a marshal of Makuran, a great power in his own right. He had grown very used to that, all those years he'd spent extending the power of Makuran through the Videssian westlands till it reached the Cattle Crossing. Being yanked back under Sharbaraz's control would have been hard on him even had the King of Kings not seen treason lurking under every pillow and behind every door.

Romezan did not dwell on the past. He looked ahead to the east. Dreamily, he said, "Do you suppose we'll lay Videssos low? How many hundred years have they and we warred? Come this fall, will the fight be over at last?"

"If the God is kind," Abivard answered.

They rode on a while in silence. Then Abivard said, "We'll muster as far forward as we can. As soon as we have word that Maniakes has landed, whether down in Lyssaion or in Erzerum, we move."

"What if he doesn't land?" Romezan said, looking eastward again, as if he could span the farsangs and see into the palaces in distant Videssos the city. "What if he decides to stay home for a year? Maniakes never ends up doing what we think he will."

That was true. Even so, Abivard shook his head. "He'll come," he said. "I'm sure of it, and Sharbaraz was dead right to assume it." Hearing him agree so emphatically with the King of Kings was enough to make Romezan dig a finger into his ear as if to make sure it was working as it should. Chuckling, Abivard went on. "What's Maniakes' chief advantage over us?" He answered his own question: "He commands the sea. What has he been doing with that command? He's been using it to take the war out of Videssos and into the realm of the King of Kings. How can he possibly afford not to keep on doing what he's done the past two years?"

"Put that way, I don't suppose he can," Romezan admitted.

"The real beauty of Sharbaraz's scheme—" Abivard stopped. Now *he* wondered if he was really talking about the King of Kings that way. He was, and in fact he repeated himself: "The real beauty of Sharbaraz's plan is that it uses Maniakes' strengths against him and Videssos. He takes his ships, uses them to bring his army back to the land of the Thousand Cities, and gets embroiled in fighting well away from the sea. And while he's doing all that, we steal a march and take his capital away from him."

Romezan thought for a while before nodding. "I like it."

"So do I," Abivard said.

He liked it better by the day. He and his escort made their way through the land of the Thousand Cities toward Qostabash. Peasants were busy in the fields, bringing in the spring harvest. Here and there, though, they were busy at other things, most notably the repair of canals wrecked in the previous fall's fighting and soon to be needed to cope with the sudden rush of water from the spring floods of the Tutub and the Tib and their tributaries.

And here and there, across the green quilt of the floodplain, fields went untended, unharvested. Some of the cities that had perched on mounds of their own rubble were now nothing but rubble themselves. Maniakes had made the land of the Thousand Cities pay a terrible price for the many victories Makuran had won in Videssos over the past decade.

Whenever he stopped at one of the surviving Thousand Cities, Abivard examined how well the city governor had kept up the local garrison. He was pleased to find most of those garrisons in better shape than they had been two years earlier, when the Videssians had first entered the floodplain. Before then both city governorships and slots in the city garrison had been the nearest thing to sinecures: but for flood or drought, what ever went wrong among the Thousand Cities? *Invasion* was not an answer that seemed to have occurred beforehand to many people.

Romezan paid the revived city garrisons what might have been the ultimate compliment when he said, "You know, I wouldn't mind taking a few thousand of these foot soldiers along with us when we go into the Videssian westlands. They really can fight. Who would have thought it?"

"That's not what you said when you came to my aid last summer," Abivard reminded him.

"I know," Romezan answered. "I hadn't seen them in action then. I was wrong. I admit it. You deserve a lot of credit for turning them into soldiers."

Abivard shook his head. "Do you know who deserves the credit for turning them into soldiers?"

"Turan?" Romezan snorted dismissively. "He's done well with them, aye, but he's still only a jumped-up captain learning how to be a general."

"He's done very well, as a matter of fact, but I wasn't thinking of him," Abivard answered. "The one who deserves the credit for turning them into soldiers is Maniakes. Without him they'd just be the same swaggering bullies they've been for the God only knows how many years. But that doesn't work, not against the Videssians. The ones who are still alive know better now."

"Something to that, I expect," Romezan said after a reflective pause.

"It's also one reason why we're not going to take any of those foot soldiers into Videssos," Abivard said. Romezan's dark, bushy brows pulled down and together in confusion. Abivard explained: "Remember, we want the Videssians heavily engaged here in the land of the Thousand Cities. That means we're going to have to leave behind a good-sized army to fight them, an army with good fighting men in it. Either we leave behind a piece of the field army—"

"No, by the God!" Romezan broke in.

Abivard held up a placatory hand. "I agree. The field army is the best Makuran has. That's what we send against Videssos the city, which will need the best we have. But the next best we have has to stay here to keep Maniakes in play while we move against the city."

Again Romezan paused for thought before answering. "This is a tricky business, gauging all the separate strengths to make sure each is in the proper place. Me, I'd sooner point my mass of troops at the foe, charge him straight on, and smash him down into the dirt."

"I know," Abivard said, which was true. He added, "So would I," which was less true. "But Maniakes fights like a Videssian, so stealth makes do for a lot of his strength. If we're going to beat the Empire so it stays beaten, we have to do it his way."

"I suppose so," Romezan said unwillingly. "But if we fight like the Videssians, we'll end up acting like them in other ways, too. And they know no caste."

He spoke with great abhorrence. Abivard knew he should have felt that same abhorrence. Try as he would, he couldn't find it inside himself. He wondered why. After a few seconds' thought he said, "I've lived so long in Videssos and here in the Thousand Cities, I don't mind that nearly so much as I used to. Up on the plateau breaking people into tight groups—the King of Kings, the Seven Clans and the servants of the God, the *dihqans*, artisans and merchants, and peasants down at the bottom—seemed a natural thing to do. Now I've seen other ways of doing things, and I realize ours isn't the only one."

"That's no sort of thing for a proper Makuraner to say." Romezan sounded almost as dismayed as if Abivard had blasphemed the God.

But Abivard refused to let himself be cowed. "No, eh? Why is it you kiss my cheek, then, instead of the other way around? You outrank me. I'm just a *dihqan*, and a frontier *dihqan* at that."

"I started giving you that courtesy because you're brother-in-law to the King of Kings," the noble from the Seven Clans answered. If he'd kept quiet after that, he would have won the argument. Instead, though, he went on, "Now I see you've earned it because—"

Abivard stuck a triumphant finger in the air. "If you grant me the courtesy because I've earned it and not because of my blood, what has that got to do with caste?"

Romezan started to answer, looked confused, stopped, and tried again: "It's—that is—" He came to another stop, then burst out, "You *have* lived among the Videssians too long. All you want to do is chop logic all day. Now I'm going to be *thinking* for the next half dozen farsangs." He made the prospect sound most unpleasant. Abivard had seen that before in many different men. It always left him sad.

Tzikas, on the other hand, actively enjoyed thinking. That wasn't necessarily a recommendation, either. The older Abivard got, the more it looked as if nothing was necessarily a recommendation for anything.

Outside Qostabash men from the field army were playing mallet and ball, galloping their horses up and down a grassy stretch of ground with great abandon. Every so often a loincloth-clad peasant, his blue-black hair bound in a bun at the nape of his neck, would look up from his labor with hoe and mattock and watch the sport for a little while before bending back down to weed or prune or dig. Abivard wondered what the peasants thought of the shouting warriors whose game was not far from combat itself. Whatever it was, they kept it to themselves.

He had sent a rider out ahead of his company to let Turan know he was near. Two years before Turan had been only a company commander himself. He'd risen fast, since Abivard had access to so few veteran Makuraner officers on whom he could rely. Now Turan had shown himself able to command an army. Very soon he'd have the chance to do just that.

Now he came riding out of Qostabash to greet Abivard and his companions—he must have had men up on the walls of the city keeping an eye out for them. The first thing he did after pulling his horse alongside Abivard's was to point over at Tzikas and say, "Isn't he supposed to be dead, lord?"

"It all depends on whom you ask," Abivard answered. "I certainly think so, but the King of Kings disagrees. As in any contest of that sort, his will prevails."

"Of course it does," Turan said, as any loyal Makuraner would have done. Then, as anyone who had made the acquaintance of Tzikas would have done, he asked, "Why on earth does he want him alive?"

"For a reason even I find . . . fairly good," Abivard answered. He spent the next little while explaining the plan Sharbaraz King of Kings had devised and the places his sovereign had designated for him and for the Videssian renegade.

When he was through, Turan glanced over at Tzikas and said,

"He had better make keeping him alive worth everyone's while or else he won't last, orders from the King of Kings or no orders from the King of Kings."

"Far be it from me to argue with you," Abivard said. Lowering his voice, he went on, "But I've decided I'm not going to do anything about it till after Videssos the city falls, if it does. Either way, the problem takes care of itself then." He explained his reasoning to Turan.

The officer nodded. "Aye, lord, that's very good. If we fail, which the God forbid, he gets the blame, and if we succeed, we don't need him anymore after that. Very neat. Anyone would think you were the Videssian, not his unpleasantness over there."

"Too many people have said the same thing to me lately," Abivard grumbled. "I thank the God and the Prophets Four that I'm not."

"Aye, I believe that," Turan agreed, "the same as I thank the God—" He broke off. He'd probably been about to say something like *for making me a man, not a woman.* Considering how much freedom Roshnani had and how well she used it, that wasn't the wisest thing to say around Abivard. Turan changed the subject: "How will you know, lord, when to leave the Thousand Cities behind and strike out for Videssos?"

"As soon as we get word Maniakes has landed, whether north or south, we go," Abivard said. "At this season of the year the badlands between the Thousand Cities and Videssos will have some greenery on them, too, which means we won't have to carry quite so much grain and hay for the horses and mules."

"Every little bit helps," Turan said. "And you'll want me to keep Maniakes in play for as long as I can, isn't that right?"

"The busier he is with you, the more time I'll have to do all I can against Videssos the city," Abivard said, and Turan nodded. Abivard added, "You may even beat him—who knows?"

"With an all-infantry army?" Turan rolled his eyes. "If I can slow him down and make his life difficult, I'll be happy."

Since Abivard had been saying the same thing to Sharbaraz over the course of the previous two campaigning seasons, he found no way to blame Turan for words like those. He said, "The two things you have to remember are not to let Maniakes get behind you and make a run for Mashiz and to make him fight as many long sieges as you can."

"He hasn't fought many long ones the past couple of years," Turan said unhappily. "Brick walls like the ones hereabouts don't stand up well to siege engines, and the Videssians are good engineers."

"I know." Abivard remembered the capable crew of artisans the elder Maniakes, the Avtokrator's father, had brought with his army when the Videssians had helped put Sharbaraz back on the throne of the King of Kings. He dared not assume that the men the younger Maniakes would have with him would turn out to be any less competent.

Romezan said, "I hope Maniakes comes soon. Every day I sit here in Qostabash doing nothing is another debt the Avtokrator owes to me. I intend to collect every one of those debts, and in good Videssian gold."

"We won't be idle here," Abivard answered. "Getting an army ready to move at a moment's notice is an art of its own and one where the Videssians are liable to be better than we are."

Romezan only grunted by way of reply. He was a good man in a fight, none better, but cared less than he might have for the other side of generalship, the side that involved getting men ready for fighting and keeping them that way. He seemed to think that sort of thing happened by itself. Abivard had needed to worry about supplies from his earliest days as a soldier, when he'd fed the *dihqans* of the Northwest as they looked Sharbaraz over at the outset of his rebellion against Smerdis the usurper. If he hadn't learned then, keeping an eye on the way the Videssians did things would have taught him.

Turan said, "When you go east, I wish I were going with you. I know the job I have to do back here is important, but—"

"You'll do it, which is what counts. That's *why* you're staying behind," Abivard told him. Turan nodded but still looked dissatisfied. Abivard understood that and sympathized with it, but only to a certain degree. The Videssians weren't so apt to tack *but* on after *important*. If something was important, they did it and then went on to the next important thing.

With a small start, he realized that all the people who'd been calling him Videssian-minded lately had a point. Having spent so much time in the Empire and among imperials, he was—always with exceptions such as Tzikas—as comfortable around them as with his own people. Was feeling that way treason of a sort or simply making the best of what life had proffered? He scratched his head. He'd have to ponder that.

A sentry brought into Abivard's presence a sweat-soaked scout who smelled strongly of horse. Abivard stiffened. Was this the man for whom he'd been waiting? Before he could speak, the scout gasped out, "The Videssians have come! They—"

Abivard waited to hear no more. All the waiting was over at last. He sprang to his feet. No matter how comfortable he had grown among the Videssians, they remained the foe. He thought he could beat them. Soon he would know. He took a deep breath and shouted out the news: "We march on Videssos!"

VIDESSOS BESIEGED

✦

THE TIME OF TROUBLES, VOL. 4

✦ 1

Outside the imperial residence in Videssos the city, the cherry trees were in bloom. Soon their pink and white petals would drift the ground and walks around the residence in much the same way as the snow had done till a few weeks earlier.

Maniakes threw wide the shutters and peered out at the grove that made the residence the only place in the palace quarter where the Avtokrator of the Videssians could find even a semblance of privacy. One of the many bees buzzing by made as if to land on him. He drew back in a hurry. When spring came, the bees were a nuisance: they were, in fact, almost the only thing he disliked about spring.

"Phos be praised," he said, sketching the good god's sun-circle above his heart, "now that good sailing weather is here again, we can get out of the city and fight another round with the men of Makuran." He made a sour face. "I *know* the Makuraners are my enemies. Here in the capital, foes come disguised, so they're harder to spot."

"Once we've beaten the Makuraners, things will go better here," said his wife, Lysia. She came over and took his hand and also looked at the flowering cherry trees. When another bee tried to fly into the chamber, she snatched up a sheet of parchment from Maniakes' desk and used it to chivvy the bee back outside. Then she smiled at him. "There. That's more use than we usually get out of tax registers."

"How right you are," he said fondly. Lysia had a gift for not taking the ponderous Videssian bureaucratic machine too seriously, while to the army of tax collectors and clerks and scribes and account reckoners it was not only as important as life itself but was in fact life itself. Better yet, she helped Maniakes not take the bureaucracy too seriously, either, a gift he often thought beyond price.

He hugged her. The two of them were not very far apart in height. They were a little stockier, a little swarthier than the Videssian norm, being of Vaspurakaner blood even if almost completely Videssian in the way they thought. Both had lustrous, almost blue-black hair, bushy eyebrows—though Lysia plucked hers to conform to imperial standards of beauty—and high-arched, prominent noses. Maniakes' thick, heavy beard covered his cheeks and chin, but under the beard that chin, he suspected, was a match for Lysia's strong one.

Their resemblance was no mere accident of having sprung from the same homeland, nor was it a case of husband and wife coming to look like each other over the course of living together—such cases being more often joked about than seen. They were not just husband and wife; they were also first cousins—Lysia's father, Symvatios, was younger brother to Maniakes' father, with whom the Avtokrator shared his name.

Lysia said, "When we sail for the west to fight the Makuraners, have you decided whether to use the northern or southern route?"

"The southern, I think," Maniakes answered. "If we land in the north, we have to thread our way through all the valleys and passes of the Erzerum Mountains. That's the longer way to have to go to aim for Mashiz, too. I want Sharbaraz—" He pronounced it *Sarbaraz*; like most who spoke Videssian, he had trouble with the *sh* sound, though he could sometimes bring it out. "—King of Kings to be sweating in his capital the way I've sweated here in the city."

"He's had to worry more than we have, the past couple of years," Lysia said. "The Cattle Crossing holds the Makuraners away from Videssos the city, but the Tutub and the Tib are only rivers. If we can beat the soldiers the Makuraners put up against us, we *will* sack Mashiz."

She sounded confident. Maniakes felt confident. "We should have done it last year," he said. "I never expected them to be able to hold us when we were moving down the Tib." He shrugged. "That's why you have to fight the war, though: to see which of the things you don't expect come true."

"We hurt them even so," Lysia said.

She spoke consolingly, but what she said was true. Maniakes nodded. "I'd say the Thousand Cities between the Tutub and the Tib are down to about eight hundred, thanks to us." He knew he was exaggerating the destruction the Videssians had wrought, but he didn't think there really were a thousand cities on the flood-plain, either. "Not only do we hurt the Makuraners doing that, but we loosen their hold on the westlands of Videssos, too."

"This is a strange war," Lysia observed.

"Maniakes nodded again. Makuran held virtually all of the Videssian westlands, the great peninsula on the far side of the Cattle Crossing. All his efforts to drive them out of the westlands by going straight at them had failed. But Makuran, a landlocked power till its invasion of Videssos, had no ships to speak of. Controlling the sea had let Maniakes strike at the enemy's heartland even if he couldn't free his own.

He slipped an arm around Lysia's waist. "You're falling down on the job, you know." She raised an eyebrow in a silent question. He explained: "The last two years, you've had a baby while we were on campaign in the Land of the Thousand Cities."

She laughed so hard, she pulled free of him. He stared at her in some surprise; he hadn't thought the small joke anywhere near that funny. Then she said, "I was going to tell you in a few more days, when I was surer, but . . . I think I'm expecting again."

"Do you?" he said. Now Lysia nodded. He hugged her, shaking his head all the while. "I think we're going to have to make the imperial residence bigger, with all the children it will be holding."

"I think you may be right," Lysia answered. Maniakes had a young daughter and son, Evtropia and Likarios, by his first wife, Niphone, who had died giving birth to Likarios. Lysia had borne him two boys, Symvatios and Tatoules. The one, a toddler now, was named for her father—Maniakes' uncle—the other for Maniakes' younger brother, who had been missing for years in the chaos that surrounded the Makuraner conquest of the westlands.

Maniakes knew Tatoules almost had to be dead, and had chosen the name to remember him.

Maniakes also had a bastard son, Atalarikhos, back on the eastern island of Kalavria. His father had governed there before their clan rose up against the vicious and inept rule of the previous Avtokrator, Genesios, who had murdered his way to the throne and tried to stay on it with even more wholesale slaughter. Now Maniakes prudently mentioned neither Atalarikhos nor his mother, a yellow-haired Haloga woman named Rotrude, to Lysia.

Instead of bringing up such a sticky topic, he said, "Shall we hold a feast to celebrate the good news?"

To his surprise and disappointment, Lysia shook her head. "What would be the point? The clan stands by us, and your soldiers do, because you've managed to make the Makuraners thoughtful about fighting Videssians, but most of the nobles would find polite reasons to be someplace else."

He scowled, his eyebrows coming down in a thick black line above his eyes. She was right, and he knew it, and he hated it. "The patriarch gave us a dispensation," he growled.

"So he did," Lysia agreed, "after you almost sailed back to Kalavria three years ago. That frightened Agathios into it. But only about half the priests acknowledge it, and far fewer than half the nobles."

"I know what will make everyone acknowledge it," Maniakes said grimly. Lysia half turned away from him, as if to say nothing would make people acknowledge the legitimacy of their union. But he found a magic word, one as potent as if spoken by a chorus of the most powerful mages from the Sorcerers' Collegium: "Victory."

Maniakes rode through the streets of Videssos the city toward the harbor of Kontoskalion on the southern side of the capital. Before him marched a dozen parasol-bearers, their bright silk canopies announcing to all who saw that the Emperor was moving through his capital. Because that thought might not fill everyone with transports of delight, around him tramped a good-sized bodyguard.

About half the men in the detachment were Videssians, the other half Halogai—mercenaries from out of the cold north. The native Videssians were little and dark and lithe, armed with swords. The Halogai, big, fair men, some of whom wore their long, pale hair in braids, carried long-handled axes that could take a head with one blow.

At the front of the procession marched a herald who shouted, "Way! Make way for the Avtokrator of the Videssians!" People on foot scrambled out of the street. People riding horses or leading donkeys either sped up or found side streets. One teamster driving a heavy wagon neither sped up nor turned. A Haloga suggested, "Let's kill him," to Maniakes.

He made no effort to lower his voice. Maniakes did not think he was joking: the Halogai had a very direct way of looking at the world. Evidently, the teamster didn't think he was joking, either. All of a sudden, the wagon not only sped up, but also moved onto a side street. No longer impeded, the procession moved on toward the harbor of Kontoskalion.

Maniakes rode past one of the hundreds of temples in Videssos the city dedicated to the worship of Phos. Perhaps drawn by the herald's cries, the priest who served the temple came out to look at the Avtokrator and his companions. Like other clerics, he shaved his pate and let his beard grow full and bushy. He wore a plain wool robe, dyed blue, with a cloth-of-gold circle representing Phos' sun sewn above his left breast.

Maniakes waved to him. Instead of waving back, the priest spat on the ground, as if rejecting Phos' evil rival, Skotos. Some of the Videssian guardsmen snarled at him. He glared back toward them, armored in his faith and therefore unafraid. After a moment, he deliberately turned his back and went into the temple once more.

"Bastard," one of the Videssian guards snarled. "Anybody who insults you like that, your Majesty—"

"We kill him." Three Halogai said it together. They cared nothing for Videssian priests; they did not follow Phos, but still cleaved to the bloodthirsty gods of Halogaland. If ever a priest needed killing, they were the men to do the job.

But Maniakes said, "No, no. I can't afford trouble with the priesthood now. Just let it go. One of these days, maybe—"

That satisfied the Halogai, whose waits for revenge could span years, even generations. Inside, though, Maniakes ached at the priest's gesture. The half of the clergy who accepted his marriage to Lysia did so grudgingly, as if against their better judgment. The ones who rejected it as incestuous, though, did so ferociously and altogether without hesitation.

"One more reason to get to Makuran," Maniakes muttered. Makuraner custom saw nothing out of the ordinary about two first cousins marrying, or even uncles marrying nieces. And the Makuraners worshiped the God, not Phos; the only Videssian priests anywhere near Maniakes would be the ones he brought along for their gift of the healing art and for enspiriting the army. All of those would be men who tolerated his family arrangements, at least nominally.

Reaching the harbor was a relief. The sailors greeted him with genuine affection; they, like his soldiers, cared more that he led them to victory than that he'd married his first cousin. He had hoped the whole Empire of Videssos would come to see things the same way. It hadn't happened yet. He was beginning to wonder if it ever would.

Most of the ships tied up to the wharfs at the harbor of Kontoskalion were beamy merchantmen that would carry his men and horses and gear to the harbor of Lyssaion, where they would disembark and begin their campaign. Almost all the war galleys that would protect the fleet of merchant vessels were moored in the Neorhesian harbor, on the northern shore of Videssos the city.

Maniakes' flagship, the *Renewal*, was an exception to the rule. The *Renewal* was neither the biggest nor the swiftest nor the newest galley in the fleet. It was, however, the galley in which Maniakes had sailed from the island of Kalavria to Videssos the city when he rebelled against Genesios, and so had sentimental value for him. It stayed in the harbor of Kontoskalion because that was where it had first landed at the capital: sentiment again.

Thrax, the drungarios of the fleet, sprang from the deck of the *Renewal* to the wharf to which it was tied and hurried toward Maniakes. "Phos bless you, your Majesty," he said. "It's good to see you."

"And you," Maniakes said, wondering for what was far from the first time whether he also kept Thrax around for sentimental reasons. The drungarios looked like a sailor: he was lean and lithe, with the sun-dark skin and carved features of a man who'd lived his whole life outdoors. He was not old, but his hair and beard had gone shining silver, which gave him a truly striking aspect.

He'd captained the *Renewal* on the journey from Kalavria to the capital. Now he headed the whole Videssian navy. He'd never done anything to make Maniakes think giving him that post was a dreadful mistake. On the other hand, he'd never done anything to make Maniakes delighted he'd given him the post. *Competent but uninspired* summed him up.

As now: he said, "Your Majesty, we'll be ready to sail on the day you appointed." When he told you something like that, you could rely on it.

"Can we be ready five days earlier than that?" Maniakes asked. "The sooner we sail, the sooner we take the war back to Makuran." *And,* he added to himself, *the sooner Lysia and I can get out of Videssos the city.*

Thrax frowned. "I'm not so sure about that, your Majesty. I've set everything up to meet the day you first asked of me. To change it would be hard, and probably not worth doing." He hadn't thought about speeding up, then, and didn't want to think about it.

"See what you can do," Maniakes told him. When Thrax knew in advance what he was supposed to do, he did it with unruffled ease. When he had to improvise, he didn't come off so well. One thing that seemed to be missing from his makeup was any capacity for original thought.

"I'll try, your Majesty," he said after a moment.

"It's not that hard," Maniakes said encouragingly. He was used to improvising; both his campaigns in the Land of the Thousand Cities had been nothing but improvisation from beginning to end, as, for that matter, had been the campaign against Genesios that had won him the throne. He'd seen, though, that not everyone had the knack for seizing what the moment presented.

A cart rattled up the wharf to one of the merchantmen. The driver scrambled down, gave his mule a handful of raisins, and started tossing sacks of grain—or possibly beans—to the sailors, who stowed them below the deck and, with luck, out of the bilgewater.

Maniakes pointed to the carter. "You need to find out where he and all the people like him are coming from, how long they travel, how long they take to unload here, and how long to get back again. Then you need to sit down with the heads of the storehouses and see if there's anything they can do to make things move faster. If they can load more carts at once than we're sending, for instance—"

He broke off there, because Thrax was clutching both hands to his head as if it were about to explode like a tightly stoppered jar left too long in a cook fire. "Have mercy on my poor wits, your Majesty!" the drungarios cried. "How am I supposed to remember all that?"

"It's not that hard," Maniakes repeated, but, by Thrax's tormented expression, it was indeed that hard, or maybe harder. He felt as if he were the ecumenical patriarch, trying to explain some abstruse theological point to a drunken peasant who didn't care about theology in the first place and was more interested in pissing on his shoes.

"Everything *will* be ready on the day you first set me," Thrax promised, and Maniakes believed that. Thrax heaved a martyred sigh, as the holy Kveldoulphios might have done when he discovered his fellow Halogai weren't going to join him in converting to the worship of Phos, but were going to slay him to stop him from preaching at them. Sighing again, the drungarios went on, "And I'll *try* to have things ready as far before then as I can, even if I have to turn this whole harbor all cattywumpus to do it."

"That's the spirit!" Maniakes slapped him on the back. "I know you'll do what needs doing, and I know you'll do it well."

What a liar I've come to be since I donned the red boots, Maniakes thought. But a Thrax who was trying to meet the demands he'd put on him was far preferable to a Thrax who was merely . . . trying.

As Thrax and Maniakes walked from one wharf to the next, the drungarios did his best to be helpful. He knew what was supposed to be happening by the original schedule, and talked knowledgeably about that. He also began thinking about what he'd have to do to make that schedule move faster. Having once rejected changes out of hand, he now took the view that any cooperation he showed afterward was bound to be reckoned an improvement. He was right, too, though Maniakes did his best not to let on about that.

Once Maniakes had done everything he could to encourage the drungarios, he remounted and rode off: Thrax wasn't the only man under whom he had to light a fire. He made a point of returning to the palace quarter by a route different from the one he'd used to go out to the harbor of Kontoskalion, not wanting to meet again the priest who had spurned him.

But it was difficult to travel more than a couple of blocks in Videssos the city without passing a temple, whether a magnificent one like the High Temple or the one dedicated to the memory of the holy Phravitas where Avtokrators and their close kin were entombed or a little building distinguishable from a house only by the spire topped by a gilded globe springing from its roof.

And so, passing by one of those temples, Maniakes found himself watched and measured by another priest, watched and measured and rejected. For a copper or two, he would have set his Haloga guards on the blue-robe this time. But, however tempting he found the notion of taking a bloody revenge, he set it aside once more. It would embroil him with the ecumenical patriarch, and he could not afford that. Being at odds with the temples would put a crimp, maybe a fatal crimp, into the war against Makuran.

And so Maniakes endured the insult. It sometimes looked as if, even if he captured Mashiz, the capital of Makuran, and brought back the head of Sharbaraz King of Kings to hang on the Mile-stone in the plaza of Palamas like that of a common criminal or a rebel, a good many clerics would keep on thinking him a sinner shielded from Phos' light.

He sighed. No matter what they thought of him while he was winning wars, they'd think ten times worse if he lost—to say nothing of what would happen to the Empire if he lost. He had to go on winning, then, to give the clergy the chance to go on despising him.

Kameas the vestiarios said, "Your Majesty, supper is ready." The eunuch's voice lay in that nameless range between tenor and contralto. His plump cheeks were smooth; they gleamed in the lamplight. When he turned to lead Maniakes and Lysia to the dining room, he glided along like a ship running before the wind, the little quick mincing steps he took invisible under his robes.

Maniakes looked forward to meals with his kin, who were, inevitably, Lysia's kin, as well. They didn't condemn him for what he'd done. The only one of his close kin who had condemned him, his younger brother Parsmanios, had joined with the traitorous general Tzikas to try to slay him by magic. Parsmanios, these days, was exiled to a monastery in distant Prista, the Videssian outpost on the edge of the Pardrayan steppe that ran north from the northern shore of the Videssian Sea.

Tzikas, these days, was in Makuran. As far as Maniakes was concerned, the Makuraners were welcome to him. Maniakes presumed Tzikas was doing his best to betray Abivard, the Makuraner commander. Wherever Tzikas was, he would try to betray someone. Treason seemed in his blood.

Kameas said, "Your family will be pleased to see you, your Majesty."

"Of course, they will," Lysia said. "He's the Avtokrator. They can't start eating till he gets there."

The vestiarios gave her a sidelong look. "You are, of course, correct, Empress, but that was not the subject of my allusion."

"I know," Lysia said cheerfully. "So what? A little irrelevance never hurt anyone, now did it?"

Kameas coughed and didn't answer. His life was altogether regular—without the distraction of desire, how could it be otherwise?—and his duties required him to impose regular functioning on the Avtokrator. To him, irrelevance was a distraction at best, a nuisance at worst.

Maniakes suppressed a snort, so as not to annoy the vestiarios. He was by nature a methodical sort himself. He used to have a habit of charging ahead without fully examining consequences. Defeats at the hands of the Kubratoi and Makuraners had taught him to be more cautious. Now he relied on Lysia to keep him from getting too stodgy.

Kameas strode out ahead of him and Lysia, to announce their arrival to their relatives. Somebody in the dining room loudly clapped his hands. Maniakes turned to Lysia and said, "I'm going to give your brother a good, swift kick in the fundament, in the hope that he keeps his brains there."

"With Rhegorios?" Lysia shook her head. "You'd probably just stir up another prank." Maniakes sighed and nodded. Even more than Lysia—or perhaps just more openly—her brother delighted in raising ruckuses.

Rhegorios flung a roll at Maniakes as the Avtokrator walked through the doorway. Maniakes snatched it out of the air; his cousin had played such games before. "Lese majesty," he said, and threw it back, hitting Rhegorios on the shoulder. "Send for the headsman."

Some Avtokrators, not least among them Maniakes' predecessor, the late, unlamented Genesios, would have meant that literally. Maniakes was joking, and obviously joking at that. Rhegorios had no hesitation in shooting back, with words this time rather than bread: "Anyone who keeps us waiting and hungry deserves whatever happens to him."

"He's right," the elder Maniakes declared, glaring at his son and namesake with a scowl too ferocious to be convincing. "I'm about to waste away to a shadow."

"A noisy, grumbling shadow," the Avtokrator replied. His father chuckled. He was twice Maniakes Avtokrator's age, shorter, heavier, grayer, more wrinkled: when Maniakes looked at his father; he saw himself as he would look if he managed to stay on the throne and stay alive till he was seventy or so. The elder Maniakes, a veteran cavalry commander, also carried a mind well stocked in treacheries and deviousness of all sorts.

"It could be worse," said Symvatios, Lysia's father and the elder Maniakes' younger brother. "We could all be in the Hall of the Nineteen Couches, lying on those silly things propped up on one elbow while from the elbow up our arms go numb." He chuckled; he was both handsomer and jollier than the elder Maniakes, just as his son Rhegorios was handsomer and jollier than Maniakes Avtokrator.

"Eating reclining is a dying ceremony," Maniakes said. "The sooner they wrap it in a shroud and bury it, the happier I'll be."

Kameas' beardless face was eloquent with distress. Reproachfully, he said, "Your Majesty, you promised early in your reign to suffer long-standing usages to continue, even if they were not in all ways to your taste."

"Suffer is just what we do when we eat in the Hall of the Nineteen Couches," Rhegorios said. He was not shy about laughing at his own wit.

"Your Majesty, will you be gracious enough to tell your brother-in-law the Sevastos that his jests are in questionable taste?"

Using the word *taste* in a context that included dining was asking for trouble. The gleam in Rhegorios' eye said he was casting about for the way to cause the most trouble he could. Before he could cause any, Maniakes forestalled him, saying to Kameas, "Esteemed sir—" Eunuchs had special honorifics reserved for them alone. "—I did indeed say that. You will—occasionally—be able to get my family and me to eat in the antique style. Whether you'll be able to get us to enjoy it is probably another matter."

Kameas shrugged. As far as he was concerned, that old customs were old was reason aplenty to continue them. That made some sense to Maniakes—how could you keep track of who you were if you didn't know who your grandparents had been?—but not enough. Ritual for ritual's sake was to him as blind in everyday life as it was in the temples.

"This evening," Kameas said, "we have a thoroughly modern supper for you, never fear."

He bustled out of the dining room, returning shortly with a soup full of crabmeat and octopus tentacles. The elder Maniakes lifted one of the tentacles in his spoon, examined the rows of suckers on it, and said, "I wonder what my great-grandparents, who never set foot outside Vaspurakan their whole lives long, would have said if they saw me eating a chunk of sea monster like this. Something you'd remember a long time, I'll wager."

"Probably so," his brother Symvatios agreed. He devoured a length of octopus with every sign of enjoyment. "But then, I wouldn't want to feast on some of the bits of goat innards they'd call delicacies. I could, mind you, but I wouldn't want to."

Rhegorios leaned toward Maniakes and whispered, "When our ancestors first left Makuran and came to Videssos the city, they probably thought you got crab soup at a whorehouse." Maniakes snorted and kicked him under the table.

Kameas carried away the soup bowls and returned with a boiled mullet doused with fat and chopped garlic and served on a bed of leeks, parsnips, and golden carrots. When he sliced the mullet open, his cuts revealed roasted songbirds, themselves stuffed with figs, hidden in its body cavity.

A salad of lettuces and radishes followed, made piquant with crumbly white cheese, lemon juice, and olive oil. "Eat hearty, to revive your appetites," Kameas advised.

Maniakes glanced over at Lysia. "It's a good thing you're not feeling any morning sickness yet."

She gave him a dark look. "Don't mention it. My stomach may be listening." Actually, she'd gone through her first two pregnancies with remarkable equanimity, which, considering that she'd been on campaign through a good part of each of them, was just as well.

Mutton chops followed the salad, accompanied by a casserole of cauliflower, broccoli, cabbage, and more cheese. Candied fruit finished off the meal, along with a wine sweeter than any of those that had accompanied the earlier courses. Maniakes raised his silver goblet. "To renewal!" he said. His whole clan drank to the toast. It wasn't merely the name he'd given his flagship, but what he hoped to accomplish for the Empire of Videssos after Genesios' horrific misrule.

It would have been ever so much easier had the Makuraners not taken advantage of that misrule to steal most of the westlands and had the Kubratoi not come within inches of capturing and killing Maniakes a few years before. He'd since paid the Kubratoi back. Avenging himself on Makuran, though, was proving a harder fight.

The commander of the garrison on the wall of Videssos the city was a solid, careful, middle-aged fellow named Zosimos. You wanted a steady man in that job; a flighty soul subject to the vapors could do untold harm there. Zosimos filled the bill.

And so, when he came seeking an audience with the Avtokrator, Maniakes not only granted it at once but prepared himself to listen carefully to whatever the officer had to say. Nor did Zosimos waste any time in saying it: "Your Majesty, my men have spotted Kubratoi spies from the wall."

"You're sure of that, excellent sir?" Maniakes asked him. "They've been quiet since we beat them going on three years ago now. For that matter, they're still quiet; I haven't had any reports of raids over the border."

Zosimos shrugged. "I don't know anything about raids, your Majesty. What I do know is that my men have seen nomads keeping an eye on the city. They gave chase a couple of times, but the Kubratoi got away."

Maniakes scratched his head. "That's—peculiar, excellent sir. When the Kubratoi come down into Videssos, they come to raid." He spoke as if setting forth a law of nature. "If they're coming to spy and nothing more . . . Etzilios is up to something. But what?"

He made a sour face. The khagan of Kubrat was an unwashed

barbarian. He was also a clever, treacherous, and dangerous foe. If he was up to something, it would not be something that benefited Videssos. If Etzilios was making his horsemen forgo their usual looting and robbery, he definitely had something large in mind.

"I'd better have a look at this for myself." Maniakes nodded to Zosimos. "Take me to where the Kubratoi have been seen."

Even a journey out to the walls of Videssos the city was inextricably intertwined with ceremony. Not only guardsmen accompanied the Avtokrator, but also the twelve parasol-bearers suitable to his rank. He had to argue with them to keep them from going up onto the wall with him and announcing his presence to whoever might be watching. Reluctantly, they admitted secrecy might serve some useful purpose.

Zosimos had taken Maniakes further south than he'd expected, most of the way down to the meadow outside the southern end of the wall that gave Videssian horse and foot a practice ground. "Are they spying on our exercises or on the city?" Maniakes asked.

"I cannot say," Zosimos answered. "If I could see into a barbarian's mind, I would be well on the way to barbarism myself."

"If you don't look into your enemy's mind, you'll spend a lot of time retreating from him," Maniakes said. Zosimos stared at him, not following that at all. Maniakes sighed and shrugged and ascended the stairs to the battlements of the inner wall.

Once up on that wall and looking out beyond Videssos the city, Maniakes felt what almost all his predecessors had felt before him: that the imperial capital was invulnerable to assault. The crenelated works on which he stood were strong and thick and eight or nine times as high as a man. Towers—some square, some round, some octagonal—added still more strength and height. Beyond the inner wall was the outer one. It was lower, so that arrows from the inner walls could not only clear it and strike the foe beyond but also could rake it if by some unimaginable mischance it should fall. It, too, boasted siege towers to make it still more commanding. Beyond it, hidden from the Avtokrator's view by its bulk, was a wide, deep ditch to hold engines away from the works.

A couple of soldiers pointed toward a stand of trees not far from the practice grounds. "That's where we spied 'em, your Majesty," one of them said. The other one nodded, as if to prove he hadn't been brought before his sovereign by mistake.

Maniakes looked out toward the trees. He hadn't expected to see anything for himself, but he did: a couple of riders in furs and leathers, mounted on horses smaller than Videssians usually rode. "We could cut them off," he said musingly, but then shook his head. "No—they haven't come down by themselves, surely. If we snag these two, the next bunch further north will know we have 'em, and that's liable to set off whatever Etzilios has in mind."

"Letting 'em find out whatever they're after is liable to do the same thing," one of the soldiers answered.

That, unfortunately, was true. But Maniakes said, "If Etzilios is willing to sneak around instead of coming right out and invading us, I'm willing to let him be sneaky for another year longer. The lesson we gave him three years ago has already lasted longer than I thought it would. After we settle with the Makuraners once and for all, which I hope to do this year, then I can try to show Etzilios that the lesson he got was only the smaller part of what he needs to learn."

He'd done some learning himself, in the years since he'd taken the throne. The hardest thing he'd had to figure out was the necessity of doing one thing at a time and not trying to do too much at once. By the time he had mastered that principle, he had very little empire left from which to apply it.

Now he reminded himself not to expect too much even if he was ever free to loose the Empire's full strength against Kubrat. No doubt, somewhere in one of the dusty archives of Videssos the city, maps a century and a half old showed the vanished roads and even more thoroughly vanished towns of the former imperial province that was presently Etzilios' domain. But Likinios Avtokrator *had* loosed Videssos' full strength against Kubrat, and all he'd got for it was the rebellion that had cost him his throne and his life.

Maniakes looked out toward the Kubratoi one last time. He wondered if any Videssian Avtokrator would ever again bring under imperial control the land the nomads had stolen. He hoped he would be the one, but had learned from painful experience that what you hoped and what you got too often differed.

"All right, they're out there," he said. "As long as they don't do anything to make me notice them, I'll pretend I don't. For the time being, I have more important things to worry about."

✦   ✦   ✦

Videssos had the most talented sorcerers in the world and, in the Sorcerers' Collegium, the finest institution dedicated to training more of the same. Maniakes had used the services of those mages many times. More often, though, he preferred to work with a wizard he'd first met in the eastern town of Opsikion.

Alvinos was the name the wizard commonly used to deal with Videssians. With Maniakes, he went by the name his mother had given: Bagdasares. He was another of the talented men of Vaspurakan who had left the mountains and valleys of that narrow country to see what he could do in the wider world of Videssos.

Since he'd kept Maniakes alive through a couple of formidable sorcerous assaults, the Avtokrator had come to acquire a good deal of respect for his abilities. Coming up to the mage, he asked, "Can you tell me what the weather on the Sailors' Sea will be like when we travel to Lyssaion?"

"Your Majesty, I think I can," Bagdasares answered modestly, as he had the past two years when Maniakes had asked him similar questions. He spoke Videssian with a throaty Vaspurakaner accent. Maniakes could follow the speech of his ancestors, but only haltingly; he was, to his secret annoyance, far more fluent in the Makuraner tongue.

"Good," he said now. "When you warned of that storm last year, you might have saved the whole Empire."

"Storms are not hard to see," Bagdasares said, speaking with more confidence. "They are large and they are altogether natural—unless some mage with more pride than sense tries meddling with them. Weather magic is not like love magic or battle magic, where the passions of the people involved weaken the spells to uselessness. Come with me, Emperor."

He had a small sorcerous study next to his bedchamber in the imperial residence. One wall was full of scrolls and codices; along another were jars containing many of the oddments a wizard was liable to find useful in the pursuit of his craft. The table that filled up most of the floor space in the little room looked to have been through several wars and perhaps an uprising or two; sorcery could be hard on the furniture.

"Seawater," he muttered under his breath. "Seawater."

Maniakes looked around. He saw nothing answering that description. "Shall I order a servant to trot down to the little palace-quarter harbor with a bucket, eminent sir?"

"What? Oh." Alvinos Bagdasares laughed. "No, your Majesty, no need for that. I was thinking out loud. We have fresh water, and I have here—" He plucked a stoppered jar from its niche on the wall. "—sea salt, which, when mixed with that fresh water, gives an excellent simulacrum of the sea. And what is the business of magic, if not simulacra?"

Since Maniakes did not pretend to be a mage, he let Bagdasares do as he reckoned best. That, he had found, was a good recipe for successful administration of any sort: pick someone who knew what he was doing—and picking the right man was no small part of the art, either—then stand aside and let him do it.

Humming tunelessly, Bagdasares mixed up a batch of artificial seawater, then, praying as he did so, poured some of it into a low, broad silver bowl on the battered table. Then he used a sharp knife with a gold hilt to cut several roughly boat-shaped chips off an oak board. Twigs and bits of cloth gave them the semblance of rigging.

"We speak of the Sailors' Sea," he explained to Maniakes, "and so the ships must be shown as sailing ships, even if in literal truth they use oars, as well."

"However you find out what I need to know," the Avtokrator answered.

"Yes, yes." Bagdasares forgot about him in the continued intense concentration he would need for the spell itself. He prayed, first in Videssian and then in the Vaspurakaner tongue to Vaspur the Firstborn, the first man Phos ever created. To the ear of a Videssian steeped in orthodoxy, that would have been heretical. Maniakes, at the moment, worried more about results. In the course of his troubles with the temples, his concern for the finer points of orthodoxy had worn thin.

Bagdasares went on chanting. His right hand moved in swift passes above the bowl that held the little, toylike boats. Without his touching them, they moved into a formation such as a fleet might use traveling across the sea. A wind Maniakes could not feel filled their makeshift sails and sent them smoothly from one side of the bowl to the other.

"The lord with the great and good mind shall favor us with kindly weather," Bagdasares said.

Then, although he did not continue the incantation, the boats he had used in his magic reversed themselves and began to sail back toward the side of the bowl from which they had set out. "What does that mean?" Maniakes asked.

"Your Majesty, I do not know." Bagdasares' voice was low and troubled. "If I were to guess, I—"

Before he could say more, the calm water in the center of the bowl started rising, as if someone had grabbed the rim and were sloshing the artificial sea back and forth. But neither Bagdasares nor Maniakes had his hand anywhere near the polished silver bowl.

What looked like a spark that flew from two iron blades clashing together sprang into being above the little fleet, and then another. A faint mutter in the air—was that what thunder might sound like, almost infinitely attenuated?

One of the boats of the miniature fleet overturned and sank. The rest sailed on. Just before they reached the edge of the bowl, Maniakes had—or thought he had—a momentary vision of other ships, ships that looked different in a way he could not define, also on the water, though he did not think they were physically present. He blinked, and they vanished even from his perception.

"Phos!" Bagdasares exclaimed, and then, as if that did not satisfy him, he swung back to the Vaspurakaner tongue to add, "Vaspur the Firstborn!"

Maniakes sketched Phos' sun-circle above his left breast. "What," he asked carefully, "was that in aid of?"

"If I knew, I would tell you." Bagdasares sounded like a man shaken to the core. "Normally, the biggest challenge a mage faces is getting enough of an answer to his question to tell him and his client what they need to know. Getting so much more than that—"

"I take it we'll run into a storm sailing back to Videssos the city?" Maniakes said in what wasn't really a question.

"I would say that seems likely, your Majesty," Bagdasares agreed. "The lightning, the thunder, the waves—" He shook his head. "I wish I could tell you how to evade this fate, but I cannot."

"What were those other ships, there at the end of the conjuration?" Maniakes asked. With the interpretation less obvious, his curiosity increased.

But Bagdasares' bushy eyebrows came down and together in a frown. "What 'other ships,' your Majesty? I saw only those of my own creation." After Maniakes, pointing to the part of the bowl where the other ships had briefly appeared, explained what he had seen, the mage whistled softly.

"What does this mean?" Maniakes asked. Then he chuckled wryly. "I have a gift for the obvious, I fear."

"Were the answer as obvious as the question, I should be happier—and so, no doubt, would you," Alvinos Bagdasares said. "But questions about meaning, while easy to ask, have a way of being troublesome to wrestle with."

"*Everything* has a way of being troublesome," Maniakes said irritably. "Very well. I assume you can't tell me everything I would know. What *can* you tell me?"

"To meet your gift for the obvious, I would say it is obviously true my magic touched on something larger than I had intended," Bagdasares replied. "As I said, you will have good weather sailing to Lyssaion. I would also say it is likely you will have bad weather sailing back."

"I didn't ask you about sailing back."

"I know that," Bagdasares said. "It alarms me. Most times, magic does either what you want or less, as I told you a little while ago. When it does more than you charge it with, that is a token your spell has pulled back the curtain from great events, events with a power of their own blending with the power you bring to them."

"What can I do to keep out of this storm?" Maniakes asked.

Regretfully, Bagdasares spread his hands. "Nothing, your Majesty. It has been seen, and so it will come to pass. Phos grant that the fleet pass through it with losses as small as may be."

"Yes," Maniakes said in an abstracted voice. As Avtokrator of the Videssians, ruler of a great empire, he'd grown unused to the idea that some things were beyond his power. Not even the Avtokrator, though, could hope to bend wind and rain and sea to his will. Maniakes changed the subject, at least slightly: "What about those other ships I saw?"

Bagdasares looked no happier. "I do not know, so I cannot tell you. I do not know if they be friends or foes, whether they come to rescue the ships from your fleet that passed through the storm or to attack them. I do not know whether the rescue or the attack succeeds or fails."

"Can you try to find out more than you do know?" Maniakes said.

"Aye, I can try, your Majesty," Bagdasares said. "I *will* try. But I make no guarantees of success: indeed, I fear failure. I was not granted the vision, whatever it might have been. This suggests it might well have been meant for you alone, which in turn suggests reproducing, grasping, and interpreting it will be extraordinarily difficult for anyone but yourself."

"Do what you can," Maniakes said.

And, for the next several hours, Bagdasares did what he could. Some of his efforts were far more spectacular than the relatively uncomplicated spell Maniakes had first requested of him. Once, the chamber glowed with a pure white light for several minutes. Shadows appeared on the walls with nothing to cast them. Words in a language Maniakes did not understand came out of thin air.

"What does that mean?" he whispered to Bagdasares.

"I don't know," the wizard whispered back. A little while later, he gave up, saying, "Whatever lies ahead is beyond my ability to unravel now, your Majesty. Only the passing of time can reveal its fullness."

Maniakes clenched his fists. If he'd been willing to wait for the fullness of time, he wouldn't have asked Bagdasares to work magic. He sighed. "I know the army will get to Lyssaion without any great trouble," he declared. "For now, I'll cling to that. Once I get there, once I punish the Makuraners for all they've done to Videssos, then I'll worry about what happens next."

"That is the proper course, your Majesty," Bagdasares said. His large, dark eyes, though . . . his eyes were full of worry.

What looked at first glance like chaos filled the harbor of Kontoskalion. Soldiers filed aboard some merchantmen; grooms and cavalrymen led unhappy, suspicious horses up the gangplanks of others. Last-minute supplies went onto still others.

"The lord with the great and good mind bless you, your Majesty, as you go about your holy work," the ecumenical patriarch Agathios said to Maniakes, sketching Phos' sun-sign above his heart.

"I thank you, most holy sir," the Avtokrator answered, on the whole sincerely. Since granting the dispensation recognizing his marriage to Lysia as licit, Agathios had shown himself willing to be seen with them and to pray with them and for their success in public. A good many other clerics, including some who accepted the dispensation as within the patriarch's power, refused to offer such open recognition of it.

"Smite the Makuraners!" Agathios suddenly shouted in a great voice. One thing Maniakes had noted about him over the years was that, while usually calm, he could work himself up to rage or down to panic with alarming speed. "Smite them!" he cried again. "For they have tried to wipe out and to pervert Phos' holy faith in the lands they have stolen from the Empire of Videssos. Now let our vengeance against them continue."

A good many soldiers, hearing his words, made the sun-sign themselves. Maniakes had punished the Land of the Thousand Cities for the outrages the Makuraners had visited upon the Videssian westlands, for the temples pulled down or burned, for the Vaspurakaner doctrine forcibly imposed upon Videssians who reckoned it heretical, for the priests tormented when they would not preach the Vaspurakaner heresy.

Maniakes recognized the irony there, even if he did not go out of his way to advertise it. He himself inclined toward what the Videssians called orthodoxy, but his father stubbornly clung to the doctrines so loathed in the westlands.

He'd gone out of his way to wreck shrines dedicated to the God the Makuraners worshiped. Having begun a war of religion, they were now finding out what being on the receiving end of it was like.

Agathios, fortunately for Maniakes' peace of mind, calmed as quick as he inflamed himself. Moments after bellowing about the iniquities of the Makuraners, he said, in an ordinary tone of voice, "If the good god is kind, your Majesty, he will let you find a way to put an end to this long, hard war once and for all."

"From your lips to Phos' ear," Maniakes agreed. "Nothing would make me happier than peace—provided they restore to us what they've stolen. And nothing would make them happier than peace—provided they keep what they took when Videssos was weak. You do see the problem, most holy sir?"

"I do indeed." The ecumenical patriarch let out a long, sad sigh. "Would it were otherwise, your Majesty." He looked embarrassed. "You do understand, I hope, that I speak as I do in the interest of Videssos as a whole and in the interest of peace rather than that of the temples."

"Of course," Maniakes answered. He'd had so much practice

at diplomacy—or perhaps hypocrisy was the better word—that Agathios didn't notice his sarcasm. Back when the fight against the Makuraners had looked as black as the gaping emptiness of the imperial treasury, he'd borrowed gold and silver vessels and candelabra, especially from the High Temple but also from the rest, and melted them down to make the gold and silver coins with which he could pay his soldiers—and with which he could also pay tribute to the Kubratoi so he could concentrate what few resources he had on fighting the Makuraners. With peace, the temples would—might—be repaid.

Thinking about the Kubratoi made him glance eastward. He was not up on the walls of Videssos the city now; he could not see the Kubrati scouts who had come down near the imperial city to see what he was doing. But he hadn't forgotten them, either. The nomads had never before sent out spies so openly. He wondered what they had in mind. Etzilios had been very quiet in the nearly three years since he'd been trounced . . . till now.

While Maniakes was musing thus, Agathios raised his hands toward the sun and spat down onto the planks of the wharf to show his rejection of Skotos. "We bless thee, Phos, lord with the great and good mind," he intoned, "by thy grace our protector, watchful beforehand that the great test of life may be decided in our favor."

Maniakes joined him in Phos' creed; so, again, did many of the sailors and soldiers. That creed linked worshipers of the good god in distant Kalavria, almost at the eastern edge of the world, with their coreligionists on the border with Makuran—or rather, on what had been the border with Makuran till the westerners began taking advantage of Videssos' weaknesses after Genesios killed Likinios and his sons.

Agathios bowed low. "May good fortune go with you, your Majesty, and may you come back wreathed with fragrant clouds of victory." Maniakes had been trained as a soldier, not as a rhetorician, but he knew a mixed metaphor when he heard one. Agathios seemed to notice nothing out of the ordinary, adding, "May the King of Kings cower like the whipped ox you have for your slaves." And, bowing again, he departed, sublimely unaware he had left meaning behind along with Maniakes.

Thrax waved from the *Renewal.* Maniakes waved back and hurried down the wharf toward his flagship. His red boots, footgear reserved for the Avtokrator alone, thudded on the gangplank. "Good to have you aboard, your Majesty," Thrax said, bowing. "Will the Empress be along soon? When everyone's here, we don't have anything left to hold us in the city."

"Lysia will be along shortly," Maniakes answered. "Do you mean to tell me Rhegorios is already aboard?"

"That he is." Thrax pointed aft, to the cabins behind the mast. On most dromons, only the captain enjoyed the luxury of a cabin, the rest of the crew slinging their hammocks or spreading blankets on the deck when they spent one of their occasional nights at sea. A ship that habitually carried the Avtokrator, his wife, and the Sevastos, though, carried them in as much comfort as was to be found in the cramped confines of a war galley.

Maniakes knocked at the door to the cabin his cousin was using. When Rhegorios opened it, Maniakes said, "I didn't expect you to be on board ahead of me and Lysia both."

"Well, life is full of surprises, isn't it, cousin your Majesty brother-in-law of mine?" Rhegorios said, stringing together with reckless abandon the titles by which he might address Maniakes. He had a habit of doing that, not least because it sometimes flustered Maniakes, which amused Rhegorios no end.

Today, though, the Avtokrator refused to rise to the bait. He said, "Lysia and I have our own reasons for wanting to be out of Videssos the city, but you're popular here. I'd think you'd want to stay as long as you could."

"Any fool with a big smile can be popular," Rhegorios said with an airy wave of his hand. "It's easy."

"I haven't found it so," Maniakes answered bitterly.

"Ah, but you're not a fool," Rhegorios said. "That makes it harder. When a fool goes wrong, people forgive him; he isn't doing anything they didn't expect. But if a man with a reputation for knowing what he's doing goes astray, they're on him like a pack of wolves, because he's let them down."

Lysia boarded the *Renewal* then, which should have distracted Maniakes but didn't. A great many people in Videssos the city reckoned he had gone wrong by falling in love with his cousin. The feeling would have been less powerful had it been more rational. Getting away from the capital, getting away from the priests who still resented the dispensation he'd haggled out of Agathios, was nothing but a relief.

Thrax shouted orders. Longshoremen ran out to cast off lines. Sailors nimbly coiled the ropes in snaky spirals. They stowed the gangplank behind the cabins; Maniakes felt the thud through the soles of his feet when it crashed down onto the deck planking.

A drum began to thud, setting the pace for the rowers. "Back oars!" the oarmaster shouted. The oars dug into the water. Little by little, the *Renewal* slid away from the wharf. Maniakes inhaled deeply, then let out a long, glad sigh. Wherever he went, and into whatever sort of battle, he would be happier than he was here.

Coming into Lyssaion was like entering another world. Here in the far southwest of the Videssian westlands, the calendar might still have said early spring, but by all other signs it was summer outside. The sun pounded down out of the sky with almost the relentless authority it held in the Land of the Thousand Cities. Only the Sailors' Sea kept the weather hot rather than intolerable.

But even the sea here was different from the way it looked in Videssos the city. Back by the capital, the seawater was green. Off Kalavria, in the distant east, it was nearer gray. You could ride out from Kastavala over to the eastern shore, and look across an endless expanse of gray, gray ocean toward the end of the world, or whatever lay beyond vision. No ship had ever come out of the east to Kalavria. Over the years, a few ships had sailed east from the island. None of them had come back, either.

Here, now . . . here the water was blue. It was not the blue of the sky, the blue enamel-makers kept trying and failing to imitate in glass paste. The blue of the sea was darker, deeper, richer, till it almost approached the color of fine wine. But if, deluded, you dipped it up, you found yourself with only a cup of warm seawater.

"I wonder why that is," Rhegorios said, having made the experiment.

"To the ice with me if I know." Maniakes spat in rejection of Skotos, whose icy hell held the souls of sinners in eternal torment.

"Phos is a better wizard than all the mages ever born put together," Rhegorios said, to which his cousin could only nod.

Against bright sky and rich blue sea, the walls of Lyssaion, and the buildings that showed over them, might have been cast of shining gold. They weren't, of course; such a test of man's cupidity could never have been built, nor survived long if by some miracle it had been. But the yellow-brown sandstone shone and sparkled in the fierce sunlight till the eye had to look away lest it be dazzled.

Till two years before, Lyssaion had been nothing but a sleepy little town that baked in the summer, mostly stayed warm through the winter, and, in times of peace, sent goods from the west and occasional crops of dates to Videssos the city. The palm trees on which the dates ripened grew both near and even within the city, as they did in the Land of the Thousand Cities. Maniakes found them absurd; they put him in mind more of outsized feather dusters than proper trees.

Lyssaion had been so unimportant in the scheme of things that the Makuraners, when they overran the Videssian westlands, hadn't bothered giving it more than a token garrison. The thrust of their invasion had been toward the northeast, toward Videssos the city. Towns on the way to the capital lay firmly under their thumb. Other towns . . .

"They didn't pay enough attention to other towns," Maniakes said happily as his men and horses left their ships and filed into Lyssaion.

"They certainly didn't," Rhegorios agreed, also happily. "And now they're paying for it."

Looking at Lyssaion, though, Maniakes thought the Makuraners could have done little to keep him from seizing it as a base no matter how much they wanted to do exactly that. It had a stout wall to hold off enemies approaching by land, but none to keep ships from drawing near. Without ships, the place had no reason to exist. Fishing boats sailed out from it; in peacetime it enjoyed modest prosperity from its dates and as a transshipment point between Makuran and Videssos. Wall off the harbor to hold out a fleet: the town would die, the people would flee, and who would feed a garrison then?

Maniakes settled Lysia in the hypasteos' residence, where the city governor's wife fussed over her: between an unexpected touch of morning sickness and a touch of seasickness, she was looking wan. "I'm glad it's only my stomach moving now," she said, "not everything around me, too."

Before long, she was going to be in a wagon, jouncing along toward the Land of the Thousand Cities and, Phos willing, toward

Mashiz. Maniakes did not mention that. He knew Lysia knew it. How could he blame her for not wanting to think about it?

His horse, Antelope, was just as glad as his wife to get back on solid ground. The beast snorted and kicked up dirt once led off the wharf. "Can you smell where we are?" Maniakes asked, stroking the side of the horse's nose. The wind smelled hot and dusty to him, but he didn't have an animal's nose. "Do you know what these smells mean?"

By the way Antelope whickered, maybe he did. Maniakes had to use his eyes. Seeing those hills—almost mountains—against the northeastern and northwestern horizon, seeing the green thread of the Xeremos River flowing through the dry desert, by Lyssaion, and into the Sailors' Sea . . . all that made him remember the fights in the Land of the Thousand Cities that had forced Sharbaraz King of Kings to dance to his tune instead of the other way round. One more year of fighting there might even bring the victory that had seemed unimaginable when he took the throne from Genesios.

His army filled Lyssaion to the bursting point and even a little beyond: tents sprang up like toadstools, out beyond the city walls. He wanted to head northwest along the banks of the Xeremos straight toward enemy country, but had to wait until not just men and horses but also supplies came off his ships. Once in the Land of the Thousand Cities, they could live off the fertile countryside. On the way there, though, much of the countryside was anything but fertile.

"Phos bless you, your Majesty, on your journey against the foe," said the local prelate, an amiable little fellow named Boinos, at supper that night. Maniakes smiled back at him; he'd never heard *Please go someplace else and stop eating us out of house and home* more elegantly expressed.

"I'll take all the blessings I can get, thank you," the Avtokrator answered. "I already think the good god is watching over us; the Makuraners could easily have tried coming down the Xeremos against Lyssaion. We'd have driven them out again, no doubt, but that might have delayed the start of the campaign, and it wouldn't have been good for your city." He beamed at Boinos, pleased with his own understatement.

The prelate sketched the sun-circle above his heart. So did Phakrases, the hypasteos, who looked like Boinos' unhappy cousin.

And so did the garrison commander, Zaoutzes, who, from his years in the sunbaked place, was as brown and weathered as a sailor. He said, "You know, your Majesty, I looked for something like that from them, but it never came. I kept sending scouts up the river to see if they were up to something. I never found any sign they were heading this way, though, for which I thank the lord with the great and good mind." He signed himself again.

"Maybe they didn't bother, knowing we could always get to the Land of the Thousand Cities by way of Erzerum if word came Lyssaion had fallen," Rhegorios suggested.

"Forgive me, your highness, but I do not like to think of my city falling back into the hands of the misbelievers," Phakrases said stiffly. "I do not like to think what happens in Lyssaion is important in Videssos the city only in the way it might make you change your plans, either."

So there, Maniakes thought. Rhegorios, for once, had no quick comeback ready; perhaps he hadn't expected the city governor to be so blunt—even if politely blunt—with him.

Lysia said, "Lyssaion is important for its own sake, and also because it is the key in the lock that, when fully opened, will set the whole Empire of Videssos free. I said the same thing when we came here two years ago, and I say it again now that it has begun to come true."

"You are gracious, Empress," Phakrases answered, inclining his head to her. Almost everyone in Lyssaion maintained a polite silence about the irregularities in her relationship with Maniakes, for which both she and the Avtokrator were grateful. Maybe it was that Agathios' dispensation sufficed, out here away from the capital, in country where people were more stolid, less argumentative. Or maybe, conversely, living so close to Makuran, where marriages between cousins and even between uncles and nieces were allowed, made the folk of Lyssaion take such unions in stride. Maniakes had no intention of asking which, if either, of those interpretations was true.

Instead, he followed Zaoutzes' thought: "What if the Makuraners *are* up to something, but it's not aimed at Lyssaion?"

The garrison commander shrugged. "I have no way to know about that, your Majesty. None of my men got deep enough into the Land of the Thousand Cities to tell for certain."

"All right," Maniakes said. "If Sharbaraz and Abivard are up to something else, I expect we'll find out when they turn it loose against us." He started to add something like, *We've stopped everything they've thrown at us so far,* but left that unspoken. If the Videssian westlands hadn't lain under Makuraner control, he wouldn't have had to sail to Lyssaion to put himself in a position of being able to carry the war to the foe.

Rhegorios said, "We've managed to stay alive this long," which came closer to summing up what the situation was really like. Rhegorios, as was his way, sounded cheerful. When mere survival was enough to make a man cheerful, though, the clouds overhead were dark and gloomy.

As Avtokrator of the Videssians, Maniakes could not afford to show that he was worried, lest by showing that he made his subjects worry, too, thus turning a bad situation worse. When he and Lysia were getting ready for bed, though, in the chamber Phakrases had given them, he said, "We've ducked so many arrows from the bows of the Makuraners, and been able to give back so few. How long can that go on?"

Lysia paused to think before she answered. As his cousin, she'd known him almost all his life. As his wife, she'd come to know him in a different, more thorough way than she had as cousin alone. At last, she said, "The Makuraners have done everything they can to Videssos, because they can't reach the imperial city. We're a long way from doing everything we can to them. The more we do, the sooner they'll come to their senses and make peace."

"Other people have said the same thing to me, ever since I got the idea of moving my army against them by sea," he answered. "The advantage you have is that you make me believe it."

"Good," she said. "I'm supposed to. Isn't that what they call wifely duty?"

He smiled. "No, that's something else."

She tossed her head, flipping her black curls back from her face. "*That's* not a duty. Duties you endure. That—"

It *was* enjoyable, not least because she didn't look on it as a duty; he thought sadly of Niphone, who had looked on it so. Afterward, he slept soundly. The next morning, the army left Lyssaion, heading northwest.

II

Where the waters of the Xeremos reached, its valley was green and fertile. Where canals and underground channels in the style of those on Makuran's western plateau could not reach, it was desert. Here and there, the locals had thrown up walls of mud brick and stone, not against human foes but to hold encroaching sand dunes at bay. Here and there, the remains of such walls sticking up through sand told of fights that had failed.

This was the second time the farmers in the valley had seen the Videssian army sally forth to attack Makuran. The first time, two years before, they'd wavered between panic and astonishment; no Avtokrator had been seen in that out-of-the-way part of the Empire for centuries, if ever. They hadn't known whether the soldiers would plunder them of their few belongings. True, they and the soldiers owed allegiance to the same sovereign, but how often did that matter to soldiers?

Maniakes had kept his men from plundering back then, and also during the fall just past, when they'd withdrawn from the Thousand Cities by way of the Xeremos. Now the peasants waved from the fields instead of running from them.

When Maniakes remarked on that, Rhegorios said, "The farmers between the Tutub and the Tib won't be so glad to see us."

"The peasants in the westlands—farmers and herders alike—

403

haven't been glad to see the Makuraners, or to have their substance stolen, or to have to pay ruinous taxes to the King of Kings, or to have the way they worship deliberately disturbed to fuel feuds among them," Maniakes returned.

"That's so, every word of it, cousin your Majesty brother-in-law of mine," Rhegorios agreed, grinning one of his impudent grins. "But it won't make the peasants in the Land of the Thousand Cities glad to see us, no matter how true it is."

"I don't want them to be glad to see us," Maniakes said. "I want them to hate us so much—I want all of Makuran to hate us so much, aye, and to fear us so much, too—that they give over their war, give back our land, and settle down inside their own proper borders. If Sharbaraz offers to do that, as far as I'm concerned he's bloody well welcome to however many of the Thousand Cities that are left standing by then."

He looked back over his shoulder. A good many of the wagons in the baggage train carried not fodder for the beasts or food for the men but stout ropes, fittings of iron and brass, and a large number of timbers sawn to specific lengths. The paraphernalia looked innocuous—till the engineers assembled the catapults from their component parts, which they could do much faster than most Makuraner garrison commanders realized.

The timbers that went into the siege engines were also useful in another way. Canals crisscrossed the flat floodplain between the Tutub and the Tib. To slow the Videssians, the Makuraners were not averse to opening the banks of the canals in their path and letting water flow out to turn roads and fields alike to mud. Plopped down into that mud, the timbers could make a passable way out of one that was not.

In a thoughtful voice, Rhegorios said, "I wonder what Abivard will try to do against us this year, now that he has some of the Makuraner boiler boys—" Videssian slang so named the fearsome Makuraner heavy cavalry, whose members did indeed swelter to the boiling point in the full armor that encased not only them but their horses, as well. "—to go with the infantry levies from the city garrisons."

"I don't know." Maniakes suspected he looked unhappy. He was certain he felt unhappy. "We would have done better the past two years if Sharbaraz had sent a worse general against us. I first got to know Abivard more than ten years ago now, and he was good then—maybe better than he knew, since he was just starting to lead campaigns. He's got better since." His chuckle had a wry edge to it. "I hardly need say that, do I, since he's the one who conquered the westlands from us?"

"This army isn't so good as the one he used to do that," Rhegorios said. "He hasn't got all the heavy horse with him, only a chunk of it, with the rest in the westlands or up in Vaspurakan. And do you know what? I don't miss the ones I won't see, not one bit I don't."

"Nor I," Maniakes agreed. They rode on in silence for a little while. Then he went on, "I wonder what Abivard thinks of me—how he plans his campaigns against me, I mean."

"What you do—what you do that most people don't, I mean—is that you learn from your mistakes," his cousin answered.

"Is that so?" Maniakes said. "Then why do I keep putting up with you?"

Rhegorios mimed being wounded to the quick, so well that his horse snorted and sidestepped under him. He brought it back under control, then said, "No doubt because you recognize quality when you see it." That wasn't bragging, as it might have been from another man; Rhegorios, in fact, did not sound altogether serious. But the Sevastos continued in a more sober vein: "You do learn. Things that worked against you two years ago won't work now, because you've seen them before."

"I hope so," Maniakes said. "I know I used to rush ahead too eagerly, without looking to see what was waiting for me. The Kubratoi almost killed me on account of that, not long after I took the throne."

"But you don't do that anymore," Rhegorios said. "A lot of people keep on making the same mistakes over and over again. Take me, for instance: whenever I see a pretty girl, I fall in love."

"No, you don't," Maniakes said. "You just want to get your hands, or something, up under her tunic. It's not the same thing."

"Without a doubt, you're right, O paragon of wisdom," Rhegorios said with a comical leer. "And how many men *ever* learn that?"

He was laughing as he asked the question, which did not mean it wasn't a good one. "Eventually you get too old to care, or else your eyes get too bad to tell the pretty ones from the rest," Maniakes replied.

"Ha! I'm going to tell my sister you said that."

"Threatening your sovereign, are you?" Maniakes said. "That's lese majesty, you know. I could have your tongue clapped in irons." This time, he leered at his cousin. "And if I do, the girls won't like you so well."

Rhegorios stuck out the organ in question. It was easy to laugh now. The campaign was young, and nothing had yet gone wrong.

The Xeremos sprang from hilly country north and west of Lyssaion. Those same hills gave rise to the Tutub, which, with the Tib, framed the Land of the Thousand Cities. Instead of flowing southeast to the Sailors' Sea, the Tutub ran north through the floodplain till it emptied itself in the landlocked Mylasa Sea.

Having traveled quickly up the length of the Xeremos, Maniakes' army slowed in the rougher country that gave birth to the river. The soldiers had to string themselves out in long files to make their way along the narrow trails running through the hill country. A small force of Makuraner troops could have made life very difficult for the advancing imperials.

No such force, though, tried to block their advance. That roused Rhegorios' suspicions. "They might have held us up here for weeks if they really set their minds to it," he said.

"Yes, but they might have had to wait for weeks to see if we were coming," Maniakes replied. He waved to the poor, rock-ribbed country all around. "What would they eat while they were waiting?"

Rhegorios grunted. As far as he was concerned, war meant fighting, nothing else but. He cared little for logistics. Maniakes could not make himself get excited about the details of keeping an army fed and otherwise supplied. But, whether those details were exciting or not, tending to them made the difference between campaigns that failed and those that won.

Maniakes went on, "You'd have to carry provisions not to starve in this country." He exaggerated, but not by much. A handful of farmers plowed fields that often seemed to run nearly as much up and down as from side to side. A few herders pastured sheep on the hills. Again, because of the steepness of those hills, the black-faced animals often looked to be grazing on a slant. A few of the trees bore nuts. That was enough to keep the small local population going. An army that didn't carry its own supplies would have eaten the countryside empty in short order.

A couple of days into the badlands, a scout came riding back toward the Avtokrator from up the track by which the army would be moving. He shouted, "Your Majesty, I've found the headwaters of the Tutub!"

"Good news!" Maniakes dug in the pouch he wore on his belt, pulled out a goldpiece, and tossed it to the soldier. Grinning, the man tucked away the coin. Maniakes wondered what the soldier would have done had he known the goldpiece was minted to a standard slightly less pure than the Videssian norm. So far as Maniakes knew, nobody outside the mint suspected that; it was one way of making his scanty resources stretch further. If he ever got the chance, he intended to return to the old standard as soon as he could. Cheapening the currency was a dangerous game.

By the look on the scout's face, he wouldn't have minded too much. It was still one goldpiece more—well, actually, almost one goldpiece more—than he would have had otherwise.

"All downhill from now on, boys!" Maniakes called, which got a cheer from the soldiers who heard him. If that proved true of the campaign as well as the line of march, he would be well pleased. The next easy campaign he had as Avtokrator would be his first. The Makuraners, now, they'd had easy campaigns, seizing the westlands while Videssos, under the vicious and inept rule of Genesios, writhed in the throes of civil war like a snake with a broken back instead of coming together to resist them.

As the army made its way through the hill country toward the Land of the Thousand Cities, it found more and larger villages. It did not find more people in them. It found hardly any people in them at all. Scouts or herders must have brought word the Videssians were coming. If he'd had that word in good time, Maniakes would have fled before his army, too.

He ordered the villages burned. He sent cavalry squadrons out to either side of his line of march, with orders to burn the more distant villages, too. Since he'd begun campaigning in Makuran, he'd done his best to make the enemy feel the war as sharply as he could. Sooner or later, he reasoned, either Sharbaraz would get sick of seeing his land destroyed or his subjects would get sick of it and revolt against the King of Kings.

The only trouble was, it hadn't happened yet.

Almost imperceptibly, the hills leveled out toward the flat, canal-pierced, muddy soil of the floodplain between the Tutub and the Tib. Peering north and west, Maniakes could see a long, long way. The nearest of the Thousand Cities, Qostabash, lay ahead.

He'd bypassed Qostabash the autumn before. He'd been retreating then, with Abivard's army harrying him as he went. He hadn't enjoyed the luxury of a few days' time in which to stop and sack the place. He promised himself it would be different now.

Qostabash, like a lot of the Thousand Cities, stuck up from the smooth land all around it like a pimple sticking up from the smooth skin of a woman's cheek. It hadn't been built where it was for the sake of the hillock on which it perched. When it was first built, that hillock hadn't been there. But the Thousand Cities were old, old. They'd sprung up between the Tutub and the Tib before Videssos the city was a city, perhaps before it was even a village. Over the long stretch of years, their own rubble—collapsed walls and houses and buildings of mud brick, along with centuries of slops and garbage—had made a hill where none had been before.

Their walls were still brick, though now mostly of fired brick, the better to resist siege engines. Better resistance was not the same as good resistance. Maniakes looked toward Qostabash the way a hungry hound was liable to look toward a butcher's shop.

But, as he approached, he discovered the town was not so defenseless as he had hoped. Its walls had not improved since the year before. But having an army between it and the Videssians did make it harder to seize.

"Well, well," Maniakes said. "Isn't that interesting?" *Interesting* was not the word he had in mind, but it was a word he could bring out without blistering everyone within earshot.

"They are getting better at reacting to us, aren't they?" Rhegorios said. "Year before last, they let us get halfway across the floodplain to Mashiz before they did anything much against us, and last year we got to have some fun when we came down from Erzerum, too. Not this time, though."

"No." Maniakes squinted, trying to sharpen his eyesight. The Makuraners were still too far away for him to be sure, but—"That's a good-sized force they have there."

"So it is," Rhegorios agreed. "They can afford to feed a good-sized force here a lot more easily than they could in the hill country." Maybe he'd been paying attention to logistics after all. He glanced toward Maniakes. "Do we try to go through them or around them?"

"I don't know yet," Maniakes answered. Hearing those words pass his lips was a sign of how far he'd come since the ecumenical patriarch had proclaimed him Avtokrator of the Videssians. He didn't charge ahead without weighing consequences, as he had only a few years before. "Let's see what the scouts have to say. When I know what's in front of me, I'll have a better chance of making the right choice."

Off rode the scouts, down toward the waiting Makuraner army. The rest of the Videssian force followed the outriders.

Maniakes wished he had some better way than eyes alone of looking at the enemy army. His eyes didn't tell him so much as he would have wished, and he didn't altogether trust what they did tell him. But magic and war did not mix; the passions war engendered made sorcery unreliable. And so he waited for the scouts. He knew more than a little relief when one of them came riding back and said, "Your Majesty, it looks to be mostly an infantry army. They have some horsemen—a few rode out to skirmish with us and hold us away from the foot soldiers—but no sign of the boiler boys from the field army."

"I thought I saw the same thing from here," Maniakes said. "I wasn't sure I believed it. No boiler boys, eh? Isn't that interesting?" Now he'd used it twice when he meant something else. "Where is the heavy cavalry, then? Abivard's gone and done something sneaky with it. I don't like that." He didn't like it at all. Not knowing where your enemy's best troops were made you look over your shoulder all the time.

He looked over his shoulder now. No force of heavy Makuraner cavalry came thundering out of the hills behind him. Had they been there, he would have discovered them.

Rhegorios rode up to hear what the scout had to say. He tossed his head. "Well, cousin your Majesty brother-in-law of mine, I'll ask you the same question again: what do we do now?"

"If you were Abivard, what would you do with the field army?" Maniakes replied, answering question with question.

"If I were Abivard," Rhegorios said slowly, thinking as he spoke, "I wouldn't know whether we were coming up from Lyssaion or down from Erzerum. I would know I could move a cavalry force faster than I could a bunch of foot soldiers. I could use infantry to slow down those cursed Videssians—" He grinned at Maniakes. "—as soon as they got into the Land of the Thousand Cities, while I stayed back somewhere in the middle of the country so I could get to wherever I was going in a hurry."

"Yes, that makes good sense," Maniakes said, and then, after a moment's reflection, "in fact, it makes better sense than anything I'd thought of myself. It tells me what needs doing, too."

"That's good," his cousin said. "What does need doing?"

Maniakes spoke with decision, pointing ahead toward the drawn-up Makuraner army. "I don't want to get bogged down fighting foot soldiers. If I do, I won't be able to maneuver the way I'd want to when Abivard comes after me. I want to beat the real Makuraner army, break past it, and strike for Mashiz. Abivard kept me from doing that last year. I don't aim to let him keep me from doing it again."

"Been a good many years since an Avtokrator of the Videssians sacked Mashiz," Rhegorios agreed in dreamy tones. Then he turned practical once more: "So you won't want to engage these fellows or to attack Qostabash, then? We'll get around them and look for more rewarding targets?"

"That's the idea," Maniakes said. "Foot soldiers have trouble engaging us unless we choose to let 'em. I don't choose that here. Let them chase us. If they get out of line doing it, we double back and punish them. If they don't, we leave them eating our dust."

Horns relayed his commands to the Videssian horsemen. In line of battle, they rode past the Makuraner army at a distance of about half a mile. That was plenty close to let his men hear the enemy shouting at them and probably calling them a pack of cowards for not coming closer and fighting.

To give the Makuraners something to yell about, he sent a few squadrons of scouts close enough to ply the mostly unarmored infantry with arrows. The enemy shot back. They put a lot more arrows in the air than had his scouts, but to less effect: they were aiming at small, armored moving targets. A couple of horses went down and one scout pitched from the saddle with an arrow in the face, but the Videssians gave better than they got.

The Makuraners also tried to use their small force of cavalry to slow down the Videssians so their infantry could move forward and come to close quarters with them. Had the force been larger, that might have worked. As things were, the Videssians used horse archers and javelin men to send their foes reeling back in retreat.

"Keep moving!" Maniakes called to his men after the Makuraner horse recoiled back onto their foot for protection. "We'll pick the field. They can't make us do it against our will."

He'd grown used to raising a cheer from the army on going into battle. Raising a cheer on escaping battle was something else again, and almost a harking back to the bad old days when the Videssians had fled the Makuraners for no better reason than that they *were* Makuraners. But the resemblance to those bad old days was only superficial. His men could have attacked the Makuraners had he given them the order. He thought they would have beaten the foe. But an army of foot soldiers was not the foe he wanted to beat, not the foe he needed to beat. He wanted Abivard's men, the best the King of Kings could throw against him. No lesser force deserved his notice.

He and his horsemen rode wide around Qostabash. On the walls of the city, more Makuraners watched. Maybe they, too, were foot soldiers. Maybe they were ordinary townsfolk imitating foot soldiers. The men of the Thousand Cities used all sorts of tricks to try to keep him from testing their inadequate walls. If this was a trick, it would work. He couldn't afford to assail Qostabash, not with that infantry army close on his heels.

On and on the Videssians went, now walking their horses, now trotting them. Maniakes dropped back to the rear guard and peered behind them. Their pursuers had dropped out of sight. He nodded to himself, well enough pleased.

When evening came, the army camped on irrigated land not far from the Tutub. The only enemies close by were mosquitoes and gnats, and they were impartial foes to all mankind. Maniakes looked east, back toward Videssos. No help would reach him from that direction, not with the Makuraners controlling the westlands. Messengers might be able to come up from Lyssaion in case of need, but the need would have to be urgent for them to risk capture by the men of Makuran. He had trouble imagining a need so urgent.

He walked over to the wagon in which Lysia had ridden. "Here we are, altogether surrounded by the foe," he said with a melodramatic wave and an even more melodramatic pause. The pause over, he added, "Isn't it wonderful?"

Lysia laughed, understanding him perfectly. "It certainly is," she said.

The Makuraners wasted no time in trying to make his life difficult. When the army began to move the next morning, it soon encountered flooded fields that came from broken canals. He faced the problem with equanimity: they'd done the same thing each of the past two years. He had enough timbers along to corduroy a road to drier ground, at which point his engineers picked up the timbers and stowed them again. Sooner or later, those infantrymen would try to follow in his footsteps. They'd have a slow, wet, muddy time of it.

Up ahead, seemingly secure on its hillock, squatted one of the Thousand Cities. No large Makuraner army lurked nearby now. Maniakes pointed to the town, whose name he did not know. "We'll take it," he said.

With practiced efficiency, engineers and soldiers went to work. The muddy timbers that had let the Videssian army make its way through muck now were reassembled as frames for catapults and rams. The catapults began lobbing big pots filled with pitch and other inflammable substances into the town. The engineers used oil-soaked rags as wicks for the pots. Before long, columns of smoke rose from burning roofs and awnings and boards inside the city.

Anywhere else, the catapults would also have flung heavy stones at the wall. In the land between the Tutub and the Tib, heavy stones were hard to come by. Forcing breaches, then, was the work of the rams. Under leather-covered wooden frames, they inched up the slope of the artificial hillock toward the city. The defenders on the wall shouted defiance at them and shot at the men who carried the frames and would swing the rams.

Anywhere else, the defenders would have dropped heavy stones down onto the frames, trying to break them and either render the rams useless or at least tear openings through which the boiling water and red-hot sand they poured down onto the attackers could find their way. Again, though, heavy stones were few and far between in the Land of the Thousand Cities.

Videssian archers filled the air with shafts, doing their best to keep the men of the city garrison from interfering with the rams. *Thud!* The pointed iron tip of one of them slammed into the wall.

Maniakes was standing just out of bowshot from the foes. The ground quivered beneath his feet, as if at a small earthquake. *Thud!* Another blow, another little tremor transmitted up through the soles of his shoes.

Thud! That one was smaller still. Off on the other side of the city, halfway round the circuit of the walls, another ram had gone into action. Now the defenders would have two things to worry about at the same time. Maniakes wondered which ram would first make the wall give way.

It proved to be the closer one. With a rumble that seemed almost like a tired sigh, some of the brick masonry came tumbling down. Through it, the screams of the defenders who came tumbling down with the wall rang high and shrill. Videssians rushed into the breach.

Surviving city garrison men met them and, for some little while, fought fiercely enough to hold them in check. But the city garrison was small, and its men neither well trained nor well armed. When a couple of its officers fell, the men began to lose heart. A few of them fell back from the breach, and then a few more. That could not go on long, not if they intended to hold back their enemies. And then, with cries of "Phos with us!" the Videssians began jumping down into the city. The defense was over. The sack had begun.

A captain asked Maniakes, "The usual rules, your Majesty?"

"Aye, the usual, Immodios," he answered. "Wreck the town, men may plunder and burn as they like, but no attacks against anyone who doesn't attack first, no murdering women and children for the sport of it. Any shrine to the Makuraner God you find, tear it down."

"As you say, your Majesty." Immodios saluted, right fist over his heart, then hurried off to spread the news.

As methodically as they had breached the wall, the Videssians went about the business of knocking down the city. A couple of the blue-robed priests who had accompanied the army urged them on, shouting, "Phos will bless you for the vengeance you inflict on his foes and the false god they worship."

Maniakes listened to that fiery talk with some regret, but made no effort to stop it. The Makuraners had turned the war into a religious struggle, not only by wrecking Phos' temples all over the westlands but also by forcing the people in the lands they occupied to follow Vaspurakaner usages rather than Videssian orthodoxy. Calling the counterattack a holy war made his men fight harder than they would have otherwise.

Eventually, the Avtokrator supposed, peace might come to Videssos and Makuran. The bitterness of the war they were fighting now would not make that peace any easier to find. Maniakes knew that. But he also knew he did not want peace to come to Videssos if it was dictated by Sharbaraz King of Kings.

With the garrison overcome, the Videssians threw open the gates and let people stream out of the city and down toward the floodplain. After a while, they would probably come back and start rebuilding. By then, of course, the rubble left from the sack would raise the artificial hillock on which the city stood another palm's breadth or so, making it that much harder for the next Videssian Avtokrator who campaigned here, ten years from now, or fifty, or five hundred, to take the place.

Well, Maniakes thought, *that will be for my successor to worry about, not me. My job is to make sure I have a successor who one day will be in a position to worry about it.*

Lysia came up to him when the sack was nearly over. Much as he loved her, he would sooner not have seen her at that moment. He knew what she was going to say. Sure enough, she said it: "I pray the lord with the great and good mind will forgive our soldiers for what they're doing to the women here. War is a filthy business."

"War is a filthy business," Maniakes agreed. "This one was forced upon us."

"I know," Lysia said; they had this argument whenever one of the Thousand Cities fell. "That doesn't mean we have to make it filthier."

Maniakes shrugged. "If they'd surrendered instead of trying to fight, they could have all left undisturbed; you know I would have let them do that. But they chose to make a fight of it. Once they did, that changed the rules and what the soldiers expected. Next time—"

"Phos forbid a next time," Lysia broke in, sketching the sun-circle above her left breast. "I've heard too many stories about all the horrid things the Makuraners did when they took our cities in the westlands; I don't want them telling horrid stories about us."

"I wish there were no need for them to tell horrid stories about us," Maniakes answered. "That's not quite the same thing, though. They've made themselves frightful to us. If we make ourselves frightful to them in return, sooner or later they'll get the idea that they can't afford to fight us anymore. That's what I'm after."

"I know that's what you're after." Lysia's face stayed troubled. "The good god grant you find it, that's all."

"What I really want to find," Maniakes said, "is Abivard's army. Once I beat him, the whole of this country falls into my hands and I can push straight for Mashiz. Taking his capital, by Phos—that would be a revenge worth having."

Now Lysia did smile, ruefully. "I don't think you've heard a word I've said. I can understand that, I suppose. I can even see that Videssos may be better off on account of what you're doing. But that doesn't mean I have to like it." She walked off, leaving him scratching his head.

From the hillock where yet another of the Thousand Cities went up in flames behind him, Maniakes peered out over the floodplain. He could see a long way from here, but seeing far was not the same as seeing clearly. Turning to Rhegorios, he said, "Drop me into the ice—" He spat in rejection of Skotos. "—if I know where Abivard and the cursed Makuraner field army are. With what we've been doing hereabouts, I thought they'd surely have come to pay us a visit by now."

"So would I," his cousin agreed. "But no sign of them so far. Outside of these worthless little city garrisons, the only Makuraner army we've seen is the one that's been following in our footsteps ever since Qostabash."

"And they're foot soldiers." Maniakes stated the obvious. "What they are, in fact, is the same kind of force Abivard used to fight us year before last. They're probably garrison troops themselves, though they've had so much action the past couple of years, they might as well be regular infantry."

"They're not the worst fighters around," Rhegorios allowed. "When they were working alongside the boiler boys, they made pretty good fighters." Now he looked around, too. "Where *are* the boiler boys?"

"If I could find them, I'd tell you," Maniakes said. "Since I can't find them, I'm going to talk with someone who can, or at least who may be able to: I'm going to see what Bagdasares can do."

"Can't hurt," Rhegorios said. "It may even do some good. Why not?"

"That's why you go see wizards," Maniakes answered, "to find out why not."

Dubious recommendations notwithstanding, he did go to consult the mage from Vaspurakan. "You have been in close contact with Abivard for years," Bagdasares said. "That will help." He looked thoughtful. "Have you got anything of his we might use as a magical source to find him?"

"I don't think so." Maniakes suddenly barked laughter. "It almost makes me wish Tzikas were in camp. He's been back and forth between me and Abivard so many times, each of us could use him as a magical source against the other."

"Contact and affinity are not necessarily one and the same," Bagdasares observed.

"The only person Tzikas has an affinity for is Tzikas," Maniakes said. "I should have taken the traitor's head when Abivard gave him back to me. Even if I did get some use out of him, I never slept easy with him around. That's why I said I almost wish he were back, not that I wish he really was. He's with Abivard again, and Abivard is welcome to worry about him or kill him, whichever he pleases."

"Aye, your Majesty." Bagdasares ran a hand through his thick, curly beard as he contemplated ways and means. "You have clasped his hand, not so?" Maniakes nodded. The wizard produced a small knife. "Let me have a bit of nail from a finger of your right hand, then. And you have spoken to him, so I shall ask for a few drops of your spittle." He quickly sketched the sun-sign over his heart. "By the lord with the great and good mind, I shall destroy these by fire when my magic is completed."

"I'll watch you do it," Maniakes said. "You I trust with my life, Bagdasares, but you're one of the few. Tzikas came too close to slaying me with sorcery for me to be easy about letting parts of myself, so to speak, get loose where other wizards might lay their hands on them."

"And right you are to be cautious," Alvinos Bagdasares agreed. "Now, if I may—"

Maniakes let him cut a bit of fingernail from his right index finger. The Avtokrator spat into a little bowl while Bagdasares bound the nail clipping to one end of a small stick with crimson thread. The mage filled the bowl into which Maniakes had spat with water from a silver ewer. He lifted the little stick with a pair of tongs and let it float in the water.

"Think about Abivard, about wanting to learn in which direction from this place he is," Bagdasares said.

Obediently, Maniakes held the image of the Makuraner marshal in his mind. Bagdasares, meanwhile, chanted first in Videssian, then in the Vaspurakaner tongue Maniakes spoke only in snatches. Maniakes hoped the Makuraner mages weren't deliberately trying to keep him from learning his opponent's whereabouts. They probably were, just as Bagdasares and the other mages accompanying the Videssian army were doing their best to keep its location from their Makuraner counterparts.

Of its own accord, the small stick began to twist in the water, sending small ripples out toward the edge of the bowl. Maniakes kept his eye on the thread tied to the nail clipping. That end of the little stick swung to the east and stayed there. Maniakes scratched his head. "I won't believe Abivard's left the Land of the Thousand Cities."

"That is what the magic suggests," Bagdasares said.

"Could the Makuraners have twisted it so that, say, the stick points in exactly the opposite direction to the proper one?" Maniakes asked.

"I suppose it is possible, so I shall investigate," the wizard replied. "I sensed no such deception, however."

"If it were done well, you wouldn't, though," Maniakes said. "The Makuraners needed quite a while to figure out how you twisted that canal back on itself last year, for instance."

"That is so," Bagdasares admitted. "And Abivard would like nothing better than to make us think he is in one place when in fact he is somewhere else."

"Somewhere else probably being a place from which he can breathe right down our necks," Maniakes said.

"No point in using such a magic unless you gain some advantage from it, now is there?" Bagdasares plucked at his beard as he thought. "Opposites, eh? Well, we shall see what we shall see."

He pulled the stick out of the water, removed Maniakes' fingernail clipping from it, and tossed the clipping into a brazier.

He smeared the end of the stick with pitch, getting his fingers stuck together in the process. Then he took a silver Makuraner arket from his beltpouch and used an iron blade to scrape several slivers of bright metal from the coin. He affixed the slivers to the pitch-smeared stick and put it back into the water.

"We shall use the bits of silver from the arket to represent Makuran's marshal in a somewhat different version of the spell," he told Maniakes.

"You know your business best," the Avtokrator answered. "I don't much care how you do what you do, as long as you get the answers I need."

"Your Majesty's forbearance is beyond price," Bagdasares said. The Vaspurakaner wizard once more began to chant and make passes over the bowl in which the stick floated. The incantations this time, especially the ones in the Vaspurakaner tongue, were different from those he'd used before, though Maniakes would have been hard-pressed to say how.

As it had during the previous incantation, the stick began to quiver in the water. And, as it had during the previous incantation, the end with the magical focus affixed swung toward the east.

Bagdasares looked from it to Maniakes and back again. "Unless I am utterly deceived, Abivard is indeed east of here."

"But that's mad," Maniakes exclaimed. "It's utterly useless. Why on earth would Abivard—and the Makuraner field army with him, no doubt—go into the Videssian westlands? Makuran holds the westlands, except for a port here and there and some holdouts in the hills of the southeast. What can he possibly do there that he didn't do years ago? He's not about to take Videssos the city—not without ships he's not, and I don't care how many soldiers he has. And for anything less important than that, he'd have been wiser to stay here and fight me instead."

"Your Majesty, my magic can tell you what is so—or what I believe to be so, at any rate," Bagdasares said. "Finding out why it is so—looking into the heart of a man that way—is beyond the scope of my art, or of any wizard's art. Often a man does not fully understand himself why he acts as he does—or have you not seen that?"

"I have," Maniakes said. "But this still perplexes me. Abivard is a great many things, but no one has ever called him stupid. He must have known we were coming back to the Land of the

Thousand Cities this year. He didn't try to stop us by seizing Lyssaion. He couldn't stop us from landing up in Erzerum and heading south. If he knew we were coming, why isn't he here to meet us? That's what I want to know."

"It is a proper question, an important question, your Majesty," Bagdasares agreed gravely. "It is also a question to which my magic can give you no good answer. May I ask a question of my own in return?"

"Ask," Maniakes told him. "Anything you can do to let Phos' light into what looks like Skotos' darkness would be welcome." He drew the good god's sun-circle above his heart.

Bagdasares also sketched the sun-circle, saying, "I have no great and wise thoughts to offer, merely this: if, for whatever reason, Abivard chose to absent himself from the land between the Tutub and the Tib, should we not punish him for his error by doing all the harm we can in these parts?"

"That's what we've been doing," Maniakes said. "That's what I aim to go on doing. If Abivard wants to go haring off on some business of his own, let him. Makuran will suffer on account of it."

"Well said, your Majesty."

Maniakes did not bother answering that. Everything he'd said made perfect sense—and not just to him, if Bagdasares had seized on it so readily. He'd told himself as much a good many times before he'd come seeking Bagdasares' sorcerous counsel. But if Abivard wasn't stupid, why had he left the almost certain scene of this year's action? What reason had he found good enough for him to do such a thing?

"No way to tell," Maniakes murmured. Alvinos Bagdasares' eyebrows rose; no doubt he hoped to learn what was in Maniakes' mind. Not likely, not when Maniakes was far from sure himself. But whatever Abivard was up to, Maniakes had the feeling he'd find out, and that he wouldn't be overjoyed when he did.

As the Videssians did with temples to Phos, the Makuraners built shrines to the God not only in cities for the benefit of merchants and artisans but also out by the roadside in the country so peasants could pray and worship and then go back to work. Maniakes had been destroying those roadside shrines ever since he first entered the Land of the Thousand Cities. If nothing else, that inconvenienced the farmers, which in a small way would help the Videssian cause.

The God was usually housed in quarters less elaborate than Phos' temples. Some of the shrines were in the open air, with the four sides of the square altar facing in the cardinal directions, each one symbolizing one of the Makuraners' Four Prophets. As the Videssians came closer to Mashiz, the shrines grew more elaborate, as Maniakes had known to be the case from previous incursions into the land between the Tutub and the Tib.

And then, as the Videssian army approached the Tib, the soldiers came upon a shrine so extraordinary, they summoned the Avtokrator to see it. "We don't know what to do with it, your Majesty," said Komentiolos, the captain of the company that had overrun the shrine. "You have to tell us, and before you can do that, you have to see it."

"All right, I'll have a look," Maniakes said agreeably, and dug his heels into Antelope's sides.

The shrine had walls and a roof. The walls were baked brick rather than plain mud brick, but that did not greatly surprise Maniakes: the Makuraners gave the God and the Four Prophets the best they had, as the Videssians did with Phos. The entranceway stood open. Maniakes looked a question to Komentiolos. The captain nodded. Maniakes went inside, Komentiolos following.

Maniakes' eyes needed a bit to adjust to the gloom within. There at the center of the shrine stood the usual foursquare Makuraner altar. Komentiolos ignored that, having seen its like many times before. He waved to the far wall, the one toward which the side of the altar honoring Fraortish, the eldest prophet, pointed.

Standing against that smoothly plastered wall was a statue of the God, the first such Maniakes had ever seen. The God was portrayed in the regalia of a Makuraner King of Kings. The sun and the moon were painted on the wall beside him in gold and silver. He held a thunderbolt in one hand and was posed as if about to hurl it against some miscreant. His plump face, mouth twisted into a rather nasty smile, said he would enjoy hurling it.

As far as Maniakes was concerned, Videssian craftsmen depicted Phos in a far more artistic and awe-inspiring way. Phos, now, Phos was portrayed as a god worth worshiping, very much unlike this petulant—

Abruptly, Maniakes realized the face the Makuraner sculptor had given the statue was not intended to be an idealized portrait of the God, as images of the lord with the great and good mind were rightly idealized. This portrait was intended to show the features of a man, and of a man the Avtokrator knew, even if he had not seen him for ten years and more.

Maniakes turned his head away from the statue. He did not want to look at it; even thinking of it gave him the feeling of having just taken a big bite of rotten meat.

"Isn't that the most peculiar excuse for a shrine you ever saw, your Majesty?" Komentiolos said. "There's a chamber back there with a lot of metal drums and stones, to make it sound like the statue of the God is thundering at whatever he's taken a mind to disliking."

"It's not a statue of the God, or not exactly a statue of the God," Maniakes answered. "What it is, exactly, is a statue of Sharbaraz King of Kings."

For a moment, Komentiolos didn't understand. Then he did, and looked as sickened as Maniakes felt. "It's a statue of Sharbaraz King of Kings *as* the God," he said, as if hoping Maniakes would tell him he was wrong.

However much Maniakes wished he could do that, he couldn't. "That's just what it is," he said.

"But don't the Makuraners—" Komentiolos spread his hands in helpless disbelief. "—don't they think this is blasphemy, too?"

"I don't know. I hope so," Maniakes told him. "But I do know one thing: Sharbaraz doesn't think it's blasphemy."

Back when he'd known Sharbaraz, more than a decade before, the King of Kings—or, as he was then, the claimant to the title of King of Kings—would never have had such a building erected. But Sharbaraz-then was not Sharbaraz-now. Through all the intervening years, he'd been unchallenged sovereign of Makuran. Everyone had sought his favor. No one had disagreed with him. The result was . . . this.

Sketching the sun-circle over his heart, Maniakes murmured, "It could have been me." The sycophancy in the court of Videssos was hardly less than that in the court of Makuran. Thanks to his father, Maniakes had taken with a grain of salt all the flattery he'd heard. Sharbaraz, evidently, had lapped it up and gone looking for more.

Komentiolos said, "Now that we've got this place, your Majesty, what do we do with it?"

"I wish I'd never seen it in the first place," Maniakes said. But that was not an answer. He found something that was: "We bring some Makuraner prisoners in here, so they can see it with their own eyes. Then we let them go, to spread the tale as they will. After that, we let some of our soldiers see it, too, to give them the idea of what sort of enemy we're fighting. Then we let them wreck the statue. Then we let them wreck the building. Then we burn it. Fire purifies."

"Aye, your Majesty. I'll see to all of that," Komentiolos said. "It sounds good to me."

"None of it sounds good to me," Maniakes said. "I wish we weren't doing it. I wish we didn't have to do it. By the good god, I wish this shrine had never been built."

He wondered how Abivard, who had always fought him as one soldier against another, no more, no less, could bear to serve under a man who was coming to believe himself on a par with his god. He wondered whether Abivard knew this place existed and, if so, what he thought of it. He filed that last question away, as possibly worth exploring later.

First things first. "Gather up the prisoners and send them through here, quick as you can. Then turn our men loose on this place. The longer it stands, the greater the abomination."

"You're right about that, your Majesty," Komentiolos said. "I'll see to it, I promise you."

"Good." Maniakes tried to imagine portraying himself as Phos incarnate on earth. Absurd. If the good god didn't strike him down, his outraged subjects would. He hurried out of the shrine, feeling a sudden need for fresh, clean air.

Maniakes looked back toward the southeast, toward Lyssaion. He couldn't see the Videssian port now, of course. He couldn't even see the hills that were the watershed between the Xeremos and the Tutub. The only hillocks making the horizon anything but flat were the artificial ones upon which perched the Thousand Cities.

His chuckle was sheepish. Turning to Lysia, he said, "When I'm back in Videssos the city, I can't wait to get away. Once I am away, I wish I had news of what's going on there."

"*I* don't miss the city," Lysia said. "We haven't heard much from it the past couple of summers, and what news they did bring us here wasn't worth having."

She spoke with great certainty, and with more than a little anger in her voice. The mockery and disapproval she'd taken in the capital for becoming her cousin's consort wore more heavily on her than they did on Maniakes. He'd already seen that, as Avtokrator, nothing he did was going to make everybody happy. That let him take scorn philosophically . . . most of the time.

"Not easy to get messengers through, anyway," he said, as if consoling himself. "Not hearing doesn't have to mean anything. They wouldn't send out dispatches unless the news was important enough to risk losing men to make sure it got to me."

"To the ice with news, except what we cause," Lysia said positively. "To the ice with Videssos the city, too. I'd give it to the Makuraners in a minute if doing that wouldn't wreck the Empire." Yes, she'd let her resentment fester where Maniakes had shrugged—most of—his off.

He stopped worrying about news from home and looked west instead. The horizon was jagged there, with the peaks of the Dilbat Mountains shouldering themselves up into view above the nearer flatlands. In the foothills of those mountains lay Mashiz. He'd been there once, years before, helping to install Sharbaraz on his throne. If he reached Mashiz again, he'd cast Sharbaraz down from that throne . . . and from his assumption of divinity. Destroying that shrine was something Maniakes had been delighted to do.

Closer than the Dilbats, closer than Mashiz, was the Tib. Canals stretched its waters out to the west. Where the canals failed, as at the eastern margins of the Tutub, irrigation failed. Irrigation, though, was only marginally in his mind now. He concentrated on getting over the river. It wasn't so wide as the Tutub, but ran swifter, and was no doubt still in spring spate. Crossing it wouldn't be easy; the Makuraners would do everything they could to keep him from gaining the western bank.

He didn't expect to capture a bridge of boats intact; that would be luck beyond any calculation. Whatever soldiers the foe had on the far side would mass against him. If they delayed him long enough, as they might well, the Makuraner infantry army he'd left behind would catch up to him. With so many soldiers mustered against his men, with the river limiting the directions in which he could move, all that might prove unpleasant.

When he grumbled about the difficulties of getting over the Tib, Rhegorios said, "If we have to, you know, we can always turn south toward the source of the river and either ford it where it's young and narrow or go round it altogether and come up along the west bank."

"I don't want to do anything like that," Maniakes said. "It would take too long. I want to go straight at Mashiz."

His cousin looked at him without saying anything. Maniakes felt his cheeks grow hot. In the early days of his reign, his most besetting fault had been moving too soon, committing himself to action without adequate preparation or resources. Rhegorios thought he was doing it again.

On reflection, though, he decided he wasn't. "Think it through," he said. "If we turn south, what will the fellow in charge of the foot soldiers from Qostabash do? Is he likely to chase us? Can he hope to catch us, foot pursuing horse? If he has any sense, what he'll do is cross the Tib himself and wait for us at the approaches to Mashiz. If you were in his sandals, isn't that what you'd do?"

Rhegorios did think it through, quite visibly. Maniakes gave him credit for that, the more so as his young cousin was inclined to be headstrong, too. "Cousin your Majesty brother-in-law of mine, I think you're likely to be right," the Sevastos said at last. "Revolting how doing something simple will spill the chamber pot into the soup of a complicated plan."

"We have to find a way to get across ourselves, once we do reach the river," Maniakes said. "The trouble is, if the defenders are even half awake, that's almost as hard a job as getting over the Cattle Crossing has been for the Makuraners. They've been trying to figure out how to manage that for years, and they haven't come close yet, Phos be praised."

"I know what you need to do," Rhegorios said suddenly. "Have Bagdasares turn the whole Tib into a Voimios strap and flip it about so that all at once we're on the west side and the cursed Makuraners are on the east."

Maniakes laughed out loud. "You don't think small, do you, cousin of mine? Except for the detail that that sounds like a magic big enough to burn out the brain of every wizard in Videssos, it's a splendid notion."

"I thought you'd like it," Rhegorios said. Now both men laughed. Rhegorios went on, "If you've got a better idea, I'd like to hear it."

"What I'd like to do," Maniakes said, "is play a trick on them like the one my father used against Smerdis' men when we were fighting alongside Sharbaraz. My father made a big, fancy, obvious move to cross a waterway—pinned the enemy's attention to it nice as you please. Then he put a force across downstream from his feint, just far enough that nobody noticed them till they were too well established to be checked."

"That sounds good," Rhegorios agreed. "How do we bring it off?"

"We're short of rafts, and this country doesn't have enough trees to make building them easy," Maniakes said. "Maybe we can try using the hide boats the locals make."

"You mean the round ones that look like soup bowls?" Rhegorios rolled his eyes. "To the ice with me if I'd be happy getting into one of those. I can't see how the people who use them keep them from spinning round and round and round. Or were you talking about the rafts that float on top of blown-up hides so they'll carry more? If those are the kinds of ideas the Makuraners get when they think of boats, it's no wonder they never tried coming over the Cattle Crossing."

"The locals *aren't* Makuraners," Maniakes reminded him. "And take a look around, cousin of mine. They do what they can with what they have: not much wood, not much of anything but mud. You can't make a boat out of mud, but you can raise beasts on what grows out of the mud and then use their hides to go up and down the rivers and canals."

"Do you really want to try putting our men into those crazy things to get to the west bank of the Tib?" Rhegorios said. "Even more to the point, do you think you can get horses into them? Men are stupid; if you order them to go and do something, they'll go and do it, even if they can see it's going to get a raft of them—" He used the term with obvious relish. "—killed. Horses, now, horses have better sense than that."

Like his cousin, Maniakes knew horses all too often showed lamentably little sense of any sort. That, however, wasn't relevant. Rhegorios' objection was. Maniakes said, "Maybe you're right. But if you are, how do you propose getting over the river?"

"Who, me? You're the Avtokrator; you're supposed to be the one with all the answers," Rhegorios said, which was highly annoying and true at the same time.

"One of the answers the Avtokrator is allowed to use is picking someone who knows more about a particular bit of business than he does and then listening to what he has to say," Maniakes returned.

"If you want to talk about the business of chasing pretty girls, I know more than you do," Rhegorios said. "If you want to talk about the business of guzzling neat wine, I know more than you do. If you want to talk about the business of leading a cavalry column, I know at least as much as you do. If you want to talk about the business of crossing a river without bridging or proper boats, neither one of us knows a bloody thing."

"You certainly made noises as if you knew," Maniakes said.

"If you want to talk about the business of making noises, I know more than you do," Rhegorios said, impudent as usual.

"I know what I'll do." Maniakes thumped himself in the forehead with the heel of the hand to show he'd been stupid. "I'd have had to do it when we got to the Tib any which way. I'll talk with Ypsilantes."

For the first time in their conversation, he discovered he had Rhegorios' complete and ungrudging approval. "That's a *good* idea," Rhegorios said. "If the chief engineer can't figure out a way to do it, it can't be done. If you want to talk about the business of having good ideas, you may know more than I do."

Being praised for an idea as obvious as it was good did not make Maniakes feel much better; the thought that it hadn't occurred to Rhegorios, either, consoled him to some degree. He wasted no time in summoning Ypsilantes. The chief engineer was nearer his father's age than his own; he had commanded the engineering detachment accompanying the Videssian army the elder Maniakes had led in alliance with Sharbaraz and against Smerdis.

"How do we get across the river?" he repeated when Maniakes put the question to him. His handsome, fleshy features did not show much of the amusement he obviously felt. "Your Majesty, you leave that to me. Tell me when and where you want to go across and I'll take care of it for you."

He sounded as confident as if he were discussing his faith in Phos. That made Maniakes feel better; he'd seen Ypsilantes was a man who delivered on his promises. Nonetheless, he persisted: "Tell me one way in which you might accomplish that."

"Here's one—first one that pops into my head," Ypsilantes said. "Suppose you want to cross somewhere near the place where a good-sized canal flows off to the northeast from the Tib—flows off behind where we already are, in other words. If we divert water from the river to the canal, what's left of the river will be easy enough to manage. Like I say, you leave all that sort of thing to me, your Majesty."

Maniakes remembered his thoughts back in Videssos the city on how best to run affairs. Here was a man who plainly knew how to do what needed doing. "When the time comes, Ypsilantes, I will," the Avtokrator said.

The engineer saluted, clenched right fist over his heart, then hurried off to ready what might need readying. Some officers of his ability would have had their eye on the throne. All he wanted was the chance to play with his toys. Maniakes was more than willing to give him that, and so could give him free rein as well. He wondered if Sharbaraz would have been so trusting, and had his doubts.

When the army was only a couple of days' ride from the Tib, a scout came galloping back to Maniakes. "Your Majesty," he called, "the King of Kings has sent you an ambassador. He's on his way here now."

"Has he?" Maniakes said, and then, a moment later, "Is he?" The scout looked confused. Maniakes knew it was his own fault. He went on, "Sharbaraz has never done that before. How can he send me an ambassador when he doesn't recognize me as rightful Avtokrator of the Videssians?"

"I don't know, your Majesty," the scout said, which had the virtue of being an altogether honest answer.

"Go back and tell this ambassador I'll listen to him," Maniakes said without any great warmth. The scout hurried off as fast as he had come. Maniakes watched his back. The most likely reason he could find for Sharbaraz to send him an envoy was to try to delay him so the Makuraners on the west bank of the Tib could shore up their defenses. But he couldn't refuse to see the fellow, because the likely reason might not be the true one.

The ambassador reached him less than half an hour later.

The fellow rode a fine gray mare and wore a striped caftan shot through with silver threads. He was about fifty, with a full gray beard and the long face, swarthy skin, and deep-set eyes that marked the Makuraners. Bowing in the saddle, he asked in fair Videssian, "You are Maniakes son of Maniakes?"

"Yes," Maniakes answered. "And you?"

"I am Rafsanj son of Shidjam," the ambassador said, "and I bring you greetings from Sharbaraz son of Peroz, King of Kings, may his years be many and his realm increase, mighty, powerful, awesome to behold, a man whom the God delights to honor—"

Maniakes held up a hand. Sharbaraz bore more titles and attributes than a stray dog had ticks; Maniakes wasn't interested in having them all trotted out. "Sharbaraz hasn't been interested in treating with me before," he remarked. "After all, he recognizes the fraud he calls Hosios son of Likinios as Avtokrator of the Videssians, not me. What has made him change his mind?" He thought he knew the answer to that: an invasion that looked like succeeding was a good way to get anyone's attention.

Rafsanj coughed delicately. "I was not bidden to treat with Avtokrator of the Videssians, but with Maniakes son of Maniakes, commander of the forces currently disturbing the realm of Makuran, who, I presume, is yourself."

"I told you yes already," Maniakes said, and then, to himself, "Presumption." Sharbaraz had a good deal of gall if he thought he could keep his own puppet Avtokrator around and treat with Maniakes at the same time. But then, any man who made a shrine where he was worshiped as a god had gall and to spare.

That he was willing to talk to Maniakes at all was a step forward. And maybe, having created the false Hosios, Sharbaraz felt he could not abandon him without losing face among his own courtiers. Rafsanj asked, "Will you hear what I have to say, Maniakes son of Maniakes?"

"Why should I?" Maniakes asked. "Why shouldn't I find some mean prison and throw you into it, the way Sharbaraz did to the eminent Triphylles, the envoy I sent to him asking for peace?"

"Because—" Rafsanj hesitated. *Because he was winning then and he's not so sure now,* was what went through Maniakes' mind. *He never thought I'd have the chance to collect the debt he owes me.* But that would have been Sharbaraz's thinking, not what was going through the mind of this Rafsanj now. The ambassador said, "Because if you imprison me, you will not hear what the King of Kings offers."

"That's not necessarily so," Maniakes answered, smiling. "I could hear the offer and then jail you, as Sharbaraz did with Triphylles."

"You are pleased to jest, Maniakes son of Maniakes," Rafsanj said. He made a good envoy; if he was nervous, he didn't let on. But he did not, would not, call Maniakes *your Majesty*.

"Let's find out if I am joking, shall we?" the Avtokrator said. "Give me Sharbaraz's terms and then we'll see how long you stay free. How does that sound to you?"

"Not good," Rafsanj answered, no doubt truthfully. "Sharbaraz King of Kings, may his years be many and his realm increase, bids you give over the devastation you are working in the Land of the Thousand Cities."

Maniakes displayed his teeth in what was not really a smile. "I'm sure he does. I wanted him to stop devastating the westlands. I was even willing to pay him to stop devastating the westlands. Did he listen to me?" That question answered itself, and suggested the next one: "Why should I listen to him?"

"He bids you bide here, that we may discuss the composition of differences between Videssos and Makuran," Rafsanj said.

"And he will, of course, hold all his armies in place while I'm doing that," Maniakes said.

"Of course," Rafsanj answered. Maniakes watched him narrowly. He was good, but not quite good enough. He went on in fulsome tones: "And once agreement has been reached, will there not be rejoicing on both sides of the border? Will voices not be raised in joy and gladness?"

"The border? Which border? The one before Sharbaraz began his war against us?" Maniakes asked. Rafsanj did not answer that question; maybe Sharbaraz had not given him an answer for it. "I don't think I'm ready to talk peace quite yet, thanks," the Avtokrator said. Strange how things had changed—a few years before, he would have fallen on such an offer with a glad cry. But not now. "I don't want to talk here, either. Tell Sharbaraz that if he still wants to discuss these things with me when I get to Mashiz, we may be able to do it there."

"Beware lest your arrogance bring you down," Rafsanj said. "Overweening pride has laid many a man low."

"I'm not the one who built a statue of the God in my own image," Maniakes retorted, raising a scowl from Sharbaraz's envoy. "I'm not the one who plans to move armies around after pledging I wouldn't, either. When is the King of Kings going to pull Abivard and his horsemen out of the sleeve of his caftan and hurl them at me? They must be around here somewhere." He still had trouble giving credence to Bagdasares' magic.

And his probe struck a nerve, too; Rafsanj jerked, as if Maniakes had jabbed a pin into his legs. But the envoy answered, "I have no obligation to speak to you of the manner in which your doom will fall and all your hopes be swallowed by the Void."

"And I have no obligation to stay here while Sharbaraz moves his pieces around the board," Maniakes returned. "I have no obligation to let myself be cozened, either. Tell Sharbaraz I'll see him in Mashiz."

"That shall never be," Rafsanj told him.

"I know better," Maniakes jeered. "Videssos has taken Mashiz before; we can do that. What will never happen is Makuran taking Videssos the city."

Again, Rafsanj started. This time, he mastered himself without saying anything. He sawed at the reins, roughly pulling his horse's head around. He rode away from Maniakes faster than he had approached him.

Maniakes watched him go. He waved to his own men, calling, "Onward!" Onward they went, toward the Tib. They did not go so fast as Maniakes would have liked. The Makuraners in front of them opened canal after canal. The harvest in this part of the Land of the Thousand Cities was liable to be scanty. The Makuraners, plainly, did not care. One of their armies would have bogged down, and might have become easy meat for raiders. The Videssians did not bog down. But corduroying a road and then recovering the timber that let them do it again was slow, hard work.

Even so, they had come within a day's—a normal day's—march of the river when a courier caught up with them from behind. That was no mean feat in and of itself. Maniakes congratulated the fellow and plied him with rough, sour army wine before asking, "What brought you here through all the Makuraners? It can't be anything small, that's certain."

"I'm the first to reach you, your Majesty?" The courier sounded dismayed but not surprised. "I'm not the first who was sent, that's certain."

"What's toward?" Maniakes demanded, worry in his voice now.

The courier took a deep breath. "Your Majesty, the Kubratoi have swarmed down over the border, heading straight for Videssos the city. For all I know, they're sitting outside the walls by now."

III

"P hos curse Etzilios to an eternity in Skotos' ice!" Maniakes
exclaimed, spitting on the muddy ground. At the same
time as he cursed the Kubrati khagan, though, he knew a
grudging admiration for him. Etzilios' spies had seen the Videssians set sail for the west. He knew, then, that the Empire's best
troops were gone. And, knowing that, he had decided to take
his revenge for the beating Maniakes had given him three years
before.

"He's hit us hard, your Majesty," the messenger said, confirming the thought in Maniakes' mind. "This isn't just a raid, or it
doesn't look like one, anyhow. The way Etzilios was storming for
the city, you'd think he aimed to take it." He grinned to show
how unlikely that was.

Maniakes grinned, too. "If that's what's in his mind, he'd better think again," he said. "The nomads have no siege engines.
He can come up to the walls. He can do all manner of horrible
things outside them. But he can't break in." That no one unwelcome could break into Videssos the city from outside had been
an article of faith, and deservedly so, for centuries. "What are
we doing against him?" he asked the courier. "Have we used our
ships to land men behind his force?"

The man took another swig of wine, then shook his head.
"Hadn't done that by the time I set out, your Majesty. Matter of

432

fact, the Kubratoi were using those single-log boats of theirs, those monoxyla, to move their own men down the coast against us."

"Yes, to the ice with Etzilios, all right," Maniakes said. "He learns his lessons too bloody well." The Avtokrator had landed troops in the rear of the Kubratoi before. Now they looked to be returning the favor.

Videssians being the sort of people they were, the courier's arrival seemed a signal for officers of all ranks to converge on Maniakes, trying to learn what news the fellow had brought. "Cheeky as sparrows, the lot of them," Rhegorios complained after he finally made it to Maniakes' side. "Haven't they got any patience?"

"Almost as much as you," the Avtokrator said, earning himself a glare from his first cousin. He turned to the courier. "Give his highness the Sevastos your message, the same as you gave it to me."

"Aye, your Majesty," the man said, and repeated himself for Rhegorios.

Rhegorios listened intently, then nodded. "Isn't that interesting?" he said when the courier was done. He raised an eyebrow and asked Maniakes, "What do you intend to do about it?"

"By the good god, not one thing," Maniakes answered. "Having the Kubratoi overrun the countryside, even if they do it all the way down to the walls of Videssos the city, isn't essential, because the city won't fall to them. What we're doing here *is* essential. If we take Mashiz, the Makuraners will have to pull troops out of the westlands to deal with that. So we'll go on doing exactly what we have been doing, and worry about Etzilios later."

"Cousin, that is an excellent plan," Rhegorios said. "For that matter, it's not only getting the Makuraners to commit troops from our westlands. Getting them to commit Abivard's force, wherever that is, has been hard enough."

"If crossing the Tib won't do it, nothing will," Maniakes predicted. He looked thoughtful. "I wonder if Abivard is hanging back on purpose, hoping we'll take out Sharbaraz and leave him a clear path to the throne. His sister is married to the King of Kings, after all, which gives him a claim of sorts."

"My sister is married to the Avtokrator of the Videssians," Rhegorios pointed out. "And I, I assure you, have no interest in claiming our throne."

Maniakes nodded. As a courtier, Rhegorios had to say that. In his case, Maniakes was convinced it was true. How true it was for Abivard, though, was liable to be a different question. "From things I've heard, I don't think Sharbaraz trusts his brother-in-law as far as I trust mine."

"Your Majesty is gracious."

"My Majesty is stinking tired of distractions, is what my Majesty is," Maniakes said, his scorn for his own title bringing a smile to Rhegorios' lips. "I am not going to let myself be distracted, not here, not now. I know where I need to go, I think I know how to get there from where I am, and I think I know what happens when I do. Stacked against all that, Etzilios is a small loaf of bread."

"No doubt you're right," Rhegorios said. "We're *that* close—" He held up thumb and forefinger, each almost touching the other. "—to paying back a decade of debt and more."

"*That* close," Maniakes echoed. He imitated his cousin's gesture and then, slowly and deliberately, brought thumb and forefinger together till they touched. Rhegorios smiled a hungry smile.

Maniakes stared across the Tib, a discontented expression on his face. The river ran strongly toward the north, blocking his way across it, blocking his way toward Mashiz. Beside him, Ypsilantes also looked unhappy. The engineer's earlier confidence now seemed misplaced. "The spring floods are strong and long this year," he remarked.

"So they are," Maniakes said. "It is as Phos wills." Even as he spoke the words, he wondered why the good god would prevent Makuran from being chastised for all its people had done to Videssos and to Phos himself. Maybe the Makuraner God held some sway here, after all. Or maybe the God was in league with Skotos against the lord with the great and good mind.

Across the Tib, parties of Makuraner foot soldiers looked to be readying a warm reception for the Videssians. Back out of sight, back behind the imperial army, that infantry force Maniakes had evaded was still dogging his heels. Their general didn't have all the resources Abivard had enjoyed the year before, but he was making the most of what he did have.

He was on Ypsilantes' mind, too. The chief engineer said, "We haven't the time to sit down in one place and work out what all it will take to cross the river with it running the way it is. If we do sit down, we'll have a battle on our hands sooner than we'd like."

"Yes." Maniakes fixed him with a sour stare. "I thought you said you could come up with any number of expedients for getting over the Tib."

"For one thing, your Majesty, like I say, I didn't figure it'd be running so high," Ypsilantes replied with some dignity. "And, for another, I did expect more time to work. An army that's digging a canal to divert the Tib can't leave off and start fighting again at a moment's notice."

"If you spoke so plain to Sharbaraz, he'd probably thank you by tearing out your tongue," Maniakes said. "Sometimes what's true matters more than what sounds good at the moment, though. I try to remember that."

"I know you do, your Majesty," Ypsilantes answered. "That's why the only people who need fear you are the ones who have done wrong."

"You're kinder than I deserve," Maniakes said, "and, if you want to see how kindly I can be, find us a way to get over the Tib no matter how it's running."

"I'll do everything I can," the engineer said. "Right now, though, I haven't got any good ideas."

"They have the bridges of boats that usually run across the river." Maniakes pointed to the far bank of the Tib. "We won't see any of them. How do we substitute without using those palm trees you hate so much? How do we make sure we don't have to use the natives' horrible boats made of skins?"

"Common sense is plenty to make sure we don't want those boats," Ypsilantes said. He looked unhappy again, now at the world rather than at Maniakes in particular.

"What's left, then?" the Avtokrator asked.

"We need boats of some sort or another, your Majesty," Ypsilantes replied. "If we can't get anything better, those hide monstrosities will have to do. We need timber. If we can't get anything better, that will have to come from date palms. And if we have to use all those things I wish we didn't, we'll also need more time to get a bridge ready than we would otherwise."

"What about using the timbers from the stone-throwers and dart-throwers as pieces of the bridge?" Maniakes said.

Ypsilantes shook his head. "We'll need at least some of those engines. When we get within a bowshot of the western bank of the Tib, we'll have to drive back the Makuraner archers so we can extend the bridge all the way out to the end."

"You know best." Maniakes took on some of the engineer's jaundiced approach to the topic. "I wish you hadn't told me we'll need more time than we might if we had better materials around here." He held up a hasty hand. "No, I'm not blaming you. But I don't want to fight those Makuraner foot soldiers slogging after us somewhere back there, not if I can help it." He turned back toward the east.

"I understand that, your Majesty," Ypsilantes said. "I'll do everything I can to push the work ahead." He rubbed his chin. "What I really worry about is Abivard coming out of whatever bushes he's using to hide himself and hitting us a lick when it hurts the most."

"I'd be lying if I said that thought hadn't also occurred to me." Maniakes looked east again. "I wish I knew where he was. Even if he were someplace where I couldn't do anything about him—the same way I can't do anything about the Kubratoi—knowing what he might be able to do to me would take a good-sized weight off my mind."

"That's it, your Majesty," Ypsilantes agreed. "You can't fight a campaign looking over your shoulder every hour of the day and night, waiting for him to pop up like a hand puppet in a show. Or rather, you can, but you'd be a lot better off if you didn't have to."

"We'd be better off if a lot of things were different," Maniakes said. "But they're not, so we're going to have to deal with them as they are."

"That's so, too, your Majesty," Ypsilantes said, sounding as if he wished he could engineer the unfortunate condition right out of existence.

Maniakes sent men up and down the length of the Tib and the major canals nearby. They came back with a few boats of various sorts—fewer than he and Ypsilantes had hoped. The Avtokrator also set men to work chopping down date palms so they could use the rather stringy timber they got from them.

That outraged the inhabitants of the Land of the Thousand

Cities more than anything else he had done up till then: more even than his having burned a good many of those cities. The farmers fought the lumbering parties as best they could, and began ambushing Videssian soldiers whenever they caught a few away from the main mass of men.

In the pavilion she shared with Maniakes, Lysia held up a jar of date wine, saying, "You'd think the local peasants would thank us for getting rid of the trees that let them make thick, sweet slop like this."

"Yes, I know," Maniakes said. "I first drank date wine when I was helping my father put Sharbaraz back on the throne. As far as I can see, the only people who like it are those who know no better."

"That's what I think of it, too," Lysia said. "But—"

"Yes, but," Maniakes agreed. "The locals are bushwhacking us, and some of my men have taken to massacring them whenever they get the chance," He sighed. "They do something, we pay them back, they do something worse—where does it end?"

Lysia didn't answer, perhaps because the answer was obvious: it ended with the two of them close by the Tib, with their gazes set on Mashiz beyond the river. Eventually, one side hit the other such a blow that it could not respond. That put an end to the fighting—for a generation, sometimes even two.

"Once we break into Mashiz," Maniakes said, "the Makuraners won't be able to stay in the field against us." He'd been saying that ever since he'd first conceived of the notion of bypassing the Videssian westlands and taking the war straight to the heart of the realm of the King of Kings. He still believed it. Before long, he hoped to find out whether he was right.

Thinking along with him as she often did, Lysia asked, "How soon can we cross the Tib and make for the capital?"

"A few more days, Ypsilantes tells me," Maniakes answered. "The squabbles with the peasants have slowed things up, but we finally have enough boats and almost enough timber. Get a little more wood, cut it to the right lengths, and then over the river we go."

Lysia looked westward. "And then it will be over." She did not speak in tones of blithe confidence. *One way or the other,* her words suggested. Maniakes did not try to reprove or correct her. After all the misfortunes he had watched as they befell Videssos, how could he? *One way or the other* was what he felt, too. Nothing was certain till it happened.

As if to prove that, one of his guards called from outside the tent: "Your Majesty, a scout is here with news."

"I'll come," he said, and did.

The scout had already dismounted. He started to perform a proskynesis, but Maniakes, impatient to hear what he had to say, waved for him not to bother prostrating himself. The scout did salute, then said, "Your Majesty, I hate to tell you this, but all those foot soldiers we bypassed back near Qostabash are about to catch up with us again."

"Oh, a pestilence!" Maniakes burst out, and spent the next couple of minutes swearing with an inventiveness that left the scout pop-eyed. The Avtokrator did not care. He'd spent more time as soldier than as sovereign and had learned how to vent his spleen.

Gradually, he calmed. He and Ypsilantes had known this might happen. Now it had. They would have to make the best of it. The scout watched him. After a moment, the fellow nodded and chuckled once or twice. "Your Majesty, I think there's going to be some Makuraner infantry out there—" He pointed east. "—sorry they were ever born."

"By the good god, I hope so." Maniakes stared east, off toward that approaching force of infantry. "You saw only foot soldiers there?" he demanded of the scout. "None of the Makuraners' boiler boys?"

"No, your Majesty, none to speak of," the scout answered. "They have a few horsemen with 'em, scouts and messengers and such, but I didn't see a sign of their heavy cavalry. If they'd been there, I'd have spotted 'em, too. You'd best believe that—those bastards can really fight, and I want to know when they're around."

"So do I," Maniakes said in abstracted tones, and then, more to himself than to the man who'd brought the unwelcome news, "To the ice with you, Abivard; where have you gone and hidden?" But even that was not the relevant question: when would Abivard emerge from hiding, and how much trouble would he cause once he did?

The Avtokrator nodded to the scout, dismissing him, then sent one of his guards after Ypsilantes. When the chief engineer arrived, Maniakes told him in a few words what had happened. Ypsilantes heard him out before loosing a long sigh. "Well, your

Majesty, they never told us this business was going to be easy, now did they?"

"I'm afraid they didn't—whoever *they* are," Maniakes agreed. "Can we protect all the timber we've cut and the boats we've collected while we're fighting these cursed foot soldiers?"

"We'd better," Ypsilantes said bluntly, which made the Avtokrator glad to have him along. He continued, "Aye, I expect we can. The Makuraner infantry moving on us won't come close to that stuff, not unless somebody really pisses in the stew pot. And if those odds and sods across the river have the nerve to try to sneak over here to this side and tear things up while most of us are busy, I'll be the most surprised man in the Land of the Thousand Cities."

Maniakes corrected him: "The second most surprised man." Ypsilantes thought that one through, blinked like a frog swallowing a fly, and barked out a couple of syllables' worth of laughter. "I'll make sure it doesn't happen, your Majesty. Count on me."

"I will," Maniakes said. "I do." He waved Ypsilantes away, then started shouting orders, preparing his force to meet the Makuraners. He had more respect for the foe's foot than he'd brought to their first clashes a couple of years before; they had rapidly turned into real soldiers. He looked around the camp, where his own men were starting to stir. He smiled. They were better warriors than they had been a couple of years before, too.

The red-lion banner of Makuran flapped lazily in a light breeze. The enemy standard-bearer was an enormous man with shoulders like a bull's. Maniakes was glad to see him used for ornamental purposes rather than as a true fighter. Every little edge helped.

The Avtokrator looked out over the battle line advancing behind the standard-bearer. The Makuraner general disposed of more men than he did. Since the fight was infantry against cavalry, that mattered less than it would have had he been facing Abivard and the field army. It did not leave him delighted with the world, even so.

Most of the foot soldiers in the enemy army were not, strictly speaking, Makuraners, but rather men from the Thousand Cities. They were shorter and stockier and a little swarthier than the boiler boys from the high plateau to the west, with hair so black it shone with blue highlights, often worn in a neat bun resting on the nape of the neck. Their chief weapon was the bow; they carried knives and clubs for fighting at close quarters. Some of them wore helmets: businesslike iron pots, or sometimes leather caps strengthened with iron bands. Past that, the only armor they bore was their wicker shields.

They could fight. Maniakes had seen that. They hadn't done much fighting in the years before the Videssians had plunged into the Land of the Thousand Cities, but, as he'd thought a little while before, they'd learned their trade since. That was partly Abivard's fault—or to his credit, if you looked at things from the Makuraner point of view. It was also partly Maniakes' fault. By fighting a series of battles against the local infantry, he'd given them a course in how to go about fighting Videssians. Some of them had learned better than he would have wished.

He nodded to Rhegorios, who sat his horse beside Maniakes and Antelope, and pointed out toward the enemy infantry. "See—they're laying down some sort of barricade to keep us from charging home against them. Thornbushes, maybe, or something like that."

"We aren't planning on charging in among them right away anyhow, though," his cousin answered. "That kind of barrier would do more against Makuraner heavy cavalry, the kind that closes on you with the lance, than it does against our horse-archers."

"It'll be a nuisance for our men, too," Maniakes said, "and they're liable to pull the barricade away if they see a good place to come charging right out at us. In the fights last fall, as we were pulling back toward Lyssaion, their infantry was as aggressive as any general could want."

"Of course, they were working alongside cavalry of their own then," Rhegorios said. "They won't be so tough without the boiler boys here."

Mention of the Makuraner heavy cavalry was plenty to make Maniakes look north and then south, wondering still where Abivard was and how and when he might appear. When the Videssian army was locked in combat with the local infantry seemed a good bet.

"You'll get the right wing," Maniakes told his cousin when Abivard once more failed to materialize. "I won't give you any detailed orders about what to do with it, but you can move faster than foot soldiers. If you can flank them out of their position, that would be a good thing to do."

"Easier if they weren't cutting more canals," Rhegorios observed. "But I will try—you know that."

"Everything would be easier if they didn't make it harder," Maniakes said, which drew a nod and a laugh from his cousin. He went on, "Keep scouts out wide on your flank, too. Abivard's lurking out there somewhere."

"Maybe he's fallen into that Void where the Makuraners are always consigning people they don't like," Rhegorios said. "But that would be too much to hope for, wouldn't it? Aye, I'll watch for him. And you, cousin, you keep a good watch on your other flank, too."

"I'll watch as carefully as a Makuraner noble checking his women's quarters to make sure nobody sneaks in." The Avtokrator slapped Rhegorios on his mailed back. "Now, let's see what kind of dance we'll have with all these lovely people, shall we?"

"They've come a long way. We wouldn't want to disappoint them." Rhegorios looked thoughtful. "We've come a long way, too."

"So we have," Maniakes said. "We wouldn't want to disappoint us, either."

Rhegorios rode off to take charge of his wing of the army. The Makuraners were leaving the choice of when and how to begin the battle to the imperials. Under most circumstances, Maniakes would also have had the option of whether to begin the battle at all, as his horsemen were more mobile than the infantry opposing them. But, having almost completed his preparations for fording the Tib, he could not abandon the timber and boats without losing them and abandoning his plans as well. Unwilling to do that, Maniakes knew he had to fight here.

He watched Rhegorios and his division ride out for the flanking maneuver they might or might not prove able to bring off. Wanting to keep his center strong, he sent a smaller force off to the left. He warned Immodios, who was commanding it, to keep an eye out for Abivard.

"I'll do that, your Majesty," the officer answered. "If he does show up, we'll stop him cold, I promise you."

"Good man," Maniakes said. If Abivard showed up with a good-sized force of boiler boys, Immodios wasn't going to stop him. The Avtokrator knew that. He hoped Immodios did, too. With luck, though, the horsemen on the left would slow down a cavalry attack from the flank enough to give the center some hope of dealing with it.

Horns brayed out orders for the advance. As the Videssians drew near, their opponents shouted curses at them in the Makuraner tongue and in the harsher, more guttural language of the Thousand Cities. "Ignore those vicious calumnies, whatever they may mean," a blue-robed priest of Phos declared. "Go forth to victory and glory, defending the true and holy faith of Phos with all the weapons of war. Go forth, and may the lord with the great and good mind shine down upon you and light your way forward."

A few men cheered. More—those who had already heard a lot of priests' homilies and seen a lot of battles won or lost or drawn—savored the rhetoric without letting it carry them away. Phos would do as he pleased, they would do as they pleased, and eventually the fight would have a winner.

The first arrows began flying soon thereafter. Whoever commanded the Makuraner army had a fine grasp of logistics, because the foot soldiers from the Land of the Thousand Cities shot and shot and shot, showing not the slightest sign that they were likely to run out of the shafts anytime soon. Such a barrage bespoke endless slow-trundling wagons filled with endless bundles of arrows. Seeing their flight was like watching a great swarm of locusts taking off from one field to descend in another.

The Videssians shot back. They were less well supplied with missiles than their foes. On the other hand, when one of their shafts struck a soldier from the Makuraner army, it usually wounded. The reverse was not true, their chain mail holding many arrows at bay.

"Get in among them and they're ours!" Maniakes shouted, urging his men forward despite the swarm of enemy arrows.

But getting in among the soldiers from the Makuraner army was anything but easy. The soldiers they had stationed immediately behind their thornbush barricades sent arrows flying out as far as they could. The second line of men from the Thousand Cities lobbed shafts high over the heads of the first line, so that those arrows came down on anyone who had reached the barricade and was trying to tear it away. All in all, it was like going forward in a rain of iron-tipped wood.

Seeing the difficulties his men were having in closing with the Makuraner force, Maniakes summoned Ypsilantes. Engineers were made for situations ordinary soldiers found impossible. Over the cries of men, the shrieks of wounded horses, through the constant whistling hiss of arrows, Maniakes pointed to the barricade and said, "What can we do about that, excellent sir?"

"They're not fools, worse luck, your Majesty," Ypsilantes answered. "They soaked the bushes well, so they won't be easy to set afire." Only after Maniakes had nodded did he think to be surprised the chief engineer had already checked about such a tiny detail—but then, that sort of attention to detail was what made Ypsilantes chief engineer. He went on, "When you look at it, it's almost like storming a city wall. Some of the same tools should answer."

Maniakes had not thought of a fight on flat, open ground as being like the climax of a siege. Once the comparison was pointed out to him, it seemed obvious enough. He shook his head. A lot of things seemed obvious—once they were pointed out. "Your detachment is ready to do what needs doing?" he asked.

"Aye, your Majesty," Ypsilantes told him. "Shouldn't be that hard to bring off." He sounded like a man studying an interesting position in the Videssian board game, not one speaking in the midst of a real war's chaos. Maniakes didn't know whether to admire him for that detachment or to be appalled by it.

Whether his detachment was admirable or appalling, Ypsilantes rapidly proved to know what he was talking about. Under the cover of portable sheds of the sort usually used to bring a battering ram up close to a wall so it could pound away, parties of engineers approached the barricades and began clearing it. For them, the work was relatively easy. No one on this field was dropping great stones or boiling oil or melted lead down onto their shelter, which, having been designed to ward against such things, all but laughed at mere arrows raining down on it.

The Makuraners also tried to shoot straight into the sheds. Soldiers standing with big, stout shields at the exposed end made that difficult. Before long, some of the enemy foot soldiers tried a more direct approach, rushing at the engineers to cut them down.

But when they did that, their comrades, of necessity, had to leave off shooting at the shed. That let the Videssian cavalry dash forward through gaps already cleared to fight the foot soldiers. It was an uneven battle. The foot soldiers were brave enough and to spare, but against armored horsemen they went down in dreadful numbers.

"You see, your Majesty," Ypsilantes said.

"Yes, I do," Maniakes answered. "You've set the enemy commander a choice of the sort I'm glad I don't have to make. Either he can send his men out to try to keep the barricade from going down—and have them slaughtered; or he can hold his men back and let the barricade be cleared—and have them slaughtered."

"If you get into a fight like this, that's the chance you take," Ypsilantes agreed. "The best answer is not to get into a fight like this."

"It would have been different if Abivard—" Maniakes made himself stop. He'd seen no sign of the Makuraner marshal, nor of the heavy cavalry Abivard had led in the last campaigning season. He didn't know where they were, but they weren't here. If Abivard hadn't shown up to support the foot soldiers, he couldn't be anywhere close by. That thought tried to touch off an echo in Maniakes' mind, but shouts from the front drowned it.

The gaps in the thornbush barricade had grown wide enough for the Videssian horsemen to begin pouring through them and attacking the Makuraner army with sword and javelin as well as with arrows. Even now, though, the enemy foot soldiers continued to show spirit. Those from the farthest ranks rushed forward to the aid of their beset comrades. They used their clubs and shortswords as much against the Videssians' horses as against the imperials themselves. The more confusion they could create, the better for them.

"Have we got enough men?" Maniakes asked the question more of Phos or of himself than of Ypsilantes, though the chief engineer sat his horse beside him.

Ypsilantes did not hesitate over replying, regardless of whether the question had been meant for him: "Your Majesty, I think we do."

He proved a good prophet; little by little, the Videssians drove their foes back from what had been the line of the thornbush barricade. By then, the sun was sinking down toward the Dilbat Mountains. The fight had gone on most of the day.

Maniakes sent messengers to the soldiers fighting at the front: "Press them with everything you have and they'll break."

He could not fault the way in which his men obeyed the order. They pressed the Makuraners, and pressed them hard. At last, after tough fighting—tougher than that at the center—Rhegorios broke through the obstacles in his path and delivered the flank attack Maniakes had awaited all day long.

But the enemy did not break. He'd hoped for a slaughter, with the Makuraners fleeing every which way and his own men gleefully hunting them down like partridges. That was, perhaps, unsporting. He didn't care. Battle was not sport; if you went into it for any other reason than smashing the foe, you were a fool.

Sullenly, the foot soldiers drew back toward the east, yielding the field to the Videssians. But they retreated in good order, holding their formation as best they could, and did not scatter and let Maniakes' army destroy them one piece at a time. Having made more fighting retreats than he cared to remember, the Avtokrator knew how hard they were to bring off.

He did not pursue so vigorously as he might have. For one thing, daylight was leaking out of the sky. For another, he thought he'd beaten the foot soldiers from the Land of the Thousand Cities so badly, they would not try to renew the struggle anytime soon. That was what he'd hoped to accomplish. With that army of foot soldiers out of the picture, he could return to the business they'd interrupted: crossing the Tib and advancing on Mashiz.

"We'll camp," he said. "We'll tend to our wounded and then we'll get back to doing what we were doing before we had to turn around and fight: taking the war to Sharbaraz so he knows what a bad idea starting it was."

Ypsilantes nodded approval. So did Rhegorios, when he came into the camp with his soldiers as twilight was giving way to night. "They're good, that they are," he told Maniakes. "A little more discipline, a little more flexibility in the way they shift from one line to the other, and they'll be quite good. If we can grab Mashiz, fine. That should end the war, so we don't have to go on teaching them how to be soldiers."

Maniakes said, "Aye." He knew he sounded as if he'd been listening to his cousin with but half an ear. Unfortunately, that happened to be true. The noise on a battlefield just after the battle was done was apt to be more dreadful than what you heard while the fighting raged. All the triumph melted away with the battle itself, leaving behind only the pain.

Men groaned and shrieked and shouted and cursed. Horses made worse noises still. Maniakes often thought on how unfair war was for horses. The men who had been hurt on the field that day had at least some idea of why they were fighting and how they had come to be injured. It was all a mystery to the horses. One moment they were fine, the next in torment. No wonder their screams tore at the soul.

Horseleeches and troopers went over the field, doing what they could for the animals. All too often, *what they could* was nothing more than a dagger slashed quickly and mercifully across a throat.

By their cries, more than a few men would have welcomed such attention. Some of them got it: most of the enemy's wounded were left behind on the battlefield. That was hard, but it was the way wars were fought. A few Videssians, too, no doubt, those horribly wounded, were granted the release of a quick slide out of this life and toward eternal judgment.

For the rest, surgeons whose skills were about on a level with those of the horse doctors aided men not desperately hurt, drawing arrows, setting broken bones, and sewing up gashed flesh with quick stitches any tailor would have looked upon with distaste. Their attentions, especially in the short run, seemed to bring as much pain as they relieved.

And a band of healer-priests wandered over the field, looking for men badly wounded who might yet be saved if something like a miracle reached them. All healers were not only priests but magicians, but not all magicians could heal—far from it. The gift had to be there from the beginning. If it was, it could be nurtured. If it wasn't, all the nurturing in the world would not bring it forth.

Heading the healers was a blue-robe named Philetos, who in times of peace—in Maniakes' recent experience, a purely theoretical conception—taught experimental thaumaturgy at the Sorcerers' Collegium in Videssos the city. He had also, not quite coincidentally, performed the marriage ceremony uniting Maniakes and Lysia, ignoring the ecumenical patriarch's prohibition against the clergy's doing any such thing. Despite the later dispensation from Agathios, some rigorist priests still condemned Philetos for that.

Maniakes found Philetos crouched beside a soldier who had a

wound in his chest and bloody froth bubbling from his mouth and nose. The Avtokrator knew the surgeons would have been powerless to save the fellow; if that wound did not prove rapidly fatal, fever would take the man in short order.

"Is there any hope?" Maniakes asked.

"I think so, your Majesty," the healer-priest answered. He had already stripped off the soldier's mail shirt and hiked up the linen tunic he wore under it to expose the wound itself. As Maniakes watched, Philetos set both hands on the injury, so that the soldier's blood ran out between his fingers.

"You must know, your Majesty, that direct contact is necessary for this healing to succeed," he said.

"Yes, of course," Maniakes said.

He was not sure whether Philetos heard him or not. "We bless thee, Phos, lord with the great and good mind," the healer-priest intoned, "by thy grace our protector, watchful beforehand that the great test of life may be decided in our favor." Philetos repeated the formula again and again, partly as a prayer, partly as a tool to lift himself out of his usual state of consciousness and onto the higher plane where healing might take place.

The moment when he reached that other plane was easy enough to sense. He seemed to quiver and then grow very firmly planted on the ground, as if fixed there by a power stronger than any merely mortal. Maniakes, standing a few feet away, felt the current of healing pass from Philetos to the wounded soldier, though he could not have said with which of his senses he felt it. He sketched the sun-circle and murmured Phos' creed himself, filled with awe at the power for which Philetos was the conduit.

The healer-priest grunted. All at once, his eyes focused on the merely mundane world once more. He took his hands away from the arrow wound and wiped them on the soldier's tunic, then used the tunic to scrub away the rest of the blood on the man's chest. Instead of a hole through which more blood came, only a white, puckered scar remained there, as if the fellow had suffered the injury years before.

He opened his eyes and looked up at Philetos. "Holy sir?" he said in tones of surprise. His voice might have been that of any young man, certainly not that of a young man who had just taken an arrow in the lung. Memory filled his face with pain, or rather with the recollection of pain. "I was shot. I fell. I couldn't breathe." His eyes widened as he realized what must have happened. "You healed me, holy sir?"

"Through me, the good god healed you." Philetos' voice came out as a harsh croak. His face was haggard, the skin stretched tight across his cheekbones. "Phos was kind to you, lad." He managed a weary chuckle. "Try not to stop any more arrows with your chest, eh?"

"Yes, holy sir." The soldier, at the point of death a few minutes earlier, scrambled to his feet. "Phos bless you." He hurried away; but for the blood still round his mouth and nose, no one would have known he'd been hurt.

Philetos, by contrast, looked about to fall over. Maniakes had seen that reaction in healer-priests before; using their talent drained them dry. The Avtokrator shouted for food and wine. Philetos gobbled and gulped, downing enough for two ordinary men. Maniakes had seen that before, too.

"Where is the next one?" the healer-priest said, still wearily but with some restored vigor. A healer-priest of extraordinary talent, such as he was, could heal two, three, sometimes even four men who would have died without his attentions. After that, the effort grew too great, and the would-be healer collapsed before being able to establish the conduit with the force that flowed through him.

"You don't want to kill yourself, you know," Maniakes told him. "I've heard that can happen if you push yourself too hard."

"Where is the next one?" Philetos repeated, taking no notice of him. But when no answer was immediately forthcoming, the healer-priest went on, "Because we can do so little, your Majesty, honor demands we do all we can. The healing art is a growing thing; healers of my generation can do more at less cost to themselves than was so in my great-grandfather's day, as surviving chronicles and texts on the art make plain. In days to come, as research continues, those who follow us will accomplish still more."

"Which is all very well," Maniakes said, "but which doesn't keep you from killing yourself if you do too much."

"I shall do all I can. If I die, it is as Phos wills," Philetos answered. He suddenly looked not just exhausted but thoroughly grim. "As is also true of those whom we try but fail to heal."

That made Maniakes' mouth twist, too. Philetos had tried to

heal his first wife, Niphone, after she'd had to be cut open to allow Likarios to be born. She'd been on the point of death when the surgery was attempted, but Philetos still blamed himself for failing to bring her back.

"You don't work miracles," the Avtokrator said.

Philetos dismissed that with a wave of his hand, as if it weren't worth refuting. "What I do, your Majesty, is I work, with no qualifiers tacked onto the end of it." His head went this way and that, taking in as much of the field as he could, looking for one more man he might restore to vigor before his own strength failed him.

"Healer!" Faint in the distance, the cry rose. Someone—maybe a surgeon, maybe just a soldier out for loot—had come across a wounded man the special power of the healer-priests might save.

"By your leave, your Majesty," Philetos said. But he wasn't really asking leave; he was telling Maniakes he was leaving. And leave he did, at a dogged trot. He might have been tired unto death, he might have been courting it himself—perhaps to make amends for Niphone and the rest of his failures—but he would fight it in others as long as he had breath in him.

Maniakes watched him go. He could have ordered the healer-priest to stop and rest. One thing he had learned, though: the most useless order was one given without any hope of its being obeyed.

"Let's see," Ypsilantes said, peering across the Tib at the foot soldiers on the western bank, "weren't we here a few days ago?"

"I think we might have been," Maniakes said. "Something or other interrupted us, though, or we'd have been busy trying to cross by now."

Both men laughed. Their humor had a touch of the macabre to it; the air was thick with the stench of corruption from the battle Maniakes had offhandedly called *something or other,* as if he couldn't remember why the attempted crossing had been delayed. He suspected Makuraners and Kubratoi cracked those same jokes. If you wanted to stay in your right mind, you had to.

Ypsilantes made a clucking noise that put Maniakes in mind of a chicken examining a caterpillar trying to decide whether it was one that tasted good or one of the horrid kind. "I don't quite like the way the river looks," the chief engineer said. "It might have one more flood surge left in it."

"So late in the year?" Maniakes said. "I can't believe that."

"It would be more likely if we were talking about the Tutub," Ypsilantes admitted. "You can't trust the Tutub. But I think the Tib here is fuller in its banks and has bigger ripples than a couple of days ago."

Maniakes examined the Tib. "Looks remarkably like a river to me," he said, thereby showing the extent of his professional knowledge.

"It's a river, all right, and any river can be trouble," Ypsilantes said. "I'd hate to try to cross and have our bridge and such swept away with half the army on this side of the river and the other half on that one."

"Could be embarrassing," Maniakes agreed, again with that dry lack of emphasis: he might not have been a professional engineer, but he was a professional soldier, and, like a lot of men in that calling, used language that minimized the sorts of things that might happen to him.

"Maybe we should wait a few days before we go looking to cross," Ypsilantes said. "Hate to say that—"

"I hate to hear it, too," Maniakes broke in. "We've already had to wait longer than I would have liked, what with having to forage for timber and boats, and what with the attack the Makuraners brought home on us."

Ypsilantes' jaw tightened. "I own, your Majesty, I don't know for certain the river is going to rise. If you want to say I'm being a foolish old woman and order me to go ahead, no one can tell you you're wrong. You're the Avtokrator. Tell me to move and I'll obey."

"And we'll both be looking over our shoulders every minute, even if no trouble comes," Maniakes said unhappily. "You can't know what's going to happen, I can't know what's going to happen . . ." He paused. "But Bagdasares might be able to know what's going to happen."

"Who?"

"Alvinos, you might know him as," the Avtokrator answered. "He knows I've got Vaspurakaner blood in me, so when we talk he usually goes by the name he was born with, not the one he uses with ordinary Videssians."

"Oh, one of those," Ypsilantes said, nodding. "Puts me in mind of that rebel a hundred and fifty years ago, the Vaspurakaner chap who would have ruled as Kalekas if he'd won. What was his real name? Do you know?"

"Andzeratsik," Maniakes told him, adding with a wry grin, "hardly a fitting name for an Avtokrator of the Videssians, is it? My clan has some sort of distant marriage connection to his. Since he didn't win the civil war, it's not anything we talk about much."

"I can see that," Ypsilantes agreed gravely. "Good enough, then—check with the wizard. See what he has to say."

"Bagdasares?" Maniakes rolled his eyes. "He always has a good deal to say. How much of it will have to do with the question I first ask him—that's liable to be another matter." The crack was unfair if taken literally, but, like most unfair cracks, held a grain of truth.

"What can I do for you, your Majesty?" Bagdasares asked after Maniakes had ridden Antelope over to his tent. The Avtokrator explained. Bagdasares plucked at his beard. "A spell much like the one we used to examine the passage of the fleet from the city to Lyssaion should serve here, I believe."

"Good enough," Maniakes said, "but can you guarantee me that it won't show more than we want to know, as that one did?"

"Could I guarantee what magic would reveal and what it would not, your Majesty, I should be Phos, or at the least Vaspur, the good god's sole perfect creation. The principal reason for casting a spell is to see what will happen, and by that I mean not only in the outer world but with the magic itself."

Having thus been put in his place, the Avtokrator spread his hands, conceding defeat. "Have it your way, then, excellent sir. Whatever your magecraft can show me, I shall be glad to view it."

Bagdasares proceeded briskly to work. He filled a bowl with dirt he dug up from close by where he was standing—"What better symbol for the local land than the local land?" He made a channel in it, and poured in water from the pitcher that rested by his bedroll—"How else to represent the water of the Tib than by the water of the Tib?"

The landscape created, he used little twigs and chips of wood to symbolize the bridge of boats that would soon stretch across the river. "You want to know whether some flood is impending, not so?"

"That's right," Maniakes said.

"Very well, then," the wizard answered, more than a little absently: he was already gathering himself for the spell proper. He began to chant and make passes over the bowl. "Reveal!" he cried in Videssian, and then again in the Vaspurakaner tongue Maniakes had trouble following.

The Avtokrator wondered if Makuraner mages were trying to interfere with Bagdasares' conjuration. He would not have been surprised to learn they were; knowing whether he could cross the Tib in safety was obviously important to him, and the magical method for determining the truth not too complex.

But Alvinos Bagdasares gave him a straight answer. The Avtokrator watched the bridge extend itself toward the western bank of the model of the Tib, then saw little ghostly, glowing specks spring into being and cross the symbolic river from east to west.

"Weather shall not hamper us, your Majesty," Bagdasares murmured.

"I see that," Maniakes answered, still looking down into the bowl. And, as he had at his friend's earlier attempt to learn what lay ahead, he saw more than he had bargained for. Those ghostly specks suddenly recrossed the Tib, this time from west to east. "What does that mean?" he asked Bagdasares.

This time, the mage had seen for himself what had happened, instead of needing to rely on his sovereign's description. "At a guess—and a guess is all it is—we are not destined to stay long in Mashiz, if indeed we succeed in reaching the seat of the King of Kings."

"That was my guess, too," Maniakes said. "I was hoping yours would be more palatable."

"I'm sorry, your Majesty," Bagdasares said. "I do not know for a fact that what I say here is true, mind you, but all other interpretations strike me as less probable than the one I offered."

"They strike me the same way," Maniakes said. "As I say, I'm just wishing they didn't." He brightened. "Maybe the magic means Sharbaraz will be so frightened after we cross the Tib, he'll make peace on our terms. If he does that, we won't have to stay west of the river long."

"It could be so," Bagdasares answered. "Trying by magic to

learn what the King of Kings might do is hopeless, or as near as makes no difference, he being warded against such snoopery as you are. But nothing in the spell I have cast contradicts the meaning you offer."

Nothing in the spell contradicted it, perhaps, but Maniakes had trouble believing it even though it came from his own mouth. The trouble was, however much he wanted to think it likely, it went dead against everything he knew, or thought he knew, of Sharbaraz's character. The next sign of flexibility the Makuraner King of Kings displayed would be the first. The envoy he had sent to negotiate with Maniakes had been sent not to make peace but to delay the Videssians till that army of foot soldiers could fall on them. Which meant . . .

"Something's going to go wrong," Maniakes said. "I have no idea what, I have no idea why, but something is going to go wrong."

He watched Bagdasares. The Vaspurakaner mage had been a courtier for a good many years now, and plainly wanted to tell him nothing could possibly go wrong with the plans of the ever-victorious Videssian army. The only trouble was, Bagdasares couldn't do that. Both he and Maniakes had seen plans go wrong before, had seen that the Videssian army was a long way from ever-victorious. Flattery worked a lot better when both sides were willing to ignore small details like truth.

"Perhaps it won't go totally wrong," Bagdasares said.

"Aye, perhaps it won't," Maniakes said. In an unsafe, imperfect world, sometimes that was as much as you could reasonably expect. He held up one finger. "No one save the two of us need know of this conjuration." Bagdasares nodded. Maniakes figured he would tell Lysia, who could be relied upon not to blab. But if the army didn't know, maybe what the magic foretold would somehow fail to come true for them.

Maniakes let out a silent sigh. He had trouble believing that, too.

Engineers ran planks and chains from one boat to the next. One piece at a time, the bridge they were building advanced across the Tib. Ypsilantes glanced over at Maniakes and remarked, "It's all going very well."

"So it is," the Avtokrator answered. He hadn't told Ypsilantes anything about the conjuration except that it showed the bridge could advance without fear of flooding. Too late, it occurred to him that too much silence might well have made the chief engineer draw his own conclusions, and that the conclusions were liable to be right. Whether Ypsilantes had his own conclusions or not, he carried out the orders Maniakes gave him.

Foot soldiers were drawn up on the west bank of the Tib to harass the engineers and, Maniakes supposed, to resist the Videssians if that harassment failed. Thanks to magic, Maniakes knew it would. The Makuraners, being more ignorant, kept trying to make nuisances of themselves.

They did a fair job of it, too, wounding several Videssian engineers once the end of the bridge moved into archery range. Not too troubled, Ypsilantes sent forward men with big, heavy shields: the same shields, in fact, that had protected the barricade-clearing engineers in the sheds in the recent battle with the Makuraners. Behind those shields, the bridge builders kept working. Surgeons tended the injured men, none of whom was hurt badly enough to need a healer-priest.

Maniakes remembered Abivard's story about the Makuraners' building a bridge across the Degird River so they could cross it and attack the Khamorth out on the Pardrayan steppe. The Makuraner expedition had come to grief: indeed, to disaster, with Peroz King of Kings dying there on the plains. The Avtokrator hoped his own luck would be better than that. He had no way of knowing whether he would become one of the little points of light Bagdasares' magic had shown recrossing the Tib.

After a while, Ypsilantes also sent archers out to the end of the bridge to shoot back at the Makuraners. The enemy, though, had more men on the bank than the chief engineer could place at the end of the bridge. Seeing that, he sent out boatloads of archers, too, and a couple of rafts with dart-throwers mounted on them. They pumped enough missiles into the unarmored Makuraner infantry, those from the dart-throwers beyond the range at which it could respond, to sow a good deal of confusion in the foot soldiers' ranks.

"Here, let's do this," Maniakes said, calling Ypsilantes over to him. The chief engineer grinned a nasty grin after they were done speaking together.

Those boats with archers in them began going rather farther

up and down the Tib, and making as if to land. That got the Makuraners running this way and that. A couple of boats did land Videssian bowmen, who stayed on the west bank of the Tib long enough to shoot a volley or two at the Makuraners, then reembarked and rowed back out onto the river.

Meanwhile, the engineers kept extending the bridge of boats till it got quite close to the western bank of the Tib. Watching their progress, Maniakes said to Rhegorios, "This is when I wouldn't mind having some Makuraner-style heavy cavalry of my own. I could send them charging over the bridge and scatter that infantry like this." He snapped his fingers.

Rhegorios said, "I think the horsemen we have will be plenty to do the job."

"I think you're right," Maniakes said. Bagdasares' magic went a long way toward persuading him his cousin was right. How much good his being right would do in the end was a different question, one Maniakes didn't want to think about. Sometimes acting was easier than thinking. He assembled a force of horsemen with javelins near the eastern edge of the bridge, ready to move when the time came.

It came that afternoon: one of the engineers reported, "Your Majesty, the water under the bridge is only three or four feet deep now."

"Then we're going to go." Maniakes shouted orders to the trumpeters. Their horn calls sent the horsemen thundering down the bridge toward the Makuraner foot soldiers. It also sent the Videssian engineers and shieldmen leaping off the bridge into the warm, muddy waters of the Tib.

He'd succeeded in surprising the Makuraners and their commander. The horses splashed down into the water, then, urged on by their riders, hurried toward the foe. Some of the cavalrymen flung their javelins at the infantry awaiting them, while others imitated the Makuraner boiler boys and used the light spears as if they were lances.

The Videssians gained the riverbank and began to push the foremost Makuraners back. That threw the ranks of the Makuraner infantry into worse disorder than they had already known, and let the Videssians gain more ground still. At Maniakes' orders, more imperials rode over the almost-completed bridge to aid their comrades.

"You're a sneaky one," Rhegorios shouted. "They figured the bridge would have to be finished for us to use it."

"You don't want to do the thing they expect," Maniakes answered. "If they know what's coming, they're most of the way to knowing how to stop it. If they haven't seen it before, though—"

He watched avidly as his men carved out a bridgehead on the western bank of the Tib. The riders who had used up their javelins slashed at the Makuraners with swords. Whoever was commanding this enemy army lacked the presence of mind of the infantry general who'd given battle against the Videssians a few days before. When he saw his troops wavering, he pulled them away from their opponents. That made them waver even more. The Videssians, sensing victory, pushed all the harder.

Little by little, Makuraner foot soldiers began to flee, some to the north, some to the south, some to the west. Once serious resistance had ended, the Videssians did not pursue as hard as they might have. Instead, they formed a perimeter behind which the engineers finished the bridge of boats. Maniakes rode across to the west bank of the Tib without having himself or Antelope get wet.

"Mashiz!" the soldiers shouted. "On to Mashiz!" They knew what they had done, and knew also what they wanted to do. Had Mashiz been only an hour's gallop distant, it might have fallen. But it was a couple of days away, and the sun was sliding down behind the Dilbat Mountains. Maniakes judged he had taken enough risks, or maybe more than enough. He ordered the army to halt for the night.

Having done that, he wondered whether he should dispense with leaving a garrison behind to protect the bridge of boats. He was tempted not to bother: after all, the magic had shown his army would come back safe over the Tib. After some thought, though, he decided idiocy might be stronger than sorcery, and so warded what obviously needed warding.

"On the far bank at last," he told Lysia once his pavilion had been set up. "Didn't come close two years ago, came close but didn't make it last year. Now—we see what we can do."

She nodded, then said, "I wish you hadn't had Bagdasares cast that spell. I'd be more hopeful than I am. Can we take Mashiz so quickly? If we do, why would we turn back so soon? What could go wrong?"

"I don't know the answers to any of those questions," he said.

"That's why we're going ahead and moving on Mashiz: to find out what can go wrong, I mean."

Lysia made a face at him. "What if nothing goes wrong? What if we go in, seize the city, and capture Sharbaraz or kill him or make him run away?"

"For one thing, Bagdasares will be very embarrassed," Maniakes answered, which made Lysia look for something to throw at him. He caught a hard roll out of the air and went on, "I don't know what then, except that I'd be delighted. I've been trying to go ahead as if I thought that was what would happen, but it's not easy. I keep wondering if something I do will make whatever is going to go wrong, go wrong."

"Better in that case not to have had the magic," Lysia said.

"I know," Maniakes answered. "I've had that thought before, every now and then. Knowing the future, or thinking you know the future, can be more of a curse than a blessing." He gave a wry shrug. "I didn't want to know as much as the spell showed me; it did more than I asked. And, of course, *not* knowing the future can be more a curse than a blessing, too."

"Life isn't simple," Lysia said. "I wonder why that isn't a text for the ecumenical patriarch to preach on at the High Temple. It doesn't work out the way you think it will. No matter how much you know, you never understand as much as you think you do."

"That's true," Maniakes said. He glanced over at her. She was glancing over at him, too. For most of their lives, they'd never expected to be married to each other. Many things would have been a good deal simpler had they not ended up married to each other. The only problem was, life wouldn't have been worth living. "How do you feel?" he asked her.

She knew what he meant when he asked that question; of itself, her left hand went to her belly. "Pretty well," she answered. "I'm still sleepy more than I would be if I weren't going to have a baby, but I haven't been sick very much this time, for which I thank the lord with the great and good mind."

Maniakes let his fancy run away with him. He knew he was doing it; it wasn't, he thought, as if he were deluding himself. "Wouldn't it be fine if we did run Sharbaraz King of Kings out of Mashiz and if Bagdasares did turn out wrong? We could spend the rest of the campaigning season there, and maybe even the

winter, too. We could have a prince—or a princess—of the Videssian imperial house born in the capital of Makuran."

"No, thank you," Lysia said at once, her voice sharp. "I know
that sounds very grand, but I don't care. I want to go home to
have this baby. If we go home after we've beaten the Makuraners,
that's wonderful—better than wonderful, in fact. But beating the
Makuraners isn't reason enough for me to want to stay here. If
you decide to do that, well and good. Send me back to Videssos
the city."

In marriage as in war, knowing when to retreat was not the
least of virtues. "I'll do that," Maniakes promised. He scratched at
his beard while he thought. "Meanwhile, though, I have to figure
out how to arrange the triumph after which I get to send you
home." He snapped his fingers. "Should be easy, shouldn't it?"

Lysia laughed. So did he.

For the next few days, Maniakes wondered whether he had
magical powers to put those of Bagdasares to shame. One snap of
the fingers seemed to have been plenty to rout all the opposition
the Makuraners had mustered against his men. The foot soldiers,
who had put up such a persistent fight for so long, now began
melting away rather than resisting as they had.

Every now and then, some of them would try to hold back
the Videssians, while others broke canals open. But these men
seldom stood in place as the other, larger, force west of the Tib
had done so often over the past couple of years; it was as if his
crossing the river had taken the spirit out of them.

And opening the canals was less effective west of the Tib than
it had been in the heart of the Land of the Thousand Cities. As
was true east of the Tutub, there was land beyond that which
the network of canals irrigated. Instead of having to slog through
fields made all but impassable by water and mud, the Videssians
simply went around them, and once or twice scooped up good-
sized bands of foes in the process.

Far more easily than Maniakes had imagined possible, his men
neared the approaches to Mashiz. There their advance slowed. The
usurper Smerdis had fortified those approaches against Sharbaraz.
Once Sharbaraz won the civil war between them and became
King of Kings himself, he'd rebuilt and improved the fortification,
though no obvious enemy threatened his capital.

"We helped break these works once," Maniakes said to Ypsilantes, "but they look a good deal stronger than they did then."

"Aye, that's so, your Majesty," the chief engineer said, nodding. "Still, I expect we'll manage. Smerdis, now, he had horsemen who would fight for him, and that made life hard for us, if you'll recall. The walls and such are better now, I'll not deny, but so what? The troops in and around 'em count for more; men are more important than things."

"Do you know," Maniakes said, "I've had a bard tell me just that. He said that as long as the people in his songs were interesting, the settings mattered little—and if the people were dull, the finest settings in the world wouldn't help."

"That makes sense, your Majesty—more sense than I'd expect from a bard, I must say. When you get down to the bottom of anything you can think of, near enough, it's about people, isn't it?" Ypsilantes looked at the fortifications ahead. "People who huddle behind thick stone are more difficult, worse luck."

"If they're trying to keep us from doing what we need to do, I should say so."

"We'll manage, never fear," Ypsilantes repeated. "With no cavalry, they'll have trouble sallying against us, too, the way Smerdis' men did."

"That's so," Maniakes said. "I'd forgotten that sally till you reminded me of it. Makuraners popping out everywhere—I won't be sorry not to see *that*, thank you very much."

The Makuraners did not sally. They did fling large stones from catapults in their fortresses. One luckless Videssian scout drew too close to one of those forts at exactly the wrong moment; he and his mount were both smashed to bloody pulps. That made Maniakes thoughtful. Even with his own stone- and dart-throwers set up to shoot back at the ones the Makuraners had in place, his army would have to run the gauntlet before breaking into Mashiz. It would be expensive, and he did not have all that many men he could spare; that he had any army that could stand against the Makuraners he took as something close to direct intervention from Phos, considering how many years of defeat Videssos had suffered.

He cast about for ways other than the most direct one to break into Mashiz. The riders he sent forth to spy out those other ways returned to him unmashed but less than optimistic: Sharbaraz had made sure getting into his capital would not be an easy business.

He lacked the Cattle Crossing to hold foes away, but had done all he could with what he had.

"Straight on, then," Maniakes said reluctantly. Ypsilantes nodded, now less enthusiastic than he had been. Even Rhegorios looked worried about the likely size of the butcher's bill. Maniakes also kept worrying about what Bagdasares' magic had meant. Should he go ahead, knowing—or thinking he knew—he could not stay west of the Tib for long?

With his usual unassuming competence, Ypsilantes readied the Videssian catapults to oppose those of the Makuraners. Maniakes mustered the army for what he hoped would be a quick, fierce descent on Mashiz. He was about to give the order for the attack to begin when a courier galloped up from out of the northeast, holding up a message tube and shouting, "Your Majesty! Your Majesty! The Makuraners are in Across, the whole great army of them, and they and the cursed Kubratoi have made common cause against Videssos the city. The city might fall, your Majesty."

✦ IV

For a long moment, Maniakes simply stared at the messenger as if he'd been spouting some incomprehensible gibberish. Then, all at once, the pieces seemed to make a new and altogether dreadful pattern. Keeping his voice under tight control, he asked, "When you say the Makuraners are back at Across, do you mean the main army under Abivard son of Godarz?"

"Aye, your Majesty, that's who I mean—who else?" the fellow answered. "Abivard and Romezan and stinking Tzikas the traitor, too. And all the boiler boys. And all the siege gear, too." He pointed toward Ypsilantes' catapults to show what he meant.

Rhegorios said, "All right, the Makuraners are back at Across again. So what? They've been there before, for years at a stretch. They can't cross over to Videssos the city."

But the messenger said, "This time, maybe they can, your highness, your Majesty. The Kubratoi have a whole great swarm of those one-trunk boats of theirs out on the water, and they've been going back and forth to the westlands. We can't stop all of that, as much as we wish we could."

"By the good god," Maniakes whispered in horror. "If they can get their stone-throwers and towers and such up against the walls of the city—"

"The walls are strong, your Majesty," Rhegorios said, for once not bothering to ring playful changes on his cousin's title. "They've

461

stood a long time, and nobody yet has found a way through them."

"That's so," Maniakes answered. "I can think of two drawbacks to it, though. For one, the Makuraners really know how to attack fortifications; they're at least as good at it as we are. We've seen that in the westlands, more times than I care to think about. And for the other, walls aren't what keep attackers out. Soldiers are. Where are the best soldiers in the Empire? No, to the ice with that. Where are the only soldiers in the Empire who've proved they can stand up to the Makuraners in battle?"

Rhegorios didn't say anything. Maniakes would have been astonished had his cousin said anything. The answer to the rhetorical question was only too obvious: he led the sole Videssian army that had proved itself against the foe. The rest of the Empire's forces, he feared, were still all too much like the armies that had lost to the boiler boys again and again and again. That would not be true in another two or three years—which, unfortunately, did him no good whatever now.

And then, to his astonishment, Rhegorios started laughing. Both Maniakes and the messenger looked at the Sevastos as if he'd lost his mind. "Beg your pardon, your Majesty," Rhegorios said after a moment, "but we've been making jokes about what might happen if we took the Makuraners' capital at the same time as they took ours. Now the jokes have turned real. If that isn't funny, what is?"

"Nothing," Maniakes said. Nothing struck him funny at the moment, that was certain. He felt like getting off his horse so he could kick himself. He'd been too headstrong again. With no sign of Abivard, he'd just charged ahead, worrying about what he himself was doing but not paying enough attention to what the enemy might be up to at the same time.

Videssos had been known to incite the steppe nomads against Makuran from time to time. He'd never expected the Makuraners to turn the tables so neatly. Etzilios, no doubt, had thirsted for revenge ever since the Videssians beat him three years before. And if Sharbaraz had somehow gotten an embassy to him . . . Maniakes hadn't thought the King of Kings possessed of such duplicity. How expensive would correcting that mistaken opinion prove?

Rhegorios said, "What happens if we *do* take Mashiz while they're sacking Videssos the city?"

Maniakes weighed that. The idea appalled him at first consideration. After he'd thought on it a little while, he liked it even less. "If we take Mashiz," he said, "the Makuraners fall back to their plateau, and we have no hope of going after them there. But if they take the city, what's to stop them and the Kubratoi from flooding across all the land we have left? No mountains like the Dilbat chain, no great rivers—nothing."

His cousin nodded. "I think you have the right of it. If we make that trade, we're ruined. The thing to do, then, is to keep from making it."

"Yes." Maniakes took a long look west toward Mashiz. He wondered when or if he would ever see the Makuraner capital again. Seeing his own again, though, suddenly counted for more. "We go back."

Seeing the bridge the engineers had forced across the Tib still intact filled Maniakes with relief. He had thought it survived; consideration of what Bagdasares' magic had shown him made it seem likely the bridge survived. But Maniakes had long since received a forceful education on the difference between what seemed likely and what turned out to be true. Seeing the makeshift ugliness of that bridge with his own eyes was like his first sight of Lysia after returning to Videssos the city from beating the Kubratoi. Now he could breathe easier and get on with the rest of the things that needed doing.

Rhegorios must have been thinking along similar lines, for he said, "I guess this means the Makuraners didn't capture any couriers who tried to bring us news out of the east. If they'd known how much harm they could do us by burning this bridge, they would have tried it."

"Can't argue with you there," Maniakes said. How much time would he have lost had the foe tried trapping him on the west bank of the Tib? It wasn't a question with a precise answer, but *too much* tolled through his head like a bell with two mournful notes.

Once the army had passed over the bridge, Ypsilantes pointed back to the structure his engineers had bled to build. "What do we do with it now?"

"Collect whatever timbers you need and burn the rest," Maniakes snapped. "That won't matter much—the Makuraners have their own bridges of boats—but it may slow them some. And why should we make life easy for them?"

Flames crackled. Smoke rose into the sky, thick and black. When the Makuraners had gone over the Degird under Peroz King of Kings to attack the Khamorth nomads, they'd thrown a bridge across that river: Maniakes remembered Abivard speaking of it. And once their survivors, the handful of them, had returned to Makuran, they'd burned that bridge. Now he understood how their engineers must have felt then.

Back on the west bank of the Tib, a few Makuraner soldiers stood watching the Videssians wreck the bridge. He wondered what they thought of his retreat. They hadn't beaten him. They hadn't come close to beating him. In the end, though, what did that matter? Regardless of the reason, he was quitting their land. If that didn't mean they had won and he had lost, he had no idea what it did mean.

"We want to move fast," he told his warriors. "We don't want to give the Makuraners the chance to delay us with skirmishes or anything of the sort. We're faster than they are; that means we mostly get to choose when to engage and whether to engage—and the answer is going to be no unless we can't possibly help it. If they offer battle, we'll go around them if we find any way to do it. If we don't—" He shrugged. "—we go through 'em."

For the first couple of days on the move through the Land of the Thousand Cities, they saw only scouts and the peasants who worked the land. One of those looked up from the garden plot he was weeding and shouted, "Thought you thieves had gone on to afflict somebody else!"

After riding past the irate farmer, Rhegorios snapped his fingers in annoyance. "Oh, a pestilence!" he burst out. "I should have told him it was his turn again. It would have been worth it, just to see the look on his face."

"Nice to know you don't always think of the right thing to say when you need to say it," Maniakes told him. "But I tell you this—you're not going to turn around and go back for the sake of watching his jaw drop. Nobody goes back for anything, not now."

Sooner than Maniakes had hoped, the Makuraner forces in the Land of the Thousand Cities realized the Videssian army was withdrawing. The enemy began trying to obstruct the withdrawal, too. That irked him; he had hoped they would be content to see him go and not seek to delay him and let him do more damage to the floodplain.

His captains took renewed skirmishing and floods ahead of them almost as a personal affront. "If they so badly want us to stay, we ought to go back to thrashing them, the way we have the past couple of years," Immodios said angrily.

"I don't think anyone in the Land of the Thousand Cities wants us to stay," Maniakes answered. "I think the King of Kings is the one who wants us stuck here. If we're fighting here between the Tutub and the Tib, even if we're beating everything they throw at us, we aren't heading back to Videssos the city and defending it against Abivard. Delaying us here helps the enemy there."

Immodios considered that, then nodded. "Sharbaraz has a long reach and a sure one, if he can keep his mind on what he does here and far away at the Cattle Crossing, both at the same time."

"This year, Sharbaraz has shown me more than in all the time before this I've had on the throne," Maniakes replied, genuine regret in his voice. "Making an alliance with Kubrat against us—no King of Kings ever thought of anything like that before. He's a good deal more clever than I dreamed he could be. But he's not so clever as he thinks he is, not if you think back to that shrine we found, the one where he was made out to be the Makuraner God. He doesn't live at the very center of the world and have it all spin round him, no matter what he thinks."

"Ah, that shrine. I'd forgotten that." Immodios sketched Phos' sun-circle above his heart. "You're right, your Majesty. Anyone who's foolish enough to think of himself as a god, well, it doesn't matter how smart he is other ways. Sooner or later, he's going to make a bad mistake. Another bad mistake, I should say."

"Sooner or later," Maniakes echoed. "I think you're right. No, I know you're right. It would be nice, though, with things as they are, to have the mistake come sooner. We could use it."

His army crossed the major north-south canal between the Tutub and the Tib. Getting over it made him smile; Bagdasares' magic had done a good job of delaying the Makuraners there the year before. Then Maniakes' smile congealed on his face. Abivard was supposed to have a Videssian wizard with him, someone he'd scooped up as he conquered the westlands. Absent that, the magic of the Voimios strap might have held the Makuraners at bay even longer than it had done.

When he'd left Videssos the city, Maniakes had been content—had been more than content, if less eager than Lysia—to leave behind reports of and from the imperial capital. Now that he moved toward the city once more, he hungered for news about it. Was he rushing back toward a town already fallen to the foe? What would he do if that turned out to be so? He did not want such macabre imaginings loose in his mind, but felt reluctant to dismiss them. If they stayed, he might come up with answers for them.

He'd been concentrating on how to go about attacking Mashiz when the messengers brought word first of the Kubratoi invasion of Videssos and then of Abivard's joining forces with the nomads. He'd seen no messengers since. Had the Makuraners captured them before they ever got to him? If they had, they would know more than he about what was going on at the heart of the Empire. Or had his own people—Phos! his own family—not sent out more men, either because they were too pressed or because they could not? Anxiety on account of his ignorance ate at him.

One day when the army was a little more than halfway across the Land of the Thousand Cities, Rhegorios rode up next to him and asked, "If you were the Makuraner commander and you knew we were leaving this country, what would you do to make things hard for us?"

"What the enemy is doing, more or less," the Avtokrator answered, "skirmishes and floods and anything else that would slow us up."

Rhegorios nodded, but then went on, "That's true, but it's not what I meant, or not all of what I meant, anyhow. What's he going to do with the men he doesn't have skirmishing with us now?"

"Ah, I see what you're saying." Maniakes' thick eyebrows came down together in a frown. When you asked the question as Rhegorios had, you also indicated the answer: "He's going to put them where they'll do the best job of blocking us: down by Qostabash and maybe in the hill country where the Tutub rises."

His cousin nodded. "That's what I thought, too. I was hoping you would tell me this heat has melted the brains right out of my head. How are we going to get through them if they do that?"

"As long as we and they are on the floodplain, it won't matter so much, because we'll be able to outmaneuver them. Up in those hills, though—" Maniakes broke off. "I'm going to have to think about that."

"Always happy to hand you something to take your mind off your worries," Rhegorios said, so blithely that Maniakes had only a little trouble fighting down the urge to punch him in the face.

Maniakes did think about what Rhegorios had suggested. The more he thought, the less he liked it. He went to check with Ypsilantes, who had such maps of the Land of the Thousand Cities as the Videssians had been able to put together, along with others dating back to an invasion several centuries before. After studying the maps for a while, he took counsel with Rhegorios, Ypsilantes, and Immodios.

He pointed to his cousin. "This is your fault, you know. It's what you get for complicating my life—no, not my life, all our lives."

"Thank you," Rhegorios said, which was not the answer Maniakes had been looking for but not one to surprise him, either.

To Ypsilantes and Immodios, Maniakes said, "His Highness the Sevastos there—the one with the tongue hinged at both ends—made me realize we ought to get to the hill country between the headwaters of the Tutub and those of the Xeremos as fast as we can." He explained why, then went on, "Unless I'm dead wrong, going back by way of Qostabash isn't the best route, either."

"Then why have we been doing it?" Immodios asked. "Going back by way of Qostabash, I mean."

Maniakes tapped two parchment maps, one new, one old. "As near as I can tell, the answer is, force of habit. Here, look: the trade route down to Lyssaion runs through Qostabash nowadays." He ran his finger along the red squiggle of ink showing the route. Then he traced it on the other map, the old one. "It's been running through Qostabash for a *long* time. But just because the trade route runs through Qostabash, that doesn't mean we have to go that way ourselves."

He traced another path with his finger, this one running well east of the town that was the southern gate to the Land of the Thousand Cities. "If we take this route, we save ourselves a day or two of travel—and, with luck, we don't have so many enemies waiting for us at the other end of it."

Immodios frowned. He had a face made for frowning, with tight, almost cramped features. "I don't follow all of that, your Majesty. Yes, we reach the hill country faster by your route, which is to the good. But what's to keep the Makuraners from shifting forces from Qostabash—if they have them there—to the east to try to block us? That would eat up the time we save."

"What's to keep them from doing it?" The smile Maniakes wore was broad but felt a little unnatural, as if he were trying too hard to be Rhegorios. "You are."

"Me?" Immodios looked splendidly surprised; no wonder, Maniakes thought, his cousin had so much fun in life.

"You," the Avtokrator said. "You're going to take a regiment, maybe a regiment and a half, of soldiers and you're going to ride to Qostabash as if you had the whole Videssian army with you. Burn the fields as you go, set out lots of fires at night, make as big a nuisance of yourself as you can."

"If you want a nuisance, you should send me," Rhegorios said.

"Hush," Maniakes told him. "You're a nuisance by yourself; for this job, I want someone who takes a little more professional approach." He turned back to Immodios. "Your task is to keep the Makuraners too busy noticing you to pay any attention to the rest of us as we slide south. Have you got that?"

"I think I have, your Majesty." Immodios pointed to one of the imperial banners, gold sunburst on sky blue, that floated not far away. "Let me have my fair share and more of those, so anyone who sees my detachment will think you're with it."

"All right," Maniakes said, fighting down misgivings. He wondered whether he shouldn't have given Rhegorios the assignment after all. If Immodios failed and the banners were captured, Videssos would be embarrassed. And if Immodios decided that bearing imperial banners gave him the right to other imperial pretensions, Videssos would be worse than embarrassed: the Empire would have a new civil war on its hands.

But Immodios was right to ask for the banners, given the role the Avtokrator had set him to play. And if Maniakes had said no, he might well have set resentment afire in a heart free of it till then. The business of ruling was never simple, and got more complicated the harder you looked at it.

Brave with banners, Immodios' detachment rode off, intent on convincing the Makuraner infantry commanders that it was the whole Videssian army. The large majority of that army, meanwhile, abandoned their journey toward Qostabash and swung south, into a region of the Land of the Thousand Cities they had never visited before.

That the region was new did not mean it was remarkable. Cities still squatted on hillocks made from millennia of rubble. Canals still crisscrossed fields of wheat and barley and beans and garden patches green with growing onions and lettuces and melons. Those absurd little boats still plied the canals. Mosquitoes and gnats still swarmed, thick as heavy rain.

Maniakes had hoped to glide through all but unnoticed. Since he was leading an army of several thousand mounted men, that hope, he admitted to himself if to no one else, was unrealistic. Getting through the untouched country cleanly and with as little fighting as he could—that he had a better chance of doing.

Scouts reported messengers pelting off to the east. Some they caught, some they could not. Those who escaped were no doubt taking word of his arrival to those in the best position to do something about it. He wondered if they would be believed. He hoped they wouldn't, not when Immodios was ostentatiously pretending to be what his army really was.

One calculation of his came true: in a land not much touched by war, the locals hesitated to open canals to slow him down. "They'd have done just that, nearer Qostabash," he said to Rhegorios.

His cousin nodded. "So they would. We'd have done some more sacking and wrecking ourselves, too. This feels as if we're traveling through their country, not fighting a war in it."

"We're here to travel," Maniakes said, and Rhegorios nodded again.

Travel they did, at a good pace. Once, not long after Immodios had separated himself from them, a delegation came out from one of the cities in the southern part of the floodplain: officials of some sort, along with yellow-robed servants of the God. Maniakes supposed they wanted to ask him not to sack their town, or perhaps not to plunder its fields. He never found out for certain, because he did not wait around for them to catch up to him. He wondered what they ended up doing. Going back into their city, he supposed, and thanking the God he'd passed it by.

He had no trouble keeping the army fed. With plenty of water, good soil, and heat the year around, the Land of the Thousand Cities bore even more abundantly than the coastal lowlands of the Empire of Videssos. Something was always ripe enough for men and horses to enjoy.

Messengers rode back and forth between Maniakes' army and Immodios' division impersonating that army. A couple of days after Maniakes didn't stop to listen to the local delegation, one of Immodios' riders brought in not only the officer's report of his position but also a message tube whose leather was stamped with the lion of Makuran. "Well, well," Maniakes said. "Where did you come by this?"

"Fellow who was using it won't need it anymore." The messenger grinned at him.

Maniakes spoke and understood the Makuraner language fairly well. In its written form, though, it used different characters from Videssian, and he'd never learned them. He found that Philetos could make sense of it. "Some interesting magical texts come out of Makuran," the healer-priest remarked, "which are well worth reading in the original."

"I don't think there's anything magical about this," Maniakes said, handing him the parchment.

Philetos unrolled it and went through it with a speed and confidence that said he was indeed fluent in the written Makuraner language. "Your Majesty, this is from the commander of the army near Qostabash—Turan is his name—to the city governors in the region through which we are passing."

"Ah," Maniakes said. "That sounds interesting. I'll wager we've caught one copy of several, then. What does he say?"

"He warns them to be alert for Videssian brigands—his phrase, I assure you—who may be operating in this area. He says their depredations are a snare and a ruse, as the main Videssian force is advancing against him, and he expects to do battle against it soon."

Maniakes smiled at Philetos. The healer-priest smiled back at him. "Isn't that nice?" the Avtokrator said. "This Turan doesn't know which end is up, sounds like." He sobered. "He doesn't, that is, unless he manages to pick off one of our messengers. That would give the game away."

"So it would," Philetos agreed. "Here as elsewhere in life, secrets are never so secret as we might like."

"That's truer than I wish it were," Maniakes said. "And, speaking of wishes, I wish I'd thought of having a code for Immodios and me to use when we write back and forth to each other. Too late now, I'm afraid: if I send him one, I'll have to worry about the Makuraners capturing it and reading things I think they can't. Best leave it alone."

Surprisingly soon, the hills from which the Tutub rose came into sight ahead of the Videssian army. Maniakes sent several messengers to Immodios, ordering him to leave off his imposture and join the main force. A rider from his division came back to Maniakes, confirming that he'd got the command. Of the division itself, though, there was for the moment no sign.

For the first couple of days, Maniakes did not worry over that. Indeed, he took advantage of it, sending scouts deep into the hill country to make sure the ways south and east remained open. And those ways *were* open; Turan had not set traps along them to slow his progress. He supposed that, whatever orders the Makuraner general might be getting from Sharbaraz, he was just as well pleased to see the Avtokrator of the Videssians abandoning the Thousand Cities.

But, when Immodios did not arrive after those couple of days, Maniakes began to fret and fume. "Curse him," the Avtokrator grumbled, "doesn't he realize this country isn't so rich as the Land of the Thousand Cities? We're going to start eating it empty pretty soon."

"He has only a division of men," Rhegorios said. "As near as I can see, this whole countryside breeds foot soldiers the way a dead dog breeds flies."

He didn't say any more. As far as Maniakes was concerned, he'd said too much already. The Avtokrator had sent out Immodios' force as a distraction. He hadn't intended to have the Makuraners swallow it up. The Makuraners could afford the losses doing that would take, but he couldn't afford those they'd inflict on him.

No messengers came from Immodios. The scouts Maniakes sent north, in the direction of Qostabash, could not find a way past Turan's infantry, which was, as Rhegorios had said, abundant, and also very alert. Maniakes found himself facing a most unpleasant choice: either abandoning Immodios' division to its fate or going north to rescue it, delaying his return to Videssos the city on account of that, and possibly losing the capital to the Kubratoi and Makuraners.

To any Avtokrator of the Videssians, the capital had to come first. Maniakes told himself that, but still could not make himself leave Immodios in the lurch. Nor could he make himself order his army to head north, away from the route to Videssos the city. For two or three days, he simply dithered.

When at last he nerved himself to order the army to forget about Immodios, he found himself saved from the consequences of his own decision, for outriders from the missing division joined up with his own scouts. Immodios' main body came into his camp half a day later.

The dour officer prostrated himself before Maniakes. Most of the time, the Avtokrator would have waved for him not to bother. Today, he let Immodios go through with the proskynesis as a sign of his displeasure. When he did signal for the captain to rise, Immodios said, "Your Majesty, you can do as you like with me. By the good god, the Makuraners had me so plugged up along a river and canal line, I thought I'd never break out and get past them."

Much of Maniakes' anger vanished. "Abivard did the same thing to us a couple of years ago—do you remember? He defied us to get onto his side of the water, but we beat him once we managed it."

"So we did, your Majesty, but we had the whole army then, and I had only a piece of it," Immodios replied. "I'm afraid I did too good a job of convincing him you were with us—he pulled out everyone under the sun to carry shield and bow and hold us away from Qostabash."

"I can see how that would have been a problem, yes," Maniakes said. "How did you finally get over the waterline?"

"The same way we did two years ago," Immodios answered. "I used part of my force to look as if I was going to force a crossing at one spot, then crossed someplace else where my scouts reported he was thinning out his garrison to cover the feint. Horses are faster than foot soldiers, so I managed to pull everyone across without too much trouble. I didn't do any more fighting afterward that I didn't have to: hurried down here to you."

"All right," Maniakes said. The dressing-down he'd planned to give Immodios died unspoken. The commander seemed to have given a good part of it to himself. "We'll head back toward Lyssaion, then."

The farmers and herders who lived in the hills from which the Tutub sprang fled into the roughest country they could find when the Videssian army made its way through their land for the second time in a relatively short interval. No doubt they stared down at the imperials with helpless resentment from their craggy refuges, wondering what had prompted Maniakes to revisit them on such short notice.

They might have been surprised to hear he was at least as unhappy about the necessity as were they. He would much sooner have been fighting outside their capital than rushing back to try to save his own.

"Next interesting question," Rhegorios observed as the army came out of the hills and into the valley of the Xeremos, "is whether any ships will be waiting for us once we get to Lyssaion."

Maniakes had entertained that same worry—had entertained it and now rejected it. "There will be ships," he said, as if he had seen them himself: and so, in a manner of speaking, he had. "Bagdasares showed them to me." Of the tempest Bagdasares had also shown him, he said nothing.

"I'd hate to have him wrong, that's all," the Sevastos murmured.

"He's not wrong," Maniakes said. "Think it through—do you think my father would send word the city was in trouble without giving us a way to get back there? I don't need magic to see that."

"Uncle Maniakes?" Rhegorios shook his head, visibly taking the point. "No, he'd never make that kind of mistake. My father calls him the most careful man he ever heard of." He pointed at the Avtokrator. "How did he ever get a son like you?"

"He was born luckier than I was, into a time where you didn't need to take so many chances," Maniakes answered. "By the time I got the crown, I had to do all sorts of desperate things to make sure I kept having an empire to rule. The trouble with desperate things is, a lot of them don't work." He sighed. "We've found out more than we ever wanted to know about *that*, haven't we?"

"So we have," Rhegorios said, adding, "Well, now we and the Makuraners are even." When Maniakes looked puzzled, his cousin condescended to explain: "Wouldn't you say throwing everything

they have into an attack on Videssos the city is about as desperate
as our throwing everything we have into an attack on Mashiz?
Maybe they're more desperate still, because the city is harder to
take than Mashiz."

"Ah, now I understand," Maniakes said. "Put that way, you're
right, of course." Some of the desperate things he'd done had been
disasters. Some of them, against the Kubratoi and Makuraners
both, had succeeded better than he'd dared hope. Now he had to
do everything he could to ensure that Abivard and Sharbaraz's
desperate attack—if that was what it was—didn't fall into the
second category.

One of the things he did, as soon as he was sure no substan-
tial Makuraner force lurked ahead of him, was to send riders
through the hill country and down the valley of the Xeremos to
make sure that the fleet he confidently expected to find waiting
for him was in fact there. He got less confident by the day till
the first rider returned. If the fleet wasn't there, he didn't know
what he'd do. Travel through the westlands by land? Go up to
Erzerum and hope to find a fleet there? Leap off a tall promontory into the sea? With the third choice, at least, the agony would
be over in a hurry.

But, by the way the returning horseman was waving at him,
he didn't have to worry about that—one down, hundreds left.
"They're there, your Majesty," the fellow shouted when he got close
enough for the Avtokrator to hear him. "A whole great forest of
masts in the harbor, waiting for us to come aboard."

"The lord with the great and good mind be praised," Maniakes
breathed. He turned to the trumpeters who were usually nearby.
"Blow the quick trot. The sooner we get to Lyssaion, the sooner
we sail."

The sooner the storm strikes us, he thought. He wondered if he
should hold back his pace in the hope the bad weather would
go by before the fleet did. He didn't think that would help. If he
held back, somehow or other the storm would manage to do the
same. And, if he held back, who could say what might happen
in Videssos the city while he was delaying?

His soldiers rode down the valley of the Xeremos as fast as
they could without foundering their horses. Blue banners with
gold sunbursts on them snapped in the breeze. Brisk as ever,
the horns called out the commands that held the army together.

As the horsemen rode by, the peasants who farmed the valley looked up from their endless labor. Did they know the soldiers were coming back too soon, too soon?

What they knew mattered little, not here, not now. Maniakes knew. Knowledge gnawed at him like a toothache.

Then, faster than he'd expected, more slowly than he would have liked, Lyssaion lay before him, baked golden under the sun. Beyond the town splashed the water. He saw, at first, only a narrow strip of that deep, implausible blue. But where there was a strip, there was a sea.

It would take him where he wanted to go. Like a mad and jealous lover, it would try to kill him. It might succeed. Bagdasares' magic hadn't shown him anything about that, not one way or the other. He rushed forward to embrace the sea just the same.

In Lyssaion waited the hypasteos and the garrison commander. They knew what was happening in Videssos the city. They had known longer than he; messengers who reached him went past them first.

In Lyssaion also waited Thrax. The drungarios' silver hair seemed out of place amidst all the golden stonework. Maniakes realized he should not have been surprised to see the commander of the fleet there, but somehow he was. The idea of Thrax's doing anything unexpected was itself unexpected.

"Aye, your father sent me and the *Renewal* here," Thrax said, which made Maniakes feel better the drungarios hadn't done anything so strange as thinking on his own, then. "You're needed back home, that you are."

"I was needed where I was, too," Maniakes answered. But saying that gained nothing. The past two campaigning seasons, he'd moved according to his own plan. This year, the will directing him belonged to Abivard and Sharbaraz. They'd outwitted him. It was that revoltingly simple. He asked the question that had to be asked: "How bad is it back there?"

"Well, Videssos the city's still standing, or was when I left," Thrax said. Maniakes wished he hadn't added that qualifier. Thrax went on, "We've spied a Makuraner or two on the eastern side of the Cattle Crossing, looking at the city the way a cat looks at a bird in a cage: it looks tasty, but they have to figure out how to get inside."

"Makuraner soldiers on our side of the Cattle Crossing,"

Maniakes murmured, and hung his head. A series of humiliations from Makuran and Kubrat had punctuated his reign, but this was the worst of all. For all the centuries of Videssian history, the strait had shielded the capital—till now.

"No siege gear on our side," Thrax said, as if in consolation— and it was consolation of a sort. "Those monoxyla the Kubratoi use, they can sneak men across easily enough, but only a few at a time, on account of our dromons still catch and sink a good many. Some of the tackle is right bulky, though."

"Less than you'd think," Maniakes said worriedly. The more he thought about it, the more worried he got, too. Ropes and metal fittings and a few special pieces of gear were all the Makuraners needed to bring over with them. They could make the rest out of green timbers, using the Kubratoi for labor . . . "Aye, we have to get back to the city as fast as we can."

"That's what I'm here for, your Majesty," Thrax said. The elder Maniakes had told him why he was here. Maniakes had a well-founded suspicion the drungarios would have had trouble figuring it out without advance instruction.

With advance instruction, he was capable enough. Wanting to use him to best advantage, Maniakes said, "You should know to expect stormy weather on the way back to Videssos the city. Bagdasares' magic warned me of it when he cast a spell to make sure we would come safe from the city to Lyssaion."

When Thrax's sun- and wind-leathered skin wrinkled into a frown, he seemed to age ten years in a moment. "I'll do all I can to make the ships ready in advance," he said. And then, anxiously, "That is the reason you're telling me this, isn't it?"

"Yes, that's the reason," Maniakes answered in a resigned voice. He and Thrax had been together for a long time. The drungarios was steady enough; that was why Maniakes had named him to his post. In most circumstances, steadiness was plenty. Every once in a while, Maniakes would have liked to see a bit of flash along with it.

As Thrax had been waiting in the harbor of Lyssaion for some time while the army returned from the Land of the Thousand Cities, he did have the fleet ready to reembark the men and horses. The men grumbled a bit filing onto the wharves to board the ships that would take them away: after hard campaigning, they'd finally returned to a Videssian city, but they weren't going to have the chance to sample such fleshpots as it held.

"Cheer up," Maniakes told a few of them. "This is just a little backwoods town. The sooner we get back to Videssos the city, the sooner you'll *really* be able to enjoy yourselves." *And the sooner you'll start fighting the Makuraners and the Kubratoi,* he added to himself—but not to them.

The horses didn't like boarding ship, either, but then horses never did. Their potential for trouble was much smaller than that of the men. In all of Videssian history, not one mutiny had ever been started by a horse.

"Phos go with you and bring you victory," Phakrases said. The hypasteos sounded worried, and well he might. If by some mischance Videssos the city fell, he would be city governor for a regime that, in effect, no longer existed. If Videssos the city fell, Lyssaion would, too, and then he would no longer be city governor at all.

If Videssos the city fell, Maniakes would hardly be Avtokrator at all, either. The key, then, was making certain the city did not fall. So he reasoned as the fleet left the harbor and set out across the Sailors' Sea.

As ships usually did, the fleet carrying Maniakes and his army back toward Videssos the city stayed within sight of land, even if, to give the ships room to maneuver when and if a storm struck them, Thrax had them sail out till the land was no more than a blur on the northern horizon. The prevailing westerlies drove them along, faster than they had gone heading out to Lyssaion.

When night came, they anchored not far offshore. Had the shore been under their control, they would have beached the ships. As things were, no telling whether a Makuraner force might try to make trouble for them if they did. No telling, for that matter, whether some of the locals might have tried to make trouble for them. The southern coast of the westlands had been a pirate haven till the imperial fleet crushed the raiders. If the Empire of Videssos collapsed, Maniakes was sure piracy would again start flourishing in these waters in a few years' time.

He paced the deck of the *Renewal* during the day. "I hate this," he said to Lysia not long after they began sailing east. "I can't do anything to change the way things are while I'm here. I can't do anything about Videssos the city because I'm far away, and I can't even do anything about how we get there because Thrax is the one in charge of the fleet."

"You've already done everything that needed doing about the fleet—you and your father, I should say," she replied. "He made sure it was there to bring you back to the city if that was what you wanted, and you decided it was and sent the men back to Lyssaion. Past that, everything else is unimportant."

He sent her a grateful look. "You're right, of course. But I want to do things, and I can't. Waiting's not easy."

She set both hands on her belly. Her pregnancy didn't show yet, but would soon. She'd had practice waiting, nine months at a time.

Maniakes suspected the folk who lived by the Sailors' Sea had practice waiting, too. Whenever the fleet drew near the limestone cliffs common there, whenever he spotted one of the inlets not big enough to support any kind of proper harbor but more than adequate as a base for a swift galley or two, he concluded that a lot of the locals were biding their time, as they had for generations. If ever Videssos grew weak, they would grow strong, and they had to know it.

He also watched the weather with a careful and dubious eye. Every speck of cloud, no matter how small, no matter how fluffy, appeared to his worried gaze as a thunderhead loaded with rain and pushed along by winds that would whip the sea to fury. But the days went by, the little puffy clouds remained little puffy clouds, and the gentle swells under the keel of the *Renewal* were not enough to make even Lysia's sensitive stomach complain.

They rounded the southeastern corner of the westlands and started the journey north toward Videssos the city. Now Maniakes stood in the bow of the *Renewal*, peering forward even though he knew the capital was still days away. He wondered if Bagdasares really was as good a wizard as he thought.

"We'll find out," Rhegorios replied when Maniakes asked that question out loud. The Sevastos was also looking north. "Nothing out there now but ocean. Plenty of time for a storm to blow up, if one has a mind to."

"Thank you, cousin of mine," Maniakes said. "No one knows how to build my spirits the way you do."

Rhegorios bowed. "Your servant," he said. Maniakes snorted,

then laughed out loud. In a perverse way, his cousin's rampant pessimism had built his spirits, after all.

The coastal lowlands were the most fertile section of the Empire of Videssos, rivaling even the Land of the Thousand Cities for abundance. This far from Videssos the city, they were not heavily garrisoned by the Makuraners. Indeed, Videssian dominance at sea had maintained a stronger imperial presence along the coasts than almost anywhere else in the westlands. All the same, the fleet did not enter any harbors or beach itself on any inviting stretches of sand. A Makuraner force might have been prowling through the countryside, looking for trouble. Wrecking the fleet carrying Videssos' best army certainly counted as trouble in Maniakes' mind.

The next day, a lookout shouted, "The Key! The Key off the starboard bow!"

Maniakes turned to see the island for himself. The Key had got its name because its position, south and east of Videssos the city, made it crucial for holding the capital in any naval campaign—any naval campaign fought by Videssian ships, anyhow. The Makuraners and Kubratoi seemed to have come up with a different idea.

Though it was merely a smudge on the horizon, seeing it also reassured him because of its two excellent harbors, Gavdos in the south and Sykeota in the north. If the storm did come, they would give the fleet more places to shelter.

They had other uses, too. Thrax came up to Maniakes and said, "By your leave, your Majesty, I'd like to put in at Gavdos, draw food there, and refill the water casks, too. We've spent more time at sea all at once than I think I've ever done, and we're lower on supplies than I'd like."

Maniakes frowned. Having come so far, he grudged any delay. But good food and water and keeping the ships and their sails in top condition counted, too. "Go ahead," he told Thrax, and did his best not to show the stop bothered him.

"We'll pick up news of the capital there," Lysia said after he'd confessed he was going to grant Thrax's request. One corner of her mouth twitched up in a wry smile. "You don't need to tell me in the tone of voice you'd use to let me know you were unfaithful."

"Oh, yes, I've had a lot of chances for *that* during this campaign," he said, holding up his hand. "'Stop the battle, please, and bring me the latest wench.'"

The cabin they shared was cramped for two; the cabin they shared would have been cramped for one. Maniakes couldn't escape when Lysia reached out to poke him in the ribs. "Who is this latest wench?" she asked darkly.

"Right now, she's carrying my child," he answered, and took her in his arms. The cabin did have a door, and shutters over the windows, but sailors still walked past it every minute or so. That meant, for dignity's sake, they had to be very quiet. To his surprise, Maniakes had found that sometimes added something. So did the gentle motion of the *Renewal* on the sea—for him, at least. Lysia could have done without it.

"Get off me," she whispered when they had finished. She looked slightly green, which made Maniakes obey her faster than he might have otherwise. She gulped a couple of times, but things stayed down. She started to dress. As she pulled her undertunic on over her head, she said in reflective tones, "It's just as well my belly will stop you from getting on top after a while. My breasts are sore, too, and you squashed them."

"I'm sorry," he answered. He'd said that during each of her pregnancies. She believed it each time—believed it enough to stay friendly, and more than friendly, at any rate. *A good thing, too,* he thought. Without her, he would have felt altogether alone against the world, as opposed to merely overmatched.

Behind Gavdos rose the mountains in the center of the Key. Thrax let out a small laugh. "I remember the first time I brought the *Renewal* into this port, your Majesty."

"So do I. I'm not likely to forget," Maniakes answered. He'd been a rebel then and had managed to bring part of the fleet that sailed from the Key over to his side. Had the rest of that fleet not gone over to him after he sailed into Gavdos . . . had that not happened, Genesios would still be Avtokrator of the Videssians.

Maniakes' mouth twisted into a thin, bitter line. Everything Genesios did had been a catastrophe—but when Maniakes overthrew him, Videssos had still held a good chunk of the westlands, and the lord with the great and good mind knew no Makuraners had come over the Cattle Crossing to stare up close at the walls of Videssos the city with hungry, clever eyes.

He cursed Genesios. He'd spent a lot of time cursing Genesios, these past half-dozen years. The incompetent butcher had left him nothing—less than nothing—with which to work.

And yet...Just before he'd taken Genesios' head, the wretch had asked him a question that had haunted him ever since: "Will you do any better?" So far, he could not say with certainty the answer was yes.

Oarsmen guided the *Renewal* alongside a quay. Sailors leapt up onto it and made the dromon fast. More sailors set the gangplank in place, to let people go back and forth more readily. When Maniakes set foot on the wharf, he wondered if he'd arrived in the middle of an earthquake: the planks were swaying under his feet, weren't they? After a moment, he realized they weren't. He'd never spent so long at sea before, and found himself without his land legs.

Waiting to greet him was the drungarios of the fleet of the Key, a plump, fussy-looking fellow named Skitzas who had a reputation for aggressive seamanship that belied his appearance. "Hello, your Majesty," he said, saluting. "Good to see you're here and not there." He pointed west.

"I wish I were there and not here, and my army, too," Maniakes answered. "But, from the messages that got through to me, Sharbaraz and Etzilios have made that a bad idea."

"I'm afraid you're right," Skitzas said. "The Kubratoi are playing it smart, may Skotos drag them down to the eternal ice. Their monoxyla aren't a match for dromons: they've learned that the hard way. So they aren't even trying to fight us. They just keep sneaking across to the westlands, mostly at night, and carrying Makuraners back toward Videssos the city. After a while, they'll have a good many of them on the side where they don't belong."

"Makuraners don't belong on either side of the Cattle Crossing," Maniakes said, and Skitzas nodded. The Avtokrator went on, "What are you doing about it?"

"What we can," the officer answered. "Every so often, we'll meet up with a one-trunk boat in the water and put paid to it. We've been scouring the coast north and east of Videssos the city, too, doing everything we can to catch the monoxyla beached. We've burned a good many." He made a sour face. "Trouble is, the cursed things are easy to drag up well out of the water and hide. Once the masts are off them, they're only tree trunks, after all. We aren't having all the luck we ought to, I own that."

"All right," Maniakes said, and then held up a hand. "All right that you've given me a straight answer, I mean; I needed one. What's going on by the city isn't all right, not even a little bit."

"I know that, your Majesty," Skitzas said. "The one thing we and the fleet in Videssos the city have done is, we've managed to keep the Kubratoi from getting a big flotilla of monoxyla over to the westlands and ferrying the whole Makuraner army over the Cattle Crossing in one swoop. To the ice with me if I ever thought I'd be happy about delaying the enemy instead of beating him, but that's how it is right now."

"They caught us with our drawers down," Maniakes said, which wrung a grunt of startled laughter out of Skitzas. "Delaying them counts; I was wondering if I'd come back only to find the city fallen."

"The good god forbid it." Skitzas sketched the sun-circle. "Anything I can do to help you along—"

"I think Thrax has that well in hand," Maniakes said. The drungarios of the fleet was bellowing instructions at the officers who had advanced to see what he required. He told them in alarming detail. When he had a chance to prepare in advance, he was a nonpareil.

Before long, laborers started carrying sacks of flour, sacks of beans, barrels of salted beef, and jars of wine aboard the ships of his fleet. Others brought coils of rope, canvas, casks of pitch, and other nautical supplies. By the time the sun went down, the fleet was in better shape than it had been since the day after it sailed out of Lyssaion.

Sunset turned clouds in the west the color of blood. Maniakes noted that, at first made nothing of it, and then turned back to look at the sunset again. He hadn't seen clouds in the west for a good long while now. Were they harbingers of the storm Bagdasares had predicted?

If they were, could he wait out the storm here at Gavdos and then sail on to Videssos the city undisturbed? He wished he thought the answer to that were yes. But he had the strong feeling that, if this was a coming storm and he waited it out, another would catch him as soon as he put to sea. He'd gain nothing that way, and lose precious time.

"We'll go on," he said aloud. "Whatever my fate is, I'll go to meet it; I won't wait for it to come to me."

The *Renewal* bounced and shook in the waves as if it were a toy boat in a washbasin inhabited by a two-year-old intent on splashing all the water in the basin onto the floor before his mother could finish washing him. Rain drummed against Maniakes' face. The wind howled like a whole pack of hungry wolves.

Thrax screamed something at him. The drungarios of the fleet stood close by Maniakes, but he had no idea what his naval commander was saying. The rain plastered Thrax's thick pelt of white hair against his skull, giving him something of the look of an elderly otter.

Whatever my fate is, I'll go to meet it. Maniakes savored the stupidity of the words. He'd been overeager again. That was easy enough to see, in retrospect. There were storms, and then there were storms. In his haste to get back to Videssos the city, he'd put the fleet in the way of a bad one.

Thrax tried again, but whatever he'd bellowed got buried in a thunderclap that made Maniakes' ears ring. The *Renewal* nosed down into a trough between two waves. It nosed down steeply, for the waves were running very high. Maniakes staggered, but managed to keep his feet. Thrax stayed upright without apparent effort. Whatever his shortcomings, he was a seaman.

Well off the starboard bow, another dromon fought its way northward. The rowers were keeping the bow into the wind and making what progress they could, as were those of the *Renewal.* At the moment, Maniakes worried little about progress. All he wanted to do was stay on top of the water till the storm decided to blow past and churn up some other part of the Sailors' Sea. Somewhere beyond the weeping gray clouds floated Phos' sun, chiefest symbol of the good god's light. He hoped he'd live to see that symbol again.

Suddenly, without warning, the other galley broke its back. One of those surging waves must have struck it exactly wrong. It went from a ship almost identical to the *Renewal* to floating wreckage in the space of half a minute. The two halves of the hull filled with water almost at once. Here and there, scattered across the ocean, men clung to planks, to oars, to anything that would bear even part of their weight for a little while.

Maniakes pointed toward the survivors. "Can we save them?" he yelled to Thrax. At first, he thought the drungarios hadn't heard him. Thrax made his way back to the stern of the *Renewal* and bawled in the ears of the men at the steering oars, pointing in the direction of the wrecked galley as he did so. The *Renewal* swung toward the struggling men.

Sailors tied themselves to the rail before throwing lines out into the heaving sea in hope some of the men who floundered there might catch hold of them. And some of those men did catch hold of them, and were pulled half-drowned from the water that had tried to take their lives.

And some of the crew from the smashed dromon could not be saved in spite of all that the men from the *Renewal* did. One luckless sailor let go of the spar to which he had been clinging to grab for a rope. A wave slapped him in the head before his hand closed on the line. He went under.

"Come up!" Maniakes shouted to him. "Curse you, come up!" But he did not come up.

Other men lost hold of whatever they were using to keep their heads above water before the *Renewal* got close enough to pluck them from the sea. Maniakes groaned every time he saw that happen. And he knew other sailors—too many other sailors—had already drowned.

A wave broke over the *Renewal's* bow. For a hideous moment, he thought the dromon was going to imitate the one that had broken up. The ship's timbers groaned under his feet. Another, bigger wave hit her—and hit him, too. The wall of water knocked him off his feet. He skidded across the deck, fetched up hard against the rail—and started to go over, out into the foaming, roaring sea.

He grabbed at the rail. One hand seized it. He hung on with everything he had, knowing he would not live above a minute if his grip failed.

A hand closed on his wrist. A sailor with a silver hoop in one ear hauled him back aboard the *Renewal.* The fellow shouted something at him. Wind and storm blew the words away. Then the sailor offered him a length of line. He tied one end around the rail, the other around his waist. That done, he shook a fist at the sky, as if defying it to do its worst.

It seemed to take up his challenge. The wind blew harder

than ever. Rain came down in sheets. Only by tasting whether the water on his lips was sweet or salt could Maniakes be sure whether storm or sea buffeted him.

A sailor pointed off to port. More wreckage drifted there, along with human forms. Maniakes started to bellow for more lines to be cast, but stopped with the words unspoken. Those luckless fellows would be walking the bridge of the separator now, to see whether their souls tumbled down into Skotos' icy hell or spent eternity bathed in Phos' light.

Maniakes turned and looked southeast, back toward the Key. They'd cleared Sykeota some while before, and he could not see very far in any case. He didn't think they would be dashed against the shore, and realized he wouldn't find out for certain till too late to stay disaster if it came.

Lysia staggered out of the cabin the two of them shared. Maniakes ran toward her, signaling with his hands for her to go back inside. He pointed to the rope around his own midsection. Lysia nodded, thrust a pot in which she'd been copiously sick into his hands, and retreated.

He poured the pot into the sea. Like everything else, its contents were scattered and swept away. He was so soaked, he hardly felt wet: it was almost as if he were immersed in a swimming bath. In the middle of summer, both sea and rain were warm, the sole blessing Maniakes could find in the present situation.

One of the broad-beamed merchantmen carrying soldiers wallowed past. It rode lower in the water than it should have; sailors and soldiers both were bailing with might and main. Maniakes murmured a prayer that the ship would survive.

Thrax came back up toward the *Renewal*'s bow. The drungarios disdained an anchoring rope. Maniakes thought that disdain a foolish display of bravado, but held his tongue; he was not Thrax's nursemaid. At the top of his lungs, Maniakes bellowed, "How long will this storm last?"

He had to repeat himself three or four times before Thrax understood. "Don't know, your Majesty," the drungarios screamed back. He, too, did not make Maniakes hear him at the first try. When he was sure the Avtokrator had gotten his first sentence, he tried another: "Maybe it'll blow itself out by nightfall."

"That would be good," Maniakes said—and said, and said. "How long till nightfall?"

"To the ice with me if I know." Thrax pointed up to the sky. One part of it was as gray and ugly and full of driving rain as the next. The only way they would be able to tell when the sun went down was by its getting dark—or rather, darker.

Nor had Thrax promised the storm would end when night came. Maniakes, then, was faced with waiting an indefinite length of time for something that might not happen. He wished he saw a better alternative. The only alternative that came to mind, though, was drowning immediately. Compared to that, waiting was better.

Not far away, a bolt of lightning lanced down out of the sky. Purple streaks dimmed Maniakes' vision. The lightning could as easily have struck the *Renewal* as not: one more thing about which the Avtokrator tried not to think.

He tried not to think at all. In the storm, thinking did him no good. He was just another frightened animal here, trying to ride out the forces of nature. On dry land, in among his soldiers or in a sturdy fortress, he could fancy himself the lord of all he surveyed. Here he surveyed little, and could control none of it.

A little while later, Rhegorios emerged from his cabin. A sailor gave him a safety line, which he accepted with some reluctance. "I thought you'd have been here on deck for the whole storm," Maniakes said. "You're always wild for adventures like this."

His cousin grimaced. "I've been puking my guts up, is what I've been doing, if you really want to know. I always thought I was a decent sailor, but I've never been in anything like—" Instead of finishing the sentence, Rhegorios leaned over the rail. When the spasm passed, he said, "I wish they hadn't given me this cursed rope. Now it's harder for me to throw myself into the sea."

"It's not that bad," Maniakes said, but all that meant was, it wasn't that bad for him. Rhegorios laughed at him—till he started retching again. Maniakes tried to hold the hair out of his face while he heaved.

"Is it getting darker?" Rhegorios asked when he could speak again. "Or am I starting to die?"

Maniakes hadn't paid much attention to the sky for a while, most likely because he'd come to assume the day would never end. Now he looked up. It *was* darker. "Thrax said the storm might blow itself out when night fell," he shouted hopefully, over the roar of the wind.

"Here's hoping Thrax is right." Rhegorios' abused stomach

rebelled again. Nothing came forth this time, but he looked as miserable as if something had. "I hate the dry heaves," he said, adding, "Bloody shame they're the only thing about me I can call dry." Water dripped from his beard, from the tip of his nose, from his hair, from his sleeves, and from his elbows when he bent his arms. Maniakes, who had stayed on deck through most of the storm, was wetter still, but the distinction would be meaningless in moments.

Darkness, having once made an appearance, quickly descended on the sea. The rain dropped from torrent to trickle; the wind ebbed. "Praise the good god, lads," Thrax shouted to the crew. "I think we've come though the worst."

A couple of sailors took him literally, either reciting Phos' creed or sending their own prayers of thanks to the lord with the great and good mind. Maniakes murmured a prayer of his own, part thanks but more a fervent hope the storm really was over and would not resume with the dawn.

"Break out a torch, boys!" Thrax yelled. "Let's find out if we have any friends left on the ocean."

Maniakes would have bet a dry torch or, for that matter, any means of setting it alight, could not be found anywhere aboard the *Renewal*. He would have lost that bet, and in short order, too. Even in darkness, more than one sailor hurried for the torches wrapped in layer on layer of oiled canvas. And the cook had a firesafe, a good-sized pot in which embers were always smoldering. Thrax took the blazing torch and waved it back and forth.

One by one, other torches came to life on the Sailors' Sea, some close by, others so far off they were hard to tell from stars near the horizon. But there were no stars, the sky still being full of clouds. The ships that had survived the storm crawled across the water toward one another. When they got within hailing range, captains shouted back and forth, setting forth the toll of those known lost and, by silences, of those missing.

"It's not so bad as it looks, your Majesty," Thrax said, somewhere getting on toward midnight. "More will join us tomorrow morning, and more still, blown so far off course that they can't see any torches at all, will make straight for the imperial city. Not everybody who isn't here is gone for good."

"Yes, I understand that," Maniakes answered. "And some, like that one transport out there somewhere—" He pointed vaguely past the bow of the *Renewal.* "—can't show torches because they haven't got any fire left. I think it's Phos' own miracle so many of our ships have been able to make lights. But still—"

But still. In any context, those words were ominous, implying lost gold, lost chances, lost hopes. Here they meant lost ships, lost men, lost animals—so many lost without any possibility of rescue, as when the dromon had broken up in the raging sea not far from the flagship.

Not all the survivors had stories like that to tell, but too many of them did. Maniakes did what he could to piece together his losses, bearing in mind what Thrax had said. They came to somewhere not far from a quarter of the force with which he'd set out from Lyssaion. He hoped not too many of the ships Thrax reckoned scattered were in fact lost.

"And speaking of scattered," he said around a yawn, "where are we, anyhow?" He yawned again; now that the storm and the crises were for the moment past, he felt with full—perhaps with double—measure how tired and worn he was.

"To the ice with me if I know exactly, your Majesty," Thrax answered. "We'll sail north when morning comes, and we'll sight land, and we'll figure out what land we've sighted. Then we'll know where we're at, and how far away from Videssos the city we are, too."

"All right," Maniakes said mildly. He was no sailor, but he'd spent enough time at sea to know that navigation was an art almost as arcane as magecraft, and less exact. Knowing how to find out where they were was nearly as good as knowing where.

He undid the rope that had been around his waist so long, he'd almost forgotten it was there. Nothing worse than gentle chop stirred the *Renewal*'s deck under his feet as he walked to the cabin. He opened the door as quietly as he could. Lysia's soft snores did not break their rhythm. He lay down in wet robes on wet bedding and fell asleep himself.

A sunbeam in his face woke him. For a moment, he simply accepted that, as he had clouds at sunset before. Then he sketched Phos' sun-circle over his heart, a sign of delight. He'd never known anything more welcome than a day of fair weather.

Still in those wet robes, he went out on deck. Sailors were busy repairing storm damage to the railing, to the rigging of the square sail, and to rips in its canvas. They'd taken it down fast when the storm struck, but not fast enough.

Thrax pointed north. "Land there, your Majesty. If I remember the shape of it aright, we're not so far from the imperial city as I would have guessed."

"Good," Maniakes said. "Aye, that's good." Spotting small sails on the sea between the fleet and shore, he pointed in his turn, off to the northwest. "Look. All the fishermen who weren't sunk yesterday are out after whatever they can get today."

"What's that, your Majesty?" Thrax hadn't noticed the sails. Now he did, and stiffened. "Those aren't fishermen, your Majesty. Those are cursed monoxyla, is what those are." His voice rose to a bellow: "Make ready for battle!"

The fleet could hardly have been less ready to fight, battered by the storm as it was. All Thrax had wanted to do, all Maniakes had wanted to do, was limp into Videssos the city, unload the warriors and animals, and take a little while to figure out what to do next. Once again, the Avtokrator wasn't going to get what he wanted. The Kubratoi in their single-trunk boats were making sure of that.

"Dart-thrower's going to be useless," Thrax grumbled, pointing to the engine at the *Renewal*'s bow. "Cords are sure to be too soaked to do any good."

Maniakes didn't answer at once. Till this moment, he'd never actually seen any of the vessels the Kubratoi had been using for years to raid his coast. They were, he discovered, more formidable than their name suggested. Each one might have been hewn from a single trunk, but the Kubratoi had taken forest giants from which to make their boats. Some of them looked to be almost as long as the *Renewal*, though of course they carried far fewer men. Along with their sails, which were made of leather, they were propelled by paddles—and propelled surprisingly fast, too.

They had spotted the Videssian ships, either before they were seen themselves or at about the same moment. Maniakes had expected that would be plenty to make them flee. Instead, they swung toward the Videssians. The paddles rose and fell, rose and fell, rose and fell. Yes, they could make a very good turn of speed.

"We'll smash them," Maniakes said.

Now Thrax didn't reply right away. He looked distinctly less happy than Maniakes would have liked to see him. At last, he said, "Your Majesty, I'm not worried about the dromons. The transports are a different game, though."

He started shouting orders across the water. Trumpeters echoed his commands. The dromons slid toward the less mobile, less protected vessels they were shepherding to the imperial city. They were none too soon in doing so, either, for the Kubratoi had no more trouble figuring out the way the game needed to be played than did Thrax. Their monoxyla were also making for the slower, beamier ships in the Videssian fleet.

"Maybe we ought to let them try to board one of the troop transports," Thrax said. "I don't think they'd be glad they'd done it."

"Something to that," Maniakes agreed, but neither one of them meant it seriously, as they both knew. Maniakes put that into words: "Too many things could go wrong. They might get lucky, or they might manage to start a fire—"

"Wouldn't be easy, not today," Thrax said, "not with the timbers soaked from yesterday's storm. But you're right, your Majesty: it could happen."

One of the dromons, oars slashing the water, rushed at a monoxylon. The Kubratoi not only managed to avoid the bronze-shod ram at the dromon's bow, they sprayed the Videssian ship with arrows. A sailor fell *splash!* into the sea.

Another single-trunk vessel got up alongside a ship transporting horses. The Kubratoi didn't try swarming aboard the vessel, but, again, shot arrows at it as rapidly as if they were shooting at Videssian soldiers from horseback.

Thrax pointed to that monoxylon. "They're so busy doing what they're doing, they aren't paying any attention to us." He shouted to the oarmaster: "Build the stroke. Give us everything you have!"

"Aye, lord," the oarmaster replied. The drum that beat time for the rowers on the two-man sweeps speeded its rhythm. The rowers responded. The wake leaping out from under the *Renewal's* hull got thicker and whiter. Thrax ran back to the dromon's stern to take charge of one of the steering oars and yell directions to the man at the other.

Maniakes, by contrast, hurried up toward the bow. He hadn't been in a sea fight since the one in the waters just off Videssos the city that let him enter the capital. This wasn't like fighting on land; ships carried a company's worth of men, but were themselves individual pieces, and valuable ones, on the game board.

The *Renewal* had closed to within fifty yards before the Kubratoi realized the dromon was there. They were close enough for Maniakes to hear their shouts of dismay when at last they spied her. They threw down their bows then and snatched up their paddles, doing their best to escape the pointed, sea-greened beak aimed square at their stem.

Their best was not good enough. They'd slowed to stay alongside the transport, and needed time to build up speed again—time they did not get. Thrax had a nice sense of aim and timing. He drove the ram home as the Kubratoi turned slightly broadside to his dromon.

The ram did not hole the monoxylon, as it would have done to a Videssian vessel. Instead, the *Renewal* rode up and over the smaller Kubratoi craft, rolling and crushing it. The collision staggered Maniakes, who almost went into the sea. What it did to the Kubratoi—

Heads bobbed in the sea, but surprisingly few of them. The Kubratoi were demons on horseback; Maniakes had never before had occasion to wonder how many of them could swim. The answer, it seemed, was *not many*. Some, who might or might not have known how to swim, clung to paddles or other floating bits of wreckage.

Videssian sailors shot arrows at the struggling Kubratoi. From what Maniakes could see, they scored few hits. It didn't matter. Either the Kubratoi would drown, or some Videssian ship would capture them once the sea fight was done. They might well have preferred to drown.

"Well done!" Thrax bellowed. "Now let's get another one." He steered the *Renewal* in the direction of the next closest monoxylon. "Keep us going there, oarmaster!" he added. The thudding drum that pounded out the strokes never faltered.

Unlike the Videssian fleet, the Kubratoi must have stayed ashore during the storm. That meant they had no trouble getting fires started. Several single-log craft bobbed in the waves near another transport. Smoke trails through the air showed they were shooting fire arrows at it.

Maniakes wished he could have seen more of how that came out, but the *Renewal* was bearing down on the monoxylon Thrax had chosen as his new target. This one, unlike the first, was not taken unawares, and the Kubrati commanding it was doing everything he could to get away. The little leather sail was raised and full of air; the paddles beat the water to froth as the nomads worked for all they were worth.

"Prepare to ram!" This time, Thrax had the courtesy to shout the warning a couple of seconds before his dromon crunched into the single-log boat. Again, Maniakes staggered at the impact. Again, the *Renewal* went right over the monoxylon. This time, though, that was a slower, more grinding business, because the difference in speed between the two vessels was much smaller than it had been before.

Again, Kubratoi spilled into the water. Again, many of them quickly sank to their deaths. But a few managed to catch hold of the *Renewal*'s planking and scramble up onto the deck.

They were dripping. By the look in their eyes, they were half-stunned and more. But none of them seemed in any mood to surrender. They wore swords on their belts. Drawing them, they rushed at the Videssian sailors—and one of them came straight for Maniakes.

He was so startled, he almost left his own sword in its scabbard till too late. He yanked it out just in time to turn aside a fierce cut at his head. The Kubrati then chose a low line, slashing at his shins. He parried again, and hopped back. The fellow might not have been an outrageously good swordsman, but enough grim energy for at least three men filled him.

One sailor was down and screaming. Others, though, fought the Kubratoi with swords and bows and clubs. Once the first surprise at being boarded began to fade, they realized how greatly they outnumbered their assailants. The fight on deck did not last long after that.

Somebody clubbed the Kubrati who was fighting Maniakes. The fellow groaned and staggered. Maniakes' sword ripped his belly open. The Avtokrator twisted his wrist to make sure it was a killing stroke. The Kubrati did not scream or clutch at himself;

the blow to the side of his head must have dazed him and given him an easy death.

He had been almost the last of his people still upright. Maniakes pulled his sword free, grabbed the Kubrati by the heels, and said, "Let's throw this carrion overboard," to the sailor with the bludgeon. The Kubrati's body splashed into the Sailors' Sea.

Thrax pointed. "Ahh, the filthy bastards, they did manage to burn one," he shouted. In spite of wet timbers, flames were spreading on one of the transports. Videssian soldiers and sailors leapt into the water. Like the Kubratoi from sunken and capsized monoxyla, they grabbed for anything they could reach to keep themselves afloat a little longer.

"Shall we pick them up or pursue the foe, your Majesty?" Thrax asked. The monoxyla still unsunk had clearly had enough of the unequal fight with the Videssian dromons. Under sail and paddle, they were heading off to the east as fast as they could go.

Maniakes hesitated not even a heartbeat. "We make pickup," he said. "Then we head on to the imperial city. To the ice with the Kubratoi; let 'em go."

"Aye, your Majesty," Thrax said. He bawled the needed orders, then turned back to the Avtokrator with a puzzled look on his face. "You usually want to finish the foe when you find the chance."

"Yes, usually." Maniakes fought hard to hold in his exasperation. Thrax sometimes had trouble seeing past the end of his nose. "Now, though, the most important thing we can do is get back to Videssos the city and make sure it doesn't fall. Those single-trunk boats were sailing straight away from it. We're not going to waste time going after them."

"Ah," Thrax said. "When you put it that way, it does make sense, doesn't it?"

To give him his due, he handled the rescue of the men who had abandoned the burning transport about as well as anyone could have done. A good many soldiers were lost, drowned before any rescuers could reach them, but a good many were pulled from the sea, too. It could have been worse. How many times had Maniakes thought that after some new misfortune?

Bagdasares' magic had shown no further trouble facing the Videssian fleet after the storm and the attack by those other ships. Maybe that meant they would reach Videssos the city with ease once they'd surmounted that attack—in the case of the *Renewal*, literally, as it rode over the Kubratoi monoxyla. Then again, maybe it meant Bagdasares had metaphorically had his elbow joggled before the sorcery showed everything it could. One way or the other, Maniakes expected he would learn soon.

Close by the imperial city, no single-log boats dared show themselves by day. The fleet based in the capital made sure of that. But, from the *Renewal*, Maniakes saw the nomads' encampments outside the double wall of the capital. That ate at him, as did knowing Makuraner engineers were teaching the Kubratoi the art of building siege engines. From now on, no Videssian city would be safe.

From the walls, Videssian defenders cheered when they saw the imperial standard flying from the *Renewal*. Maniakes did not flatter himself that all those cheers were for him. He had taken to Makuran the best soldiers the Empire of Videssos had. Getting those soldiers back made Videssos the city likelier to hold. Had he been a defender hopefully awaiting them, he would have cheered their return, too.

"We'll land as many ships as we can in the little harbor for the palace quarter," he told Thrax. "That will include the *Renewal*."

"Aye, your Majesty," the drungarios said, nodding in obedience. "You'll want to send the rest around to the Neorhesian harbor in the north?"

"That's right," Maniakes agreed.

"When we tie up at that little harbor, you'll be able to get a good look at what's going on in Across," Thrax said, as if the idea had only just occurred to him. It probably *had* only just occurred to him; that saddened Maniakes, who was used to looking further ahead. Thrax could, of course, have been the sort of man who did not look ahead at all; too many men were like that. But in that case he would not have been drungarios of the fleet.

Across looked to be buzzing. The red-lion banner of Makuran flew from a silk pavilion situated barely out of range of dart-throwers mounted on dromons. Yes, Abivard would know exactly how far that was, having spent so much time on the wrong—or, from the Videssian perspective, the right—side of the Cattle Crossing from Videssos the city.

Maniakes wondered whether the Makuraner marshal remained on the western side of the Cattle Crossing, or whether the Kubratoi had sneaked him over the narrow strait so he could gauge the land walls of the imperial city with his own eyes. Suddenly and rather sharply, the Avtokrator wondered which side of the Cattle Crossing Tzikas was on these days. Before he began his treacheries, Tzikas had been a Videssian general, and a formidably good one. If anyone knew of weaknesses in the walls—if there were any weaknesses to know—he was likely to be the man.

The Makuraners saw the imperial standard, too, when the *Renewal* drew near Across to give Maniakes a closer look at them. The curses they sent his way warred with the cheers from Videssos the city. Their whole camp was much closer to the Cattle Crossing than had been their way during earlier stays in Across. Then they had seemed content merely to have come so close to Videssos' capital. Now they had the notion they could cross, could reach the goal so long denied them.

"They're wrong," Maniakes murmured. Saying that and ensuring it was true, though, were two different things. Maniakes turned back to Thrax. "Take us to the harbor. I've seen enough here."

With his father, and with Rhegorios and Symvatios, Maniakes passed through the Silver Gate's opening in the inner wall of Videssos the city and strode out toward the lower outer wall. "By the lord with the great and good mind, the parasol-bearers are still fuming because I wouldn't let them come out here with me," he said, fuming himself. "That would be all I needed, wouldn't it? Showing the Kubratoi exactly whom to shoot, I mean."

"That's the kind of nonsense you don't have to put up with in the field," the elder Maniakes agreed. "I don't blame you for getting out of Videssos the city whenever you can, son. You don't have idiots getting in the way of what needs doing."

"No," the Avtokrator said. Escaping the stifling ceremonial of the imperial court *was* one reason he was glad to get out of Videssos the city. He noticed his father did not mention the other one. The elder Maniakes did not approve of his marriage to Lysia, either, but, unlike so many in the city, was at least willing to keep quiet about it.

The massive portals of the Silver Gate's entryway through the outer wall were shut. The even more massive bars that held those portals closed were in place in their great iron brackets. Behind the gate, the iron-faced portcullis was lowered into its place in the gateway. Up above it, murder holes let defenders pour boiling water and heated sand down on the heads of warriors who might try to break down the defenses. Maniakes would not have cared to assault the Silver Gate, were he besieger rather than besieged.

But, if the Makuraners taught the Kubratoi how to build and use siege engines, they would not have to attack the gate. They might choose instead to try to break down some less heavily defended stretch of wall. If they had any sense, that was what they would do. But who could say for certain what lay in Etzilios' mind? Maniakes wondered whether the Kubrati khagan himself knew.

The Avtokrator climbed the stone stairway to the walk atop the outer wall. His father, cousin, and uncle followed. He tried to make himself climb slowly out of consideration for the elder Maniakes and Symvatios, but they were both breathing hard by the time they gained the walkway.

Maniakes peered out toward the Kubratoi camp nearby. Etzilios had chosen to set his own tent opposite the Silver Gate, the chief way into Videssos the city. The horsetail standards that marked his tent were unmistakable. Also as near unmistakable as made no difference was the banner fluttering next to that standard. White and red . . . Maniakes could not make out the lion of Makuran on the flag, but had no doubt it was there.

Kubratoi rode back and forth, out beyond the ditch in front of the wall. They weren't doing much: he didn't see any of them shooting arrows at the Videssians defending the city, for instance. But they were alert enough to make a sally look like a bad idea.

"How are we fixed for grain?" Maniakes asked. He looked back over his shoulder. The bulk of the inner wall hid Videssos the city from his view. He could feel the weight of its populace pressing out at him all the same. How many people did the city hold? A hundred thousand? A quarter of a million? Twice that? He didn't know, not even within such a broad range. What he did know was that, however many of them there were, they all needed to eat and to keep on eating.

"We're not too bad off," Symvatios answered. "The granaries were fairly full when the siege started, and we've been bringing in more from further south and east, where the Kubratoi haven't reached. We can last . . . a while."

"Other question is, how long can the Kubratoi last out there?"

The elder Maniakes pointed toward Etzilios' encampment. "What do they do for food once they've eaten the countryside empty?"

"Starve or go home," Rhegorios said. "Those are the choices they have."

"Those are two of the choices they have," Maniakes said, which made his cousin look puzzled. Wishing he didn't have to, the Avtokrator explained: "They can also try breaking into the city. If they do that, it doesn't matter how much grain we have left or how little food they have. If they break in, they win."

Rhegorios nodded, now unwontedly serious. "Do you know, cousin of mine—" He didn't string titles together now, either. "—that never crossed my mind. In spite of everything they've gathered out there, I have trouble making myself believe they might break in."

"We all have trouble believing it," the elder Maniakes said. "That may be good or bad. It's good if the Kubratoi have doubts in the same proportion as we have confidence. But if we're slack because we know Videssos the city has never fallen and they're all eager and zealous to make a first time, we're in trouble."

"That's so," Maniakes said. "They haven't tried storming the walls?"

His father shook his head. "No. Some days they aren't quiet like this, though. They'll come up into archery range and shoot at our people on the walls. They haven't done that so much lately. It's as if they're—waiting."

"And we know what they're waiting for, too," the Avtokrator said unhappily. "They're waiting to see what the Makuraners can show them and how much help it will be. The boiler boys are good at what they do, too. I wish they weren't, but they know as much about siege warfare as any Videssian."

"Abivard will probably want to get more of his people over to this side of the Cattle Crossing before any serious attack on the walls," Symvatios said. "He won't fancy the Kubratoi taking all the spoils if we fall."

"And they won't want him taking any—Etzilios sucked in treachery at his mother's breast." Maniakes grew thoughtful. "I wonder if we can make the allies distrust each other more than they hate us."

"That *is* an interesting notion," the elder Maniakes said. He, too, stared out toward the Kubrati camp. "I have to say I'd guess the odds are against it. We might as well try, though. The worst they can tell us is no."

"The world doesn't end if you get your face slapped," Rhegorios remarked. "You just ask another girl the same question. Or sometimes you ask the same girl the same question a little later on, and you get a different answer."

"Hear the voice of experience," Maniakes said dryly. His cousin coughed and spluttered. His father and uncle both laughed. The world looked a little brighter, giving him three, maybe even four, heartbeats' worth of relief—till he thought about the Kubratoi again.

A postern gate swung open. Despite all the grease the soldiers had poured onto the hinges, they still squeaked. Maniakes wondered when anyone had last oiled them. Had it been a year ago, or five, or ten? Till this year, no one had expected Videssos the city to be besieged, and a siege was the only time when a postern gate was useful.

"Curse it, we don't want to let all the Kubratoi and Makuraners know we're doing this," the Avtokrator hissed. "The idea is to keep it secret—otherwise we wouldn't have chosen midnight."

"Sorry, your Majesty," the officer in charge of the gate answered, also in a low voice. "That's as quiet as we could manage." He peered out into the darkness. "Here comes the fellow, so he is on time. I wouldn't have thought it, not with a barbarian."

No shouts from the wall above warned of any other Kubratoi moving forward with the single emissary Maniakes had suggested to Etzilios. The khagan was keeping his end of the bargain, most likely because he didn't think he could wring any great advantage from betraying it now. At Maniakes' command, the soldiers at the postern gate ran a long plank out over the far side of the ditch.

"Mind you don't fall off," one of the men called softly to the newcomer. "It's a goodish way down."

"I shall beens very carefuls, thank youse," the Kubrati answered in Videssian fractured but fluent. His footfalls thudded confidently on the gangway. When he came into Videssos the city, the guardsmen pulled back the plank and shut the postern gate once more.

"Moundioukh, isn't it?" Maniakes said. No torches burned

nearby—that would have given away the parley. But the Avtokrator had heard only one man capable of mangling Videssian as this fellow did.

And, sure enough, the Kubrati nodded in the darkness and said, "Whose else would the magnifolent Etzilios sends to treat against youse?" Maniakes wondered whether that *against* was more slipshod grammar or a slip of the tongue. He'd find out.

With the gate closed, a couple of torchbearers came hurrying up. Yes, that was Moundioukh, in the flesh as well as in the voice. His scraggly beard had more gray in it than Maniakes remembered. "Your master is a treacherous man," the Avtokrator said severely.

To his surprise, Moundioukh burst out laughing. "Of courses him are," the Kubrati answered. "Otherwisely him never talkings at youse."

"I daresay," Maniakes said. "All right—what does he want from me for him to give over his alliance with the Makuraners? I presume there must be something I can give him, or he wouldn't have sent you to me."

Moundioukh's large, square teeth flashed in the torchlight as he laughed again. "The magnifolent Etzilios tell me, 'Go to this Maniakes. See him crawl. See him slithither'—is word, yes, slithithering? 'Then youse tells he what me tells youse.'"

"And what did the magnifolent Etzilios tell you?" Maniakes knew a certain amount of pride at bringing the epithet out with a straight face.

"Not seen enough of slithitherings yettish times," the Kubratoi replied pointedly.

Maniakes exhaled through his nose in exasperation. "To the ice with him, and to the ice with you, too. I don't know what else I can do but tell you I'll do whatever you and the khagan want." He couldn't say *magnifolent* again, no matter how hard he tried.

"You prostitute yourselves for I, like youse always having I prostitute myselves to youse?" Moundioukh said.

The guards growled. "He means 'prostrate,'" Maniakes said quickly. He wondered if that made the demand any more bearable. He was vicegerent of Phos on earth; who was this nasty barbarian envoy to demand that he go down on his belly before him? *The man with the whip hand*—the answer was painfully plain. "I said *anything*, and I was not lying." Maniakes did the deed. He'd seen it performed before him countless times, but hadn't done it himself since Likinios Avtokrator sat on the Videssian throne. His body, he discovered, still remembered how.

"Youse really doing this things." Moundioukh sounded amazed.

"Yes, I really did it. Have I slithithered enough for you now?" After performing a proskynesis, desecrating the Videssian language came easy.

"Is enoughly, yeses," Moundioukh admitted. "Now we tells youse what the magnifolent khagan tell we. He tell, nothing in all these world youse does—" He made it sound like *yooz dooz*. "—am enoughs to make he go buggering Makuraners. Us, theys see chance to slaughterize you, and usses takes it."

"You and the Makuraners would quarrel afterward, even if you won," Maniakes said. "We have a saying—'thieves fall out.'"

"We quarrels?" Moundioukh shrugged. "Then we quarrels. Not having mores of quarrels with Videssians, not nevers again. Magnifolent Etzilios sezzing, that worths any sizes of quarrelings with Makuran."

The khagan was probably right, too, when you looked at things from the Kubrati point of view. If Videssos the city fell, it would be a frontier province to the Makuraners, far from their center. But Videssos the city was the very heart of the Empire of Videssos. Cut it out and the Empire had no heart left. Free rein hereabouts, near enough—that was the stake for which Etzilios was playing.

"And beside," Moundioukh added, "you beat Etzilios. He pay youse back how youse am deservings."

For a barbarian, the khagan was a rational man. But a hunger for revenge, coupled with sound reasons of policy, could make him unreasonable—and apparently had made him so. "If I hadn't beaten him, he would have been down here by the city years before," Maniakes pointed out.

"Should has beed," Moundioukh said. "Should has killed you in trick making treaty. Save Kubrat shitpot full troubles, that beed happening."

"I'm so sorry," Maniakes said dryly. "I should have killed Etzilios, that last fight where I landed troops behind your raiders. That would have saved me a lot of trouble."

"Now youse gots troubles, Etzilios gots troubles, all gots troubles,"

Moundioukh said, apparently in agreement. "Am time of troubles."

"No agreement from the khagan, then?" Maniakes said unhappily.

"Nones," Moundioukh said. "He says I says no. Youse pushing, I says no and futter yourself, youse pushings hard and I tells youse something really with lots of juices in it. You wants I should?" He sounded delighted to oblige.

"Never mind," Maniakes told him. He didn't bother waving the torchbearers away from the postern gate now—if any Makuraners saw Moundioukh coming back, maybe they'd think the Kubratoi were betraying them even when they weren't. "Let him out," he said to the men in charge of the gate. "We're not going to be able to come to terms."

Having opened once, the gate proved more willing to do so quietly the second time—when Maniakes would have preferred it noisy. The Videssian soldiers slid the gangway out across the ditch. Moundioukh walked across it. This time, no one urged him to be careful. If he fell down and broke his neck in the ditch now, what difference would it make? None Maniakes could see.

"I think that was worth a try, your Majesty," the officer in charge of the gate said. "We're no worse off now than we were before."

"That's true." Maniakes remembered throwing away his crown and the rest of the imperial regalia to escape the Kubratoi when they'd ambushed him in that treaty ceremony. "Aye," he said, half to himself, "I've had worse from the nomads. This time, Moundioukh didn't cost me anything but my dignity."

"I kept hoping it wasn't true," Maniakes said, looking out from a tower thrusting up from the inner wall.

"Well, it bloody well *is* true," Rhegorios answered. He was looking in the same direction. "You're not going to try and tell me the Kubratoi could build those all on their lonesome, are you?"

Those were siege engines, some of them stone- and dart-throwers, others the skeletal beginnings of towers to overtop the outer wall. On the timber frames, the Kubratoi would soon add raw hides to make the towers harder to burn. If they could bring them up to the wall, they'd be able to put men on the walkway. If they did that, anything could happen.

"You're right, of course—they couldn't," Maniakes said unhappily. "Abivard, Skotos curse him to the ice—" He turned his head and performed the ritual expectoration. "—did sneak one of his engineers, or maybe more than one, over the Cattle Crossing. Those are Makuraner-style engines, or else I'm a wolf with a purple pelt."

"Nothing would surprise me, not anymore," his cousin said. "The only worse thing would be having to try handstrokes with all those heavy-armored Makuraners."

"That mail is better for horseback," Maniakes said.

"I know," Rhegorios replied. "But it's not so heavy they can't use it afoot, either, and I wouldn't want to be in their way if they tried."

"Well, neither would I," the Avtokrator admitted. "The key to making sure that doesn't happen is keeping them on . . . the far side of the Cattle Crossing." He scowled, angry at himself. "I almost said, keeping them on their own side of the Cattle Crossing. It's not theirs. It's ours. I aim to get it back, too."

"Sounds fine to me," Rhegorios said "How do you propose to do that?"

"Which? Keep them on that side of the Cattle Crossing or get the westlands back?"

"Whichever you'd rather tell me about. You're the Avtokrator, after all." Rhegorios gave him a saucy grin.

"And you're incorrigible," Maniakes retorted. "We've got drom-ons prowling up and down the coast, north and east from the city. Whenever they find any of the Kubrati monoxyla, they burn them or sink them. The trouble is, they don't find that many. The cursed things are too fornicating easy to hide. We're doing what we can. I console myself with that."

"Something," his cousin agreed. "Maybe not much, but something. How about getting the westlands back?"

"How about that?" Maniakes said, deadpan, and then made as if not to go on. When Rhegorios was somewhere between lese majesty and physical assault, the Avtokrator, chuckling, deigned to continue: "Once this siege fails, I don't think they'll be able to mount another one for a long time. That gives the choice of what to do next back to me. How does another trip to the Land of the Thousand Cities sound? Better that Sharbaraz should worry about his capital than that we worry about ours."

"That's the truth." Rhegorios sent him a respectful look. "You really do have it figured out, don't you?"

Maniakes coughed, spluttered, and finally laughed out loud. "I know what I'd *like* to do, yes. How much I'm going to be *able* to do is another question, and a harder one, worse luck."

Rhegorios looked thoughtful. "Maybe we ought to use our ships against the Kubratoi the way we did three years ago: land troops behind their army and catch 'em between hammer and anvil."

"Maybe," Maniakes said. "I've thought about it. The trouble is, Etzilios is looking for it this time. The dromon captains report that he's got squads posted along the coast every mile or so, to bring him word if we do land. We wouldn't catch him by surprise, the way we did then. And the likeliest thing for him to do would be trying to storm the city as soon as he heard we'd pulled out some of the garrison."

"That makes unfortunately too much sense," Rhegorios said. "You're quite sharp when you get logical, you know. You should have been a theologian."

"No, thank you," Maniakes said at once. "I've had so much trouble from the theologians, I wouldn't want to inflict another one on the world. Besides, I'd be an indifferent theologian at best, and I'm vain enough to think I make something better than an indifferent Avtokrator."

"I'd say so," Rhegorios agreed. "Of course, if I said anything else, I'd get to find out how the weather is up at Prista this time of year." He was joking; he didn't expect to be sent into exile across the Videssian Sea. The joke, though, illustrated the problem Maniakes had in getting straight answers from his subjects, no matter how much he needed them.

And some of the answers he got from his subjects he didn't like for other reasons. As he was riding back to the palace quarter from the walls, a fellow in a dirty tunic shouted to him, "This is your fault, curse you! If you hadn't married your cousin, Phos wouldn't be punishing all of Videssos and letting Skotos loose here for your sins!"

Some of the Avtokrator's guardsmen tried to seize the heckler, but he escaped them. Once away from Middle Street, he lost himself in the maze of lanes and alleys that made up most of the city's roads. The guards came back looking angry and disappointed.

"Don't worry about it," Maniakes said resignedly. "Skotos will have his way with that fellow. I hope he enjoys ice, because he's going to see an eternity of it."

He hoped that, by making light of the incident, he would persuade the guards it wasn't worth mentioning. Otherwise, they would gossip about it with the serving women, and from them it would get back to Lysia. He was also glad Rhegorios had stayed back at the wall and hadn't heard the heckler. Predicting that such troubles would be long-lasting, his cousin had proved himself a better prophet than Maniakes.

The Avtokrator didn't stay at the imperial residence long. Likarios, his son by Niphone and the heir to the throne, asked him seriously, "Papa, when they're bigger, will my little brothers throw me out of the palaces?"

"By the good god, no!" Maniakes exclaimed, sketching the sun-circle over his heart. "Who's been filling your head with nonsense?"

Likarios didn't give a direct answer; he'd very quickly learned to be circumspect. "It was just something I heard."

"Well, it's something you can forget," Maniakes told him. His son nodded, apparently satisfied. Maniakes wished he were satisfied himself. Though Likarios was his heir, the temptation remained to disinherit the boy and place the succession in the line of his sons by Lysia.

She had never urged that course on him. Had she done so, he would have worried she was out for her own advantage first and the Empire's only afterward. But that did not keep the idea from cropping up on its own.

He went out to the seawall to escape it. A dromon glided over the water of the Cattle Crossing. The sight, though, was far less reassuring than it had been when the Makuraners were encamped in Across before. Monoxyla crept out at night and made nuisances of themselves, just as mice did even in homes where cats prowled.

Then a different image occurred to him. Two or three times, in barns and stables, he'd seen snakes with their coils wrapped around rats or other smaller animals. The rats would wiggle and kick and sometimes even work a limb free for a little while, but in the end that wouldn't matter. They'd be squeezed from so many directions, they ended up dead in spite of all their thrashing.

He wished that picture hadn't come to mind. In it, the Empire of Videssos was rat, not snake.

What did Abivard plan, over there in Across? He couldn't

smuggle his whole army to this side of the Cattle Crossing ten and twenty men at a time, not if he aimed to take Videssos the city before winter came. Maniakes' guess was that he wanted to take the city as fast as he thought he could. The Kubratoi couldn't indefinitely maintain the siege on their own. They'd eat the countryside empty, and then they'd have to leave.

That meant . . . what? Probably an effort on Abivard's part to get a good-sized chunk of the Makuraner field force over here to the eastern side of the Cattle Crossing fairly soon now. If the fleet managed to stop him, the siege would probably collapse of its own weight. If the fleet didn't stop him, Videssos the city was liable to fall, all past history of invincibility notwithstanding. For the Makuraners to teach the Kubratoi siegecraft was bad enough—worse than bad enough. For the Makuraners to conduct the siege would be worse still. Unlike the nomads, they really knew what they were doing.

"I wish I had a better drungarios of the fleet," Maniakes murmured. Erinakios, the prickly former commander of the fleet of the Key, would have been ideal . . . had Genesios' chief wizard not slain him by sorcery while the tyrant was trying to hold off Maniakes.

A guardsman came trotting toward him. "Your Majesty, there's a messenger from the land wall waiting for you in the imperial residence," the fellow called.

"I'll come," Maniakes said at once. "Has the attack begun?" The Kubrati siege towers weren't finished yet, but that might not figure. If the attack had begun, all Maniakes' worries about what might be would vanish, subsumed into worries over what was. Those, at least, would be immediate, and—with luck—susceptible to immediate repair.

But the guardsman shook his head. "I don't think so, your Majesty—we'd hear the racket from here, wouldn't we? The fellow acts like it's important even so."

"You're probably right about the racket," Maniakes admitted. He followed the soldier at a pace halfway between fast walk and trot. As he hurried along, he scratched his head. He'd been at the wall only a little while before the guard arrived. What had changed of such importance, he had to find out about it right away? He forced a shrug, and forced relaxation on himself as well. He was only moments from learning.

The messenger started to prostrate himself. Maniakes, losing the patience he'd cultivated, waved for him not to bother. The man came straight to the point: "Your Majesty, Immodios, who knows him well, has spotted Tzikas out beyond the wall."

Maniakes stiffened and twitched, as if lightning had struck close by. Well, maybe that wasn't so far wrong. "Spotted him, has he?" he said. "Well, has he tried killing him yet?"

"Uh, no, your Majesty," the messenger said.

"By the good god, why not?" Maniakes demanded. He shouted for Antelope—or, if his warhorse wasn't ready, any other animal that could be saddled in a hurry. The gelding he ended up riding lacked Antelope's spark, but got him out to the wall fast enough to keep him from losing all of his temper.

The messenger led him up to the outer wall, close by one of the siege towers. Immodios stood there. He pointed outward. "There he is, your Majesty. Do you see him? The tall, lean one prowling around with the Kubratoi?"

"I see him," Maniakes answered. Tzikas stalked out beyond archery range. He wore a Makuraner caftan that billowed in the breeze, and had let his beard grow fuller than the neatly trimmed Videssian norm, but was unmistakable nonetheless. His build, as Immodios had said, set him apart from the stocky nomads who kept him company, but Maniakes thought he would have recognized him even among Makuraners, whose angular height came closer to matching his. All you had to do was wait till you saw him point at something, at anything. *I want it* radiated from every pore of his body.

A dart-thrower stood a few paces away, ready to fling its missiles at the Kubratoi when they attacked in earnest. Darts waited ready beside it, in wicker baskets that did duty for outsized quivers. It would hurl those darts farther than the strongest man could shoot a bow.

Maniakes' father had made sure Maniakes knew how to operate every sort of engine the Videssian army used. The Avtokrator could almost hear the elder Maniakes saying, "Learning doesn't do you any lasting harm, and every once in a while some piece of it—and you never know which one beforehand—will come in handy."

After sketching a salute to his father, Maniakes remarked, "I make the range out to the son of a whore to be about a furlong and a half. Does that seem about right to you, Immodios?"

"Uh, aye, your Majesty," Immodios replied. Though the question had caught him by surprise, he'd considered before he spoke. Maniakes approved of that.

He seized a dart, set it in the catapult's groove, and said, "Then perhaps you'll do me the honor of serving on the other windlass there. I don't know if we can hit him, but to the ice with me if I don't intend to try."

Immodios blinked again, then worked the windlass with a will. For a range of a furlong and a half, you wanted fifteen revolutions of the wheel; more would wind the ropes too tight and send the dart too far, while fewer and it would fall short. The wooden frame of the catapult creaked under the building tension of the rope skeins.

The dart-thrower didn't point in quite the right direction. Maniakes used a handspike to muscle it toward Tzikas. He checked his aim with two pins driven into the frame parallel to the groove. Still not quite right. He levered the engine around a little further with the handspike, then grunted in satisfaction.

Tzikas paid no attention to the activity of the wall. He was pointing to something at ground level, something to which the Kubratoi were paying rapt attention. Maniakes hoped they would go right on paying rapt attention to it. He looked over to Immodios. "Are we ready?"

"Aye, your Majesty, I believe we are," the somber officer answered.

Maniakes picked up a wooden mallet and gave the trigger a sharp whack. That released the casting arms, which jerked forward, sending the dart on its way. The engine that had propelled it bucked like a wild ass. Half the frame jounced up in the air. It crashed back down to the walkway a moment later.

The dart flew straight toward Tzikas, faster and on a flatter trajectory than any archer could have propelled a shaft. "I think we're going to—" Maniakes' voice rose in excitement.

A Kubrati strode in front of the Videssian renegade. The nomad must have spied the dart, for he flung his arms wide an instant before it struck him. Before he had a chance to do anything more, he himself was flung aside by the terrible impact.

"Stupid fool," Maniakes snarled. "To the ice with him—it was Tzikas I wanted." He seized another dart and thrust it into the catapult's trough.

Too late. Even as he and Immodios worked the windlasses on either side of the engine, he knew it was too late. Tzikas and the Kubratoi were scattering, all except the luckless fellow the dart had slaughtered. He lay where he had fallen, as a cockroach will after a shoe lands on it.

Maniakes sent that second dart whizzing through the air. It nearly nailed another nomad, and missed Tzikas by no more than ten or twelve feet. The traitor kept right on going till he was out of range of the engines on the wall. He knew to the foot how far they could throw. *He ought to,* Maniakes thought bitterly.

"Close," Immodios said.

"Close, aye," Maniakes answered. "Close isn't good enough. I wanted him dead. I thought I had him. A little bit of luck—" He shook his head. He hadn't seen much of that during his reign, and whatever he had, he'd had to make for himself. A timely error by the enemy, a truly important Makuraner message falling into his hands . . . the next time he saw anything like that would be the first.

"I wonder what the traitor was showing the Kubratoi," Immodios remarked.

"I have no idea," Maniakes said. "I don't much care, either. The trouble is, he can still show it to them whenever he wants, whatever it may be. He wouldn't be showing them anything if it hadn't been for that one miserable nomad, may Skotos clutch him forever." That the Kubrati had paid with his life for moving into the wrong place at the wrong time seemed to Maniakes not nearly punishment enough.

Immodios persisted: "What does Tzikas know about the way the city walls are built?"

"Quite a lot, worse luck for us," Maniakes answered. "He's not going to get close enough to use whatever he knows, though, not if I have anything to say about it."

But how much would he have to say about it? Immodios, being alert, sharp-eyed, and a former colleague of Tzikas', had recognized the traitor at long range. How many other officers were likely to do the same tomorrow, or the day after, or in a week? The longer Maniakes thought about that, the less he liked the answer he came up with.

Whatever Tzikas knew, he'd probably have the chance to show it to the men he now called his friends . . . unless he decided to betray them again. If Tzikas did that, Maniakes decided, he would welcome him with open arms. And if that wasn't a measure of his own desperation, he didn't know what was.

Watching the Kubrati siege towers grow and get bedecked with hides and with shields on top of those was almost like watching saplings shoot up and put out leaves as spring gave way to summer. Maniakes found only two differences: the towers grew faster than any saplings, and they got uglier as they came closer to completion, where leaves made trees more beautiful.

The Kubratoi were being more methodical about the entire siege than Maniakes would have thought possible before it began. He credited that to—or rather, blamed it on—the Makuraners the nomads' monoxyla had smuggled over from the westlands. Abivard and his officers knew patience and its uses.

Well out of range of Videssian arrows or darts or flung stones, the Kubratoi practiced climbing up into their siege towers and rushing up the wooden stairs they'd made. They also practiced moving the ungainly erections, with horses and mules on ropes and then by men inside the towers.

"They're going to find out that's not so easy as they think," the elder Maniakes remarked one day as he and his son watched a siege tower crawl along at a pace just about fast enough to catch and mash a snail—always provided you didn't give the snail a running start.

"I think you're right, Father," the Avtokrator agreed. "Nobody's shooting at them now. No matter what they do, they won't be able to keep all our darts and stones from doing them damage when the fighting starts."

"That does make a bit of a difference, doesn't it?" the elder Maniakes said with a rheumy chuckle. "You know it, and I know it, and Etzilios has been too good a bandit over the years not to know it, but does your ordinary, everyday Kubrati know it? If he doesn't, he'll learn quick, the poor sod."

"What do we do if the nomads manage to get men on the wall in spite of everything we've done to stop 'em?" Maniakes asked.

"Kill the bastards," his father answered at once. "Until Etzilios rides into the palace quarter or the Mobedhan-Mobhed chases the patriarch out of the High Temple, I'm too stubborn to think I'm beat. Even then, I think I'm going to take some convincing."

Maniakes smiled. He only wished things were as simple as his father, a man of the old school, still reckoned them to be. "I admire the spirit," he said, "but how do we go on if that happens?"

"*I* don't know," his father answered, a little testily. "Best thing I can think of is to make sure it doesn't."

"Sounds easy, when you put it that way," Maniakes said, and the elder Maniakes let out a grunt undoubtedly intended for laughter. The Avtokrator went on, "I wish they weren't guarding all their siege engines so closely. I told Rhegorios I wouldn't, but now I think I would sally against them and see how much damage we could do."

His father shook his head. "You were right the first time. Biggest advantage we have is fighting from the inside of the city and the top of the wall. If we sally, we throw all that out the window." He held up a hand. "I'm not saying, never do it. I am saying that the advantage of surprise had better outweigh the disadvantage of giving up your position."

Weighing that, Maniakes rather regretfully decided it made good sense. "So long as they stay alert, then, a sally's not worthwhile."

"That's what I'm telling you," the elder Maniakes agreed.

"Well, people on the wall will just have to keep their eyes open, that's all," Maniakes said. "If the chance comes, I want to take it."

"Different matter altogether," his father said.

"It all depends on how you look at things," Maniakes said, "same as anything else." He made a face that suggested he'd been sucking on a lemon. "I must say, I am tired of people screaming at me that the siege is my fault because I married Lysia."

"Aye, I can see how you might be," the elder Maniakes said steadily. "But that's not surprising, either, is it? You knew as soon as you decided to marry her that people would be yelling that sort of thing at you. If you didn't know it, it's not because I didn't tell you. The question you've had to ask yourself all along, same as if we were talking about sallying against the Kubratoi, is, does the trouble outweigh everything else you get from the marriage?"

"Cold-blooded way of looking at things," Maniakes remarked.

"I'm a cold-blooded sort of fellow," his father replied. "So are you, come to that. If you don't know what the odds are, how can you bet?"

"It's been worth the trouble. It's been more than worth the trouble." The Avtokrator sighed. "I had hoped, though, that things would die down over the years. That hasn't happened. That hasn't come close to happening. Every time anything goes wrong, the city mob throws my marriage in my face."

"They'll be doing the same thing twenty years from now, too," the elder Maniakes said. "I thought you understood that by now."

"Oh, I do," Maniakes said. "The only way I know to make all of them—well, to make most of them—shut up is to drive away the Makuraners and the Kubratoi both." He pointed out toward the siege towers. "You can see what a fine job I've done of that."

"Not your fault." The elder Maniakes held up a forefinger. "Oh, one piece of it is—you beat Etzilios so badly, you made him wild for revenge. But that's nothing to blame yourself about. We were trying to hit Sharbaraz where he lives, and now he's trying to return the favor. That makes him clever. It doesn't make you stupid."

"I should have worried more about why Abivard and the boiler boys had disappeared," Maniakes said. Self-reproach came easy; he had been practicing all the way from the outskirts of Mashiz.

"And what would you have done if you'd *known* he'd left the Land of the Thousand Cities?" his father asked. "My guess is, you'd have headed straight for Mashiz and tried to take it because you knew he couldn't stop you. Since that's what you did anyway, why are you still beating yourself because of it?"

Maniakes stared at him. He'd found no way to forgive himself for failing to grasp at once what Abivard and Sharbaraz had plotted. Now, in three sentences, his father had shown him how.

As if sensing his relief, the elder Maniakes slapped him on the back. "You couldn't have counted on this, son. That's what I'm saying. But now that it's here, you still have to beat it. That hasn't changed, not one single, solitary, miserable bit it hasn't."

Off in the distance, the Kubratoi were still hauling their siege towers back and forth, trying to learn how to use them and what to do with them. On another tower, one that wasn't moving, a crew of workmen nailed hides ever higher on the frame. Before long, that tower would be finished, too.

"I know, Father," Maniakes said. "Believe me, I know."

Splendid—*perhaps even magnifolent,* Maniakes thought wryly—in his silk vestments shot through with gold and silver thread and encrusted with pearls and other gems, Agathios the ecumenical patriarch paraded up Middle Street from the procession's starting point close by the Silver Gate and the embattled land walls of Videssos the city. Behind him marched lesser priests, some swinging censers so the sweet-smelling smoke would waft the prayers of the people up to the heavens and to the awareness of the lord with the great and good mind, others lifting trained voices in songs of praise to Phos.

Behind the priests came Maniakes, riding Antelope. Almost everyone cheered Agathios. Everyone without exception cheered the more junior priests. Though all of them had been chosen at least in part because they vigorously supported the dispensation Agathios had granted Maniakes for his marriage to Lysia, that was not obvious to the city mob. Priests who entertained them—anyone who entertained them—deserved praise, and got it.

The parade would not have come off at all had Maniakes not instigated it. The city mob paid no attention to that. Some people booed and heckled him because the Kubratoi and Makuraners had laid siege to Videssos the city. Those were the ones who remembered nothing earlier than the day before yesterday. Others booed and heckled him because they reckoned his union with his cousin Lysia to be incestuous. They were the ones, almost as common as the other group, who remembered everything and forgave nothing.

And a few people cheered him. "You beat the Kubratoi," someone shouted as he rode by, "and you beat the Makuraners. Now you get to beat them both together." More cheers followed, at least a few.

Maniakes turned to Rhegorios, who rode behind him and to his left. "Now I get to beat them both together. Doesn't that make me a lucky fellow?"

"If you're a lucky fellow, you *will* beat them both together," his cousin returned. "It's what happens if you aren't lucky that worries me."

"You're always reassuring," Maniakes said, to which Rhegorios laughed.

When the chorus wasn't chanting hymns to the crowd, Agathios called an invitation to the people on the colonnaded sidewalks who stood and stared at the procession as they would have stood and stared at any entertainment: "Come join us in the plaza of Palamas! Come join us in praying for the Empire's salvation!"

"Maybe we should have done this at the High Temple, after all," Maniakes said. "It would have given the ceremony a more solemn air."

"You want solemn air, find a polecat," Rhegorios said, holding his nose. "Only the nobles and a handful of ordinary people can get into the High Temple. Everyone else has to find out secondhand what happened in there. This way, all the people will know."

"That's so," Maniakes said. "If everything goes well, I'll say you were right. But if things go wrong, all the people will know about that, too."

As far as he was concerned, the ecumenical patriarch was doing his best to make things go wrong. "Come pray for the salvation of the Empire!" Agathios cried again. "Come beg the good god to forgive our sins and make us pure again."

"I'll purify him," Maniakes muttered. "I'll bake him for two weeks, till all the grease runs out of him." When the patriarch spoke of forgiving sins, to what were the minds of the people likely to turn? To their own failings? Maniakes let out a snort of laughter. Not likely. They would think of him and Lysia. He would have suspected anyone else of deliberately inciting the people against him. He did suspect Agathios, in fact, but only briefly. He'd seen that the ecumenical patriarch was as a sucking babe when it came to matters political.

He wondered what sort of crowd they would draw to the plaza of Palamas, which was not commonly made the scene of religious gatherings. While wondering, he looked back over his shoulder. Behind the Imperial Guards, behind a couple of regiments that had distinguished themselves in the Land of the Thousand Cities, came a swelling tide of ordinary Videssians intent on hearing what the patriarch and the Avtokrator had to say. The plaza would be full.

The plaza, in fact, was packed. Agathios had trouble making his way to the platform that had been set up for him, a platform more often used by emperors to address the city mob. Maniakes looked back over his shoulder again. This time he waved. The guardsmen came trotting up through the ranks of the priests. Efficiently using elbows, spear shafts, and sheathed swords to clear a path, they got the patriarch to the platform in minimum time while also leaving people minimally angry—no small feat in Videssos the city, where everyone was touchy even when not under siege.

"We bless thee, Phos, lord with the great and good mind," Agathios intoned, "by thy grace our protector, watchful beforehand that the great test of life may be decided in our favor." Reciting the good god's creed was the blandest thing the patriarch could possibly have done. Picking the blandest thing to do was altogether in character for him.

As he must have known they would, the crowd joined him in the creed; many of them sketched Phos' sun-circle above their hearts as they prayed. Sometimes the blandest choice was also the wisest. Agathios had his audience as receptive as he could have hoped to get them for whatever else he planned to say.

"We need to come together, to remember we all follow Phos and we are all Videssians," the ecumenical patriarch declared. Maniakes' lips moved along with Agathios'. He knew the sermon to come at least as well as the patriarch did: not surprising, since he'd written most of it. Agathios had not argued it was unsound doctrine. *A good thing, too*, Maniakes thought. *I wouldn't want to have to change patriarchs at a time like this.*

Agathios gestured out beyond the wall. "There, encircling us, lie the tents of the Makuraners, who revere their false God and who have forced Phos' temples in the lands they have stolen from Videssos to conform to the erroneous usages of the Vaspurakaners; and there, also encircling us, lie the tents of the Kubratoi, who worship only their swords and the murderous power of sharpened iron. May the good god keep our disunion from granting our foes victory against us, for such victory would surely extinguish the light of our true faith throughout the world."

Applause started close by the platform and rippled outward. Maniakes and Rhegorios exchanged an amused glance. At functions of this sort, you didn't want to leave anything to chance. A couple of dozen men with goldpieces in their belt pouches could create a good deal of enthusiasm and transmit it to the crowd.

Telling Agathios about such chicanery would have been—*pointless* was the word Maniakes found. If the ecumenical patriarch was gratified at the response he received, he would preach better. So the Avtokrator told himself, at any rate.

And so it proved. Voice all but oozing sincerity, Agathios went on: "And so, fellow seekers after truth and after Phos' holy light and the enlightenment springing therefrom, let us for the time being exercise the principle of economy and agree to disagree. Let us lay aside all issues now dividing us until such time as they may be considered without also considering the threat of imminent extermination under which we now lie."

Again, the paid claque began the applause. Again, it spread beyond the claque. As far as Maniakes was concerned, Agathios was only talking plain sense. How Videssos, on the edge of falling to its foes, could be exercised about whether he'd married within limits proscribed by the temple hierarchy was beyond him.

It was not, however, beyond some Videssians. "Traitor!" they shouted, safe in the anonymity of the crowd. "Capitulator!" "Better to die in the sack and go to Phos' light than to live in sin and pass eternity in Skotos' ice!" They shouted things at Maniakes, too, and at Lysia—who was not there—things for which he would have drawn sword had he known upon whom to draw it.

He took a couple of steps toward Agathios. Rhegorios set a hand on his arm. "Careful," the Sevastos warned. "Are you sure you know what you're doing?"

"I'm sure," the Avtokrator growled.

His tone made his cousin look more worried still. "Whatever it is, are you sure you won't be sorry about it this time tomorrow?"

"I'm fairly sure," Maniakes said, sounding more like his usual self. Rhegorios, still looking unhappy, had no choice save stepping aside and letting his sovereign do whatever he would do.

Agathios looked surprised to see the Avtokrator approaching; had things gone according to plan, Maniakes would not have spoken till after the patriarch had finished. *Well,* Maniakes thought, *things don't always go according to plan. If they did, I'd be in Mashiz right now, not here.*

As the Sevastos could not restrain him, so the ecumenical patriarch could not keep him from speaking now, since he had shown the desire to do so. "Your Majesty," Agathios said, and, bowing, withdrew.

Maniakes stood at the edge of the platform and looked west. The crowd packing the plaza of Palamas filled his vision, but there at the far side of the plaza was Middle Street, up which the procession had come from close to the land walls of the city.

And out beyond the walls, apparently discounted by many city folk, remained the Kubratoi and the Makuraners.

For a couple of minutes, Maniakes simply stood in the place that had been Agathios'. A few taunts flew his way, but most of the throng waited to hear what he would say. That made the jeers seem thin and empty, isolated flotsam of sound on a sea of silence.

At last, the Avtokrator did speak, pitching his voice to carry as if on the battlefield. "I don't much care whether you love me or not." That was a thumping lie, but it was also armor against some of the things people had called him and Lysia. "What you think of me is your concern. When my soul walks the bridge of the separator and I face the lord with the great and good mind, I'll do it with a clear conscience.

"But that doesn't matter, as I say. When Midwinter's Day comes around, you can rail at me however you like. And you will. I know you, people of the city—you will. Go ahead. In the meanwhile, we have to make certain that we *can* celebrate Midwinter's Day in the Amphitheater. You need not love me for that to happen—soldiers need not love their captain, only do what he requires of them and keep from making things worse. After we've defended the city, we can attack one another to our hearts' content. Till then, we'd be wiser to wait."

Silence. From the whole crowd, silence. A few members of the paid claque applauded, but their clapping seemed as lost in emptiness as the earlier jeers had been. Maniakes thought he'd won abeyance, suspension of judgment, if not acceptance. He would gladly have settled for that. And then, out of the silence, a cry: "Phos will let the city fall, on account of *your* sin." And after that, more cries, hot, ferocious, deadly.

Were the worse enemies outside the walls, or within? He wanted to cry out himself, to scream for the soldiers to slaughter the hateful hecklers. But, having done that, what matter if he threw back the Makuraners and Kubratoi? Over what would he rule then, and how?

He held up a hand. Slowly, silence returned. "If the city does not fall, then, the holy ecumenical patriarch's dispensation must be valid. And the city shall not fall." Silence again, now lingering.

Challenge. Accepted.

✦ VI

O ut beyond the walls, a horn blew. Maybe, once upon a
time, it had been a Videssian horn. The Kubrati who
winded it, though, knew nothing of Videssian notions
of music. What he wanted was to make noise with the horn, as
much noise as he could, as a child will make noise to hearten
his army of wooden soldiers when they march out to war.

But only in a child's imagination will wooden soldiers charge
and fight and, of course, bravely sweep all before them. What
the Kubrati called into being was real, so real and so frightening that he might almost have been sorcerer rather than mere
horn player.

Yelling like demons, the Kubratoi burst from their encampments and rushed toward Videssos the city, some mounted, others
afoot. They started shooting arrows at their foes atop the walls
even before they were in range, so that the first shafts fell into
the ditch at the base of the great stone pile and the ones coming
just after smacked the stone and mostly shivered.

But, like raindrops at the start of a storm, those were only the
first among many. Soon as could be, the arrows walked up the
side of the outer wall and flew among the defenders at the top.
One hummed past Maniakes' face and men down to strike the
inner wall near its base.

Not all shafts flew *among* defenders. Not twenty feet from the

Avtokrator, a man tumbled to the walkway, writhing, weeping, cursing, screaming. A couple of his comrades, braving more arrows themselves when they could have crouched behind crenellations, hustled him to a siege tower. Surgeons waited inside there to do what they could for the wounded. Healer-priests waited, too, to fling their own faith and strength against the wounds of war.

A catapult bucked and thudded. A dart flew out, flat and fast. It pinned a nomad's leg to his horse. The horse fell as if poleaxed, pinning the fellow's other leg between its kicking corpse and the ground. The Kubrati's cries, if he raised them—if he lived—were lost, buried, forgotten in the tumult.

Stone-throwers on the wall cast their fearful burdens at the attackers, too. A man hit by a stone weighing half as much as himself and traveling like an arrow ceased to be a man, becoming instead in the twinkling of an eye a red horror either lying still, smeared along the ground, or wailing like a broken baby bereft of breast, bereft of brother, bereft of hope.

And Maniakes, seeing what he would have mourned had it befallen one of his own subjects, even one who hated him as an incestuous tyrant, clapped his hands with glee and shouted to the crew that had launched the fatal stone: "Give 'em another one just like that, boys!"

And the crew did their best to obey, and cried out in fury and disappointment when their next missile fell harmlessly to earth. Maniakes moaned when that happened, too. Only later did he think on what a strange business war was.

He had no leisure for such thoughts in any case, for some of the Kubratoi, instead of pausing at the ditch in front of the outer wall, dropped down into it along with ladders tall enough to reach from that depression to the top of the wall. Not many of those ladders ever went up, though. A stone dropped straight down rather than flung from a catapult crushed a man as thoroughly, if not so spectacularly, as one actually discharged from a stone-thrower. The Videssian defenders also rained arrows and boiling water down on the heads of the Kubratoi directly below them.

Wearing an ordinary trooper's mail shirt and a much-battered helmet, the elder Maniakes came up beside his son. He peered down into the ditch for a moment, then nodded in somber satisfaction. "I don't think they'll try that again any time soon," he said. "Bit of a slaughter down there."

"This is the high ground," Maniakes agreed. "If they let us keep it, they'll pay the price." He frowned. "If they let us keep it high, they'll pay the price." He pointed to show what he meant.

Maybe Etzilios, in spite of the better advice the Makuraners undoubtedly must have given him, had thought Videssos the city would fall to direct assault, and never mind all the fancy engines he'd spent so much time and effort building. Maybe he'd believed that the imperials huddled inside their walls from fear alone and lacked the spirit to resist his ferocious warriors. If that was so, he'd received an expensive lesson to the contrary.

And now he was going about things as he should have done from the beginning. The ladders lay in the ditch; after a while, the Videssians set them afire, to be rid of them.

Meanwhile, though, Etzilios' warriors and teams of horses dragged his own stone-throwers, the ones the Makuraners had taught him to make, up to where they would bear on the walls. More men—Maniakes thought them Videssian prisoners, not Kubratoi—carried stones up and piled them beside the engines.

"Knock them down!" he shouted to his own catapult crews. But at long range, that was not so easy. The Kubratoi had only to hit the wall, a target they could hardly miss. Hitting specific stone-throwers, as the Videssians needed to do, was a different proposition.

Every once in a while, by the curious combination of good shooting and luck so necessary for success in war, a Videssian catapult crew would manage to land a stone square on an enemy engine, with results as disastrous for that engine as for a man unfortunately in the path of such a missile. The stricken stone-thrower would go from engine to kindling in the course of a heartbeat, and the Videssian catapult crew would caper and pound one another on the backs and brag to anyone who listened or, more often, to anyone nearby, listening or not.

And the Kubratoi would make their prisoners haul away the wreckage of the ruined stone-thrower, the said wreckage sometimes extending to the men who served the engine and were injured when a piece flying off it smote them. And they would drag up another stone-thrower and go back to pounding away at the walls of Videssos the city.

Up on the walkway of the outer wall, Maniakes felt caught in an unending medium-sized earthquake. Stones crashed against the stonework of the wall, which brought every impact straight to the soles of his boots. The roar of stone striking stone put him in mind of an earthquake's fearsome rumble, too.

But earthquakes, no matter how fearsome they were, stopped in a minute or two. This went on and on, the continuous motion underfoot almost making him seasick. Many of the stones the engines cast bounded away from the walls without effect; the masons who had built those works centuries before knew their business.

Every so often, though, the Kubratoi let fly with a particularly hard stone, or with one hurled particularly hard, or with one that hit in a better spot or at a better angle. Then stone on the face of the wall shattered, too.

"How much pounding can we stand?" Maniakes asked his father.

"Haven't the foggiest notion," the elder Maniakes replied. "Never had to worry about it quite this way before. Tell you what, though—knowing where to find the answers is nearly as good as knowing what they are. Anything Ypsilantes can't tell you about the walls isn't worth knowing."

"That's true, by the good god," Maniakes agreed, and summoned his chief engineer.

"We should be able to hold out against pounding like this a good long while, your Majesty," Ypsilantes said. "Only a few stretches of the wall have a rubble core; most of it is either solid stone all the way through or else double-thick stone over storerooms and kitchens and such."

"That's what I'd hoped," the Avtokrator said. "Nice to have hopes come true every now and again."

"I am pleased to have pleased you, your Majesty," Ypsilantes said. "And now, if you will please excuse me—" He hurried away on missions more vital than reassuring his sovereign.

After Ypsilantes had left, the elder Maniakes tapped his son on the arm. "Come back to the palaces," he said. "Get some rest. The city isn't going to fall to pieces while you go to bed, and you're liable to fall to pieces if you don't."

Maniakes shook his head. "As long as I'm here, the men on the wall will know I'm with them. They'll fight harder."

"Maybe a little, but not that much," his father replied. "And I tell you this: if you're the only prop holding the defenders up, then the city *will* fall. They're fighting for more reasons than just your being here. For one thing, they're good soldiers already, because you've made them into good soldiers over the past few years. And for another, believe me, they like staying alive as much as anyone else does. Now come on."

He put some roughness into his voice, as he had when Maniakes disobeyed him as a boy. The Avtokrator laughed. "You sound like you'll take a belt to my backside if I don't do what you tell me."

The elder Maniakes looked down at the belt he was wearing. As befitted the Avtokrator's father, he had on a gold one with a fancy jeweled buckle. He undid the buckle, took off the belt, and hefted it speculatively. "I could give you a pretty fair set of welts with this one, son," he remarked.

"So you could," Maniakes said. "Well, if that's not lese majesty, to the ice with me if I know what is." He and his father both laughed. When the elder Maniakes started down from the wall, the Avtokrator followed him. They rode back to the palaces together.

All the way there, though, Maniakes heard heavy stones thudding against the wall. He didn't think he'd get much rest.

"A sally, that's what we need," Rhegorios said. "A sally to scatter some of their archers and put paid to some of their engines. The stone-throwers would do, I suppose, but I'd really like to be rid of those siege towers. That would be something worth doing."

Maniakes eyed his cousin with amusement. "How did you manage to slide from *what we need* to *I suppose* in a couple of sentences there? What you mean is, you feel like going out and fighting Kubratoi and you want me to tell you it's all right."

Rhegorios gave him a glance respectful and resentful at the same time. "Anyone would think we'd grown up together, or something like that," he said. "How can I sneak anything past you? You know me too well. For that matter, how do you sneak anything past my sister? She knows you too well."

"How do I try to sneak anything past Lysia?" Maniakes said. "Mostly I don't. It doesn't work well, for some reason. But that has nothing to do with whether we ought to sally against the Kubratoi."

"I suppose not," his cousin agreed. "But are we just going to sit here and let them pound on us?"

"That was exactly what I had in mind, as a matter of fact," the Avtokrator said. "Whenever I've got in trouble, all through my reign, I've tried to do too much. I'm not going to do that this time. I'm going to do as little as I can, and let the Kubratoi and Makuraners wear themselves out, banging their heads on our walls. That's why the walls went up in the first place."

"What kind of battle plan is that?" Rhegorios said indignantly.

"A sensible one?" Maniakes suggested.

"Where's the glory?" Rhegorios demanded. "Where are the heroes parading down Middle Street singing songs of victory?"

"As for the heroes," Maniakes said, "more of them will be left alive if we play the game cautiously. As for the glory, the Kubratoi and the Makuraners are welcome to it, for all of me. Now wait." He held up a hand to check his cousin's expostulation. "Whoever wants glory for glory's sake can have it, as far as I'm concerned. If I can win the war by sitting here like a snail pulled back into its shell, I'll do that, and gladly."

"Cold-blooded way to look at things," Rhegorios said. Then, after a moment, he admitted, "Your father would tell me the same, though; I will say that much. Which leaves me with only one question: what does a snail do when somebody tries to smash in his shell?"

"That's simple," Maniakes said. "He twists around and bites him from the inside." Rhegorios went off, dissatisfied.

Maniakes' attitude toward warfare might well have been more typically Videssian than that of his cousin. Only the Imperial Guards, for instance, had a name and reputation stretching over generations. When the Avtokrator went out to the wall a few days later, then, he was surprised to find a stretch of it defended by a unit of stone-throwers decorated with graffiti proclaiming, THE BITING SNAILS! DON'T CRACK OUR SHELLS!

"Did my cousin put you up to this?" he demanded with mock severity.

"His highness the Sevastos might have mentioned it, your Majesty, but he didn't put us up to it, like," their commanding officer said. "The lads and I, we liked the name, so we decided to wear it."

"May your teeth be sharp, then," Maniakes said, and the soldiers cheered.

As he walked along the walls, he realized all the defenders, not just the Biting Snails, were going to need sharp teeth. The Kubratoi were dragging their siege towers, one after another, into position for an assault on the city. They stood just beyond the range of the engines the Videssians had mounted on the outer wall.

Immodios was studying the towers, too, and not looking very happy while he did it. Maniakes consoled himself by remembering how seldom Immodios looked happy about anything. The officer said, "Your Majesty, I fear we're going to have a hard time stopping them or even slowing them down much before they reach the wall."

"I think you're wrong," Maniakes answered. "I think the darts and the stones and the fire we'll hurl at them from the wall will make sure they never reach it. I think most of them will burn up or be smashed before they get within bowshot of the wall."

"If the Kubratoi had figured out siege towers on their own, your Majesty, I'd say you were likely to be right," Immodios said. "They wouldn't build them strong enough. But the Makuraners know what they're doing, same as we do."

"They just did the showing," Maniakes said. "The Kubratoi did the building. They've never tried anything like this before. My bet is, they haven't built strong enough."

"The lord with the great and good mind grant that you have the right of it," Immodios said. He didn't sound as if he believed it.

He had reason to worry, too, as the Avtokrator soon discovered. Maniakes had even dared hope that the Kubratoi would try to use beasts of burden to haul the siege towers up close to the wall. The Biting Snails, the other dart- and stone-thrower crews, and the archers would have enjoyed targets to dream of, even if massacring beasts of burden was a stomach-turning business in and of itself.

But Etzilios, perhaps having ignored one set of instructions from his Makuraner tutors, did not ignore two. No horses or mules ever came within range of the engines on the outer wall. The nomads led the animals away and disconnected the ropes with which they'd been harnessed. Then they herded ragged men—Videssian prisoners again—into the towers, treating them not much differently from the way they used any other beasts of burden. Kubrati warriors went into the towers, too, a few to make the prisoners propel them forward, most for the assault on Videssos the city.

Very slowly, the towers began to advance.

"Now we find out," Maniakes said. To his dismay, the closer the towers got, the sturdier they looked.

When he said as much, Immodios nodded. "That's so, your Majesty," he agreed. It wasn't quite I told you so, but it would do.

"Well, well," Maniakes murmured. "How stupid was I?" He held up a hand before Immodios could speak. "Never mind. You don't have to answer that. In fact, I'd be happier if you didn't answer that."

Whatever Immodios' opinions were, he dutifully kept them to himself. Foot by foot, the siege towers moved forward. When they came into range of the engines on the walls, the Videssians let fly with everything they had. Some of their darts did pierce the hide covering and shields on the front of the siege towers. Some, no doubt, pierced warriors and haulers in the towers. Such pinprick injuries, though, did little to make the Kubratoi give over their assault.

Stone-throwers hurled their missiles at the towers, too. They hit with loud crashes, but they bounced off without doing any visible damage. Maybe the Kubratoi had listened to the Makuraner engineers, after all. Instead of looking just somber, Immodios looked somber and vindicated. Maniakes did his best not to notice.

But the stone-throwers could throw more than stones. Their crews loaded them with jars full of a nasty mix of tallow and rock oil and naphtha and sulfur, then lighted the mix with torches before flinging it at the foe. Fire dripped down the fronts of the towers. The harsh smoke stank. When it got into Maniakes' eyes, it made them water and burn. Inhaling some, he coughed. "What vile stuff!" he said, coughing some more.

Fire the Kubratoi could not ignore, as they had the darts and stones. Some of them came up onto the tops of the towers and poured water down onto the flames. That did less good than they might have hoped. Instead of putting out the fires, the water only made them run faster down the fronts of the towers.

That sufficed, though, for the flames had trouble igniting the hides that faced the siege towers. Maybe the Kubratoi had soaked them to leave them wet and slimy and hard to burn. Whatever the reason, they did not catch fire. Inch by slow inch, the towers advanced.

Looking north and south, Maniakes spied seven or eight of them. Three moved on the Silver Gate, near which he stood. The others crawled singly toward the wall. Kubrati stone-throwers flung boulders at the outer wall and at the walkway atop it, making it hard and dangerous for the Videssians to concentrate their defenders where the attacks would come.

Maniakes bit his lip. Somewhere back at one of the Kubrati encampments, those Makuraner engineers had to be hugging themselves with glee. The towers were doing everything they wanted, which meant they were doing everything Maniakes didn't want them to do.

Off to the north, cheers rang out from the wall. The Avtokrator stared to see why his men were cheering in the middle of what looked like disaster. He needed a while, peering in that direction, before he understood: one of the towers wasn't moving forward any more. Maybe it had tried to go over damp ground and bogged down. Maybe a wheel or axle had broken under the strain of the weight the tower carried. Maybe the ground sloped ever so slightly, so it had to try to go uphill. Whatever the reason, it wasn't going anywhere now.

Maniakes felt like cheering himself. He didn't, though, not with only one threat gone and so many remaining. And then, right before his eyes, one of the siege towers bearing down on the Silver Gate began to burn at last. The flames and smoke rising from it were no longer solely from the incendiary liquid with which the Videssians had been bombarding it. The timbers of its frame had also caught fire.

So did the Kubratoi inside the tower. Enemies though they were, Maniakes pitied them then. Above the snap of catapults discharging, above the thud of stones and darts striking home against the wall and against the siege tower, rose the screams of the warriors in that inferno.

What was it like in there? Maniakes tried to imagine himself a nomad on the stairs between, say, the fourth and fifth floors. It would be packed and dark and frightening even without fire; every stone that slammed into the tower had to feel like the end of the world. The odor of smoke would have been in the air for some time already, what with jars of blazing grease striking the tower along with the stones.

But what happened when the odor changed, when the Kubratoi

smelled unmistakable woodsmoke and saw flames above them? Worse, what happened when they smelled unmistakable woodsmoke and saw flames *below* them?

Warriors streamed out of the base of the siege tower and fled away from the walls of Videssos the city back toward their encampment. Stones and darts and ordinary arrows took a heavy toll among them. At that, though, they were the lucky ones: that was a quicker, cleaner way to die than they would have found had they remained in the tower.

At the very peak of the siege tower, a doorway opened and a gangway was thrust forth, as if a boy had stuck out his tongue. With the tower more than half a bowshot from the wall, it was a gangplank to nowhere. But that did not mean no one used it.

Kubratoi desperate to escape the flames and smoke inside the siege tower dashed out onto the gangway. Maniakes got the feeling that a lot of them would have been content simply to stand there, to rest for a moment after getting away from the fire. But that was not to be, could not be. For one thing, smoke poured out of the doorway from which the long plank had emerged. And for another, more and more Kubratoi, men who could not use the stairs and ladders down to the ground, tried to get out on the gangway.

What happened after that was grimly inevitable. Some nomads, crowded off the plank by their comrades, fell to the ground nearly forty feet below. Others jumped, no doubt thinking it better to propel themselves off into space than to be forced off at a time and attitude not of their choosing.

A few of the nomads were lucky, getting up apparently uninjured from their falls. A few, as unlucky as they could be, lay unmoving. More dragged themselves away, hurt but alive. A couple of those, at least partly lucky at first, were unlucky later, when other Kubratoi, either forced off or springing from the gangway, landed on top of them or when a stone from a Videssian engine finished them where the fall had not.

And then fire reached the end of the gangway still inside the siege tower. Maniakes could hear the wood crack, and the board, burning, crashed to the ground along with the nomads left on it.

The siege tower collapsed in on itself a minute or two later, flames flaring brighter and higher in the breeze of the collapse for a little while and then beginning to subside once more.

"There's one we don't have to worry about any more," Maniakes said.

That, unfortunately, left all the siege towers about which the Videssians did still have to worry. Several of them were going to reach the wall: that seemed revoltingly obvious, despite the Avtokrator's earlier optimism. The places where they would reach the wall seemed obvious, too—they could hardly change their paths, twisting and dodging like rabbits chased by hounds.

"That means we'll just have to give them a nice, warm reception," Maniakes said, more than half to himself. But the stream of orders he sent forth after that was meant for the men on the wall. Soldiers around the Silver Gate got those orders straight from his lips. Couriers dashed off to give his ideas to men on other stretches where the towers were advancing.

When one of the couriers returned, he said, "Begging your pardon, your Majesty, but the officers I talked to said they'd already thought of that for themselves."

"No need to beg my pardon," Maniakes answered. "I'm not angry if the soldiers who serve me think for themselves. The reverse, in fact."

Archers and stone- and dart-throwers from the inner wall rained missiles down on the siege towers as those drew near the lower outer wall. A few of the missiles they rained down fell short, wounding defenders instead of attackers.

An arrow from behind Maniakes shattered against a battlement only a couple of feet to his left. An assassin could slay him so easily, and then say it was an accident. He made himself shrug. He couldn't do anything about that.

Closer and closer to the Silver Gate crawled the two towers still unburnt. The bombardment they took from the Videssian catapults on the walls was harsher than any Maniakes had seen. The Avtokrator wished the Makuraner engineers who had taught the Kubratoi the art of making such towers into Skotos' coldest icepit.

Videssians in mail shirts crowded the walkway by the spots where the towers would send forth their gangplanks. The Kubratoi on the ground did everything they could to keep the imperials from concentrating against the towers, redoubling their own barrage of arrows and catapult-flung stones. Hale men hauled their wounded comrades to the siege towers on either side of the Silver Gate. More soldiers took the places of those hurt or slain.

"We have to beat them back," Maniakes called to his men. "No foreign foe has ever set foot inside Videssos the city. And besides," he added practically, "if we don't kill them, they'll kill us, and enjoy themselves doing it, too."

A few of the soldiers laughed. More, though, simply nodded. He'd phrased his words as a joke, but that didn't mean they weren't true.

Now the first tower almost touched the wall. Maniakes could see that a couple of the shields mounted on it had burned when his men hurled fire at it, but the hides below those shields had kept the fire from turning to conflagration. His nostrils twitched. Those hides weren't fresh. He hoped the Kubratoi inside the tower were good and sick. It would make them easier to beat.

The doorway in the upper story of the siege tower opened. Like the rest of the tower, it was armored with shields and hides. The Kubratoi waiting inside let out a cheer at seeing the light of day once more and shoved the gangway out toward the wall.

"Now!" Maniakes shouted, as loud as he could to make himself heard over the din of battle.

He wasn't sure afterward, but he didn't think the catapult crew waited for his command before letting fly. As soon as the doorway came open, they launched a great jar full of the Videssian incendiary mix straight at it. The jar smashed against the foremost couple of Kubratoi, knocking them over and drenching them and the inside of the tower with clinging flames.

The inside of the tower, of course, was made of wood. In moments, it began to burn. Smoke billowed out of the door. The gangway remained perhaps a third extended, several feet shy of the wall.

"They're not going to come at us that way, by the good god!" Maniakes said. The soldiers around him yelled themselves hoarse and him deaf. He didn't care. The Kubratoi had only one limited way of getting at the Videssians on the wall. Turn that way into a seething mass of fire, and the whole immense siege tower, on which they'd labored so long and hard, all at once became useless.

Not so many Kubratoi were trapped here as had been in the

other tower that burned. With the fire at the top, the warriors packing this tower had the chance to flee out the bottom. The Videssians killed and wounded many of them with stones and darts and arrows, but many also fled back out of range of those missiles without taking any hurt.

Maniakes dismissed them from his mind even as they ran: if they were running away from Videssos the city, they were for the time being no threat. He also dismissed the burning siege tower, except insofar as the smoke now pouring from it made him cough and his eyes stream tears. The tower that had not yet opened its door posed the greater threat.

"Be ready!" he shouted to the crews of the catapults facing that second tower. "We'll treat this one the same way we did the other, and then we'll go and help our friends farther up along the wall."

"That's right, your Majesty!" the Biting Snails yelled. "We'll lick 'em, same as we'll lick anybody you turn us loose against."

"Good men!" he said, and a couple of the warriors turned their heads to grin at him. Even after returning to Videssos the city, they didn't care whom he'd married. That he'd led them to victory counted for more. He wished the same held true for people he hadn't led into battle.

The second siege tower assaulting the Silver Gate crawled forward slowly, ponderously. Maniakes thought it was taking a very long time to reach the wall. Maybe it had slowed when some of the men inside saw what had happened to its companion. Maybe, too, time simply seemed to have slowed down for him, as it often did in battle.

Whatever the truth there, at last it came close enough for the Kubratoi inside to open the door. "Now!" Maniakes shouted, as he had before.

And, as the other catapult had done, this one flung a jar full of the Videssians' incendiary liquid straight into the doorway. But the Kubratoi must have thought on what went wrong when the first tower tried extending its gangway toward the wall. All the men crowding forward thrust big shields up against the impact of the jar.

They were so tightly jammed into that little space up there, the impact did not, could not, tumble them backward, as it otherwise would have done. The jar shattered against the upthrust shields, and probably broke arms and ribs in so doing, but most of the burning stuff dripped down over the shields and hides and did not start a great, inextinguishable blaze inside the top of the tower.

Out came the gangway, snaking toward the wall. A Videssian with an axe he must have taken from a Haloga guardsman chopped at it, once, twice, before an arrow caught him in the face. He dropped the axe and reeled back with a groan.

Even before the gangway reached the stones of the outer wall, several Kubratoi charged out onto it. *Snap!* The crew at a dart-thrower smote the engine's trigger. Those darts could slay a man at a quarter of a mile. At such short range, this one drove through two Kubratoi and skewered a third behind them. All three tumbled to the ground, which they struck a second later with heavy, meaty thuds.

No one who had faced the Kubratoi, weapons in hand, had ever claimed they were anything less than brave. After having fire hurled at them, after a dart had hurled to their doom the first three bold enough to try the gangway, the warriors who came after could hardly have been blamed had they hesitated. They did nothing of the sort. Shouting fierce war cries, they shoved one another aside in their eagerness to rush at the Videssians.

Arrows thudded into the shields they held up to protect their vitals. An arrow caught one of them in the thigh. He stumbled and fell, screaming, to the ground below. Another one went down on the gangway, whereupon the Kubrati behind him tripped and also fell.

But the rest came on. The Videssians at the end of the gangway met them not with swords or even spears, but with long, stout poles. They swept a couple of Kubratoi off the narrow way and into that long, deadly drop. The nomads chopped at the poles with their swords. One of the poles split. A Kubrati grabbed another by the end and, instead of trying to fend it off, pulled with all his might. Caught by surprise, the Videssian wielding it did not let go before overbalancing. "Phooooos!" he shrieked all the way down. His cry cut off abruptly when he hit.

With a shout of triumph, the first Kubrati leapt off the gangway and onto the stone of the wall. That shout turned to a scream of agony moments later; beset by three imperials, he went down under spear and sword. So did the next Kubrati, and the next.

After that, even the nomads' fierce courage faltered. A Videssian, caught up in the same unthinking battle fury as his foes, jumped up onto the gangway and ran at the Kubratoi, slashing as he went.

"No!" Maniakes shouted. "Come back! Don't throw yourself away!"

The soldier paid no heed. He cut down the first nomad he faced, but was pierced by an arrow a moment later. Leaping over the Kubrati he'd just slain, he seized the fellow behind that one by the waist and then leapt off the narrow plank, taking his foe down with him.

Maniakes sketched the sun-circle above his heart. The Videssian hadn't thrown himself away; the Avtokrator silently admitted as much to himself. He'd made the Kubratoi pay two to get one—and, in the way he'd done it, he'd made them think, too.

They kept coming, but the moment's hesitation the soldier's self-sacrifice bought let more Videssians rush up toward the gangway. The Kubratoi did manage to put men on the wall every so often, but none of the men they put there lived more than moments. Maniakes' greatest fear was that they would be able to force the Videssians back and create a perimeter behind which more and more of their men would gain the wall.

It did not happen, not by the Silver Gate. "Phos be praised," Maniakes murmured, and anxiously looked up and down the wall to see if the Kubratoi had gained lodgments with any of their other towers. Seeing no signs of that, he said "Phos be praised" again and gave his attention back to the fighting close by him.

The stone-thrower crew had finally managed to load another jar of incendiary liquid into their engine. They could not shoot it at the Kubratoi, though, or at their tower, because too many Videssian soldiers crowded round the machine, which stood near the forefront of the fighting. At last, seeing their moment, they loosed the jar.

It smashed a Kubrati on the gangway near the tower. He fell spinning to the ground below, some of the burning sticky stuff clinging to him. More splashed onto Kubratoi directly behind him. Screaming, they tried to run back into the siege tower, but could make no progress against the stream of warriors trying to come forward. Indeed, those warriors fended them off weapons in hand, not wanting to burn along with the couple of unfortunates.

And some of the mixture of oil and fat and sulfur and naphtha dripped down on the gangway and set the wood afire. The burning Kubratoi kept the others from dousing it, not that it would have been easy to douse with water. The men closer to the wall than the two on fire were so intent on pressing ahead against the Videssians, they did not notice the flames till far too late to stamp them out.

The gangway burned, then, till it broke in two. Both halves, and all the men on them, tumbled down, down, down. Maniakes let out a cry of triumph when that happened. "Come ahead!" he shouted, shaking his fist at the Kubratoi staring out of the siege tower. "Come ahead and get what we just gave your friends!"

He'd hoped they had but a single gangway and would be stuck in the siege tower after losing it. But they, or more likely the Makuraner engineer from whom they'd learned how to build the tower, had planned better than that. Out snaked another plank toward the wall of Videssos the city.

"Here!" Maniakes bawled to his men. "To me!" He snapped orders. Videssian soldiers carried yet another jar of inflammable liquid up to the very edge of the wall. At his command, they poured some of the stuff onto the stone where the gangway would reach the wall, then thrust a torch into it.

Yellow flames sprang up. Thick clouds of black, choking smoke made the Videssians pull back from the fire they'd started. That might have worked to the advantage of the Kubratoi, had they been able to put men on the wall then. But the nomads in charge of the gangway halted with it half-extended, not daring to push it forward into the flames.

"Come on!" Maniakes shouted again. "Don't you want to see the rest of the welcome we have waiting?"

He didn't know whether they heard him or not. If they did hear, he didn't know whether they understood. What he did know was that the gangway advanced no farther. Through the blowing smoke, he saw the Kubratoi pull it back into the tower. And then, so slowly that at first he did not believe what his eyes told him, the tower drew back from the Silver Gate. The other surviving towers were also moving away from the wall.

Now, for the first time that whole mad, terrifying day, Maniakes spoke softly, in tones of wonder: "By the lord with the great and good mind, we've won."

And one of his veterans, a fellow with a scar on his forehead and a kink to his nose, shook his head and said, "No, your Majesty. They've just had enough for today, that's all."

"You're right, of course," the Avtokrator said, recognizing truth when he heard it. Also for the first time that day, he laughed. "And do you know what else? That will do nicely, thank you very much."

No one disagreed with him. He did not think the soldiers deferred to his views because he was their ruler. He thought they kept silent because they, like he, were glad to be alive and not driven from the outer wall.

"What will they do next?" That was the elder Maniakes, taking the question his son addressed to the council of war and doing his best to answer it: "Whatever it is, I hope it won't be as bad as what they threw at us today."

"I expect it will be worse," Maniakes answered. "In today's fight, they were seeing what they could do. Now, curse them to the ice, they have a pretty good notion."

Symvatios said, "The khagan will have a rare old time trying to get them to bring the towers forward again, after what we did to them this time. A warrior who's just watched a good many of his friends go up like so many joints of beef isn't going to be dead keen on heading up to the wall to cook himself afterwards."

"Something to that," Maniakes said. "A lot to it, I hope."

Rhegorios said, "What worries me most of all is that these were the Kubratoi. No sign that many Makuraners were in the fighting today." He pointed westward. "Best we know, they're still over on the other side of the Cattle Crossing. If they once reach this shore—"

"We have more troubles," the Avtokrator broke in. "That wouldn't be the worst move for Etzilios to make, either. It would make his own men happier, because their allies are helping them, and it would make the attack stronger, too, because—"

The elder Maniakes took a father's privilege of interrupting his sovereign: "Because the Makuraners really know what they're doing." That hadn't been what Maniakes intended to say, but it fit well enough. His father went on, "If we could, we really ought to find out what the Kubratoi and Makuraners are planning, not what we'd be doing in their sandals. It's not battle magic, not precisely . . ."

"They'll be warded," Maniakes said glumly. "I'd bet a goldpiece against a copper that their mages are trying to listen in on us right now. If they learn anything, some heads that are in the Sorcerers' Collegium ought to go up on the Milestone instead."

"If we don't try, it's sure we won't do it," the elder Maniakes said.

"That's so," Maniakes agreed. "Let it be as you say, Father. I'll summon Bagdasares."

Alvinos Bagdasares said something startled in the throaty Vaspurakaner tongue. Maniakes, though of the same Vaspurakaner blood as the mage, understood that language only haltingly. He did not think, though, that Bagdasares had thanked him for the sorcerous assignment.

"Your Majesty, this will be a difficult conjuration at best, and may well prove impossible," Bagdasares warned, returning to Videssian.

"If it were easy, I could pick a wizard off a street corner to do it for me," Maniakes returned. "I know you may not get the answers I want, but I want you to do everything you can to find out what Abivard and Etzilios are plotting against us now."

Bagdasares bowed. "It shall be as you command, of course, your Majesty." He tugged at his bushy black beard, muttering in both Videssian and Vaspurakaner. When Maniakes caught a word—*affinities*—he nodded to himself. Yes, the mage would do his best.

To symbolize Abivard, Bagdasares came up with a shiny silver arket. "I have nothing similar for the Kubrati khagan," he said unhappily.

"Why not just use one of our goldpieces, then?" Maniakes answered, sounding anything but gleeful himself. "We were going to pay Etzilios enough of them—but not enough to suit him."

"The analogy needs to be more exact." Bagdasares didn't notice that Maniakes was indulging in a wry joke—or else whipping himself for past failures. The mage finally chose a Kubrati saber. Its blade shone, too, though with a different sort of gleam from that of the Makuraner coin. Bagdasares looked almost pleased with the world after that. "Now I need but one thing more: you."

"Me?" Maniakes heard himself squeak, as if he were a youth whose voice broke every other word.

"Certainly, your Majesty," the wizard said. "You shall be the element transmuting the general to the specific. This is not Etzilios' sword, only a Kubrati weapon. The odds are long against this coin's ever having been in Abivard's beltpouch. But you have met both men. By the working of the law of contagion, you remain in touch with both of them. And that contact strengthens the action of the law of similarity here, linking these artifacts not only with their respective nations but also with the individuals whose plans we are trying to learn."

Maniakes had hoped to get back to the wall in case Etzilios, instead of conferring with Abivard, simply decided to attack again. If that happened, though, a messenger would no doubt bring him word of it. He could leave when that happened. The urgent needs of battle would give him a good excuse for interrupting Bagdasares' magic. Meanwhile, he resigned himself to wait.

"Take the arket in one hand, your Majesty, and the sword in the other," Bagdasares said. "Think on the two men whom the objects represent. Think on them talking with each other, and on what they might say in the situation in which they find themselves."

"I've been doing nothing but thinking on what they *might* say," Maniakes answered. "I want to find out what they *did* say or *will* say."

Bagdasares did not reply. Maniakes was not sure Bagdasares even heard. The mage had begun the chanting invocation he would use for the spell and the passes that would accompany it. If a wizard did not fix his mind on the essential, his magic would surely fail.

It might fail even if he did everything perfectly. Bagdasares' frown made him look older. "Wards," he said to Maniakes in a moment when his hands were busy but he did not need to incant orally. "I am resisted." His forehead corrugated in thought. When he began to chant again, the rhythm was subtly different from what it had been.

Different, perhaps, but not better. Frown darkened into scowl. "They have a Videssian mage with them," he said, releasing the words as if from a mouth full of rotting fish. "He has foreread-ied charms against many things I might try. Many, aye, but not all."

Once more, the rhythm of the chant shifted. This time, so did the language: from archaic Videssian, he turned to the Vaspurakaner tongue. Now his eyes brightened, his voice firmed—progress, Maniakes judged.

A moment later, he was able to judge progress for himself. He began to feel . . . something pass between silver coin and iron sword. He did not think he was feeling it with any of the five ordinary senses. It was more akin, or so he judged, to the current that passed from a healer-priest to the person he was helping: as indescribable as that, and as real.

"We have to do this together," a voice said from out of the air in front of him. "The delay hurts my men, too—half of them want to go north tomorrow."

"Get enough of my soldiers over the Cattle Crossing and we'll lead the way up the towers and onto the wall," another voice replied, apparently from that same empty place.

Maniakes started in surprise. It was not so much at hearing Etzilios and Abivard: he'd required that Bagdasares make him able to hear them. Having the mage succeed though he'd doubted whether success was possible gratified the Avtokrator without astonishing him. What he had not expected, though, was that both the khagan of Kubrat and the marshal of Makuran would be speaking Videssian. What did it say when the Empire's two greatest foes had only its language in common?

"And while they're busy fighting the towers—" Maniakes was surprised again, not having expected to hear a third voice there. But, whether Bagdasares had given him anything to mark it or not, he had an affinity for Tzikas, an affinity of longtime common cause soured into near-murder and endless betrayal. Oh, yes, the two of them were connected.

But what did Tzikas know? What had he been trying to show the Kubratoi when Maniakes almost put a dart through him?

The Avtokrator did not find out. Abivard said, "Get the monoxyla over to us. You know the signal to use to let us know when they're coming?"

"I know the one you gave me," Etzilios answered. "Why that in particular?"

"Because it—" Abivard undoubtedly went on talking, but Maniakes heard no more. The arket and the hilt of the sword he was holding went hot in his hands. Weapon and coin both fell to the floor, the one with a clatter, the other chiming sweetly from the stone.

Bagdasares staggered slightly, then caught himself. "I crave pardon, your Majesty," he said. "The wizards warding them became aware that I had threaded my way through their defense, and cut off the thread after me."

"I wish they hadn't done it right then," Maniakes said. "If we'd learned what the Kubratoi signal is, our dromons would be waiting to pounce on their one-trunk boats. We'd slaughter them."

"No doubt you are right," Bagdasares said. "I promise you, I shall do everything I can to learn what this signal may be. But I cannot do it now; the enemy's wizards almost made me lose a good-sized piece of my soul in the escape."

"Go rest, then," Maniakes said. "You look like you need it." What Bagdasares looked as if he needed was something more than rest. Maniakes said nothing of that, in the hope rest would also restore what else was missing from the Vaspurakaner mage. And, on leaving, Bagdasares did indeed yawn enormously, as if his body, not his spirit, had put in a hard day.

Maniakes waited till Bagdasares was well clear of the room in which he'd worked before muttering a ripe oath. That might not have done him any good, if Bagdasares was listening with senses beyond those mundane five. The Avtokrator cursed again, more ripely yet.

"*So* close!" Maniakes said, slamming a fist down on a tabletop. Another sentence, two at the most, would have told him what he so desperately wanted—so desperately needed—to learn. Now all he knew was that the Kubratoi would in fact swallow their pride and get help from the men of Makuran, who were more experienced when it came to sieges.

He wished—how he wished!—Etzilios had been too headstrong to share what he hoped would be his triumph with his allies. But Etzilios was too practical for that, worse luck. Trim his beard and take him out of his furs and he would have made a pretty fair Videssian. On that depressing note, Maniakes also left the chamber where Bagdasares had worked his successful spell. *If only it had been a little more successful,* the Avtokrator thought.

Thrax rose from his prostration, eyeing Maniakes warily. "How may I serve your Majesty?" he asked. The ceremonial of the Grand Courtroom weighed on him, as it was meant to do.

"I summoned you here to make certain you have the fleet at

the highest pitch of readiness over the next few days," Maniakes said from the throne, staring down at the drungarios of the fleet with no expression whatever on his face. The only way he could have sounded more imposing would have been to use the royal *we*, as Sharbaraz did—*probably even when he goes in unto his wives*, Maniakes thought, which amused him enough to make him have trouble holding his face still.

"The fleet is always at the highest pitch of readiness, your Majesty," Thrax said. "If the cockroaches come away from the wall, we'll step on 'em."

"I know you're ready to fight," Maniakes said. "That isn't quite what I meant."

"Well, what did you mean, then?" the drungarios of the fleet asked. A couple of courtiers muttered to one another at the imperfectly respectful way in which he framed the question.

Maniakes felt like muttering, too, but held onto his patience by main force. He knew how Thrax was. Knowing how Thrax was had made him convoke this ceremony. If the drungarios knew ahead of time exactly what he was supposed to do, he would do it, and do it well enough. If taken by surprise, he still might do well—but he also might do anything at all, with no way to guess beforehand whether for good or ill.

"I summoned you here to explain just that," the Avtokrator answered. "I expect that the Kubratoi will try to send a good many monoxyla over to the west side of the Cattle Crossing to bring back enough Makuraners to man the siege towers against us. Are you with me so far?"

"Aye, your Majesty," Thrax said confidently. Under that shock of shining silver hair, his bronzed, lined face was a mask of concentration.

"Good." Maniakes did his best to sound encouraging. Since he hadn't found anyone better than Thrax, he had to work as best he could within the man's limitations. He went on, "Before they sail, they'll signal, to let the Makuraners know they're coming. If we can spot that signal, too, we'll be able to get a running start on them, you might say. Wherever the main body of the fleet is, whether tied up at the piers or on patrol a little way off from the city, you have to be ready to get it out and covering the Cattle Crossing on the instant. Now do you understand what I'm saying?"

"I think so," the drungarios said. "You're saying you don't only want us ready to fight at a moment's notice, you want us ready to move at a moment's notice, too."

"That's it! That's perfect!" Maniakes felt like leaping down from the throne and planting a kiss on Thrax's cheek. Only the suspicion that that would fluster the drungarios more than it pleased him kept the Avtokrator in his seat. "Can you do it?"

"Oh, aye, I can, no doubt about that," Thrax said. "I'm still not sure I see the need, but I can."

"Seeing the need is my job," Maniakes said.

"Oh, aye," Thrax repeated. Unlike a lot of officers, he had no secret ambition to set his fundament on the throne Maniakes occupied. He might well have lacked the imagination to picture himself enjoying the power that would accrue to him on the seat. Cocking his head to one side, he asked, "How will you know what signal the Kubratoi are using?"

That was a good question. It was, in fact, *the* question of the moment. It wouldn't have been, had Etzilios' wizards—or perhaps Abivard's—not discovered Bagdasares' sorcery till another few moments had gone by. But they had discovered it, and now Maniakes had to live with—or perhaps die from—the consequences.

He said, "Our wizards are working on that," which had the twin virtues of being true and of satisfying Thrax. Also true was that the wizards had not had any luck whatever, but Maniakes did not tell the drungarios that.

The wizards' failure ate at the Avtokrator. So did the feeling they shouldn't have failed, or rather that their failure shouldn't have mattered. But matter it did. The Kubratoi, curse them, were not fools. Their wizards knew he'd been eavesdropping on Etzilios and Abivard. They knew he knew they intended to signal Abivard before their one-trunk boats dashed over the Cattle Crossing to ferry the Makuraners back to the eastern side of the strait to attack the walls of Videssos the city.

They also knew, or perhaps hoped, Maniakes did not know what the signal was supposed to be. And so they gave him every kind of signal under the sun. Fires sent columns of dense black smoke into the air by day. Fires crackled on the beach near the city by night. Kubratoi on horseback carried enormous banners of different colors back and forth. In among that welter of decoys the nomads might almost have hung out a sign—HERE WE COME, say, in letters fifty feet high—and had it pass with no special notice.

For the Videssians, in the frustrating absence of any sure knowledge of what the true signal would be, had to react to each and every one of them as if it was the real thing. Time after time, dromons would charge out into the Cattle Crossing, oars whipping the waves to foam, only to find no sign of the monoxyla they'd hoped to trap.

Inevitably, the false alarms began corroding the fleet's readiness. Maniakes had expected that to be a worse problem than it was. After a while, he realized why it wasn't so bad. He'd told Thrax he wanted the dromons ready to move at a moment's notice, no matter what. *No matter what* turned out to be more complicated and difficult than he'd expected. But he'd given Thrax an order, and the drungarios of the fleet was going to make sure that order got obeyed—period. Every once in a while, dogged mediocrity had its advantages.

Had Rhegorios suggested a sally now, Maniakes might have been more inclined to listen to him. The notion did not tempt him enough to order one on his own. He had more patience than his cousin—or so he kept telling himself, at any rate, though his record of moving too soon made it a dubious proposition.

The Kubratoi kept Videssos the city under blockade by land, and, away from it, their monoxyla picked off some of the merchantmen bringing supplies to the defenders. Grain did not grow scarce, but looked as if it would soon, which drove up the price in the markets.

Maniakes summoned a couple of the leading grain merchants. One of them, Boraides, was short and plump and smiled all the time. The other, Provhos, was tall and thin and doleful. Their looks and temperaments might have been different, but they thought alike.

Boraides said, "Not right to keep a man from turning an honest profit, heh heh."

"We are in a risky business, your Majesty," Provhos agreed. He cracked his knuckles with careful attention, one after another, his two thumbs last of all. The popping noises were startlingly loud in the small audience chamber of the imperial residence.

"I called you here to ask you to keep your prices down of your own free will," Maniakes said, "and to ask you to ask your colleagues to do likewise."

Boraides' eyes flicked left to Provhos, whose eyes were flicking right to him. Both men coughed at the same time. "Can't be done, your Majesty," Provhos said.

"Wish it could, but it can't," Boraides agreed. "Us grain sellers, we don't trust anybody. Why, I don't trust myself half the time, heh heh. I tell the other boys what you've just told me, they're liable to bump up prices on account of what you said, no better reason than that."

"They would be well advised not to do anything so foolish," Maniakes said.

Boraides started another breezy story. Provhos held up a hand. His fingers were long and, except at the joints, thin. Maniakes wondered whether that was because he cracked his knuckles. The lean grain merchant asked, "Why is that, your Majesty?"

"Because if they try to make an unfair profit off the people during this time of trouble—which is something the two of you would never even think of doing, of course—I would decide I had no choice but to open the imperial granaries to bring prices down again."

"You wouldn't do such a thing, your Majesty," Boraides said. "Why, it'd cost the grain merchants' goodwill for years to come."

Maniakes angrily exhaled through his nose. Some people's self-importance never failed to amaze him. He said, "Shall I have the soldiers take you out to the wall, distinguished sir? Do you want to go up there and see the Kubratoi and Makuraners with your own eyes? If that will convince you they're really there, I'll be happy to arrange it."

"I know they're there, your Majesty, heh heh," Boraides said. "It's only that—"

"If you know they're there, why don't you act like it?" Maniakes interrupted. "I don't want people going hungry while we're besieged, and I don't want people hating the men who sell them grain, either. Both those things are liable to make them fight worse than they would otherwise, and that's all I'm worried about. If the city falls, we're dead—for true, not metaphorically. Next to that, gentlemen, having the grain merchants angry at me is something I don't mind risking."

"But—" Boraides was ready to go on arguing.

Provhos seemed to have a better grip on reality. "It's no good, Bor," he said sadly. "He can do more things to us than we can do to him, and that's all there is to it." He bowed to Maniakes. "We'll keep prices down as low as we can, your Majesty. If you open the imperial granaries, you can always knock them down lower. That's what being Avtokrator is all about."

"That's right," Maniakes said. "I'm glad one of you has the wit to realize it, anyhow."

"Bah," Boraides said. "If we put enough people on the streets—"

"A lot of them will end up dead," Maniakes promised. "So will you. You may perhaps have noticed that we have an army's worth of soldiers in the city. If merchants protest now because they can't gouge, they will be sorry, as I said earlier. How long do you think they'll be able to go before soldiers start looting the shops of merchants who've been . . . troublesome, especially if they didn't think anyone would punish them afterward?"

Boraides still didn't seem ready to keep his mouth shut. Provhos hissed at him. They put their heads together. Maniakes let them mutter for as long as they liked. When they finished, he had trouble deciding which of them looked less happy. Provhos' long face had probably seemed mournful on the most joyous day of his life, and he wasn't joyous now. Boraides usually looked jolly even when he wasn't. He didn't look jolly at the moment.

"You're doing a terrible thing to us, your Majesty, keeping us from earning an honest return on our work," he said. "You can make us do it—Provhos is right about that—but you can't make us like it."

"I've never said you can't make your usual profit. I've said you can't gouge," Maniakes answered. "Think back. Pay attention to my words. I don't like the idea of food riots. I have enough trouble and to spare outside the city. If I can stop trouble inside the city before it starts, you'd best believe I'm going to do that."

Both grain merchants shook their heads. He'd overawed them. He hadn't convinced them. He was willing to settle for that. He was not the lord with the great and good mind, to reach inside a man's head and change the way he thought. If he could make his subjects act as he wished them to act, he'd be content.

He scowled. Up till now, he hadn't had much luck making the Makuraners and Kubratoi act as he wished them to act.

Provhos and Boraides took his frown as dismissal. He hadn't intended it that way, but it would do. As they rose, Kameas appeared in the doorway to escort them out of the imperial residence.

"How do you do that?" Maniakes asked when the vestiarios returned to see if he needed anything else.

"How do I do what, your Majesty?" Kameas asked in return.

"Know exactly when to show up," the Avtokrator said. "I've never caught you snooping, and neither has anyone else, but you're always in the right place at the right time. How do you manage?"

"I have a good notion of how long any particular individual is likely to require your attention," the eunuch said, which was not really an answer.

"If your sense of timing is as good as that, esteemed sir, maybe you belong on the battlefield, not in the palace quarter."

Maniakes hadn't meant it seriously, but Kameas sounded serious as he replied, "A couple of chamberlains with my disability have served their sovereigns as soldiers, your Majesty. I am given to understand that they did not disgrace themselves, perhaps for the very reason you cited."

"I didn't know that," Maniakes said, bemused. Eunuch generals would have to gain respect from their men by different means from entire men, that was certain. It wouldn't be easy, either; he could see as much. "I must say I admire them."

"Oh, so do we, your Majesty," Kameas replied. "Their memory is yet green within the palaces." Maniakes pictured old chamberlains telling young ones of the great deeds of their warlike predecessors, and then those young eunuchs growing old in turn and passing on the tales to those who came after them. Then Kameas rather spoiled his vision by adding, "And several historians and chroniclers also note their martial accomplishments."

"Do they?" Maniakes' reading, aside from endless parchments from the bureaucrats and soldiers who made the Empire of Videssos keep running even in the face of the dislocations of the Makuraner and Kubrati invasions, ran more to military manuals than to histories. And soldiers like Kalokyres, in explaining how a general was to go about doing the things he needed to do, never bothered mentioning whether testicles were essential for the job.

"They certainly do, your Majesty." The vestiarios showed more enthusiasm for the subject than Maniakes usually saw in him, no doubt because it touched him personally. He went on, "Should you so desire, I could show you some of the relevant passages. I have several of these scrolls and codices myself, copied out by very fine scribes, and I am gradually accumulating more as I discover documents in the archives."

"Is that what you do in your free time—search the archives, I mean?"

"One of the things, yes, your Majesty." Kameas drew himself straight with a pride that was liable to be twisted. "After all, things being as they are, I am hardly in a position to chase women."

Maniakes walked over and punched him in the shoulder, as he might have done with Rhegorios. "To the ice with me if I think I could joke about it," he said. "You're a good man, esteemed sir—and you don't need a pair of balls for most of the things that make a good man."

"I have often thought as much myself, your Majesty, but I must tell you that it gives me a great deal of satisfaction to hear it from an entire man," Kameas said. "Some, I assure you, are less generous than that."

His mouth stretched out into a thin, hard, bleak line. He had been vestiarios for Genesios before Maniakes managed to rid Videssos of the tyrant. Every so often, Kameas let slip something that suggested Genesios' reign of terror had been even worse within the palace quarter than anywhere beyond. Maniakes had never questioned him or any of the other palace eunuchs about that, partly because he was as well pleased not knowing and partly because he did not want to pain the eunuchs by making them remember.

The vestiarios bowed. "Will there be anything further, your Majesty?"

"I don't think so," Maniakes said. As Kameas turned to go, the Avtokrator changed his mind. "Wait." The eunuch obediently stopped. Maniakes dug in his beltpouch. He found no gold there, only silver: a telling comment on the state of the Empire's finances. He tossed a couple of coins to Kameas. They shone in the air till the eunuch caught them. "For your copyist," Maniakes said.

Kameas bowed again, this time in a subtly different way: as himself now, not as vestiarios. "Your Majesty is gracious."

"What my Majesty is, is sick and tired of being hemmed into

the city and waiting for the Makuraners to try swarming over the Cattle Crossing," Maniakes said. "We should know when they're going to do it, but we can't steal the signal that warns they're truly moving."

"If we keep responding to all the signals the Kubratoi have been putting forth—" Kameas began.

"We end up not responding well enough to any one of them," Maniakes broke in. "It will happen, sooner or later. It has to. But one day soon, one of those signals will be real, and, if we don't take that one seriously, we'll have a Makuraner army on this side of the . . ."

His voice trailed away. When he didn't go on after a minute or so, Kameas cleared his throat. "You were saying, your Majesty?"

"Was I?" Maniakes answered absently. His eyes and his thoughts were far away. "Whatever I was saying—" He had no memory of it. "—that doesn't matter any more. Had I had gold to give you, esteemed sir, I might not have known. But I do. Now I know."

"Your Majesty?" Kameas' voice was plaintive. Maniakes did not reply.

✦ VII

Your Majesty!" The messenger spoke in high excitement. He smelled of lathered horse, which likely meant he'd galloped his mount through the streets of Videssos the city to bring his word to Maniakes. "Your Majesty, the Kubratoi are flashing sunlight from a silver shield over the Cattle Crossing to the Makuraners!"

"Are they?" Maniakes breathed. As he had with Kameas, he reached into his beltpouch for money. He'd made sure he had gold there now, against this very moment. The messenger gaped when the Avtokrator pressed half a dozen goldpieces into his hand. Maniakes said, "Now give Thrax the word. He knows what to do." He hoped—he prayed—the drungarios knew what to do.

"Aye, your Majesty, I'll do that," the messenger said. "Immodios sent a man to him, too, but I'll go, in case poor Vonos fell off his horse and cracked his hard head or something." He hurried away.

His boots rang against the mosaic tiles on the hallway floor of the imperial residence. Rhegorios rose from his chair, stiffened to attention, and gave Maniakes a formal salute, right clenched fist over his heart. "You knew," he said, nothing but admiration in his voice.

Maniakes shook his head. "I still don't *know*," he answered. "But I think I'm right, and I think so strongly enough to gamble

547

on it. When Abivard first came to Across and I parleyed with him, he asked me if the Imperial Guards carried silver shields, and he seemed disappointed when I said no. And then there was Bagdasares' magic—"

"Yes, you told me about that the other day," his cousin answered. "He managed to capture the words some Makuraner seer had given Abivard?"

"That's right, or I think that's right," Maniakes said. "Wherever they came from, the words were clear enough." He shifted into the Makuraner tongue: "'Son of the *dihqan*, I see a broad field that is not a field, a tower on a hill where honor shall be won and lost, and a silver shield shining across a narrow sea.'" Returning to Videssian, he went on, "Wherever the words came from, as I say, they meant—and mean—a great deal to Abivard. If he asked Etzilios for any one signal to start his army moving, that would be the one—or that's my guess, at any rate."

"I think you're right," Rhegorios said. "And so does your father. I've never seen Uncle Maniakes looking so impressed as he did when you set your idea in front of him—and he doesn't impress easily, either."

"Who, my father?" Maniakes said, as if in surprise. He gave that up; he couldn't bring it off. "I had noticed, thanks."

"I thought you might have," his cousin agreed.

Maniakes said, "I couldn't decide for the longest time whether I'd watch the sea fight from the palace quarter here or from the deck of a ship. At last I thought, if I was there on the land wall, I ought to be there on the sea, too. I've ordered Thrax to pick me up at the palace harbor. Will you come, too?"

"Aboard the *Renewal*?" Rhegorios asked. Maniakes nodded. His cousin said, "If I didn't drown in that one storm, to the ice with me if I think the Kubratoi can do me any harm. Let's go. We'd better hurry, too. If you've told Thrax to pick you up there, he'll wait around and do it even if you don't show up till next month, and he won't care a rotten fig for what that does to the plans for the sea fight."

Since Rhegorios was undoubtedly right, Maniakes wasted no time arguing with him. The two men hurried out of the imperial residence. A few guards peeled off from the entranceways to the building and trotted along with them, complaining all the while that they should have waited for more men to accompany them.

Maniakes wasted no time arguing with the guards, either. He was reveling in having escaped his dozen parasol-bearers. He wondered how they would have done standing at the bow of the *Renewal* when it climbed up and over a one-trunk boat. With any luck, half of them would have gone into the drink and drowned.

He and Rhegorios reached the quays by the palaces none too soon. Here came the *Renewal*, oars rising and falling in perfect unison. The sun shining off Thrax's hair was almost as bright as it would have been, reflected from a silver shield.

As the imperial flagship picked up the Avtokrator and the Sevastos, more dromons—many more dromons—dashed out into the middle of the Cattle Crossing, ready to keep the Kubratoi from reaching the western shore and picking up their Makuraner allies. "If you're right, your Majesty, they've fallen into our hands," Thrax declared. He sounded confident. Maniakes had told him it would be thus and so. He was going to act on that assumption. If Maniakes was right, all would be well. If Maniakes was wrong, Thrax's blind obedience would make him wronger.

"Let's go get them," Maniakes said. He would assume he was right, too, and would keep on assuming it for as long as he could. If he was wrong, he hoped he'd notice quickly, because Thrax wouldn't.

One of the dromons far enough south for its captain to be able to see around the bulk of Videssos the city sent a horn call back toward the rest of the fleet. Other ships echoed it, spreading the word as fast as they were able. "That's *enemy in sight*," Rhegorios breathed.

"Yes, it is, isn't it?" Maniakes said. He looked up into the heavens and sketched Phos' sun-circle above his breast. He felt taller, quicker, more agile, as if an enormous weight had just fallen from his shoulders.

Thrax shouted to the oarmaster. The deep drum picked up the beat. The *Renewal* fairly leapt over the waves, speeding toward the foes who had shown themselves at last. Maniakes peered south and east, for once regretting Videssos the city's seawall, because for some little while it kept him from learning how great a threat he, the city, and the Empire faced.

"By the good god," he said when the *Renewal*, like that first dromon, had come far enough to let him get a good look at the foe. Dozens of monoxyla bobbed in the chop of the Cattle

Crossing. Their paddles rose and fell, rose and fell, in almost the same rhythm as the dromons' oars. Since the wind came out of the west, their masts were down.

Thrax shouted again, this time to the trumpeter: "Blow *each ship pick its own foe.*" The call rang out and quickly went through the fleet.

Spying the Videssian warships between them and their allies, the Kubratoi shouted to one another. "If you were in one of those boats, what would you do?" Rhegorios asked Maniakes.

"Me?" The Avtokrator considered. "I'd like to think I'd have the sense to go back to dry land and try again some other day." He shook his head. "I'd probably press on, though, figuring I'd come too far to turn back. I've made a lot of mistakes like that, so I expect I'd make one more."

"Here's hoping it *is* a mistake," Rhegorios said, to which his cousin could only nod.

Mistake or not, the Kubratoi kept coming. Now they shouted not just back and forth among themselves but also at the Videssians. Maniakes did not understand their language. He did not need to understand it to get the idea that they weren't paying him compliments. If the fists they shook at the Videssian dromons hadn't given him a clue, the arrows arcing toward his fleet would have.

Those first arrows fell short, splashing into the sea like flying fish. Most of the dromons carried dart-throwers that could shoot farther than any archer. When their darts missed, they kicked up bigger splashes than mere arrows. When they hit, as they did every so often, a couple of Kubratoi would suddenly stop paddling, slowing their monoxyla by so much.

As the one-trunk boats and the dromons drew nearer to one another, the Kubrati archers began scoring hits, too. Here and there, Videssians crumpled to the decking of their ships. One or two of them fell into the water. Maniakes saw one wounded man bravely strike out toward the shore less than half a mile away. He never found out whether the fellow made it.

More and more arrows rained down on the dromons. More and more men cried out in pain. "Is this going to give us a lot of trouble?" Maniakes asked Thrax.

The drungarios of the fleet shook his head, then brushed disarrayed silver locks back from his forehead. "This is like a mosquito bite, your Majesty. It itches. It stings. So what? Fights on the sea aren't like your fights on land. A bunch of silly arrows don't decide anything, not here they don't."

He sounded perfectly confident. Maniakes, knowing himself only a spectator on this field, could but hope the drungarios had reason for confidence.

Up ahead, the dromon that had first spotted the monoxyla raced straight toward one, seawater slicing aside from its ram. It struck the one-log boat amidships. The crunch of the bronze-shod ram striking home was audible across a couple of furlongs. The dromon backed oars. Water flooded into the monoxylon through the gash the ram had torn. The Videssian vessel rowed off toward another victim.

"That one!" Thrax pointed at a one-trunk boat. The men at the steering oars swung the *Renewal* in the direction he had ordered. He called out course corrections with calm certainty. He'd done this before, after the storm on the Sailors' Sea. Anything he'd done before, he did well.

But, however well he did, the monoxylon escaped him. Maybe its Kubrati captain had as much experience dodging dromons as Thrax had in running down the smaller vessels. As the one-log boat and the war galley closed on each other, the monoxylon put on a sudden burst of speed, so that the dromon's ram slid past its stern.

Thrax cursed foully. "He was lucky," Maniakes said, which was not strictly true—the Kubrati had shown both nerve and skill. The Avtokrator went on, "We have plenty of monoxyla left to hunt, and they can't all get away." *They'd better not all get away,* he added to himself.

"Phos bless you, your Majesty, for your patience," the drungarios of the fleet said.

While Thrax swung the *Renewal* toward the next nearest one-trunk boat, Maniakes turned to Rhegorios. "I've been patient with him, all right—patient to a fault. If I had anyone better—"

"You would have put him in Thrax's place a long time ago," Rhegorios broke in. "You know that. I know that. Maybe even Thrax knows that. But you don't. Sometimes there aren't enough good men to go around, and that's all there is to it. He's not bad."

Maniakes didn't answer. Having the fate of the Empire depend on a man who wasn't bad gnawed at him. But the sea fight, as it developed, didn't really depend on Thrax alone. It was every Videssian captain for himself, trying to crush enemy vessels that seemed as small and quick and elusive as cockroaches scuttling from one side of a room to the other.

One of those cockroaches would not get away. The *Renewal* rode up and over a monoxylon, capsizing it and spilling most of its warriors into the green-blue waters of the Cattle Crossing. The collision had slowed the dromon. Would it be able to reach the next nearest one-trunk boat before the latter could speed off? Maniakes shouted in delight as the ram bit into the monoxylon near the stern.

"Back oars!" Thrax shouted. The *Renewal* pulled free. The one-log boat filled rapidly. It did not sink—it was, after all, only wood. But the Kubratoi aboard, regardless of whether they eventually managed to reach Across, would bring back no Makuraners to attack Videssos the city.

Monoxylon after monoxylon was holed or capsized by the Videssian fleet. The imperials did not quite have it all their own way. Some of the Kubratoi shot fire arrows, as they had in Maniakes' earlier encounter with them. They managed to set a couple of dromons afire. And four monoxyla converged on a war galley that had trouble freeing its ram from the one-log boat it had struck. The Kubratoi swarmed onto the dromon and massacred its crew.

"Ram them," Maniakes said, pointing to the nomads who exulted on the deck of the dromon. Thrax, for once, did not need to be told twice. The *Renewal* had not been too near the captured galley, but quickly closed the distance. Thrax guided the flagship between two of the one-log boats still close by the dromon. The Kubratoi had barely got the unfamiliar ship moving by then. It moved no more after the *Renewal*'s ram tore a gaping hole in its flank.

Maniakes peered toward the western shore of the Cattle Crossing. A couple of monoxyla had managed to make the crossing despite all the Videssian fleet could do. Makuraner soldiers were running toward them and scrambling inside. A lot of Makuraners stood drawn up over there, awaiting transport over the narrow strait to Videssos the city. By the way the sea fight was going, most of them would wait a long time.

Together, Kubratoi and Makuraners shoved into the sea once

more one of the boats that had made the crossing. Before Maniakes could order the *Renewal* to the attack, two other Videssian dromons raced toward the eastbound monoxylon. Abivard's men, being armored in iron, went to the bottom faster than Etzilios'. Otherwise, there was not much difference between them.

"It's a slaughter!" Rhegorios shouted, slapping Maniakes on the back.

"By the good god, it is," Maniakes said in some astonishment. Few uncapsized monoxyla still floated. Some of those that did, having managed to escape the fighting, were paddling back toward the shore from which they had come. Kubratoi bobbed in the water, a few still swimming or clinging to wreckage but most of them dead.

"Haven't I said all along, your Majesty," Thrax boomed proudly, "that if we ever got the chance to fight a big sea battle, dromons against monoxyla, I mean, we'd smash them to flinders? Haven't I said that?"

"So you have," Maniakes said. "It seems you were right." That Thrax had also said a fair number of things that had turned out to be wrong, he did not mention. The drungarios had redeemed himself today.

"I didn't think it would be *this* easy," Rhegorios said. He was looking at bobbing bodies, too.

"I did," Thrax said, which was also true. "These one-trunk boats, they're good enough to carry raiders, but they've always taken lumps when they went up against real war galleys. The Kubratoi know it, too; they aren't in the habit of getting into stand-up fights with us. They tried it here this once, and they've paid for it."

"That they have," Maniakes said. "If they haven't thrown away more men here on the sea than they did trying to storm the city's walls, I'll be astonished."

A ripple showed near one of the corpses floating in the Cattle Crossing. A moment later, it floated no more. Land battles quickly drew ravens and buzzards and foxes. Sea fights had their scavengers, too.

"Remind me not to eat seafood for a while," Rhegorios said.

Maniakes gulped. "I'll do that. And I won't do that for a while myself." His cousin nodded, having no trouble sorting through the clumsy phrasing.

The Avtokrator gauged the sun. It wasn't that far past noon, and it hadn't been long before noon when he and Rhegorios boarded the *Renewal*. In the space of a couple of hours, Etzilios' hopes, and those of Sharbaraz, too, had gone to ruin in the narrow sea between Videssos the city and Across.

"I wonder how much gold we've spent on the fleet over the years—over the centuries, by Phos," the Avtokrator said musingly. "So much of it must have looked like nothing but waste. However much we spent, though, what we did here today made every copper of it worthwhile."

"That's right, your Majesty. That's exactly right," Thrax said. "And so next year, when I ask for gold for new ships and for keeping the old ones in the shape they should be, you'll give me all I ask for, won't you?"

Scratch a drungarios, find a courtier. In a mock-fierce voice, Maniakes growled, "If you ask me for so much as one Makuraner silver arket, Thrax, I will beat you with a club studded with nails. Is that plain?"

"Yes, your Majesty." Not even Thrax, naive and stolid as he was, could take the threat seriously.

Rhegorios said, "Etzilios' plans have gone down the latrine, and so have those of Sharbaraz King of Kings, may his days be long and his arse covered in boils. What about Abivard's plans?" The Sevastos pointed over toward Across, where Makuraner soldiers still waited near the shore for boats that would never come.

"I don't know," Maniakes said. "We'll have to find out. He can't do anything to the capital now. That, I think, is certain. He can still do quite a lot to the westlands—or he may pull back to the Land of the Thousand Cities against a move from us. No way to tell till it happens."

"I suppose not," Rhegorios said. "I wish we could pry him loose from Sharbaraz, the way he pried Tzikas loose from you."

"He didn't pry Tzikas loose from me. Tzikas pried himself loose from me," Maniakes answered. "When he didn't manage to kill me, taking refuge with the Makuraners looked like the best way to keep me from prying his head loose from his shoulders." He made a sour face. "It worked too bloody well."

"Abivard seems loyal." Rhegorios made it sound like a disease. Maniakes felt the same way, at least where Abivard was concerned. A disloyal Makuraner marshal would have been a great boon to the Empire of Videssos. Thinking of loyalty in such disparaging terms made Maniakes realize how completely a Videssian he'd become in spite of his Vaspurakaner heritage. His great-grandparents surely would have praised loyalty even in a foe. He shrugged. His great-grandparents hadn't known everything there was to know, either.

"What now, your Majesty?" Thrax asked.

Having thought himself a true Videssian, Maniakes had an idea of truly Videssian duplicity. "Let's go over to the shore near the Kubrati camp," he answered. "I want to deliver a message to Etzilios."

As he'd guessed, the sight of the *Renewal* cruising not far away brought a crowd of Kubratoi to the seaside to see why he was there. "What youse am wantings?" one of them shouted in Videssian so mangled that he recognized the speaker at once.

"Moundioukh, take my words to your khagan, the magnifolent Etzilios." Full of triumph, Maniakes used the contorted epithet without hesitation. "Tell him that, since my fleet has disposed of those poor, sorry toys he called boats, nothing now prevents me from shipping a force to the coast north of Videssos the city, landing it there, and making sure he never escapes from the Empire of Videssos."

"Youse am bluffing," Moundioukh shouted across the water. He did not sound confident, though. He sounded frightened.

"You'll see. So will Etzilios," Maniakes said, and then, to Thrax, "Move us out of bowshot now, if you'd be so kind."

"Aye, your Majesty," the drungarios replied. For a wonder, he understood exactly what Maniakes had meant, and said "Back oars!" loud enough to let the oarmaster know what was required but not so loud as to alert the Kubratoi on the shore.

"That's—demonic, cousin of mine," Rhegorios said admiringly. "By the good god, we really could do it, too."

"I know we could," the Avtokrator said. "Etzilios has to know it, too. We did it once, three years ago, and we almost put paid to him. He has to think we'd try it again. I'm not going to ship an army out of Videssos the city, on the off chance that he'd try using his siege towers again instead of retreating, and get inside because we'd weakened the garrison. But he won't know that, and I'm going to make it look as much as if we *are* moving troops as I can."

"What now, your Majesty?" Thrax asked again.

"Now we go back to Videssos the city," Maniakes answered. "We've sown the seed. We have to see what kind of crop we get from it."

Agathios the ecumenical patriarch called for a service of thanksgiving in the High Temple. He sent the call through Videssos the city without the least urging from Maniakes, who was almost as surprised as he was pleased. Agathios displayed initiative only a little more often than Thrax did.

Maniakes was also surprised at the fervor of the Videssians who flocked to the Temple to worship and to give thanks to the good god. A fair number of them also seemed willing to give him some credit for having smashed the Kubratoi at sea. They knew how desperate their situation had been, and knew also that, while the Kubratoi still besieged them, the risk of the Makuraners' joining the assault was gone.

And then, with timing Maniakes could not have hoped to emulate, a messenger rushed into the High Temple just as the service was ending and before more than a handful of people had filed out. "Your Majesty!" the fellow cried out in a great voice. "Your Majesty, the Kubratoi are withdrawing! They're burning their towers and engines and riding away!"

"We bless thee, Phos, lord with the great and good mind!" Agathios exclaimed, and his voice came echoing back from the dome wherein the great mosaic image of Phos stern in judgment looked down on his congregation. Even Phos' majestic face seemed less harsh at that moment, the Avtokrator thought.

"This I will see for myself," Maniakes declared. For the first time since marrying Lysia, he left the High Temple accompanied by cheers. Though judging those cheers aimed less at himself than at the news the messenger brought, Maniakes was glad of them all the same.

He saw long before reaching the city wall that the messenger had spoken the truth. Black clouds of smoke rose into the sky to the east. Maniakes had seen such clouds before, when the Kubratoi came down to raid as far as the wall. Then they had been Videssian fields and farmlands going up in flames.

This time, the Kubratoi had not merely come up to the wall. They had set foot on it, which no invaders in all the history of the Empire of Videssos had done before them. But, though they had done so much, they had done no more; the defenders and the great strength of the walls themselves had made sure of that. What they burned now was of their own substance, which they could not take with them lest it slow them in their retreat, and which they did not care to leave lest the Videssians take it and use it against them.

When Maniakes went up onto the wall, the picture became sweeter still. The siege towers the Videssians had not been able to set afire burned now. So did the stone-throwers the Makuraner engineers had taught the Kubratoi to build. "We would have saved those, had this been our campaign," a Videssian officer said, pointing out toward them.

"Aye, so we would," Maniakes answered. He'd carried a baggage train full of the parts needed for siege engines throughout the Land of the Thousand Cities. "They're nomads, though. They didn't bring supply wagons along with them, and they've been living off the countryside."

"They won't be back soon, not after this," the officer said. "They've failed against us twice running now, and they can't be happy about it. With any luck, they'll have a nice little civil war over what went wrong and who was to blame."

"From your mouth to Phos' ear," Maniakes said fervently. It didn't look as if any stone-throwers at all were going back north with the Kubratoi. He wondered if their artisans would be able to make new ones without models before them. They probably would, he thought with no small regret. Underestimating how clever his foes were did no good.

"Are we going to pursue, your Majesty?" the officer asked, avid as any Videssian to pick up news that was really none of his business.

"Right now, I think I'm willing to let them go," the Avtokrator said. The officer's disappointed look would have drawn applause had he been a mime in a Midwinter's Day show. So would the way he brightened with excitement when Maniakes added, "And I'll tell you why." He went on, "I don't want my soldiers chasing the Kubratoi away from what has to be the main center of action. The most important thing we can do is get the westlands back from the Makuraners. Chasing the Kubratoi, however delightful it might be, distracts us from what needs doing more."

"Ah." The captain saluted. "This I can understand." Videssians could be, and often were, ruthlessly pragmatic when it came to war.

Maniakes watched the Kubratoi engines smolder. The wind shifted, blowing harsh smoke into his face. His eyes stung. He coughed several times. And then he started to laugh. The officer stared at him for a moment. He started laughing, too. The sweet sound spread up and down the wall, till every soldier in the garrison seemed to be letting out his relief in one long burst of hilarity. Maniakes hoped the Kubratoi had not fled too far to hear that laughter. It would have wounded them almost as badly as the Videssians' stalwart defense had done. *Take that, magnifolent Etzilios*, the Avtokrator thought.

The elder Maniakes raised a silver winecup high. "Here's to half the battle won!" he said, and drained the cup.

Maniakes drank that toast without hesitation. It was exactly how he viewed the situation himself. Lysia, however, spoke with some asperity: "It's more than half the battle, I'd say. The Kubratoi and the Makuraners had the one chance to work together, and we've ruined it. They'll never put that alliance back together again, because we'll never let them."

"You're right, lass, you're right," the elder Maniakes said, making a placating gesture. "Every word you say is true—and far be it from me to argue with my daughter-in-law. My son would probably put my head up on the Milestone for that, with a big placard saying what a naughty fellow I'd been." He made as if to shrink from the Avtokrator.

"It would need to be a very big placard, to get all that on," Maniakes said with a snort. But even his father's drollery had calculation in it. Lysia had been the elder Maniakes' niece all her life. He did not mention that family tie now, as Rhegorios often did. He would not speak out against the marriage Maniakes had made, but he did not speak for it, either.

"You're right, Lysia—and you're wrong," Symvatios said. "Yes, we've forced the Kubratoi and the Makuraners apart again, and that's a very great triumph again. I don't say it isn't. But—" He pointed west. "—there's Abivard still, practically close enough to spit on. Till we drive him back where he belongs, we're missing a good piece from a whole victory."

"Will we sail back to Lyssaion, or through the Videssian Sea to Erzerum?" Rhegorios asked. "Getting late in the year to do either, worse luck."

"I'd like to," Maniakes said. "Now that we don't have to worry about the Kubratoi any more—or don't have to worry about them sacking the city, anyhow—we could."

He looked from his father to his uncle to his cousin to his wife. None of them seemed to think much of the idea. After a brief pause, the elder Maniakes said, "It's late in the year to hope to accomplish much unless you intend to winter in the Land of the Thousand Cities."

"I could," Maniakes said. "They bring in crops the year around. The army would eat well enough."

"Late in the year for a fleet to be setting out, too," Rhegorios observed. "We've been through one bad storm already this campaigning season. That's plenty for me."

"If I order Thrax to sail west, he will sail," Maniakes said.

"You can order Thrax to do whatever you please, and he will do it," the elder Maniakes put in. "That doesn't make him smart. It only makes him obedient."

"The Avtokrator of the Videssians can command his subjects as he pleases," Symvatios added, "but I've never heard that even the Avtokrator can order wind and wave to obey his will."

Maniakes didn't have such an inflated view of his own place in the world as to disagree with that. Had he had such an inflated view, the storm he and his cousin and the entire fleet barely survived would have made him revise it. He said, "I'll have Bagdasares check what sort of weather we'll have if we sail. He warned me of this storm coming home, and we couldn't get away from it no matter what we did. If he says the sailing will be good, we'll go. If not, not. Does it please you?"

Everyone beamed at him.

Bagdasares prostrated himself when Maniakes came into his sorcerous study. Having risen, the Vaspurakaner wizard said, "How may I serve you, your Majesty?"

If he did not know what Maniakes had in mind, the Avtokrator would have been astonished. Bagdasares would have needed no divination to know; palace gossip was surely plenty. But the forms had to be observed. Formally, Maniakes said, "I want to know if the fleet will enjoy good weather sailing west to Lyssaion later this campaigning season."

"Of course, your Majesty," Bagdasares said, bowing low. "You have seen how this spell is performed. If you will be good enough to bear with me while I assemble the necessary ingredients—"

He did that with such quick efficiency as to remove all doubt from Maniakes' mind as to whether he'd known this visit was coming. He even had several little wooden ships already made to symbolize the vessels of the fleet. Maniakes hid his smile. Had everyone served him as well as Bagdasares, he would have been the most fortunate Avtokrator in Videssian history.

Into the bowl went the ships carved from chips of wood. They rode the ripples there, as real ships would ride over the waves of the Sailors' Sea. Bagdasares began to chant; his hands moved in swift passes above the bowl.

Developments were not long in coming. Maniakes vividly remembered the storm the mage's spell had predicted for the return journey from Lyssaion. The miniature tempest Bagdasares raised this time was worse, with lightning like sparks and thunder like a small drum. One of the little lightning bolts smote a sorcerous ship, which burned to the waterline.

"Your Majesty, I cannot in good conscience recommend that you undertake this course," Bagdasares said with what struck Maniakes as commendable understatement.

"A pestilence!" Maniakes muttered under his breath. "All right—suppose we sail the Videssian Sea to Erzerum, then?" He didn't want to do that. It made for a longer journey to Mashiz, and one in which the Makuraners would have plenty of chances to slow and perhaps even stop him before he ever brought his army down into the Land of the Thousand Cities.

"I shall attempt to see what may be seen, your Majesty," the wizard replied. Like most in his art, he had a sober countenance, but now his eyes twinkled for a moment. "As this route would bring you close to Vaspurakan, so will the sorcery become more precise, more accurate."

"Really?" Maniakes asked, intrigued in spite of his annoyance at the earlier prediction; Bagdasares had never claimed anything like that before.

The Vaspurakaner mage sighed. "I wish it were true. Logically, it should be true, Vaspur the Firstborn and his descendants being the primary focus of Phos' activity here on earth. But if you order me to prove to you it is true, I fear I cannot."

"Ah, well," Maniakes said. "If you could, you'd have a lot of mages in the Sorcerers' Collegium—and in Mashiz, too, I shouldn't wonder—hopping mad at you. All right, you can't be more accurate about what happens on the Videssian Sea. If you can be as accurate, I'll take that."

What he meant was, *If you can show me how to do what I want to do, even if I have to do it in this inconvenient way, I'll take that.* Bagdasares spent some little while incanting over the bowl and the water and the little ships he had made—except for the one that had burned—sorcerously persuading them they now represented a fleet on the Videssian Sea, not one on the Sailors' Sea.

When he was satisfied the components of his magic understood their new role, he began the spell proper. It was almost identical to the one that had gone before, name and description of the new sea and new landing place being substituted for those he had previously used.

And, to Maniakes' dismay, the results of the incantation were almost identical to those that had gone before. Again, the Avtokrator watched a miniature storm play havoc with the miniature fleet. None of the little chip ships caught fire this time, but more of them capsized than had been true in the previous conjuration.

He asked the only question he could think to ask: "Are you certain you took off all the influence from the earlier spell?"

"As certain as may be, yes," Bagdasares answered. "But if it pleases you, your Majesty, I can begin again from the beginning. Preparing everything from scratch will take a bit more time, you understand, but—"

"Do it," Maniakes said.

Do it, Bagdasares did. He chose a new bowl, he prepared fresh—or rather, new—symbolic seawater, and he made a new fleet of toy ships. It did seem to take quite a while, though Maniakes reflected that his wizard was much swifter than his shipwrights. "I shall also use a different incantation this time," Bagdasares said, "to reduce any possible lingering effects from my previous spells." The Avtokrator nodded approval.

Bagdasares went about the new spell as methodically as he had with the preparations for it. The incantation was indeed different from the one he'd used before. The results, however, were the same: a tiny storm that sank and scattered most of the symbolic fleet.

"I am very sorry, your Majesty." Bagdasares' voice dragged with weariness when the spell was done. "I cannot in good conscience recommend sending a fleet to the west by way of the Videssian Sea, either." He yawned. "Your pardon, I crave. Three conjurations of an afternoon will wear a man down to a nub." He yawned again.

"Rest, then," Maniakes said. "I know better than to blame the messenger for the news he brings." Bagdasares bowed, and almost fell over. Wobbling as if drunk, he took his leave. Maniakes stood alone in the sorcerous workroom. "I know better than to blame the messenger for his news," he repeated, "but, by the good god, I wish I didn't."

With a screech of rusty hinges, the postern gate opened. It was not the gate through which Moundioukh had come when Maniakes tried to detach the Kubratoi from their alliance to Makuran. That one had been made quiet. Now silence and stealth no longer mattered. Maniakes could leave Videssos the city without fear, without worry; no enemy stood nearby.

Maniakes could not leave Videssos the city, however, without his guardsmen or without his full complement of twelve parasol-bearers. He might have vanquished Etzilios, he might have kept the Makuraners on the west side of the Cattle Crossing, but against entrenched ceremonial he struggled in vain.

Rhegorios said, "Don't worry about it, cousin your Majesty brother-in-law of mine." That he was using his whimsical mix of titles for Maniakes again said he thought the crisis was over for the time being. He went on, "They won't get in your way very much."

"Ha!" Maniakes said darkly. But, even with the demands of ceremony oppressing him, he could not hold on to his foul mood. Being able to leave the imperial city, even with his escort, felt monstrous good.

Seeing the wreckage of Etzilios' hopes up close felt even better. Videssian scavengers were still going over the engines and towers for scraps of timber and metal they could use or sell. Before long, nothing would be left.

"On this side of the Cattle Crossing, we're our own masters

again," Rhegorios said, thinking along with him. The Sevastos' grin, always ready, got wider now. "And from where we are, the wall keeps us from looking over the Cattle Crossing at the Makuraners on the other side. We'll worry about them next, of course, but we don't have to do it now."

For once, Maniakes didn't try to peer around the wall to glare at Abivard's forces. He wasn't worrying about them now, but not for the reason Rhegorios had put forward. His worries, for the moment, were closer to him. Pointing toward the base of the wall, he said, "It was right around here somewhere."

"What was right around here?" asked Rhegorios, who hadn't asked why the Avtokrator was leaving Videssos the city before coming along with him.

"That's right," Maniakes said, reminding himself. "You weren't up on the wall then. Immodios and I were the ones who served the dart-thrower."

"What dart-thrower?" Rhegorios sounded like a man doing his best to stay reasonable but one unlikely to stay that way indefinitely.

"The one we used to shoot at Tzikas," the Avtokrator answered; he hadn't intended to thwart his cousin. "The renegade, may the ice take him, was showing the Kubratoi *something*—probably something he wanted them to know so they could hurt us with it. Whatever it is, I want to find it so we won't have to worry about it again."

"How could it be anything?" Rhegorios sounded calm, logical, reasonable—more like his sister than the way he usually sounded. "If something were here, wouldn't we know about it?"

"Who can say?" Maniakes replied. "We spent years in exile, our whole clan. Good thing Likinios sent us away, too, as it worked out; if we had been anywhere Genesios could have reached us, our heads would have gone up on the Milestone. But Tzikas was here in the city at least part of the time, before he went off to the westlands to fight the Makuraners and play his own games."

"Well, maybe," Rhegorios said grudgingly. "But if you're right, wouldn't *somebody* here besides Tzikas know about this whatever-it-is?"

"Well, maybe," Maniakes said, as grudgingly. "But maybe not, too. A lot of heads went up on the Milestone when Genesios held the throne. A lot of men died other ways, too, murdered or in battle or even in bed. And this thing would have been very secret. Not many people would have known about it in the first place, or we would have heard of it years ago."

"There's another explanation, you know," Rhegorios said: "How can you know about something that's not there?"

The guards and the parasol-bearers and Maniakes and even Rhegorios kept on going over the area again and again. Maniakes began to think his cousin was right. He shrugged. If that was so, it was so. Knowing it rather than merely hoping it would be a relief.

One of the guards, a big blond Haloga who wore his hair in a braid halfway down his back, called to Maniakes: "Lord, here the ground feels funny under my feet."

"Funny, Hafgrim?" The Avtokrator came over and stomped where the guardsman was standing. "It doesn't feel funny to me."

Hafgrim snorted. "One of me would make two of you, lord." That wasn't true, but it wasn't so far wrong, either. The Haloga went on, "I say it feels funny. I know what I know." He folded his arms across his broad chest, defying Maniakes to disbelieve him.

With nothing better found—with nothing else found at all— Maniakes was willing to grasp at straws. "All right, to you it feels funny," he said agreeably. "Let's break out the spades and mattocks and find out why."

The guards set to work with a will. The parasol-bearers stood around watching. Maniakes didn't say anything about that, but he suspected several of those parasol-bearers would suffer accidents—accidents not too disabling, he hoped—around the palace in the near future.

He also suspected the diggers would find nothing more than that Hafgrim's weight had made damp ground shift under his feet. That made him all the more surprised when, after penetrating no deeper than a foot and a half, the diggers' tools thumped against wood. "What did I say, lord?" Hafgrim said triumphantly.

"What did I say, cousin of mine?" Maniakes said triumphantly.

Rhegorios, for once, said nothing.

"It is a trapdoor, lord," the Haloga guardsman said after he and his companions had cleared more of it. "It is a trapdoor—and what would a trapdoor have under it?"

"A tunnel," Maniakes breathed, even before one of the guards dug the tip of a spade under the door and levered it up. "By the good god, a tunnel."

"Now, who would have wanted to dig a tunnel under the wall?" Rhegorios said. No possible doubt where the tunnel went: it sloped almost straight down, to dive beneath the ditch around the outer wall, and was heavily shored with timbers on all four sides.

An answer leapt into Maniakes' mind: "Likinios. It has to be Likinios. It would have been just like him to build a bolt-hole—the man could see around corners on a straight line. And Tzikas could easily have known about it." Maniakes shivered. "Good thing it came up so near the wall, where all our weapons would bear on it. Otherwise, Tzikas would have had the Kubratoi dig it open right away."

"He should have done it anyhow," Rhegorios said. "Getting the enemy inside the city would have been a dagger stabbing at our heart."

"When it comes to scheming, there's nobody to match Tzikas," Maniakes answered. "But when it comes to fighting, he's always been on the cautious side. We've seen that before. Me, now, I think you're right, cousin of mine. If that had been me out there, I'd have tried to break in no matter what kind of losses I took doing it. But I'm Tzikas' opposite. I can't plot the way he does, but I'll stick my neck out when there's a battle going on."

"Yes, and you've almost had a sword come down on it a time or two, too," Rhegorios said, which would have made Maniakes angry had he not known it was true. In musing tones, the Sevastos went on, "I wonder why Likinios never got to use the hole he made for himself."

"I wonder if we'll ever know," Maniakes said. "I have my doubts about that. We were just saying how most of the people who served Likinios are dead. Genesios made sure they were dead after he took over." He blinked. "Kameas was around, though, and he's still here." He snapped his fingers. "By the good god, I wonder if he's known about this tunnel all along. Have to ask him when we get back to the palaces."

"What do we do about it in the meantime?" Rhegorios asked, pointing down into the black mouth of the tunnel.

"Fill it up," Maniakes said at once. "It's more dangerous to us than it's ever likely to be useful."

Rhegorios plucked at his beard while he thought that over. After a few seconds, he nodded. "Good," he said.

"A tunnel, your Majesty?" Kameas' eyes grew round. The soft flesh under his beardless chin wobbled as he drew back in surprise. "No." He sketched Phos' sun-sign above his heart. "I never heard of such a thing. But then, you must remember, Likinios Avtokrator was always one to hold what he knew as close as he could."

"That's so," Maniakes said. Rhegorios looked to him for the agreement: the Sevastos had never known Likinios himself. The Avtokrator continued, "If the secret was so good even you didn't know it, esteemed sir, why didn't Likinios use it when he saw Genesios was going to overthrow him?"

"That, your Majesty, I may perhaps be able to answer," Kameas replied. "Throughout Genesios' rebellion, Likinios never took him seriously enough. He would call him 'commander of a hundred,' as if to say no one with such small responsibility could hope to cast down the Avtokrator of the Videssians."

"He must not have realized how much the army on the Astris hated him, there at the end," Maniakes said.

"And everyone else, there at the end," the vestiarios agreed. "The guards at the Silver Gate opened it to let Genesios' soldiers into Videssos the city. Nothing, they said, could be worse than Likinios." His eyes were far away, looking back across the years. "Soon enough, Genesios let them—let all of us—know they were mistaken."

"Likinios was clever," Maniakes said. "He had to have been clever, or he wouldn't have ruled the Empire for twenty years, he wouldn't have convinced a man as able as my father that he had no chance for the throne, and he wouldn't have used the war to restore Sharbaraz to the Makuraner throne to gain so much. But he was clever about things, about ideas, not so much about people and feelings. In the end, that cost him."

"We used to say, your Majesty—we of his court, I mean—that he thought like a eunuch," Kameas said. "It was neither compliment nor condemnation. But he seemed somewhat separated from most of mankind, as we are, and divorced from the passions roiling mankind as well."

"I suspect my father would agree with you," Maniakes answered.

"I doubt he ever would have said so while Likinios was alive, though."

"The trouble with what Likinios did was that it needed him on the throne to keep it working," Rhegorios observed. "Once we had Genesios instead, it fell apart faster and worse than it would have if it were simpler." He turned toward Maniakes with that impudent look on his face. "I'm glad you're nice and simple, cousin of mine your Majesty."

"I'll simple you," Maniakes said. He and his cousin both laughed. The Avtokrator suddenly sobered. "Do you know, all at once I think I begin to understand Tzikas."

"I'm so sorry for you!" Rhegorios exclaimed. "Here, sit down and stay quiet, you poor fellow. I'll send for Philetos from the Sorcerers' Collegium and for Agathios the patriarch, too. Between the two of them, they ought to be able to exorcise whatever evil spirit's got its claws in you."

Maniakes laughed again, but persisted: "By the good god, I mean it. Tzikas must have learned a lot, serving under Likinios. He couldn't have helped it, sly as he was—still is, worse luck. I don't know whether he decided to be just like Likinios the way sons decide to be like their fathers, but I'd bet it was something like that. And he *is* just like Likinios—or rather, he's just what Likinios would have been without integrity."

"Your Majesty, I believe you are correct," Kameas said. "I admit, however, that my experience with Tzikas is limited."

"I wish mine were." But Maniakes refused to let himself get downhearted. "He's not my worry now, Phos be praised. He's Abivard's worry, there on the far side of the Cattle Crossing. Abivard's welcome to him, as far as I'm concerned."

The mention of Abivard brought silence in its wake, as it often did. "Why is he still sitting in Across?" Rhegorios said at last. "What will he do now that he knows he can't get over the strait and attack us?"

He and Maniakes and their kin had been asking one another the same question since they'd crushed the Kubratoi on the sea. "We still don't know, curse it," Maniakes said. "I've been trying to figure it out, these past few days. Maybe he thinks Etzilios will be able to bring the Kubratoi south again and start up the siege once more."

"He cannot be so foolish, can he, your Majesty?" Kameas

said, at the same time as Rhegorios was vehemently shaking his head.

Maniakes spread his hands. "All right. I didn't really believe that myself. Etzilios is going to be lucky if someone doesn't take his head for leading the nomads into disaster." He spoke with the somber satisfaction any man can feel on contemplating his enemy's discomfiture. "But if that's not the answer, what is?"

Rhegorios said, "As long as he's over there—" He nodded west, toward the suburb of Videssos the city. "—he blocks our easiest way into the westlands."

"That's true," Maniakes said. "Still, with us having a fleet and him not, we can bring our men in wherever we want, whenever we want—if the weather lets us, of course. But even in the dark days, before we had any kind of army worth mentioning, we were using ships to put raiders into the westlands and get them out again."

"Not that we've stopped since," Rhegorios said.

"Hardly," Maniakes agreed. "We've had rather bigger things going on beside that, though." Rhegorios and Kameas both nodded. Maniakes went on, "Cousin of mine, you hold a piece of the truth, but I don't think you have all of it. As I say, I've been thinking about this ever since we saw that Abivard wasn't going anywhere."

"We all have," Rhegorios said. He grinned. "But do enlighten us, then, O sage of the age."

"I'll try, cousin of mine, though after that buildup whatever I say won't sound like much," Maniakes answered. He and Rhegorios both laughed. The corners of Kameas' mouth slid upward, too, slowly, as if the vestiarios didn't want that to happen but discovered he couldn't help himself. Maniakes continued, "The frightening thing about this siege is how close it came to working. The other frightening thing is that we didn't see it coming till it was here. Sharbaraz King of Kings—may the ice take him—prepared his ground ever so well."

"All true," Rhegorios said. "The lord with the great and good mind knows it's all true. If that messenger hadn't made it through the Land of the Thousand Cities—" He shivered. "It was a *good* plan."

"Aye," Maniakes said. "And Abivard did everything he could to make it work, too. He got engineers over the Cattle Crossing. He got Tzikas over the Cattle Crossing. By the good god, he crossed over himself. The only thing he couldn't do was get a good-sized chunk of his army across, and that wasn't his fault. He had to depend on the Kubrati fleet, and we smashed it."

"All true," Rhegorios said. "And so?"

"The planning was splendid. We all agree about that," Maniakes said. The Sevastos and the vestiarios both nodded. "Abivard did everything possible to get it to work." More nods. "But it didn't." Still more nods. Maniakes smiled, once more enjoying a foe's predicament. "When Sharbaraz King of Kings, being who he is, being what he is, finds out it didn't work, *what will he do?*"

"Phos," Rhegorios whispered.

"Not exactly," Maniakes said. "But he is the fellow who had a shrine for the God made over in his own image, remember. Anyone who'd do that isn't the sort of fellow who's likely to stay calm when things go wrong, is he? And who knows Sharbaraz King of Kings better than Abivard?"

"Phos," Rhegorios said again, this time most reverently. "He doesn't dare go home, does he?"

"I don't know whether I'd go that far," Maniakes answered. "But he has to be thinking about it. We would be, if that were us over there. The Makuraners may play the game a little more politely than we do, but it's the same game. Sharbaraz will be looking for someone to blame."

"He could blame Etzilios, your Majesty," Kameas said. "The fault, as you pointed out, lay in the Kubrati fleet."

"Yes, he could do that," Maniakes agreed. "He probably even does do that, or will when the news reaches him, if it hasn't got there yet. But how much good will that do him? Even if he blames Etzilios, he can't punish him. He was lucky to get an embassy to Kubrat. He'd never get an army there."

Rhegorios said, "Half the fun of blaming someone is punishing him for whatever he did wrong."

Maniakes hadn't thought of it as fun. He'd worried about what was practical and what wasn't. But his freewheeling cousin had a point. When you were King of Kings of Makuran—or, for that matter, Avtokrator of the Videssians—you could, if you wanted, do exactly as you wanted. Punishing those who failed you was one of the perquisites—sometimes one of the enjoyable perquisites—of the position.

Musingly, Kameas said, "I wonder how we could best exploit whatever disaffection may exist between Sharbaraz and Abivard, or create such disaffection if none exists at present."

Maniakes clapped the vestiarios on the back. "The Makuraners are always complaining about how devious and underhanded we Videssians are. Esteemed sir, if they heard that, it would prove their point. And do you know what else? You're exactly right. That's what we have to do."

"Send a messenger—secret but not *too* secret—to Abivard," Rhegorios said. "One of two things will happen. He may go along with us, which is what we have in mind. Or he may say no, in which case Sharbaraz will still get word he's been treating with Videssians. I don't think Sharbaraz would like that."

"I don't, either," Maniakes said. "I'll do it."

The messenger sailed out of Videssos the city the next day. He went behind a shield of truce. Abivard was better about honoring such shields than most officers on either side. Maniakes had reason to expect the messenger, a certain Isokasios, would return intact, if not necessarily successful.

Return Isokasios did, by noon that day. He was tall and lean, with a close-trimmed gray beard fringing a face thin to gauntness. After prostrating himself, he said, "Your Majesty, I failed. Abivard would not see me, would not hear my words, would have nothing to do with me whatever. He did send one message to you: that, since the westlands are, in his words, rightfully Makuraner territory, any Videssian warriors caught there will be treated as spies henceforth. Fair warning, he called it."

"Killed out of hand instead of slowly, you mean," Maniakes said. "They work their war captives to death, a digit at a time." He wondered if that had happened to his brother Tatoules, who had vanished in the Makuraner invasion of the westlands and not been seen since.

"I'm afraid you're right, your Majesty," Isokasios said.

"By Phos, I shall put a stop to that before it starts." Maniakes shouted for a scribe, saying, "I'd write this myself, but I don't want whoever he has reading Videssian for him puzzling over my scrawl." When the secretary arrived, the Avtokrator told him, "Take my words down exactly: 'Maniakes son of Maniakes to Abivard son of Godarz of Makuran: Greetings. Know that, should any Videssian soldier taken by your army within the bounds of the Videssian Empire at the time of the death of Likinios Avtokrator be slain as spies, any Makuraner soldiers captured by Videssos within those same bounds shall likewise be slain as brigands. My actions in this regard shall conform to those shown by you and your men.'" He made a slashing gesture to show he was finished. "Make a fair copy of that if the one you have there isn't, then bring it to me for my signature and seal."

"Yes, your Majesty." The scribe hurried away.

To Isokasios, Maniakes said, "When he comes back with that, you take it straight to Abivard. No secrecy this time. I want the Makuraners to know exactly what kind of trouble they're playing with and what we think about it."

"Aye, your Majesty," the messenger replied. Moments later, the scribe returned. Maniakes set down his name on the fair copy in the crimson ink reserved for the Avtokrator alone. He stamped his sunburst signet into hot wax, handed the message to Isokasios, and sent him off once more.

The messenger came back to Videssos the city at sunset with a written message from Abivard. When Maniakes broke the seal, he grunted in surprise. "It's in the Makuraner tongue. He doesn't usually do that." He clicked his tongue between his teeth. "I wonder if this is something he couldn't trust to a Videssian-speaking scribe. If it is, it might be interesting."

Since he did not read Makuraner himself, he summoned Philetos the healer-priest, who did. When the blue-robe arrived, Maniakes gave him the square of parchment. Philetos read through it once, his lips moving, then translated it: "'Abivard son of Godarz, servant to Sharbaraz King of Kings of Makuran, good, pacific, beneficent—'"

"You can skip the titles," Maniakes said dryly.

"As you say, your Majesty. I resume: 'to Maniakes son of Maniakes: Greetings.'"

Before he could go on, Maniakes interrupted again: "He still won't admit I'm the legitimate Avtokrator, but at least he isn't calling me a usurper anymore." Sharbaraz maintained a puppet who pretended to be Likinios' eldest son, Hosios. Having seen the true Hosios' head, Maniakes knew Genesios had liquidated him along with the rest of Likinios' clan. The Avtokrator added,

"Come to think of it, the Makuraners don't have the false Hosios along with them. I wonder if he's still alive."

"An interesting question, I am certain," Philetos said, "but would you not like to hear that which you summoned me to read?" Having regained Maniakes' attention, he went on, "'The policy you question was instituted at the command of Sharbaraz King of Kings, may his years be many and his realm increase. I shall not put it into effect until after I have sent your response to the King of Kings for his judgment thereon.'"

Maniakes scowled in reluctant admiration. "I'd hoped for more," he said at last. "All he's saying is, 'This isn't my fault, and maybe I'll be able to get it changed. Meanwhile, don't worry about it.'"

"I should have thought that was exactly what you wanted to hear, your Majesty," Philetos said.

"No." The Avtokrator shook his head. "This gives me nothing I can grab, nothing I can use to separate Abivard from Sharbaraz. He's obeying the King of Kings and referring the question back to him. That's not what I need. I'd rather have him tell me Sharbaraz is flat-out wrong. Then I could either use that to detach him from the King of Kings or else send it on to Sharbaraz and detach him from Abivard."

"Ah. Now I understand more fully, your Majesty," the healer-priest said. "But if the brute fact of Abivard's failure to capture Videssos the city will not cost him the favor of the King of Kings, why should anything smaller have that effect?"

"I'd hoped for this failure to cost him that favor," Maniakes said, pronouncing the words with care; he wouldn't have liked to try it after a couple of cups of wine. "Since it doesn't seem to have done the job, I'm not too proud to try tossing pebbles onto the big boulder, in the hope that they'll tip the scale where it didn't. But Abivard didn't hand me any pebbles."

"Compose yourself in patience." Philetos sounded more like a priest than he usually did. "These things take time."

"Yes, holy sir," Maniakes said dutifully. On the one hand, he'd been patient throughout his entire reign—a necessity during much of it, when he was either desperately weak, beset on two fronts, or both. On the other hand, when he had seen chances to act, he'd often moved too soon, so perhaps he still needed instruction on the art of waiting.

"Will there be anything more, your Majesty?" Philetos asked.

"No. Thank you, holy sir," Maniakes answered. The healer-priest departed, leaving Abivard's letter behind. Maniakes stared in frustration at the document he could not read unaided. He consoled himself by remembering Abivard had written it himself, in the Makuraner script, so as not to have to reveal its contents to anyone else. That was something. It was not enough.

Philetos proved a fairly frequent visitor at the imperial residence over the next few weeks. The Videssian raiders who prowled the westlands had not the numbers to take on Makuraner armies. They observed and used shipborne messages to report back to Maniakes. They were, in fact, a good deal like spies if not the veritable beasts, a point on which the Avtokrator chose not to dwell.

They also made a habit of ambushing Makuraner couriers whenever they could. That always had the potential of being useful, as it had in the Land of the Thousand Cities. A lot of the messages they captured and sent back to Videssos the city were in the Makuraner tongue. The healer-priest had no trouble making sense of them.

Most, unfortunately, were not worth having, once captured. "Your Majesty, how do you profit by learning the garrison commander at Aptos has asked the garrison commander of Vryetion for the loan of some hay?" Philetos asked after translating a captured dispatch wherein the commander at Aptos had done just that.

"I could make a fancy speech about how learning that any one Makuraner garrison is low on supplies might be important," Maniakes replied. "I won't bother. The plain truth is, it doesn't do me any good I can see. They can't all be gems. When you're rolling dice, you don't get Phos' little suns—" Double ones counted as the winning throw in the Videssian game. "—every time out. But you never know what you'll get till you do throw the dice."

"I suppose so, your Majesty." Philetos sounded obedient but less than delighted. Whenever new messages from the westlands came into Videssos the city, he was called away from his sorcerous researches to translate them. "I might wish the Makuraners had the courtesy to write in Videssian."

"It would make our lives easier, wouldn't it?" Maniakes grinned at the healer-priest. "It would certainly make your life easier."

Every few days, one ship or another would bring in a dispatch or a handful of dispatches from out of the westlands. The hill country in the southeastern part of the peninsula had never been so firmly in Makuraner hands as the rest: it lay well away from the line of march toward Videssos the city. Makuraner commanders in the area were always howling about Videssian harassment and complaining to Abivard or to one another that they needed more men if they were not to be overwhelmed.

In the northern part of the westlands, Videssian land forces were weaker, but the fleet, now that pressure on the imperial city had eased, could swoop down and seize a port whenever it liked. The captured messages that came back to Videssos the city from that area were mostly warnings for Makuraner officers to remain ever alert and, again, unending and apparently unanswered pleas for reinforcements.

Studying Philetos' translations, the elder Maniakes said, "They haven't got enough men to do everything they have to do, not if they keep their field army at Across."

"True, but if they split up, they'll have a hard time putting it back together again," the Avtokrator said.

"The more I look at their position, the more I like ours," his father remarked. "They're sinking a little at a time, and the only way they can plug one hole is to let another one leak."

"And we've convinced them they don't dare bring any more troops forward out of the Land of the Thousand Cities," Maniakes said. "If they try that, we *will* end up taking Mashiz, the way we could have this past campaigning season if Sharbaraz hadn't had his cursed clever idea."

"Too late in the year to send the fleet out now, even if your omens hadn't all been bad," the elder Maniakes said. "But there's next year, and the year after that if need be. The Kubratoi will leave us alone for a while. We can concentrate against Makuran."

"Sooner or later, though, we'll have to go up against the Makuraner field army," Maniakes said. "That's a lot of boiler boys to take on at once."

"Maybe you can split them up so you won't have to," his father answered. "And maybe you'll just beat them. Videssian armies *can* beat them, you know. If that weren't so, Makuran would have owned the westlands for hundreds of years by now."

"I understand that," Maniakes said. "But still—"

Throughout Genesios' unhappy reign, and throughout the

opening years of his own, the Makuraners had regularly routed all the forces Videssos threw against them. The Makuraners had become convinced they could do it whenever they pleased—and so had the Videssians. Back in the Land of the Thousand Cities, Maniakes' troops had shown they could face the fearsome Makuraner heavy cavalry on something close to even terms. Facing the entire Makuraner field force, though, was different from facing a detachment from it. If something went wrong . . .

Kameas stuck his head into the chamber where the two Maniakai were talking and said, "Your Majesty, I beg pardon, but another handful of captured dispatches has just come in."

"Thank you, esteemed sir," Maniakes said. "Have them brought here and send someone to fetch Philetos, if you'd be so kind."

"I have taken the liberty of doing that already," the vestiarios said with the slightest hint of smugness.

Philetos arrived about a quarter of an hour later. After bowing to the elder Maniakes and prostrating himself before the younger, he went to work on the parchments Kameas had set on an alabaster tabletop. When he came to one of them, he stiffened and grew alert. "Your Majesty," he said in a tightly controlled voice, "we have something of importance here. This is from Sharbaraz King of Kings to Romezan son of Bizhan."

"Abivard's second-in-command," Maniakes breathed. "You're right, holy sir; that *is* important. What does it say?"

Philetos read through the parchment. When he looked up again, his eyes were wide and wondering. He said, "The gist is, Sharbaraz blames Abivard for failing to capture Videssos the city. This letter orders Romezan to take Abivard's head, send it back to Mashiz, and assume command of the field army himself."

✦ VIII

Maniakes, his father, and Philetos stared at one another. The Avtokrator said, "I never imagined having anything so big fall into my lap. It's almost *too* big. How do we use it to best advantage?"

In a dry voice, the elder Maniakes said, "We've been looking for something that would pry Abivard loose from Sharbaraz. If an execution order won't do it, to the ice with me if I know what will."

Philetos said, "Might it not be best to refrain from interfering? The natural course of events, so to speak, would then remove Abivard from matters concerning us."

"And put Romezan in his place." Maniakes shook his head. "I've fought against Romezan. He's very good, and the soldiers like him. The Makuraners would be as dangerous with him in command as they are now."

"That's so," the elder Maniakes agreed. "By what I've seen, this Romezan is as nasty as Abivard commanding troops in battle, maybe worse, because he presses harder. Abivard is better at seeing past the nose on his face, though."

"Every word of that is true, Father, and it tells me what we need to do," Maniakes said. "If Abivard gone hurts Makuran only a little, what we have to have is Abivard angry at Sharbaraz."

"Like I say, showing him that letter ought to do the trick," the elder Maniakes rumbled.

"Just what I intend to do," the Avtokrator said. "I'll invite him into Videssos the city on the pretext of discussing a truce between his troops and mine. When he's in here—out comes the parchment."

"Will he not fear to come into Videssos the city?" Philetos said, "being worried lest you treat him as in fact his own sovereign intends to do?"

"I think he'll come," Maniakes said. "No matter what Sharbaraz has done, Abivard and I have fought hard but fair: no treachery on either side I can think of. And he must know we know how good Romezan is, and how little we'd gain by murdering him."

Philetos, still looking shaken at the magnitude of what he'd discovered, sketched Phos' sun-circle above his heart. "The good god grant that it prove as you desire."

A shield of truce at her bow, the *Renewal* bobbed in the chop within hailing distance of the beach at Across. Before long, a Makuraner soldier came forward and hailed the dromon in accented Videssian: "Who are you, and what do you want?"

Maniakes, gorgeous in full imperial raiment, stepped forward to show himself to the Makuraner. "I am Maniakes son of Maniakes, Avtokrator of the Videssians. I would speak with Abivard son of Godarz, your commander here. I want to invite him into Videssos the city, that we may confer on ways to end the war between us."

The Makuraner stared at him. "How do I know you're really Maniakes, not just some guy in a fancy suit?"

"Sharbaraz is the one who keeps imposters around his court—all the false Hosioi he's trotted out, for instance," Maniakes answered tartly. "Will you take my words to your commander? Tell him I promise his safety in the city and his free and safe return here the instant he requests it from me. Tell him also that I will give hostages if he doubts my word."

"I'll tell him," the Makuraner said, "or tell someone who'll tell him, anyhow." He hurried away.

Aboard the *Renewal*, Thrax breathed a sigh of relief. So did the shieldmen who had been poised to spring in front of Maniakes at the first sign of danger: a ship within hailing distance of the shore was also within easy arrow range. Abivard did not seem prone to murder even if it might help his cause, but what of his soldiers?

More and more of those soldiers came to stare at the dromon. At Thrax's order, the crew of the *Renewal* had a dart in the catapult at the bow. They'd done good work before, against Makuraners straying too close to the edge of the sea. Now, like Maniakes, they waited before moving.

Waiting ended when Abivard came riding up, sand spurting out from under the hooves of his horse. He swung down from the big, broad-shouldered animal—well suited for carrying a man in full armor, though the marshal wore a Makuraner caftan now—and peered out toward the *Renewal*. When he spied the imperial raiment, he called, "If you are the true Maniakes, what is my wife named?" He spoke in Makuraner so his men could understand.

"Her name is Roshnani," Maniakes replied in the same tongue. He knew he was mispronouncing the name, as he habitually did with Sharbaraz's: Videssian tongues would not wrap themselves around the *sh* sound.

"You are yourself, or else well coached," Abivard said. After a moment, he went on, "You are yourself; I know your voice, and your look. We've met often enough for that, over the years. What would you?"

"What I told your man." Of necessity, Maniakes kept his Makuraner simple. "I invite you to come to Videssos the city. I will give hostages, if you want hostages. What I want is to end the war between Makuran and Videssos. I think I see a way to do that."

"Tell me here and now." Abivard spoke more simply, responding to Maniakes' rusty use of his language.

"I have something you must see. It is in the city." Maniakes waved back over the Cattle Crossing to the imperial capital, the city Abivard had been unable to enter by force of arms. "Will you come?"

"I will come," Abivard declared. "Shall I swim to your ship, or will you send a boat?" He made as if to pull the caftan off over his head, as if expecting to have to swim.

"Get a boat in the water," Maniakes hissed to Thrax, who relayed the command to the sailors. To Abivard, Maniakes spoke in some surprise: "No hostages, marshal of Makuran? I will give them."

"No hostages." Abivard laughed. "If you make away with me, you have to deal with Romezan. I do not think you want the wild boar of Makuran rampaging through what you call the westlands." Maniakes waved to him across the strip of water between them, a gesture of respect: he and Abivard had made the identical calculation.

The boat grated up onto the beach. Abivard, after a few words to his men, got into it. One of the sailors pushed it back into the sea. The men rowed to the *Renewal* with remarkable celerity, as if delighted to get away from all the Makuraners by the seaside. Maniakes did not blame them for that. He helped them and the man they had come to fetch clamber back up into the *Renewal*.

Maniakes studied the Makuraner marshal. Abivard was not far from his own age, perhaps a few years younger, with a long, thoughtful face, bushy eyebrows and liquid dark eyes, a nose straighter than Maniakes' but hardly less formidable, and a black beard into which the first strands of silver were working. Bowing to Maniakes, he said, "I would have treated the city differently if I had come into it without an invitation." He spoke Videssian now, using it more fluently than Maniakes did Makuraner.

The Avtokrator shrugged. "And the city would have treated you differently, too."

"That is also probably true," Abivard replied with an easy insouciance Maniakes had to admire. "But since I am not entering Videssos the city as a conqueror, why exactly am I entering it?"

"I can tell you that, if you like," Maniakes said. "I'd sooner show you, though. Can you wait? It's not far." He gestured over the water of the Cattle Crossing toward the imperial city, now visibly closer than it had been from the shore of the strait. He had not brought Sharbaraz's letter with him, lest a chance wave splash up over it and blur the evidence he needed to persuade Abivard.

"I have placed myself in your hands," the Makuraner general said. "I shall wait and see whatever it is. If I do not accept it, I rely on you to return me to my soldiers once more. You have fought hard against the armies of Sharbaraz King of Kings, may his years be many and his realm increase, but you have for the most part shown yourself honorable."

"For which I thank you," Maniakes said. "I've thought the same of you, by the bye. Had we started on the same side, I think we might have been friends."

"This thought has also crossed my mind," Abivard said, "but the God—" He dropped back into Makuraner to name his deity. "—chose my sovereign as he willed, not as I might have willed. Being only a mortal, I accept the God's commands."

"Your sovereign certainly knows you're only a mortal," Maniakes remarked. Abivard sent him a curious look. He pretended not to notice it. He did not need to pretend for long, for the *Renewal* came up to the little harbor in the palace quarter. Men stood on the quays to catch the ropes the sailors threw to them and to make the dromon fast to the pier.

Abivard watched the process with interest. "They know their business," he observed.

"They'd better," Maniakes answered. He waited till the gangplank led from ship to pier, then strode up it, waving for Abivard to follow. "Come, eminent sir," he said, granting Abivard the highest rank of Videssian nobility. "Have a look at what you could not take."

Abivard did, with lively curiosity that grew livelier as they pressed into the palace quarter toward the imperial residence. "So this is what I could not see," he said when they turned a corner and a building hid the sea from sight. "Till now, I gained more detail on things I gazed at from afar. This, though, this is new to me."

Waiting at the residence stood Rhegorios, Symvatios, and the elder Maniakes. Abivard bowed to all three of them. The elder Maniakes held out his hand, saying, "Good to see you again when we're not trying to kill each other."

Abivard accepted the handclasp. "Indeed. Were it not for the army you once commanded, Sharbaraz would not be King of Kings today."

"He is King of Kings today, though, worse luck," the elder Maniakes growled. "But whether he'll be King of Kings tomorrow . . ." His voice trailed away.

Abivard's face went stiff, masklike. "If you have summoned me here to seek to make me rebel against Sharbaraz King of Kings, may his days be long and his realm increase, please take me back over the Cattle Crossing now. I will not betray my sovereign."

"No?" Maniakes led the Makuraner into the residence. Kameas came up to them, carrying a silver tray. Abivard looked at the vestiarios without curiosity; the Makuraner court used eunuchs, too. Considering the way the Makuraners so often mewed up their women, that was anything but surprising. Maniakes took the parchment off the tray and handed it to Abivard. "No?" he repeated. "Not even after this?"

Watching Abivard read it through, he could tell exactly when the Makuraner marshal came to the passage ordering his own elimination. Abivard did not shout or bellow or grow visibly angry. His face just set more firmly into nonrevelation. When he was through, he looked up at Maniakes. "How did you come by this?"

"Luck," the Avtokrator answered. "Nothing but luck. One of our raiding parties happened to run into the messenger before he got to Across."

"Before I do anything about it," Abivard said, "I will want proof it is genuine, you know."

Maniakes nodded. "I thought you would say as much. You leave as little to chance as you can—I've seen that fighting you. I don't suppose you'll trust my wizards: I wouldn't, in your place. If you want to bring a Makuraner mage over here to test the truth, you may do so."

"That you make the offer goes a long way toward telling me this letter is genuine." Abivard let out a long sigh. "It doesn't surprise me. Sharbaraz has come close to taking my head before, as you may or may not have heard. But I will know for certain before I decide what to do next. One of my two chief mages is a Makuraner. The other is of Videssian blood."

"I knew that—or thought as much, anyhow," Maniakes broke in. "If it weren't so, the Voimios strap conjuration we used last year would have confused you longer than it did."

"Bad enough as things were." Abivard shook his head. "Ride into a canal, head for the other side, and come back out where you started—as I say, bad. But does the truce hold for Panteles, too?"

"Aye, it does," Maniakes answered. "He'll have to stay with you always, though. If he ever comes back into the Empire when he's not under your protection, his head goes up on the Milestone."

"I agree," Abivard said. "I would say the same if you had a Makuraner traitor in your midst, as Videssians have been known to do."

"Speaking of traitors, how's Tzikas these days?" Rhegorios asked.

"Alive," Abivard said. "Unfortunately. Sharbaraz thinks well of him, since he can't possibly aim to set his fundament on the throne of Mashiz."

"That may matter less in the way you look at the world than it did a little while ago," Maniakes observed.

"It may," Abivard agreed. "And, then again, it may not." He looked down at the parchment he was still holding and read through it again. "We shall see."

Bringing the wizards over the Cattle Crossing without arousing undue suspicion proved easier than Maniakes had expected. When his envoy said they were needed for the truce talks, the Makuraners accepted that not only without hesitation but also without further questions. Panteles and Bozorg hopped into a Videssian boat, were rowed out to the *Renewal*, and traveled back to Videssos the city in the course of a couple of hours.

"If you're vague enough," Maniakes said, watching the dromon tie up at the little palace-quarter harbor, "you can get away with anything."

"What do you mean, vague?" Rhegorios' voice rose in mock indignation. "We didn't even tell any lies."

Like Abivard, Maniakes was determined to observe the tests the Makuraner marshal's mages would use on the captured parchment. That meant he had to have his own mages present, lest those working for the other side try to turn their sorcery against him. He would have summoned Bagdasares and Philetos in any case, to make sure Panteles and Bozorg did not try to feed Abivard results that were not true.

Bozorg examined the parchment with the air of a man looking over a fish several days out of water. He was tall and thin and clever-looking, with the perfectly upright posture a column would have envied. At last, in grudging tones, he said, "It does have the look of a document that may perhaps—perhaps, I say, mind you—have come from the court of the King of Kings." As he himself had come from the court of the King of Kings to serve Abivard, that was no small admission.

Panteles said nothing at all. Though he'd been promised safety while in Videssos the city, he had the air of a man ready to flee at any moment. Coming to the imperial capital seemed to have reminded him he was a Videssian, and therefore an embarrassment to other Videssians.

His conscience is still breathing, Maniakes thought. *Coming here wouldn't bother Tzikas a bit.*

Abivard told his mages, "I want you to let me know whether Maniakes is being more clever than he has any business being—" He sent the Avtokrator a look full of mistrustful warmth. "—or whether Sharbaraz really does want Romezan to drop me into the Void."

"Lord, my own provenance will aid us in that," Bozorg said, speaking elegant Makuraner. "By the law of contagion, both this letter and I are in contact with the court of the King of Kings, and thus with each other."

"Go ahead, then. Do whatever you need to do," Abivard said. Maniakes nodded. His heart sped up in his chest. Once Abivard was convinced—if Abivard was convinced—Sharbaraz wanted to be rid of him . . . All manner of interesting things might happen then.

Bozorg set the captured letter on a table, then strode across the chamber in the imperial residence till he stood next to the wall farthest from that table. "Once in contact, always in contact," he said. "If this letter in fact emanates from the court of the King of Kings, the spell I am about to use will draw it to me once more. I begin."

Maniakes could follow spoken Makuraner, but caught only the occasional word of the wizard's chant. Philetos, though, was paying close attention, alert for any discrepancy from a spell and a type of spell evidently familiar to him.

Bozorg raised his hands and made a few passes with them: nothing complicated or ornate, which suggested to Maniakes that the spell was as basic as the arrogant Makuraner mage claimed. Bozorg called out in a loud, commanding voice—and the parchment flew across the room and came to rest on his right hand.

He looked from it to Maniakes to Abivard. Voice cautious, he said, "This does appear to indicate that the letter came from the court at Mashiz, as the Avtokrator of the Videssians has asserted." That was no small admission; coming from the court himself, he was more likely to be a creature of Sharbaraz's than of Abivard's.

Panteles walked over to him and took the parchment. Speaking Videssian, the mage said, "There is a simple test to see whether the letter is to be directly associated with the King of Kings." He fumbled in his beltpouch, eventually drawing forth a new-minted silver arket. "Using this coin with Sharbaraz's image, we can apply the law of similarity to determine the relationship of the parchment to the King of Kings."

"That is sound sorcery," Bagdasares said. Philetos nodded. After a moment, so did Bozorg.

Maniakes glanced at Bagdasares with a certain amount of amusement. Not so long before, Bagdasares had used a Makuraner coin himself when he sorcerously spied on Abivard's conference with Etzilios. Though in his person far away in Mashiz, Sharbaraz played a vital role here.

The Videssian wizard in Abivard's pay went about his business with matter-of-fact competence. His spell, though carried out in Videssian, seemed closely related to the one Bozorg had used. He set the coin on the table where the Makuraner mage had placed the letter. Holding the sheet in his left hand, he began to chant.

"Wait," Bagdasares said suddenly. He, too, produced a coin from his pouch: a goldpiece of Maniakes' minting. He put it on the table not far from the silver arket. "This will provide a check. If the parchment goes to it, you will know we seek to lead you astray."

Panteles nodded his agreement to the change in the sorcery. So did Abivard, who said quietly, "If you are so sure you can prove your own innocence here, that is no small sign of it."

Again, the Videssian mage began his chant. He let the parchment drop from his hand—but it did not fall to the floor. Floating in the air as if it were a wisp of smoke, it drifted toward the table on which rested the two coins, one Videssian, the other Makuraner. Even though Maniakes knew he had captured the message rather than fabricating it, he tensed. Maybe Panteles was clever enough to fool both Bagdasares and Philetos. Or maybe the magic would simply go wrong.

Softly, softly, the parchment descended on the arket blazoned with Sharbaraz's imperious profile. Maniakes heaved a sigh of relief. Abivard sighed, too: the sigh of a man who now had to choose a course he might have hoped to avoid. And all four mages in the chamber sighed as well, having shown their masters what was so and what was not.

Turning to Bozorg, Abivard spoke in his own language: "Tell me, my friend—do I deserve such treatment from Sharbaraz King of Kings?" He did not wish his overlord either long days or many years.

The Makuraner mage licked his lips. If he was from the court in Mashiz, he had to have risen under Sharbaraz's eye. And yet, by the way Abivard asked the question, Bozorg also seemed to have been with the Makuraner marshal for some time. Had that not been so, Abivard would have got rid of him on the instant—or Maniakes would have, in Abivard's position, to keep the mage from upsetting whatever plans he might make.

"Lord, I have seen you in war for some years now," Bozorg said slowly. "All that Sharbaraz has asked of you, all that a man could do: this you have done. For him to pay you back by ordering you treacherously slain . . . lord, there is no justice in that. Tell me what to do. In any way I can, I shall aid you. By the God and the Prophets Four I swear it. May I be lost forever in the Void if I lie."

"I stand with you, too, lord," Panteles said quickly. Abivard nodded in absentminded acknowledgment. The Videssian who served him had little choice but to stay loyal: he couldn't return to his homeland, and who else among the Makuraners was likely to want him?

Abivard spoke wonderingly: "So it comes to this at last. I could have rebelled against the King of Kings half a dozen times, and always I held back, out of loyalty and because my sister Denak is his principal wife. Now I have no choice, not if I want to go on breathing."

"Your sister had a son last year, I hear," Maniakes said.

"At last," Abivard agreed, "and, I daresay, to everyone's astonishment."

"As may be," Maniakes said "You might go further among your own people as uncle and protector to the infant King of Kings than as an out-and-out usurper seizing power for no one but yourself."

"Mm, so I might," Abivard cocked his head to one side. "May I speak with you alone, your Majesty?"

"You may." Maniakes spoke without hesitation, finding Abivard a most unlikely assassin. The Avtokrator gathered up Philetos and

Bagdasares by eye. They led their thaumaturgical counterparts out of the chamber in which they had proved the parchment genuine. Bagdasares closed the door behind him. Maniakes gestured for Abivard to say whatever he had in mind.

After coughing a couple of times, the Makuraner marshal came out with it: "Your Majesty, will you be so good as to invite my principal wife Roshnani—she may as well be my only wife, as I've not set eyes on any of the others for ten years and more—to Videssos the city? No one would think that odd in the least; everyone knows how fond she is of the easier way between men and women you Videssians have."

"Yes, I'll do that," Maniakes said at once. "By the way you ask, though, you sound as if you don't want me to invite her just for the sake of banquets where she can eat with you without scandalizing three quarters of your comrades."

"Half of them, I'd say." Abivard's eyes twinkled. "We have come a little way, we Makuraners, from what we were when we crossed the Videssian border as refugees all those years ago, Sharbaraz and Denak and Roshnani and I." He grew intent once more. "But the reason we crossed to Videssos—that was Roshnani's idea, not Sharbaraz's or mine."

"Really?" Maniakes said in genuine surprise. Abivard nodded. "Isn't that interesting?" the Avtokrator murmured. "So the real reason you want her here is so the two of you can do a better job of plotting, is it?" Abivard nodded again. Maniakes went on, "There is, of course, the chance I take that you'll be plotting against me, but I'll risk it. She ought to get on well with Lysia, as a matter of fact."

"I can see that," Abivard agreed. "By all accounts, your marriage is as far removed from your customs as mine is from ours."

"Further, maybe," Maniakes said, with a bitterness that would not fade. After a moment, he tried for a more judicious view: "And maybe not, too. I look at mine from the inside and yours from the outside, so my view of the two is different. But I didn't bring you here to talk philosophy. I brought you here to talk rebellion. And if having your lady here will help that, eminent sir, have her you shall."

Roshnani's round, pleasant face proved to conceal a mind convoluted enough to have made her a great success as a Videssian logothete. "Romezan isn't going to want to believe this or to revolt on account of it," she said when Maniakes and Abivard had brought her up to date on why her husband and she had been asked to Videssos the city. "He's a high noble of the Seven Clans, the great families that support the King of Kings."

Maniakes looked at Abivard. "And you're not."

"Not even close." Abivard's smile had knives in it. "I'm just a jumped-up frontier *dihqan*—a minor noble, but one to whom Sharbaraz happens to owe his life, his freedom, his throne . . . minor details. To be just, Romezan doesn't fret about class the way so many Seven Clan nobles do. A good many officers under him would like to think of me as a cursed upstart, but I've started up so high, you might say, that they don't dare."

Roshnani's eyes lit up. "And you know who those officers are, too. You could make a long list of them."

"I could, yes, without any trouble," Abivard said. Roshnani reached out and let her hand rest on his for a moment. Maniakes nodded thoughtfully. Yes, the Makuraner marshal and his wife were as isolated from their army as he and Lysia were from the people and clergy of Videssos the city.

In a small, innocent voice, Roshnani went on, "And you could add that list of officers from the high nobility—and some officers you know the King of Kings doesn't favor—to Sharbaraz's letter to Romezan, so that it would look as if he were supposed to kill every last one of them, not you alone."

"That's—fiendish," Maniakes said, his own voice full of astonished admiration. He turned to Abivard. "If a lot of Makuraner women are like this, I can see why you keep so many of them under lock and key—they'd be dangerous if you let them run around loose."

"Thank you, your Majesty," Roshnani said. "Thank you very much."

"I was right," the Avtokrator said. "You will get on well with Lysia. Will the two of you dine with us tonight?"

"Of course," Abivard said.

"We've grown fond of Videssian cooking," Roshnani added. "We've spent so much time at Across—"

Maniakes smiled back at her, but it wasn't easy. He'd thought he was making a joke with Abivard. Now, abruptly, he wasn't so sure.

When the only seafood the cook served that evening was raw oysters, Roshnani said, "Did you think we were only being polite when we said we liked Videssian food?"

"By no means," Maniakes answered. "I'm not eating fish or crabs or prawns myself these days." He explained why, and had the small satisfaction of watching Roshnani and Abivard turn green.

They recovered, however, to do justice to seethed kid and roast mutton with garlic. The only thing they would not do was pour fermented fish sauce over the mutton. "Has nothing to do with the sea fight," Abivard said. "But I found out how the stuff was made, not long after I came into the Empire of Videssos. I haven't been able to stomach it since."

Lysia said, "Some things are better if you don't look at them too closely. Politics are like that, a lot of the time."

"They certainly are in Makuran," Roshnani agreed. "Here, too?" Lysia nodded. Maniakes immediately thought of the bargain he'd made with Agathios the patriarch to get him to recognize the validity of his marriage to his cousin. He also thought of the scheme for altering Sharbaraz's letter that Roshnani had come up with. Neither of those would have stood examination in the clean, bright light of day, but the one had been extremely effective and the other gave every sign of equaling that.

He raised his goblet of wine in salute. "To Abivard son of Godarz, protector of his tiny nephew."

Abivard drank, but looked unhappy. He'd emptied his goblet once or twice already. "This isn't what I'd sooner be doing, you know," he said, as if the notion was likely to surprise Maniakes.

It didn't. "I understand that—you'd sooner take my head," the Avtokrator said, to which Abivard gave a jerky, startled nod. Maniakes went on, "But since Sharbaraz would sooner take your head . . ." He let his guest complete the sentence for himself.

"Sharbaraz has never given Abivard his due," Roshnani said bitterly. "If it weren't for Abivard, Sharbaraz would be dead or locked up in Nalgis Crag stronghold, and Smerdis would still be King of Kings." *And Makuran and Videssos wouldn't have had this war,* Maniakes thought. Roshnani pushed ahead in a different direction: "Whatever victories we've won in the fight against your people, Abivard's led our armies. And what thanks does he get from the King of Kings?"

"The same thanks Maniakes gets from the priests and the

people of Videssos the city for whatever success he's had against Makuran," Lysia answered, every bit as bitterly. At least in the matter of the husbands they saw slighted, the two women did understand each other well.

Roshnani pointed to Lysia's swollen belly. "How are you feeling?"

"Pretty well," Lysia answered. "If I had my choice, though, I'd sooner be pregnant in winter, not through the hottest time of the year."

"Oh, yes," Roshnani exclaimed. That made Abivard smile; Maniakes guessed he'd heard the same complaint from her a time or twelve.

"As soon as you have that list ready, I'm going to want to see it," Maniakes told the Makuraner marshal.

"I expected you would," Abivard said. "I'll have it for you in a couple of days at the latest, I promise. Names have been running around my head all this time I've been eating your excellent food. One I know will top it, and that's Kardarigan. He stands next after me and Romezan."

"That's very good." Maniakes felt like clapping his hands together. "If Romezan thinks Sharbaraz wants him to purge all your officers—"

"—and if the officers think Sharbaraz wants Romezan to purge them," Roshnani interrupted.

"Yes," Maniakes said. "If that happens, Romezan won't be happy with the King of Kings, and the officers won't be happy with Romezan or the King of Kings." He nodded toward Abivard. "You should be able to pick up a few pieces from that, don't you think?"

"What do you have in mind?" Lysia asked. "Once Abivard makes the list of officers, are you going to have Bagdasares sorcerously splice it into the letter Sharbaraz sent, so it looks as if he wants Romezan to do away with all of them?"

"That's exactly what I want Bagdasares to do," Maniakes said. "If it turns out he can't, life gets more complicated."

"Life is liable to get more complicated anyhow," Lysia said. "Abivard's two wizards know what the letter looked like when we got it. If they want to, they can make liars of us."

"You're right," Maniakes said. "If they want to, they can do that." He turned to Abivard. "How do we keep them from doing that?"

"I'm not worried about Panteles," Abivard said. "His first loyalty is to me, not to Sharbaraz. But Bozorg, now—he could be trouble."

"What does he want?" Lysia asked with brisk practicality. "Gold? Titles? Whatever it is, promise he'll get all he ever dreamt of if he keeps his mouth shut at the right time."

"I can arrange that side of it," Abivard said. "I can also put him in fear. Wizards are stronger than soldiers—when they have the leisure to prepare their spells. When they don't, soldiers can skewer them before they're able to do anything about it."

"And, maybe most important of all, you can convince him he's doing the right thing for Makuran," Roshnani said. "By what you've told me, husband of mine, he didn't want to believe Sharbaraz could stoop so low as to send out orders for your murder."

"Sharbaraz has stooped lower than that," Maniakes said.

"I'd like to know how!" Roshnani said indignantly.

Maniakes told her and Abivard about the shrine to the God his soldiers had come across in the Land of the Thousand Cities—or rather, the shrine to Sharbaraz in the role of the God. The two Makuraners exclaimed in their own language and made signs Maniakes presumed were meant to ward off evil. Slowly, sadly, Abivard said, "This is the curse of the court of the King of Kings, who never hears the word *no* and who comes to decide he can do exactly as he pleases in all spheres. I shall pass it on to Bozorg. If he needs one more reason to reject Sharbaraz, he'll have it."

Roshnani said, "If you'd known about that, you would have rebelled against the King of Kings a long time ago."

"Maybe I would have, but I didn't know," Abivard answered; Maniakes got the feeling this was an old argument between them. Abivard went on, "It doesn't matter any more. I have to go into rebellion now."

Roshnani muttered something. Maniakes wasn't quite sure he heard it, but thought it was *about time.*

Abivard nodded to him. "I'll have that list for you as fast as I can write it. The longer we delay, the more it looks as if we're plotting something. Since we are, we can't afford to look like it." Maniakes gave him a thoughtful nod. With a bit of practice, he would have made a good Videssian himself.

✦   ✦   ✦

Late the next afternoon, Abivard handed Maniakes a large sheet of parchment. "Here you are, your Majesty," the Makuraner marshal said. "If this doesn't do the job, nothing will."

"I thank you for your diligence," the Avtokrator answered. He looked down at the list Abivard had compiled. Because it was written in the Makuraner script, he could read not a name, not a title. Somehow that made it more impressive, not less: thanks in no small measure to its unintelligibility, it seemed magical to him.

But he knew the difference—and the distance—between what seemed magical and what was. Abivard had given him a tool through which he might accomplish his ends. To get the most from the tool, he had to understand how best to use it. He summoned Philetos from the Sorcerers' Collegium.

The healer-priest arrived promptly, no doubt expecting he would be called. He studied Abivard's list for a little while, then looked up at Maniakes and said, "He has been most thorough, your Majesty."

"I thought so," Maniakes said. "There's a lot of writing here, even if I can't make sense out of any of it."

"He begins with Kardarigan, who ranks just after Romezan, and continues through division commanders and regimental commanders, and he gets all the way down to troop leaders." Philetos looked awed. "If it is made to appear that Sharbaraz intended Romezan to execute all these officers, your Majesty, he would barely have enough high-ranking men left alive to let him lead the army."

"Good," Maniakes said. "That's the idea."

He carried the parchment to Bagdasares. The Vaspurakaner mage studied it. "It's longer than I thought it was going to be, your Majesty," he said. "That complicates things, because I'll have to sorcerously stretch the substance of the parchment on which Sharbaraz wrote so that it can accommodate all these names."

"Not a difficult spell, thanks to the law of similarity," Philetos murmured, which earned him a venomous glance from Bagdasares: like men of any other trade, mages did not appreciate being told how to do their jobs.

"It may not matter," Maniakes said. "We still have to see if Panteles and Bozorg will play along."

Leaving Bagdasares to prepare his spell, Maniakes approached the two wizards who had come to confirm for Abivard that the letter ordering his execution truly had come from the King of Kings. As he'd expected, Panteles gave no trouble; his loyalty and hopes rested with Abivard, for whom he was prepared to say almost anything.

Bozorg proved a tougher nut to crack. He stood stiff and erect, wearing not only his caftan but also a nearly palpable cloak of virtue. "A wanton lie is the surest way for a man's soul to fall into the Void and be lost forever," he said. "If Romezan son of Bizhan asks me whether the King of Kings included all these names on the letter, I shall have to tell him no."

He had spirit. He also, perhaps, had confidence that Maniakes could not afford to get rid of him before he'd spoken to Romezan. In that, he was unfortunately—at least from Maniakes' point of view—correct. Eyeing his stern face, Maniakes got the idea he would not be so amenable to bribery as Roshnani had suggested. Again, he wished a foe's principles more flexible.

Picking his words with care, the Avtokrator said, "If Romezan doesn't ask that exact question, you don't have to blurt out all you know, do you? You can truthfully say Sharbaraz did send this letter. You can say he ordered Abivard killed." He realized he should have brought a priest of Phos, to discuss with Bozorg the propriety of telling only part of the truth and lying by omission.

The Makuraner mage chewed on the inside of his lower lip. At last, he said, "I am of the opinion that Sharbaraz has acted unjustly in the matter of Abivard. If my silence helps justice be restored, then I am willing to be silent. But I tell you once more: I shall not lie."

Maniakes ended up agreeing to that, having no better choice. It left him discontented. It left him worse than discontented—it left him nervous. The whole plan rested on a gamble now: the gamble that Romezan would not ask the damning question. What they would do if Romezan did ask that question was something he knew he'd have to worry about, but not yet. Bagdasares' magic came first.

When the Avtokrator returned to the mage's chamber, Bagdasares had already succeeded in expanding the strip of parchment on which the order for Abivard's death was written to a size that would also let it hold the names from the Makuraner marshal's list.

"Not a difficult sorcery, your Majesty," he said when Maniakes praised him. He'd grown angry when Philetos had said the same thing, but now he was extolling his own skill, which was a different matter altogether. "Instead of changing the substance of the parchment, as I had first planned, I merely fused its edge with another, having taken care to secure a good match in appearance."

Picking up the extended sheet, Maniakes nodded. Neither his eyes nor his fingernail could detect the join. A sorcerer probably would have been able to do so, but he counted on no sorcerers analyzing the document till it was too late to matter.

"And now," Bagdasares said, "if you will forgive a homely metaphor, I aim to cut the list of names and ranks from the parchment whereon Abivard wrote it and to paste it into the appropriate place on the one written by Sharbaraz's scribe. I shall attend to the cutting first, as is but fitting."

The parchment Abivard had given to Maniakes lay on a silver tray. Bagdasares had set a silver arket with a portrait of Sharbaraz on top of the parchment. Now he began to chant and to make passes above it. Some of the chanting was in the old-fashioned Videssian of the divine liturgy, the rest in the Vaspurakaner tongue.

Sweat ran down Bagdasares' face. Pausing for a moment, he turned to Maniakes and said, "I have created the conditions wherein cutting is possible and practical. Now for my instrument."

Instead of producing an ensorceled knife, as Maniakes had expected, the mage walked over to a cage and pulled out a small, gray mouse. The little animal sat calmly in his hand, and did not try to escape even when he dipped its tail into a bottle of ink.

"You understand, your Majesty, that the animal is acting under my sorcerous compulsion," Bagdasares said. Maniakes nodded. The wizard went on, "It will—the good god and Vaspur the Firstborn willing, it will—precisely pick out the text to be shifted from one document to the other."

He removed the arket from Abivard's list, then set the mouse at the head of the parchment. Whiskers twitching, the mouse ran down to the bottom of the list. Maniakes feared its inky tail would smear Abivard's writing. Nothing of the sort happened. Bagdasares' sorcery must have kept anything of the sort from happening. Instead, the unintelligible—at least to Maniakes—characters Abivard had written now turned a glowing white, while the parchment beneath them went black as soot.

Bagdasares let out a sigh of relief. Evidently, that was the effect he had wanted to achieve. Maniakes let out a sigh of relief, too, because he had achieved it. The mage said, "Now to paste."

He coaxed the mouse back up into the palm of his hand. It stared at him with beady little black eyes. Maniakes wondered what, if anything, it thought of its role in the sorcery. One more thing he'd never know.

Bagdasares carried the silver arket of Sharbaraz over to the letter the King of Kings had sent to Romezan. "I have learned enough of the Makuraner script to be able to recognize Abivard's name," he said, "and I am going to set this coin immediately after it, so as to indicate the insertion point for the text to be shifted."

That done, he put the mouse back in its cage. It began to lick the ink off its tail with a tiny pink tongue. Bagdasares began another incantatory chant. His long-fingered hands moved in swift passes. His tone went from beseeching to serious to demanding. He shifted into throaty Vaspurakaner, a good language for demanding if ever there was one.

Maniakes exclaimed. There, starting where the arket lay, were the names and titles to be shifted to Sharbaraz's letter. The characters in which those names and titles were written remained white, though, and the portion of the parchment on which they appeared, black.

"Here," Bagdasares said, "we have an exact copy of the list Abivard wrote."

"Too exact, maybe," Maniakes observed, examining the document. "For one thing, the margins of the added text are different from those of the letter from Sharbaraz to Romezan."

"I have not yet completed the sorcery," Bagdasares said with a touch of annoyance. The Avtokrator waved for him to go on. He did, muttering now in Videssian, now in the Vaspurakaner tongue. When he stabbed out his forefinger at the parchment, the region of white characters on black grew longer and narrower; names and titles seemed to crawl downward to accommodate themselves to the change.

Watching words move made Maniakes vaguely seasick. Once having written, he expected what he wrote to stay put. But the result was no small improvement over what had been there before.

It was, however, not yet perfect. Pointing, Maniakes said, "I don't read Makuraner, but even I can tell two different hands did the writing here."

Bagdasares exhaled through his nose—and a fine nose he had for exhaling, too. With the air of a man clutching for patience as it slipped through his fingers, he said, "I am aware of this, your Majesty. I have a remedy for it." He walked over to the cage to which he had returned the mouse. After he took it out once more, he let out another exasperated exhalation. "A pestilence! The foolish creature has done too good a job of cleaning itself. I shall have to reink it."

He dipped the mouse's tail into the jar of ink again, all the while murmuring the cantrips that made the black liquid part of his sorcery rather than a messy nuisance. That done, he set the mouse at the top of the document, allowing its sorcerously inked tail to slide across a couple of lines of text there.

"That should do it," he said, and picked up the little beast again. "Now we apply the law of similarity to the names pasted onto the parchment . . ."

He set the mouse down at the top of the area where the words were still white and the parchment black. His magic made it walk down the black area to the very end, its tail twisting this way and that till it touched all the names and titles in Abivard's pasted list. And as its tail touched them, they—changed. Now they were written in the same style as the words of the document to which they had been appended.

Once the change of scripts was complete, Bagdasares again caged the mouse. He turned to Maniakes. "Is this indeed how you wish the final document to appear, your Majesty?"

"Well, I'd be happier if it were all black on white instead of half the other way around," the Avtokrator answered.

Bagdasares snorted. "The reversal shows that part of the text still remaining mutable. Has it now been changed to your satisfaction?"

"Yes," Maniakes said. "I hope turning it back into black on white isn't too complicated for you."

"I think I can manage that, your Majesty," Bagdasares said with a smile. Tongue between his teeth, he made a single sharp clicking sound. All at once, white letters turned black, black parchment white. "There you are: one long, bloodthirsty letter, ready to befuddle Romezan."

Maniakes studied the letter. As far as he could tell, it might have come straight from the chancery of the King of Kings. The only trouble was, he couldn't tell much. "We'll let Abivard have a look at it and see what he thinks," Maniakes said. Bagdasares nodded.

When the Avtokrator stepped out of the wizard's workroom, Kameas stood waiting for his command. Half of him was surprised to find the vestiarios there; the other half would have been surprised had Kameas been anyplace else. "I shall bring him here directly," the eunuch said, almost before Maniakes could tell him what he wanted.

Bozorg came up the hallway of the imperial residence with Abivard. Maniakes was glad both of them would be reviewing the document before Romezan set eyes on it. Abivard looked at it first. He read it through, read it again, and then read it a third time. Having done that, he delivered his verdict: "Romezan will have kittens."

"May I see, lord?" Bozorg asked. Abivard passed him the altered letter. He studied it even longer than the Makuraner marshal had done. When he was finally finished, he looked not to Maniakes but to Bagdasares. "This is very fine work," he said, admiration in his voice.

Bagdasares bowed. "Your servant."

"You must tell me how you achieved such a perfect match of the script between the original and that which was written afterward," the Makuraner mage said. "I do not slight my own skill, but I am far from certain I could do the like."

"I'd be delighted," Bagdasares said, preening; he was never shy about receiving praise. "The method employs—"

Maniakes coughed. Bagdasares checked himself. Had he not checked himself, Maniakes might have trodden on his toes. The Avtokrator said, "It might be better if the details remain private." That seemed a politer way of putting it than, *If our magic is better than theirs, let's keep it that way, since we've been at war with them for the last ten years or so.*

Abivard coughed in turn. That worried Maniakes. If the Makuraner marshal insisted that his wizard learn Bagdasares' document-altering technique, Maniakes would have an awkward time gainsaying him. But Abivard contented himself with remarking, "We have our secrets, too, which we would be well advised not to let you Videssians learn."

"Fair enough," Maniakes said. Abivard was dead right in that, and the Empire of Videssos had almost died because Sharbaraz had kept his alliance with the Kubratoi secret so long.

Bagdasares said, "The document does meet with full approval, then?"

"Oh, yes," Abivard answered. "It will serve in every particular."

Bozorg said, "It is the best forgery I have ever seen." Bagdasares preened again. The Makuraner mage went on, "It will make me look at new techniques, it truly will, for nothing with which I am now familiar could produce such a fine linkage between two documents. The joining of new parchment to old is also quite good, but that I know I can equal."

Bagdasares bristled, offended at the notion any other mage was sure he could equal him at anything. Maniakes hid a smile. When he'd first met Bagdasares at the start of the uprising against Genesios, the Vaspurakaner mage had been a journeyman back in Opsikion, and, though proud of his skill, hadn't reckoned it extraordinary.

He'd come a long way since. So had Maniakes. Rising with the Avtokrator had let—had sometimes made—Bagdasares deal with sorceries more elaborate than those he would have seen had he stayed in Opsikion. It had also let him largely discard *Alvinos*, the Videssian-sounding name he'd been in the habit of using then. Now he truly was a sorcerer as good as any in the world—and ever so aware of it.

Maniakes sobered. Bagdasares' blind spot was easy enough for him to recognize. What of his own? He'd noted his habit of moving too soon and too hard in the direction he wanted to go. But if he didn't spot his own weaknesses, who would tell him about them? He was the Avtokrator, after all. And how could he hope to notice his own blind spots if he was blind to them?

Lost in that unprofitable reverie, he realized he'd missed something Abivard had said. "I'm sorry?"

"You were thinking hard about something there," Abivard remarked with a smile. "I could tell. What I said was, I want to see the expression on Romezan's face when he looks at this letter."

"That will be interesting," Maniakes agreed. "The other thing that will be . . . interesting is the expressions on the faces of all the other officers you've added to the list." His attention suddenly sharpened. "Did you put Tzikas' name there, by any chance?"

"Tzikas' name is on your list, your Majesty, and the God knows he's on my list, but he'd never, ever be on Sharbaraz's list, so I left him off," Abivard said, real regret in his voice. "Sharbaraz trusts him, remember."

"You could tell that story as a joke in every tavern in the Empire of Videssos, and you'd get a laugh every time," Maniakes said. "I'll tell you this: the notion of *anyone* trusting Tzikas is pretty funny to me."

"And to me," Abivard said. "But, in some strange ways, it does make sense. As I said before, Sharbaraz is the one person in the whole world Tzikas can't hope to overthrow. Anyone below Sharbaraz—me, for instance—certainly. But not the King of Kings. Besides, Tzikas knew, or claimed he knew, something that would have given us a better chance to take Videssos the city."

"He did know something," Maniakes said. "I can even tell you what it was." He did, finishing, "It doesn't matter that you know, because the tunnel is filled in by now."

"It does sound like Likinios to have made such a thing," Abivard said. "If Likinios had ever told me about it, I would have used it against you—and then, with Tzikas no longer useful to me . . ." He smiled again, this time as cynically as any Videssian might have done.

"What we ought to do next," Maniakes said, "is get Romezan over here as fast as may be. One of the things we don't know is how many copies of that letter Sharbaraz sent to him. If the authentic version falls into his lap before he's seen this one . . ."

"Life gets difficult," Abivard said. "All those years ago, when Sharbaraz and I came into Videssos, I wondered if we were going into exile. If Romezan sees the authentic letter, I know perfectly well I am." His face clouded. "And my children are all on the far side of the Cattle Crossing."

"We'll attend to it," Maniakes said.

Isokasios rose from his prostration and said, "Your Majesty, Romezan won't come to this side of the Cattle Crossing. I asked him every way I could think of, and he flat-out won't do it."

Maniakes stared at his messenger in dismay. "What do you

mean, he won't do it? Did he tell you why? Is it that he doesn't trust us?"

"Your Majesty, that's exactly what it is," Isokasios answered. "He said that, as far as he was concerned, we were just a pack of sneaky, oily Videssians trying to separate the Makuraner field army from its generals. Said he didn't like the chances of his coming back to Across in one piece, and so he'd stay where he was."

"To the ice with him!" Maniakes exclaimed. "I'm not the one who mistreats envoys from the other side—that's Sharbaraz."

Abivard coughed. "Your Majesty, what I've seen since we came into the Empire of Videssos is that there are two kinds of Makuraners. Some of us, like me—and like Roshnani more than me—have grown fond enough of your ways to ape some of them. The rest of us, though, keep all our old ideas, and cling to them harder than ever so we don't have to look at anything different. Romezan is in the second bunch. He's smoother about it than a lot of the other officers who think that way, but he is one."

"He would be," Maniakes said, a complaint against the way the world worked, a complaint against the way the world had worked against him since he'd had the Avtokrator's crown set on his head.

"What do we do now?" Rhegorios asked.

Abivard said, "I will go back over to the western side of the Cattle Crossing and tell him that he needs to come here with me."

"That's—one idea," Maniakes said. Romezan did not want to come to Videssos the city, for fear of what the Videssians might do to him and Abivard. Maniakes was less than keen on Abivard's return to the Makuraner field army, for fear of what he might do with it. He'd finally succeeded in splitting Abivard from Sharbaraz—or rather, Sharbaraz had done it for him—and he neither wanted the breach repaired nor for Abivard to go off on his own rather than acting in concert with him.

He found no way to say any of that without offending Abivard, which was the last thing he wanted to do. He wondered if he could find any polite way to use Roshnani as a hostage against the Makuraner marshal's return. While he was casting about for one, Rhegorios said, "If Romezan will come here, I'll go there. That should convince them we're serious about this business."

"If he wants hostages, he has my children," Abivard said, in a way anticipating Maniakes. He sounded serious, serious to the point of bleakness.

"They don't matter," Rhegorios said, and then, before Abivard could get angry, "As far as he knows, you and he are still on the same side. If he wants one of us over there while he's over here, I'll go."

"He doesn't need you, cousin of mine," Maniakes said. "If he wants a hostage against Videssos, he has the westlands."

"That doesn't matter, either," Rhegorios insisted. "As far as he knows, the westlands belong to Makuran by right. You offered hostages when Abivard came here. Why not now?"

Maniakes stared at him. "You *want* to do this."

His cousin nodded. "I do. Right now, it's the most useful thing I can do, and it's something *only* I can do: I'm a hostage Romezan has to take seriously. That means I'd better do it."

What he said wasn't strictly true. The elder Maniakes or Symvatios would have made as fitting a hostage. Maniakes, however, would not have sent his father or uncle into the hands of the Makuraners, not when they'd proved themselves liable to mistreat high-ranking Videssians. He would not have sent his cousin, either, but Rhegorios plainly thought the risk worth taking.

Abivard said, "Romezan is a man of often fiery temper, but he is also, on the whole, a man of honor."

"On the whole?" Maniakes did not like the qualification. "What if he gets an order from Sharbaraz to execute every hostage he has? Wouldn't he be as likely to obey that order as the one that called for him to kill you?"

Abivard coughed and looked down at his hands, which led Maniakes to draw his own conclusions. But Rhegorios laughed, saying, "What are the odds the King of Kings will send just that order at just this moment? It's a gamble, but I think it's a good one. Besides, as soon as Romezan sees what we've cooked up here—" He pointed to the augmented parchment. "—he's not on Sharbaraz's side any more, right? From then on, he's ours. By the good god, he'd better be ours from then on."

Maniakes hadn't even thought what might happen if Romezan read the altered documents and said something like, *Well, if that's what Sharbaraz wants me to do, I'd better do it*. Thrax might have done something like that, if faced with an order from Maniakes.

But Abivard said, "Romezan might well carry out an order aimed at me alone. He will not try to carry out an order aimed at me and half the officers in the army. He is headstrong, but he is no fool. He could see for himself that in moments we would be fighting among ourselves harder than we ever fought you Videssians."

That did make sense, and went a long way toward easing Maniakes' mind—at least about the prospect of Romezan's turning once he saw the letter. About Rhegorios' going over to Across . . . he felt no easier about that, not even a little.

With his cousin determined to go, though, the Avtokrator saw no way to stop him, not if his going made Romezan agree to come over the Cattle Crossing in return. "I'll send Isokasios back to Romezan," Maniakes said. "If he agrees to cross . . ." He sighed. "If he agrees to cross, you may go over there."

Rhegorios looked surprised, as if needing Maniakes' permission had not occurred to him. It probably hadn't; Rhegorios was used to doing as he pleased. Evidently concluding this was not the moment to argue for his own freedom of action, he said, "Very well, your Majesty," as if he were in the habit of obeying his cousin without question all the time.

When Maniakes ordered Isokasios back to Across yet again, the messenger gave him an impudent grin. "You ought to pay me by the furlong, your Majesty," he remarked.

"I'll pay your tongue by the furlong," Maniakes retorted. Back in his days of exile on the island of Kalavria, a messenger would have stuck out the organ in question after a crack like that. Maniakes watched Isokasios' eyes light up. He wanted to be difficult; Maniakes could see as much. But he didn't dare, not when he was dealing with the Avtokrator of the Videssians. Maniakes sighed to himself. The ceremonial upon which the Empire was founded made life less interesting in a multitude of ways.

Traveling openly in the *Renewal*, Isokasios went off to visit Romezan the next morning. Rhegorios stood with Maniakes at the foot of the piers in the palace quarter, watching the imperial flagship glide over the waters of the Cattle Crossing, oars rising and falling in smooth unison.

Rhegorios said, "When I get over there, I'll feel as if the reconquest of the westlands has started."

"You can feel any number of different things," Maniakes replied. "If feeling them made them real, life would be easier."

"Ah, wouldn't it?" his cousin agreed. "And if what we felt about Tzikas could make him feel what we feel he ought to feel..."

"I dare you to say that again," Maniakes broke in. "In fact, I defy you to say that again."

Rhegorios started to, but tripped on his tongue before he made it through. Unlike Isokasios, he was of rank exalted enough to be rude to the Avtokrator. Both men laughed.

Maniakes, though, soon grew serious. "If we do manage to drive a wedge between Sharbaraz and his field army, we also need to figure out how we can take best advantage of that." He listened to his own words, then shook his head in bemusement. "By the good god, I sound like poor Likinios." He sketched the sun-circle over his heart to avert any possible omen connecting his fate to that which his unfortunate predecessor had suffered.

His cousin also made the sun-sign. "You're right," he said. His eyes narrowed in thought. "Maybe I will be the first step in taking back the westlands—taking them back without losing a man."

"You're right with me," Maniakes said. "I don't know if that will work; I don't know what Abivard will choose to do. But we have our best chance now. Which reminds me—I ought to have our army ready to move whenever it needs to. The Makuraners may take more convincing than words can give."

"They always have up till now, that's certain," Rhegorios said. "That's another reason I need to go over to Across." Maniakes grimaced, annoyed at his cousin for making a connection he hadn't seen himself.

The *Renewal* brought Isokasios back, with the sun not far past noon. The messenger said, "Your Majesty, you and Romezan have a bargain. When I said his Highness—" He glanced over to Rhegorios. "—would come to Across to guarantee his safety, he looked at me as if I'd started speaking the Haloga language. I needed a little while to convince him I meant it."

Maniakes turned to Rhegorios. "There. You see? Romezan thinks you're crazy, too." Rhegorios laughed at him.

Isokasios went on, "Once Romezan understood you were serious, he swore by his heathen God that no harm would come to the Sevastos in Across, so long as no harm came to *him* in Videssos the city. And he said he'd sail back here on the *Renewal* as soon as the Sevastos got there."

"He won't wait long, then," Rhegorios said. "I'm ready now, which means Romezan will be here this afternoon." He grinned at Maniakes. "And won't he have himself a surprise when he gets here?"

The Avtokrator embraced his cousin. "I still wish you weren't going. The lord with the great and good mind go with you." He and Rhegorios—and Isokasios, too—sketched Phos' sun-circle above their hearts.

Watching the *Renewal* glide west over the Cattle Crossing with Isokasios on board had been easy enough. Watching the dromon sail west with Rhegorios on board was something else entirely. Had Maniakes not had such a desperate need to see Romezan, he would not have let his cousin go. Had he not had desperate needs of one sort of another, he would not have done a lot of the things he had done since the ecumenical patriarch set the crown on his head. He was sick of acting from desperation rather than desire.

When the *Renewal* came back toward the imperial city, Maniakes shaded his eyes with his hand, half hoping he would see Rhegorios in the bow, a sign Romezan had decided not to keep the bargain, after all. He didn't see his cousin. He did see a large caftan-clad man who did not look familiar, though the Avtokrator might have seen him on one battlefield or another.

Sailors made the *Renewal* fast to a wharf. Abivard came up beside Maniakes. "They're very quick and smooth at what they do," he remarked. "They put me in mind of well-trained troops—which in their own way I suppose they are."

"Etzilios would think so," Maniakes agreed absently. He waited for the sailors to run the gangplank out between the dromon and the shore. Romezan came across it first. When he did, Maniakes could see why his countrymen called him the wild boar of Makuran: he was not only tall but, unusual for a Makuraner, thick through the shoulders as well. He had a fierce, handsome, forward-thrusting face, with his mustache and the tip of his beard waxed to sharp points.

Politely, he prostrated himself before Maniakes, then kissed Abivard on the cheek, acknowledging the marshal's higher rank: no small concession for a noble of the Seven Clans to yield to a man raised over him from the lower nobility. "Lord," he said to Abivard before turning to Maniakes, whom he addressed in the Makuraner tongue: "Majesty, you've made my curiosity itch as much as a flea in my drawers would do for my bum. What can be so important that you'd use your cousin as surety for my safe return? The sooner I know, the happier I'll be."

Having at last lured Romezan over the Cattle Crossing, the Avtokrator now temporized. "Come to my residence," he said. "What you need to learn is there, and I have food and wine waiting, too."

"To the Void with food and wine," growled Romezan, who would have been blunt-spoken as a Videssian and made a truly startling Makuraner. Had Maniakes' Haloga guardsmen understood his tongue, they would have reckoned him a kindred spirit.

Once back at the residence, though, he did accept wine and honey cakes, and greeted Symvatios and the elder Maniakes with the respect their years deserved. To the latter, he said, "When I was first going to war, you taught me Videssians are enemies not to be despised."

"I wish you'd remembered the lesson better in later years," Maniakes' father answered, at which Romezan loosed a deep, rolling chortle.

The Makuraner general soon grew restless again. He prowled along the corridors of the residence nodding approval at the hunting mosaics on the floor and the trophies of victories past. Maniakes and Abivard accompanied him, the Avtokrator answering questions as they walked. When Maniakes judged the time ripe, he handed Romezan Sharbaraz's altered orders. "Here," he said without preamble. "What do you plan to do about this?"

✦ IX

Romezan read through the entire document with the headlong intensity he seemed to give to everything. He kept his face as still as he could, but the more he read, the higher his eyebrows rose. "By the God," he said when he was through. He looked up at Maniakes. "Majesty, I crave pardon for doubting you. You were right. This is something I had to see."

"Now you have seen it," Abivard said before the Avtokrator could reply. "What *do* you plan to do about it?" His voice had an edge that required no pretense; Sharbaraz truly had ordered his execution.

"I'm not going to yank out my sword on the spot and carve slices off you, if that's what you mean," Romezan answered. "If this is real, Sharbaraz has fallen over the edge." His gaze sharpened, as if, on horseback, he had spotted a new target for his lance. "*Is* this real, or is it some clever forgery the Videssians have cooked up?"

He spoke without regard for Maniakes, who stood only a couple of feet away from him. Maniakes was better at holding his features quiet than the Makuraner. Behind the stillness, he was laughing. The only true answer to Romezan's question was *both*; part of the parchment was real, part clever forgery, though Abivard had had as much to do with that as any Videssian.

"It's real," Abivard said, playing the part that benefited Videssos

605

because it also benefited him. "My mages have shown that's so—it's why I summoned them to this side of the Cattle Crossing."

"I will hear as much from them," Romezan said.

Maniakes nodded to Kameas. Bowing to Romezan, the vestiarios glided out of the audience chamber. He returned in short order with Panteles and Bozorg. Bowing again, he said, "Here they are, eminent sir."

To Abivard, Romezan said, "That's right, you brought your tame Videssian along, didn't you?" He dismissed Panteles with a wave of his hand. "Go on, sirrah; what you have to say interests me not at all, for you'll say whatever your master wants you to say."

"That is not so," the Videssian mage replied with dignity.

Since Maniakes knew perfectly well it was so, he was not surprised to discover Romezan did, too. The Makuraner general said, "Go on, I tell you," and Panteles perforce went. Romezan turned his attention to Bozorg. "Do you really mean to tell me Sharbaraz was this stupid?"

The Makuraner mage nodded. "Can you reckon wise any man who would treacherously seek to compass the death of his finest marshal?" He did not say anything about the deaths of all the other officers whose names had been transferred to the King of Kings' letter. Maniakes noted the omission. He had to hope Romezan would not.

"He truly did send that order?" Romezan sounded thoughtful and, unless Maniakes read him wrong, sad.

Bozorg nodded. "He did. My magic—and also that of Panteles— confirmed it." What the wizard said was the truth, as he had promised it would be. What he did not say, and would not say unless specifically asked . . .

No doubt intending to keep Romezan from asking the questions Bozorg was liable to answer truthfully, Abivard said, "You still haven't answered the question I put to you when I first showed you this. What do you plan to do about it?"

"If I do as the King of Kings commanded me, this whole army goes straight into the Void," Romezan observed, and Abivard nodded. "But if I don't do as the King of Kings commanded me," Romezan went on, "that by itself makes me into a traitor, and means some other officer—"

"Tzikas," Abivard interrupted. By the way he said it, he didn't expect Romezan to like Tzikas. Maniakes wondered whether any-one in the civilized world besides Tzikas liked Tzikas.

"Some other officer will get a letter like this one," Romezan finished, as if Abivard had not spoken. "But he won't have orders to get rid of you. He'll have orders to get rid of me." Romezan sighed. Those broad shoulders sagged. "I never thought I would have to turn away from Sharbaraz King of Kings, may his—" He broke off the honorific formula in the middle. "And to the Void with that, too. May his fundament be removed from the seat of the chair he occupies in Mashiz." He went down on his belly before Abivard. "Majesty," he said. "There. Now my rebellion is official."

"I hadn't planned to—" Abivard broke off. The logical conse-quences of being in the situation came crashing down on him. If he stayed loyal to Sharbaraz, he offered his neck to the chopping block. Beside that, rebellion became the more attractive choice.

Maniakes offered the alternative he'd suggested before: "If you don't care to be King of Kings in your own name, there's still your baby nephew to protect."

Still down on hands and knees, Romezan laughed wolfishly, an effect enhanced by his posture. "I've heard a lot of stories about men who rebel in the name of babies," he said. "Maybe I've heard one where the baby lived and got to rule when he grew up. Maybe I haven't, too."

"I don't have to decide that right away," Abivard answered. "What matters is that I'm in rebellion against Sharbaraz King of Kings—and so are you." He bent down and tapped Romezan on the shoulder. "Get up."

Romezan rose, that wolfish look still in his eye. "By this time tomorrow, the whole field army will be in arms against Sharbaraz. We'll march back to Mashiz, throw him out, get rid of him, put you on the throne, and—" His vision of the future ran out at that point. "And everything will be fine then," he finished.

Abivard did indeed look farther ahead than the noble from the Seven Clans. He glanced toward Maniakes. "It's . . . not going to be quite that simple, I don't think," he said.

"No, it's not," Maniakes agreed. He had been hoping for, and been planning for, a moment like this ever since he became Avtokra-tor of the Videssians. He had also spent a large stretch of time wondering if it would ever come. He spoke not to Abivard but to Romezan: "What do you propose to do with your garrisons in the westlands while the field army goes up against Sharbaraz?"

"Leave them there," Romezan answered at once. "Why not? We'll be back next year, and—" The difficulty Abivard had seen at once now became apparent to him, too. He looked at Maniakes with no great warmth. "Oh. If we leave, you'll start taking those cities back."

The Avtokrator shook his head. "No, I won't do anything of the sort," he answered. Romezan stared at him, angrily suspicious. Even Abivard looked surprised. He didn't blame them. Liberating the cities in the westlands after the Makuraner field force pulled out had been his first plan. Instead of using it, though, he said, "If you leave the garrisons behind, I'll burn everything in front of the field army and I'll attack it the first chance I get."

"Why would you want to do a stupid thing like that?" Romezan burst out. "If you do, our campaign against Sharbaraz goes into the latrine."

"He knows that," Abivard said, as if to a child. "He doesn't care—or he doesn't care much. What he wants is to get the westlands back under Videssian rule."

"That's right," Maniakes said. "Agree to put the border back where it was before Likinios Avtokrator got murdered, and I'll help you every way I can. Try to fight your civil war and hold on to the westlands, too, and I'll hurt you every way I can—and I can hurt you badly now."

"Suppose we don't march on Mashiz?" Romezan said. "Suppose we just stay where we are? What then?"

"Then Sharbaraz finds out you didn't execute Abivard," Maniakes said, a touch of wolf in his own smile. "Then somebody— Kardarigan, maybe, or Tzikas—gets the order to execute *you*, not for failure, but for rebellion. You said as much yourself."

Already swarthy, Romezan darkened further with anger. "You dare to take advantage of our squabbles among ourselves and use them to steal from us?"

Maniakes threw back his head and laughed in Romezan's face. The noble from the Seven Clans could not have looked more astonished had Maniakes dashed a bucket of cold water over him. The Avtokrator said, "By the good god, Romezan, how do you think you got the westlands in the first place? You marched into them when Videssos looked more like a catfight than an empire, after Genesios murdered Likinios and every general thought he could steal the throne for himself, or at least keep his neighbor from having it. Taking back what was mine is not stealing, not here it isn't."

"He's right," Abivard said, and Maniakes inclined his head to him, respecting his honesty. "I don't like him getting the west-lands back, and if I can find any way to keep him from getting them back, I will use it. But trying to get them back doesn't make him a thief."

"I don't think you can find such a way," Maniakes said. "I don't think you have very long to spend looking for one, either of you. You can bargain with me or you can try to bargain with Sharbaraz. If you have any choices past those two, I don't see them."

"You are enjoying this," Romezan said, as if he were accusing the Avtokrator of lapping soup from a bowl like a dog.

Again, Maniakes met the challenge straight on. "Every minute of it," he agreed. "You Makuraners have spent my whole reign, and the one before mine, humiliating Videssos. Now I get a chance to get my own back—literally. You can either give it up and go back to your own land to deal with the King of Kings who put you in this predicament, or you can try to keep it, try to go back, and get chewed up along the way. The choice is yours."

"We have no choice," Abivard said. "Let the borders be as they were before Likinios Avtokrator was murdered." Romezan looked mutinous but said nothing.

"That was the start of the trouble between us," Maniakes said.

But Abivard shook his head. "No. Likinios paid gold to the Khamorth tribes north of the Degird to raid into Makuran. When Peroz King of Kings, may the God cherish his spirit, moved against them, he was defeated and slain, which let Smerdis usurp Sharbaraz's throne, which let Likinios interfere in our civil war, which . . . You know the tale as well as I. Finding a beginning for the strife between us is not easy."

"Nor will finding an end to that strife be easy," Romezan rumbled: a plain note of warning.

"For now, though, on these terms, we can stop," Maniakes said.

"For now." Abivard and Romezan spoke together.

✦　　✦　　✦

Abivard and Roshnani scrambled down into a boat from the *Renewal*. The sailors swiftly rowed them over the narrow stretch of water separating the imperial flagship from the beach at Across. When they got out of the boat on the beach, Rhegorios got into it. The sailors brought him back to the dromon.

"I am well," he said to Maniakes. "Is all well here?"

"Well enough," his cousin answered.

The Avtokrator nodded to Romezan. "Your turn now."

"Aye, my turn now," the noble from the Seven Clans said heavily. "And I shall make the most of it." He got down into the boat. So did Bozorg and Panteles. The Videssian mage in Makuraner pay looked as if he wished he could sit farther from Romezan than the boat permitted.

After Romezan and the two wizards had got out of the boat again and strode up the beach toward Across, Thrax spoke up: "I expect you'll want to get back to the imperial city now, eh, your Majesty?"

"What?" Maniakes said. "No, by the good god. Hang about here—a bit out of bowshot, if that suits you. This is where things that matter are going to happen today. I want to be here when they do."

"Why not just hop out of the dromon and go on into the Makuraners' camp yourself, then?" Thrax laughed.

All Maniakes answered was, "No, not yet. The time isn't ripe." The drungarios of the fleet stared at him; Maniakes was used to having Thrax stare at him. After the fleet had kept the Kubratoi from getting over the Cattle Crossing to join with the Makuraners, he begrudged Thrax his limitations less than he had.

"I presume we're waiting for the cheers that mean Abivard is reading the letter to a joyous and appreciative audience?" Rhegorios asked, grinning at his own irony.

"That's what we're waiting for, all right," Maniakes said. "I asked Abivard to meet with his officers by the seaside, but he said no. He doesn't care to remind them they're going to be cooperating with us any more than he has to, not right now he doesn't. Put that way, he has a point."

"Aye, likely so," Rhegorios agreed. "I'll be glad when we do get back to the city, though; I'll tell you that. They wanted to honor me, so they gave me a Makuraner cook. I've been eating mutton without garlic ever since I traded myself for Romezan. I think the inside of my mouth has fallen asleep."

"If that's the worst you suffered, you came through well," Maniakes said. "I'm just bloody glad the Makuraners let you go again."

Thrax pointed toward Across. "Looks like something's going on there, your Majesty. To the ice with me if I can make out what, though."

Trees and bushes and buildings—some standing, others ruins—screened most of the interior of the suburb from view from the sea, but Thrax was right: something was going on there. Where things had been quiet, almost sleepy, before Abivard and Romezan returned to the Makuraner field force, now suddenly men were moving through the streets, some mounted, others afoot. As Maniakes watched, more and more soldiers started stirring.

Shouts rang out, someplace he could not see. To his annoyance, he could not make out the words. "Move closer to shore," he told Thrax. Reluctantly, the drungarios obeyed the order.

A couple of horsemen came galloping out of Across. Maniakes and Rhegorios looked at each other. No way to tell what that meant. Had the *Renewal* come any closer to the shore, she would have beached herself. Maniakes should have been able to make out what the Makuraners were shouting. The trouble was, they weren't shouting anything after that first brief outcry. Only the slap of waves against the dromon's hull broke the quiet.

He waited, wishing he could be a fly on the wall wherever the Makuraners had gathered instead of uselessly staying here on the sea. After a moment, he thumped his forehead with the heel of his hand. Bagdasares' magic might have let him be that fly on the wall, as he had been for a little while listening to Abivard and Etzilios and, unexpectedly, Tzikas.

Mages on the other side had soon blocked his hearing then. But two of the chief mages for the other side were at least partly on his side now. On the other hand, magic had a way of falling to pieces when dealing with, or trying to deal with, inflamed passions—that was why both battle magic and love magic worked so seldom. And he suspected that passions at the Makuraner assemblage, if not inflamed now, would be soon.

Hardly had the thought crossed his mind when a great, furious roar arose somewhere near the center of Across. He could make out no words in it, but found himself less annoyed than he had been before. He did not think that angry baying *had* any words in it, any more than a pack of hounds cried out with words when they scented blood.

On and on went the roar, now getting a little softer, now rising again to a new peak of rage. Rhegorios chuckled. "What do you want to bet they're reading through the whole list Abivard came up with?" he said.

"You're likely right," Maniakes answered. "When they shout louder it must be because they've just come across some especially popular officer."

Abivard had come up with more than three hundred names. Reading them all took a while. At last, silence fell. A moment later, fresh outcry broke out. Now, for the first time, Maniakes could make out one word, shouted as part of a rhythmic chant: the name of the Makuraner King of Kings.

"If that's not 'Dig up Sharbaraz's bones!' in Makuraner, I'm a shave-pated priest," Rhegorios exclaimed.

Maniakes nodded. "Aye, that's the riot call, no doubt about it." He did several steps of a happy dance, right there on the deck, and slammed his fist into his open palm. "By the good god, cousin of mine, we did it!"

Where he was uncharacteristically delighted, Rhegorios was as uncharacteristically restrained. "We may have done it," he said. "We've done part of it, anyhow. But there are still thousands of boiler boys sitting right here next to the Cattle Crossing, only a long piss away from Videssos the city. Getting the buggers out of the westlands and back where they belong is going to take a deal of doing yet."

A Makuraner burst out from among the buildings of Across and ran along the beach. He utterly ignored the presence of the *Renewal* not far offshore—and well he might have, for three of his countrymen were at his heels, their caftans flapping about them like wings as they ran. The swords in their hands glittered and flashed in the sun.

The fleeing Makuraner, perhaps hearing them gaining on him, turned at bay, drawing his own sword. As with most fights of one against three, this one did not last long. He lay where he had fallen, his blood soaking the sand.

"Maybe their whole army will fall apart," Rhegorios said dreamily. "Maybe they'll have their civil war here and now."

"Maybe," Maniakes said. "I don't think enough Makuraners will stay loyal to Sharbaraz to make much of a civil war, though."

"Mm, something to that," Rhegorios admitted. "For so long, though, we've got less than our due that I don't think the good god will be angry with me if I hope for more than our due for a change." He shifted from theology to politics, all in one breath: "I wish I knew which side the dead man was on, and which the three who killed him."

Maniakes could not grant that wish, but the three Makuraners did, almost as soon as it was uttered. They waved to the *Renewal*, and bowed, and did everything they could to show they were well inclined to Videssos. One of them pointed to the body of the man they had killed. "He would not spit on the name of Sharbaraz Pimp of Pimps!" he shouted, his voice thin across the water of the Cattle Crossing.

"Sharbaraz Pimp of Pimps." Now Maniakes, echoing the Makuraners, sounded dreamy, his mind far away across the years. "When Sharbaraz was fighting Smerdis, that's what his men called the usurper: Smerdis Pimp of Pimps. Now it comes full circle." He sketched Phos' sun-sign, a circle itself, above his heart.

"We have the rebellion," Rhegorios said. Solemnly, he and Maniakes and Thrax clasped hands. As Rhegorios had said, success seemed strange after so many disappointments.

The Makuraners on the beach were still shouting, now in bad Videssian instead of their own language: "You Avtokrator, you come here, we make friends. No more enemies no more."

"Not yet," Maniakes shouted back. "Not yet. Soon."

A little breeze flirted with the scarlet capes of the Halogai and Videssians of the Imperial Guard as they formed three sides of a square on the beach near Across. The sun mirrored off their gilded mail shirts. Almost to a man, they looked wary, ready to fight: all around them, drawn up in far greater numbers, stood the warriors of the Makuraner field force.

The waters of the Cattle Crossing formed the fourth side of the square. Sailors decked out in scarlet tunics for the occasion rowed Maniakes and Rhegorios from the *Renewal* to the shore. One of them said, "Begging your pardon, your Majesty, but I'd sooner jump in a crate full of spiders than go over there."

"They won't do anything to me or the Sevastos." Maniakes kept his voice relaxed, even amused. "If they do, they'll have our fathers to deal with, and they know it." That was true. It was, however, the sort of truth that would do him no good if it came to pass.

Sand grated under the planks of the boat. Maniakes and Rhegorios stepped out. As they did so, the Makuraner army burst into cheers. Rhegorios' grin was wide enough to threaten to split his face in two. "Did you ever imagine you'd hear that?" he asked.

"Never once," Maniakes replied. The Imperial Guards, without moving, seemed to stand easier. They might yet have needed to defend the Avtokrator against being trampled by well-wishers, but not against the murderous onslaught they'd dreaded, knowing they were too few to withstand it if it came.

Out among the Makuraners, deep drums thudded and horns howled. The axe-bearing Halogai and the Videssians with swords and spears tensed anew: that sort of music commonly presaged an attack. But then an iron-lunged Makuraner herald cried: "Forth comes Abivard son of Godarz, Makuran's new sun now rising in the east!"

"Abivard!" the warriors of the field army shouted over and over again, ever louder, till the marshal's name made Maniakes' head ring.

Only a handful of his own soldiers understood what the outcry meant. Not wanting fighting to start from panic or simple error, the Avtokrator called to them: "They're just announcing the marshal."

Slowly, Abivard made his way through the crush of Makuraners till he stood before the Imperial Guards. "May I greet the Avtokrator of the Videssians?" he asked a massive Haloga axeman.

"Let him by, Hrafnkel," Maniakes called.

Without a word, the Haloga stood aside. So did the file of guardsmen behind him. Abivard strode past them into the midst of the open space their number defined. As the Makuraner field force could have overwhelmed the Imperial Guards and slain Maniakes before help could reach him, so the guards could have slain Abivard before his men could save him. Maniakes nodded, appreciating the symmetry.

Abivard came up to him and held out his hand for a clasp. That was symmetry of another sort: the greeting of one equal to another. The only equals in all the world the Avtokrators of the Videssians acknowledged were the Kings of Kings of Makuran.

Maniakes clasped Abivard's hands, acknowledging that equality.

As he did so, he asked, "What was your herald talking about—the new sun of Makuran? What's that supposed to mean?"

"It means I still haven't decided whether I'm going to overthrow Sharbaraz on my own account or in the name of my nephew," Abivard answered. "If I call myself King of Kings now, I've taken the choice away from myself. This way, I keep it."

"Ah," Maniakes said. "Fair enough. The more choices you have, the better off you are." He inclined his head to Abivard. "Over the years, you've given me too bloody few of them."

"As you well know, I am not excessively burdened with choices myself at the moment," Abivard answered tartly.

"Shall we get on with the ceremony, your Majesty, your—uh—Sunship?" Rhegorios said with a grin. "The sooner we have it out of the way, the sooner we can find someplace quiet and shady and drink some wine."

"A splendid notion," Abivard agreed. Till then, he, the Avtokrator, and the Sevastos had been speaking quietly among themselves while the Imperial Guards and the Makuraner warriors peered in at them and tried to make out what they were saying. Now Abivard raised his voice, as he might have on the battlefield: "Soldiers of Makuran, here is the Videssian Avtokrator, who has dealt honestly and honorably with us. Who is a better friend for us, Maniakes or that mother of all assassins, Sharbaraz Pimp of Pimps?"

"Maniakes!" the soldiers shouted. Again, the Avtokrator had the bewildering sensation of hearing himself acclaimed by men who, up till a few days before, had bent all their efforts toward slaying him and sacking his city.

"If Sharbaraz Pimp of Pimps wants to slaughter half our officers, what do we tell him?" Abivard asked.

A majority of the men in the field force shouted, "No!" That was the one word Maniakes could make out clearly. The other answers to Abivard's question were far more various, and blurred together into a great din. But, although Maniakes could make little sense of them, he did not think they would have delighted the heart of Sharbaraz back in Mashiz.

Abivard asked the next question: "Shall we make peace with Videssos, then, and go home and settle the man who's tried to ruin all Makuran with this war?"

"Aye!" some of the warriors shouted. Others cried, "Peace!"

Other shouts mixed in with those, but Maniakes did not think any of them were cries of dissent.

"On going home," Abivard continued, "is it agreed that we empty out our garrisons to secure the peace and do no more harm to this country than we must to keep ourselves fed?"

"Aye!" the Makuraners shouted again, not with the heartfelt enthusiasm they'd put into the first couple of questions, but, again, without any complaints Maniakes could hear.

"There you have it," Abivard said to the Avtokrator. "What you and I agreed to in Videssos the city, the army agrees to as well. Peace lies between us, and we shall evacuate the westlands to seal it."

"Good enough," Maniakes said, "or rather, almost good enough. Can you give me one present?—an advance payment on the peace, you might say."

Abivard might have styled himself the new sun of Makuran, but his face clouded over. "I have carried out our bargain in every particular," he said stiffly. "If you are going to add new terms to it now—"

"Hear me out," Maniakes broke in. "I don't think you'll object."

"Say on." Every line in Abivard's face expressed doubt.

Smiling, Maniakes made his request: "Give me Tzikas. You have no need to withhold him from me now. Since he's Sharbaraz's creature, you ought to be all the gladder to yield him up, in fact."

"Ah." Abivard relaxed. "Yes, I could do that in good conscience."

He said no more. He had already shown he spoke Videssian well, and could get across subtle shades of meaning in the language of the Empire. Taking note of that, Maniakes said, "You *could* yield him up, eh? Not, you *can* yield him up?"

"Just so." Abivard spread his hands in angry regret. "As soon as I learned Sharbaraz had betrayed me, I realized his protection over the traitor mattered no more—the reverse, as you say. One of the first things I did, even before I announced to the assembled soldiers what Sharbaraz had done, was to send two men to seize him. I would have dealt with him myself, you understand. The two men did not come back. I have not seen Tzikas since that day."

"Did he slay them?" Rhegorios asked.

"Not so far as I know," Abivard answered. "I meant exactly

what I said—the two men did not come back. Neither did Tzikas. The only thing I have thought of is that he and they escaped together."

"That is not good," Maniakes said, one of his better understatements since assuming the imperial throne. "If he's escaped with them—"

"Very likely he's on his way to Sharbaraz, to let him know I'm on my way, too," Abivard broke in. Maniakes started to glare: how dared this fellow interrupt him? But if Abivard was a sovereign, too, he was not interrupting a superior, only an equal, which might have been rude but wasn't lese majesty. Abivard went on, "I've sent riders after the three of them. The God willing, they'll pull them down."

"And if they don't?" Maniakes asked. "Tzikas, may Skotos torment him in the ice forevermore, has got out of more trouble than anyone in his right mind would ever get into."

Abivard shrugged. He waved in the direction of the bearded men in caftans staring in at him from beyond the thin cordon of Maniakes' Imperial Guards. "This is the field force of Makuran. It is, I think, the finest army we have ever put in the field. Do you deny it, Maniakes Avtokrator?"

"I'd be a fool if I did," Maniakes answered. "It's taken me my whole reign to build my army up to the point where it can stand against your cursed boiler boys." He finally had troops who could do that, too, but not so many of them as Abivard had gathered here.

"Just so," Abivard said, waving again. "These are the best warriors of all Makuran. Since that is so, where will Sharbaraz Pimp of Pimps come up with their like? We may start the fight against him a little farther east than otherwise, but what of it?"

"Something to that," Maniakes admitted.

"Something," Rhegorios said, "but not enough. If you're not worried about what Tzikas is doing or where he's going, why did you send men after him?"

"Because I wanted him dead," Abivard snapped, sounding very much like a man who would be King of Kings. "And," he added grudgingly, "because with Tzikas and Sharbaraz, you never know, not for certain, not till too late."

"*I* certainly found that out about Sharbaraz," Maniakes said with feeling.

"He was a good man, or as good a man as a pampered prince could be, when he got his throne back a dozen or so years ago." Abivard sighed. "The court and the eunuchs and the women's quarters all worked together to ruin him."

"He had something to do with it, too—what he is, I mean," Maniakes said. "My court is as stifling as the one in Mashiz; you've seen my eunuch chamberlains, and how many women you can choose from doesn't matter all that much, I don't think."

"You give me hope," Abivard said.

"Take it where you find it," Maniakes said. "Plenty of times when I've had to look for it under flat stones myself, so to speak. But Tzikas, now . . . whatever Tzikas does, it will be for himself first. As long as you understand that, you have a portrait of the man."

"This I have seen with my own eyes, I assure you," Abivard answered. For the second time, he waved out to the men of the Makuraner field army. "Do you want to say something to them? They'd like to hear you, I think. The times we've met before haven't been times for talk."

"Haven't been for talk, indeed." Maniakes snorted; Abivard had an unsuspected gift for understatement himself. "My Makuraner is only fair at best." Abivard shrugged, as if to say, *So what?* Maniakes took a deep breath and raised his voice: "Men of Makuran!" Silence rippled outward from the warriors closest to the Imperial Guards. "Men of Makuran!" Maniakes called again. "For years, I have pursued and chased after peace. I fought, but I never wanted this war. Sharbaraz forced it on me—and on you. Now, then, let us take up weapons against each other no more. Let us welcome the peace we have found. Let us put out the flame of war, before it burns us all."

He wondered how that would go over. The Makuraners were proud and fierce; they might take the longing for peace as an admission of weakness. When they stayed quiet after he finished speaking, he feared that was what they had done.

Then the cheering started. The Makuraners pressed harder on the Videssian guards than they had when tension curdled the air. They pressed so hard, they broke through, which they might not have done so fast had they and the guardsmen used weapons against one another. They swarmed toward Maniakes, Rhegorios, and Abivard.

Maniakes wore at his side the sword he commonly carried into battle. He did not draw it: what point to drawing it? With so many Makuraners bearing down on him, if one of them was a murderer, the fellow would have his way. If Tzikas had planned for this very moment, Maniakes was in peril.

No blows came. Tzikas, never popular himself, had apparently failed to imagine an outpouring of affection from the Makuraners for a Videssian Avtokrator. Maniakes had trouble thinking him obtuse for that. He'd never imagined such a thing, either.

A Makuraner shouting his name grabbed him around the waist. The fellow was not trying to wrestle him to the ground. Instead, grunting, he hoisted Maniakes up onto his shoulders. Once up there, the Avtokrator discovered that Rhegorios and Abivard had been similarly elevated. The cheering got louder than ever.

The Makuraners passed the two Videssians and their own almost King of Kings back and forth among themselves. It would have been scandalous if... Maniakes shook his head. It *was* scandalous, but he, like the soldiers, was having too much fun to care.

Presently, he discovered he was riding atop one of his own Haloga guards rather than a Makuraner. "Put me down!" he shouted, trying to make himself heard through the din.

The Haloga shook his big blond head. "No, your Majesty," he boomed in slow, sonorous Videssian. "You need this. Soldiers need this." As if Maniakes weighed nothing, he tossed him through the air to a couple of Makuraners who caught him and kept him from smashing to the ground below.

They, in turn, threw him to some of their friends. He nearly did fall then; one of the Makuraners grabbed him around the waist in the nick of time. "Careful, Amashpiit!" exclaimed another Makuraner nearby. "Don't drop him."

"I didn't," Amashpiit answered. "I won't." The fellow who'd warned him helped him lift Maniakes up above them once more. Then the two of them—and other eager, shouting, grinning Makuraners—propelled the Avtokrator through the air again.

In the course of his wild peregrinations, he passed close enough to Rhegorios to yell, "If Kameas saw me now, he'd fall over dead." His cousin laughed—or so he thought, though the crowd swept him away almost before he could be sure.

At last, when he was certain every boiler boy had bounced him through the air at least one and most of them two, three, or four times, his feet touched the ground. The couple of men closest to him, instead of seizing him and hurling him up onto yet another bumpy road, helped straighten him. "I thank you," he told them, most sincerely.

Someone was shouting his name: Abivard. By what had to be luck, the Makuraner marshal had alighted not far from him. "Whew!" Maniakes said when they clasped hands again. "As part of our ritual for crowning the Avtokrator, his soldiers lift him onto a shield—but they don't throw him around afterward."

"That wasn't part of our ritual, either," Abivard answered. "Just something that happened. That's what life is, you know: just one cursed thing after another."

"I wouldn't call this a cursed thing," Maniakes said in judicious tones. "More on the lines of—interesting. There's a good word." He looked around. "What happened to Rhegorios? Did they fling him into the Cattle Crossing?"

He and Abivard—and, soon, the men around them—raised their voices, calling for his cousin. Rhegorios turned out to be about as far from them as he could have been while remaining on the same beach. When they finally rejoined one another, the Sevastos said, "Now I know how a horse feels when it's ridden for the first time. All jumps and bounds and hard landings—have we got an imperial masseur?"

"I've never asked for one," Maniakes said, "but one of the eunuchs or another will know who the best in the city is." Taking stock of his body, he realized he was going to be bruised and sore in some unusual places. "Cousin of mine, that's not a bad idea."

Abivard brought matters back to the business at hand. "For the moment, we are friends, you and I, you and my army," he said. "If we Makuraners are going to leave the westlands, we had best do it quickly, while that friendship holds. Will you in your turn do all you can to keep us supplied as we travel, or will you understand when we take what we may need from the countryside?"

"As Videssos hasn't held most of the westlands since before I became Avtokrator, I don't know how much I can do to resupply you," Maniakes said. "As for the other, you know the difference between requisitioning and plundering, or I hope you do."

"Certainly," Abivard said at once. "Requisitioning is what you do when someone is watching you." He dipped his head to Maniakes.

"Since we are friends—for the moment—and since you will be watching, we shall requisition. Does that suit you?"

Maniakes opened his mouth, then closed it again on realizing he had nothing to say. He had, for once, met his match in the cynicism that came with ruling or aspiring to rule a great empire.

Later, sailing back to Videssos the city, Rhegorios remarked, "Smerdis King of Kings didn't suit us, so we helped the Makuraners get rid of him and put Sharbaraz King of Kings on the throne. Sharbaraz turned out to be more dangerous than Smerdis ever dreamt of being, which meant he didn't suit us, either. So now we're helping the Makuraners get rid of *him* and put Abivard King of Kings, or whatever he ends up calling himself, on the throne. And Abivard is liable to turn out to be . . ." He let Maniakes finish the progression for himself.

"Oh, shut up," Maniakes said loudly and sincerely. Rhegorios laughed. So did the Avtokrator. They both sounded nervous.

The Videssian army exercised on the meadow near the southern end of the city wall. The soldiers rode and hurled javelins and shot arrows from horseback into bales of straw with more enthusiasm than Maniakes had ever known them to show. Immodios said, "They didn't care for being cooped up in the siege, your Majesty. They want to be out and doing."

"So I see," the Avtokrator said. "They would have been doing in Mashiz, if only Sharbaraz hadn't turned out to be more clever than we thought." Rhegorios' comment went through his mind. Resolutely, he ignored it. If Genesios hadn't overthrown Likinios, Sharbaraz would have been a good enough neighbor to the Empire of Videssos. Since no one was going to overthrow *him* . . . He laughed, though it wasn't very funny. He knew how lucky he was to remain on his own throne.

Immodios said, "We won't have quite the numbers the boiler boys do, once we go over into the westlands."

"I know we won't," Maniakes answered. "Their army will get bigger as they go, too, because they'll be adding garrison troops to it. But that'll make them slow, less likely to up and strike at us: not that they aren't already aimed at Sharbaraz. And besides, I expect we'll recruit a few men of our own once we get over there."

"Oh, aye, no doubt," Immodios said, "men who used to be

Videssian soldiers, but who've been making their living as bandits and robbers while the Makuraners held the westlands. The ones who can recall what they used to be will be worth having. The others—"

"The others will end up short a hand, or maybe a head," Maniakes broke in. "That will be what they deserve, and it'll help the better ones remember what they're supposed to be."

He put his horse through its paces. Antelope was glad to run, glad to rear and lash out with iron-shod hooves, glad to halt and stand steady as a rock while Maniakes shot half a quiver of arrows into a hay-bale target. Since other riders gave way for Maniakes, Antelope was convinced their horses gave way for *him*. For all Maniakes knew, they did.

Maniakes enjoyed putting himself through his paces, too. As long as he was up on Antelope, using his body as he'd been trained to do from as far back as his memory reached, he didn't have to think about how best to shepherd the Makuraners out of the westlands. He didn't have to remember the scorn so much of the city mob and so much of the ecclesiastical hierarchy felt for him. He didn't have to do any thinking, and he didn't. His body did what needed doing without his worrying about it.

He came back to himself some while later, returning to awareness when Antelope started breathing hard. His next conscious thought was startlement at how far the sun had moved across the sky. "Been at it for a bit," he remarked to Immodios.

"Yes, your Majesty, you have." Immodios was a sobersides, and sounded full of somber approval. If he reckoned anything more important than readying himself for war, Maniakes didn't know what it was.

Having stopped, the Avtokrator realized how tired he was. "I'll be stiff and sore tomorrow, too," he grumbled, "even if it's not from being thrown all over the landscape. I don't do this often enough to stay in the shape I should." After a moment's reflection—thought, once back, would not be denied—he added, "I'm not so young as I used to be, either." He was tempted to start exercising again, to drive that thought away. But no. The alternative to getting older was *not* getting older, which was worse.

Accompanied by a squad of guardsmen, Maniakes rode up to the Silver Gate and then back along Middle Street toward the palace quarter. The guards were there only to protect him. They took no special notice of the hot-wine sellers and the whores, the scribes and the thieves, the monks and the mendicants who filled the street. But the crowds noticed them. They were the nearest thing to a parade Videssos the city had at the moment, which of itself made them worthy of attention.

A few people, safely anonymous among others, shouted obscenities at the Avtokrator. He ignored them. He'd had plenty of practice ignoring them. Several men in the blue robes of the priesthood turned their backs on him, too. Agathios might have granted him his dispensation, but lacked the will for the ecclesiastical civil war enforcing it on the clergy would have required. Maniakes ignored the priests' contempt, too.

And then, to his astonishment, a blue-robe standing under a colonnade bowed to him as he rode past. Some priests did acknowledge Agathios' dispensation, but few till this moment had been willing to do so publicly. The Avtokrator waited for some outraged rigorist, layman or priest, to chuck a cobblestone at this fellow.

Nothing of the sort happened. Perhaps a furlong farther up Middle Street, someone shouted, "Good riddance to those Makuraner bastards, your Majesty!" The fellow waved to Maniakes.

He waved back. He'd always hoped success in war would bring him acceptance. Till recently, he hadn't had enough success in war to put the idea to the test. Maybe, earlier appearances to the contrary notwithstanding, it was true after all.

Someone yelled a lewd joke that suggested Lysia was his own daughter, not a cousin close to his own age. For a moment, he wanted to draw his sword and go after the ignorant loudmouth as fiercely as he'd practiced earlier in the day. But he surprised his bodyguards, and himself, too, by throwing back his head and laughing instead.

"You are well, your Majesty?" one of the Halogai asked.

"By the good god, I *am* well," he answered. "Some of them still hate me, aye, but most of those are fools. The ones who know what I've done know I haven't done too badly." It was, he thought, the first time he'd not only said that but also believed it.

"How a man judges himself, this lies at the heart of things," the northerner said with the certainty his people commonly showed. "A man who will let how others judge him turn how he judges himself—that is the man whose judgment is not to be trusted."

"If only it were so easy," Maniakes said with a sigh. The Haloga stared at him, pale eyes wide in perfect incomprehension. For him, it *was* that easy; to the Halogai, the world seemed a simple place. Maniakes saw it as much more complex than he could ever hope to understand. In that, even if not in blood, he was very much a Videssian.

The Haloga shrugged, visibly putting the matter out of his mind. Maniakes worried about it and worried at it all the way back to the imperial residence. There, he supposed, both he and his guardsman were true to the pictures they had built up of their world. But which of them was right? And how could you judge? He didn't know.

Videssian soldiers began filing out of merchantmen onto the beaches near Across. Sailors began persuading horses to leave barges and ships they'd persuaded the animals to board not long before. They'd had trouble getting the horses on; they had trouble getting them off. Curses, some hot as iron in a smith's forge but more resigned, floated into the morning sky.

Not far away, a detachment of Makuraner heavy cavalry stood waiting, watching. When Maniakes, Lysia on his arm and Rhegorios behind him, walked down the gangplank from the *Renewal* to the sandy soil of the westlands, the Makuraners swung up their lances in salute.

Rhegorios let out a soft whistle. "Here we are, landing in the westlands with the boiler boys watching," he said in slow wonder.

"I never thought it would be like this," Maniakes agreed.

"No," Lysia said. "Otherwise, you would have made me stay in the *Renewal* till you'd beaten them back from where you landed."

Was that resentment? Probably, Maniakes thought. He glanced over at his wife's bulging belly. "You wouldn't be at your best right now, not shooting the bow or flinging javelins from horseback," he remarked.

"I suppose not," Lysia admitted. In tones suggesting she was trying to be just, she went on, "You use that sort of excuse less than most men, from all I've seen and heard. You don't leave me behind when you go on campaign."

"I never wanted to leave you behind, going on campaign," he answered.

A single Makuraner in full armor rode toward the Videssians. All Maniakes could see of his flesh were the palms of his hands, his eyes, and a small strip of forehead above those eyes. Iron and leather encased the rest of him, from gauntlets extending up over his fingers to a chain-mail veil protecting most of his face.

Coming up to Maniakes, he spoke in his own language: "Majesty, you know that Tzikas the traitor fled our encampment, accompanied by two others he suborned to treason."

"Yes, I know that," Maniakes answered. Emerging from behind that metal veil, the Makuraner's voice took on iron overtones, too. And hearing his words without seeing his lips was disconcerting; it was almost as if he were disembodied and reanimated by sorcerous arts. But all that paled before the possible import of his message. "I know that," Maniakes repeated. "Are you telling me you've caught the son of a whore?"

"No, Majesty. But one of the patrols sent out by Abivard King of Kings, may his days be long and his realm increase—" Though Abivard did not yet claim the Makuraner royal title, this soldier was doing it for him. "—did run down a confederate of his. The wretch now stands before the God for consignment to the Void."

"That's good news, though not so good as I would have hoped," Maniakes said.

"Wait," Rhegorios put in. "This patrol caught only one of the men who went west with Tzikas?"

"Just so, lord," the Makuraner messenger replied.

Maniakes saw the import there as readily as his cousin. "They've split up to make it harder for your men to catch them," he said, "and easier for them to get the word through to Sharbaraz. That is not good." Tzikas had a way of making his life—and evidently Abivard's life, too—difficult.

"Abivard judges this in the same way," the Makuraner said. "His view is that he will reckon himself rid of Tzikas for good when he sees the traitor's head on a pole—provided it does not answer when he speaks."

"Mm, yes," Maniakes said. "If anyone could bring that off, Tzikas is the man. Your task is the same, either way, though: whether or not Tzikas gets to Mashiz ahead of you, you still have to beat Sharbaraz."

"This is also true, Majesty," the messenger agreed. "But I can swim the Tutub naked, or I can swim it, or try to swim it, in my corselet here. Swimming it naked is easier, as taking Sharbaraz unawares is also easier."

Now Maniakes nodded, yielding the point. "The faster Abivard moves, then, the better his chances of doing that."

"Again I think you speak the truth," the Makuraner said. "The bulk of his army has already headed west." He waved back to his comrades. "We are a guard of honor for your men—and a force that can harm you if you go against the agreement you have made. You are Videssians, after all."

"We are your comrades in this, since it works for our good as well as yours," Maniakes said.

The Makuraner nodded; that was logic he could understand. "And we are your comrades. Know, *comrade,* that we shall always watch you to make sure we stay friends and you do not try to move into a position where you can harm us."

Maniakes smiled at him, none too sweetly. "Even after you drove our armies out of the westlands, we've always watched you. We'll keep on doing it. And tell Abivard for me that I am not the one who has harmed him and I am not the one who intends to harm him."

"I shall deliver your words, just as you say them." The Makuraner rode back toward the force of heavy cavalry waiting for him.

Lysia sighed. "I wish we could come to trust each other."

"We've come further now than we ever did before," Maniakes answered. "If I had to guess, I'd say we've come about as far as we can. Abivard is welcome to keep an eye on me, I'll keep an eye on him, and maybe we can stretch two generations of peace out of that instead of one. Worth hoping for, anyhow." In earnest of that hope, he sketched the sun-circle over his heart.

Close by Across, the countryside had been fought over several times, and looked it. Many little farming villages were nothing but charred ruins, many fields full of nothing but weeds because the peasants who should have worked them were dead or fled. Seeing the wreckage of what had been prosperous farmland saddened Maniakes without surprising him.

What did surprise him was how normal things seemed as soon as his army moved away from areas war had ravaged. The Videssian force traveled behind and a bit north of Abivard's army;

had it followed directly in back of the Makuraners, it would have found the land largely eaten bare before it arrived.

As things were, the quartermasters attached to the Videssian army had a harder time keeping it fed than they'd expected. "The cursed peasants get word we're on the way, your Majesty," one of them said indignantly, "and they light out for the nearest hills they can find. And what's worse, they lead all their livestock with them and bury their grain in the ground in jars. How are we supposed to find it then?"

"Magic?" Maniakes suggested.

The quartermaster shook his head. "We've tried it, your Majesty. It does no good. Passion is magic's foe. When the peasants hide their food, they aren't thinking kind thoughts about the people from whom they're hiding it—"

"I wonder why that is," Maniakes said.

"I don't know," the quartermaster answered, showing he was better suited to counting sacks of beans than to understanding the people who grew them. "The net result, though, is that we haven't got as much as I wish we did."

"Have we got enough?" Maniakes asked.

"Oh, aye, a sufficiency," the quartermaster sniffed, "but we should do better than that." Even in matters of supply, he wanted to turn a profit.

"A sufficiency will, uh, suffice," Maniakes said. "After all, if everything goes as we want, after this campaign—which isn't even a fighting campaign, at that—we'll have the westlands back. If we can't get a surplus with the whole Empire restored, that will be time enough for worry." The quartermaster's nod was reluctant, but it was a nod.

Everything went smoothly till the army came to Patrodoton, a good-sized village a couple of days' ride east of the Eriza, a south-flowing tributary of the Arandos, the biggest river in the westlands. Patrodoton, though not large enough to boast a city wall, had hosted a Makuraner garrison, a couple of dozen men who'd made sure the local peasants gave a share of their crops and animals, and the handful of local merchants a share of their money, to support the Makuraner occupation.

Getting the garrison to leave Patrodoton was not the problem. The Makuraners had already pulled out by the time Maniakes' outriders neared the village. Three of the occupiers had married

Videssian women, apparently intending to settle down in the area for good. Two of those brides headed back toward Makuran with their husbands, and the father of one of them left with the garrison, too. That was the start of the problem, right there.

The village *epoptes*, or headman, was a gray-bearded miller named Gesios. After performing a proskynesis before Maniakes, he said, "It's a good thing you're here, your Majesty, to settle all the treason that's gone on in this town while the heathen Makuraners were running things. If Optatos hadn't run off with Optila and the heathen she gave herself to, I expect you'd already have shortened him by a head. He was the worst, I reckon, but he's a long way from the only one."

"Wait." Maniakes held up a warning hand. "I tell you right now, a lot of this I don't and won't want to hear about. Once the westlands are in our hands again, we're all going to have to live with one another. If someone turned his neighbors over to the Makuraners to be killed, that's treason, and I'll listen to it. If people went on quietly living their lives, I'm going to let them keep on doing it. Have you got that?"

"Aye, your Majesty." Gesios sounded more than disappointed. He sounded angry. "What about the priest, then? These past years, Oursos has been preaching the worst nonsense you ever did hear, about Vaspur the Firstborn and all sorts of heresy, enough to make your beard curl. Boiler boys made him do it."

Maniakes didn't bother mentioning that his own father still clung to the Vaspurakaner beliefs that Makuraners had tried to impose on Videssos. What he did say was, "Now that the boiler boys are gone, will the holy Oursos return to the orthodox faith? If he will, no one will punish him for what he preached under duress."

"Oh, he will," Gesios said. "He's already done it, matter of fact. Thing of it is, though, he's been preaching the other way for so long now, about one in four has decided it's the right way to believe."

You could plunge a burning torch into a bucket of water. That would put out the fire. What it wouldn't do was restore the torch to the way it had been before the fire touched it. And having the Makuraners pull out of the westlands would not restore them to what they had been, either. They'd been tormented for years. They wouldn't heal overnight.

"Have the holy Oursos talk with them," the Avtokrator said with as much patience as he could find. "The good god willing, he'll bring them back to orthodoxy in a while. And if he doesn't—well, that's something to worry about later. Right now, I've got more to worry about than I can hope to handle, and as for later—" He laughed, though he didn't think Gesios saw the joke.

Not only he, but also Rhegorios and nearly every other officer above the level of troop leader, was bombarded with claims from the locals while the army spent the night outside Patrodoton. The officers dismissed a lot of claims out of hand—which meant Maniakes found out about them only afterward, and was sure he never found out about them all—but some got passed up the line till they came to him.

Next morning, he looked at the villagers, all of them in the best tunics that were too often the worst and only tunics they owned. "I am not going to punish anyone for fraternizing with the Makuraners," he said. "I wish that hadn't happened, but the boiler boys were here for years because we were so weak. So—if those are the complaints you have to make, go home now, because I will not hear them."

An old man and his wife left. Everyone else stayed. Maniakes listened to charges and countercharges and to peasants calling one another liars till long after he should have been in bed. But that was the price that came with the return of Videssian authority, and he was Videssian authority personified.

The hardest and ugliest case involved a man named Pousaios and his family. What made it even harder and uglier than it would have been otherwise was that he was obviously the richest man in Patrodoton. By the standards of Videssos the city, he would have been a small fish, but Patrodoton was farther from Videssos the city than the few days' travel getting from one to the other took. That had been true before the Makuraners seized the village, and was all the truer now.

Everyone loudly insisted Pousaios had got his wealth by licking the occupiers' boots or some other, more intimate, portions of their persons. As loudly, the prosperous peasant denied it. "I didn't do anything the rest of you didn't," he insisted.

"No?" Gesios questioned. "What about those two troopers—*our* troopers—who rode into town in the middle of the night six or eight years ago? Who told the Makuraners which house they were hiding in? Who's living in that house today, because it's finer than the one he used to have?"

Pousaios said, "Blemmydes was my wife's cousin. Why shouldn't I have moved into his house after he died?"

That produced fresh outcry. "He didn't just die," Gesios said shrilly. "A boiler boy killed him, and nobody ever saw those two soldiers again."

"I don't know anything about it," Pousaios insisted. "By Phos the good god, I swear I don't. Nobody ever proved a thing, and the reason's simple: nobody can prove a thing, because there's nothing to prove. Your Majesty, you can't let them do this to me!"

Maniakes bit his lip. The case cried out for slow, careful investigation, but that was the last thing the people of Patrodoton wanted. They were out for vengeance. The question was, did they deserve to get it?

Since he couldn't be sure, not on what he'd heard so far, he didn't give it to them, saying, "I'll be gone from here tomorrow, but from this day forth the land here is under Videssian rule once more. I swear by the good god—" He sketched the sun-circle over his heart. "—to send in a team of mages to learn the truth here by sorcery. When they do, I shall act as their findings dictate, with double punishment for the side that turns out to have been lying to me."

Both Gesios and Pousaios complained about that, loud and long. At last, Maniakes had to turn his back on them, a bit of dramatic rudeness that silenced them where nothing else had.

When he got up the next morning, one of his guardsmen, a Videssian named Evethios, said, "Your Majesty, half the people from this little pisspot of a town have been trying to wake you up since a couple of hours before sunrise. Finally had to tell 'em I'd shoot arrows into 'em if they didn't shut up and go away and leave you alone till you decided all by your lonesome to get out of bed. Nothing—" He spoke with great conviction. "—*nothing* that happens here is worth getting you out of bed two hours before sunrise."

"You're probably right, but don't tell the Patrodotoi I said so," Maniakes answered. Through Evethios' laughter, he went on, "I'm up now, so bring them on. I expect the army can get ready to move out without my looking at everything every moment."

"If we can't, we're in trouble, your Majesty, and not just with you," Evethios said, the last few words delivered over his shoulder as he went off to fetch the contingent from Patrodoton.

They came on at a dead run, almost as if they were so many Makuraner boiler boys charging with leveled lances. As soon as Maniakes saw Gesios baying in the van, he knew what must have happened. He could have delivered the village headman's speech for him, idea for idea if not word for word. He tried to tell that to the local, but Gesios was in no mood to listen.

"Your Majesty, Pousaios has run off, the son of a whore!" the headman cried.

"Run off!" the villagers behind him echoed, as if he were soloist and they chorus.

"His house is empty, and his stable's empty, too."

"Empty," the villagers agreed.

"He's fled to the Makuraners, may the ice take them, him, and all his worthless clan."

"Fled to the Makuraners."

"That proves what I was telling you last night was so, don't it?"

"Don't it?"

The choral arrangement got disconcerting in a hurry. Maniakes' head kept whipping back and forth between Gesios and his followers. But the message, delivery aside, was clear enough. He didn't even have to turn his back to get Gesios to stop; holding up a hand sufficed.

"By his own actions, Pousaios has proved himself a traitor," he said. "Let his lands and house and other property be divided equally among all those who have plots adjoining his, with no tax on those lands for two years."

"You can catch him now!" Gesios exclaimed, clenching his fists with bloodthirsty glee. "Catch him and kill him!" The chorus broke down. Instead of speaking as one, the villagers each suggested some new and different way to dispose of Pousaios. Before long, they got ingenious enough to have horrified Sharbaraz's executioners.

"Wait," Maniakes said again, and then again, and then again. Eventually, the Patrodotoi waited. Into something resembling silence, save that it was a good deal noisier, the Avtokrator went on, "As far as I'm concerned, the Makuraners are welcome to as many of our traitors as they want to keep. Sooner or later, they'll be sorry they have them. Traitors are like adulterers: anyone who cheats on one wife will likely cheat on another one, too."

What that got him was an earful of village gossip, some of it going back a couple of generations. The scandals of Patrodoton, he discovered without any great surprise, were much the same as those that titillated Videssos the city. The only differences he noted were that less money was involved here and that fewer people talked about these.

Thinking of traitors, inevitably, made him think of Tzikas. Every couple of days, Abivard would send a courier up to the Makuraner army with news of what he'd learned of the location of the Videssian renegade and the Makuraner Tzikas had talked into riding with him. Every couple of days, the answer was the same: nothing. That didn't strike Maniakes as answer enough.

Although the Patrodotoi would cheerfully have gone on telling him who'd been sleeping with whom and why and sometimes for how much till everything turned blue, he brought that to a halt, saying, "I'm sorry, my friends, but this isn't the only town in the Empire whose affairs—however you want to take that—I have to settle." They gaped at him: surely he could see they were the true center of the world?

He couldn't. The army moved out on time, and he rode with it. Pousaios had given the villagers some tasty new scandal with which they could regale visitors a hundred years from now. And, for all he knew, a couple of his cavalry troopers might have caused some adultery during their brief stay here, women being no more immune to it than men.

West of Patrodoton, a wooden footbridge had spanned the Eriza. Only burned remnants on either side of the river stood now. He didn't think the retreating garrison had torched the bridge; it looked to have been down longer than that. Ypsilantes was of the same opinion. "Aye, your Majesty," the chief engineer said. "Likely tell, some band of Videssian irregulars did the job, one of those years when the boiler boys were lording it over the westlands. Well, no matter."

Some of the timbers his men used to build the temporary bridge were still stained with the mud of the Land of the Thousand Cities. Since it wasn't being built against opposition, the bridge swiftly crossed the Eriza. Waiting, Maniakes reflected that he could have listened to more gossip from Patrodoton, after all.

Ypsilantes was the first to cross by the temporary bridge, to show it could be safely done. The rest of the army followed. Antelope snorted and shied, as he always did when setting foot on a bridge, especially one where the timbers shifted under his hooves as these did. But, having let his master know what he thought of things, he crossed when he found out Maniakes insisted. Maniakes looked back over the Eriza with something like amazement. "One corner of the westlands ours again," he said, and rode on.

Abivard's army, on reaching the Eriza at a place a couple of days' march south of Patrodoton, did not cross the river. Instead, it proceeded south along the Eriza's eastern bank till it came to Garsavra, which lay at the confluence of the Eriza and the Arandos, where the lush coastal lowlands gave way to the westlands' central plateau.

Maniakes hovered northwest of Garsavra, waiting to see what the garrison there would do. It was one of the shackles the Makuraners had used to bind the westlands to them; if the soldiers in the town declared for Sharbaraz, the Makuraners were liable to start fighting their civil war on Videssian soil, which was not what Maniakes wanted.

But the messenger Abivard sent to the Videssian encampment was all smiles. "The garrison unites in denouncing and renouncing Sharbaraz Pimp of Pimps," he said, spitting on the ground in a gesture of rejection he'd surely learned inside Videssos. "Nowhere has anyone a good word to say for the tyrant who sent us forth in this useless war."

"Good news, and I'm glad to hear it," Maniakes said. The phrase *this useless war*, though, would not leave his mind once heard. Had the Makuraners taken Videssos the city along with their Kubrati allies, no one among them, not even Abivard, would be cursing Sharbaraz now. They cared nothing about the injustice of his invasion of Videssos. All that mattered to them was his angry reaction when they failed to bring the war to a satisfactory end. And even that, unbeknownst to them, Maniakes had needed to amplify.

He shrugged, not feeling the least bit guilty about his own chicanery. When he tossed the Makuraner messenger a goldpiece, the fellow praised him as if he were somewhere in rank between the King of Kings and one of the Four Prophets. That was chicanery, too, designed to squeeze another goldpiece—or maybe even two—out of him at the messenger's next visit. Pretending to believe it, Maniakes waved the rider out of his camp.

He stayed in that camp for the next several days. While there, he got another reassuring sign, for Abivard recalled to his own army the force that had been shadowing the Videssians as the Videssians had shadowed his main body. Augmented by those men and by the Garsavra garrison, Abivard began his journey up the Arandos toward Amorion. "When he gets to Amorion—better yet, when he leaves the place—we'll truly have come full circle," Maniakes told Rhegorios.

"Aye, that's the truth," his cousin answered. "That's the town that held the Makuraners out of the Arandos valley for so long. Once it's in our hands, where it belongs, we can hold them out again if they ever try to come back."

"That's so," Maniakes said. "And the general who held them out before was Tzikas. He's bound to have friends there still. I wonder if he'll be waiting for Abivard—or for us."

"Now there's an interesting thought." Rhegorios raised an eyebrow. "Whom do you suppose he hates worse, you or Abivard?"

"Good question." Maniakes plucked at his beard as he thought. "I have the title he wanted most, of course, but, to balance that, Abivard is going after a title he can't hope to claim. Both of us should have executed him when we had the chance, and neither one of us did it, the bigger fools we. Dishonors are about even, I'd say."

"I'd say you're right," his cousin answered. "I'd also say that means you and Abivard had both better watch yourselves."

"Oh, yes." Maniakes nodded vehemently. "Phos only knows what would happen to the Makuraner army if Abivard came down with a sudden case of loss of life."

He didn't know what would happen in Videssos if he himself

vanished from the scene without warning, either. He didn't bring that up with Rhegorios for a couple of reasons. For one, he wouldn't be around to worry about it if that did happen. For another, the succession would be disastrously complicated. Likarios was his legal heir, but Likarios' mother was years dead. Lysia might push her children's claims instead. But they were all young, young. And Rhegorios, as cousin to the Avtokrator, brother to the Empress, and Sevastos in his own right, would have a formidable claim of his own: certainly more formidable in law than Abivard's to the throne of Makuran.

Rhegorios said, "Here's hoping he's not lurking there. Here's hoping he's not lurking anywhere. Here's hoping his horse slipped on a mountainside road and he broke his snaky neck in a fall. Here's hoping you never have to worry about the two-faced son of a whore again."

"Aye, here's hoping," Maniakes said. "But something tells me that's too much to hope for. Tzikas is too much of a nuisance to disappear just because we wish he would."

Abivard's army stuck close to the northern bank of the Arandos, eating their way along the river like a swarm of locusts. His riders were not the only ones who came north bringing news to Maniakes. Several peasants and herders came up, begging him to keep the Makuraners from emptying the countryside of everything edible.

He sent them away unhappy, saying, "Abivard's men are our allies now, and I do not begrudge our allies the supplies they need." Having to answer in that way left him unhappy, too. *How many times have the Makuraners despoiled the westlands since Likinios fell?* he wondered. At last, though, his distress eased. *However many times, this is the last.*

He kept his army a couple of days' march north of the Arandos. Up on the plateau, that meant making sure he had enough grain and water before he crossed one south-flowing tributary to be certain he could reach the next. The country was scrubby between streams.

In spite of complaints from his countrymen, he admitted to himself that Abivard could have done far worse than he was doing. The Makuraner wanted to give Maniakes no excuse to attack him, just as the Avtokrator wanted to give him no excuse to break their partnership. Mutual fear might have made a strange foundation for an alliance, but it seemed to work.

The Arandos and the Ithome joined east of a range of hills, the Arandos flowing up from the southwest, the Ithome down from the northwest. Amorion lay on the north bank of the Ithome, three or four days' travel west of the meeting place of the two rivers. It was the most important town in the westlands, even if the Garsavrans probably would have argued the distinction. It had anchored Videssian possession of the Arandos valley and, once lost to Makuran, anchored the invaders' occupation.

For all those reasons, and also because of its central location, it held the largest Makuraner garrison in the westlands. Maniakes worried that the garrison would stay loyal to Sharbaraz and require a siege to make it yield. The siege wouldn't be Abivard's problem, either—the Makuraner marshal would no doubt keep on moving west against the King of Kings he'd renounced. Amorion was Maniakes' city, and it would likely be Maniakes' job to take it back.

And so, when a rider from Abivard came up to the Videssian army, the Avtokrator tensed. But the horseman cried, "Good news twice, your Majesty! The garrison of Amorion joins everyone else in rejecting Sharbaraz. And the soldiers of the garrison captured the second Makuraner rider who went with Tzikas the traitor to let the Pimp of Pimps know his murderous wickedness has been laid bare before the entire world."

"That *is* good news," Maniakes agreed. "What happened to this second rider?"

"Nothing lingering or unusually interesting." The messenger sounded almost disappointed. "The garrison commander, knowing Abivard's reputation for leniency, questioned him for a time and then took his head. Very simple, very neat."

Maniakes wasn't used to thinking of the esthetics of executions. "All right," he answered, faintly bemused. "Did he learn by which roads Tzikas was going, so we can send pursuit down them?"

"Not in all the detail he should have liked, Majesty," the Makuraner answered. "The two of them had separated some time before. The rider believed Tzikas was traveling south of the Arandos, but knew no more than that."

"All right," Maniakes said. It wasn't, but he couldn't do anything about it. He knew too well how little Tzikas could be relied upon once out of sight. Like as not, the renegade had headed north as soon as he thought his departing comrade thought he was going south. He was a connoisseur of deceit, as some men were connoisseurs of wine, and had a fine and discriminating palate for it.

Or, of course, knowing Maniakes knew of his deceitfulness, he might have thought to deceive by doing exactly what he'd said he would do, reckoning the Avtokrator would assume he'd done the opposite. Or . . . Maniakes shook his head. Once you started floundering in those waters, the bewildering whirlpool would surely drag you under.

Maniakes did move down to Amorion once Abivard's forces and the Makuraner garrison abandoned it. Not only did he intend to place a small garrison of his own there, he also wanted to see the town for the first time since becoming Avtokrator. His previous push up the Arandos toward Amorion had been rudely interrupted by Abivard's capture of the place.

Finding the wall intact was the first surprise. The Makuraners had breached it, after all; otherwise, they never would have taken the city. Afterward, they'd repaired the breaches with new stone, easy to tell from what had been there before because it was so much less weathered. One of the city gates was also new, and arguably stronger than the Videssian work it replaced.

Once inside Amorion, though, Maniakes saw what several years of occupation by hostile masters had done. A good many buildings had been burned or otherwise wrecked in the sack. If any of them had been repaired since, he would have been astonished. And many of the buildings that had survived the Makuraners' entry were simply empty. Maybe the people who had lived in them had fled before the Makuraners stormed in. Maybe they had been expelled afterward, or simply left. Maybe they were dead.

"We're going to have to rebuild," Maniakes said. "We're going to have to bring in people from parts of the Empire that haven't taken such a beating."

"We're going to have to find parts of the Empire that haven't taken such a beating," Rhegorios said, exaggerating only a little.

"There'll always be Vaspurakaners trickling out of their mountains and valleys, too," Maniakes said. "The Makuraners don't treat them well enough to make them want to stay . . . and after a while, they start turning into Videssians."

"Can't imagine what you're talking about," his cousin said with a chuckle.

Here and there, people did come out and cheer the return of Videssian rule—or at least acknowledge it. "Took you long enough!" an old man shouted, leaning on his stick. "When Tzikas was here, things was pretty good—not perfect, mind you, but pretty good. You'll have to go some to beat him, whatever your name is, and that's a fact."

"I'll do my best," Maniakes answered. Riding along next to him, Rhegorios giggled: not the sort of noise one would expect to come from the august throat of a Sevastos. The Avtokrator ignored him.

When he got to what had been the *epoptes'* palace, he found it in better shape than any other building he'd seen. The servants who trooped out to greet him looked plump and prosperous, where everyone else in the city seemed skinny and shabby and dirty. In answer to Maniakes' question, one of them said, "Why, yes, your Majesty, the Makuraner garrison commander did live here. How did you know?"

"Call it a lucky guess," Maniakes answered dryly.

Across the central square from the residence, the chief temple to Phos seemed to have taken all the abuse and neglect the residence had avoided. Like a lot of chief temples in provincial towns, it was modeled after the High Temple in Videssos the city. It hadn't been the best of copies before; now, with weeds growing all around, with the stonework of the exterior filthy and streaked with bird droppings, and with every other windowpane bare of glass, it was nearer nightmare vision than imitation.

A blue-robed priest came out of the temple and looked across the square at Maniakes. Recognizing the Avtokrator's raiment, he dashed over the cobblestones toward him, sandals flapping on his feet. When he got close, he threw himself down on the cobblestones in front of Maniakes in a proskynesis so quick and emphatic, he might almost have fallen on his face rather than prostrating himself.

"Mercy, your Majesty!" he cried, his face still pressed down against the paving stones. "Have mercy on your holy temple here, so long tormented by the savage invaders!"

"Rise, holy sir," Maniakes said. "You are—?"

"I am called Domnos, your Majesty," the priest replied, "and I have had the honor—and, I assure you, the trial—of being prelate of Amorion these past three years, after the holy Mavrikios gave up this life and passed to Phos' eternal light. It has not been an easy time."

"Well, I believe that," Maniakes said. "Tell me, holy Domnos—did you preach Vaspurakaner dogmas when the Makuraners ordered our priests to do that?"

Domnos hung his head. He blushed all the way up to the top of his shaven crown. "Your Majesty, I did," he whispered. "It was that or suffer terrible torment, and I—I was weak, and obeyed. Punish me as you will." He straightened, as if eagerly anticipating that punishment.

But Maniakes said, "Let it go. You'll preach a sermon on things you had to do under duress, and then you and your fellow priests will talk to the people who've accepted the Vaspurakaner doctrines as better than our own—I know you'll have some. We won't push them back into orthodoxy all at once. After that, you can go on with life as it was before the invasion." He knew it wouldn't be that easy. If Domnos didn't know, he'd find out soon enough.

Now Domnos stared at the Avtokrator. He'd asked for mercy. Maniakes had given it to him, a large dose of it, but he didn't seem to want it as much as he'd claimed. "Yes, your Majesty," he said, rather sulkily.

Maniakes, however, had more important things to worry about than a priest put out of temper. He chose a question touching on the most important of those things: "Has Tzikas, the former commander here, passed through this town in the last few days?"

Domnos' eyes widened. "No, your Majesty." After a moment, he qualified that: "Not to my knowledge, at any rate. If he came here in secret, I might not know it, though I think I should have heard. But why would he have needed to come in secret?"

"Oh, he'd have had his reasons," Maniakes answered, his voice drought-dry. He reflected that Amorion under Makuraner rule had been a town wrapped up in wool batting, a town caught in a backwater while the world went on around it. By the look on Domnos' face, he still thought of Tzikas as the stubborn general who had held Abivard away for so long, and he had no reason to think otherwise. Yes, sure enough, the world had passed Amorion by.

"You will know better than I, your Majesty," Domnos said. "Will you come see the temple and learn the relief we need?"

"I'll come," Maniakes said, and followed Domnos across the square.

He had not gone more than a couple of paces before his guardsmen, Videssians and Halogai both, formed a square around him. "No telling who or what all's waiting in there, your Majesty," a Videssian guard said, as if defying him to order the warriors to step aside. "Might even be this Tzikas item you're worrying about."

That comment, delivered in the streetwise dialect of Videssos the city, might have been one of Bagdasares' magic words, so effectively did it shut off any argument the Avtokrator might have made. The plain truth was, the guardsman was right. If Tzikas struck, it would have to be from ambush. What more unexpected place to set an ambush than one of Phos' holy temples?

Up the steps and into the exonarthex, Domnos led Maniakes. The priest pointed to a mosaic of a bygone Avtokrator presenting Amorion's temple to Phos as a pious offering. "Do you see, your Majesty?" the priest said. "The infidel Makuraners chiseled out every gold tessera from the costume of Metokhites II."

"I do see." Maniakes didn't know how much gold the Makuraners had realized from their chiseling, but they must have thought the results worth the labor.

In the next chamber in from the entrance, the narthex, Domnos sadly pointed out where silver lamps had been torn from the ceiling. "They took the great candelabrum, too," he said, "thinking its polished brass gold. Even after they found they were wrong, they did not return it."

"Brass is useful," Maniakes said. He didn't need to say much to keep the conversation going. Domnos talked enough for any two ordinary people, or possibly three.

Tzikas had not lurked in the exonarthex or narthex. Maniakes' guardsmen preceded their charge into the main worship area. No renegade, no band of bravos, crouched in ambush behind the pews. The guards gave their permission for Maniakes to enter. He was sovereign in the Empire of Videssos, but hardly in his own household.

"You see?" Domnos said again. "Gold, silver, brass, semiprecious gems—all gone."

"Yes," Maniakes said. Even before the Makuraners had come, the temple here in Amorion had been a copy of the High Temple in the capital, but a poor man's copy. Despoiled by the invaders, it was, as Domnos had claimed, poorer still.

Maniakes glanced upward toward the dome in the central altar. The mosaic image of Phos in the dome was not perfectly stern in judgment, as it was in Videssos the city; here, he looked more nearly petulant. And the gold tesserae that had surrounded his image were gone, survived only by the rough gray cement in which they had been mounted. That made Phos' image seem even more lifeless than it would have otherwise.

"Aye, they even stripped the dome," Domnos said, following Maniakes' gaze. With a certain somber satisfaction, he added, "And three of their workmen died in the doing, too; may Skotos freeze their souls forevermore." He spat on the marble floor in rejection of the dark god.

So did Maniakes. He asked, "How much money do you think you'll need to restore the temple to the way it was?"

Domnos clapped his hand. A less senior priest in a plainer blue robe came running. "The accounts list," the prelate snapped. His subordinate hurried off, returning shortly with three leaves of parchment held together at one corner by a small iron ring. Domnos took it from him, then presented it to Maniakes with a flourish. "Here you are, your Majesty."

"Er—thank you," Maniakes said. He flipped through the document. His alarm grew with every line he read. Domnos had the cost of full repairs calculated down to the last copper, in materials and labor both. The sum at which he'd finally arrived looked reasonable in light of the damage done to the temple—and altogether appalling in light of the damage done to the Empire's finances.

"Well, your Majesty?" Domnos said when Maniakes gave no sign of pulling goldpieces out of his ears.

"Well, holy sir, all I can say right now is that yours isn't the only temple to have suffered, and I'll have to see what other needs we have before I can think of paying you this entire sum." Maniakes knew he sounded weak. He didn't know what else to say, though. Tzikas hadn't been lurking inside the temple, no, but he'd been ambushed just the same.

Domnos' acquisitive instincts aside, reestablishing Videssian control over Amorion proved easier than Maniakes had expected. Most of the locals who had collaborated with the Makuraner occupiers had fled with them. The ones who were left were loudly repentant. As he had elsewhere, Maniakes forgave more than he punished.

Being a good-sized town, Amorion had had its own small Vaspurakaner community before it fell to the Makuraners, a community with its own discreetly sited temple. That let the Avtokrator send the Videssian locals who had converted to Vaspurakaner usages during the occupation and now refused to abandon them to a place where they could continue to worship in the fashion they had come to find fitting.

"But, your Majesty," Domnos protested, "the goal is to return them to orthodoxy, as you said, not to confirm them in their error. One Empire, one true faith: it is a law of nature."

"So it is," Maniakes said. "As time goes by, holy sir, I think almost all of them *will* return to orthodoxy. We make that the easier path, the preferred path, just as the Makuraners made the dogma of Vaspur the Firstborn the way to move ahead. You lay under the Makuraner yoke for years; you've been free a few days. Not everything happens at once."

"I certainly see *that*, your Majesty," Domnos said, and stalked off, robe swirling about him.

Rhegorios eyed his retreat with amusement. "Do you know, cousin of mine, I don't think you're one of his favorite people right now."

"I noticed that, thanks." Maniakes made a sad clucking sound. "I wouldn't empty the treasury to repair the temple here this instant, and I wouldn't burn heretics without giving them a decent chance to come back to orthodoxy, either. See what a wicked fellow that makes me?"

"Sounds bloody wicked to me," Rhegorios agreed. "Not giving someone all the money he wants the instant he wants it—why, if that doesn't rank right up there for wickedness with ordering your best general executed, I don't know what does." He paused, looking thoughtful. "But since you're your own best general, that would complicate the whole business a bit, wouldn't it?"

"Complicate? That's one way to put it, anyhow." Maniakes sighed. "Here's Amorion back under Videssian rule. I didn't have to fight to get it back, so the town isn't burned or wrecked any worse than it was before I got here. The Makuraners didn't take anybody with them who didn't want to go. And what thanks do

I get? I haven't made everything perfect right away, so of course I'm nothing but a tyrant."

Rhegorios plucked at his beard. "If it's any consolation, cousin your Majesty brother-in-law of mine, I'll bet the people here were grumbling about the Makuraners the same way till the day the boiler boys pulled out." His voice rose to a high, mocking falsetto: "'The nerve of that cursed Abivard. To the ice with him, anyway! He has gall, he does, going off to try and conquer Videssos the city when his supply wagons have left such big potholes in *our* streets.'" He looked and sounded like an indignant chicken.

Maniakes opened his mouth to say something, but he'd already started laughing by then, and almost choked to death. When he could speak, he pointed an accusing forefinger at his cousin: "You, sirrah, are a demon from a plane of being the Sorcerers' Collegium hasn't yet stumbled onto, the reason being that it's too absurd for such calm, careful men to contemplate."

"Why, thank you, your Majesty!" Rhegorios exclaimed, as if the Avtokrator had just conferred a great compliment upon him. From his point of view, maybe Maniakes had done just that.

"It's a good thing Uncle Symvatios passed all the silliness in his line of the family down to you and not to Lysia," Maniakes said.

"Oh, I don't know about that." Rhegorios studied him. "My sister puts up with you, doesn't she?"

Maniakes considered. "You may have something there," he said at last, and flung his arm over his cousin's shoulder. They walked back to the *epoptes'* residence together.

While Maniakes settled affairs in Amorion to his satisfaction, if not always to that of the town's inhabitants, Abivard kept marching steadily to the west, and took a good-sized lead on the Videssian force that had been following him. On the day when Maniakes was finally ready to head west from Amorion himself, a courier from Abivard brought a message to the Avtokrator.

"Majesty," the fellow said, "the general has decided to swing up a bit to the northwest, to pick up some detachments on garrison duty in Vaspurakan. It won't cost but a couple of days of time, and will add some good soldiers to his army."

"Whatever he thinks best," Maniakes said, though he would not have been diverted from the shortest road to Mashiz. "I hope the soldiers turn out to be worth the delay."

"Through the Prophets Four, we pray the God they so prove," the messenger replied, and rode back toward Abivard's army. Maniakes stared after him.

So did Rhegorios, who said, "I wouldn't have done that. I'd have gone for Sharbaraz's throat with what I have here."

"I was thinking the same thing," Maniakes agreed. "That's what I'd have done. So would my father. I have no more doubt of that than I do of the truth of Phos' holy creed. And yet—" He laughed ruefully. "When Abivard and I have met each other on the battlefield, he's come off the winner as often as I have, so who's to judge which of us is wiser?"

"Something to that—I hope," his cousin said. "The other side of the goldpiece is, if Abivard has swung to the northwest, we're going to have to swing farther northwest than we thought we would, or else we'll be feeding ourselves from the crumbs the Makuraners leave behind."

"That's so," Maniakes said. "You've thought of it sooner than I did, for which I thank you. I'll change the marching orders. You're right; we'd get hungry in a hurry if we came straight down the path the Makuraners had just used."

The first settlement of decent size northwest of Amorion was Aptos, which, like Patrodoton farther east, lay on the border between town and village. Unlike Patrodoton, Aptos knew it wanted to be a town: when Maniakes and the Videssian army arrived, the folk of the area had started running up a rammed-earth core for what would be a wall around it.

The headman, a baker named Phorkos, was proud of the initiative his town was showing. "Your Majesty, we never imagined the Makuraners would come so far or stay so long," he said. "If that ever happens again—which Phos prevent—they won't find us so ripe for going into their oven."

"Good," Maniakes said. "Excellent, in fact. I have to tell you, I don't have a lot of money right now. I'll do what I can to help you pay for your work, but it won't be much and it may not be soon."

"We're taking care of it, your Majesty," Phorkos said. "One way or another, we'll manage."

"I wonder if you could go down to Amorion and talk with

Domnos the priest for a while," Maniakes murmured. Phorkos' blank look said he didn't know what the Avtokrator was talking about. That, Maniakes decided, was probably as well: if Phorkos did talk with Domnos, the priest was liable to persuade him he deserved an enormous subsidy.

That Phorkos and his fellow townsfolk were undertaking this labor on their own, that they'd presented Maniakes with what they were doing rather than asking permission of him to do it, said they'd got used to being out from under the stifling weight of Videssian bureaucracy, one of the first good things the Avtokrator had found to say about the Makuraner invasion. He didn't think he'd come up with many more.

From Aptos, the army continued northwest for another couple of days to the town of Vryetion. Vryetion, already having a wall, was what Aptos aspired to be. Having a wall, however, had not kept it from falling to the Makuraners. Maybe it had made seizing the place more difficult, and cost the boiler boys more wounded and dead. Maniakes hoped so.

He lodged in what had been the *epoptes'* residence, a house a medium-sized linen dealer in Videssos the city would have rejected as inadequate. The Makuraner garrison commander had made his home there during the occupation, and left several graffiti expressing his opinion of the place. So Maniakes guessed, at any rate, though he didn't read the Makuraner language. But the scribbled drawings accompanying a couple of the inscriptions were anything but complimentary.

Like it or not, though, that garrison commander had been forced to make the best of it. So did Maniakes, who spent a day hearing petitions from the locals, as he'd done in other towns through which he passed.

Those were, for the most part, straightforward. As had happened in other towns farther east, few collaborators were left; however many there had been, they'd fled with the Makuraner garrison. The officer who'd led that garrison seemed to have done a more conscientious job than many of his peers, and the folk of Vryetion tried to get the Avtokrator to overturn only a couple of his rulings.

"To the ice with me if I know whether I like that or not," Maniakes said behind his hand to Rhegorios. "He didn't torment them, and most of them were as happy with him in charge as with one of their own."

"He's gone now," Rhegorios answered, to which Maniakes nodded.

A woman a few years younger than the Avtokrator came before him along with her son, who was a little older than the eldest of his own children. She and the boy both prostrated themselves, a bit more smoothly than any of the other locals had done.

"Rise," Maniakes said. "Tell me your name, and how I may help you."

"My name is Zenonis," the woman said. She looked from Maniakes to Rhegorios and back again. She would have been attractive—she might even have been beautiful—had she not been so worn. "Forgive me, your Majesty, but why is my husband not with you?"

"Your husband?" Maniakes frowned. "Who is your husband?"

Zenonis' eyebrows flew upward. He'd either astonished or insulted her, maybe both. Probably both, from her expression. "Who is my husband, your Majesty? My husband is Parsmanios—your brother. And this—" She pointed to the boy. "—this is your nephew Maniakes."

Beside the Avtokrator, Rhegorios softly said, "Phos."

Maniakes felt like making the sun-sign himself. He didn't, schooling himself to stillness. Parsmanios had mentioned that he'd married in Vryetion, and mentioned his wife's name as well. But Parsmanios had not been anyplace where he could speak to Maniakes for four years and more, and the Avtokrator had spent all that time trying to forget the things his younger brother had told him. He'd succeeded better than he'd guessed.

"Why is Parsmanios not here with you?" Zenonis asked again. She probably had some Vaspurakaner blood in her—not surprising, this close to the princes' land—for she was almost as swarthy as Maniakes and Rhegorios. Beneath that swarthiness, she went pale. "Is my husband dead, your Majesty? If he is, do not hide it from me. Tell me the truth at once." Her son, who looked quite a bit like Likarios, started to cry.

"By the good god, lady, I swear Parsmanios is not dead," Maniakes said. He got reports from Prista, on the peninsula depending from the northern shore of the Videssian Sea, several times a year. When last he'd heard, at any rate, his brother had been well.

Zenonis' smile was as bright as her frown had been dark. "Phos be praised!" she said, sketching the sun-circle and then hugging little Maniakes. "I know how it must be: you have left him back in the famous city, in Videssos the city, to rule it for you while you take the westlands back from the wicked Makuraners."

Rhegorios started to have a terrible coughing fit. Maniakes kicked him in the ankle. The woman before him was plainly no fool and would realize how badly she was mistaken. Maniakes wanted to give her that news as gently as he could; what her husband had done was not her fault. The Avtokrator would not lie to her, though: "No, he is not back in Videssos the city. My father—his father—has the authority there while I am in the westlands."

Zenonis' frown returned, though it was not so dark as it had been a moment before. "I do not understand," she said.

"I know you don't," Maniakes told her. "The explanation will take a while: no help for that. Come here at sunset for supper with me and Lysia, my wife, and with Rhegorios here—my cousin, the Sevastos."

"Both of you have something of the look of Parsmanios," Zenonis said. "Or maybe he has your look, I don't know." Her frown got deeper. "But if your cousin is Sevastos, what rank does Parsmanios hold?"

Exile, Maniakes thought. Aloud, he replied, "As I said, the explanation isn't quick or simple. Let me handle the matters here that are simple. At supper, I promise I'll tell you everything you need to know. Is that all right?"

"You are the Avtokrator. You have the right to command," Zenonis said with considerable dignity. "As you say, so shall it be." She led her son away. The next petitioner stepped forward.

Before dealing with the fellow, Maniakes sent Rhegorios a stricken glance. "I'd forgotten all about this," he said. "It won't be easy."

"You aren't the only one who forgot," his cousin answered, which did not make him feel any better. Rhegorios went on, "You're right. It won't be easy."

Lysia grimaced. She spoke severely to her belly: "Stop that." The baby in there didn't stop wiggling; Maniakes could see movement where her swollen middle pressed against her gown. She grimaced again. "He's kicking my bladder. Excuse me. I need to use the pot again."

"It won't be long now," Maniakes remarked when she came back.

"No, not long," Lysia agreed.

Silence fell. Maniakes broke it with a sigh, and then said, "I'd sooner have an aching tooth pulled than go through with this supper, but I don't see any way not to do it."

"Neither do I," Lysia answered. "We'll tell her the truth and see how things go from there, that's all. I don't know what else we can do."

"Send her into exile to keep my brother company?" Maniakes suggested. But he shook his head and held his hands out in front of him before Lysia could say anything. "No, I don't mean it. What Parsmanios did wasn't her fault."

"No, it wasn't." Lysia sighed, too. "And we'll have to explain about ourselves again: better she should hear it from us than from anyone else. I get tired of explaining sometimes."

"I know. So do I." Maniakes spread his hands once more. "We fell in love with each other. I didn't expect it, but . . ." His voice trailed off.

"I didn't, either," Lysia said. "I'm not saying it hasn't been worth the fight over the dispensation and the explanations and everything else. But I do get tired."

Rhegorios knocked on the door of the chamber they were sharing and said, "Zenonis is here. She's nervous as a cat. I gave her a big cup of wine. I hope that will settle her down. If it doesn't, she'll jump up to the ceiling when the two of you come down to the dining hall."

"We'd better get on with it." Maniakes stood aside to let Lysia precede him through the door. Hand in hand, the two of them followed Rhegorios downstairs.

Zenonis did jump when Maniakes came into the dining hall, enough to make a little wine slop out of the cup she was holding. She'd left young Maniakes at home. She started to prostrate herself before the Avtokrator. He waved for her not to bother. "Your Majesty is gracious," she said, her voice under tight control. She wanted to scream questions at him—Maniakes had heard that kind of restraint before, often enough to recognize it here.

To forestall her, at least for a bit, the Avtokrator said, "Zenonis, let me present you to my wife, the Empress Lysia, who is sister to the Sevastos Rhegorios." There. There it was, all in a lump.

At first, she simply heard the words. Then she figured out what they meant. Rhegorios was Maniakes' cousin. Lysia was Rhegorios' sister. That meant . . . Zenonis took a deep breath. Maniakes braced himself for trouble—thought there would surely be trouble of one sort or another tonight. "I am allied with this family by marriage," Zenonis said after a visible pause for thought. "I am allied with all of it."

"Well said, by the good god!" Rhegorios exclaimed.

Lysia took Zenonis' hands in hers. "We do welcome you to the family," she said. "Whether you'll be so glad of us after a while may be another question, but we'll get to that."

The cooks brought in bread and a roasted kid covered with powdered garlic and a sharp, pungent cheese. They also presented the diners with a bowl of golden mushrooms of a sort Maniakes had never seen before. When he remarked on them, one of the cooks said, "They don't grow far from Vryetion that I know of, your Majesty. We've sautéed them in white wine for you."

They were delicious, with a flavor half nutty, half meaty. The kid was falling-off-the-bone tender, no easy trick with goat. And yet, however good the supper proved, Maniakes knew he was enjoying it less than he should have. He kept waiting for Zenonis to stop picking at the lovely food and start asking the unlovely questions he would have to answer.

She lasted longer than he'd thought she would. But, when he showed no signs of volunteering what she wanted to know, she took a long pull at her cup of wine and said, "Parsmanios lives, you tell me." Maniakes nodded, taking advantage of a full mouth to say nothing. His new-met sister-in-law went on, "He is not here. You said he was not in Videssos the city." She paused, like a banister building a case in a law court. Maniakes nodded again. Zenonis asked the first of those blunt questions: "Where is he, then?"

"In Prista," Maniakes answered, giving blunt for blunt.

But he was not blunt enough. "Where is that?" Zenonis said. "I never heard of it. Is it important? It must be. Is he your viceroy there?"

"No, he is not my viceroy there," Maniakes said. "Prista is a little town on the northern shore of the Videssian Sea." It was, in its way, an important place, for it let the Empire of Videssos keep an eye on the Khamorth tribes wandering the Pardrayan steppe. But that wasn't what Zenonis had meant, and he knew it.

"That's—at the edge of the world," she exclaimed, and the Avtokrator nodded yet again. "Why is he there and not here or in the capital?"

Yes, that was *the* blunt question, sure enough. "Why, lady?" Maniakes echoed. He found no way to soften his reply: "Because he and one of my generals conspired to slay me by magic. The general got away; I still haven't caught up with him. But Parsmanios—"

"No." Zenonis' lips shaped the word, but without sound. Then she said it again, aloud this time: "No." She shook her head, as if brushing away a buzzing fly. "It's not possible. When Parsmanios was here in Vryetion with me after you became Avtokrator, your Majesty, he would talk about going to Videssos the city so he and you and your brother Tatoules could run things the way they—"

Maniakes held up his hand. "I don't know where Tatoules is. He never came to Videssos the city, and no one knows what's happened to him. If I had to guess, I'd say the Makuraners captured him in the early days of their invasion, while Genesios was still Avtokrator. Most of my family was in exile on Kalavria then. To the boiler boys, he'd have been just another officer, just another prisoner. They probably worked him to death."

"I am sorry," Zenonis said; she'd already shown she had good manners. "I didn't know. Parsmanios didn't know, either, of course. He would go on and on about how you three brothers would set the Empire to rights and get rich doing it, too."

"He was welcome to help me set the Empire to rights," Maniakes said. "By the good god, it's needed setting to rights. He did help, some. But he wanted to be promoted without having earned it, just because he was my brother. When I told him no, he didn't like that."

Rhegorios wriggled in his seat, then held up his winecup. A servant hurried to fill it. Rhegorios hurried to empty it. The title Parsmanios had wanted was Sevastos, the title he owned. The Avtokrator had kept him in preference to his own brother. No wonder he felt a little uneasy here.

Zenonis said, "I can't believe he would turn on his own flesh and blood."

"I couldn't believe it, either," Maniakes answered. "Unfortunately, it happens to be true, and I nearly died from it. He always claimed he did it because he thought my marriage with Lysia was wrong and wicked. Maybe he was even telling the truth; I don't know. It doesn't matter. What he did matters, and that's all. Phos, I wish he hadn't done it."

Zenonis' gaze flicked from him to Lysia and back again. Parsmanios' wife had spirit; Maniakes could tell she was going to challenge him. When she did, she picked her words with great care, but challenged nonetheless: "By the teachings of the holy temples, the two of you are within the prohibited degrees of kinship, and so—"

"No." Maniakes made his voice flat. "We have a dispensation from Agathios, the most holy ecumenical patriarch. My father—Parsmanios' father—has accepted the wedding." That was true, as far as it went. The elder Maniakes didn't like the wedding, but he accepted it. "Lysia's father has accepted it, too." That was also true, with the same reservations. "None of them tried to overthrow me or take the throne for themselves." Most important of all, that was true, too. "Neither did Rhegorios here."

"Me?" Rhegorios' eyebrows shot upward. "I've seen what all the Avtokrator has to do. Looks too much like work for my taste."

Lysia snorted. So did Maniakes. Rhegorios had a hard time keeping his own face straight. He enjoyed affecting the role of a useless, gilded fop. When he was younger, the affectation might have covered some truth. No more, though. Maniakes knew that, if he fell over dead tomorrow, his father and Rhegorios would keep the Empire running as smoothly as it could in these troubled times.

He also knew Rhegorios would do nothing to try to make him fall over dead, and everything in his power to keep him from falling over dead. There, in a sentence, was the difference between his cousin and the brother he'd had to exile.

"If the ecumenical patriarch says it is acceptable, then it is," Zenonis said, as if stating a law of nature. If it was a law of nature, Maniakes wished more clerics and citizens were familiar with it. His sister-in-law bowed her head. "Thank you for sparing his life."

"You're welcome," Maniakes answered. He started to say something more, but stopped. He started again, and again left it unspoken. Whatever comments he might make about not having the stomach to spill a brother's blood would only cause him to seem smug and self-righteous, because Parsmanios had shown he had the stomach to try doing just that.

"What will you do with me?" Zenonis asked.

"I don't intend to do anything with you," Maniakes answered. "And, in case you're still wondering, I don't intend to do anything to you, either. If you want to stay here in Vryetion, you may do that. If you want to come to Videssos the city, you may do that. If you want to go into exile with Parsmanios, you may do that, too. But think carefully before you choose that road. If you go to Prista, you will never come back."

"I don't know what to do now," Zenonis said. "These past few years, I've wondered whether my husband was alive. To find out he is, to be raised to the heights by that, and then to learn what he'd done and to plunge into the depths again . . . I don't know where I am now." She looked down at her hands again.

Gently, Lysia said, "After this, you may not want anything to do with our clan any more. If you should decide to dissolve the marriage, the clerics will give you no trouble, not with your husband a proved traitor. None of us would hold it against you, I know that." She glanced to Maniakes and Rhegorios for confirmation. Both quickly nodded.

"I don't know," Zenonis repeated.

"You don't have to decide right away," Maniakes said. "Take your time to find what you think is best. The Makuraners aren't going to run us out of Vryetion again tomorrow, nor even the day after." He sketched the sun-circle above his heart to make sure Phos was paying attention to his words.

"What's best for me may not be best for Maniakes—my Maniakes, I mean," Zenonis said, thinking out loud. "And what's best for me may not be best for Parsmanios, either." She looked up at Maniakes, half-nervous, half-defiant, as if daring him to make something of that.

Before he could reply at all, Rhegorios asked, "What was it like, living here under the Makuraners when you were the Avtokrator's sister-in-law?"

"They never knew," Zenonis answered. "Half the people in Vryetion know who my husband is, but none of them ever told the boiler boys. I was always afraid that would happen, but it never did."

"Interesting," Maniakes said. That meant Zenonis was widely liked in the town. Otherwise, someone eager to curry favor with the occupiers would surely have betrayed her, as had happened so often at so many other places in the westlands. It also meant no one had hated Parsmanios enough to want to strike at him through his family, a small piece of favorable information about him but not one to be ignored.

"You are being as kind to me as you can," Zenonis said. "For this, I am in your debt, so much I can never hope to repay."

"Nonsense," Maniakes said. "You've done nothing to me. Why should I want to do anything to you?"

That question answered itself in his own mind as soon as he spoke it. Genesios would have slaughtered Parsmanios in the name of vengeance, and disposed of Zenonis and little Maniakes for sport. Likinios might have got rid of them merely for efficiency's sake, to leave no potential rivals at his back. Not being so vicious as Genesios nor so cold-blooded as Likinios, Maniakes was willing to let his sister-in-law and nephew live.

"You will let me think a while on what I should do?" Zenonis said, as if she still had trouble believing Maniakes. After he had reassured her yet again, she rose and prostrated herself before him.

"Get up," he said roughly. "Maybe people whose great-grandfathers were Avtokrators before them got used to that, but I never have." The confession would have dismayed Kameas, but Kameas was back in Videssos the city. The vestiarios had accompanied Maniakes on his ill-fated journey to buy peace from Etzilios. Maniakes had almost been captured then. Kameas had been, though Etzilios later released him. Since then, he'd stuck close to the imperial city.

With still more thanks, Zenonis made her way out of the city governor's residence. Maniakes looked at Rhegorios. Rhegorios looked at Lysia. Lysia looked at Maniakes.

Being the Avtokrator, he had the privilege of speaking first. He could have done without it. "That," he said, "was ghastly. If I'd known it was coming, that would have been hard enough. To have it take me by surprise this afternoon . . . I knew Parsmanios had lived in Vryetion. I didn't think about everything that would mean."

"You did as well as you could," Lysia said.

"Yes, I think so, too," he answered without false modesty. "But I think I'd sooner have been beaten with boards."

Thoughtfully, Rhegorios said, "She's nicer than I thought she'd be. Not bad-looking at all, a long way from stupid . . . I wonder what she saw in Parsmanios."

"No telling," Maniakes said wearily. "He wasn't a bad fellow, you know, till jealousy ate him up from the inside out."

A servant came in with a platter of pears, apricots, and strawberries candied in honey. He looked around in some surprise. "The lady left before the sweet?" he said in faintly scandalized tones.

"So she did." Maniakes' imperturbability defied the servitor to make something of it After a moment, the Avtokrator went on, "Why don't you set that tray down? We'll get around to it sooner or later. Meanwhile, bring us a fresh jar of wine."

"Meanwhile, bring us two or three fresh jars of wine," Rhegorios broke in.

"Yes, by the good god, bring us two or three fresh jars of wine," Maniakes exclaimed. "I hadn't planned to get drunk tonight, but then, things can change. Till this afternoon, I hadn't planned on entertaining the wife of my traitorous brother tonight, either."

Lysia yawned. "I've had enough wine already," she said. "I'm going upstairs to bed. I'll see what's left of the two of you in the morning."

"She's smarter than either one of us," Maniakes said. That judgment didn't keep him from using a small knife to scrape the pitch out from around the stopper of one of the wine jars with which the servant had presented him. Once the stopper was out, the fellow took the jar from him and poured his cup and his cousin's full.

Rhegorios lifted the goblet, spat on the floor in rejection of Skotos, and drank. "Ahh," he said. "That's good." He took another pull. "You forget, your magnifolent Majesty—" He and Maniakes both laughed at that. "—I grew up with Lysia. I've known for a long time that she's smarter than I am. And while I wouldn't commit lese majesty for anything . . ."

"I get your drift." Maniakes drank, too, and ate a candied strawberry. Then he shook his head. "What a night. You know how the laundresses batter clothes against rocks to get the dirt out? That's how I feel now."

"Life is full of surprises," Rhegorios observed.

"Isn't it, though?" Maniakes drained his cup and filled it again before the servant could. "I'd thought the Kubratoi and the Makuraners—to say nothing of Tzikas, which is generally a good idea—had long since taught me all I needed to know of that lesson. I was wrong."

"I don't think Zenonis is out to kill you or overthrow the Empire—or to kill you *and* overthrow the Empire," Rhegorios said.

"I don't think so, either," Maniakes agreed. "But when you've been wrong before, you can't help wondering. I've given her a powerful reason to dislike me."

"That's so," his cousin admitted. "Times like this, you almost begin to understand how Genesios' ugly little mind worked."

"I had that same thought not very long ago," Maniakes said. "Frightening, isn't it?" He looked down into his goblet. It was empty. *How did that happen?* he wondered. Since no drunken mice staggered across the floor, he must have done it himself. He filled the cup again. "If I'd had some warning, I would have handled it better."

"You did fine, cousin of mine," Rhegorios said. "If you won't listen to Lysia, listen to me. I don't see what else you could have done. You explained what Parsmanios did, you explained what you did afterward, and you explained why. You didn't get angry during any of it. I would have, I think."

"I doubt it," Maniakes said. "You probably would have pardoned Parsmanios, too. I'm sterner than you are."

"Not for things like that," Rhegorios declared. "I would have advised you to take his head—but it wasn't my place to advise you of anything, not with him wanting my job and being blood of my blood both. I thought you'd do right on your own, and you did."

"Poor Zenonis, though," the Avtokrator said. "If her being here took me by surprise, what I told her must have hit like a—like a—" He began to feel the wine, which made groping for a simile hard. He found one anyhow: "Like a jar of wine in a tavern brawl. Life shouldn't work that way."

"A lot of things that shouldn't happen, happen to happen." Rhegorios stared reproachfully at the winecup he was holding, as if shocked that the ruby liquid it contained had betrayed him into saying something so absurd. Then he giggled. So did Maniakes. They both let loose gales of laughter. With enough wine, the world looked pretty funny.

When Maniakes woke up the next morning, nothing was funny any more. He felt as if a thunderstorm were rattling his poor abused brains. Every sound was a crash, every sunbeam a bolt of lightning.

Lysia, who'd had a full night's sleep and only a little wine, was less than properly sympathetic. "You look like you're going to bleed to death through your eyes," she said. "And you ought to comb your beard, or maybe iron it—it's pointing off to one side."

"Oh, shut up," he mumbled, not very loud.

His wife, heartless creature that she was suddenly revealed to be, laughed at him. "Remember, you've got another full day ahead of you, sorting through who was doing what to whom here and why, all the way through the Makuraner occupation."

He groaned and sat up in bed. That prompted another groan, more theatrical than the first. Then he groaned yet again, this time in good earnest. "Phos, Zenonis is going to be back here this morning, telling me what she wants to do."

"If she sees you like this—" Lysia hesitated. "No, come to think of it, maybe she went home and got drunk after dinner last night, too. You could hardly blame her if she did."

"No, but she'll blame me," Maniakes said. "I'm the Avtokrator. That's what I'm for—getting blamed, I mean."

He breakfasted on a little bread and honey and a cautious cup of wine. Splashing cool water on his face helped. So did combing the tangles out of his beard. Lysia studied him, then delivered her verdict: "Amazingly lifelike." Maniakes felt vindicated. He also felt human, in a glum sort of way.

Sure enough, by the time he came downstairs, petitioners were lined up in front of the city governor's residence. He dealt with them as best he could. Approving some and denying others made some people glad and others angry, but no one seemed to think the decisions he made especially idiotic.

Rhegorios bravely stuck his head into the chamber where Maniakes was passing his judgments. "I wondered if you could use some help," he said, his voice a rasping croak.

"I'm managing," Maniakes answered.

"I see you are," his cousin said. "In that case—" He withdrew. Whatever he'd done to fight his hangover, the hangover had won the battle.

Zenonis and little Maniakes came into the chamber about half-way through the morning. They both prostrated themselves before the Avtokrator, even though he waved for them not to bother. In a way, that relieved his mind, as a sign that Zenonis took his sovereignty seriously . . . unless, of course, she was dissembling. Life, he decided with the mournful clarity the morning after a drunken night could bring, was never simple.

"Have you decided what you would like to do?" he asked after his sister-in-law and nephew had risen.

"Yes, your Majesty," Zenonis said. "By your leave, we—" She put her arm around little Maniakes' shoulder. "—will travel to Videssos the city." She hesitated. "Maybe, later on, we will sail across the sea to Prista. I still have to think on that."

"Good enough," Maniakes said. "I think you are wise not to go to Prista at once, but I wouldn't have stood in your way if that was what you wanted to do. I'll give you an escort to go to the city, and I'll send a courier ahead to let my father know you're coming and to ask him to show you every kindness. He would anyway, for your husband's sake."

He watched Zenonis' eyes when he spoke of Parsmanios. As best he could tell, she looked sad, not angry. All the same, he'd also quietly ask his father to keep an eye on her while she was in the capital.

Zenonis said, "Your father is also Maniakes, not so?"

Maniakes nodded. "Yes. I suppose he's the one for whom your son is named, not me."

"No," Zenonis said, "or not altogether. When Maniakes—or little Maniakes, I should say—was born, my husband named him for the two of you. Now he's met one of his namesakes, and soon he'll meet the other."

"What do you think of that?" Maniakes asked his nephew.

"I don't know," little Maniakes answered. "It's all right, I guess, but I want to see my papa. That's what I really want to do."

Beside him, Zenonis began, very quietly, to weep. Obviously, she hadn't told her son what Parsmanios had done. Maniakes found himself unable to blame her for that. Sooner or later, little Maniakes would have to find out. It didn't have to be right away, though. To him, Maniakes said, "Maybe you will, one of these days. You *will* meet your grandfather, though. Isn't that good?"

"I don't know," his nephew said again. "Is he nicer than Gramps here in Vryetion?"

Maniakes hadn't even thought about Zenonis' father. Taken aback, he said, "Well, you can ask him for yourself when you get to Videssos the city. I'll bet he tells you yes." His nephew gravely puzzled away at that. Though tears still streaked her face, Zenonis managed a smile.

More claims about collaboration and treason kept the Avtokrator busy the rest of the day. Vryetion hadn't been occupied so long as some of the other Videssian towns up on the plateau, and it had been fortunate in having a relatively decent Makuraner overlord. Maybe that was why so many people had, or were accused of having, collaborated with the occupiers. Maniakes fought through the cases, one by one.

As in other Videssian towns through which he'd passed in the wake of the retreating Makuraners, temple affairs were in turmoil here. Vryetion wasn't far from the border with Vaspurakan. Some of the locals had Vaspurakaner blood; even some of those who didn't had looked kindly on Vaspurakaner doctrines before those were imposed on them.

A priest named Salivas said, "Your Majesty, your own clan reveres Vaspur the Firstborn. How can you condemn us for doing the same?"

"I follow the orthodox creed of Videssos," Maniakes answered, which was not a thorough denial of what the priest had said. He went on, "And you, holy sir, you were orthodox before the Makuraners ordered you to change the way you preached. You were happy enough then, not so? Why doesn't orthodoxy content you any more?"

"Because I believe with all my heart the doctrines I preach now are Phos' holy truth." Salivas drew himself up to his full height. He was tall, and also thin, which made him look even taller. "I am ready to die to defend the truth of the dogma of Vaspur."

"Nobody said anything about killing you, holy sir," Maniakes replied, which seemed to surprise and disappoint the priest—not the first time the Avtokrator had seen that, either. He went on, "I have another question for you: if you're so bloody eager to martyr yourself for faith in Vaspur the Firstborn, why didn't you let the boiler boys slaughter you when they made you change from orthodoxy?" *Then I wouldn't have had to deal with you,* he added to himself.

Salivas opened his mouth and closed it without saying anything. As far as Maniakes was concerned, that was a triumph almost as satisfying as holding the Kubratoi and Makuraners out of Videssos the city. Then, dashing it, Salivas tried again to speak, and succeeded. What he said, though, made the Avtokrator feel victorious after all: "Your Majesty, I don't know."

"May I offer a suggestion?" asked Maniakes, who had observed this phenomenon a couple of times before, too. Since Salivas could hardly refuse his sovereign, the Avtokrator continued, "You were orthodox all your life. You took orthodoxy for granted, didn't you?" He waited for Salivas to nod, then pressed ahead: "The Vaspurakaner doctrines are new to you. They're exciting on account of that, I think, as a man will find a new mistress exciting even though there's nothing whatever wrong with his wife except that she's not new to him any more."

Salivas flushed to the shaven crown of his head. "That is not a comparison I would have chosen to use," he said stiffly. Reminding Videssian priests of the celibacy required of them was bad manners.

Maniakes didn't care about bad manners, except insofar as he preferred them to religious rioting and other civil strife. "Use whatever comparison you like, holy sir. But think hard on it. Remember that you'd been perfectly content while you were orthodox. Remember that the other priests here—" *Most of them, anyhow,* he qualified mentally, and the couple of others who still inclined to Vaspurakaner views were wavering. "—have gone back to orthodoxy now that the Makuraners have left."

"But the Vaspurakaner views are—" Salivas began.

He was probably going to be stubborn. Maniakes didn't give him the chance. "Are imposed on you by foreigners who wanted to ruin Videssos," he said firmly. "Do you want to help Sharbaraz King of Kings win this fight even after his soldiers have left the Empire?"

"No," Salivas admitted, "but neither do I want to spend eternity in Skotos' ice for having misbelieved."

What Maniakes wanted to do was punch the stubborn priest, or possibly hit him over the head with a large stone in the hope of creating an opening through which sense might enter. With more patience than he'd thought he owned, he asked, "Didn't you believe you would be bathed in Phos' holy light before the Makuraners made you change your preaching?"

"Yes, but I have changed my mind since then," Salivas answered.

"If you changed it once, do you think you might change it again?" the Avtokrator said.

"I doubt that," Salivas told him. "I doubt that very much."

"Before the boiler boys made you reject orthodoxy, did you ever think you would change your mind about that?" Maniakes asked.

"No," the cleric said.

"Well, then—" Maniakes waited for Salivas to make the connection. He waited, and waited, and waited some more. The connection remained unmade. Salivas remained convinced that what he believed now, he would believe forever. Maniakes became convinced the priest was a perfect blockhead, but the only thing he could do about that was hope the people of Vryetion would notice it, too.

Seeing his discontent without fully recognizing its source, Salivas said, "I shall pray for you, your Majesty."

"For that much I thank you," Maniakes said wearily. Vryetion was going to be a town with Vaspurakaner-style heretics in it for some time to come. There were a lot of towns like that in the westlands. The ecumenical patriarch wouldn't be happy about it. Maniakes wasn't happy about it himself; it disturbed his sense of order. But plunging the westlands back into strife just after getting them back from the Makuraners disturbed his sense of order even more. He dismissed Salivas, who departed with the air of a man who, having nerved himself for the worst, was more angry than relieved at not having suffered it. The next case that came before the Avtokrator was a complicated stew of forgery, where property bounds lay, and whether Makuraner officials had been bribed to make them lie there. It involved no theology, just skulduggery. Maniakes attacked it with great relish.

XI

Abivard bowed in the saddle to Maniakes. "If the God is kind," the Makuraner marshal said, "the next message you have from me will be that Mashiz has fallen into my hands."

"May it be so," Maniakes said. "Then we shall be equals: two jumped-up generals sitting on the thrones of our lands."

"Yes," Abivard said. "I suppose so." He still had his little nephew with whom to concern himself. Denak's son had a more nearly legitimate claim to the Makuraner throne than he did. Had the boy been Sharbaraz's get by another woman, the answer would have been easy. Disposing of his sister's child, though . . .

Judging it wiser to shift the subject a bit, Maniakes said, "So you have the men you need out of Vaspurakan?"

"Oh, yes," Abivard answered. "And I have three regiments of Vaspurakaners, all of them eager to cast down Sharbaraz."

"You'll take their help, but you won't take me?" Maniakes jabbed.

"Of course," Abivard said easily. "They are our subjects. If you were a Makuraner subject now, Sharbaraz would be well pleased with me, and I'd have had no need to rebel against him. The Vaspurakaners weren't invading the Land of the Thousand Cities earlier this year, either."

"A point," Maniakes said. "Two points, as a matter of fact. Good

662

luck go with you. Cast down Sharbaraz; give him everything he deserves for all the sorrows he's brought to Videssos and Makuran both. And then, by the good god, let's see how long we can live in peace."

"Long enough to rebuild everything that's been destroyed, here and in Makuran," Abivard said. "That should take a few years, or more than a few—you weren't gentle between the Tutub and the Tib."

"I can't even say I'm sorry," Maniakes said. "The only way I could find to get you out of my land—where you weren't always gentle, either—was to ravage yours."

"I understand," Abivard said. "It worked, too. Maybe, if the God is kind, we'll have got out of the habit of fighting each other once we have everything patched. And the two of us, we know what this war was like, and why we don't want another one."

"Maybe we can even make our sons understand," Maniakes said hopefully. Abivard's nod was tighter and more constrained than the Avtokrator would have liked to see. The hesitation worried him till he remembered that Abivard was still pondering whether to rule as King of Kings or as regent for his nephew.

Maniakes drew the sun-circle, lest his thinking past Abivard's victory prove a bad omen for winning that victory. He rode forward, holding out his hand. The Makuraner marshal clasped it. Then Abivard surprised him, saying, "I want you to tell your father something for me."

"What's that?" the Avtokrator said.

"Tell him that if the Khamorth nomads hadn't killed Godarz— my father—I think the two of them would have got on famously together."

"I'll remember," Maniakes promised. "They might even have fought against each other, back when we were small or before we were born."

"That's so." Abivard looked bemused. "They might have. I hadn't thought of it, but you're right. And we certainly have. If the God is kind, our sons won't." He gave what might have been a sketched Videssian salute or might as easily have been a jerky wave, then used his knees and the reins to turn his horse and ride back toward his own army. His guards, who, like Maniakes', had halted out of earshot of their masters, fell in around him.

After watching him for most of a minute, Maniakes turned

Antelope in the direction of the Videssian army. He heaved a long sigh as he trotted up to Rhegorios, who had ridden out a little way to meet him.

"It's over," Maniakes said in wondering tones. "It's really over. After all these years, the Makuraners really are leaving the westlands. We're at peace with them—unless Sharbaraz beats Abivard, of course. But even then, the King of Kings would have to think three times before he dared a new war with us. The Kubratoi aren't going to fight us any time soon, either. We're at peace, and we have the whole Empire back."

"Well, don't let it worry you too long," his cousin said. "The Khatrishers may decide to get bold, or the Halogai might gather a fleet together and attack Kalavria, or, for that matter, some people none of us has ever heard of might appear out of nowhere, for no better reason than to cause Videssos trouble."

"You do so relieve my mind," Maniakes said.

Rhegorios laughed. "Happy to please, your Majesty. You were looking so bereft there without anybody to fight, I thought I'd give you someone."

"People appearing out of nowhere? In the middle of the Empire, I presume? No, thank you," Maniakes said with feeling. "If you're going to wish for something absurd, wish for the Halogai to invade Kubrat instead of Kalavria. That would actually do us some good."

"You've won the war," Rhegorios said. "What will you do now?"

"What I'd like to do," Maniakes answered, "is go back to Videssos the city, enjoy my children and the rest of my family for a while, and have the people in the city not throw curses at me when I go out among 'em. Too much to ask for, I suppose."

"Now you're feeling sorry for yourself," Rhegorios said. "I'm not going to let you get away with that. I need to remind you that you just drove the invincible Makuraner army out of the westlands, and you didn't lose a man doing it. Go ahead and blubber after *that*."

Maniakes chuckled. "There you have me. Only goes to show, I suppose, that forgery beats fighting."

Rhegorios whipped his head around in sudden anxiety, or an excellent simulation thereof. "You'd better not let any Makuraners hear you say that."

"Of course not," Maniakes said. "If Romezan ever finds out all those other names weren't on the order Sharbaraz sent him, the whole civil war over there—" He pointed in the direction of the withdrawing army. "—might still unravel."

"That isn't what I mean," his cousin said. "You were talking like one of the sneaky Videssians they always complain about."

"Oh," the Avtokrator said "I *am* a sneaky Videssian, but I don't suppose they have to know about that. They can think of me however they like—as long as they do it from a great distance."

"Do you plan on going back to the capital right away?"

"No." Maniakes shook his head. "Once I'm sure the boiler boys are gone for good—or at least for this campaigning season—I'll send back half, maybe even two thirds, of the army. Until I find out how the fight between Abivard and Sharbaraz goes, though, I'm going to stay in the westlands myself. If you can't stand being away from the fleshpots of the city, I'll send you back with the part of the army I release."

"What, and let you find out who wins the Makuraner civil war a couple of weeks before I do?" Rhegorios exclaimed. "Not likely. Send Immodios. If he's not killing Makuraners himself, he hasn't got the imagination to worry about what happens to 'em."

"All right, I'll do that," Maniakes said with a laugh. "My father and yours will be jealous of both of us, because we'll know when they don't."

"So they will." Rhegorios' eyes twinkled. "And they'll both say it's the first time in the history of the world we ever knew anything they don't already, even for a little while. That's what fathers are for."

"So it is," Maniakes said. "And pretty soon I'll be able to treat my boys the same way. See how life goes on?"

As Rhegorios had predicted, Immodios made not the tiniest protest when Maniakes ordered him to take half the imperial army back toward Videssos the city. The Avtokrator had decided not to give him more than half, on the off chance that he might take whatever he had into rebellion with him. Maniakes trusted him further than anyone not of his own immediate family; but someone inside his own immediate family had conspired against him, so that said little.

And no sooner had Immodios led the detachment back toward

Videssos the city than Maniakes wished the army reunited. That, though, had nothing to do with fears about Immodios' loyalty or lack of same. It had to do with news a messenger brought up from the south.

"I'm sorry to have to tell you this, your Majesty," the fellow said, "but the Makuraner garrison in Serrhes hasn't pulled out of the town. They keep insisting they're loyal to Sharbaraz."

"Oh, they do, do they?" Maniakes sounded half-angry, half-resigned. "Well, I suppose I should have expected that would happen somewhere. I wish it hadn't happened at Serrhes, though." The garrison town's main reason for existing was to plug that stretch of frontier between Makuran and the Empire of Videssos. He and his father had set out from Serrhes along with Abivard and Sharbaraz to return the latter to the Makuraner throne. That seemed a lot longer before than twelve or thirteen years.

"What will you do, your Majesty?" the messenger asked.

"What can I do?" Maniakes returned. "I'll go down to Serrhes and pry the Makuraners out of it." He paused. "How big a Makuraner garrison does the place have in it?"

"About a thousand men, or so I hear," the messenger said.

"I still have four times that many with me," the Avtokrator mused aloud. Having sent Immodios' detachment back toward the capital, he did not want to recall those troops. "Maybe I can get away with just using what I've got."

Intending to try it, he moved south with his half of the army. They hadn't had to march quickly since they'd left the Land of the Thousand Cities; the journey through the westlands had been a parade. The roads down toward Serrhes weren't good, and had been little traveled during the Makuraner occupation. The Videssians pressed rapidly along them nonetheless.

Before they got to Serrhes, the corrugated central plateau of the westlands began to give way to the scrubby semidesert lying between Videssos' western border and the Tutub River. Back in the long-ago days of his reign, Likinios Avtokrator had complained about almost every expense he ever had to meet. Trying not to meet one, finally, had cost him his throne and his life. So far as Maniakes knew, he'd never complained about keeping Serrhes supplied.

Approaching the town, Maniakes wondered how—or if—the Makuraners had managed that. Had they fed Serrhes off the countryside? The countryside yielded little. A few cattle grazed it, but not enough grew nearby to support more than a few. Over the dry country from the Land of the Thousand Cities? If so, the supply line was either already broken or easily breakable.

Looking at Serrhes' thick walls, looking at the citadel on the high ground in the center of town, Maniakes quickly decided he did not want to try storming the place. He rode forward behind a shield of truce to parley with the garrison commander.

Tegin son of Gamash came to Serrhes' western gate and looked down at the Avtokrator of the Videssians. He was a solidly built man with a gray beard and an impressive nose. "You're wasting your time," he called to Maniakes. "We won't yield to you."

"If you don't, you'll be sorry after I break into Serrhes," Maniakes said, threatening to do what he least wanted to do. "We outnumber you at least six to one. We'll show no mercy." *Assuming we're lucky enough to get onto or through those works,* he thought. Serrhes had been built with admirable skill to hold the Makuraners at bay. Now it threatened to do the same to the folk who had built it in the first place.

"Come do your worst," Tegin retorted. "We're ready for you."

Maniakes concluded he was not the only one running a noisy bluff. "What do you propose to eat in there?" he demanded.

"Oh, I don't know," Tegin said airily. "We have a deal of this and that. What do you propose to eat out there?"

It was, Maniakes had to admit, a good question. Supplying an army surrounding Serrhes had all the drawbacks of supplying the town itself. He wasn't about to let the Makuraner know he'd scored a hit, though. "We have all the westlands to draw on," he said. "Yours is the last Makuraner garrison hereabouts."

"All the more reason to hold it, then, wouldn't you say?" Tegin sounded as if he was enjoying himself. Maniakes wished he could say the same.

What he did say was, "By staying here, you violate the terms of the truce Abivard made with us."

"Abivard is not King of Kings," Tegin said. "My ruler is Sharbaraz King of Kings, may his years be many and his realm increase."

"All the Makuraners in the westlands have renounced Sharbaraz," Maniakes said.

Tegin shook his head. "Not all of them. This one hasn't, for instance."

"A pestilence," Maniakes muttered under his breath. He should have expected he'd come across a holdout or two. Things could have been worse; Romezan could have stayed resolutely loyal to Sharbaraz. But things could also have been better. The Avtokrator had no intention of letting Serrhes stay in Makuraner hands. He said, "You know Sharbaraz ordered Abivard and most of his generals slain when they failed to take Videssos the city."

"I've heard it said," the garrison commander answered. "I don't know it for a fact."

"I have seen the captured dispatch with my own eyes," Maniakes said. He had also seen the document transformed into one more useful for Videssian purposes, but forbore to mention that, such forbearance also being more useful for Videssian purposes.

Tegin remained difficult. "Majesty, begging your pardon, I don't much care what you've seen and what you haven't seen. You're the enemy. I expect you'd lie to me if you saw any profit in it. Videssians are like that."

Since Maniakes not only would lie but to a certain degree was lying, he changed the subject: "I point out to you once more, excellent sir, that you are at the moment commanding the only Makuraner garrison left in the westlands."

"So you say," Tegin replied, still unimpressed.

"If there are others all around, how have I fought my way past them to come to you?" Maniakes asked.

"If they've all gone over to Abivard, you don't need to have done any fighting," Tegin said.

"That's true, I suppose," Maniakes said. "And what it means is, I can concentrate my entire army—" He did not think Tegin needed to know that Immodios was leading half of it back to Videssos the city. "—against you holdouts in Serrhes." He waved back toward his encampment. It was as big as . . . an army. He did not think Tegin was in a position to estimate with any accuracy how many men were in it.

And, indeed, the garrison commander wavered for the first time. "I am surrounded by traitors," he complained.

"No, you're surrounded by Videssians," Maniakes answered. "This is part of the Empire, and we are taking it back. You've probably heard stories about what we've done to the walls of the Thousand Cities. Do you think we won't do the same to you?"

He knew perfectly well they couldn't do the same to Serrhes.

The walls of the towns between the Tutub and the Tib were made of brick, and not the strongest brick, either. Serrhes was fortified in stone. Breaking in wouldn't be so easy. If Tegin had time to think, he would realize that, too. Best not give him time to think, then.

Maniakes said, "Excellent sir, I don't care how brave you are. Your garrison is small. If we once get in among 'em, I'm afraid I can't answer for the consequences. You'll have made warnings of that sort yourself, I expect; you know how soldiers are."

"Yes, I know how soldiers are," Tegin said somberly. "If I had more men, Majesty, I would beat you."

"If I had feathers, I'd be a tall rooster," Maniakes replied. "I don't. I'm not. You don't, either. You'd better remember it." He started to turn away, then stopped. "I'll ask you again at this hour tomorrow. If you say yes, you may depart safely, with your weapons, like any other Makuraner soldiers during the truce. But if you say no, excellent sir, I wash my hands of you." He did not give Tegin the last word, but walked off instead.

At his command, Videssian engineers began assembling siege engines from the timbers and ropes and specialized metal fittings they carried in the baggage train, as if they were intending to assault one of the hilltop towns in the Land of the Thousand Cities.

"We'd be able to run up more, your Majesty," Ypsilantes said, "if the countryside had trees we could cut down and use. We can only carry so much lumber."

"Do the best you can with what you have," Maniakes told the chief engineer, who saluted and went back to his work.

From the walls of Serrhes, Makuraner soldiers watched dart- and stone-throwers spring up as if by magic, though Bagdasares had nothing whatever to do with them. They watched the Videssian engineers line up row upon row of jars near the catapults. They no doubt had their own store of incendiary liquid, but could not have been delighted at the prospect of having so much of it rained down on their heads.

Seeing all those jars, Maniakes summoned Ypsilantes again. "I didn't know we were *that* well supplied with the stuff," he said, pointing.

Ypsilantes coughed modestly. "If you must know, your Majesty, most of those jars used to hold the wine we've served out to the troops when we weren't drawing supplies from a town. They're empty now. We know that. The Makuraners don't."

"Isn't that interesting?" Maniakes said with a grin. "They fooled me, so I expect they'll fool Tegin, too."

Ypsilantes also put ordinary soldiers to work dragging stones into piles. Those were perfectly genuine, though Maniakes wouldn't have put it past the chief engineer to have a few deceptive extras made of—what? stale bread, perhaps—lying around in case he needed them to befuddle an opponent.

A little before the appointed hour the next day, Tegin threw wide the gates of Serrhes. He came out and prostrated himself before Maniakes. "I would have fought you, Majesty. I wanted to fight you," he said. "But when I looked at all the siege gear you have with you, my heart failed me. I knew we could not withstand your army."

"You showed good sense." Maniakes made a point of not glancing toward Ypsilantes. The veteran engineer had served him better in not fighting this siege than he had in fighting a good many others. "As I told you, you may depart in peace."

Out filed the Makuraner garrison. Seeing it, Maniakes started to laugh. He wasn't the only one who'd done a good job of bluffing. If Tegin had even three hundred soldiers in Serrhes, he would have been astonished. He'd thought the garrison commander led three times that many, maybe more. Tegin might have fought an assault, but not for long.

Seriously, respecting the foe who had tricked him, Maniakes said, "If I were you, excellent sir, I'd keep my men out of the fight between Sharbaraz and Abivard. You can declare for whoever wins after he's won. Till then, find some little town or hilltop you can defend and stay there. That will keep you safe."

"Did you find 'some little town or hilltop' during Videssos' civil wars?" Tegin's voice dripped scorn.

But Maniakes answered, "As a matter of fact, yes." Tegin's jaw dropped. The Avtokrator went on, "My father was governor of the island of Kalavria, which is as far east as you can go without sailing out into the sea and never coming back. He sat tight there for six years. He would have thrown himself and his force away if he'd done anything else."

"You and your father took the course you judged wise," Tegin said tonelessly. "You will, I hope, forgive me if I say that this course goes straight against every Makuraner noble's notion of honor."

"Makuraner notions of honor didn't stop you people from kicking Videssos when we were down," Maniakes said.

"Of course not," Tegin replied "You are only Videssians. But I cannot sit idly by in a fight among my countrymen. The God would judge me a faintheart without the will to choose, and would surely drop my soul into the Void after I die."

"There are times," Maniakes said slowly, "when I have no trouble at all dealing with Makuraners. And there are other times when I think we and you don't speak the same language even if we do use the same words."

"How interesting you should remark on that, Majesty," Tegin said. "I have often had the same feeling when treating with you Videssians. At times, you seem sensible enough. At others—" He rolled his eyes. "You are not to be relied upon." That sounded as if he were passing judgment.

"No, eh?" Maniakes knew his smile was not altogether pleasant. "I suppose that means nothing would stop me from ignoring the truce we agreed to and scooping up your men now that they're out from behind the walls of Serrhes." Tegin looked appalled. Maniakes held up his hand. "Never mind. *I* think I have honor, whether you do or not."

"Good," Tegin said. "As I told you, sometimes Videssians are sensible folk. I am glad this is one of those times."

At the head of his little army, the garrison commander rode off to the west. He had a jauntiness to him that Maniakes didn't usually associate with Makuraners. Maniakes hoped he wouldn't have to throw his small force into the fight between the King of Kings and his marshal.

Like many other provincial towns, Serrhes centered on a square with the city governor's residence and the chief temple to Phos on opposite sides. Maniakes settled down in the residence and, as he had in so many other towns, began sorting through the arguments left behind after Tegin and his troopers were gone.

Some of those quarrels were impressively complicated. "He cheated me, your Majesty!" one plump merchant exclaimed, pointing a finger at another. "By Phos, he diddled me prime, he did, and now he stands there smooth-faced as a eunuch and denies every word of it."

"Liar," the second merchant said. "They were going to make you a eunuch, but they cut off your brain instead, because it was smaller."

"Ahem, gentlemen," Maniakes said, giving both the benefit of a doubt neither seemed likely to deserve. "Suppose, instead of insulting each other, you tell me what the trouble is."

"Actually," Rhegorios murmured from beside him, "I wouldn't mind hearing them insult each other a while longer. It has to be more interesting than the case, don't you think?"

"Hush," Maniakes said, and then, to the first merchant, "Go ahead. You say this other chap here cheated you. Tell me how." The second merchant started to howl a protest before the first could begin to speak. Maniakes held up a hand. "You keep quiet. I promise, you'll have your turn."

The first merchant said, "I sold this whipworthy wretch three hundred pounds of smoked mutton, and he promised to pay me ten and a half goldpieces for it. But when it came time for him to cough up the money, the son of a whore dumped a pile of trashy Makuraner arkets on me and said I could either take 'em or stick 'em up my arse, because they were all I'd ever see from him."

Maniakes' head started to ache. He'd run into cases like this before. With many parts of the westlands in Makuraner hands for more than a decade, it was no wonder that silver coins stamped with the image of the King of Kings were in wide circulation thereabouts. The methodical Makuraners had even made some of the provincial mints turn out copies of their coins rather than those of Videssos.

"May I speak now, your Majesty?" the second merchant asked.

"Go ahead," Maniakes said.

"Thank you," the merchant said. "The first thing I want to tell you is that Broios here can give himself piles when he sneezes, his head is so far up his back passage. By the lord with the great and good mind, your Majesty, you must understand what money of account is. Am I right, or am I right?"

"Oh, yes," Maniakes answered.

"Thank you," the merchant said again. "When I told this chamber-pot-sniffing jackal I'd give him ten and a half goldpieces, that was money of account. What else could it be? When was the last time anybody in Serrhes saw real goldpieces? Whoever has 'em, has 'em buried where the boiler boys couldn't find 'em. We all buy and sell with silver these days. We coin our silver at twenty-four to the goldpiece, so if I'd given Broios two hundred and fifty-two pieces of silver—Videssian silver, mind you—for his smoked mutton, that would have been right and proper. You see as much, don't you, your Majesty?"

Maniakes had a good education—for a soldier. He would sooner have given himself over to a torturer than multiplied twenty-four by ten and a half in his head. But, since Broios wasn't hopping up and down like a man who needed to visit the jakes, the Avtokrator supposed the other merchant—whose name he still didn't know—had made the calculation correctly.

"If Vetranios had given me two hundred and fifty-two of our silverpieces, I wouldn't be fussing now," Broios said, thereby giving Maniakes the missing piece.

"I couldn't give you that many of our silverpieces, because I didn't have them, you ugly twit," Vetranios said. "I gave you as many as I had, and paid the rest of the scot in Makuraner arkets—I had plenty of those."

"Of course you did," Broios shouted. "All the time the boiler boys were here, you did nothing but lick their backsides."

"Me? What about you?" Vetranios swung at the other merchant, awkwardly but with great feeling. Broios swung back, with rather greater effect. A couple of Haloga guards grabbed them and pulled them away from each other.

"Gently, gentlemen, gently," Maniakes said. "Did you come before me to fight or to get this dispute settled?" The question was rhetorical, but neither of the merchants quite had the nerve to say he would sooner have fought the other. Maniakes took their silence as acquiescence. "Let us continue, then. You, Vetranios, how many Videssian silverpieces did you pay to Broios here?"

"Forty," Vetranios answered at once. "That was all the Videssian silver I had. I made up the other two hundred and twelve with arkets. They're silver, too."

"You only gave me seventy-seven of them," Broios howled.

"That's how many I was supposed to give you, you boil on the scrotum of stupidity," Vetranios retorted. The Haloga who was holding him let go to clap his hands together to applaud the originality of the insult. The merchant ignored that, saying, "It takes eleven Videssian silverpieces to make four arkets, weight for weight, so I gave you the proper payment; you're just too stupid to see it."

Maniakes would have needed pen and parchment and infinite patience to be sure whether Vetranios had done his calculations right. He decided for the time being that they were when Broios didn't protest. "This *was* the correct pay, then?" he asked the merchant who claimed he'd been defrauded.

"No, your Majesty," Broios answered. "This *would have been* the right pay, if this dung beetle who walked like a man hadn't cheated me. All the arkets he gave me were so badly clipped, there wasn't sixty arkets' worth of silver in the seventy-seven."

"Why, you lying sack of moldy tripes!" Vetranios said.

"To the ice with me if I am," Broios said, "and to the ice with you if I'm not." He handed Maniakes a jingling sack of silver. "Judge for yourself, your Majesty. The cursed cheat's clipped the coins, and kept for himself the silver that was round the rim."

Opening the sack, Maniakes examined the silver arkets it held. They were indeed badly clipped, one and all. "May I see those, your Majesty?" Vetranios asked. When Maniakes showed them to him, his face darkened in anger—or, perhaps, in a convincing facsimile thereof; Maniakes could not for the life of him tell which. The merchant said, "These aren't the coins I gave to Broios. I gave him perfectly good silver, by Phos. If anybody clipped them, he did it himself."

Now Broios turned purple, as convincingly as Vetranios had done a moment before. "By the lord with the great and good mind, your Majesty, hear how this sack of manure farts through his mouth." Vetranios tried to punch him again; the Haloga guards kept them apart.

"Each of you says the other is a liar, eh?" Maniakes said. Both merchants nodded vehemently. Maniakes continued, "Each of you says the other clipped these coins, eh?" Both men nodded again. The Avtokrator's face went stern. "Both of you no doubt know that clipping coins comes under the same law as counterfeiting and carries the same unpleasant penalties. If I have to get all the way to the bottom of this, I fear that one of you will regret it very much."

Both merchants nodded again, as vigorously as before. That surprised Maniakes. He'd expected one of them—he didn't know which—to show some sign of alarm. They had nerve, these two.

He said, "If whichever of you is lying makes a clean breast of it now, I swear by the lord with the great and good mind to make the penalty no greater than a fine of seventeen Makuraner arkets and an oath binding you never to clip coins again on penalty of further punishment."

He waited. Vetranios and Broios both shook their heads. Each glared at the other. Maniakes didn't know whether to be annoyed or intrigued at their stubbornness. He would sooner have had no trouble from the newly reoccupied westlands. That hadn't happened. He hadn't thought it would. Here, at least, was a dispute more interesting than the common sort, where truth was easy to find.

"Very well, gentlemen," he said. "For the time being, I shall keep these arkets, since they are evidence—of what sort remains to be seen—in the case between you. Come back here tomorrow at the start of the eighth hour, after the midday meal. We shall see what my sorcerer makes of this whole strange business."

Before the merchants returned the next day, Rhegorios came up to Maniakes and said, "I've done some of my own investigating in this case, cousin of mine."

"Ah?" Maniakes said. "And what did you find?"

"That Broios has a very tasty daughter—not shaped anything like him, Phos be praised." Rhegorios' hands described curves in the air. "Her name's Phosia. I think I'm in love." He let out a sigh.

"What you're in, cousin of mine," Maniakes retorted, "is heat. I'll pour a bucket of water on you, and you'll feel better."

"No, wetter," Rhegorios said. He ran his tongue across his lips. "She really is beautiful. If her father weren't a thief . . . Maybe even if her father is a thief . . ." Since Rhegorios had made similar noises in almost every town the Videssian army visited, Maniakes took no special notice of these.

Broios and Vetranios returned to the city governor's residence within a couple of minutes of each other at the eighth hour. Maniakes had looked for that; to merchants, punctuality was hardly a lesser god than Phos. What the Avtokrator had not looked for was that each of the men from Serrhes brought his own wizard with him.

Broios' champion, a certain Sozomenos, was as portly as his principal, and resembled him enough to be his cousin. Phosteinos, who represented Vetranios' interests, was by contrast thin to the point of emaciation, as if whoever had invented food had forgotten to tell him about it.

Bagdasares looked down his long nose at both of them. "Have you gentlemen—" As Maniakes had with the merchants, he sounded like a man graciously conferring the undeserved benefit of the doubt. "—been involved in this matter from the outset?"

"Of course, we have," Phosteinos said in a thin, rasping voice. "Vetranios hired me to keep Broios from cheating him, and the wretch countered by paying this charlatan here to help him go on bilking my client."

"Why don't you blow away for good?" Sozomenos demanded. Phosteinos responded with a skeletal smile. Sozomenos ignored it, turning to Maniakes and saying, "See how they misrepresent me and my principal both?" He shrugged his plump shoulders, as if to say, *What can you do?* The Avtokrator was suddenly certain each merchant had spent a great deal more on this case than the seventeen arkets' worth of silver allegedly at issue.

Bagdasares took Maniakes aside and whispered, "Your Majesty, getting to the bottom of this will be harder than we thought. These two bunglers will have muddied the waters till no one can hope to tell where the truth lies and where the lies start."

"Just go ahead," the Avtokrator answered. "Make it as impressive as you can." He looked from merchant to merchant. "Makes you wonder if we shouldn't have let the Makuraners keep this place, doesn't it?"

Bagdasares let out a loud sniff, perhaps at the notion of having to associate with wizards who, in Videssos the city, would surely have starved for lack of trade; Phosteinos looked to be on the point of starving anyhow, but Maniakes blamed that on personal asceticism rather than want of business: his robe looked expensive.

"Very well," Bagdasares said, that sniff having failed to make his sorcerous colleagues vanish. "We have to determine two things today: whether the coins Broios presented to his Majesty—" He had them in a bowl. "—are in fact those Vetranios paid to him, and, if so, who was responsible for clipping the aforesaid coins."

"We know *that*," Broios and Vetranios said in the same breath with the identical intonation. They glared at each other.

"First," Bagdasares went on as if they had not spoken, "we shall use the law of similarity to determine whether Broios is honestly representing these arkets to be the ones he received from Vetranios."

"Now see here," Sozomenos said, "how can we trust you not to have it in for Broios? When the Makuraners were here, by the good god, a little coin in the right places would make magic turn out any way the chap who was paying had in mind."

Bagdasares started to answer. Maniakes cut him off, saying, "*I* will deal with this." He glowered at the mage. "Do you think either of your clients is important enough in the scheme of things to buy off the Avtokrator of the Videssians and his chief sorcerer?"

Before Sozomenos could say anything, Phosteinos broke in with a loud, startled cackle of laughter. Sozomenos glowered at his thin colleague, then coughed a couple of times. "Put that way, probably not, your Majesty," he said.

"Good. See that you remember it." Maniakes nodded to Bagdasares. "Proceed, eminent sir. These fellows here are welcome to watch you to make sure you do nothing to favor Broios or Vetranios—not that you would—but they are not to interfere with your magic in any way." He gave Phosteinos and Sozomenos a severe look. "Is that understood, sorcerous sirs?"

Neither of the mages from Serrhes said no. Maniakes nodded again to Bagdasares. The Vaspurakaner wizard said, "The first thing I intend to do, as I said a little while ago, is to find out whether Broios presented to his Majesty coins he actually received from Vetranios. Vetranios, if you have an arket in that pouch on your belt, please hand it to Broios. Broios, you will then hand it to me."

"I just might have an arket or two," Vetranios said, chuckling. "Yes, sir, I just might." He opened the pouch and took out a shiny silver coin. "Not clipped at all, you'll note," he remarked as he handed it to Broios.

The other merchant took it from him as if it smelled bad. He handed it to Sozomenos, who in turn passed it to Bagdasares.

Bagdasares looked pained. "We'll do that again, with a new arket," he said, tossing the first one aside. Vetranios' eyes hungrily followed it. So did Broios'. So did those of both local wizards.

"No more foolishness," Bagdasares told them. "Anyone who fails to follow my instructions will be deemed to have forfeited his case."

Under Bagdasares' watchful eye, Vetranios got out another arket. This one was also unclipped, but he didn't boast about it. He gave it to Broios. Broios gave it to Bagdasares without presuming to let another wizard handle it in between.

"That's better," Bagdasares said. Maniakes hid a smile; the mage spoke with the authority of a provincial governor. The Avtokrator was suddenly thoughtful. He would need new governors for the provinces of the westlands—he would need to repair the whole system of provincial administration here, in fact. He could do much worse than Bagdasares.

Muttering to himself, the Vaspurakaner mage dropped Vetranios' arket in among the coins Broios claimed to have received from the other merchant. It clinked sweetly; the Makuraners coined little gold, but their silver was as pure as anything from a Videssian mint.

Bagdasares began to chant. Phosteinos and Sozomenos both pricked up their ears. They evidently knew the spell he was using. Maniakes watched as the mage made several swift passes over the coins. Phosteinos nodded what looked like approval of Bagdasares' technical skill.

After one final pass, Bagdasares cried out in a commanding voice. Some of the coins in the bowl began glowing with a soft, bluish radiance. Others remained simply—coins. "Your Majesty," Bagdasares said, "as you may judge for yourself, some of this money has indeed passed from Vetranios to Broios, as we see by the aid of the law of similarity. Some of the coins, however, did not take this route."

"Isn't that interesting?" Maniakes studied Broios, who seemed to be doing his best to disappear while remaining in plain sight. Gloating glee filled Vetranios' chuckle. The Avtokrator turned a mild and speculative eye on the merchant who'd brought the charges against his fellow in the first place. "Well, Broios, what have you got to say for yourself?"

"Y-y-your M-majesty, maybe I—I mixed in a few arkets that weren't from Vetranios by—by mistake." Broios' voice firmed. "Yes, that's it. I must have done it by mistake."

Vetranios walked over to look at the arkets more closely. "Likely tell," he jeered. "You can see that all of these 'mistaken' coins are clipped." He struck a pose so overblown, Maniakes wondered if he'd gotten it from some mime in a Midwinter's Day troupe.

Broios said, "They're not the only ones that are clipped, though, by Phos!" He came up to the bowl and pointed to some of the shining coins. "Look at that arket there, and that one—and that one. That one's cut so bad, you can hardly see the King of Kings' face at all. They were like that when I got 'em, too."

"Liar!" Vetranios shouted. He turned to Maniakes. "You hear with your own ears, you see with your own eyes, what a liar he is. I don't think there's any bigger liar in the whole Empire than Broios."

"Liar yourself," Broios retorted. "You have your wizard here, your Majesty. He can show you who stuck the silver from the rims of these arkets into his pouch."

"Yes, why don't you go ahead and show me that, Bagdasares?" Maniakes said. "I confess, by now I'm curious. And nothing about this case would surprise me any more, except perhaps finding an honest man anywhere in it."

Phosteinos stirred. "Your Majesty, I resent the imputation. You have proved nothing illicit about my actions."

"That's true," Maniakes admitted, and the scrawny wizard preened. Then the Avtokrator brought him down to earth: "I haven't proved anything yet." That got a laugh from Sozomenos, a laugh that cut off very sharply when Maniakes glanced over at the sorcerer who'd been helping Broios.

At a nod from Maniakes, Bagdasares handed Vetranios a small sharp knife and said, "I presume you have in your pouch yet another unclipped arket." Most unhappily, the merchant nodded. "Excellent," Bagdasares declared. "Be so good as to trim the silver from the edges, then, that we may have a comparison against which to set these arkets in the bowl."

Vetranios looked as if he would sooner have stuck the knife into Bagdasares. He shot Phosteinos a hunted glance. Almost imperceptibly, the emaciated mage shook his head: he could do nothing—or, more likely, nothing Bagdasares wouldn't detect. Vetranios deflated like a popped pig's bladder. "Never mind," he mumbled. "You don't need to go through the rigmarole. I clipped some of those arkets—*just like every other merchant around.*" Now he might have wanted to stab Broios.

Broios took no notice of his hate-filled glare. "Who's the biggest liar in the Empire now?" he said, for all the world like one small boy scoring a point against another.

"You're both wrong," Maniakes said. "Neither one of you knows the biggest liar in the Empire. His name is Tzikas."

Broios pointed at Vetranios. "*He* knows this Tzikas. I've heard him talk about the fellow, plenty of times."

Suddenly, everyone in the room was staring at Vetranios. "So you know Tzikas, do you?" Maniakes said in a soft voice. "Tell me about Tzikas, Vetranios. When did you see him last, for starters?"

Vetranios knew something was wrong, but not what, nor how much. Serrhes was far from Videssos the city, and had been in Makuraner hands since the earliest days of Genesios' disastrous reign. The merchant answered, "Why, it must have been about three weeks before you came, your Majesty. He's been through the town now and again, these past few years. I've sold him this and that, and we've drunk wine together every now and then. That's about the size of it, I'd say."

Maniakes studied not him but Broios. If Vetranios' enemy accepted that tale, it was likely to be true. If, on the other hand, Broios found more to say . . . But Broios did not find more to say. Maniakes didn't know whether to be glad or disappointed.

"I can understand why you wouldn't like having a Videssian working for the boiler boys," Vetranios said, sympathy oozing from him like sticky sap from a cut spruce. "He's not the only one, though."

"He's the only one who's tried to overthrow me," Maniakes said. "He's the only one who's tried to murder me. He's the only one who's betrayed both sides in this war more times than I can count. He's the only one who's—" He made a disgusted gesture. "Why go on?"

Broios and Vetranios were both staring at him. He could see exactly what was going on behind Broios' eyes as the merchant realized he should have done a more thorough job of slandering Vetranios. He could also see Broios realizing that now was too late, and growing furious at his own lapse.

"Why did Tzikas come here?" Maniakes asked Vetranios.

"I don't know for certain," the merchant answered. "He spent a lot of time closeted with Tegin, I know that much. It had something to do with the squabbles the Makuraners are having, didn't it? They both favored Sharbaraz King of Kings, may his days be long and his realm increase." He spoke the honorific formula without noticing he'd done so. Serrhes *had* been in Makuraner hands a long time.

Letting that ride, Maniakes said, "So you know about whom Tzikas favored, do you?" Vetranios gave a tiny nod, as if expecting hot pincers and thumbscrews to follow upon the admission. Maniakes asked the next question: "What exactly did he say to you when the two of you talked?"

"Let's see." Vetranios was ready to cooperate freely, if for no better reason than to keep himself from having to cooperate any other way. "He bought ten pounds of the smoked mutton I had of this wretch here." He pointed to Broios. "Then he said something about how hard life had been lately, and how nobody appreciated his true worth. I told him I did. For some reason, he thought that was funny."

Maniakes thought it was funny, though he didn't say so. If a cheat of a merchant was the only one who appreciated Tzikas, what did that say about the overversatile Videssian officer? Idly, the Avtokrator asked, "When you sold him the ten pounds of mutton, how badly did you bilk him?"

"Not a barleycorn's worth," Vetranios answered, wide-eyed. "He killed a man here who gave him short weight last year."

"I remember that!" Broios exclaimed: such a calamity had obviously created a lasting impression on the merchants of Serrhes. "I didn't know the name of the fellow who did it."

Thoughtfully, Bagdasares said, "Ten pounds of smoked mutton? That's traveler's food, something somebody would want if he was going on a long journey."

"So it is." Maniakes was thoughtful, too. "The timing strikes me odd, though. You're sure he was here only three weeks before I came to Serrhes, Vetranios? It wasn't longer ago than that?"

"By the lord with the great and good mind I swear it, your Majesty." To emphasize his words, Vetranios sketched Phos' sun-circle over his heart.

"I wish you'd said longer." Maniakes wondered if Vetranios, like a lot of merchants, would change his story to suit his customer better. But the plump trader shook his head and drew the sun-sign again. Maniakes drummed the fingers of one hand on a tabletop. "It doesn't fit. He wouldn't have dawdled here in the westlands so long, not if he was all hotfoot to warn Sharbaraz. Phos, he could have gone to Mashiz and come back here in that time. But why on earth would he do that?"

It was a rhetorical question. He hoped Bagdasares, one of the mages from Serrhes, or one of the merchants would answer it nonetheless. No one did. Instead, Bagdasares added more questions of his own: "And if he did do it, what need would he have for smoked mutton? He could have stayed here with Tegin and gone west with the Makuraner garrison. We'd be none the wiser."

"I didn't see him here after he bought the mutton from me," Vetranios said. "If he'd stayed with the garrison, I might not have seen him, but I think I would."

Phosteinos coughed to draw attention to himself and then said, "I also know this man somewhat. I agree with my principal in this matter: the visit to Serrhes was but a brief one."

Maniakes' glance toward the local wizard was anything but mild and friendly. "You know Tzikas, eh?" he asked. Phosteinos nodded. The Avtokrator interrogated him as he had with Vetranios: "Did you ever perform any magical service for him?" Phosteinos nodded again. Maniakes pounced: "And what sort of service was that, sirrah?"

"Why, to use the laws of similarity and contagion to help him find one of a pair of fancy spurs early this year, your Majesty," Phosteinos answered.

"Nothing else?" Maniakes' voice was cold.

"Why, no," Phosteinos said "I don't understand why—"

"Because when the son of a whore tried to murder me, he did it with a wizard's help," the Avtokrator interrupted. Phosteinos' eyes went big in his pinched face. Maniakes pressed on: "Now, are you sure this was the only sorcerous service he ever had of you?"

Phosteinos was as eager to swear by Phos as Vetranios had been. Maniakes reckoned both those oaths as being worth only so much: a man might easily prefer risking Skotos' ice in the world to come to the Avtokrator's wrath in the world that was here. But then Sozomenos spoke up: "May it please your Majesty, I have no great love for my scrawny colleague here, but in all our years of acquaintance I have never known him to work magic to harm a man's health, let alone seek his death."

To Bagdasares, Maniakes said, "I'd sooner have your word on that than the word of someone I don't know if I can trust."

Sozomenos looked affronted. Maniakes didn't care. Bagdasares looked troubled. That worried the Avtokrator. Bagdasares said, "Judging a wizard's truthfulness by sorcerous means is different from gauging that of an ordinary man. Mages have too many subtle ways to confuse the results of such examinations."

"I was afraid you were going to say something like that," Maniakes said unhappily. He studied Phosteinos and Sozomenos. Both of them fairly radiated candor; had they been lamps, he would have had to shield his eyes against their glow. What Bagdasares told him meant he would have to gauge whether they were telling the truth by his usual, mundane complement of senses—either that or try to drag truth out of them by torture. He wasn't fond of torture; under the lash or more ingenious means of interrogation, people were too apt to say whatever they thought likeliest to make the pain stop.

Reluctantly, he decided he believed the two sorcerers from Serrhes. That left one last thing to do. Turning to Broios and Vetranios, he said, "And now to deal with the two of you."

Both merchants started. Both, Maniakes guessed, had hoped he'd forgotten about them. "What—what will you do with us, your Majesty?" Broios asked, his voice trembling.

"I don't know which of you is worse," Maniakes said. "You're both liars and cheats." He stroked his beard while he thought, then suddenly smiled. Broios and Vetranios quailed under that smile. Maniakes took an ignoble but very real pleasure in passing sentence: "First, you are fined fifty goldpieces each—or their weight in *perfect* silver—for tampering with the currency. The money is due tomorrow. And second, both of you shall be sent out to the center of the square here between the city governor's residence and Phos' holy temple. There in the square, a Haloga will give each of you a sturdy kick in the arse. If you can't get honesty through your heads, maybe we can send it up from the other direction."

"But, your Majesty, publicly humiliating us will make us laughingstocks in the city," Vetranios protested.

"Good," Maniakes said. "Don't you think you deserve to be?"

Neither merchant answered that. If they agreed, they humiliated themselves. If they disagreed, they contradicted the Avtokrator of the Videssians. Given those choices, silence was better.

Maniakes escorted them out of the room where Bagdasares had performed his sorcery. When he told the guardsmen outside about the sentence, they shouted approval and almost came to blows in their eagerness to be the two who would deliver the kicks.

The Avtokrator came back into the chamber. He found Bagdasares talking shop with Phosteinos and Sozomenos. That convinced him the wizards shared his view of the two merchants from Serrhes. To those two, he said, "I presume you were doing nothing to threaten me. Because of that, you may go."

They thanked him and left in a hurry, giving him no chance to change his mind. "What was Tzikas doing here so recently?" Bagdasares asked again as soon as they were out of earshot.

"To the ice with me if I know," Maniakes answered. "It makes no more sense to me now than it did when we first found out about it." He scowled at Bagdasares even more fiercely than he had at Vetranios and Broios. "But I'm sure of one thing."

"What's that?" Bagdasares asked.

"It makes sense to Tzikas."

For as long as Maniakes stayed in Serrhes, he heard no more from his squabbling merchants. That suited him fine; it meant they were on their best behavior. The other alternative was that it meant they were cheating so well, no one was catching them and complaining. Maniakes supposed that was possible, but he didn't believe it: neither Broios nor Vetranios was likely to be that good a thief.

Rhegorios did keep sighing over Phosia. Maniakes kept threatening him with cold water. After a while, his cousin fell silent.

As long as Abivard had stayed in the Videssian westlands, he'd sent streams of messengers to Maniakes. Once he crossed back into territory long Makuraner, though, the stream shrank to a trickle. Maniakes worried that something had gone wrong.

"What's likely wrong," Rhegorios said, one day when the Avtokrator had been fretting more than usual, "is that Tegin has got between us and Abivard. The little garrison force couldn't do anything much against Abivard, mind you, but it's big enough to pick off a courier or two."

"You're right about that, of course," Maniakes said. "And you're probably right that that's what's causing the trouble. I should have thought of it for myself." Thinking of everything was part of what went with the Avtokrator's job. That it was impossible didn't make it any less necessary. Every time Maniakes missed a point, he felt bad for days.

He cheered up when a rider did come from out of the west. The fellow wore the full panoply of a Makuraner boiler boy; either he'd worried about running into Tegin's men or about running into Maniakes'. His armor clattered about him as he prostrated himself before the Avtokrator of the Videssians.

"Majesty," he said, rising with noisy grace, "know that the forces led by Abivard the new sun of Makuran have encountered those foolishly loyal to Sharbaraz Pimp of Pimps in the Land of the Thousand Cities. Know further that Abivard's forces have the victory."

"Good news!" Maniakes exclaimed. "I'm always glad to hear good news."

The messenger nodded. His chain-mail veil rattled. Above that veil, all Maniakes could see of the man himself were his eyes. They snapped with excitement. "We have Sharbaraz on the run now, Majesty," he said. "A good part of his army came over to ours, which made him flee back to Mashiz."

"That's better than good news," Maniakes said. "Press hard and he's yours. Once his forces start crumbling, they'll go like mud brick in the rain."

"Even so, or so we hope," the messenger said. "When I was detached to come east to you, the field force was making ready to follow Sharbaraz's fugitives to the capital."

"Press hard," Maniakes repeated. "If you don't, you give Sharbaraz a chance to recover." From behind the messenger's veil came an unmistakable chuckle. "What's funny?" the Avtokrator asked.

"Majesty, you speak my language well," the messenger answered. Maniakes knew he was politely stretching a point, but let him do it. The fellow went on, "No one, though, would ever take you for a Makuraner, not by the way you say the name of the man Abivard will overthrow."

Maniakes proved his command of the Makuraner tongue left something to be desired by needing a moment to sort through that and figure out what the messenger meant. "Did I say *Sarbaraz* again?" he demanded, and the man nodded. Maniakes snapped his fingers in chagrin. "Oh, a pestilence! I've spent a lot of time learning how to pronounce that strange sound you use. His name is . . . is . . . *Sarbaraz!*" He started to raise a hand in triumph, then realized he'd failed again. Really angry now, he concentrated hard. "Sar . . . Sar . . . *Shar*baraz! There."

"Well done!" the messenger said. "Most of you hissing, squeaking Videssians never do manage to get that one right, try as you will."

"You can tell a Makuraner by the way he speaks Videssian, too," Maniakes said, to which the messenger nodded. Maniakes went on, "You haven't—or Abivard hasn't—by any chance got word of where Tzikas is lurking these days?"

"The traitor? No, indeed, Majesty. I wish I did know, though I'd tell Abivard before I told you. He's offering a good-sized reward for word of him and a bigger one for his head."

"So am I," Maniakes said.

"Are you?" The Makuraner's eyes widened. "How much?" His people claimed to scorn Videssians as a race of merchants and shopkeepers. Maniakes' experience was that the men of Makuran were no more immune to the lure of gold and silver than anyone else. And when Maniakes told him how much he might earn for finding Tzikas, he whistled softly. "If I hear anything, I'll tell you and not Abivard."

"Tell whichever of us has the best chance of catching the renegade," Maniakes said. "If he is caught thanks to you, get word to me and I'll make good the difference between Abivard's reward and mine, I promise. Tell all your friends, too, and tell them to tell their friends."

"I'll do that," the messenger promised.

"Good," Maniakes said. "If I had to guess, I'd say he's somewhere not far from here, but I know that could be wildly wrong." He explained what he'd learned from Vetranios and Phosteinos.

"He is more likely to be here than he is in the Land of the Thousand Cities or in Mashiz, I think," the messenger said. "Here, at least, he can open his mouth without betraying himself every time he does it."

"When Tzikas opens his mouth, he betrays other people, not himself," Maniakes said, which made the messenger laugh. "You think I'm joking," the Avtokrator told him. He was, but only to a degree. And the Makuraner's comments made him thoughtful. If Tzikas wanted to disappear in the westlands, he could. Maniakes had found it impossible to imagine a Tzikas who wanted to disappear. He admitted to himself he might have been wrong.

He gave the messenger a goldpiece, warned him about Tegin's small force of men still loyal to Sharbaraz, and sent him back to Abivard with congratulations. That done, he went outside the city governor's residence instead of getting on to the next order of business in Serrhes.

Everything looked normal. A few peasants from the surrounding countryside were selling sheep and pigs and ducks. Some other peasants, having made their sales, were buying pots and hatchets and other things they couldn't get on their farms. One of them was showing a harlot some money. The two went off together. If the peasant's wife ever found out about that, Maniakes could think of at least one thing the fellow wasn't likely to get on the farm.

So many people: tall, short, bald, hairy, young, old. And, if Tzikas had decided to disappear instead of trying to get his revenge, he might have been about one out of three of the men. The thought was disquieting, freighted as it was with a heavy burden of anticlimax.

Maniakes had needed to hold off the Kubratoi and Makuraners. He'd done that. He'd needed to find a way to get the Makuraners out of the westlands. Thanks to some unwitting help from Sharbaraz, he'd done that, too. And now, either Abivard would beat Sharbaraz or the other way round in the Makuraner civil war he'd helped create. Whichever happened, he'd know, and handle what came next accordingly.

Sharp, decisive answers—like anyone, he was fond of those. He already had ambiguity in his life: he'd never found out, and doubted he ever would find out, what had happened to his brother Tatoules. He knew what was most likely to have happened to him, but that wasn't the same.

Getting rid of Tzikas would be a sharp, decisive answer. Even knowing what had happened to Tzikas, regardless of whether he'd had anything to do with it, would be a sharp, decisive answer. Never learning for certain whether Tzikas was alive or dead, or where he was or what he was doing if he was alive . . . Maniakes didn't care for that notion at all.

He understood only too well how dangerous ambiguity could be when connected to Tzikas. He might be riding down a street in Videssos the city ten years from now, having seen or heard nothing of the renegade in all that time, having nearly forgotten him, only to be pierced by an arrow from a patient enemy who had not forgotten *him*. Or he might spend those ten years worrying about Tzikas every day when the wretch was long since dead.

"No way to know," he muttered. A writer of romances would not have approved. Everything in romances always came out neat and tidy. Avtokrators in romances were never foolish—unless they were wicked rulers being overthrown by someone who would do the job right. Maniakes snorted. He'd done exactly that, but, somehow, it hadn't kept him from remaining a human being.

"No matter how much I want the son of a whore dead, I may never live to see it." That was another matter, and made him as discontented as the first. If Tzikas chose obscurity, he could cheat the headsman. Would obscurity be punishment enough? It might have to be, no matter how little Maniakes cared for the notion.

He kicked at the dirt, angry at himself and Tzikas both. This should have been the greatest triumph of his career, the greatest triumph any Avtokrator had enjoyed since the civil wars the Empire had suffered a century and a half before cost it most of its eastern provinces. Instead of being able to enjoy the triumph, he was still spending far too much of his time and energy fretting over the loose end Tzikas had become.

He knew one certain cure for that. As fast as he could, he went back to the city governor's residence. "The Empress, your Majesty?" a servant said. "I believe she's upstairs in the sewing room."

Lysia wasn't sewing when Maniakes got up there. She and some of the serving women of the household were spinning flax into thread and, by the laughter that came from the sewing room as Maniakes walked down the hall toward it, using the work as an excuse for chat and gossip.

"Is something wrong?" Lysia asked when she saw him. She set the spindle down on the projecting shelf of her belly. The serving women exclaimed in alarm: he wasn't supposed to be there at this time of day.

"No," he answered, which was on the whole true, his worries notwithstanding. He amplified that: "And even if it were, I know how to make it better."

He walked over to her and helped her rise from the stool on which she sat: the baby wouldn't wait much longer. Then, standing slightly to one side of her so he wouldn't have to lean so far over that great belly, he did a careful and thorough job of kissing her.

A couple of the serving women giggled. Several more murmured back and forth to one another. He noticed all that only distantly. Some men, he'd heard, lost desire for their wives when those wives were great with child. Some of the serving women had made eyes at him, wondering if he felt like—and perhaps trying to provoke him into feeling like—amusing himself elsewhere while Lysia neared the end of her pregnancy. He'd noticed—he'd never lost his eye for pretty women—but he hadn't done anything about it.

"Well!" Lysia said when the kiss finally ended. She rubbed at her upper lip, where his mustache must have tickled her. "What was that in aid of?"

"Because I felt like doing it," Maniakes answered. "I've seen how many layers the bureaucracy in the Empire has, but I've never yet seen anything that says I have to submit a requisition before I draw a kiss from my wife."

"I wouldn't be surprised if there was such a form," Lysia answered, "but you can probably get away without using it even if there is. Being Avtokrator has to count for something, don't you think?"

If that wasn't a hint, it would do till a real one came along. Maniakes kissed her again, even more thoroughly than he had before. He was so involved in what he was doing, in fact, that he was taken by surprise when he looked up at the end of the kiss and discovered the serving women had left the room. "Where did they go?" he said foolishly.

"It doesn't matter," Lysia said, "as long as they're gone." This time, she kissed him.

A little later, they went back to their bedchamber. With her so very pregnant, making love was an awkward business. When they joined, she lay on her right side facing away from him. Not only was that a position in which she was more comfortable than most others, it was also one of the relatively few where they *could* join without her belly getting in the way.

The baby inside her kicked as enthusiastically then as at any other time, and managed to be distracting enough to keep her from enjoying things as much as she might have done. "Don't worry about it," she told Maniakes afterward. "This happened before, remember?"

"I wasn't worried, not really," he said, and set his hand on the smooth curve of her hip. "We'll have to make up for things after the baby's born, that's all. We've done that before, too."

"Yes, I know," Lysia answered. "That's probably why I keep getting pregnant so fast."

"I've heard the one does have something to do with the other, yes," Maniakes said solemnly. Lysia snorted and poked him in the ribs. They both laughed. He didn't think about Tzikas at all. Better yet, he didn't notice he wasn't thinking about Tzikas at all.

✦ XII

Having settled affairs in Serrhes, Maniakes rode west with about half his army, so as to be in a position to do something quickly if the civil war in Makuran required. He sent small parties even farther west, to seize the few sources of good water that lay in the desert between Videssos' restored western frontier and the Land of the Thousand Cities.

"See, here you are, invading Makuran the proper way, the way it should be done, instead of sneaking up from the sea," Rhegorios said.

"If we didn't have control of the sea, we wouldn't be here on land now," Maniakes said. "Besides, what could be better than coming up from an unexpected direction?"

"The last time I asked a question like that, the girl I asked it of slapped my face," his cousin said.

Maniakes snorted. "I daresay you deserved it, too. When we go back to Videssos the city, I'm going to have to marry you off, let one woman worry about you, and put all the others in the Empire out of their fear."

"If I'm as fearsome as that, brother-in-law of mine, do you think being married will make any difference to me?" Rhegorios asked.

"I don't know if it will make any difference to you," Maniakes said. "I expect it will make a good deal of difference to Lysia, though. If you tomcat around while you're single, you get one kind of name for yourself. If you keep on tomcatting around after you're married, you get a name for yourself, too, but not one you'd want to have."

"You know how to hit below the belt," Rhegorios said. "Considering what we're talking about, that's the best way to put things, isn't it? And you're right, worse luck: I wouldn't want Lysia angry at me."

"I can understand that." Maniakes looked around. "I wonder if we could put a town anywhere around here, to help seal the border."

"Aye, why not?" Rhegorios said. "We can call it Frontier, if you like." He waved a hand, as if he were a mage casting a spell. "There! Can't you just see it? Walls and towers and a grand temple to Phos across the square from the *hypasteos'* residence, with barracks close by."

And Maniakes *could* see the town in his mind's eye. For a moment, it seemed as real as any of the cities in the westlands he'd liberated from the Makuraners. It was, in fact, as if he *had* liberated the hypothetical town of Frontier from the Makuraners, and spent a couple of days in that *hypasteos'* residence digging through the usual sordid tales of treason, collaboration, and heresy.

But then Rhegorios waved again, and said, "Can't you see the dust-herders bringing their flocks into the market for coughing—I mean, shearing? Can't you see the rock farmers selling their crops to the innkeepers to make soup with? Can't you see the priests of Phos, out there blessing the scorpions and the tarantulas? Can't you see the vultures circling overhead, laughing at the men who set a town three weeks away from anything that looked like water?"

Maniakes stared at him, stared at the desert through which they were traveling, and then started to laugh. "Well, all right," he said. "I think I take your point. Maybe I could put a town not too far from here, somewhere closer to water—though we're less than a day from it, not three weeks—to help seal the border. Does that meet with your approval, your exalted Sevastosship, sir?"

Rhegorios was laughing, too. "That suits me fine. But if I'm going to be difficult, wouldn't you rather I had fun being difficult, instead of looking as if I'd just had a poker rammed up my arse?" He suddenly assumed an expression serious to the point of being doomful.

"Do you know what you look like?" Maniakes looked around to make sure no one could overhear him and his cousin, then went on, "You look like Immodios, that's what."

"I've been called a lot of hard names in my time, cousin of mine, but that's—" Rhegorios donned the stern expression again, and then, in lieu of a mirror, felt of his own face. As he did so, his expression melted into one of comically exaggerated horror and dismay. "By the good god, you're right!"

He and Maniakes laughed again. "That feels so good," Maniakes said. "We spent a good many years there where nothing was funny at all."

"Didn't we, though?" Rhegorios said. "Amazing how getting half your country back again can improve your outlook on life."

"Isn't it?" Instead of examining the ground from which the town of Frontier would never sprout, Maniakes looked west toward Makuran. "Haven't heard from Abivard in a while," he said. "I wonder how he's doing in the fight against Sharbaraz."

"I'm not worrying about it," Rhegorios said. "As far as I'm concerned, they can hammer away at each other till they're both worn out. Abivard's a good fellow—I don't deny that for a moment—and Sharbaraz is a right bastard, but they're both Makuraners, if you know what I mean. If they're fighting among themselves, they'll be too busy to give us any grief."

"Which is, I agree, not the worst thing in the world," Maniakes said.

"No, not for us, it's not." Rhegorios' grin was predatory. "About time, don't you think, some bad things happen to the Makuraners? Things ought to even out in this world, where we can see them happen, not just in the next, where Phos triumphs at the end of days."

"That would be fine, wouldn't it?" Maniakes' tone was wistful. "For a long time, I wondered if we'd ever see things even out with the boiler boys."

Rhegorios pursued his own thought: "For instance, we might even be able to cast down that villain of an Etzilios and do something about the Kubratoi. The good god knows what they've been doing to us all these years."

"Oh, wouldn't that be sweet?" Maniakes breathed. "Wouldn't that be fine, to get our own back from that liar and cheat?"

The memory of the way Etzilios had deceived him, almost captured him, and routed his army came flooding back, as if the years between that disaster and the present were transparent as glass. The Makuraners had done Videssos more harm, but they'd never inflicted on him a humiliation to match that one.

"We did give him some," the Avtokrator said. "After our fleet crushed the monoxyla, the way he fled from the city was sweet as honey to watch. But he's still on his throne, and his nomads are still dangerous." He sighed. "Getting the westlands back in one piece counts for more, I suppose. I rather wish it didn't, if you know what I mean."

"Oh, yes," Rhegorios said. "The pleasure of doing what you want to do—especially of paying back somebody who's done you wrong—can be more delicious than just doing what needs doing."

"That's it exactly." Maniakes nodded. "But I'm going to do what needs doing." His grin was wry. "I'd better be careful. I'm in danger of growing up."

The Makuraner heavy cavalryman dismounted, walked toward Maniakes in a jingle of armor, prostrated himself before the Avtokrator, and then, with a considerable display of strength, rose smoothly despite the weight of iron he wore. "What news?" Maniakes demanded. "Is Sharbaraz overthrown?" He would have paid a pound of gold to hear that, but didn't tell the boiler boy in front of him. If the word was there, that would be time enough for rewards.

Regretfully, Abivard's messenger shook his head. "Majesty, he is not, though we drive his forces back toward Mashiz and though more and more men from the garrisons in the Land of the Thousand Cities declare for us each day. That is not why the new sun of Makuran sent me to you."

"Well, why did he send you, then?" Maniakes said, trying to hide his disappointment. "What news besides victory was worth the journey?"

"Majesty, I shall tell you," the Makuraner replied. "In the Land of the Thousand Cities, in a barren tract far from any canal, we found another of the blasphemous shrines such as the one you described to my master." The man's eyes were fierce behind the chain-mail veil that hid the lower part of his face. "I saw this abomination for myself. Sharbaraz may act as if he is the God in this life, but the God shall surely drop him into the Void in the next."

"I burned the one my men came across," Maniakes said. "What did Abivard do with this one?"

"The first thing he did was send every squadron, every regiment of his army through the place, so all his men could see with their own eyes what kind of foe they were facing," the messenger said.

"That was a good idea," Maniakes said. "I used the one we discovered to rally my men's spirits, too."

"If a blasphemy is so plain that even a Videssian can see it, how did it escape the notice of the King of Kings?" the messenger asked rhetorically. He failed to notice the casual contempt for Videssians that informed his words. Instead of getting angry, Maniakes wondered how often he'd offended Makuraners without ever knowing it. The messenger finished, "Once everyone had seen that the Pimp of Pimps reckoned himself the God of Gods, the shrine was indeed put to the torch."

"Best thing that could have happened," Maniakes agreed. "Pity Abivard couldn't have taken Sharbaraz's soldiers through the place instead of his own. I wonder how many would have fought for Sharbaraz after they saw that. Not many, I'd wager."

"Aye, that would have been most marvelous." The Makuraner sighed in regret. "In any case, Majesty, the balance of this message is that, while Abivard the new sun of Makuran did not reckon you a liar when you told him of a shrine of this sort, he did reserve judgment until he saw such with his own eyes. Now he knows you were correct in every particular, and apologizes for having doubted you."

"For one thing, he hid the doubt very well," Maniakes replied. "For another, I can hardly blame him for keeping some, because I had trouble believing in a place like that even after I saw it."

"I understand, Majesty," the messenger said. "If the God be gracious, the next you hear from us will be when the wretch has been ousted from the capital and the cleansing begun."

"I hope that news comes soon," Maniakes said, whereupon the messenger saluted him and rode back toward the west. Maniakes smiled at the Makuraner's armored back. So Abivard intended to cleanse Mashiz, or perhaps only the court at Mashiz, did he? That struck Maniakes as a project liable to go on for years. He liked the idea. As long as the Makuraners were concentrating on their internal affairs, they would have a hard time endangering Videssos.

When he told Rhegorios of the message from Abivard, his cousin's smile might almost have been that of a priest granted a beatific vision of Phos. "The boiler boys can cleanse, and then countercleanse, and then countercountercleanse, for all of me," the Sevastos said. "They're welcome to it. Meanwhile, I expect we'll head back to Serrhes."

"Yes, I suppose so." Maniakes gave Rhegorios a sharp look. "You're not usually one who wants to go backward."

His cousin coughed. "Well—er—that is—" he began, and went no further.

Seeing Rhegorios tongue-tied astonished Maniakes—but not for long. He thought back to the conversation he'd had with his cousin not long before. "Have you found a woman there?"

Knowing his cousin's attitude, he hadn't intended the question as more than a probe. But then Rhegorios said, "I may have."

Maniakes had all he could do not to double over with laughter. When someone like Rhegorios said he might have found a woman, and especially when he said it in a tone of voice suggesting he didn't want to admit it, even to himself, it was likely he'd fallen hard. Maybe Maniakes wouldn't have to worry about his tomcatting through the Empire, after all. "Who is she?"

Rhegorios looked as if he wished he'd kept his mouth shut. "If you must know," he said, "she's that Phosia I was telling you about, Broios' daughter."

"The larcenous merchant?" Now Maniakes did laugh. "If it hadn't been for you, I'd never have known he had a daughter."

"I make a point of investigating these things." Rhegorios did his best to sound dignified. His best was none too good. "The lord with the great and good mind be praised, she takes after her mother in almost everything—certainly in looks."

"Well, all right. All I can say is, she'd better." Thinking of Broios still irked Maniakes. "She doesn't want to slide a knife between your ribs because I had her father's backside kicked in public?"

"Hasn't shown any signs of it," Rhegorios said.

"Well, good enough, then." Maniakes reached out and gave his cousin an indulgent poke in the shoulder. "Enjoy yourself while we're in Serrhes, and you can find yourself another friend, or another cartload of friends, when we get back to Videssos the city."

By everything Maniakes knew of his cousin, that should have made Rhegorios laugh and come back with a gibe of his own. Instead, the Sevastos said, "I may have my father talk with Broios when we get back to the city."

If Maniakes had been startled before, he gaped now. "What?" he said again. "I've never heard you talk like that before." He wondered if his cousin had taken their earlier conversation to heart and resolved to marry. Then he wondered if this Phosia, or maybe Broios himself, had prevailed upon their wizard to work love magic on—or maybe against—Rhegorios. He would have found that easier to believe had such sorcery been easier to use. Passion made magic unreliable.

"Maybe it's time, that's all," Rhegorios said. His wry grin was very much his own. "And maybe, too, it's just that I'm fascinated by the idea of a girl who says no. I don't see that every day, I'll tell you."

"Mm, I believe you," Maniakes said. His cousin was handsome, good-natured, and the man of second-highest rank in the Empire of Videssos. The first two would have been plenty by themselves to find him lots of female friends. The prospect of the riches and power his position added didn't hurt his persuasiveness, either.

"I think she's what I want," Rhegorios said.

Maniakes wondered if she was what he wanted precisely because she hadn't let him have her. Was her reluctance altogether her own? The Avtokrator doubted Broios was clever enough to come up with such a scheme. He knew nothing about the merchant's wife, though. Not trusting his own judgment, he asked, "Have you told Lysia about this?"

"Some if it," Rhegorios answered. "Not the whole."

"I think you should do that," Maniakes said. "She will have a clearer view about Phosia and her family than either one of us. She's not assotted with the girl, as you are." He ignored his cousin's indignant look. "And she's—not quite—so worried about the Empire as a whole as I am."

"By the good god, though, she's my sister," Rhegorios said.

"How can I talk about matters between man and woman with my sister? It wouldn't be decent."

"For one thing, I daresay she has more sense than either one of us," Maniakes replied. "And, for another, if you can't talk about these things with her, with whom can you talk of them? I know what you were thinking of doing, I'll wager, and never mind this yattering about having Uncle Symvatios talk with Broios: go ahead and marry this girl and then tell me about it afterward, when I couldn't do anything. Am I right or am I wrong?"

Rhegorios tried for dignified silence. Since he wasn't long on dignity under most circumstances, nor, for that matter, on silence, Maniakes concluded he'd read his cousin rightly.

"We'll be heading back to Serrhes soon—as you guessed, cousin of mine," the Avtokrator said. "It'll have to do as our frontier outpost for now. And while we're waiting there to hear from Abivard, we won't have anything better to do than sort through this whole business. Doesn't that put your mind at ease?"

"No," Rhegorios snarled. "You're taking all the fun out of it. The way you're treating it, it's a piece of imperial business first and a romance afterward."

Maniakes stared again. "Cousin of mine, everything we do is imperial business first and whatever else it is afterward."

"Oh, really?" Rhegorios at his most polite was Rhegorios at his most dangerous. "Then how, cousin of mine your Majesty brother-in-law of mine, did you happen to end up wed to your own first cousin? If you tell me that was good imperial business, by Phos, I'll eat my helmet. And if you get to have what you want for no better reason than that you want it, why don't I?"

Maniakes opened his mouth, then shut it again in a hurry on realizing he had no good answer. After a bit of thought, he tried again: "The one thing I can always be sure of with Lysia is that she'll never betray me. Can you say the same about this woman here?"

"No," Rhegorios admitted. "But can you say you wouldn't have fallen in love with Lysia if you weren't so sure of that?"

"Right now, I can't say anything about might-have-beens," Maniakes answered. "All I can say is that when we get back to Serrhes, we'll see what we have there, I expect."

✦   ✦   ✦

After a while out in the semidesert that marked the Empire's western frontier, Serrhes seemed almost as great a metropolis as Videssos the city, a telling measure of how barren that western country really was. Maniakes did not invite Broios and Phosia and her mother to dine with him right away. Instead, he did some quiet poking around.

So did Lysia, who said, "What your men don't hear, my serving women will, in the marketplace or from a shopkeeper or from a shopkeeper's wife."

"That's fine," Maniakes said. "You're right, of course; women do hear any number of things men miss." He grinned. "Some of those things, some of the time, might even be true."

Lysia glared at him, showing more anger than she probably felt. "You know I'll remember that," she said. "You know I'll make you pay for it one of these days, too. So why did you say it?"

"If I give you something you can sharpen your knives on," he said, as innocently as he could, "you won't have to go out looking for something on your own." The dirty look he got for that was more sincere than the earlier one. He went on, "You never have said much about what you think of your brother's choice. Does that mean what I'm afraid it means?"

Lysia shook her head. "No, not really. It means I paid no attention to this Phosia when we were here before." Now she sank a barb of her own, aimed not so much at Maniakes in particular as at his half of the human race: "A pretty face is less likely to distract me."

"Less likely to distract you than what?" he asked, and then held up a hasty hand. "Don't answer that. I don't think I want to know." By the dangerous gleam that had come into his wife's eye, he knew he'd changed course in the nick of time.

Sure enough, gossip about Phosia, about Broios, and about Broios' wife—whose name was Zosime—began pouring in. A lot of it had to do with the way Broios ran his business. Vetranios had been able to cheat him, but he'd evidently managed to be on the giving as opposed to the receiving end of that a good many times himself. Maniakes didn't quite know how much weight to give such reports. A lot of merchants thought first of themselves and then, if at all, of those with whom they dealt. He couldn't gauge whether Broios was typical of the breed or typical of the breed at its worst.

His men and Lysia's serving women also brought in a lot of reports claiming Broios had been hand in glove with the Makuraners while they held Serrhes. Again, he had trouble deciding what those meant. If Broios hadn't cooperated with the occupiers to a certain degree, he wouldn't have been able to stay afloat. No one said he'd betrayed any of his fellows, and the Avtokrator had consistently forgiven those who'd done nothing worse than get on with their lives regardless of who ruled the westlands. But did that mean he wanted such people in his family? That was a different question.

No one seemed to say anything bad about Phosia. People who disliked her father thought she was nice enough. People who liked her father—there were some—thought she was . . . nice enough. Everyone agreed her mother talked too much. "If that's a vicious sin, Skotos' ice will be even more crowded than the gloomiest priests claim," Lysia said.

"True enough," Maniakes said. "Er, true." His wife laughed at him for editing his own remarks.

Once he was back in Serrhes, he naturally started judging cases again. His first stay in the city had scratched the surface of what had gone on in better than a decade of Makuraner rule, but had not done much more than that. As he lingered in the westlands waiting for word from Abivard, he had time to look at cases he had not considered before. And, seeing him do that, others who had not presented matters to him in his earlier stay now hauled them out, dusted them off, and brought them to his notice.

Enough new cases and accusations and suits came before him to make him hand some of them over to Rhegorios. His cousin, instead of making his usual protests about doing anything resembling work, accepted the assignment with an alacrity Maniakes found surprising. After a little thought, it wasn't so surprising any more. When Rhegorios was fighting his way through the intricacies of a case involving fine points of both Videssian and Makuraner law, he wasn't thinking about Phosia.

His decisions were good, too: as thoughtful as the ones Maniakes handed down. As day followed day, the Avtokrator grew more and more pleased with the Sevastos. Rhegorios had been a good second man in the Empire even when he grumbled about having to do his job. Now that he was doing it without the grumbling, he was as fine a second man as anyone could have wanted.

As day followed day, he also grew more confident in his decisions and made ever more of them on his own, without checking with Maniakes till after the fact. Thus he startled the Avtokrator when he came in one afternoon and said, "Your Majesty, a matter has come to my notice that I think you should handle in my place."

"It will have to wait a bit," Maniakes said. "I'm in the middle of an argument here myself." He nodded at the petitioner standing before him. "As soon as I'm done, I'll deal with whatever perplexes you. You ought to know, though, that I think you're up to fixing it, whatever it happens to be."

"Your Majesty, it would be better to your hands," Rhegorios said with unwonted firmness. Maniakes shrugged and spread those hands, palms up, in token of puzzled acquiescence.

Having disposed of the petitioner—and having annoyed him by denying his request for land that had belonged to a monastery till the Makuraners razed it to the ground and slaughtered most of the monks—Maniakes sent a secretary to Rhegorios to let him know he could bring his unusual case, whatever it was, up into the chamber the Avtokrator was using.

As soon as the Sevastos and the man who had come before him walked into the room, Maniakes understood. Broios walked up to the high-backed chair Maniakes was using as a throne and prostrated himself before his sovereign. "Rise," the Avtokrator said, at the same time sending his cousin an apologetic look. Had he been assotted of Broios' daughter, he wouldn't have wanted to deal with a case involving the merchant, either. He asked Broios, "Well, sir, how may I help you today? Not more clipped arkets, I hope."

"No, your Majesty," Broios said. "I don't fancy another week with a sore fundament, thank you very kindly all the same."

"Good," Maniakes said. "What *can* I do for you, then?"

"Your Majesty, I beg your pardon if I give you great offense, but I hear from a lot of people that you've set men and women to asking questions about me and my family," Broios said. "You can say whatever you like about me, Emperor; Phos knows you have the right. But if you're going to say I have treason in mind, it isn't so, and that's all there is to it. All the men and women you sent out won't find it when it's not there. Remember, your Majesty, Vetranios is the one who took a shine to that Tzikas item, not me."

Maniakes turned to Rhegorios. "Well, cousin of mine, you had the right of it after all: this one wasn't for you to judge." He gave his attention back to Broios. "I wasn't trying to find out about you because I think you're a traitor. I'm trying to make certain you aren't."

"I don't understand, your Majesty," Broios said.

Sighing, Maniakes found himself explaining what he would rather have kept dark a while longer. "My cousin here, his highness the Sevastos Rhegorios, has . . . conceived an interest in your daughter, Phosia. I need to know if there are any scandals in your family that would keep it from being joined to mine."

Broios wobbled on his feet. For a moment, Maniakes feared he would faint. The merchant coughed a couple of times, then found words: "Your Majesty, I crave your pardon in a different way. I know his Highness has seen my daughter, but—" His voice broke like that of a youth whose beard was beginning to sprout. What he was probably thinking was something like, *I knew Rhegorios wanted to dally with her, but . . .* "—I had no idea that—that—" He ran down again.

"Since you are here, since you have come to me," Maniakes said, "I want you to tell me anything that might be an impediment to this union. If you tell me here and now, no penalty and no blame will come to you, even if we decide not to make the match. But if you conceal anything and I learn of it for myself, not only is the match forfeit, you will regret the day you were born for having lied to me. Do you understand, Broios?"

"Yes, your Majesty." Broios drew himself to his full unimpressive height. "Your Majesty, to the ice with me if I can think of any reason—except the late kick in the arse, of course—for you not to take my tender chick under your wing." His voice rang with sincerity.

His voice had also rung with sincerity when he denied having mixed in some arkets Vetranios hadn't given him before taking the coins to the Avtokrator. He'd been lying then. Was he lying now? Maniakes couldn't tell. A successful merchant got to the point where he could dissemble well enough to deceive anyone who didn't have a sorcerer at his side.

The Avtokrator wondered if he should summon Bagdasares. For the moment, he decided against it. He'd given Broios the warning. "Remember what I said," he told the merchant. "If you don't speak now—"

"I have nothing to say," Broios answered, a statement normally so improbable that Maniakes thought it stood some chance of being true,

He dismissed the merchant and then asked Rhegorios, "And what do you think of your prospective father-in-law?"

"Not bloody much," his cousin replied at once. "But I'm not interested in marrying him, the lord with the great and good mind be praised. He's Zosime's problem, which suits me down to the ground."

"Only shows you've never been married," Maniakes said. "Your wife's family is your problem." He grinned at Rhegorios. "Take my brother-in-law, for instance."

"Who, him? He's a prince among men," Rhegorios said, laughing. "Why, he's even a prince among princes." The reference to the Vaspurakaner blood the two of them shared made Maniakes laugh, too.

But he did not laugh long. He said, "Do we really want Broios in the family with us?"

"No, that's not the question," Rhegorios said. "The question is, is Broios so revolting, we can't stand to have him in the family no matter how much I want Phosia in it?"

As far as Maniakes could tell, the question wasn't how much Rhegorios wanted Phosia in it, the question was how much he wanted it in Phosia, the *it* being different in the two cases. He didn't say that, for fear of angering his cousin instead of amusing him. Taken on its own terms, what Rhegorios asked was reasonable. Recognizing that, Maniakes said, "We shall see, cousin of mine. We shall see."

Excitement on his face, a Videssian trooper led one of Abivard's boiler boys before Maniakes. "He's got news for you, your Majesty," the imperial exclaimed as the Makuraner went down on his belly in a proskynesis.

"Rise, sir, rise," Maniakes said. "Whatever you tell me, I am certain it will be more interesting than the endless arguments I've been hearing here in Serrhes."

"I think this is small praise, not great," the Makuraner said, his dark eyes sparkling with amusement above the chain-mail veil he wore. "But yes, Majesty, I have news indeed. Know that Abivard son of Godarz, the new sun of Makuran, now holds Mashiz in the hollow of his hand, and know further that he also holds in the hollow of his hand Sharbaraz Pimp of Pimps, and awaits only the decree of the Mobedhan-Mobhed concerning the said Sharbaraz's infamous and impious practices in regard to religion before ending his life and consigning him to the Void forevermore." The Mobedhan-Mobhed, the leading servant of the God, held a place in the Makuraner hierarchy close to that of the ecumenical patriarch in Videssos.

Maniakes clapped his hands together. "He has the capital and he has his foe, eh?" The Makuraner messenger nodded. Maniakes went on, "That's very wise, getting your chief cleric to condemn him. Taking his head won't seem so much like murder then: more as if he's getting his desserts."

"Majesty, he is," the Makuraner said angrily. "To start so great a war and then to lose it, to leave us with nothing to show for so much blood and treasure spent—how can a man who fails so greatly deserve to live?"

Again, none of the Makuraners blamed Sharbaraz for starting the war against Videssos. They blamed him for losing it. Had Videssos the city fallen, no one would have lifted a finger against the victorious, all-conquering figure Sharbaraz would have become. He would have ruled out his span of years with unending praise from his subjects, who might even have come to think he deserved deification as much as he did. He probably would have found some convenient excuse to get rid of Abivard so no one shared the praise. Success would have concealed a multitude of sins; failure made even virtues vanish.

"It's over, then," Maniakes said in wondering tones. He would still have to see if and how he could live at peace with Abivard. But even if they did fight, they wouldn't go to war right away. The struggle that had begun when Sharbaraz used Genesios' overthrow of Likinios as an excuse to invade and seek to conquer Videssos was done at last.

Abivard's messenger construed Maniakes' three words in the sense in which he'd meant them. "Majesty, it is," he said solemnly, giving back three words of his own.

"I presume your master is tying up loose ends now," Maniakes said, and the messenger nodded. The Avtokrator asked, "What of

Abivard's sister—Denak, was that her name? She was Sharbaraz's wife, not so?"

"His principal wife, yes," the messenger answered, making a distinction about which the monogamous Videssians did not need to bother.

"What does she think of the changes in Mashiz?" Maniakes chose his words with care, not wanting to offend either the messenger or Abivard, to whom what he said would surely get back.

The Makuraner boiler boy replied with equal caution: "Majesty, as pledges have been given that no harm shall come to her children, and as these past years she had not always been on the best of terms with him who was King of Kings, she is said to be well enough pleased by those changes."

Maniakes nodded. Abivard, then, was not inclined simply to dispose of his little nephew. Maniakes liked him better for that. Still, he wondered how happy Denak would be when she fully realized the child of her flesh would not succeed to the throne. But that was Abivard's worry, not his own. He had plenty that were his, and chose to air one: "Any sign of Tzikas in Mashiz?"

"The Videssian traitor?" The Makuraner spoke with unconscious contempt that would have wounded Tzikas had he been there to hear it. "No. I am told he was in Mashiz at some earlier time, but Abivard the new sun of Makuran—" *Abivard the man with a new fancy title,* Maniakes thought wryly. "—finds no trace of him there at present, despite diligent searching."

"What a pity." Maniakes sighed. "It can't be helped, I suppose. For the good news you do bring—and it's very good news indeed—I'll give you a pound of gold."

"May the God and the Prophets Four bless you, Majesty!" the Makuraner exclaimed. Coming from a nation that coined mostly in silver, he, like most of his countrymen, held Videssian gold in great esteem.

When Maniakes went to tell Rhegorios that Sharbaraz had been cast down, he discovered his cousin already knew. He was flabbergasted for a moment, but then remembered the grinning Videssian soldier who had brought the messenger into his presence. That grin said the Videssian had already heard the news—and what one Videssian knew, a hundred would know an hour later, given the imperials' unabashed love for gossip.

By sunset tomorrow, all of Serrhes would have all the details of Abivard's entry into Mashiz. Some of the people might even have the right details.

"It doesn't matter that I heard it from other lips than yours," Rhegorios said soothingly. "What matters is that it's so. Now we can start putting the pieces back together again."

"True," Maniakes said. With more than a little reluctance, he added, "I still haven't heard anything out-of-the-way about Phosia."

"Neither have I," Rhegorios said. "I don't expect to hear anything bad about her, either. What I do worry about is hearing something so bad about Broios that I wouldn't want him in the family if he had ten pretty daughters."

"Ten pretty daughters!" Maniakes exclaimed. "What would you do with ten pretty daughters? No, wait, don't tell me—I see the gleam in your eye. Remember, cousin of mine, the Makuraners are trying to get away from the custom of the women's quarters. What would your sister say if she found out you'd started that custom on Videssian soil?"

"Something I'd rather not hear, I'm sure," Rhegorios answered, laughing. "But you needn't worry. Having a whole raft of wives may sound like great fun, but how is any man above the age of eighteen—twenty-one at the outside—supposed to keep them all happy? And if he doesn't keep them all happy, they'll be unhappy, and whom will they be unhappy about? Him, that's whom. No, thank you."

The grammar in there was shaky. The logic, Maniakes thought, was excellent. Idly, he said, "I wonder what will happen to all of Sharbaraz's wives now that he isn't King of Kings anymore. For that matter, if I remember rightly, Abivard has a women's quarters of his own, up at Vek Rud domain, somewhere off in the far northwest of Makuran."

"Yes, he does, doesn't he?" Rhegorios said. "He never talks about his other wives back there, though. He and Roshnani might as well be married the way any two Videssians are."

"Which is all very well for the two of them, no doubt," Maniakes said. "But Abivard has spent most of his time the past ten years and more here in Videssos, and none of it, so far as I know, up in Vek Rud domain. I wonder what the other wives have to say about him, yes, I do."

"That could be intriguing." Rhegorios got a faraway look in his eyes. "He's not in Videssos any more. He's not going to come back here, either, not if Phos is kind. Now that he's the new lead horse in Makuran, wouldn't you say he's likely to be going through the plateau country, to make himself known to the *dihqans* and such up there? Wouldn't you guess he'll probably find his way back to his own domain one day?"

"I wouldn't mind being a fly on the wall when he did." Maniakes wondered if Bagdasares could make magic stretch that far. After a moment, he realized it didn't matter: he would have no way of knowing exactly when Abivard returned to his old domain. *Too bad*, he thought. *Too bad*.

Fat and sweating with nervousness as well as heat, Vetranios prostrated himself before Maniakes. "I pray that you hear me out," he said to the Avtokrator after he had risen. "It is true, your Majesty, isn't it, that you've been trying to find out what sort of games Broios has been playing with his daughter?"

"Yes, that is true," Maniakes said, "and what's also true is that I'll land on you like an avalanche if you're lying to score points off your rival. If you know something I should hear, why didn't I hear it two weeks ago?"

"I got back into Serrhes only day before yesterday," Vetranios answered with some dignity. "I went over to Amorion to see if I could collect on a debt owed me since before the Makuraners took the town."

"Any luck?" Maniakes asked, genuinely curious.

"Alas, no. The merchant who owed me the payment walked the narrow bridge of the separator during the years of the Makuraner occupation, and is now settling up accounts with either Phos or Skotos." Vetranios sounded sad, not so much because his debtor had died but because he'd died without paying him back. As if to prove that, the merchant went on, "I was unable to locate any of his heirs or assigns, either. Most distressing, and a most slipshod way of doing business, too."

"War does have a habit of making people's lives difficult," Maniakes said. Vetranios nodded; the Avtokrator's irony sailed right past him. Reflecting that he should have known better, Maniakes returned to the matter at hand: "Very well. You haven't been in Serrhes for a bit. I thought the town seemed quieter than usual. What do you know about Broios and Phosia that I haven't already heard?"

"Since I don't know what you've already heard, your Majesty, how can I tell you that?" Vetranios asked. Given his past record, the question struck Maniakes as altogether too reasonable to have come from his lips. Vetranios went on, "I can tell you, though, that Broios betrothed Phosia to Kaykaus, Tegin's second-in-command, while the Makuraners were occupying Serrhes."

"What?" Maniakes stared. "By the good god, sir, you'd better give me a good answer as to how you know that when no one else in this city has breathed a word of it to me. If you're lying, the Halogai may be kicking your head through the city square, not your arse."

"I am not lying." Vetranios sketched the sun-circle above his heart. Of course, he'd done the same thing during his earlier dispute with Broios. He'd been lying then. So had Broios, who had sworn just as hard he was telling the truth. "As for how I know . . . Your Majesty, I have a daughter, too. Her name is Sisinnia. Kaykaus and I were dickering over an engagement when all at once he broke off the talks, saying he preferred Phosia—by which I take it he meant her dowry. So news of this will not have got round the town."

"I—see," Maniakes said slowly. "Don't leave Serrhes again without getting my consent first, Vetranios. I may have to use magic to find out whether you're telling the truth."

"Your Majesty!" The merchant assumed an expression of injured innocence. "How could you possibly doubt me?"

"Somehow or other, I manage," Maniakes said, another shot that sailed over Vetranios' head. "Never mind. Go home. Stay there. If I need you again, I'll summon you."

After the merchant left the city governor's residence, Maniakes hunted up Rhegorios and gave him the news. "That doesn't sound good, does it?" Rhegorios said with a scowl. "Not that he wanted to make the marriage—that would be easy enough to forgive. But trying to make it and then not telling us about it . . . Master Broios has some explaining to do, I fear."

"So he does. And unless he's got a bloody good explanation . . ." Maniakes strode over and set his hand on Rhegorios' shoulder. "I know you're sweet on this girl, cousin of mine, but unless her

father has a bloody good explanation, I don't want to be connected with him."

"I'm not arguing with you," Rhegorios said. "I wish I could argue,
but I can't." He laughed in self-mockery. "If I were fifteen years
younger, I'd be sure as sure I couldn't possibly live without her,
and my life would be ruined forever. And I'd probably yank out
my sword and try and make you change your mind—either that
or I'd run off with her the way I was thinking of doing anyhow,
get a priest to say the words over us, and leave you to make the
best of it. But do you know what, cousin your Majesty brother-
in-law of mine? If what Vetranios says is true, I'm not dead keen
on having an old reprobate like Broios in the family."

"Don't despair," Maniakes said. "There may be a perfectly innocent explanation for this."

"So there may," Rhegorios said. "To the ice with me if I can
think of one, though." Maniakes thumped him on the shoulder
again. He couldn't think of an innocent explanation, either.

Broios' proskynesis was so smooth, he must have been practicing
back at his own home. The robes he wore were of a cut, and of a
quality of silk, above those to which even a prosperous merchant
might normally aspire. Maniakes didn't know where he'd gotten
them, but he looked to be ready for his role as father-in-law to
the Sevastos of the Empire of Videssos.

"Good evening, your Majesty," he wheezed to Maniakes as he
rose. "A pleasure to be in your company, as always."

Maniakes raised an eyebrow. "As always. As I recall, you weren't
so glad to see me the second time we met."

"Only a misunderstanding," Broios said easily. The impression
he gave was that Maniakes had done the misunderstanding, but
that he was generously willing to overlook the Avtokrator's error.
He let a little petulance creep into his voice as he went on, "I
had hoped, your Majesty, that you might have chosen to honor
my wife and daughter with an invitation to this supper tonight.
After all—" He gave Maniakes a coy, sidelong glance. "—you'll
be seeing a lot of them in times to come."

"No need to hurry, then, wouldn't you say?" Maniakes
replied.

Broios looked to Rhegorios for support. Finding none, he said,
"Well, however you like, of course." Again, he managed to make

it sound as if the Avtokrator was obviously in the wrong, but he, out of his splendid magnanimity, was willing to overlook the breach in decorum.

One of the servants at the city governor's residence came in and announced that supper was ready. Maniakes found himself unenthusiastic about breaking bread with Broios, but he knew he would have to endure it. "Do try the wine," the servant urged.

Everyone did. Broios' eyes widened. "That's potent stuff," he said, and tossed back his cup. "Good, mind you, but potent. Are you planning on serving supper *under* the table tonight, eh, your Majesty?" He laughed loudly at his own joke.

"I hope not," Maniakes answered, although he would not have minded seeing Broios drunk so his tongue would wag freer. To further that end, he'd ordered the cooks to do up a salty casserole of mutton and cabbage, the better to encourage thirst.

Broios was not shy about drinking wine. Broios, as well as Maniakes could tell, was not shy about anything, whether that meant making deals or telling lies. But the merchant, while refilling his cup several times, gave no sign the wine was doing anything to him water would not have done.

"It is a pity, your Majesty, that Phosia couldn't taste this vintage," he said. "I don't know where in town you found it, but it's very fine."

"I'm glad you like it," Maniakes said, and then, given an opening of sorts, went on, "You must be very proud of your daughter."

"Oh, I am," Broios said with the same fulsome sincerity with which he invested every pronouncement. "Nothing too good for my little girl, that's the truth. Not that I've spoiled her, you understand," he added hastily. "Nothing like that. She won't be difficult for his Highness the Sevastos, not in any way she won't." He glanced over toward Rhegorios. "You've not said much tonight, your Highness."

Rhegorios went on saying not much. Broios looked puzzled, but then shrugged and went back to his supper.

"Nothing too good for Phosia, you say?" Maniakes asked, as if unsure he'd heard correctly. Broios' emphatic nod said he had no doubts on that score. Thoughtfully, Maniakes went on, "Not even the Sevastos of the Empire of Videssos?"

"Your Majesty has been generous and gracious enough to let me believe such a match might not be impossible," Broios said.

Since that was true, Maniakes nodded meditatively. And, meditatively, he asked, "Nothing is too good for Phosia, eh? Not even the—" He plucked the perfect word out of the air. "—magnifolent Kaykaus, second-in-command of the Makuraner garrison here?"

Broios stared at him. When the merchant spoke, he might almost have had reproach in his voice: "Ah, your Majesty, where could you have heard about that?"

"Never you mind where I heard about it," Maniakes answered. "That is not the point. The point, sirrah, is why I didn't hear of it from you weeks ago, when I asked if any obstacles or embarrassments stood between your daughter and my family. Wouldn't you say that an engagement to a Makuraner officer is an embarrassment of sorts?"

"If she'd been married to him, your Majesty, that would have been an embarrassment," Broios said. Whatever he knew of embarrassments, he plainly knew at second hand, for he was impervious to them himself.

Maniakes said, "Having her engaged to this officer may not be so much of a much; you're right about that." Broios looked relieved. But then the Avtokrator went on, "Not telling me about the engagement, though, is something else again. I asked you if there were problems. You said no. That was a lie. I don't think we want liars in our clan."

"Your Majesty!" Broios cried. He turned to Rhegorios. "Your Highness!"

Rhegorios shook his head. "No. You have a lovely daughter, Broios, and I think she's a sweet girl, too. If I were marrying just her, I'd be more than happy enough. But you don't marry just a girl—you marry her whole family." Maniakes had to keep himself from clapping his hands in glee. His cousin had listened to him after all! Rhegorios went on, "While I'd like to have Phosia for a wife, I'd sooner have a snake in my boot than you for a father-in-law."

Maybe the strong wine Broios had drunk had loosened his tongue, after all. He shouted, "You're the Avtokrator's cousin, so you think you can pick any girl you want and she'll be glad to have you. If you weren't his cousin, there's not a woman in the Empire would look at you twice."

"Yes, I am the Avtokrator's cousin," Rhegorios agreed, "and you're right, the rules for me are different because of it. If I weren't the

Avtokrator's cousin, I might even put up with the likes of you for the sake of getting Phosia. But I can pick and choose, and so I will." He stood up and looked down his nose at Broios. "But I will say this, sir: when I was an exile on the island of Kalavria, I had no trouble at all getting women to look at me twice—or getting them to do more than that, either, when the mood took them. And it did."

Maniakes knew that was true. One of the reasons Rhegorios remained unwed was precisely that he did so well for himself without making any permanent promises. "You are dismissed, Broios," the Avtokrator said, more than a little sadly. "We'd have to watch you closer than the Makuraners, and that's all there is to it. If you like, once things settle down in Mashiz, you have my leave to write Kaykaus and see if you can bring that match back to life."

"Bah!" Pausing only to empty his winecup one last time and pop a couple of candied apricots into his mouth, Broios stormed out of the dining hall. The city governor's residence shook as if in a small earthquake as he slammed the door behind him.

"I'm sorry, cousin of mine," Maniakes said.

"So am I," Rhegorios answered. "I am going to be a while finding someone who suited me as well as Phosia. But Broios—" He shook his head again. "No, thank you." He suddenly looked thoughtful. "I wonder what Vetranios' daughter is like." Seeing Maniakes' expression, he burst out laughing. "I don't mean it, cousin of mine. If Broios is a snake in my boot, Vetranios is a scorpion. We're well shut of both of them."

"Now you're talking sense." Maniakes sketched the sun-circle to emphasize how much sense Rhegorios was talking. Then he eyed the wine jar. "That *is* a good vintage. Now that we've started it, we may as well finish it. After all, you're drowning your sorrows, aren't you?"

"Am I?" Rhegorios said. "Well, yes, I suppose I am. And by the time we get to the bottom of *that*, I expect they'll be so drowned, I'll have forgotten what they are. Let's get started, shall we?"

Broios was not seen in public for the next several days. The next time he was seen, he sported a black eye and a startling collection of bruises elsewhere about his person. When Maniakes heard the news, he remarked to Lysia, "I'd say his wife wasn't very happy to have the betrothal fall through—or do you suppose Phosia was the one who did the damage?"

"I'd bet on Zosime," Lysia said. "She knows what she lost, and she knows who's to blame for losing it, too."

By her tone, she would have given Broios the same had she been married to him rather than to Maniakes. The Avtokrator suspected it wasn't the last walloping the merchant would get, either. Videssians breathed the heady atmosphere of rank almost as readily as they breathed the ordinary, material air. To have a chance at a union with the imperial family snatched away . . . no, Broios wouldn't have a pleasant time after that.

Maniakes kept waiting for news out of the west. He wondered again if one or more of Abivard's messengers had gone missing—if, perhaps, Tegin's garrison force, heading back toward Makuran from Serrhes, had waylaid the riders. If that was so, Tegin would have to know the King of Kings whose cause he still espoused had failed, and that he would be well advised to make whatever peace he could with the new powers in his land.

Tegin, at least, would know. Not knowing, Maniakes kept coming up with fresh possibilities in his own mind, each less pleasant than the one before. Maybe Sharbaraz had somehow rallied, and civil war raged across the Land of the Thousand Cities. That would account for no messengers' having reached Serrhes in a while.

Or maybe Abivard had won a triumph so complete and so easy that he repented of his truce with the Videssians. Maybe he'd stopped sending messengers because he was gathering the armies of Makuran with a view toward renewing the war against the Empire.

"I don't think he'd do that," Rhegorios said when Maniakes raised the horrid prospect aloud. The Sevastos looked west, then went on thoughtfully, "I don't think he *could* do that, not this campaigning season. We're too close to the fall rains. His attack would bog down in the mud before it got well started."

"I keep telling myself the same thing." Maniakes' grin conveyed anything but amusement. "I keep having trouble making myself believe it, too."

"That's why you're the Avtokrator," Rhegorios said. "If you believed that all of Videssos' neighbors were nice people who wanted to do us a favor, you wouldn't be suited for the job."

"If I believed that all of Videssos' neighbors were nice people who wanted to do us a favor, I'd be out of my bloody mind," Maniakes exclaimed.

"Well, that, too," Rhegorios said. "Of course, if you believe all our neighbors are out to get us all the time, the way it must sometimes look if you're sitting on the throne, that's liable to drive you out of your bloody mind, too, isn't it?"

"I expect it is," the Avtokrator agreed. "And yes, it does look that way a lot of the time, doesn't it? So what have we got? If believing an obvious falsehood means you're out of your bloody mind, and if believing an equally obvious truth can send you out of your bloody mind, what does that say about sitting on the throne in the first place?"

"It says you have to be out of your bloody mind to want to sit on the throne, that's what." Rhegorios studied Maniakes. "Judging from the specimen at hand, I'd say that's right enough. Cousin of mine, I want you to live forever, or at least until all your sons have beards. I don't want the bloody job. Sevastos is bad enough, with leeches like Broios trying to fasten on to me."

"Fair enough," Maniakes said. "I—" Before he could go on, one of his Haloga guardsmen came in from outside. "Yes? What is it, Askbrand?"

"Your Majesty, a boiler boy waits in the plaza," the big blond northerner answered. "He would have speech with you."

"I'll come," Maniakes said happily. "About time we've had some news from Abivard. Phos grant it be good."

"Just hearing from him is good news," Rhegorios said. "Now you can stop having dark suspicions about what he's up to."

"Don't be silly," Maniakes said. "I'm the Avtokrator, remember? It's my job to have dark suspicions."

"One more reason not to want it, as I said before," Rhegorios replied.

Maniakes walked out of the city governor's residence and onto Serrhes' central square. After the gloom of indoors, he blinked several times against the bright sunshine. The messenger bowed in the saddle when he saw the Avtokrator; the rings of his chain-mail veil rattled faintly. "Majesty," he said in the Makuraner.

"What word?" Maniakes asked.

The messenger rode closer. "Majesty, the word is good," he said. "Abivard bids me tell you that he has at last decided the fate of Sarbaraz Pimp of Pimps. Sarbaraz is to be—"

Maniakes had been listening intently for the news, so intently that he missed the first time the horseman mispronounced the name of the overthrown King of Kings. When the fellow made the same mistake twice in two sentences, though, he blurted, "You're a Videssian, aren't you?"

By then, the messenger had come quite close, almost alongside him. With a horrible curse, the fellow yanked out his sword and cut at Maniakes. But the Avtokrator, his dark suspicions suddenly roused, was already springing away. The tip of the blade brushed his robe, but did not cleave his flesh.

Cursing still, the messenger pressed forward for another slash. That fell short, too. The boiler boy wheeled his horse and tried to get away. Askbrand's axe came down on the horse's head. The animal was wearing the scale mail with which the Makuraners armored their chargers. Against arrows, the mail was marvelous. Against a stroke like that, it might as well not have been there. The horse crashed to the cobblestones. Guardsmen swarmed over the rider.

"Don't kill him!" Maniakes shouted. "We'll want answers from him."

"So we will," Rhegorios said grimly. "If Abivard is sending murderers instead of messengers, we have a new war on our hands right now."

"I don't think he is," Maniakes said. "Didn't you hear the way the fellow talked?"

"I didn't notice," his cousin answered. "You speak Makuraner better than I do. I was just trying to understand him."

The guards had gotten the would-be assassin's sword away from him. Roughly, one of them yanked off his helmet. Maniakes knew well the furious, clever, narrow face that glared at him. "Almost, Tzikas," he said. "Almost. You might have managed to let the air out of me and then get away—if I didn't make the same mistakes speaking Makuraner that you do."

"Almost." The renegade officer's mouth twisted bitterly. "The story of my life. Almost. I almost held Amorion. I almost got you the first time, as I should have. Once I went over to the other side, I almost had Abivard's position. And I almost had you now."

"So you did," Maniakes said. "I admit it—why not? If you think you can take it with you for consolation when you go down to Skotos' ice, I'd say you're wrong. The dark god robs the souls he gets of all consolation." He spat on the cobblestones in rejection of Phos' eternal foe, and shivered a little on reflecting how easily his blood rather than his spittle might have flowed among them.

"I prefer to believe I'll fall into the Void and be—nothing—forevermore." Tzikas still had a smile left in him. "I worshiped the God of the Makuraners as fervently as ever I prayed to Phos."

"I believe that." Maniakes held up one hand, palm out flat, then the other. "Nothing here—and nothing here, either. It's not *almost* that's the story of your life, Tzikas, it's *nothing*. You were always good at seeming to be whatever you liked, because it was all seeming and nothing real, nothing at the bottom of you to make you truly any one particular kind of person."

"Oh, I don't know," Rhegorios put in. "He's always been a particular kind of bastard, if anyone cares about what I think."

"Make your jokes. Take the last word," Tzikas said. "You can. You're the Avtokrator and the Sevastos. You've won. You even got away with swiving your cousin, Maniakes. Aren't you proud? My dying curse on you."

"As a matter of fact, I *am* proud," Maniakes said. "I've done what I've done, and I've never tried to hide it, which is more than you could say if you lived another thousand years—which you won't." He raised his voice: "Askbrand!"

The Haloga's axe rose and fell. Blood gushed from the great gash that split Tzikas' head almost in two. *Almost,* Maniakes thought. The renegade's feet drummed a brief tattoo and then were still.

Rhegorios sketched the sun-circle. "Don't fear his curse, cousin of mine," he said. "You had the right of it, and that curse won't stick, because it has nothing behind it."

"Nothing now." Blood flooded down through Tzikas' gray beard. Maniakes shook his head. "I feared him alive—feared him as much as anyone, because I never knew what he would do. He was quicksilver come to life: bright, shiny, able to roll any which way, and poisonous. And now he's gone, and I'm not, and I'm bloody glad that's the way things turned out."

"Now you can go through doors without checking behind them first to make sure he's not lurking there," Rhegorios said.

"Now I can do all sorts of things," Maniakes said. "I would have done them anyway, I think, but slower, always looking over my shoulder. Now I can live my life a free man." *Or as free from custom and danger as the Avtokrator ever gets, which isn't very far.*

The first thing he did to celebrate his new freedom was order Tzikas' head, already badly the worse for wear, hewn from his body and mounted on a spear for the edification of the people of Serrhes. At least he didn't have to do the hewing himself, as he had with Genesios when his vicious predecessor was captured. Askbrand and his axe took care of the business with a couple of strokes. Tzikas wasn't moving or fighting any more, which made things easier, or in any case neater.

The next thing Maniakes did was give Askbrand a pound of gold. The Haloga tried to decline, saying, "You already pay me to guard you. You do not need to pay me more *because* I guard you."

"Call it a reward for doing a very good job," Maniakes said. Askbrand's fellow guardsmen who happened to be Videssians urgently nodded, whispered in the northerner's ears, and seemed on the point of setting fire to his shoes. No imperial in his right mind—and bloody few out of it—turned down money for no reason, and the Videssians feared that, if one bonus was turned down, no more would be forthcoming. At last, reluctantly, Askbrand agreed to let himself be rewarded.

Drawn by the commotion in the square, Lysia came out then. She listened to the excited accounts, took a long look at Tzikas' still-dripping and very mortal remains, said, "Good. About time," and went back into the city governor's residence. At times, Maniakes thought, his wife was so sensible, she was unnerving.

A moment later, he sent one of the guardsmen into the residence, after not Lysia but a secretary. The fellow with whom the guard emerged did not take a headless corpse, an impaled head, and a great pool of blood on the cobbles in stride. He gulped, turned fishbelly pale, and passed out.

Gleefully, the guards threw a bucket of water over him. That brought him back to himself, but ruined the sheet of parchment on which he'd been about to write. When at last both the scribe and his implements were ready, Maniakes dictated a letter: "Maniakes Avtokrator to Abivard King of Kings, his brother: Greetings. I am pleased to tell you that—"

"Excuse me, your Majesty, but is 'King of Kings' Abivard's proper style?" the secretary asked.

Maniakes hid a smile. If the fellow could worry about such minutiae, he was indeed on the mend. "I don't know. It will do," the Avtokrator said, as much to see the scribe wince as for any other reason. "I resume: Greetings. I am pleased to tell you that Tzikas will trouble our counsels no more. He tried to murder me while in the guise of one of your messengers, and suffered what failed assassins commonly suffer. If you like, I will send you his head, so you can see it for yourself. I assure you, he looks better without it." He held up a hand to show he was done dictating. "Give me a fair copy of that for my signature before sunset. This is news Abivard will be glad to have."

"I shall do as you require, your Majesty," the scribe said, and went back indoors—*where he belongs,* Maniakes thought—in a hurry.

"By the good god," the Avtokrator said, taking another long look at what was left of Tzikas, "here's another step toward making me really believe the war is over, the westlands are ours again, and that they're liable to stay that way."

"If that's what you think, why don't we head back toward Videssos the city?" Rhegorios said. "The fall rains aren't going to hold off forever, you know, and I'd much sooner not have to slog through mud on the road."

"So would I," Maniakes said. "So would Lysia, no doubt." He didn't want her giving birth on the road. He knew she didn't want to give birth on the road, either. Having done that before, she did not approve of it.

"And besides," Rhegorios went on, "by now the people of Videssos the city are probably itching for you to get back so they can praise you to the skies. Phos!" The Sevastos sketched the sun-circle. "If they don't praise you to the skies after this, I don't know when they ever will."

"If they do not praise the Avtokrator to the skies after this—" Askbrand began. He didn't finish the sentence, not in words. Instead, he swung through the air the axe he'd used to take Tzikas' head. The suggestion was unmistakable.

"I'll believe it when I see it." Maniakes' laugh held less bitterness than he'd expected. "As long as they don't riot in the streets when I ride by, I'll settle for that."

"You may be surprised," his cousin said. "They were starting to give you your due back there before you went into the westlands."

"*You* may be surprised," Maniakes retorted. "That was just

because they were glad they had me in the city instead of Etzilios and Abivard. If a goatherd saves a pretty girl who's fallen down a well, she might go to bed with him once to say thanks, but that doesn't mean she'd want to marry him. And the city mob in the capital is more fickle than any pretty girl ever born."

"Which only goes to show, you don't know as much about pretty girls as you think you do," Rhegorios said.

"I'm sure there are a great many things you can teach me, O sage of the age," Maniakes said. "I'm sure there are a great many things you can teach most billy goats, for that matter." Rhegorios made a face at him. He ignored it, continuing, "But one thing you can't teach me about, by the good god, is the mob in Videssos the city."

"We'll see," was all his cousin said. "If I'm wrong, I may ask to borrow Askbrand's axe."

"Honh!" the guardsman said. "An these stupid city people give not the Avtokrator his due, maybe he will turn all the Halogai loose on them. They would remember that a long time, I bet you." He swung the axe again. His pale, intent eyes lit up, perhaps in anticipation.

"I don't think so," Maniakes said hastily. "There are ways to be remembered, yes, but that's not one I care for. We'll go home and see what happens, that's all. Whatever it is, I can live with it."

✦ XIII

I t rained on Maniakes' parade. It had rained the day before, and the day before that, too. It was liable to keep on raining for the next week.

He didn't care. He'd returned to Videssos the city before the fall rains began, which meant traveling had been easy. He'd ordered the parade more because he thought the city mob expected one than because he had anything spectacular to display. The sole disadvantage of having peacefully reacquired the westlands was the absence of captured siege gear, dejected prisoners in chains, and most of the other elements that made a procession dramatic and worth watching.

Without prisoners and booty, Maniakes paraded his own soldiers. Without those soldiers, he never would have been able to take the war to Makuran or to defend Videssos the city against the Makuraners and Kubratoi. They deserved the credit for the victories that would go down in the chronicles as his.

He'd thought the rain and the relatively mundane nature of the parade—which he'd taken pains to announce beforehand—would hold down the crowd. He didn't mind that. If only dedicated parade-goers came out, he'd reasoned, fewer of the people lining Middle Street would be of the sort who amused themselves by hissing him and shouting obscenities at Lysia.

Looking at the way men and women packed the capital's chief

thoroughfare, though, he turned to Rhegorios and remarked, "More folk came out than I expected. Must be the colonnades—I'd forgotten how they let people stay dry even in wet weather."

Rhegorios didn't answer right away. Like Maniakes, he was busy waving to the people as he rode along. Unlike Maniakes', most of his waves seemed aimed at the pretty girls in the crowd; he hadn't let his disappointment over Phosia dishearten him for long. At last, he said, "Cousin of mine, you may as well get used to it: they've decided they like you after all."

"What? Nonsense!" Maniakes exclaimed. He'd grown so used to being an object of derision in Videssos the city that any other role seemed unnatural.

"All right, don't listen to me," Rhegorios said equably. "You're the Avtokrator; you don't have to do anything you don't want to do. But if you don't pay attention to what's going on around you, you're in a pretty sorry state, wouldn't you say?"

Stung by that, Maniakes did listen harder. A few shouts of "Incest!" and "Vaspurakaner heretic!"—this despite his orthodoxy—did come out of the crowd. He always listened for shouts like that. Because he always listened for them, he always heard them.

Now, though, along with them and, to his amazement, nearly drowning them out, came others: "Maniakes!" "Huzzah for the restorer of the westlands!" "Maniakes, conqueror of Kubrat and Makuran!" "Thou conquerest, Maniakes!" He hadn't heard that last one since his acclamation as Avtokrator. It was shouted during acclamations as a pious hope. Now he'd earned it in truth.

"Maybe I really have convinced them," he said, as much to himself as to Rhegorios. He'd hoped victory would do that for him—hoped and hoped and hoped. Up till this past campaigning season, he hadn't won enough victories to put the theory to a proper test.

"You're a hero," Rhegorios said with a grin. "Get used to it." The grin got wider. "So am I. I like it."

"There could be worse fates," Maniakes admitted. "We almost found out about a good many of them, these past few months."

"Didn't we, though?" Rhegorios said. "But it came right in the end. Why, the mime troupes may even leave you alone this Midwinter's Day."

Maniakes considered that. He didn't need long. "I don't believe it for a minute," he said. "The mime troupes don't ever leave any-body alone: that's what they're for. And if you're the Avtokrator, you have to sit on the spine of the Amphitheater and pretend it's funny. On Midwinter's Day, that's what the Avtokrator's for." After a moment, he added in a wistful, almost hopeful voice, "Maybe they won't bite quite so hard this year, though."

He didn't even believe that, not down deep. Midwinter's Day was still a couple of months away. By then, renewed familiarity would surely have blunted the respect the city mob felt for him now.

Rhegorios said, "Enjoy this while it lasts, anyhow." By the way he spoke, he didn't think it would last indefinitely, either.

In the crowd, a man held up a little baby in one hand, pointed to it with the other, and shouted, "Maniakes!"—he'd named the boy for the Avtokrator.

"Take him home and get him out of the rain, before he comes down with the croup," Maniakes called. Several nearby women—including, by the look of things, the infant Maniakes' mother—expressed loud and emphatic agreement with that sentiment.

Agathios the patriarch, who was riding a mule just behind Maniakes and Rhegorios, said, "Today, everyone delights in honoring you, your Majesty."

"Yes. Today," Maniakes said. But being honored was better than being despised; he couldn't deny that. Having experienced both, he could compare them.

And he was still despised, here and there. From the margins of the crowd, a priest cried, "Skotos' ice still awaits you for your lewdness and the travesty you have made of the marriage vow."

Maniakes looked back over his shoulder toward Agathios. "Do you know, most holy sir," he said in thoughtful tones, "just how badly we need priests to preach against the Vaspurakaner heresy in the towns and villages of the westlands? A passionate fellow like that is really wasted in Videssos the city, wouldn't you say? He would do so much better in a place like, oh, Patrodoton, for instance."

Agathios was not an astute politician, but he knew what Maniakes had in mind when making a suggestion like that. "I shall do my utmost to find out who that, ah, intrepid spirit is, your Majesty, and to translate him to a sphere where, as you rightly remark, his zeal might be put to good use."

"Speaking of good use, you'll get that out of the westlands," Rhegorios murmured to his cousin. "Now that we have them back, you've got a whole raft of new places to dump blue-robes who get on your nerves."

"If you think that's a joke, cousin of mine, you're wrong," Maniakes said. "If priests don't care to deal with sinful me in this sinful city, they can—and they will—go off somewhere quiet and out of the way and see how they like that."

A certain bloodthirsty gleam—or maybe it was just the rain— came into Rhegorios' eyes. "You ought to send the really zealous ones up to Kubrat, to see if they can convert Etzilios and the rest of the nomads. If they do, well and good. If they don't, the lord with the great and good mind will have some new martyrs, and you'll be rid of some old nuisances."

He'd intended only Maniakes to hear that. But he spoke a little too loudly, so that it also reached Agathios' ears. In tones of reproof, the ecumenical patriarch said, "Your Highness, mock not martyrdom. Think on the tale of the holy Kveldoulphios the Haloga, who laid down his life in the hope that his brave and glorious ending would inspire his people to the worship of the good god."

"I crave your pardon, most holy sir," Rhegorios said. Like any other Videssian, he was at bottom pious. Like any other Vides- sian high in the government, he also thought of the faith as an instrument of policy, holding both views at the same time without either confusion or separation.

Maniakes turned back and said to Agathios, "But the Halogai follow their own gods to this day, and the holy Kveldoulphios lived—what?—several hundred years ago, anyhow. Long before the civil wars that tore us to pieces."

"Your Majesty is, of course, correct." The patriarch let out a sigh so mournful, Maniakes wondered if he shed a tear or two along with it. In the rain, he could not tell. Agathios went on, "But he went gloriously to martyrdom of his own free will, rather than being hounded into it by the machinations of others."

"Very well, most holy sir. I do take the point," Maniakes said. Patriarchs were, in their way, government functionaries, too. Each one of them, though, had a point beyond which his obligations to Phos took precedence over his obligations to the Avtokrator. Maniakes realized the talk of deliberately creating martyrs had pushed Agathios close to that point.

"Thou conquerest, Maniakes!" "Maniakes, savior of the city!" "Maniakes, savior of the Empire!" Those shouts, and more like them, kept coming from the crowd. They didn't quite swallow up all the other shouts, the ones that had been hurled at Maniakes since the day he married his first cousin, but there were more of them and fewer of the others. If he hadn't won any great love, the Avtokrator had gained respect.

Pacing the floor, Maniakes said, "I hate this." In the Red Room, Zoïle the midwife was with Lysia, and custom binding as manacles kept him from being there. Having lost his first wife in childbed, he knew only too well the dangers Lysia faced.

His father set a hand on his shoulder. "Hard for us men at a time like this," the elder Maniakes said. "Just don't let your wife ever hear you say so, or *you* won't hear the last of it. It's the difference between watching a battle and going through one yourself, I suppose."

"That's probably about right," Maniakes said. "How many people here were watching from the seawall when our fleet beat the Kubratoi? They could drink wine and point to this and that and say how exciting it all was, but they weren't in any danger." He paused. "Of course, they would have been if we'd lost the sea fight instead of winning it."

"Nobody's going to lose any fights, by the good god," Symvatios said. "Lysia's going to give you another brat to howl around this place so a man can't get a decent night's sleep here."

"Ha!" The elder Maniakes raised an eyebrow at his brother. "You're more likely to be looking for an indecent night's sleep, anyhow."

Symvatios growled something in mock high dudgeon. Maniakes, his own worries forgotten for a moment, grinned at his father and uncle. They'd been bickering like that since they were boys, and enjoying it, too. Maniakes and Rhegorios bickered and bantered like that. Maniakes had done the same with Parsmanios . . . when they were boys. But between the two of them, the jealousy that had grown up was real.

As if picking the thought from his son's mind, the elder Maniakes said, "Your nephew, the little fellow who's named for the two of us, seems a likely lad."

"I hope so, for his sake," Maniakes said. "Zenonis and her boy have been here a good deal longer than I have, so you'll have seen more of them than I have. They don't seek me out, either." The corners of his mouth turned down. "You're her father-in-law, but in her mind—and I suppose in the boy's mind, too—I'm the chap who sent her husband into exile across the sea."

"Couldn't be helped, son," the elder Maniakes said heavily. "After he did what he undoubtedly did to you, I don't see that you had any choice. I've never held it against you—you know that."

His heavy features got a little heavier. He'd had three sons. One, his namesake, was a great success. But one was a proved traitor, and one long years missing and surely dead. A great weight of sorrow had to lurk there, though he spoke of it but seldom.

Symvatios said, "Sometimes there isn't any help for the things that happen, and that's all there is to it. You do the best you can with what you've got and you go on."

One of the things that had happened, of course, was Lysia and Maniakes falling in love with each other. Symvatios tolerated Maniakes as son-in-law as well as nephew, as the elder Maniakes was resigned to having Lysia as daughter-in-law. The marriage had been one of the things—though jealousy of Rhegorios played a bigger role—pushing Parsmanios away from the rest of the family and toward Tzikas' plot. Neither Maniakes' father nor his uncle had ever blamed him for that, not out loud. He was grateful to them for so much.

With a sigh, he said, "We always were a tight-knit clan. Now we're knitted tighter than ever." That was his doing, his and Lysia's. But the world, as far as he was concerned, wasn't worth living in without her.

Kameas came in. "Wine, your Majesty, your Highnesses?" he said.

"Yes, wine," Maniakes said. Wine would not take away the worry. Nothing would take away the worry. But, after three or four cups, it got blurry around the edges. That would do.

The vestiarios glided away, looking as he always did as if he propelled his vast bulk without moving his feet up and down when he walked. He returned a few moments later with that same ponderous grace. "I have an extra cup here, if his Highness the Sevastos should join you," he said.

"You think of everything," Maniakes said. Kameas nodded slightly, as if to say that was part of his job. Suddenly Maniakes wished this were his fourth cup of wine, not his first. He forced out a question: "Have you seen to Philetos?"

"Oh, yes, your Majesty. One of the prominent sirs—" He used the palace term for a lower-ranking eunuch. "—is attending to him, down by the Red Room." Kameas sketched Phos' sun-circle above his breast. "We all pray, of course, that the holy sir's presence shall prove unnecessary."

"Aye, we do, don't we?" Maniakes said harshly. That Philetos was a priest was not why, or not precisely why, he'd been summoned to the imperial residence when Lysia's pangs began. He was also a healer-priest, the finest in Videssos the city. If anything went wrong . . . If anything went wrong, he might be able to help, and then again he might not. He hadn't been able to help when Niphone died giving birth to Likarios.

With a distinct effort of will, the Avtokrator forced his thoughts away from that track. He spat on the floor in rejection of Skotos, at the same time raising his cup toward Phos and his holy light The elder Maniakes and Symvatios did as he did. Then Maniakes drank. The wine, golden in a silver cup, slid down his throat smooth as if it were sunlight itself.

"Well," Rhegorios said indignantly, walking into the little dining hall where his kinsfolk waited. "Shows the importance *I* have around here, when people start drinking without me."

Maniakes pointed to the extra cup Kameas had left behind. "We don't have a long start on you, cousin of mine—not like the one Abivard got on us when he moved against the city while we were sailing to Lyssaion. If you apply yourself, I expect you can catch up."

"Apply myself to wine?" Rhegorios raised an eyebrow. "Now there's a shocking notion." He used the dipper to fill the cup.

"*I'm* not shocked at it," Symvatios said. Rhegorios winced, rhetorically betrayed by his own father. After a perfectly timed pause, Symvatios went on, "I daresay you get it from me."

The elder Maniakes said, "It's a gift that runs in the family, I expect. Father certainly had it." Symvatios nodded at that. The elder Maniakes went on, "He had so much of it, sometimes he needed two or three tries before he could make it through a door."

"He was right when it mattered, though," Symvatios said. "When he did his drinking, it was when he didn't have to do anything else." He paused again. "Well, most of the time, anyhow."

"You're scandalizing your children, you know, the two of you," Rhegorios told his father and uncle. "Maniakes and I don't remember Grandfather all that well, so if you tell us he was an old soak, we'll believe you."

"What else will you believe if we tell it to you?" Symvatios asked. "Will you believe *we're* as wise and clever as we say?"

"Of course not," Rhegorios replied at once. "We *do* know you."

Both Maniakai, father and son, laughed. So did Symvatios. Kameas brought in a tray full of little squid sautéed in olive oil, vinegar, and garlic. They went well with the wine. Before too long, the jar was empty. The vestiarios fetched in another of the same vintage. For a little while, Maniakes managed to enjoy the company of his kin enough to take his mind off what Lysia was going through in the Red Room.

But time stretched. If Maniakes didn't intend to emulate his grandfather—or the account of his grandfather his father and uncle gave—he had to keep from drinking himself blind. And if he slowed his drinking so as to keep his wits about him, those wits kept returning to his wife.

Lysia had begun her labor around midmorning. The sun was sinking toward late autumn's early setting when Zoïle strode into the little dining hall and thrust a blanket-wrapped bundle at Maniakes. "Your Majesty, you have a daughter," the midwife announced.

Maniakes stared down at the baby, who was staring up at him. Their eyes met for a moment before those of the tiny girl wandered away. She was a dusky red color, and her head wasn't quite the right shape. Maniakes had learned all that was normal enough. He asked the question uppermost in his mind: "Is Lysia all right?"

"She seems very well." If Zoïle disapproved of his having married his cousin, she didn't show it. Since Maniakes had the strong impressions she was as frank as a Haloga, he took that for a good omen. The midwife went on, "She has been through this business a time or two, you know."

"Three, now," Maniakes corrected absently. "May I see her?" When it came to matters of the Red Room, even the Avtokrator of the Videssians asked the midwife's leave.

Zoïle nodded. "Go ahead. She'll be hungry, you know, and tired. I think Kameas has already gone to get her something." She pointed toward the baby Maniakes was still holding. "What will you name her, your Majesty?"

"Savellia," Maniakes said; he and Lysia had chosen the name not far into her pregnancy.

"That's pretty," Zoïle said, as quick and sharp in approval as in everything else. "It's the Videssian form of a Vaspurakaner name, isn't it?"

"That's right." The elder Maniakes spoke for his son, whose command of the language of his ancestors was sketchy. "The original is Zabel."

"Forgive me, your highness, but I like it better in Videssian disguise," Zoïle said—no, she wasn't one to hide her opinions about anything.

Maniakes carried Savellia down the hall to the Red Room. The baby wiggled in the surprisingly strong, purposeless way newborns have. If he stepped too hard, it would startle his daughter, and she would try to throw her arms and legs wide, though the blanket in which she was wrapped kept her from managing it. Frustrated, she started to cry, a high, thin, piercing wail designed to make new parents do whatever they could to stop it.

She was still crying when Maniakes walked into the Red Room with her. "Here, give her to me," Lysia said indignantly, stretching out her arms but not rising from the bed on which she lay. She looked as exhausted as if she'd just fought in a great battle, as indeed she had. She didn't sound altogether rational, and probably wasn't. Maniakes had seen that before, and knew it would last only a couple of days.

He handed her Savellia. She set the baby on her breast, steadying the little head with her hand. Savellia didn't know much about the way the world worked yet, but she knew what the breast was for. She sucked greedily.

A serving woman wiped Lysia's face with a wet cloth. Lysia closed her eyes and sighed, enjoying that. Other maidservants cleaned up the birthing chamber. They'd already begun that before Maniakes got there. Even so, the place still had an odor to it that, like Lysia's worn features, put him in mind of the aftermath of a battle. It smelled of sweat and dung, with a faint iron undertone of blood he tasted as much as he smelled it.

Being here, smelling those smells—especially the odor of blood—also made him remember Niphone, and how she had died here. To put his fears to rest, he asked, "How do you feel?"

"Tired," Lysia answered at once. "Sore. When I walk, I'm going to walk all bowlegged, as if I've been riding a horse for thirty years like a Khamorth nomad. And I'm hungry. I could eat a horse, too, if anyone would catch me one and serve it up with some onions and bread. And some wine. Zoïle wouldn't let me have any wine while I was in labor."

"You'd have puked it up," the midwife said from the doorway, "and you'd have liked giving it back a lot less than you liked drinking it down."

She stood aside then, for Kameas came gliding into the Red Room, carrying a tray whose delicious aromas helped cover the ones that had formerly lurked in the birthing chamber. "Tunny in leeks, your Majesty," he said to Lysia, "and artichokes marinated in olive oil and garlic. And, of course, wine. Congratulations. Savellia—did I hear the name rightly?"

"Yes, that's right," Lysia said. The eunuch set the tray down beside her on the wide bed. She smiled at him. "Good. Now I won't have to eat the horse, after all." He looked confused. Maniakes hid a smile. Lysia went on, "Oh, and you've gone and cut everything up into little bite-sized bits for me. Thank you so much." She sounded on the edge of tears with gratitude. Maybe she was. For the next little while, her emotions would gust wildly.

"I am glad your Majesty is pleased," Kameas said. The Avtokrator wondered how he felt about being in the presence of new life when he could never engender it himself.

"Here." Maniakes sat down on the bed, carefully, so as not to jar Lysia. "Let me do that." He picked up the spoon and started feeding his wife.

"Well!" she said after he'd given her a few bites. "You're the one who's supposed to have beautiful slaves dropping grapes into your mouth whenever you deign to open it, not me."

"I'm afraid beautiful is rather past my reach," Maniakes said, "and it's too late in the year for fresh grapes, but if Kameas will bring me some raisins, I'll see what I can do for you."

Kameas started to leave the Red Room, no doubt on a quest for raisins. "Wait!" Lysia called to him. "Never mind. I don't want any." She laughed, which made her wince. "Aii!" she said. "I'm still very sore down there." Her eyes traveled to Savellia, who had fallen asleep. "And why do you suppose that is?"

Rhegorios, Symvatios, and the elder Maniakes made themselves visible in the hall outside the open door to the Red Room. Maniakes waved for them to come in. "Ha!" Rhegorios said when he saw his cousin feeding Lysia. "We've finally gone and run out of servants, have we?"

"You be quiet," Lysia told him. "He's being very sweet, which is more than you can say most of the time." Maniakes knew Rhegorios would give him a hard time about that in due course, but he couldn't do anything about it now.

"Are you all right?" Symvatios asked his daughter.

"Right now? No," Lysia answered. "Right now I feel trampled in every tender place I own, and every time I have a baby, I seem to discover a couple of tender places I never knew I did own before. But if everything goes the way it should, I will be all right in a few weeks. I don't feel any different from the way I did the first two times I went through this."

"Good. That's good," Symvatios said.

"'Went through this,' eh?" the elder Maniakes rumbled. He nodded to his son. "Your own mother talked that way, right after she had you. It didn't keep her from having your brothers, mind you, but for a while there I wondered if it would."

Maniakes did his best to make his chuckle sound light and unforced. Even what was meant for family banter could take on a bitter edge, with one of his brothers in exile and the other likely dead. He went back to feeding Lysia. Rhegorios' teasing him about that would not bite so close to the bone.

Lysia finished every morsel of tunny and every chunk of artichoke heart. She also drank down all the wine. Maniakes wondered if she would ask Kameas for raisins, after all. Instead, she yawned and pulled Savellia off her breast and said, "Will someone please put the baby in a cradle for a while? I'd like to try to sleep till she wakes up hungry again. It's been a busy day."

Both grandfathers, her husband, and her brother reached for Savellia. She gave the new baby to Symvatios, who smiled as he held his granddaughter, then laid her in the cradle so gently, she did not wake.

"You could have a wet nurse deal with her," Maniakes said.

"I will, soon," Lysia answered. "The healer-priests and physicians say mother's milk is better for the first week or so, though. Babies are funny. They're tough and fragile, both at the same time. So many of them don't live to grow up, no matter what we do. I want to give mine the best chance they can have."

"All right," Maniakes said. She was right, too. But mothers were also tough and fragile, both at the same time. He leaned over and kissed her on the forehead. "Get what rest you can, then, and I hope she gives you some."

"She will," Lysia said. "She's a good baby." Maniakes wondered how she could tell. He wondered if she could tell. One way or the other, they'd find out soon enough.

Savellia was a good baby. She slept for long stretches and wasn't fussy when she woke. That helped Lysia mend sooner than she might have. The new princess's brothers and half brother and half sister stared at her with curiosity ranging from grave to giggly. When they realized she was too little to do anything much, they lost interest. "She doesn't even have any hair to pull," Likarios remarked, like a judge passing sentence.

"She will," Maniakes promised. "Pretty soon, she'll be able to pull yours, too." His son by Niphone—his heir, as things stood—looked horrified that anyone could presume to inflict such an indignity on him. Maniakes said, "She's already done it to me," which surprised Likarios all over again. "So did you, for that matter," the Avtokrator added. When a baby got a handful of beard . . . His cheeks hurt, just thinking about it.

Likarios went off. Maniakes watched him go. He plucked at his own beard. He'd wondered how Abivard would handle the problem of Denak's son by Sharbaraz. But Abivard was not the only one with family problems relating to the throne. Maniakes wondered what he'd do if Lysia ever suggested moving her sons ahead of Likarios in the succession. She never had, not yet. Maybe she never would. Succession by the eldest son born of the Avtokrator was a strong custom.

But strong custom was not the same as law. What if he saw young Symvatios, or even little Tatoules, shaping better than

Likarios? He sighed. The answer suggested itself: in that case, when he hoped above all else for simplicity, his life would get complicated once more, in new and incalculable ways.

His mouth twisted. Parsmanios hadn't cared anything for the strong custom of rule by the eldest. That made a disaster for Parsmanios, and nearly one for the whole clan. It was liable to be as nothing, though, next to what could happen if his sons got to squabbling among themselves.

Later that day, he wondered if his thinking of Parsmanios was what made Kameas come up to him and say, "Your Majesty, the lady Zenonis requests an audience with you, at your convenience." The eunuch's voice held nothing whatsoever: not approval, not its reverse. Maybe Kameas hadn't made up his mind about Parsmanios' wife. Maybe he had and wasn't letting on, perhaps not even to himself.

"I'll see her, of course," Maniakes said.

Formal as an ambassador, Zenonis prostrated herself before him. He let her do it, where for other members of the family he would have waved it aside as unnecessary. Maybe he hadn't made up his mind about Zenonis, either. Maybe she was just tarred with Parsmanios' brush.

"What can I do for you, sister-in-law of mine?" he asked when she'd risen.

She was nervous. Seeing that was something of a relief. Had she been sure of herself, he would have been sure, too: sure he needed to watch his back. "May it please your Majesty," she said, "I have a favor to beg of you." She licked her lips, realized she'd done it, and visibly wished she hadn't.

"You are of my family," Maniakes answered. "If a favor is in my power to grant, you must know I will."

"I am of your family, yes." Zenonis licked her lips again. "Considering the branch of it I'm in, how you must wish I weren't."

Speaking carefully, Maniakes answered, "I have never put my brother's crimes on your page of the account book, nor on your son's. That would be foolish. You did not know—you could not have known—what he was doing."

"You've been gracious, your Majesty; you've been kind and more than kind," Zenonis said. "But every time you see me, every time you see little Maniakes, you think of Parsmanios. I see it in your face. How can I blame you? But the thing is there, whether you wish it or not."

Maniakes sighed. "Maybe it is. I wish it weren't, but maybe it is. Even if it is, it won't keep me from granting you whatever favor you ask."

"Your Majesty is also just." Zenonis studied him. "You work hard at being just." The way she said it, it was not altogether a compliment: mostly, but not altogether. She took a deep breath, then brought out her next words in a rush: "When spring comes and ships can cross the Videssian Sea without fearing storms, I want you to send my son and me to Prista."

"Are you sure?" Maniakes asked. Regret warred in him with something else he needed a moment to recognize: relief. That he felt it shamed him, but did not make it go away. Fighting against it, he said, "Think three times before you ask this of me, sister-in-law of mine. Prista is a bleak place, and—"

To his surprise, Zenonis laughed. "It's a provincial town, your Majesty, not so? All I've ever known my whole life long is a provincial town." She held up a hand. "You're going to tell me that, if I go, I can't come back. I don't care. I never set foot outside Vryetion till I came to Videssos the city. If I'm in Prista with my husband, that will be company enough."

Maniakes spoke even more carefully than he had before: "Parsmanios will have been in exile some little while by the time you arrive, sister-in-law of mine."

"He'll be the gladder to see me, then, and to see his son," Zenonis replied.

She didn't see what Maniakes was aiming at. Having been several years in Prista, Parsmanios was liable to have found another partner. Why not? He could hardly have expected his wife to join him, not when, up till this past summer, Vryetion had been in Makuraner hands. Maniakes got reports on his banished brother's doings, but those had to do with politics, not with whom Parsmanios was taking to bed. Maniakes expected he could find out whom, if anyone, Parsmanios was taking to bed, but that would have to wait till spring, too.

He said, "Don't burn your boats yet. If, when sailing season comes, you still want to do this, we can talk about it then. Meanwhile, you and your son are welcome here, whether you believe me or not."

"Thank you, your Majesty," Zenonis said, "but I do not think my mind will change."

"All right," he answered, though it wasn't all right. He was settled into being Avtokrator, too, and taken aback when anyone met his will with steady resistance. "Only remember, you truly can't decide now. If, come spring, you want to go to Prista, I will give you and your son a ship, and to Prista you shall go, and to . . . to my brother. But you and little Maniakes and Parsmanios will never come back here again. I tell you this once more, to make certain you understand it."

"I understand it," she said. "It gave me pause for a while, but no more. I am going to be with my husband. Little Maniakes is going to be with his father."

"If that is what you want, that is what you shall have," Maniakes answered formally. "I do not think you are making the wisest choice, but I will not rob you of making it."

"Thank you, your Majesty," Zenonis told him, and prostrated herself once more, and went away. Maniakes stared at her back. He sighed. He thought—he was as near sure as made no difference— she was making a bad mistake. Did he have the right to save his subjects from themselves, even when they wouldn't thank him for it? That was one of the more intriguing questions he'd asked himself since he took the throne. He couldn't come up with a good answer for it. Well, as Zenonis had time to think on her choice, so did he.

Courtiers, functionaries, bureaucrats, soldiers, and, for all Maniakes knew, utter nonentities who chanced to look good in fancy robes packed the Grand Courtroom. The Avtokrator sat on the throne and stared down the long colonnaded hall to the entranceway through which the ambassador from Makuran would come and make obeisance before him.

When Makuran and Videssos changed sovereigns, they went through a ritual, as set as the figures in a dance, of notifying each other. In the scheme of things, that was necessary, as each recognized only the other as an equal. What the barbarians around them did was one thing. What they did with each other was something else again, and could—and had—set the civilized world on its ear.

No hum of anticipation ran through the assembled Videssian dignitaries when the ambassador appeared in the doorway. On the contrary: the courtiers grew still and silent. They looked straight ahead. No—their heads pointed straight ahead. But their eyes all slid toward that small, slim figure silhouetted against the cool winter sunshine outside.

The ambassador came gliding toward Maniakes, moving almost as smoothly—no, a miracle: moving as smoothly—as Kameas. At the proper spot in front of the throne, he prostrated himself. While he lay with his forehead pressed against the polished marble, the throne rose with a squeal of gearing till it was several feet higher off the ground than it had been. The effect sometimes greatly impressed embassies from among the barbarians. Maniakes did not expect the Makuraner to be overawed, but custom was custom.

From his new altitude, the Avtokrator said, "Rise."

"I obey," Abivard's envoy said, coming to his feet in one smooth motion. His face was beardless, and beautiful as a woman's. When he spoke, in good Videssian, his voice was silver bells. He must have been gelded early in life, for it never to have cracked and changed.

"Name yourself," Maniakes said, continuing the ritual, though the ambassador had already been introduced to him in private.

"Majesty, I am called Yeliif," the beautiful eunuch answered. "I am come to announce to Maniakes Avtokrator, his brother in might, the accession of Abivard King of Kings, may his years be many and his realm increase: divine, good, peaceful, to whom the God has given great fortune and great empire, the giant of giants, who is formed in the image of the God."

"We, Maniakes, Avtokrator of the Videssians, vicegerent of Phos on earth, greet with joy and hope the accession of Abivard King of Kings, our brother," Maniakes said, granting Abivard the recognition Sharbaraz—who had claimed the Makuraner God was formed in *his* image—had consistently refused to grant him. "Many years to Abivard King of Kings."

"Many years to Abivard King of Kings!" the assembled courtiers echoed.

"Majesty, you are gracious to grant Abivard King of Kings the boon of your shining countenance," Yeliif said. However lovely and well modulated his voice, it held no great warmth. He spoke, not with Kameas' impassivity, but with what struck Maniakes as well-concealed bitterness. He was, of course, a eunuch, which certainly entitled any man—or half man—to be bitter. And his features, however beautiful, had the cold perfection of statuary, not the warmth of flesh.

"May we live in peace, Abivard King of Kings and I." That was also part of the ritual, but Maniakes spoke the words with great sincerity. Videssos and Makuran both needed peace. He dared hope they might find some small space of it.

Abivard King of Kings, he thought. The man who was, or could have been, his friend, the warrior who had made such a deadly foe, and now the ruler who had in the end chosen to reign in his own name, not that of his nephew, his sister's son by Sharbaraz.

That brought to mind another question: "What has befallen Sharbaraz the former King of Kings, esteemed sir?" the Avtokrator asked, giving Yeliif the title a high-ranking eunuch in Videssos would have had.

"Majesty, the God judges him now, not mortal men," Yeliif answered. "Not long before I set out for this city, his successor had his head stricken from his body." Was that regret? Yeliif had presumably been at court throughout Sharbaraz's reign. However little use most Makuraners might have had for Sharbaraz at the end, he might have been sorry to see his sovereign overthrown.

Well, Maniakes thought, *that's not my worry.* Aloud, he said, "I have gifts for you to take to Abivard King of Kings on your return to Makuran." That, too, was ritual.

But then affairs in Makuran became Maniakes' worry, for Yeliif broke with ritual by prostrating himself again. "Majesty, may it please you, I cannot return to Makuran, save only that my head should answer for it, as Sharbaraz's did for him," the beautiful eunuch said. "Abivard King of Kings sent me here not only as embassy but also as exile." He sighed, a wintry sound. "He was, in his way, merciful, having had it in his power to slay me out of hand."

"*I* won't slay you out of hand," Maniakes promised. "I'm sure I'll be able to learn a great deal about Makuran from you." *I'll squeeze you dry,* was what he meant. Yeliif nodded to show he understood and assented—not that he had much choice. Maniakes went on, "For now, esteemed sir, you may reckon yourself enrolled among the eunuchs of the palaces."

"Majesty, you are gracious to an exile," Yeliif said. "I shall have a great deal to say about everyone I know, I assure you."

"I'm sure you will," Maniakes said. "I'm sure you will." Betrayal was the coin with which the beautiful eunuch would buy his welcome in Videssos the city. Abivard must have known as much and exiled him anyhow, which was . . . interesting. And Yeliif did not have to have it spelled out for him. Maniakes studied the limpid dark eyes, the elegant cheekbones, the sculptured line of jaw. Though a man only for women himself, he recognized the danger in that loveliness. Yes, Yeliif would know about betrayal. And, of course, someone in Yeliif's early days had given him over to be castrated. What worse betrayal than that?

The Avtokrator bowed his head, signifying the audience was ended. Yeliif prostrated himself, rose, and backed away from the throne till he could turn around without showing disrespect. A great many eyes followed him as he withdrew from the Grand Courtroom.

"Yes," Yeliif said, "of course, the lady Denak was furious when Abivard chose to rule as King of Kings rather than as regent for Peroz, her son by Sharbaraz. Before that, she was furious with him for overthrowing Sharbaraz just when she'd finally gained influence over the then-King of Kings by bearing a son. Before that, she was furious with Sharbaraz for not giving her the influence she reckoned her due as principal wife." The eunuch sipped wine and nodded first to Maniakes and then to the secretary who was taking down his words for further study.

"And what of Sharbaraz?" Maniakes asked. "How did he take it when he learned Abivard was moving against him?"

"He bellowed like a bull." Yeliif's lip curled in scorn. "And, like a bull, he raged this way and that, neither knowing nor caring how he might best meet the threat before him, so long as he could bellow and paw the ground."

With a faint *scrape-scrape*, the secretary's stylus raced over the waxed surface of his three-leaved wooden tablet. Maniakes slowly nodded. He hoped Yeliif would take that for agreement and understanding. Both were there, but so was something else, something that grew with every conversation he had with the beautiful eunuch: wariness. The next complimentary word Yeliif said about anyone at the Makuraner court would be the first. What was in a way worse was that the eunuch didn't seem to notice he was casually savaging everyone he mentioned. His view was so jaundiced, Maniakes had trouble deciding how much reliance he could place in it.

Experimentally, the Avtokrator said, "And what of Romezan? He's a noble of the Seven Clans. How does he feel about serving a sovereign born a mere *dihqan*?"

"It's no great difficulty." Yeliif's gesture was elegant, scornful, dismissive. "Give Romezan something to kill and he's happy. It could be Videssians, it could be wild asses, it could be those who followed Sharbaraz. So long as he welters in gore, he cares not what gore it is." *Scrape-scrape* went the stylus.

"He fights well," Maniakes observed.

"He should. He's had practice enough. He'd fight himself, I daresay, till the bruises got too painful even for him to bear." Somehow, malice was all the more malicious when expressed in that sweet, sexless voice. If Romezan had practice fighting, Yeliif had the same in backbiting—but he'd never wounded himself.

"And Abivard?" Maniakes said.

"I warned Sharbaraz of him long ago," the beautiful eunuch said. "I told him Abivard had his eye on the throne. Did he heed me? No. Did anyone heed me? No. Should he have heeded me? Majesty, I leave that to you."

"Suppose Sharbaraz had got rid of him," Maniakes said—actually, he said *Sarbaraz*; here in the city, he didn't care if his accent was imperfect. "Who would have led Makuran's armies against us this past spring?"

Yeliif returned a perfect shrug. "Romezan. Why not? He might have done better, and could hardly have done worse—worse for Makuran, I mean, as he made quite a good thing for himself out of failure."

Such cynicism took the breath away, even for an Avtokrator of the Videssians. Coughing a little, Maniakes said, "I begin to see why Abivard doesn't want you coming back to Mashiz."

"Oh, indeed," Yeliif agreed. "I remind him of the time when the world did not turn at his bidding, when he was small and weak and impotent."

For a eunuch to use that particular word, and to use it with such obvious deliberation, was breathtaking in its own way. Maniakes got the idea Yeliif had done it to throw him off balance. If so, he'd certainly succeeded. "Er—yes," the Avtokrator said, and dismissed the exiled ambassador from Makuran.

"I thought you'd want to go on longer, your Majesty," the secretary said after Yeliif had gone.

"So did I," Maniakes said, "but I'd had about as much spite as I could stomach of an afternoon, thank you very much."

"Ah." The scribe nodded understanding. "You listen to him for a while and it does kind of make you want to go home and slit your own wrists, doesn't it?"

"Either your own or your neighbor's, depending on whom he's been telling tales about," Maniakes answered. He glanced over to the scribe in some relief. "You thought so, too, did you? Good. I'm glad I'm not the only one."

"Oh, no, your Majesty. Any milk of human kindness that one ever had, it curdled a long time ago." The secretary sounded very sure. But then, in meditative tones, he added, "Of course, losing your stones, now, that's not the sort of thing to make you jolly and ready for a mug of wine after work with the rest of the lads, is it?"

"I shouldn't think so," Maniakes said. "Still, I haven't known any of the eunuchs here to be quite so—" At a loss for words to describe Yeliif's manner, he gestured. The secretary nodded once more. Having heard the beautiful eunuch, he did not need to hear him described.

Maybe his beauty had something to do with the way he was, Maniakes thought. He would surely have been pursued at the court of Mashiz, very likely by men and women both, his loveliness being of a sort to draw and hold the eye of either sex. What had being the object of desire while unable to know desire himself done to his soul?

When the Avtokrator wondered about that aloud, the scribe nodded yet again. But then he said, "The other chance is, your Majesty, you don't mind my saying so, he might be a right bastard even if he had his balls and a beard down to here and a voice deeper than your father's. Some people just are, you know."

"Yes, I had noticed that," the Avtokrator said sadly. He dismissed the scribe: "Go have yourself a cup of wine, or maybe even two." The man left with fresh spring in his step. Watching him go, Maniakes decided to have a cup of wine himself, or maybe even two.

When Kameas started to prostrate himself before Maniakes, the Avtokrator waved for him not to bother. To his surprise, the eunuch went through the full proskynesis anyhow. To his greater surprise, he saw a bruise on the side of Kameas' face when the vestiarios rose. "What happened?" Maniakes asked. "Did you walk into a door, esteemed sir?"

"Your Majesty," Kameas began, and then shook his head, dissatisfied with himself. He took a deep breath and tried again: "Your Majesty, may I speak frankly?"

"Why, yes. Of course, esteemed sir," Maniakes answered, thinking that might have been the most unusual request he'd ever had from a court eunuch. He wondered whether Kameas *could* speak frankly, however much he might wish to do so.

By all appearances, such unwonted effort wasn't easy for the vestiarios. But then, after touching his bruised cheek, Kameas seemed to steady on the purpose for which he had approached the Avtokrator. He drew in another deep breath and said, "No, your Majesty, I did not walk into a door. I received this . . . gift at the hands of another of your prominent servitors."

At the hands of another eunuch, he meant, *prominent* being the next step below *esteemed* in their hierarchy of honorifics. Maniakes stared. Eunuchs' squabbles were commonly fought with slander, occasionally with poison, but . . . "Fisticuffs, esteemed sir? I'm astonished."

"So was I, your Majesty. I must say, though," Kameas added with a certain amount of pride, "I gave as good as I got."

"I'm glad to hear it," Maniakes said. "But by the good god, esteemed sir, what on earth set you and your colleagues to boxing one another's ears?" That sort of display of bad temper was a vice of normal men upon which eunuchs usually looked with amused contempt.

"Not *what*, your Majesty, *who*," Kameas replied, his voice going surprisingly grim. "The reason I have come before you, the reason I am violating propriety and decorum, is to request that you—no, to beg that you—find some way of removing this serpent of a Yeliif from the palaces, before it comes to knives rather than fists. There. I have said it." It couldn't have been easy for him, either; his breath came in little gasps, as if he'd forced his fat frame to run a long way.

"What on earth has he done, esteemed sir, to make you ask something like that only a couple of weeks after he got to the city?"

"Your Majesty, that Makuraner eunuch is a snake with a skin of honey, so that, his bite being at first sweet, one does not feel the venom till too late. He has, in the little space of time you named, set all who dealt with him in any way at odds with one another, playing with the imperial eunuchs as cat plays with mouse, making some hate the rest—" Kameas touched his cheek again. "—and every one of us suspect everyone else. Had Skotos risen from the eternal ice—" Kameas and Maniakes both spat. "—he could have worked no greater mischief among those who serve."

"What is he up to?" Maniakes asked. "Does he think that, by sowing discord, he'll make me want to supplant you as vestiarios? If he does, esteemed sir, believe me, he's mistaken."

"Your Majesty is gracious." Kameas bowed. "In point of fact, though, I would doubt that. As best I can see, Yeliif stirs up hatreds for no better reason than that he enjoys stirring up hatreds. It being winter, there are no flies whose wings he can pull off like a small, nasty boy, so he torments the servitors around him instead."

That was franker speech than Maniakes had ever imagined from Kameas. "We'll get to the bottom of this," he assured the vestiarios. "Summon the esteemed Yeliif. I will not condemn him without hearing what he says in his own behalf."

"Guard your ears well against his deceits, your Majesty," Kameas said, but he went off happier than he had approached the Avtokrator.

As they had been whenever Maniakes saw him, Yeliif's manners were impeccable. After prostrating himself with liquid grace, he inquired, "In what manner may I serve you, Majesty?"

"I am told," Maniakes said carefully, "you may have something to do with the recent discord among the palace eunuchs here."

Yeliif's large, dark eyes widened. He looked convincingly astonished. "I, Majesty? How could such a thing be possible? I am but the humblest of refugees at your court, beholden to you for all the many kindnesses you have been generous enough to show me. How can you imagine I would so repay that generosity?"

"Considering the way you talk about everyone you knew back in Mashiz, esteemed sir, I must tell you these reports don't altogether astonish me," Maniakes said. "The next good word you have for anybody will be the first."

The beautiful eunuch shook his head in vigorous disagreement. "Majesty, like so many others, you misunderstand me. I speak nothing but the truth, the plain, unvarnished truth. If this pains people, am I at fault?"

"Maybe," Maniakes said. "Probably, in fact. Have you ever known anyone who prides himself on what he calls frankness but only uses that frankness to tear down those around him, never to build them up?"

"Oh, yes," Yeliif replied. "I have suffered at the hands of such scorpions many times—and now, it would seem, again, or why would you have called me before you to tax me with these base-less calumnies?"

Had Maniakes been listening to Yeliif in isolation, he might well have been convinced the beautiful eunuch was telling the truth. He was convinced Yeliif thought he was telling the truth. Mus-ingly, he said, "One measure of a man is the enemies he makes. Among yours, esteemed sir, you seem to number both Abivard King of Kings and my vestiarios, the esteemed Kameas."

"They are prejudiced against me," Yeliif replied.

"It may be," Maniakes said. "It may be. Nevertheless . . ." Unlike Yeliif, he was not so frank as to declare that he trusted Abivard and Kameas' opinions further than those of the beautiful eunuch. Instead, still in musing tones, he went on, "Perhaps we would all be better served if you were to take a position somewhat removed from the contentious air of the palaces."

"I do not believe this to be in any way necessary," Yeliif said, more than a little asperity in that bell-like voice. After a moment, he realized he'd gone too far. "You are, of course, the sovereign, and what pleases you has the force of law."

"Yes." Maniakes drove that point home before turning concilia-tory. "The post I have in mind is in no way dishonorable. I have received word that the city governor of Kastavala died of some illness this past summer. I think I shall send you there, complete with a suitable retinue, to take his place. Kastavala, you should know, is the capital of the province of Kalavria, where my father served as governor before I became Avtokrator."

"Ah." Yeliif bowed. "That is indeed a post of honor. I thank you, Majesty; I shall do everything in my power to ensure you have no cause to regret the trust you repose in me."

"I'm sure I won't," Maniakes answered. Being a Makuraner, Yeliif would not be overfamiliar with the geography of Videssos, especially that of the eastern portions of the Empire. Maniakes hadn't lied, not in any particular. He also had not mentioned that Kalavria was the easternmost island under Videssian rule: the easternmost island under anyone's rule, so far as anyone knew. No ship had ever sailed out of the east to Kalavria. No ship sailing east from Kalavria had ever come back. Once Yeliif went east to Kalavria, he was not likely to come back, either. Maniakes didn't think he would have any cause to regret that.

"Since this is a position of such importance, I do not think it should long remain vacant," the beautiful eunuch said. "If, Majesty, you are serious about entrusting it to me—" He made it sound as if he did not truly believe that. "—you will send me to it forthwith, permitting no delays whatever."

"You're right," Maniakes said, to Yeliif's evident surprise. "If you can be ready to depart from the imperial city tomorrow, I shall have an armed escort to convey you to Opsikion, from which place you can take ship to Kastavala."

"Take—ship?" Yeliif said, as if the words weren't any part of the Videssian he'd learned.

"Certainly." Maniakes made his voice brisk. "It's too far to swim from Opsikion, and the water's much too cold for swimming this time of year, anyhow. I dismiss you now, esteemed sir; I know you'll have considerable packing to do, and you'll need an early start tomorrow, with the days so short now. Thanks again for your willingness to fill the post on such short notice."

Yeliif started to say something. Maniakes turned away from him, signifying that the audience was over. Trapped in the web of court etiquette, the beautiful eunuch had no choice but to withdraw. From the corner of his eyes Maniakes noted Yeliif's expression. It was more eloquently venomous than any of his sweet-sounding words.

Kameas came into the audience chamber a few minutes later. "Is it true, your Majesty? The island of Kalavria?" Maniakes nodded. The eunuch sighed. His kind might not know physical ecstasy, but this came close. "From the bottom of my heart, your Majesty, I thank you."

"You *thank* me," Maniakes demanded, "for doing *that* to poor, sleepy, innocent Kastavala?"

Avtokrator and vestiarios looked at each other for a moment. Then, as if they were two mimes taking the same cue, they both began to laugh.

✦　　✦　　✦

Midwinter's Day dawned clear and cold. The cold had nothing to do with why Maniakes would sooner have stayed in bed. "There was a time," he said in wondering tones, "when I used to look forward to this holiday. I remember that, but I have trouble making myself believe it."

"I know what you mean," Lysia said. "No help for it, though."

"No, not when you're the Avtokrator," Maniakes agreed. "One of the things by which the city mob judges you is how well you can take the flaying the mime troupes give out." That they had extra reason to flay him because he was wed to Lysia went without saying. His wife who was also his cousin understood that as well as he did.

"As long as we're not in the Amphitheater, we can try to enjoy the day," she said, and Maniakes nodded.

"Well, yes," he admitted. "The only trouble with that is, we have to be in the Amphitheater a good part of the day."

"But not all of it." Lysia sounded determined to make the best of things. The past few years, that had been Maniakes' role, with her reluctant to go out in public. But now she tugged at his arm. "Come on," she said.

He came, then suddenly stopped. "I know what it is," he said. "You're so glad you can be up and about after you had Savellia anything but the inside of the imperial residence would look good to you."

"I suppose you're right," she said. Then she stuck out her tongue at him. "So what?" She pulled him again. This time, he let himself be dragged along.

When he and Lysia left the hypocaust-heated residence, breath puffed from their mouths and noses in great, soft-looking clouds of fog. Frost glittered on the dead, yellow-brown grass of the lawns between buildings. As if to fight the chill, a big bonfire blazed on the cobbles of the path leading east toward the plaza of Palamas.

A crowd of palace servants and grooms and gardeners, plus a leavening of ordinary city folk in holiday finery, stood around the fire. Some huddled close, spreading out their hands to warm them. Then a laundress dashed toward the flames, long skirts flapping about her ankles. As she leapt over the bonfire, she shouted, "Burn, ill-luck!" She staggered when she landed; a groom in a gaudy tunic caught her around the waist to steady her. She repaid him with a kiss. His arms tightened around her. The crowd whooped and cheered and offered bawdy advice.

Lysia's eyes sparkled. "Anything can happen on Midwinter's Day," she said.

"I know what that fellow hopes will happen," Maniakes answered. He tilted Lysia's face up to his for a brief kiss. Then he made his own run at the bonfire. People shouted and got out of his way. He leapt. He soared. "Burn, ill-luck!" he shouted. All over Videssos the city, all over the Empire of Videssos, people were leaping and shouting. Priests called it superstition and sometimes inveighed against it, but when Midwinter's Day came, they leapt and shouted, too.

The sound of determined running feet made Maniakes look back. Here came Lysia, her shape shifting oddly when seen through the heat-ripples of the fire. "Burn, ill luck!" she shouted as she sprang. Making sure nobody beat him to it, Maniakes eased her landing. "Why, thank you, sir," she said, as if she'd never seen him before. The crowd whooped again when he gave her another kiss. The suggestions they called were no different from the ones they'd given the groom and laundress.

Arm in arm, Maniakes and Lysia strolled toward the plaza of Palamas. An enterprising fellow had set up a table with a big jar of wine and several earthenware cups. Maniakes glanced toward Lysia, who nodded. The wine was no better than he'd expected it to be. He gave the wineseller a goldpiece. The fellow's eyes went big. "I'm s-sorry, your Majesty," he said, "but I can't change this."

"Don't be foolish," Maniakes told him. "It's Midwinter's Day. Anything can happen on Midwinter's Day." He and Lysia strolled on.

"Phos bless you, your Majesty," the wineseller called after him. He smiled at Lysia. He hadn't heard that in the city, not often enough.

Lysia must have been thinking along with him, for she said, "After that, it seems a shame to have to go on to the Amphitheater."

"It does, doesn't it?" the Avtokrator said. "No help for it, though. If I don't sit up there on the spine and watch the mime troupes mocking me, half the city will think I've been overthrown and the other half will think I ought to be. I rule every day of the year but one, and I can't—or I'm not supposed to—complain about what goes on then. Anything can happen on Midwinter's Day." Now he gave the saying an ironic twist.

The plaza of Palamas, out beyond the palace quarter, was packed with revelers—and with winesellers, foodsellers, and harlots to help them enjoy themselves more . . . and, no doubt, with cutpurses and crooked gamblers to help them enjoy themselves less. Maniakes and Lysia leapt over several more fires. No one cursed them. Maniakes saw a couple of priests in the crowd, but one was falling-down drunk and the other had his arm around the waist of a woman who was probably not a lady. The Avtokrator shrugged and kept on toward the Amphitheater. He supposed even priests deserved a day off from holiness once a year.

People streamed into the Amphitheater, the enormous soup bowl of a building where horse races were held through most of the year. Just before Maniakes and Lysia got to the gate through which, on most days, the horses entered, the Empress let out an indignant squeak. "Someone," she said darkly, "has hands that need a lesson in manners, but, in this crowd, to the ice with me if I know who." She sighed in something approaching resignation. "Midwinter's Day."

"Midwinter's Day," Maniakes echoed. Men had no shame during the festival. For that matter, neither did women. A fair number of babies born around the time of the autumnal equinox bore no great resemblance to their mothers' husbands. Everyone knew as much. Remarking on it was bad form.

Kameas, Rhegorios, the elder Maniakes, Symvatios, Agathios the patriarch, assorted courtiers and functionaries, a squad of Imperial Guards in gilded mail and scarlet cloaks, and the full twelve imperial parasol-bearers stood waiting by the gate. Rhegorios patted Kameas on the shoulder. "There. You see, esteemed sir? I told you they'd be here."

"They had no business wandering off on their own and leaving me to fret," the vestiarios said petulantly, giving Maniakes a severe look.

"Anything can happen on Midwinter's Day—even an escape from ceremonial," the Avtokrator said. Kameas shook his head, plainly disagreeing. He would have his way now; Maniakes was caught in the net once more. With a gesture more imperious than any to which the Avtokrator could aspire, Kameas ordered the procession into the Amphitheater.

The crowd in there fell silent for a moment, then burst into loud cheers, knowing the day's main entertainment was about to begin. Maniakes' father and Lysia's both drew prolonged applause; they'd made themselves popular in the city. So did Rhegorios, who was popular wherever he went. Marching along behind the parasol-bearers, Maniakes knew a moment's jealousy. Had Rhegorios wanted to usurp his place, he probably could have done it.

Then, Lysia beside him, the Avtokrator strode out into full view of the crowd. He was braced for the curses and jeers to come cascading down on the two of them, as they had on Midwinter's Days past. And there were curses and jeers. He heard them. But, to his delighted astonishment, a great torrent of cheers almost drowned them out.

Lysia reached out and squeezed his hand. "We've finally managed it, haven't we?" she said.

"Maybe we have," Maniakes answered. "By the good god, maybe we have."

Behind the parasol-bearers, they stepped up onto the spine of the Amphitheater. The Avtokrator's seat, set in the center, had a special property: a trick of acoustics let everyone in the enormous structure hear the words he spoke there. The converse was that he heard, or thought he heard, all the racket inside the Amphitheater, every bit of it seeming to be aimed straight at him. Sitting in that seat, he sometimes wondered if his head would explode.

When he held up his hand for quiet, he got . . . a little less noise. After a bit, he got still less, and decided that would have to do. "People of Videssos the city!" he called, and then, taking a chance, "My friends!" No great torrent of hisses and catcalls rained down on him, so he went on, "My friends, we've been through a lot together these past few years, and especially this past summer. The good god willing, the hard times are behind us for a while. In token of that, and in token of Phos' sun turning once more to the north after this day, let us rejoice and make merry. Anything can happen on Midwinter's Day!"

The applause almost took off the top of his head. He had to lean away from the exact focus of sound to save his ears. Then the first troupe of mimes swaggered out onto the race track. The frenzied cheers they got made what he'd received seem tepid by comparison. His grin was wry. That showed him where he stood in the hearts of the city—better than ever before, but still behind the entertainment.

He knew that would slip if he didn't at least look amused at every skit the mime troupes presented, regardless of whether it was aimed at him. The first one wasn't: it showed Etzilios fleeing up to Kubrat like a dog with its tail between its legs, and pausing to relieve himself as he went. It was crude, but Maniakes was glad enough to laugh at any portrayal of an old foe's discomfiture.

The next skit seemed to be about tavern robberies. The crowd ate it up, though it went past Maniakes. "That happened while you were in the westlands," his father said.

After that troupe came several men with shaved faces, one of whom set about poisoning the others and stabbing them in the back. Kameas and the rest of the eunuchs on the spine of the Amphitheater laughed themselves silly over that one. Yeliif was already on the way to Opsikion. Maniakes doubted he would have been amused. The Avtokrator wondered how much the eunuchs had paid the mimes to get them to cut off their beards for their roles.

Another skit suggested that Sharbaraz, rather than thinking himself the God incarnate, thought he was the ecumenical patriarch, a dignity the mummers reckoned much more impressive. What he did when he discovered the patriarch had to be celibate made Agathios wince and giggle at the same time. Everyone was fair game on Midwinter's Day.

A new troupe came on and presented the spectacle of the Kubrati monoxyla being sunk and going up in flames. The mimes really did set one of their prop boats on fire, then leapt over it as if it were a good-luck blaze out on the plaza of Palamas.

Yet another troupe had a boiler boy obviously supposed to be Abivard trying to decide whether he should put on robes like those of the Videssian Avtokrator or the Makuraner King of Kings. When he decided on the latter, the mime who had been wearing the Videssian getup chased him around the track, to the loud delight of the crowd. Maniakes leaned over to Lysia and said, "I wish it had been that easy."

"Everything is easy—if you're a mime," she answered.

Maniakes thought he and Lysia would get away scot-free, but one mime troupe did lampoon them—and Agathios, too, for good measure. Glancing over at the patriarch, Maniakes saw him fume. That made it easier for the Avtokrator to sit and pretend he enjoyed the insults that made the city mob chortle.

But his good mood was quite restored when, in the next—and last—skit, he realized the nasty little man who kept getting kicked back and forth between mimes dressed as Videssians and others intended to be Makuraners, neither side wanting him, was Tzikas. The crowd laughed louder at that than they had at the lewd skit skewering him.

And then it was over. He got cheers when he dismissed the crowd: cheers, no doubt, from many of the people who'd jeered him during the mimes' mockery a few minutes before. He moved away from the seat at the acoustical heart of the Amphitheater and said, "That wasn't too bad—and now it's over for another year."

"Phos be praised!" Lysia said. "But you're right; it wasn't too bad." As they were making their way out of the great arena behind the parasol-bearers, she asked, "What do you want to do now?"—their ceremonial duties for the day were over.

He slipped his arm around her waist. "I know it's a *little* early after Savellia was born, but it *is* Midwinter's Day. People will be too busy looking for their own good times even to think of bothering us," Maniakes said hopefully.

"Maybe." Lysia didn't sound as if she believed that, but her arm went around his waist, too. Together, they walked through the plaza of Palamas and the palace quarter, back toward the imperial residence.